The Canadian Jewish Studies Reader

edited by RICHARD MENKIS & NORMAN RAVVIN

The Canadian Jewish Studies Reader

edited by RICHARD MENKIS & NORMAN RAVVIN

Red Deer PRESS

Chaire de l'Université Concordia
en études juives canadiennes
The Concordia University Chair
in Canadian Jewish Studies

THE PUBLISHERS
Red Deer Press
813 MacKimmie Library Tower
2500 University Drive N.W.
Calgary Alberta Canada T2N 1N4
www.reddeerpress.com

CREDITS
Edited for the Press by Richard Menkis & Norman Ravvin
Cover and text design by Erin Woodward
Cover illustration courtesy of Angela Grossmann
Printed and bound in Canada by Friesens for Red Deer Press

ACKNOWLEDGEMENTS
Financial support provided by the Canada Council, the Department of Canadian Heritage, the Alberta Foundation for the Arts, a beneficiary of the Lottery Fund of the Government of Alberta, the University of Calgary and Concordia University.

THE CANADA COUNCIL | LE CONSEIL DES ARTS
FOR THE ARTS | DU CANADA
SINCE 1957 | DEPUIS 1957

NATIONAL LIBRARY OF CANADA CATALOGUING IN PUBLICATION
The Canadian Jewish studies reader / edited by Richard Menkis & Norman Ravvin.
Includes bibliographical references.
ISBN 0-88995-295-7
1. Jews—Canada—Identity. 2. Jews—Canada—History. 3. Jews—Canada. I. Menkis, Richard II. Ravvin, Norman, 1963–
FC106.J5C394 2004   305.892'4071   C2004-904904-6

5 4 3 2 1

The Canadian Jewish Studies Reader is part of a series devoted to Canadian Jewish Studies, which is co-published by Red Deer Press and the Institute for Canadian Jewish Studies at Concordia University. The series editor is Norman Ravvin.

PREVIOUS TITLES:

Not Quite Mainstream: Canadian Jewish Short Stories, ed. Norman Ravvin.
Mordecai & Me: An Appreciation of a Kind, by Joel Yanofsky.

Acknowledgements

I would be amiss if I did not thank the scholars in this volume for dedicating their time to understanding the Canadian Jewish experience. I wish to thank Linda Pasquale for her hard work and good cheer throughout this project. I also want to try to thank Cathie, Aviva and Lavi for helping me to feel and understand many things more clearly. This book is dedicated to the memory my father, Sidney (Siegfried) Menkis, for whom deep inclusivity was a way of life. I hope that ideal is reflected, somewhat, in this book.

Richard Menkis

I dedicate this volume to the memory of my maternal grandfather, Yehuda Yoseph Eisenstein, a cultural worker in any number of fields, who, after World War II, maintained an old world view in the most new world of cities, Vancouver.

I would also like to acknowledge the crucial editorial and administrative help of Linda Pasquale, without whom this text could not have taken such orderly shape.

Norman Ravvin

Editorial Methods

The essays and excerpts included in this *Reader* are drawn from sources that include books, journals, and unpublished scholarship. In the latter case, the editors were careful to shape the authors' work to this volume's needs. In the case of previously published work, the materials are presented much as they appeared in their original setting. Errors and oddities in the texts have been corrected, but no effort has been made to get the collected contributions to attend to a boilerplate style. As much as was possible, citation style has been made similar from essay to essay, although some variations do remain. This decision allows the reader, by checking the original source for these materials, to appreciate how work in the field of Canadian Jewish Studies has appeared, and in what way publication and editorial styles have varied. The collaborative nature of the work, then, is furthered, as the original editorial stamp is not removed from many of the contributions.

NR

Contents

Jewish Rag Picker; bearded man with sleigh, Bloor Street West (Toronto), 1911
Photo by William James.
Photo courtesy of the City of Toronto Archives, Fonds 1244, Item 616.

Introduction:
Jewish Cultures, Canadian Cultures

RICHARD MENKIS

We begin, as did so many Jewish communities, with a Jewish peddler. Doubled over under a heavy pack, or, perhaps, dragging his wares behind him on a cart or sled, he ventured out to unfamiliar territory, not knowing when or where he would find a customer. But he was not just *shlepping* items for sale or barter. He carried a world inside him, and he confronted unfamiliar worlds when he left the Jewish immigrant neighbourhoods for Canadian cityscapes and rural land-scapes. In his own Jewish community, he found some of his fellow Jews strange, such as those who had been in Canada longer, or who had a different political or religious outlook than himself. And the suspicion was mutual: the newcomer was often viewed with a mixture of brotherhood and disdain.

One aim of this volume is to examine the habits of thinking and the behaviour of this peddler and other Jews. First, however, we want to offer a declaration of indebtedness to our colleagues in the area of Canadian Jewish Studies. Why wait until the end of the chapter when the research of our colleagues is our point of departure? It's a wonderful time to be compiling this volume. In the past two decades, historians, sociologists, students of literature and others have created superb studies, which allow us to better understand the Canadian Jewish experience. Gerald Tulchinsky's magisterial two volume history of Canadian Jewry provides an expert guide through the demographic and political history of the Jews, as well as a portrait of the changes in attitudes toward Jews.[1] Morton Weinfeld's recent review of the contemporary Jewish community engagingly communicates how Canadian Jews have succeeded economically, socially and politically.[2] Michael Greenstein's survey of English Canadian Jewish literature is a point of departure for attempts to understand the lives and themes of some of Canadian Jewry's most prominent writers.[3] Excellent studies have enhanced our understanding of the involvement of Jews in the labour movement. Canadian Jewish historiography has even spawned some debates on the nature of anti-Semitism in Canada, such as the studies by Pierre Anctil and Esther Delisle on Quebec, and Janine Stingel's investigation of the Social Credit Party in Alberta.[4] In their minor masterpiece, *None is Too Many,* Irving Abella and Harold Troper portrayed a wartime Canada rendered heartless, if not worse, by racial hierarchies, political machinations and callous bureaucrats.[5] Theirs is a book that has affected many Canadians, both Jewish and non-Jewish.

These books offer a rich harvest indeed. Many of them excel at revealing the explicit political struggles between Jewish communal groups and non-Jewish governmental agencies, as well as the organizational struggles within the Jewish community. We find less research, however, on the creation, maintenance and transformations of Canadian Jewish cultures. In this volume, we hope to encourage thinking along the latter lines. Some of the readings we have selected have received a fair bit of attention; others less so. What is new is our grouping of these articles, and the juxtapositions we have created within those categories.

Our own personal canonization of these materials has been informed by the insights of modern critical cultural studies. From the thicket of theoretical speculation in this area, we have untangled three useful strands. First, we understand that culture can be seen as the very anvil on which the crucial issues of our lives, such as relationships of power, are hammered out. Second, we work with the assumption that we develop meanings by challenging, negotiating and testing the meanings of others, and that it is important to identify various sites of conflict. And finally, we believe that there is much to be gained by having a broad notion of text, so that we use our tools of critical analysis not just for words on paper, but also for images and rituals, among other artifacts.

In less abstract terms, we have chosen categories and methods that will offer insight into the creation of Jewish communal identities in Canada. In our first section, we have brought together essays that suggest why Jews have had trouble accepting some of Canada's iconic figures. Could Canadian Jews accept as the source of inspiration a Goldwin Smith?[6] Or, in a very recent development, how would Jewish feminists treat a figure who fought for women's rights in Canada, but also penned an anti-Semitic letter?[7] These examples are less familiar parallels to the well-rehearsed controversy surrounding Lionel Groulx. Smith imagined a Canadian society that he thought would be better off without Jews, while Jews proffered their own heroes, who were either implicitly or explicitly a response to the exclusion of Jews. For Jews in Victorian Canada, Moses Montefiore was the counterexample, the famous English Jew who remained Jewish but who was benevolent towards all Englishmen.[8] Benjamin Sack, an early historian of Canadian Jewry, insisted on the heroic presence of Jews in the history of New France, even though there were no professing Jews in the colony, and thus challenged the exclusion of the Jew from the French Canadian nationalist foundation narrative.[9] Within the Jewish community, the promotion of certain figures could be an attempt to strengthen one subgroup's identity. Thus, Jews from North Africa now living in Montreal have fortified their own minority culture within a largely Ashkenazic and English Jewish community, by reviving the memories of saintly figures whose graves were pilgrimage sites.[10]

In subsequent chapters, we identify other arenas of cultural contest. Time is a scarce commodity: if used for one purpose, it cannot be used for another. Some Christians in the early twentieth century looked to inculcate or reinforce Christian values in Canada, and aimed to inscribe a mandatory Lord's Day on Sunday for the whole country. Within the Jewish community, rabbis looked to reinvigorate lax Sabbath observance. In the case of Rabbi Yudel Rosenberg of Montreal, this led to a form of literary experimentation.[11] Some Jews, looking to de-Judaize the Jewish community, aimed to subvert the observance of the holiest day of the Jewish year and announced a Yom Kippur Ball, as a kind of burlesque of religious observance.[12] The effort failed, and most Jews have brokered, in a less ideological fashion, their own Jewish calendar out of multiple attachments to work, recreation and religion. Furthermore, factions in the community have inscribed new days, to reflect new occasions, both joyous and mournful. Thus, we see Jews promoting Zionism by parading on Balfour Day, then Israeli Independence Day. For those on the left, May Day was also a day of parading, when Jews proudly identified themselves with signs in Yiddish or Hebrew, in addition to English. In the post-war period, Holocaust Commemoration Day (*Yom Hashoah*) observances have assumed a greater role in Jewish consciousness, although its rituals and liturgy are in flux. On the related matter of the Jewish life cycle—another cycle of Jewish time, in addition to the Jewish calendar—we also see significant developments, as the ritual of the wedding ring ceremony becomes one arena for defining and redefining gender roles.[13]

The Jewish attitude to place is complex. Jews have historically identified themselves as living in a diaspora. They are thus faced with a dual challenge: to mark their place in their new homeland while deciding whether they still believe in an *axis mundi*—or centre of the world—elsewhere. In his article in this collection, Etan Diamond shows how the modern Orthodox Jew attempted to sanctify suburban space in post-war Toronto. Throughout the Jewish presence in Canada, there are, of course, those who have viewed the synagogue as the sacred centre of the community. Many of the socialist secularists felt no attachment to the synagogue, and replaced it with a Jewish public library, or, as in the case of Miriam Waddington, a literary salon.

But Canada, for many Jews, was only one homeland. In traditional Jewish society, the longing for a return to Zion was a clear expression of the inseparable nature of traditional Jewish ethnoreligiosity. In the nineteenth century, however, some Jews excised this longing from their cultural repertoire and defined Jews as only a religious group, while other Jews proposed a modern Jewish nationalism through Zionism. Recent research has emphasized the non-verbal means of fostering a modern attachment to Zion. For example, photographs and films of the new Jewish pioneers in Palestine were used to create emotional and political solidarity between diaspora Jews and the Jewish settlements in Palestine. In this volume, we have included an analysis of community-sponsored trips to Israel, a recent transformation of the pilgrimage.[14] Some Jewish communists, who were anti-Zionist in orientation, looked to the Soviet Union for a solution and believed that the promise of an autonomous Jewish region there deserved support from Canadian Jews. This was a short-lived venture, but, like the Yom Kippur Balls, such rejected attempts to redefine the Jewish community highlight the dominant discourses within the community.

As an avalanche of recent research demonstrates, memory is a hotly contested subject. Several essays in this volume address the issue of the pliability of memory and the search for a usable past.[15] In the section dedicated to memory, we emphasize the active choice to encourage a kind of forgetting, as well as a graphic attempt by a historical society to revive what others insist should be forgotten.[16] Of all the contemporary challenges to memory, however, none looms as large as the Holocaust. In this *Reader*, Franklin Bialystok examines the rise of public memory of the Holocaust and the forces that have shaped it. In an illuminating case study, Barb Schober addresses problems related to commemoration, by analyzing reactions to both the content and medium of Arnold Belkin's representation of the Warsaw Ghetto uprising.

In the last section, we have chosen to focus on the Jewish engagement with the very Canadian question of cultural pluralism and multiculturalism. Pierre Anctil examines how A.M. Klein tried to understand French Canada on its own terms, in an attempt to create a more harmonious future. In two case studies, we bring together authors who show the potentially incendiary conflicts that may arise when ethnic groups have competing interests and claims.[17] In the final essay, Norman Ravvin addresses the issue of Matt Cohen's own complex relationship to being Jewish and being Canadian.

We have chosen to arrange this volume thematically, and not chronologically. Every era of the standard periodization of Canadian Jewish history is, however, represented, and it may be useful to review these eras as background. The first stratum consisted of Jews who were English in orientation. As late as 1881, their numbers did not amount to more than a few thousand, and they lived, by and large, in Montreal, Toronto, Hamilton, Victoria and a few other small settlements. The contribution of Moses Montefiore spoke to them most strongly.

Between 1881 and the mid-1920s, when the Canadian government essentially cut off immigration, waves of Jews from eastern Europe arrived in Canada. During this period, about eighty percent of Canadian Jews lived in Montreal, Toronto and Winnipeg. In the immigrant quarters, secular Jews battled against religious Jews (as exemplified in the extreme case of the Yom Kippur Balls), and the struggle between Zionists and anti-Zionists was largely a heated debate within the eastern European Jewish communities. Collectively, however, Jews had to fight a hardening of attitudes. Some Canadians sought to transform Canada into "His Dominion," which in fact meant Christianizing Canada. We can also trace an increasingly exclusivist language used to describe Canadian Jews, with the work of Goldwin Smith being but one example of this development.

After World War Two, the major waves of immigration consisted of Holocaust survivors, North African Jews, and more recently, Israelis and Russians. It took some time for the Canadian Jewish community to recognize the significance of the Holocaust and to allow the survivors to express their stories,[18] while North African Jews had to struggle to assert their identity in an Ashkenazic milieu. The period was characterized by a departure from the old neighbourhoods and the dramatic suburbanization of the community.[19] Canadian society looked to transform the old hostilities and reinvent itself as multicultural, which has presented both promise and challenges.

This is a rough chronology, but again, our main task is to look at the ways in which Jews have created meanings, and thus our thematic approach. A close reader will notice underdeveloped areas, and we are certainly aware of them. Lamentably, there is little published research on the Jews of Atlantic Canada, or on the Jewish communities west of Winnipeg. As a result, many of our readers in the east and west may agree with Eli Mandel's correspondent, who claimed that he had left out far too much. Work also needs to be done on the meanings of masculine and feminine within the Canadian Jewish community, thus we offer few explicit discussions on gender issues.

This *Reader* is clearly not a book of primary sources. We have made, however, one major exception. Photographs and other images are texts, therefore, they are not self-explanatory but require close analysis. With the illustrations included in this *Reader*, we have supplied analyses rather than short captions. In addition to the chapter introductions and the introductions to the individual articles, these photographs and captions are integral to the issues we wish to highlight in each chapter.

This *Reader* raises questions about one minority, with some emphasis on the struggles within that community. These inner struggles have often been hidden from the majority of historical writing, but we feel that they are integral to a deeper understanding of Canada. Even more directly, some of the articles included here discuss how Jews negotiated the majority cultures of English and French Canada, while others reflect on the implications of multiculturalism. We can learn a great deal about dominant cultures by studying their impact on minorities. If this collection engages more readers in the study of the Canadian Jewish experience, and therefore helps spark new research, then we will be very pleased indeed.

NOTES

1 Gerald Tulchinsky, *Taking Root: The Origins of the Canadian Jewish Community* (Toronto, 1992) and *Branching Out: The Transformation of the Canadian Jewish Community* (Toronto, 1998).

2 Morton Weinfeld, *Like Everyone Else . . . But Different: The Paradoxical Success of Canadian Jews* (Toronto, 2001).

3 Michael Greenstein, *Third Solitudes: Tradition and Discontinuity in Jewish-Canadian Literature* (Kingston, 1989).

4 Pierre Anctil, *Le rendez-vous manqué: les Juifs de Montréal de l'entre deux guerres* (Québec, 1988); Esther Delisle, *The Traitor and the Jew: Anti-semitism and Extreme Right-Wing Nationalism in Quebec from 1929 to 1939*, trans. by Madeleine Hébert et al, Montreal, 1993); Janine Stingel, *Social Discredit: Anti-Semitism, Social Credit and the Jewish Response* (Montreal, 2000).

5 Irving Abella and Harold Troper, *None is Too Many: Canada and the Jews of Europe, 1933–1948* (Toronto, 1982).

6 See Gerald Tulchinsky's article in this volume.

7 See Brenda Cossman and Marlee Kline.

8 See Michael Brown.

9   See Richard Menkis.

10   See Janice Rosen.

11   See Ira Robinson.

12   See Rebecca Margolis.

13   See Marlene Bonneau.

14   See Faydra L. Shapiro.

15   See articles by Menkis, and by Cossman and Kline.

16   See Norman Ravvin on Eli Mandel, as well as the illustration on page 278.

17   See articles by Harold Troper and Morton Weinfeld, and by Howard Adelman.

18   See articles by Frank Bialystok and by Barb Schober.

19   See Etan Diamond.

Heroes and Counterheroes

Some of the essays in this section address the lives and legacies of mainstream figures who proved problematic for Canadian Jews. Contrasting essays present examinations of cultural heroes that Canadian Jews sought out for themselves. The authors convey a strong sense of cultural divide between Jewish Canadians and their fellow citizens, and though they tend to focus on centuries- or decades-old issues, they help us understand how Jews and non-Jews view one another today. There is a wealth of material in this area, and one figure who has been explored in detail elsewhere is Lionel Groulx. A religious and intellectual leader, Groulx had an enormous impact on the French sense of national identity and culture before World War Two. However, his rightist and tribalist inclinations presented a foundation on which anti-Jewish rhetoric was supported. Today, a major Montreal metro station is named for this divisive figure. The cityscape, then, continues to be marked by a troubled narrative from the past.

Among the articles included here, the piece by Brenda Cossman and Marlee Kline parallels the Groulx narrative, but focuses on less familiar material. In 1992 the *Canadian Journal of Women and the Law* examined discussions aroused by Clara Brett Martin, a pioneer in Canadian legal history. Martin, in historian Constance Backhouse's words, was "the first white Protestant woman admitted to the profession of law in the then British Empire." This took place in 1897. Martin viewed her struggle for admission as a fight for women in general, and feminists saw much to admire in her. In 1989, however, a letter was discovered from Clara Brett Martin to the Attorney-General of Ontario, dated 1915, in which she complains bitterly about the shady behaviour of Jews in real estate, and calls on the government to take action. In the wake of a debate over whether a building should be named after her, a number of articles appeared in *Canadian Journal of Women and the Law*. Cossman and Kline's article examines and furthers this debate.

The other articles in this section take up a variety of important figures, as well as the fascinating subject of the role of Moroccan Jewish "saints" in the transplanted Moroccan Jewish community.

NR

Historiography, Myth and Group Relations: Jewish and Non-Jewish Québécois on Jews and New France

RICHARD MENKIS

In January 1947, Saul Hayes, the Executive Director of the Canadian Jewish Congress, forwarded a copy of B.G. Sack's *History of the Jews in Canada* as a gift to A. L. Jolliffe, the Director of the Immigration Branch of the federal government.[1] Hayes sent the book at a time when the Jewish community was valiantly attempting to pry open Canadian immigration gates for Jewish refugees, often in the face of resistance to these efforts from various quarters, including Jolliffe's department.[2] Hayes favoured quiet diplomacy over confrontation, and evidently hoped that Sack's book would be one small tool in improving the situation for the Jews by convincing Jolliffe and his department of the valuable contribution of the Jews to Canada.[3] Whatever may have been Jolliffe's reaction to the book—if he ever read it— Hayes's action does reveal that Sack's book could be called upon to serve the Jewish community.

Professional historians have often labelled historical writing such as Sack's filiopietism, ancestor-worship in the guise of history. While partly true, the comment is also unsatisfying, as filiopietism is a descriptive rather than analytical term. Analysis of historical writing can contribute to ethnic studies not only by demanding competent research and methodological rigor, but by analyzing the discourse of historical writing for what it tells of concerns far more general than any specific historical issue. This type of scrutiny has certainly been carried out by historians interested in the writing of majority history. A recent work has argued that early English-Canadian historical writing was motivated first by a desire to promote Canada in the eyes of the inhabitants of Great Britain, then a perceived need to foster a sense of national destiny which, in reaction, led to historians of various regions and causes to challenge these national historians.[4] Carl Berger has demonstrated how English-Canadian historical writing changed after World War I, when historians stressed Canada's autonomy over its imperial connections.[5] Historical writing in Quebec has attracted the attention of Serge Gagnon, who has illustrated that in the mid-twentieth century, Québécois historiography detached itself from the clerical moorings which had characterized it from the mid-nineteenth century. This transformation occurred both as a result of changes in the historical profession and the emergence of the non- (and anti-) clerical nationalism of the mid-twentieth century.[6]

Canadian Jewish historical writing has not received the equivalent critical analysis. Gerald Tulchinsky reviewed the historical literature of the late 1970s and early 1980s, and noted a greater degree of professionalism in recent Canadian Jewish historical writing than had previously been evident.[7] It was not, however, Tulchinsky's intention to analyze the earlier historical writing by placing it in its larger cultural context. In this essay, I shall analyze the historical treatment of the so-called first chapter of Jewish history in Canada, namely the relationship between Jews and New France, especially the role of the Gradis family of Bordeaux in provisioning New France before it fell. Sack's treatment of the issue, its incorporation by the Jewish community, and the response by non-Jewish Québécois historians, can tell us a great deal about cultural creativity, Jewish communal concerns, and the shifting image of the Jew in Quebec.

BENJAMIN SACK ON THE GRADIS FAMILY

Benjamin G. Sack (1889–1967) was born in Lithuania of an orthodox Jewish family. Shortly after his arrival in Montreal in 1905, he dedicated himself to Yiddish journalism, writing under a variety of pen names for newspapers in New York, Montreal as well as overseas, and dealing with a wide variety of themes. Sack was associated with the *Keneder Adler (The Jewish Daily Eagle)* from its first issue in 1907, served briefly as editor (1914–1916), but ultimately settled into the role of associate editor (1927–1957).[8] When not pressed with his heavy journalistic responsibilities—his editor-in-chief wondered how he found the time—Sack pursued his interest in Canadian Jewish history. The research of some twenty years culminated in the *History of the Jews in Canada,* first published in English in 1945. It was a pioneering study, gathering for the first time a large selection of primary sources, and offering a survey of Canadian Jewish history. This was a remarkable feat for a self-schooled man incapacitated from childhood with muscular dystrophy.[9] From at least the early 1920s, Sack was interested in the question of the presence of Jews in New France, especially in the Gradis family and its place in Canadian Jewish historiography.[10] He consulted with Benjamin Sulte in 1922, asking him for information about the Jews of New France, and shortly thereafter corresponded with historians in France specifically about the Gradises.[11] This interest culminated in two chapters devoted to the Gradises in his *History,* a rather generous allocation of space considering that no family member ever set foot on Canadian soil during the French regime.

The most significant Gradis for our purposes is Abraham Gradis (1695–1780), a Portuguese Jew whose predecessors had settled in Bordeaux in the second half of the seventeenth century, and who established themselves as shippers to the French colonies in the first decades of the eighteenth century. In 1728, Abraham's father, David, established the firm *David Gradis et fils,* and by the 1740s Abraham took control of the firm from his ailing father. It was Abraham who moved the firm into the trade with New France, most notably in the context of the *Société du Canada,* a partnership formed in 1748 between Gradis and two colonial officials, François Bigot, the intendant of New France, and the controller of the Marine, Jacques-Michel Bréard. Gradis also served as a major provisioner to New France in the last years before it fell, often in conjunction with colonial officials.[12] In the aftermath of the fall of New France, the French Crown set up a commission to investigate the participation of the colonial officials in this trade, more as a measure of finding scapegoats, rather than out of a concern about public officials engaged in private enterprise.[13] The firm *David Gradis et fils* had a selection of its commercial papers seized during this *Affaire du Canada,* and was ultimately held responsible for some of the debts which the commission determined Bigot and Bréard ought to pay the Crown, but the damage was controlled by the protection of the Minister of the Marine, the Duc de Choiseul.[14]

Sack was uncompromising in his depiction of Abraham Gradis as a patriotic Jew who risked all to help France protect its interests in New France. Sack treated the private partnership agreement between Gradis and Bigot and Bréard as a selfless attempt to maintain the shipping connection between France and New France.[15] He suggested that the *Société du Canada* could have succeeded in delaying the English conquest "had France been represented in Canada by officials other than Bigot and Bréard."[16] Sack treated the topic as if Gradis was the only merchant shipping to New France, and as if the Jewish merchant did not associate with these officials willingly. When the French Crown investigated Bigot, the historian claimed that Gradis "was invited by the Versailles government to testify against him," which he used as proof that "Gradis was extremely popular in government circles where great faith was placed in him."[17] This is certainly an unusual way to view the confiscation of the relevant commercial papers of *David Gradis et fils.*[18] In discussing Gradis's shipments in the years immediately before the fall of New France, Sack's prose is unbridled in its enthusiasm. For Sack, Abraham Gradis became the "right hand man" to Montcalm, the French general in charge of troops in New France at the end of the French regime, and Gradis provided the "sole support" that Montcalm would receive from France.[19]

This enthusiasm was, in part, inherited as previous historians of the Gradises had portrayed the family in a very favourable light. The earliest chroniclers of the Gradises were members of the family. In the nineteenth century, the head of the firm *David Gradis et fils,* Henri Gradis, published a variety of historical works and wrote an unpublished history of the Gradises. In the latter, he stressed the close connections of the family with colonial officials and the appreciation of the Crown towards the family, and minimized the humble origins of the Gradises, although he had access to this information in the Gradis archives.[20] This glowing self-portrayal found its way into other works. The great Jewish historian of the nineteenth century, Heinrich Graetz, was drawn to the history of the Gradis family, and published an article enthusiastically describing the achievements of its members.[21] Graetz relied heavily on notes sent to him by the aforementioned Henri Gradis,[22] although Graetz did not stress the high connections of the Gradises. Writing at a time when anti-Jewish animus was intensifying in an economically depressed Germany, particularly with respect to the claim that the Jews were threatening Germany with their supposedly corrupt commercial ethic,[23] Graetz emphasized the upright behaviour of the family, and ascribed its business success in large part to this rectitude.[24]

Historians primarily interested in the history of Bordeaux described the Gradis family in highly laudatory terms as well. In fact, one of the leading historians of Bordeaux, Camille Jullian, believing that the glory of Bordeaux lay in its many merchants,[25] attempted to convince Henri Gradis to write a detailed history of his family and its great services to the city and the Crown.[26] Jullian went so far as to claim that a family like the Gradises seemed to be more interested in the fate of France than the Crown itself.[27] This enthusiasm eventually affected the *Académie de Bordeaux,* which decided in 1910 to hold a contest for the best essay on the subject: *"Un grand armateur bordelais au XVIIIe siècle: Abraham Gradis."* It is likely that this contest inspired Jean de Maupassant to write his major biography of Abraham Gradis. While Maupassant made substantial contributions to the understanding of the Gradis family's arrangements with the Crown, and used documents from both the Gradis archives (albeit selectively) as well as other records, a strong apologetic motif persists in Maupassant's biography. He patently subscribed to Jullian's view of the majesty of the great merchant families of Bordeaux, and chose to end his biography by including Abraham Gradis in this group.[28] More specifically, Maupassant's discussion of the *Affaire du Canada* is apologetic, the major thesis being that Gradis was innocent of any offence.[29]

Sack, in his description of the Gradis family, absorbed the enthusiasm for the family of some of the historians described above, and for Sack, as for many popular historians, their authority constituted proof. He was in awe of Graetz, and assumed that his readers would be as well, and thus Sack noted in his *History* that many of the characteristic acts of generosity for which Gradis was known had already been noted by that German-Jewish historian.[30] Sack was, however, disappointed that one such act noted by Graetz in the German original of his *Geschichte* was not included in the English and Hebrew translations.[31] Sack also relied heavily on Maupassant's work, and corresponded with that author.[32] Maupassant in turn put Sack in touch with Raoul Gradis,[33] who was in charge of *David Gradis et fils* in the early twentieth century, and controlled the family archives. In a subsequent exchange, Raoul Gradis forwarded copies of selected documents from the Gradis collection, such as one that "showered Gradis with compliments" from a Minister of the Marine.[34]

Thus, either directly or indirectly, Sack was influenced by the apologetic tendencies of earlier historians. But Sack provided strong local colouring to the descriptions offered by others. His predecessors, especially Graetz, did not focus on New France, whereas Sack's primary interest was the contribution of the Jews to New France. Reasons for this interest derive, in part, from Sack's historical circumstances. Sack correctly sensed that a wall existed between Jews and French-Canadians. In the introduction to his *History*, Sack recounted how in his consultation with a leading French-Canadian historian of his time, Benjamin Sulte, on the issue of Jews during the French Regime, Sulte's response was *"Je ne me rappelle rien concernant les Juifs au Canada durant le régime français."*[35] Sack claimed that the reason for this ignorance was "not necessarily for an ulterior motive,"[36] a curious circumlocution. Not necessarily, but, it did seem to Sack that there was a strong likelihood that an ulterior motive could be found. Moreover, Sack perceived that antisemitism had increased in Quebec society during the depression and war years.[37] He had, in fact, co-authored a short article on hostility towards Jews in Quebec shortly before the publication of his *History*.[38]

Sack's emphasis on the presence of Jews in New France, and especially the activities of the Gradis family of Bordeaux, reflected his desire to challenge the mutual isolation of Jew and French-Canadian by elaborating on the myth of profound Jewish roots in French-Canadian society. This example of "the intellectual steeplechase to prove longevity in the land" is a commonplace in Jewish historiography and ethnic historiography in general.[39] But the location was new, with specific uses. The function of this myth in Quebec was to represent the Jewish community as a patriotic part of the French-Canadian community. Although few Jews ever set foot in New France (according to law, at least, non-Catholics were not permitted in New France),[40] by emphasizing Gradis's Jewishness and what Sack saw as the great contribution of the family to the defence of New France, Sack was implicitly claiming that Jews would have been good settlers if they could have come, as they even loved New France from a distance. By highlighting Gradis's connection with General Montcalm,[41] Sack also intended to prove that there was enthusiastic Jewish support for the French forces in the War of Conquest, a war with great symbolic value to the French-Canadians. Thus, rather than emphasize the fact that an organized Jewish community in Canada only began with the British conquest, Sack attempted to show that Jews were not aligned exclusively with the English. In fact, Sack rather downplayed the connection of the arrival of the first Jews with the British conquest, calling it simply a "sort of by-product of the struggle for the country."[42]

But Sack was not cynical, and did not believe that dropping the walls between Jews and Québécois would prove only the value of the Jews to French-Canadians. Sack evinced true respect for Quebec's resilience in the face of the English challenge, and called upon other Jews to respect it. In the introduction to his *History,* Sack reminds his readership that after Lord Durham's report, the population of Quebec responded nobly by focussing on their history.

> Over a century ago Lord Durham, in his famous Report on conditions in Canada, referred rather disparagingly to the history of the French-Canadians. The latter rightly regarded his remarks as an insult which to this day has not been forgiven him. But their national pride has reacted constructively as well: it has found expression in the work of a series of prolific historians who, beginning with Francois [sic]-X. Garneau, have with love and earnest care put together the monument of their recorded national

history. No people has shown greater sincerity or painstak-
ing vigor in bringing to light the story of its past.[43]

Sack was thus one of a small group of Jewish intellectuals who tried to understand the French-Canadians on their own terms. Another example from the middle of the 1940s was A.M. Klein, who composed poems depicting French Canada. As was the case with Klein, if Sack could not always grasp the deeper cultural concerns of French Canada, he was at least one of the few to attempt to bridge the isolation between Jewish and non-Jewish Québécois. Sack, like Klein, combined respect for the culture of French-Canadians with a desire to improve social relations.[44]

Sack made this appeal not just in his written work, but in actual contacts with French-Canadians. In the late 1930s and early 1940s, H.M. Caiserman, the Executive Director of the Canadian Jewish Congress, believed that the only way to improve relations between French-Canadians and Jews was by direct dealings between the two, either by correspondence or by meetings. At a time when Jews and French-Canadians rarely met face-to-face, a meeting of the Canadian Jewish Historical Society was convened in February 1944, and among those who attended as "special guests" was Léon Trépanier, a past president of the nationalistic *Société Saint-Jean Baptiste* and a journalist who had earlier in the century published pieces with an antisemitic slant.[45] On that occasion, Sack's paper on Gradis's relationship with Montcalm was read, and while the exact talk has not been preserved, the minutes of the meeting indicate that Sack emphasized the great services that Gradis rendered to Montcalm, and the General's appreciation.[46]

The integrationist apologetic of Sack certainly provided raw material for the self-portrayal of a Jewish community anxious for contact with non-Jewish Québécois, as was the case with Klein's "French-Canadian" poetry.[47] As noted above, the Canadian Jewish Congress made political use of Sack's work in the immediate post-war period, when Jews were arguing for a loosening of the immigration quotas.[48] In 1959, the Jewish community was faced with the ideologically similar, if less harrowing, problem of how to celebrate the bicentennial of the settlement of Jews in Canada, without associating itself with the Conquest. As the Executive Director of the National Joint Public Relations

Committee of the Canadian Jewish Congress wrote to his chairman in 1958, in anticipation of the problem:

> The bicentenary of the Jewish settlement in Canada is to be marked in 1959. As you know, Congress will have its Plenary session at that time and a committee has been set up to plan bicentenary celebrations and events throughout Canada. A factor that is of the utmost importance to the Jewish community of the Province of Quebec is the somewhat embarrassing coincidence that the settlement of the Jews in Canada coincides with what to us in Ontario is the coming of the British, but in Quebec is equated to the conquest or subjugation of the French. *Although Jews were not tolerated in New France* . . . to stress the identification of Jewish settlement in Canada with the British conquest, would tend to underline the role of the Jews as those who accompanied the foreign invader.
>
> . . . My thinking on this . . . is that the events of 1759 need not be the focal centre of attention in the bi-centenary. There are certainly enough milestones in the 200 year period which can be dwelt upon quite aside from the Plains of Abraham and its accompanying events . . . . In any case, it is our feeling that these considerations can be overcome with some planning and do not warrant the cancellation of the whole project.[49]

Among the materials distributed at the Plenary was an outline of Canadian Jewish history published by the National Bicentenary Commission of the Canadian Jewish Congress.[50] In this pamphlet, the Conquest by the British received scarcely any mention, but the role of Abraham Gradis is mentioned four times in the fifteen years before the Conquest. The author of the chronology was clearly inspired by Sack's view of the relations between Montcalm and Gradis, and thus made a long separate entry for the date 9 June 1757, when the

General received provisions from the ships of *David Gradis et fils*. The apologetic message rings clear at the end of this entry:

> Although the Gradis Family did much to stimulate trade between France and Quebec, and helped to maintain and defend the French Colonists in Canada, it was not possible for any Huguenot or Jew to make his home in New France until 1759, when the rule of the King of France in Canada came to an end.[51]

HISTORIANS OF QUEBEC RESPOND

When Sack decided to express his views on the Gradises, and concomitantly, on the last years of New France, the Jewish historian entered into an emotionally charged fray with many partisans and a forum of excitable observers. Sack's portrayal of the Gradises was not accepted by French-Canadian scholars with enthusiasm. Two works stand out for their discussion of the Gradises; first, the biography of one of Abraham Gradis's business partners, François Bigot, by Guy Frégault, a leading French-Canadian historian and intellectual of the mid-twentieth century; the other, a monograph devoted to the study of the Jews and New France by Denis Vaugeois, who held political office during the reign of the Parti Québécois in Quebec.

Frégault's work is characterized by a thoroughness of research, although he was hampered by his scrutiny of copies of documents at the Public Archives in Ottawa, rather than the French originals. But the most important flaws in the work had little to do with the documentary evidence. While Frégault occasionally was willing to admit that blaming Bigot for the fall of New France is an exaggeration,[52] Frégault ultimately used strong language to portray Bigot as a powerful villain. Frégault distrusted Bigot partly because he was a metropolitan official, who, like most others in Versailles or those sent to Quebec, did not consider "*le Canada comme une nation . . . à leurs yeux, le Canada n'est qu'une colonie.*"[53] In fact, for Frégault, Bigot became the very embodiment of the evils of the metropolitan regime. While writing the work on Bigot, Frégault was under the influence of a vision of history that placed great emphasis on the personalities in history. Frégault's early mentor, Lionel Groulx, emphasized the heroes of New France. Frégault continued with the biographical approach, but added what one reviewer of historical writing on New France has justly labeled an obsession with anti-heroes.[54] Moreover, although Frégault did not adopt uncritically all that Groulx said, he did believe that the society of New France was one founded on the family and the parish,[55] and was rather disdainful of the spirit of enterprise and businessmen.

Associated with these problems of bias was another: historical context. Although distrusting French metropolitan politics, Frégault evinced little suspicion that metropolitan justice might be self-serving.[56] Did eighteenth-century France have a developed sense of conflict of interest, and did Bigot violate any clearly defined guidelines? Is the timing of the commission not somewhat suspicious, since there were reports about Bigot's activities while still in office, but nothing was done to remove him from it?[57] In the drive to portray Bigot as a villain, Frégault ignored the two important contexts of French administrative practice and the nature of eighteenth-century justice, as he himself realized later.[58]

In part, Frégault's portrayal of Gradis reflected his disdain of metropolitan figures, and he mocked all those who attempted to portray Gradis in heroic terms. He called the Maupassant work too sympathetic because of his love of Bordeaux and the pressures of the family. Frégault was deeply suspicious of the panegyric of an editor of the Gradis letters, and bluntly accused Sack of "*vanité raciale*" in writing fantasies about Gradis,[59] not at all understanding the reasons behind Sack's apologetic. To Frégault, Gradis was intimately involved in all the activities of the Bigot group in New France, and as such was a rapacious merchant aligned with rapacious administrators.

By the time Frégault had published his work on Bigot, Québécois historiography was changing. Historians were divorcing themselves from the idealization of New France as clerical, rural, and conservative, and looking at issues such as the class structure of early French Canada, an historiographic shift that reflected the transformation of the concerns of Québécois intellectuals in general. In fact, by 1955 Frégault would also become a leading exponent of this new school, and a marked difference can be noted in his discussion of Bigot. He no longer viewed the intendant as the embodiment of all that was evil. Instead, Frégault saw Bigot as belonging to an oligarchy of government officials and businessmen that could also be found in other colonial administrations.[60] Although Frégault still believed that Bigot was rapacious, the historian argued that Bigot and his group could hardly be considered responsible for the downfall of New France,[61] and that the intendant was a scapegoat for the Minister of the Marine in France.[62] There is also a transformation in Frégault's analysis of Abraham Gradis's relations with New France, insofar as the latter is mentioned. The historian only alluded to the merchant's involvement in the Canada trade in the context of the competition for business with other merchants of Bordeaux, and the profits that accrued from this business.[63] Nor did Frégault refer to Gradis's Jewishness, an implicit argument that the issue was of no intrinsic significance.[64]

While Frégault revealed little systematic interest in the "Jewish aspect" of the fall of New France, Denis Vaugeois took up the issue explicitly in his *Les Juifs et la Nouvelle-France,* based on his graduate thesis at Laval.[65] Vaugeois went to several of the archival collections that could throw light on the participation of the Gradises in the commerce to New France, including the *Archives départementales de la Gironde* in Bordeaux, and he spent some time in the private archives of the Gradis family.[66] But more significant in determining his outlook than these primary sources was his historiographical model. Vaugeois was influenced by Frégault in the manner that Sack was swayed by Graetz; his authority constituted proof.[67] Vaugeois, however, was influenced by Frégault's earlier outlook on Bigot. While superficially entertaining the possibility that the intendant was a scapegoat for the French Crown, Vaugeois worked with the assumption that Bigot and his clan were guilty of corruption, not questioning seriously the motives of the Crown in the *Affaire du Canada.* Vaugeois believed that even if these colonial officials were not responsible for the fall of New France, "*ils ont été étroitement associés à la défaite française et ils l'ont certes rendue plus tragique encore.*"[68]

Unlike Frégault, however, Vaugeois's focus was on the history of the Jews, and he devoted several chapters to Abraham Gradis. Vaugeois attempted to establish that the merchant should hardly be considered the lover of New France as portrayed by Sack and others. Some of Vaugeois's arguments are factually correct. He discovered a financial link between Gradis and Bigot after the latter had been banished from France,[69] and thus successfully challenged the views of Maupassant and Sack, which downplayed the bonds between Gradis and Bigot. Vaugeois's inferences from these facts, however, are questionable. He saw the financial link as proof that Gradis promised to reward Bigot if the latter did not implicate the Jewish merchant in the *Affaire du Canada*.[70] The financial arrangement was made by a Reynack, and Vaugeois highlights at this point that this man's father "*était issu d'une famille juive de Suisse,*"[71] and he thus appears as an *iudaeus ex machina* to link the corrupt Bigot with his Jewish banker.

Vaugeois's *Les Juifs et la Nouvelle-France* betrays an unresolved tension. On the one hand, Vaugeois was engaged in an effort to confront antisemitism, particularly the antisemitism that feared the "international connections" of the Jew.[72] After writing a chapter on Gradis, Vaugeois described the activities of the Franks family, Jewish merchants from England who provisioned the English troops during the Seven Years War. Vaugeois expressed concern that this section of his work could provide ammunition for antisemites who believed that Jews were behind all wars, or interpreted it as proof that international Jewry and freemasonry were at work.[73] (On this point Vaugeois was, incidentally, correct, as in the same year that Vaugeois submitted his M.A. thesis to Laval, the newsletter of the antisemitic radical right in Quebec published a four-page article on the Gradises, blaming Abraham Gradis for the fall of New France.[74]) Vaugeois recognized that antisemitism had deep roots, and pointed out that the antisemites had produced "*ouvrages étonnants de recherche et de popularité,*" and in revealing some of his own preconceptions, argued that this antisemitism "*trouve facilement sa nourriture dans l'activité inlassable des Juifs de la Diaspora.*" He assured his readers, however, that it was simply as merchants that the Jews had profited from the events surrounding the war, and that there were probably Jews who went bankrupt at the same time. He also informed his readers that there was no reason to think the Jews were responsible for provoking the war.[75]

While Vaugeois was trying to force his readership to reject antisemitic myths, he made other curious remarks. He pointed out that there was, of course, no relationship of cause and effect between the Jews and the War of Conquest, but he did add that the Franks family did provision the English troops, "*tandis que les Gradis, bien involontairement certes, favorisaient aussi une victoire anglaise par leur complicité avec le clan Bigot.*"[76] If Vaugeois were truly anxious to reject antisemitic interpretations, he would not have suggested, even mildly, that Jews on the French side facilitated English victory. It would appear from this inconsistency that Vaugeois had taken on the antisemitic myth of the international control of finance by the Jews as a working hypothesis for approaching the topic, a hypothesis that he rejected but which retained residual force in his thinking.[77] This hypothesis tells very little about the eighteenth century; it speaks eloquently, however, about inherited myths regarding the Jews, and the process of dismantling them in mid-twentieth century Quebec.[78]

If Vaugeois's inconsistency on the issue indicated a transitional point in antisemitic attitudes, a more recent work reveals that a rapprochement may be taking place. In 1986, a history of the relations between Jewish and French Québécois appeared, with the subtitle "200 *ans d'histoire commune,*" jointly authored by a priest, Jacques Langlais, and David Rome, a Jew who has been active in Jewish communal affairs in Montreal from the early 1940s.[79] An intense ecumenical spirit animates the book, and the section on the Gradises reflects this. While wisely acknowledging that Abraham Gradis was motivated, in part, by commercial interests, the authors focus on the apparent patriotism of Gradis. The position of Sack is largely assumed, and the latter is cited favourably as suggesting that the great investment of the Gradises in New France prolonged the reign of France in Canada. In attempting to explain why Gradis's enormous contribution was not known among "*Français canadiens*"—evidently thereby preventing an early opportunity for French-Jewish rapprochement—Langlais and Rome explain that Bigot "*détournait à son profit les arrivages de Bordeaux.*"[80]

CONCLUSION

The myth of Abraham Gradis in Canada had its parallel in English Canada. For the Jews of twentieth-century Toronto, the culture of the elite was Anglo-Saxon, which proffered a different set of cultural roots—and prejudices—from those in French Canada. A patrician of twentieth-century Toronto Jewry, Sigmund Samuel, began his autobiography by arguing that which is impossible to prove; that members of his family lived in England before the expulsion of the Jews in 1290, and that one branch of the family may even have been allowed to stay after that royal decree![81] Even more blatant is an American example, where arriving on the Mayflower was not good enough. In the late nineteenth century, the wealthy American Jew, Oscar Straus, approached the Jewish historian, Meyer Kayserling, with the request that he explore the notion that the discoverers of America included a number of Jews, as Straus sensed that "this fact would be an answer for all times to come to antisemitic tendencies in this country."[82]

The depictions of Abraham Gradis in Canada have had little to do with his historical context, and thus shed very little relevant light on the eighteenth century. This frenetic search for deep roots in the immigrant's country has all too frequently diverted the energy and attention of ethnic historians from more important issues, as Roberto Perin has cogently argued.[83] In the case of Canadian Jewry, for example, the proper background for Canadian Jewish history rests more in the historical experiences of the Jews in England, central and eastern Europe, and more recently North Africa, than in the presence—and in our case, the nonpresence—of some early settlers. But as a touchstone for analyzing the insecurities surrounding the social integration of a minority, and the receptivity of the majority to minority aspirations, the marginal issue (from the point of view of Canadian Jewish history, that is) of the Gradises becomes the primary source, and the historiographer a cultural and social historian.

Notes

1   National Archives of Canada, Records of the Immigration Branch, RG 76, vol. 391, file 541782, pt. 6, A.L. Jolliffe to Saul Hayes, 23 January 1947, acknowledging the latter's letter and gift of 13 January 1947. The full title of the work is Benjamin G. Sack, *History of the Jews in Canada: From the Earliest Beginnings to the Present Day. Volume One: From the French Regime to the End of the Nineteenth Century* (Montreal, 1945). The work was translated by Ralph Novek: The Yiddish original appeared in print three years after the translation.

2   The story of the attempt to loosen immigration quotas, and the resistance of the Immigration Branch, has received authoritative treatment in Irving Abella and Harold Troper, *None is too Many: Canada and the Jews of Europe, 1933–1948* (Toronto, 1982). On the postwar period, see chapters 7 and 8.

3   Ibid., pp. 210–211 on Jolliffe and Hayes.

4   M. Brook Taylor, *Promoters, Patriots and Partisans: Historiography in Nineteenth Century English Canada* (Toronto, Buffalo and London, 1989).

5   Carl Berger. *The Writing of Canadian History: Aspects of English-Canadian Historical Writing, 1900–1970* (Toronto, 1976).

6   Serge Gagnon, *Quebec and its Historians,* trans. Jane Brierly (Montreal, 1985), esp. pp. 165–166.

7   Gerald Tulchinsky, "Recent Developments in Canadian Jewish Historiography," *Canadian Ethnic Studies* 14, 2 (1982): 114–125. Harold Troper and Morton Weinfeld discuss the conflicting historical memories of Jews and Ukrainians in Canada as pertain to their respective European experiences in *Old Wounds: Jews, Ukrainians and the Hunt for Nazi War Criminals in Canada* (Markham, 1988), especially pp. 1–24.

8   On Sack, see Saul Hayes, "Benjamin Gutl Sack," preface to *Canadian Jews—Early this Century* by Benjamin G. Sack (Montreal, 1975), unpaginated. This is the posthumous second volume of Sack's history. Hayes drew extensively on Sack's unpublished autobiographical notes "Sack, Benjamin Gutman, son of (Iseah [*sic*] Lipe) Journalist," B.G. Sack Papers, Canadian Jewish Congress, National Archives, Montreal (hereafter CJC-M). See also the two notes on Sack, by Ch. L. Fox and Yoseph Gala, in Ch. L. Fox, ed., 100 *Years of Yiddish and Hebrew Literature in Canada* (Montreal, 1980), pp. 118–121 (in Yiddish) and Yaacov Zipper, "B.G. Sack (1889-1967)," *Canadian Jewish Anthology/Anthologie juive canadienne,* ed. Chaim Spilberg and Yaacov Zipper (Montreal, 1982), pp. 490–496 (in Yiddish). On the *Adler,* see Jean Hamelin et André Beaulieu, eds., *La presse québécoise des origines à nos jours* 8 vols. to date (Quebec, 1973–), 4:253–256, and more recently the excessively brief description in Lewis Levendel, *A Century of the Canadian Jewish Press* (Ottawa, 1989), pp. 17–22.

9   Hayes, "Sack."

10 Among the articles published by Sack, Benjamin G. Sack, "The Society of Canada, Founded by a Jew 180 Years Ago," *Canadian Jewish Chronicle,* 14 September 1928, also published in Yiddish in the *Jewish Daily Eagle* and the *Israelite Press* of Winnipeg; "Les Juifs durant le régime français," *Jewish Daily Eagle Jubilee Edition* (Montreal, 1932) and "The Jew who once helped to Defend Canada," *Jewish Daily Eagle*, 20 September 1933 (in Yiddish), and a variation in "A Jew, defender of French Canada" *Canadian Jewish Chronicle*, 30 October 1933. See also below for a discussion of his correspondents.

11 See below.

12 On the Gradis family and the *société du Canada,* see Jean de Maupassant, *Un grand armateur de Bordeaux: Abraham Gradis (1699?–1780)* (Bordeaux, 1931). pp. 38–44: 52–118, esp. pp. 113–118 on the *affaire du Canada.* This is the second edition of the work, identical to the first edition of 1917 except for the addition of several articles on Gradis, which Maupassant wrote before he published the biography of Abraham. The biography itself was originally published in the *Revue historique de Bordeaux* 6 (1913) and 7 (1914). See also Guy Frégault, *François Bigot, Administrateur français.* 2 vols. (Montréal, 1948) and more recently Richard Menkis. "Patriarchs and Patricians: The Gradis Family of Eighteenth-Century Bordeaux," in *From East and West: Profiles of Jews in a Changing Europe, 1750–1870,* ed. Frances Malino and David Sorkin (Oxford and

Cambridge, MA., 1990), pp. 11–45 for biographical information and "The Gradis Family of Eighteenth Century Bordeaux: A Social and Economic Study," (unpublished Ph.D. dissertation, Brandeis University, 1988), pp. 178–245 for a discussion of the commercial ties with New France.

13   See the two excellent articles by J.F. Bosher, "Government and Private Interests in New France," *Canadian Public Administration* 10 (1967): 244–257, and "The French government's motives in the *Affaire du Canada, 1761–1763*," *English Historical Review* 96 (1981): 59–78, and, more recently, his monograph *The Canada Merchants, 1713–1763* (Oxford, 1987).

14   Menkis, 'The Gradis Family," pp. 178–179 and pp. 244–245.

15   Sack, *Jews in Canada*, p. 29.

16   Ibid.

17   Ibid., p. 27.

18   Sack would have known that this was a confiscation of papers from Maupassant, *Gradis*, pp. 180–182.

19   Ibid., p. 39.

20   Henri Gradis, "Notice sur la Famille Gradis et sur la maison Gradis et fils de Bordeaux," is preserved in the Private Archives of the Gradis Family, Box 31, file 354. The organizer of the catalogued section of the Gradis archives also emphasized the "great deeds" of the Gradises, and their connections with high-ranking officials in the French bureaucracy.

21   Heinrich Graetz, "Die Familie Gradis," *Monatsschrift für Geschichte und Wissenschaft des Judentums* (hereafter *MGWJ*) 24 (1875): 447–459; 25 (1876): 78–85.

22   Graetz, "Die Familie Gradis," *MGWJ* 24 (1875): 447. The connection between Graetz and the Gradis family was probably through Hippolyte Rodrigues, whom Graetz acknowledges as his friend in the article itself, "Die Familie Gradis," *MGWJ* 25 (1876): 84. Rodrigues was a relative of Henri Gradis, and a friend of Graetz's associate, Moses Hess. There are many references to Rodrigues in the correspondence of Graetz with Moses Hess. See Heinrich Graetz, *Tagebuche und Briefe*, ed. Reuven Michael (Tübingen, 1977).

23   On the growing hostility, see Fritz Stern, *Gold and Iron: Bismarck, Bleichröder and the Building of the German Empire* (New York, 1977), pp. 501–502, and Jacob Katz, *From Prejudice to Destruction: Anti-Semitism, 1700–1933* (Cambridge, MA., 1980), pp. 249–252.

24   Graetz, "Gradis," *MGWJ* 24 (1875): 447: "[Die Familie Gradis] verdankte ihre Blüthe nicht blos dem Zufall, sondern dem hoen Sinne, der Energie, der strengen Rechtlichkeit und ganz besonders auch dem innigen Zusammenhang ihrer Glieder..."

25   Camille Jullian, Preface to Maupassant, *Abraham Gradis,* pp. vi–vii.

26   See his comments in Ibid., p: viii:

> Je crois bien que j'aurais décidé à la fin Henri Gradis à écrire les annales de sa famille, qui, par les huit générations de travailleurs fournis à Bordeaux, par la grandeur des services rendus à la cité et à la patrie dans les temps de crise, doit être mise au premier plan de l'histoire, je dis de

l'histoire de la ville et l'histoire de la nation. Mais Henri Gradis n'eut pas eu le temps de réaliser ce rêve. Il n'a pu que réunir de précieuses notes.

27 Camille Jullian, *Histoire de Bordeaux* (Bordeaux, 1895), p. 542: "*la maison Gradis parut protéger la France plus que la Royauté elle-même.*" This is a phrase that has been repeated by subsequent historians.

28 Maupassant, *Gradis*, p. 165, in the closing remarks to the volume:

Nous ne voyons pas que les plus célèbres négociants de Bordeaux au temps de sa splendeur, Bethmann, Jauge, Nairac, Bonnaffé ou les frères Raba, présentent de pareils titres au souvenir de leurs compatriotes, et l'on peut dire d'Abraham Gradis qu'il ne fut pas seulement l'une des gloires de notre ville, un "bon et vertueux citoyen", comme l'écrit Choiseul, mais aussi l'une des personnalitiés de son siècle.

29 Ibid., pp. 113–118.

30 Ibid., p. 40, n. 2 and p. 41.

31 Ibid., p. 41, n. 2.

32 Maupassant to Sack, 22 January 1924, B.G. Sack Papers.

33 Raoul Gradis to Sack, 10 April 1924, B.G. Sack Papers, and Sack, *Jews in Canada*, p. v.

34 Ibid., p. 40.

35 Cited in Sack, *Jews in Canada*, p. xvi.

36 Ibid. I did not find the letter in the Sack papers, but the letter was sent on 29 June 1922. A copy of the letter was read at a meeting of the Canadian Jewish Historical Society on 8 February 1944. The minutes of that meeting have been preserved in the uncatalogued papers of B.G. Sack.

37 On the interwar period, see Pierre Anctil, *Le rendez-vous manqué: les Juifs de Montréal face au Québec de l'entre-deux guerres* (Québec, 1988). On the antisemitism of the radical right during this period, see Lita-Rose Betcherman, *The Swastika and the Maple Leaf: Fascist Movements in Canada in the Early Thirties* (Toronto, 1975).

38 See the *Universal Jewish Encyclopedia,* s.v. "Quebec," by Louis Rosenberg and Benjamin G. Sack, where the authors refer explicitly to the increase in antisemitism in Quebec. The encyclopedia was published in 1943, and the article included information on that same year.

39 The quote is from Robert F. Harney, " 'So Great a Heritage as Ours': Immigration and the Survival of the Canadian Polity," *Daedalus* 17,4 (Fall, 1988): 81, who refers briefly to the phenomenon in ethnic historiography in Canada. For some earlier examples in Jewish historiography, see Joseph Shatzmiller, "Politics and the myths of Origins: the case of the Medieval Jews," *Les Juifs au regard de l 'histoire. Mélanges en l'honneur de Bernhard Blumenkranz* (Paris, 1985), pp. 49–61, especially the literature cited on p. 60 nn. 45–46. Mordecai Richler's novel, *Solomon Gursky was Here* (Markham, 1989) portrays and mocks the fabrication of lineage in Canada; see especially p. 187 and pp. 226–7. See also below, n. 80 and n. 81. For a searing attack on filiopietism in general, and the "whitewashing" of Canadian Jewish biographies, see Richler's review of Stuart

Rosenberg's *Jewish Community in Canada,* reprinted in Mordecai Richler, *Shovelling Trouble* (London, 1973), pp. 143–148, especially pp. 145–146 as background for *Gursky.*

40 The *de iure* and *de facto* statuses of Jews and Protestants in French colonies are as complex as the Bourbon legal system and administration from which they derive. For a useful synthesis, see Cornelius J. Jaenen, "The Persistence of the Protestant Presence in New France," *Proceedings of the Meeting of the Western Society for French History* 2 (1974): 29–40. I have attempted to evaluate the meaning of these restrictions for the Jews in "Antisemitism and Anti-Judaism in pre-Confederation Canada," (unpublished paper), with full references.

41 Sack, *Jews in Canada,* chapter 3. Sack had published a short note on the topic, "Abraham Gradis and General Montcalm," *YIVO Bleter* 15 (1940): 134–139 (in Yiddish).

42 Sack, *Jews in Canada,* p. 50.

43 Ibid., p. iii.

44 Pierre Anctil, "A.M. Klein: du poète et de ses rapports avec le Québec français," *Revue d'études canadiennes/Journal of Canadian Studies* 19,2 (Summer, 1984); 118 emphasizes both these motivations; the respect for the other with a similar concern for "survival" and the attempt to approach Francophones in Quebec.

45 Jacques Langlais et David Rome, *Juifs et québécois français: 200 ans d'histoire commune* (Montréal, 1986), p. 110. After that meeting, Trépanier was challenged by a Jewish woman to explain why hatred of Jews was so prevalent in Quebec. CJC-M, DA 1 Box 3, File 40, Trépanier to H.M. Caiserman, 13 March 1944. In a private letter, David Rome of the Canadian Jewish Congress listed Trépanier among those "prominent vicious anti-Semites who later dramatically and publicly and profoundly converted and became militant friends of the Jewish people." CJC-M, ZB "Vaugeois, Denis," David Rome to Zvi Loker, 6 July 1979.

46 Minutes of Canadian Jewish Historical Society, meeting of 8 February 1944, B.G. Sack collection, CJC-M. Although Sack was present at the meeting, he did not deliver the paper, perhaps because of his physical ailment. The talk was based on his short article in the *YIVO Bleter,* see above n. 41.

47 Anctil, "A.M. Klein: du poète et de ses rapports avec le Québec français," pp. 119–121.

48 Hayes, "Sack."

49 Toronto Jewish Congress/Canadian Jewish Congress, Ontario Regional Archives. F.M. Catzman papers, uncatalogued collection, B.G. Kayfetz [Executive Director of JPRC] to F.M. Catzman [Chairman of JPRC], 14 February 1958.

50 Louis Rosenberg, *Chronology of Canadian Jewish History* (n.p., n.d.). Although undated, this pamphlet was certainly published in 1959, the year of the Plenary.

51 Ibid., p. 2.

52 Frégault, *Bigot,* 1: 391–392.

53 Ibid., p. 394.

54 Jean Blain, "Économie et société en Nouvelle-France," *Revue d'histoire de l'Amérique française* 28,2 (Sept., 1974): 175.

55 Yves F. Zoltvany, *The Government of New France: Royal Clerical or Class Rule?* (Scarborough, Ont., 1971), pp. 70–75, p. 91.

56 It was a hypothesis that had already been raised, as Frégault acknowledged in the introduction to *Bigot*, 1: 36–37, but which he did not, in the end, accept.

57 Although not the first to raise these questions, they have been recently explored with great insight by J.F. Bosher in the two articles and the book listed above, n. 13.

58 See below.

59 Frégault, *Bigot*, 1: 285–286, n. 10.

60 Guy Frégault, *Canada; the War of the Conquest,* trans. Margaret M. Cameron (Toronto, 1969), especially pp. 33–34. The book was originally published in French in 1955 as *La Guerre de la conquête.* The argument voiced in a nascent form here was elaborated by another leading historian of the new approach to the history of New France, Michel Brunet, who stated about Bigot and the group around him that "These men, who have been so maligned, were also great businessmen, similar to those who built the capitalist economies of all the western countries. If the conquest of the colony and the defeat of France had not brutally put an end to the career of these rich Canadian capitalists, their names would to-day rank with our great men." The quote is taken from Michel Brunet, *La Présence anglaise et les Canadiens* (Montréal, 1958). as translated in Zoltvany, *The Government of New France,* pp. 91–92.

61 *Frégault, War of the Conquest,* pp. 30–31.

62 Ibid., p. 234.

63 Ibid., p. 240 and p. 325. Some of the acid tone of the Bigot volume is retained; see, for example, from the latter reference: "The 'sacrifice' of Canada touched these citizens [the merchants of Bordeaux] to the bottom of their cash boxes."

64 In 1973, Frégault delivered a paper to the Institut Canadien on Bigot, where he stated explicitly that he would reword the conclusion of his biography to minimize the uniqueness of Bigot, ("Il y a 25 ans, je concluais ainsi ma biographie de Bigot: 'Le dernier intendant du Canada participe à l'avilissement de son siècle.' Aujourd'hui . . . j'écrirais: 'Bigot, en son temps, participa à la médiocrité de son milieu.'") Frégault also stated unambiguously that he viewed the Bigot–Gradis association as "un épisode normal de la vie administrative." University of Ottawa, Centre for Research on French Canadian Culture, P168/2 Boîte 13, "François Bigot intendant de la Nouvelle-France, Allocution de M. Frégault le 24 septembre 1973, à l'Institut Canadien," p. 8 and pp. 20–21.

65 Denis Vaugeois, *Les Juifs et la Nouvelle-France* (Trois-Rivières, 1968), based on his "Les Juifs et la guerre de Sept Ans (1756–1763)," (Thesis for Diplôme d'études supérieures en histoire, Université Laval, 1967).

66 Vaugeois, *Les Juifs et la Nouvelle-France,* p. 18. It is, however, unclear what he exactly viewed in the Gradis collection, as he does not cite a single document from it.

67 In discussing the partnership document of 1748 founding the *Société du Canada*, rather than describe it from the primary source, a copy of which he cites from the collection of documents on the Bibliothèque nationale, and which was also published from the

Gradis collection in Maupassant, *Gradis*, pp. 167–169, Vaugeois quotes Frégault's summary of it. Ibid., pp. 67–68.

68 Ibid., p. 77.

69 Ibid., p. 82.

70 Ibid., p. 78–82. If there were any protection to be had, it undoubtedly would have come from the Minister of the Marine, Choiseul. Vaugeois does not even mention his name.

71 Ibid., p. 78. The evidence of Reinach's Jewishness—even that he came from a Jewish family—is flimsy. Frégault referred to it in his *Bigot.* 1: 67, n. 97, but Vaugeois has taken it one step further by emphasizing Reinach's Jewishness in the context of the events of the *affaire du Canada*.

72 In fact, Vaugeois studied at the Hebrew Union College in Cincinnati in the 1960s and seems to have had pleasant contact with Jacob R. Marcus. See "avant-propos" to ibid., and the apology he offers for Marcus's explanation of the Gradis family in a manner similar to Sack, ibid., pp. 64–65. The book is also dedicated to "deux amis juifs."

73 Ibid., pp. 103–104.

74 Antoine de Longual, "Une page de notre histoire," *Serviam* 2,5 (avril–mai, 1967): 5–8. The newsletter reflected the views of its editor, Adrien Arcand, the most influential fascist in Canada in the 1930s, who was interned during World War II. On Arcand, see Betcherman, *The Swastika and the Maple Leaf,* passim.

75 Vaugeois, *Les Juifs et la Nouvelle-France*, pp. 103–104.

76 Ibid., p. 141.

77 David Rome, who had contact with Vaugeois while the latter was working on his thesis at Laval, related to a correspondent that in the penultimate draft of the thesis Vaugeois's hypothesis was patently antisemitic, but had been changed by hand with pro-Jewish sentiments, so that the prejudicial remarks were removed by the final version. CJC-M, ZB "Vaugeois, Denis," David Rome to Zvi Loker, 6 July 1979. Although I did not see the earliest version, Rome's comments are consistent with my reading of Vaugeois's working assumptions, and how he himself challenged these assumptions.

78 This process of dismantling the mythic thinking about the Jews has yet to find its historian. In the interim, however, see Pierre Anctil, *Le Devoir, les Juifs et l'immigration: de Bourassa à Laurendeau* (Québec, 1988), pp. 135–141; Anctil, "A.M. Klein: du poète et de ses rapports avec le Québec français," pp. 125–129; Langlais and Rome, *Juifs et Québécois*, pp. 206–213.

79 Langlais et Rome, *Juifs et Québécois*. This volume appears in the series "Rencontre des cultures," itself a modest indication of an openness to the "other" in Quebec.

80 Ibid., pp. 26–29.

81 Sigmund Samuel, *In Return: The Autobiography of Sigmund Samuel* (Toronto, 1963). p. 3.

82 Cited in Naomi W. Cohen, *A Dual Heritage: The Public Career of Oscar S. Straus* (Philadelphia, 1969), p. 71.

83 Roberto Perin, "Clio as Ethnic: The Third Force in Canadian Historiography," *Canadian Historical Review* 64 (1983): 448.

Goldwin Smith:
Victorian Canadian Antisemite

GERALD TULCHINSKY

Most of those who read the works of Goldwin Smith are impressed by the brilliance of his intellect and the enormous range of his interest in and knowledge of the political and intellectual world of Britain, the United States and Canada during the last half of the nineteenth century. A reformer and a liberal of the Manchester school, he fought throughout his life for the separation of church and state, the liberalization of trade and the termination of British imperialism, as well as for the union of Canada with the United States. Above all, Goldwin Smith pursued the liberalization of the intellect from the shackles of the past. In his voluminous writings of nearly 70 years, he championed these causes with remarkable tenacity and single-mindedness in three countries: England, where he was born (in 1823) and educated, and where he became Oxford's Regius Professor of History; the United States, where he was one of the founders of Cornell University; and Canada, where he settled in 1871 (Toronto), becoming one of the nation's leading intellectuals until his death in 1910. An assessment of Smith by the Canadian historian Frank Underhill stresses these liberal views as well as Smith's "enlightening . . . criticism of the nature of Canadian nationality, and . . . far-reaching conception of the place of Canada in the English-speaking world."[1] Placing him in the wider sphere of Victorian liberalism, Elizabeth Wallace writes as follows: "As the champion of a liberal creed [Smith] tried to shape opinion and thus the course of events."[2] One of a small group engaged in a vigorous debate over Canadian identity, as well as a leading writer and reformer, he enjoyed enormous prestige among the city's intelligentsia—a prestige enhanced by his marriage to Harriet Boulton, a wealthy widow who owned "the Grange," one of Toronto's great houses. Professors Maurice Hutton and James Mavor of the University of Toronto were regular members of the Round Table circle that met at the Grange for dinner and conversation.[3] As an undergraduate at the University of Toronto in 1906, Vincent Massey, the son of one of the city's wealthiest families, was in transports of awe when he walked through its gates to be ushered into the presence of the great man.[4] When leaving the University of Toronto for Harvard in 1897, William Lyon Mackenzie King carried a letter of introduction from Smith, a family friend.[5]

While Smith always has been regarded as a leading liberal spirit of his era, Ramsay Cook points out that his liberalism was highly selective, even by nineteenth-century standards.[6] Although he advocated colonial emancipation, free trade, an extended franchise and reform on numerous other imperial and economic questions,[7] he harboured a "faith in the superiority of Anglo-Saxon civilization that is his most striking trait."[8] Smith was also an outspoken Jew-hater, one of the most prominent of his day in the English-speaking world. Many of the "Professor's" antisemitic tirades are recounted in the memoirs of his secretary, Arnold Haultain; for example, his claims that the cause of the Boer War was Britain's demand that the franchise be extended to "the Jews and gamblers of Johannesburg"; that Jews were gaining greater control over the world's press and influencing public opinion; that "the Jews have one code of ethics for themselves, another for the Gentile"; that Disraeli was a "contemptible trickster and adventurer. He couldn't help it because he was a Jew. Jews are no good anyhow"; and that "the Jew is a Russophobe," etc.[9]

These were not merely the ruminations of an elderly and bitter social critic; Smith had embraced antisemitic views at least since the late 1870s, expressing them often in print with force, conviction, persuasiveness and skill. His anti-Jewish articles were published in some of the most prestigious journals of the English-speaking world, such as the *Nineteenth Century,* the *Contemporary Review* and the *Independent,* as well as in his own Canadian papers, *The Bystander, The Week* and the *Weekly Sun.* While he had an astonishingly wide range of interests, and several other long-standing hatreds, antisemitism was a major preoccupation.[10] In Smith's mind, the very presence of Jews in society posed serious problems that required urgent resolution. Their removal from Europe, he asserted ominously in 1878, would remove a "danger from western civilization."[11] Four years later, he prophesied that unless Jews turned to "the grand remedy" of assimilation, "there is further trouble in-store . . . collisions which no philanthropic lecturing will avert. . . Coheleth's [the Jews'] end will come."[12]

THE HISTORIANS

It is remarkable that such a prominent aspect of Smith's thought has received practically no attention from Canadian historians concerned with his contribution to the intellectual life of the English-speaking world, particularly that of Canada during the post-Confederation debate over nationhood. Neither Underhill nor Wallace even mentions Smith's antisemitism. In his doctoral thesis, written in 1934, Ronald McEachern notices that Smith drew heavily on the "research" of a paid agent in London, and concludes that his antisemitism was essentially social and economic, not religious: Smith was only opposed to "Jewish tribalism . . . [the Jews'] refusal to coalesce with the rest of the population, their business habits and the type of employment to which they usually devoted themselves." Moreover, since his antipathy was directed "only against the Jewish nation, parasitical, separatist, and . . . un-English," his anti-Jewish views are dismissed as xenophobia or nativism, essentially harmless and, in their context, understandable—after all, he was opposed to the influx of almost any foreign group.[13] In his study of Canadian imperialism, Carl Berger briefly mentions Smith's antisemitism when dealing with the latter's opposition to the Boer War, which, the 'sage of the Grange' had alleged, was "instigated on behalf of

Jewish financiers."[14] Malcolm Ross's otherwise insightful and sensitive essay on Smith says only that he "looked a-squint at Jews," and that it is "disturbing to find the Oxford apostle of the Christian brotherhood of man brought finally to such a view as this: 'Two greater calamities have never befallen mankind than the transportation of the negro to this hemisphere and the dispersion of the Jews'."[15] In his extended discussion of Smith's contribution to the late nineteenth-century debate in Canada on the role of religion in modern society, Ramsay Cook makes no mention of Smith's antisemitism.[16] The only real examination of the latter is provided by non-Canadian histories.[17] Steven G. Bayme, an American who studied the reaction of Jewish leadership to antisemitism in Britain from 1898 to 1918, places Smith among those English liberals to whom Jews as universal citizens were acceptable, but Jews as Jews were not.[18] Why Anglo-Canadian historians have neglected to discuss Smith's antisemitism is puzzling, since it was well known to some of his Canadian contemporaries.[19]

Wallace's omission of this subject from her intellectual biography was not an oversight. In a letter to the Canadian Jewish historian Benjamin Sack, who had expressed surprise, she admitted that she had done so deliberately: while "it must be admitted that among the groups against which he was prejudiced were the Jews. . . . It seems to me to be going a bit far to say that he used any of his journals as a forum for anti-Semitic propaganda. . . . He certainly did not descend to anything approaching our modern 'hate literature'."[20] However, these conclusions are in need of revision. At least in part, his ideas were derived from the epicentre of antisemitic propaganda in western Europe, chiefly Germany and France, making him a major disseminator of Jew-hatred at the end of the nineteenth century.

NATIVISM AND ANTISEMITISM

The special nature of antisemitism, as distinct from the opprobrium generally felt for immigrants, is not always easy to detect. In the popular views of journalists, members of the House of Commons and many other Canadians preceding World War I, Jews were usually seen as undesirable settlers, but Ukrainians (known then as Ruthenians or Galicians) also frequently received unfavourable mention on grounds of their racial "inferiority," their dress or other habits.[21]

James Shaver Woodsworth, whose book about immigrants, *Strangers Within Our Gates,* was suffused by the racism characteristic of some turn-of-the-century Social Gospellers, preferred Jews to Ukrainians, Italians, Chinese or blacks because, in his opinion, they were more adaptable, assimilable and culturally suitable.[22] The Winnipeg general strike of 1919 witnessed more anti-Ukrainian than anti-Jewish sentiment, even though the strike probably had as much support among the Jewish working class as among Ukrainians, and even though Abraham Heaps—an English Jew—was among its major leaders.[23]

Moreover, notwithstanding popular prejudices, Jewish immigrants found entry into the country comparatively easy before 1914, whereas only a trickle of East Asians, Japanese and Chinese immigrants managed to enter during the same period. Riots and bloodshed against Orientals occurred on the west coast, but nothing comparable happened to Jews.[24] The latter, in fact, may have enjoyed certain advantages over other immigrants during the early 1900s. After all, the Jewish community was an old one, having been a feature of the Montreal scene since 1768, Toronto since the 1840s, and Victoria since the 1860s; by the early twentieth century, it had established an economic, social and political presence in Canada. Whereas the nation's Jewish population was only 6501 in 1891, 10 years later it was 16,401 and by 1911 numbered 74,564.[25] Also, the Canadian response to Jewish sufferings at various times during the late nineteenth century had been empathetic and generous;[26] for example, on the part of Protestant laymen and church leaders in Montreal and Winnipeg during the Russian pogroms of the early 1880s.[27] Subsequently, Jewish organizations in western Europe, the United States and Canada had collected funds, and, with varying success, interceded with political authorities to facilitate immigration and settlement.[28] The scholarly investigations of Jaroslav Petryshyn, John Zucchi and Anthony Rasporich suggest that Ukrainian, Italian and Croatian immigrants before World War I had fewer political and social mechanisms of support than Canada's Jews possessed.[29] By 1917, Canadian Jewry also had a representative in the House of Commons, as well as aldermen on the Montreal and Toronto municipal councils.[30] A small number with sufficient wealth and political connections succeeded in exerting some influence in federal and provincial affairs on issues directly affecting the Jewish community; most other ethnic communities had no such power. During the late nineteenth- and early twentieth-century period, Jews probably suffered less from serious discrimination than most ethnic groups in Canada. Antisemitism, therefore, cannot be abstracted entirely from the fairly generalized distrust of and dislike for foreigners prevalent at this time.

Yet, in certain respects, it remains significantly different from xenophobic nativism. Unlike other minorities, even those regarded with contempt or fear on other grounds, Canada's Jews were the only sizeable immigrant community before 1914 outside the Christian communion. Furthermore, they continued to suffer the disadvantages of that self-imposed exclusion even after the secularization of the state during the nineteenth century. There is no better proof of this liability and of the perpetuation of ancient prejudices in the modern world than that provided by Goldwin Smith.

SMITH AND DISRAELI

The origins of Goldwin Smith's antisemitism are not entirely clear. Some of his writings indicate that he shared popular medieval notions about Jews that persisted in early nineteenth-century England.[31] The controversy in the 1840s and 1850s over the civil emancipation of the Jews in Britain may have inflamed deep-seated resentments even among political liberals, although Smith was willing to accept Jews as members of the House of Commons.[32] In 1848, as a young correspondent for London's *Morning Chronicle,* he wrote a series of articles attacking Benjamin Disraeli. A critic of the Tories, Smith did not make an issue of Disraeli's Jewish origins immediately, but "there was an acrimonious feud between them which led each to seize every opportunity for personal attacks on the other"; at one point, Smith referred to Disraeli as an "adventurer."[33] Their mutual antipathy simmered in the 1860s over various foreign policy issues, such as the cession of the Ionian Islands and Smith's advocacy of domestic legal reforms.[34] Disraeli described Smith contemptuously in 1863 as a "rhetorician," "prig" and "pedant"—rebukes that Smith apparently never forgave. During the debates over the second Reform Bill, he attacked Disraeli again, provoking the bemused and disdainful reply that Smith must have spent his life "in a cloister."[35] In 1870, Disraeli referred to his enemy in his novel *Lothair* as a "social parasite," causing Smith to call him a "coward" in return.[36] While it caused a stir for a few months, the contretemps seems to have fizzled out.[37] Smith not only disliked Disraeli's political style but detested him personally, confiding to a friend in 1880 that "Dizzy's life had been one vast conspiracy, the first object of which was the gratification of his own devouring vanity, the second the subversion of Parliamentary government."[38] To another friend, he wrote of his antagonist in 1896: "It is surprising that his [Disraeli's] Hebrew flashiness should have so dazzled a practical nation."[39] Smith's antisemitism may have begun with his hatred of Disraeli. But by the end of the 1870s, it began to develop into a broad belief that Judaism posed a "danger" to the kind of "civilization" that Smith aspired to achieve.

Early in 1878, while visiting England, Smith published an article attacking Disraeli for risking war with Russia by supporting Turkey over the Bulgarian uprising.[40] Not only did Smith castigate the Turks for their cruelties, but he also condemned Islam, which he described contemptuously as "not a religion of humanity." Then he turned his attention to Judaism and the Jews, whom he described as "another element originally Eastern [which] has, in the course of these events, made us sensible of its presence in the West." He contended further that, during the debate over the Bulgarian issue, "for the first time perhaps Europe has had occasion to note the political position and tendencies of Judaism. . . . In fact, had England been drawn into this conflict it would have been in some measure a Jewish war, a war waged with British blood to uphold the objects of Jewish sympathy, or to avenge Jewish wrongs."[41] Providing no evidence to support this assertion, which, however, was widely believed by opponents of Disraeli's pro-Turkish policies,[42] Smith went on to say that Judaism was not "like any other form of religious belief." The nations of Europe "have acted on the supposition that by extending the principle of religious liberty they could make a Jew a citizen, as by the same policy citizens have been made of ordinary Nonconformists," but they are in error. Jewish monotheism is "unreal" because the Jewish God "is not the Father of all, but the deity of His chosen race." After

> the nobler part of the Jewish nation, the real heirs of David
> and the Prophets, heard the Gospel, and became the
> founders of a human religion: the less nobler part . . .

rejected Humanity, and . . . fell back into a narrower and harder tribalism than before . . . bereft of the softening, elevating, and hallowing influences which . . . link patriotism with the service of mankind.

"Wanderers," "plutopolitans" and "partners of royal and feudal extortion" for 18 centuries, Jews "have now been everywhere made voters," he continued, "[but] to make them patriots, while they remain genuine Jews, is beyond the legislator's power . . . patriots they cannot be; their only country is their race, which is one with their religion."

JEWISH TRIBALISM

Smith's position became clearer a few months later when he also attacked Herman Adler, Britain's Chief Rabbi, who had responded to Smith's allegations by asserting that Jews can be and, in fact, are patriots in their countries of residence. On the contrary, Smith insisted that Jews are like Catholics, whose primary allegiance was to another country, i.e. Rome. They cannot yield undivided political allegiance to Britain because their highest loyalty is to their race or religion:

> Judaism is not, like Unitarianism or Methodism, merely a religious belief in no way affecting the secular relations of the citizen; it is a distinction of race, the religion being identified with the race, as is the case in the whole group of primaeval and tribal religions, of which Judaism is a survival. A Jew is not an Englishman or Frenchman holding particular tenets: He is a Jew, with a special deity for his own race. The rest of mankind are to him not merely people holding a different creed, but aliens in blood.[43]

While recognizing that the spirit of Judaism is universal in character, Smith maintained that in reality the Jewish religion is "confined to the tribe."[44] Why else do Jews pray only to the God of Israel ("Jehovah"), fail to proselytize, practice the "primaeval rite" of male circumcision (in order to separate themselves from other peoples), shun intermarriage with non-Jews (whom they call gentiles) and regard themselves as the chosen people? Furthermore, they crucified Christ and persecuted his followers. As a liberal, Smith professed to tolerate as full members of society those Jews willing to integrate into "the full element of European civilization . . . by putting off their Judaism." But the "hard-shell Jew," the strictly-observant, religious, orthodox or "genuine" Jew, was anathema because of his "primaeval and tribal" resistance to "the sun of modern civilization."[45] Such a Jew's public morality is tribalistic in the worst sense; if he possesses patriotism, the "object is not England, France, or Germany, but the Jewish race."[46] To Smith, Jews were also guilty of "wealth worship, stock-jobbing, or any acts by which wealth is appropriated without honest labour."[47] This trait was explained as follows:

> Among the great calamities of history must be numbered
> the expatriation of the Jews and their dispersion through
> the world as a race without a country, under circumstances
> which intensified their antagonism to mankind and forced
> them more and more as objects of aversion and proscrip-
> tion to live by arts such as were sure at once to sharpen the
> commercial instinct and to blunt the conscience, the more
> so as they were placed beyond the healthy pale of public
> opinion and could look to no moral judgment but that of
> their tribe.[48]

In uttering these accusations, Smith was echoing the latest wave of antisemitism in central and western Europe. From distant Canada, where there was no public perception of a "Jewish problem," Goldwin Smith began his entry into the international brotherhood of antisemitic propagandists. Heralded in Germany in 1879 by the publication of Wilhelm Marr's *Der Sieg des Judenthums über das Germanenthum*, a series of articles by University of Berlin history professor Heinrich von Treitschke, and the establishment of Pastor Adolph Stöcker's antisemitic *Christlichsoziale Arbeitspartie*, this movement alleged that the

German economy, judiciary, legislature and press were controlled by Jews.[49] Its proponents called on "non-Jewish Germans of all confessions, all parties, all positions in life to one common and close union, that will strive towards one goal . . . to save our German fatherland from complete Judaization."[50] In this way, all evil in society was ascribed to Jewish influence; hence, if the cause were removed, the consequences would disappear as well. Marr, a political radical who espoused democracy, emancipation and anticlericalism, reviled Jews—he actually coined the term 'antisemitism'—for their "innate tribal peculiarity."[51] Stöcker claimed that the emancipation of the Jews in Germany had induced them to think that they were the equals of Germans; therefore they must be put in their place and reminded that they were no better than tolerated strangers. Treitschke declared that the Jews were Germany's "misfortune."[52] In spite of its occasional religious overtones, this recent antisemitism was secular in mood, repudiating Jews not for traditional Christian reasons but because they were politically, socially and culturally alien. While reviving old images of the foes of Christendom, it also possessed a new and radical nationalistic dimension.[53] The German economist, Eugen Dühring, went a significant step further by arguing that the Jews were a unique human species with distinctive physical and moral qualities, all of them negative.

In his views on Jews and Judaism, Smith was especially indebted to Ernest Renan, a leading French intellectual tainted with racism, who disparaged what he regarded as the "fanatical spirit of prophetic Judaism" and its negative influence on Christianity. This must be combatted, Renan believed, "in order that the spirit of the Indo-European race predominate in its bosom,"[54] an idea that originated with Count Arthur de Gobineau, whose *Essai sur l'inégalité des races humaines* (1853–55) enjoyed considerable, if delayed, influence among European intellectuals. By 1870, Renan had despaired of liberalism and democracy, while attributing Germany's recent victory to the preservation of its virility as founded upon its blood, notably the blood of its aristocracy.[55] Smith referred often to Renan's critique of the modern Jew, particularly his notion that "He who overturned the worldly by his faith in the Kingdom of God believes now in wealth only."[56] Smith also drew from contemporary German and Russian antisemitism, and actively solicited fashionable new European anti-Jewish ideas.[57]

He absorbed these notions and propagated them throughout Britain, the United States and Canada, in some of the most potent antisemitic compositions in the English language. He issued periodic warnings of "dangers," "troubles" and "collisions." He was not simply a critic of Jewish "tribalism"; he challenged the legitimacy of Judaism and the right of the Jewish people to survive as a distinct cultural group in the modern world. This was antisemitism of the most fundamental and dangerous kind.

JOSEPH LAISTER

Aside from his abiding suspicion and dislike of Disraeli—in his mind a Jew who used England as a "gaming table" for Jewish interests—Smith nurtured his anti-Jewish passions during the late 1870s and the 1880s by means of a long personal association with a publicist in London, Joseph Laister. A minor government employee, Laister was obsessed with hatred for Jews and Judaism—he referred to them as "the enemy"—and wrote blatant antisemitic articles with titles such as "The Imperishable Jew" that argued that Jews "deserved what they had suffered."[58] From at least as early as December 1881, Laister wrote regularly to Smith, informing him about Jewish religious beliefs, the differences between Talmud Jews and Bible Jews, the "real" reasons for the outbreak of anti-Jewish rioting in Russia during the early 1880s, the "barbaric rites" of the Jews, various aspects of Jewish sexuality and a number of other Jewish-related matters. He was probably Smith's most important source of antisemitic material, sending him countless pamphlets and articles from all over Europe, as well as his chief avenue of contact with the leading European antisemites of the day. Smith's replies have not been preserved in his papers at Cornell University, but it can be inferred that the Canadian pundit wrote frequently to offer advice, ask questions and remit cheques (sometimes referred to by Laister as "encouragement") in payment for the services rendered.[59] Clearly, Smith regarded Laister as an indispensable supplier of information that he could not easily obtain by himself. He incorporated much of this material into his own articles.

One of Laister's most laboured themes was that Jewish religious works, chiefly the Hebrew Bible and the Talmud, as well as the oral traditions based on these texts, allow, and even encourage, Jews to treat their non-Jewish neighbours "immorally."[60] Allegedly, Jewish hostility toward non-Jews in the ancient world was so deeply ingrained that usury and slaveholding became widespread and normative. The Old Testament, according to him, is so replete with "immorality" that it "is responsible for the low tone of morals prevailing among Bible reading Christians."[61] Smith enlarged this claim by recommending, in Marcionite terms, the elimination of the Old Testament from the Christian canon. "There was a Judaism of the Prophets, and a Judaism of the Law, . . . the first broadened into Christianity, while the second was narrowed into Pharisaism and the Talmud," he solemnly informed the readers of *The Bystander* in 1882.[62]

Laister combed the *Jewish World* and the *Jewish Chronicle* for reports and editorials on interesting Jewish matters, and was in touch with continental anti-semitic publications, such as the Paris newspaper *L'anti-Juif,* and the pronouncements of Treitschke and Stöcker, copies of which he began sending to Smith in 1882.[63] He also attempted to help Smith by writing replies to London newspapers that published letters critical of the latter's antisemitism.[64] Laister's most important contact was probably Stöcker in Berlin, with whom he regularly corresponded. One of the leading demagogues of the day, the Kaiser's court preacher tirelessly popularized anti-Jewish ideas during the 1880s.[65]

An important feature of Laister's Judeophobia was his conviction that the Jews secretly exercised control or, at least, undue influence over much of the English press.[66] Pressing further, he reached other disturbing conclusions, such as the belief that the Jews had "got at" various Church papers.[67] Fully as worrisome was Jewish control over the news elsewhere as well. As pogroms raged in Russia, Laister reminded Smith that "the great News Agent Baron Reuter is himself a Jew," thereby raising doubts about the veracity of reports concerning the outrages.[68] Also sensitive to possible Jewish interference in the book industry, he informed Smith that "Green's history is often quoted in favour of the Jews. Green is a name commonly assumed by Jews." "Is he one?" he asked.[69] He objected even to the existence of the Yiddish press in London. "Why is this," he complained to Smith in 1891, "and why is the national [Jewish] language [such at least as it has degenerated to be] kept up if not for a *nation*?"[70]

Obviously tutored by Laister, Smith, in almost every article he composed on Jewish matters, alleged Jewish control over the press to explain why the real truth could not reach the public. "What organs can they not command," he asked rhetorically in July 1883, when dealing with Jewish claims of persecution in Europe.[71] In July 1897, he informed the readers of the *Weekly Sun* that "the Jews control the European press. They are sometimes found behind even Christian religious journals."[72] Like Laister, Smith was always on the *qui vive* for Jews in journalism and was quick to report his findings. In April 1897, for example, he informed the readers of Toronto's *Weekly Sun* that "the originator of this style" (the "yellow press") of journalism was "not a native American but a Hungarian Jew, reckless, as men of that tribe often are."[73] Whenever the London papers were less than favourable to Jewish complaints of persecution in Russia, or whenever "Jewish domination" of the fourth estate was being resisted, Laister passed the news to Smith who passed it on. "Evidently here is strong anti-Jewish feeling on the staff of the *Spectator*. Probably elsewhere as well, only they dare not speak their minds—at present."[74] "Is there such a thing as a paper or periodical which is not controlled by Jews or afraid to print the truth . . . about them?" he lamented to a friend in May 1906. "They seem to be behind the press everywhere, or at least be able to muzzle it."[75]

THE JEWISH CHARACTER

The Talmud, the great storehouse of Jewish law and commentary, held for Smith, as for many antisemites, an enormous fascination. Laister seems to have devoted considerable time gleaning 'insights' on the subject from Dr. Alexander McCaul's book, *Old Paths,* as well as the hostile writings of Jacob Brafman, a Russian Jewish apostate, and P. I. Hershon, another Jewish apostate and a compiler of Talmudic miscellany.[76] The Talmud, he explained to Smith, "is really translated according to taste," meaning that Jews are not obliged to treat gentiles in the same way as other Jews, and that robbery and possibly even murder are condoned, as well as a host of other horrible depravities.[77] The Talmud and "Talmud Jews" were frequent objects of Smith's derision as well, and he repeated the same myths about biblical Judaism, which he regarded as legitimate, and Talmudic Judaism, which he excoriated as evil.[78] In a lengthy article for the *Nineteenth Century* in November 1882, Smith wrote that:

> Talmudism is the matter from which the spirit has soared
> away, the lees from which the wine has been drawn off. It is
> a recoil from the Universal Brotherhood of the Gospel in a
> Tribalism . . . which . . . built up ramparts of hatred. . . . It
> is a recoil from the moral liberty of the Gospel in a legalism
> which buries conscience under a mountain of formality,
> ceremony and casuistry. . . . It is a recoil from the spiritual-
> ity of the Gospel . . . to a religious philosophy which . . .
> makes the chief end of man consist in the pursuit of wealth,
> as the means of worldly enjoyment.[79]

The Talmud, he informed the readers of *The Bystander* in 1883, is "a code of casuistical legalism [and] . . . of all reactionary productions the most debased, arid, and wretched."[80] Non-Talmudic Jews were better than Talmudic Jews. Smith, less of a racist than Laister, regarded the religion as the source of the offence, arguing that Jews would be acceptable if they assimilated into the surrounding cultures.[81] Yet, in demanding the eradication of all their religious and cultural traces, he was really demanding the eradication of the Jewish people as a distinctive entity. This, in effect, was tantamount to an anti-Jewish crusade, and it is difficult to see much difference between the two men at this point.

Laister also evinced considerable interest in Jewish sexuality, and wrote to Smith on this subject. While Smith seems to have avoided explicit sexual allusions, he poured contempt on Jewish claims that Jewish women were raped during the 1881–82 pogroms. Using reports from British consular officials in southern Russia in a selective and polemical manner, he stated that these complaints were ridiculous, and repeated canards current among Russian antisemites that Jews lacked "civic honesty," exploited their female servants sexually, corrupted the Russian peasants with drink, abused Christian burgesses, raised prices of food unjustly, mixed vodka with impure substances, traded on the Christian sabbath and holidays, and put peasants into debt.[82] While never sinking to quite the poisonous levels of some contemporary antisemites, Smith made frequent oblique references to "facts," such as "the fact that the Oriental character, in its leading features, is inferior to the European . . . race."[83] It was his view that assimilation was essential in order to avert "danger to western civilization"; Jews who wished to remain fully Jewish should emigrate to Palestine. However, "those who refuse to mingle with humanity must take the consequences of their refusal. They cannot expect to enjoy at once the pride of exclusiveness, and the sympathies of brotherhood."[84] He believed that the Jews and their religion would disappear in the course of time—the sooner the better. In a viciously humorous piece for the *Weekly Sun,* July 1897, he wrote:

> The discovery of the Ten Lost Tribes is another religious fancy of which we ought to have heard the last. "I am very much out of funds," was the reply of one who had been asked to subscribe for that object, "and I really cannot afford at present to give any thing to your association for finding the Ten Tribes, but if you have an association for losing the Two Tribes, poor as I am, I will try to contribute."[85]

The major threat was Jewish financial power. Smith alluded frequently to Jews as exploiters and extortionists. It was probably his favourite allegation, and he waxed eloquent on the theme. "Their usurious oppression of the people" would have to be given up before they could be absorbed into their host societies.[86] Smith feared the effects of public sympathy in light of the Russian atrocities. Many of Laister's reports concerned the reaction in Britain to these events, including sermons by leading clergy.[87] Thus in February 1882, he argued that the early information from Russia was unreliable, and that vigorous British protests were unnecessary.[88] More than a year later, he wrote to Smith to complain that "the news agencies have never ceased to let the world know how the Jews were being persecuted."[89] Smith gave the consular findings large play in Britain and Canada, claiming that Jewish losses "were in most cases exaggerated, and in some to an extravagant extent."[90] In any case, he claimed, the troubles started over "bitterness produced by the exactions of the Jew, envy of his wealth, jealousy of his ascendancy, combined in the lowest of the mob with the love of plunder."[91] He repeated these allegations over 20 years later, after anti-Jewish pogroms broke out in Romania in 1907. "Any race," he avowed, "let its religion and its historical record be what they might, which did what the Jews have done would have provoked the same antipathies with the same deplorable results."[92]

Laister and Smith

The relationship between Laister and Smith was reciprocal; although Smith paid for Laister's research, he regarded him as a friend and a valuable source of information about Jews.[93] Laister, of course, was a visceral antisemite—he regarded Jews as disgusting—with his own special agenda. He agreed with Smith's observation that the newspapers were not reproving the Jews for their "immoral doings."[94] On occasion, Laister wrote simply to raise a technical question: in January 1882, he asked whether it was true—as Jews often asserted—that throughout European history they had always been prevented from owning land. "These [historical questions] are peculiarly your province and I wished to put the matter for your consideration. . . . Please think it over. It seems to me very important to get this point cleared up authoritatively."[95] Smith took Laister's suggestion and incorporated some discussion of this subject in the article he was preparing for the *Nineteenth Century*.[96]

Laister's major aim was the fostering of antisemitism through willing associates. Sometimes, he suggested that Smith adopt a certain line of attack: "a telling retort to the . . . boasted superiority of the Jewish race by reason of its hygienic and other regulation. . . wd. be why don't the Jews ask us to participate why don't they condescend to teach us something if they have something good to teach?"[97] On one occasion, he recommended that Smith buttress his arguments with biblical references.[98] He not only advised the latter on what points to cover, but also on what subjects to focus. For example, Smith's reply to Rabbi Adler's counterattack to the former's first major antisemitic foray drew advice concerning "points that seem to still want answering, omitting those of course which you are quite sure to have dealt with."[99] He rushed fresh material to Smith to "read . . . before the opportunity passes for incorporating something in the Jewish article."[100] He also offered suggestions on the drafts of articles that Smith sent him for comment,[101] asking his correspondent to help him track down information in turn.[102] When Smith requested the name of a certain antisemitic

German writer, Laister replied that it was Richard Andrée, whose book *Zur Volkskunde der Juden* was "creating much attention in Germany."[103] Although he welcomed his collaboration with the famous Canadian, and made use of his ideas, Laister was nevertheless anxious to establish himself as his own man:

> I regret to find that both the Jewish *Chron* and *World* have fixed me as a disciple of yours; I thought that I had struck out all references to you, but they have fastened on one quotation apparently to justify their conjecture. I will take the next opportunity of disclaiming this connection. Meanwhile I hope it may not have caused you any annoyance.[104]

Their correspondence reveals that Smith reciprocated by confiding his own dark thoughts, such as his view on the link between Jewish money and nihilism.[105] Smith, too, was a regular reader of the London *Jewish World,* as well as the antisemitic literature published in the United States during the 1880s, such as the pamphlet *Conquest of the World* (St. Louis).[106] Hence, he was able to contribute material of his own. "Pray let me know where I can get particulars," Laister wrote to Smith in November 1882 concerning the latter's statement that certain Italian newspapers belonged to Jews.[107] Like Laister, Smith was interested in circumcision, and wrote about it.[108] Despite this reciprocity, however, the evidence suggests that Laister was mostly the tutor and the "Professor" mostly the pupil. As a pupil, moreover, Smith was particularly valuable, because of the fame of his articles on religion and the Irish question.[109] Laister also regarded Smith's social and political connections in Britain as useful, urging him, on the eve of his departure from London in May 1882, to "make me acquainted with any sympathisers here in England so that I may not be entirely isolated when you go."[110] So anxious was Laister for Smith's continued collaboration that he implored him to accept "anything I think worth your while to see, and to write when needful—for which, please, I shall take no remuneration whatever."[111] In fact, he sent drafts of his antisemitic essays.[112] Moreover, the two men shared their feelings as well as their ideas.[113]

Stöcker's London visit brought Laister directly into contact with other potentially useful Germans.[114] He described the visitor's address on Jews in Germany as a "parting shot for the trouble they [the Jews] have given him." By this time also, he was in touch with Canon August Rohling, a German Catholic priest whose antisemitic tract *Der Talmudjude* (1871) had aroused considerable public controversy in Germany.[115] He sent the pamphlet, which purported to show the depravity of the Jews on the basis of extracts from the Talmud, to Smith for his edification.[116]

SMITH'S GOALS

While Smith's writings on the Jewish question did not reflect all of Laister's beliefs in the essential immorality of Judaism, he saw the Jews as a most serious social menace nonetheless. Between 1878, when he charged that Jewish influence was "strong both in the money-world and in the press," and 1906, when he wrote his last essay on the subject, he remained consistent.[117] Because Jews could not be loyal to the countries in which they lived, this influence created a political danger.[118] "The political tendencies should be watched with solicitude, not only with reference to special questions like the present where the separate objects or sentiments of their race seem likely to conflict with the interests of the nation or of mankind, but with reference to the general progress of civilisation," because "they now seem disposed as plutopolitans, to cast into the scale of reaction a weight which would be that of mere wealth untempered by any larger consideration either national or European."[119] Later, he elaborated this thesis: "Few greater calamities perhaps have ever befallen mankind than the transportation of the negro and the dispersion of the Jew."[120] Following Renan, Smith had no doubt that the Jews were fully responsible for their own troubles:

> Take any race you please, but with an intensely tribal spirit; let it wander in pursuit of gain over the countries of other nations, still remaining a people apart, shunning intermarriage, shrinking from social communion, assuming the attitude assumed by the strict and Talmudic Jews toward the Gentiles, plying unpopular, perhaps oppressive,

trades and gleaning the wealth of the country without much adding to it by productive industry; you will surely have trouble.[121]

If there was persecution, Jews had invited it by persecuting others. "To pronounce the antipathy to the Jews utterly groundless is in fact to frame an indictment against humanity."[122] Had not Tacitus and Juvenal written about Jew-hatred in the ancient world, and did not Gibbon find evidence of it in his research? In medieval times, Jews "provoked the hatred of the people by acting as the regular and recognized instrument of royal extortion";[123] Jews avoided military service; they bought land and thereby undermined the feudal system; they attacked Christian religious processions; they loaned money at high interest; they sympathized with and supported the forces of Islam, notably in medieval Spain; they showed themselves to be intolerant of religious dissenters like Spinoza and Acosta within Judaism. Jews like Disraeli and the merchants of Johannesburg foster war for their own financial gain. In Russia, Jews are "eating into the core of her Muscovite nationality," while in Germany they "lie in wait for the failing Bauer" and in the southern United States "a swarm of Jews" have engaged in "an unlawful trade with the simple negroes . . . [thus] driving out of business many of the old retailers."[124] In short, Smith proclaimed in 1874, "the cruel maltreatment which they often received was caused less by hatred of their misbelief than by their rapacity."[125] To prove this claim, he pointed to the situation in Germany in the late 1870s. "History in fact shows, that, of all the European nations, the Germans have been the most free from the vice of persecution." It was merely the struggle of the people against

the progress of an intrusive race, which is believed by its patient Oriental craft, to be getting into its hands not only the money of the nation but the newspaper press and other organs of influence, while it is said to avoid manual labour, seldom to produce or even to organize production, to decline as much as possible public burdens, to retain its exclusive nationality, and to be little more attached to the

particular country in which it happens to sojourn than is
the caterpillar to the particular leaf on which it feeds.[126]

For Smith, there were only two possible solutions to the Jewish problem:
repatriation and assimilation. Until the end of his life, he favoured returning
their own land to the Jews once the Turkish empire was dissolved. He even suggested that Britain surrender Cyprus to Turkey in payment for Turkey's granting
Palestine to the Jews.[127] If this occurred, the most "exclusive" Jews might return
to Palestine, and "their withdrawal might facilitate the fusion of the more liberal element into European society."[128] Consequently, either assimilation or, "what
the Zionists desire, repatriation, is the cure."[129] He was doubtful, however, that
more than "a few of the race" would desert the stock exchanges for the "courts
of Zion."[130] "To propose to him (the Jew) to change New York, London or
Amsterdam for Zion is little better than mockery."[131] The second option included the acceptance of Christian and patriotic values. Jews should be invited to

cease to cling to this miserable idolatry of race . . . [and]
accept Humanity, and in its service find again a nobler
exercise for those ancestral gifts which, since they rejected
that service, have been employed mainly in money-getting
by means often low, and sometimes inhuman.[132]

Only by eliminating all aspects of Jewish exclusiveness, such as the concept that the Jewish God is the "deity of his chosen race," and only by abandon-
ing barbaric "tribal" practices such as circumcision and economic pursuits, such
as money-lending, could Jews become full, equal and truly patriotic members of
any of the European civil societies in which they had been granted equal rights.
In short, Jews had to reject their Jewishness, their social and economic habits,
and adopt "the softening, elevating, and hallowing influences which, in such a
patriot as Mazzini, link patriotism with the service of mankind" in order to
merit this status.[133] They must be willing to "melt into the general population
of the West"—in effect, to disappear. Clearly, Smith never wavered from his pri-
mal conviction of Judaism as a danger to Western civilization.

The exact nature of this danger was pointed out in 1878, and in a series of subsequent articles. First was the possibility that Disraeli, a Jew masquerading as an Englishman while secretly representing Jewish interests, would involve Britain in a war with Russia over the Balkans. "Let the electioneering agents, who are Lord Beaconsfield's chief counsellors and the real framers of his policy, tell him what they will," he thundered, "the nation has declared, for peace. . . . England must have sunk low indeed before she can allow herself to be tricked by a political intriguer, to whom she is a gambling table, not a country, for the purposes of his game, into a needless, iniquitous, dishonourable, and ruinous war."[134] Smith raised the same allegation in 1882 when, during the controversy over the pogroms, he asserted that "an attempt is being made to drag us into a Russian war."[135] Jews, in Smith's view, were the enemies of the state. In an article for the *North American Review* in 1891, he stated that "the Jew is detested not only because he absorbs the national wealth, but because, when present in numbers, he eats out the core of the nationality."[136] To the readers of the *Weekly Sun,* he declared that the Jews were "a cosmopolitan tribe of money-dealers whose influence threatens to be baleful to our civilization."[137]

CONCLUSION

These were most serious charges and, coming from a person of Smith's stature in the intellectual life of the English-speaking world, they must have inflicted considerable damage. It is impossible to estimate the true effect of his antisemitic declarations on public opinion or public policy in Canada. There appears to have been little reaction. One prominent Canadian did react strongly, however. In a review of Smith's *Essays on Questions of the Day,* George Munro Grant, Principal of Queen's College, pointed out that Smith's explanation for the rise of antisemitism amounted to blaming the victims: "The fault is thrown wholly upon the Jews and not upon those who treat them with brutal violence."[138] While his antisemitic views do not appear to have had any discernible influence on Canadian immigration policy during his life, his disparagement of Jews (and other Europeans) in some of the articles he wrote for the *Weekly Sun* during the 1890s and 1900s possibly contributed to general tensions over immigrant issues during those decades.[139] Smith received many letters from readers of his articles in support of his antisemitic writings. However, he wrote only sporadically and without much fervour in criticism of reigning practices. "What is the use of excluding the Chinaman when we freely admit the Russian Jew?" he asked despondently in July 1897. Ten years later, he lamented: "We have been welcoming a crowd of . . . Russian and Polish Jews, the least desirable of all possible elements of population."[140] Nor did Smith, a prolific writer of letters to prime ministers Sir John A. Macdonald and Sir Wilfrid Laurier, even raise this question with them, though he did protest against proposals to establish Jewish farm colonies in western Canada.[141] The major manifestations of antisemitism in that era were either related to French-English political conflicts, or bound up with the nativism current during the great wave of immigration into Canada after 1900. This was insufficient for a successful antisemitic movement in Canada, and, unlike some of his European counterparts, Smith never attempted to form one.

Still, he was a confirmed antisemite, reviling Jews with an animus that far surpassed mere dislike. He mounted nothing less than an outright assault on the right of the Jewish people to live as Jews in European civil society. He sought out and paid for professional assistance on this subject, and pursued a vigorous literary campaign across the English-speaking world for over thirty years, serving as a leading conduit for some of the worst forms of European antisemitism to the New World and providing those prejudices with his imprimatur.[142] In his correspondence with some of the English-speaking world's leading intellectuals, Smith frequently injected his views of the "Jewish question." Therefore, he merits special attention in the history of modern antisemitism, even if he lacked the political ardour and ambition of his continental mentors. Most likely, Smith would not have wished to lead an overt antisemitic political party or movement in any of the English-speaking countries, even if this had been possible. He was ultimately too much of a mid-Victorian believer in the existing British party system to advocate such measures, and he might have sensed the revolutionary dangers of single-interest parties. Yet he made no secret of his views to all who would listen, and his influence on at least one young student was profound. Writing in his diary in February of 1946 about the threat of communism, Prime Minister King confided these thoughts:

I recall Goldwin Smith feeling so strongly about the Jews. He expressed it at one time as follows: that they were poison in the veins of a community . . . the evidence is very strong, not against all Jews . . . that in a large percentage of the race there are tendencies and trends which are dangerous indeed.[143]

Contempt for Jews, therefore, was intrinsic to a most illiberal Goldwin Smith, whose antisemitism filled only one compartment in a valiseful of hatreds. He also reviled the Irish, the Roman Catholics and the French-Canadians, and held distinctly reactionary views on the question of female suffrage.[144] These passions in themselves raise serious reservations about his reputation as a liberal. Yet, paradoxically, his liberalism was genuine and pervasive. Smith's antisemitism was not only personal, as his hatred for Disraeli—ironically, the personification of the assimilated Jew that Smith idealized—demonstrates, since Disraeli died in 1881, and Smith continued to publish anti-Jewish articles almost until his own death in 1910. It was general and theoretical, arising from the very nature of the philosophy he so keenly espoused. The liberal deity of the nineteenth century was a most jealous god. His creed, and that of continental radicalism, brooked no dissenters and no deviation, especially from those who, like the Jews after their emancipation, were expected to leap joyfully into the brave new world of freedom and toleration, with its opportunities for total assimilation into a higher culture. That most Jews declined this invitation astonished, dismayed and disgusted his liberal mind, just as it had enraged Marr and Renan. Antisemitism was integral to this part of the liberal worldview. Interestingly, Smith did not pursue his other enemies with nearly the zeal he invested in the Jewish question, nor did he challenge other minorities as fundamentally as he did the Jews. For the latter alone, a special detestation was nurtured, based on such strong personal feelings and imported revulsion that their very right to exist was in effect annulled. That antisemitism was inherent to his liberalism was confirmed by Smith himself: "Our Liberalism," he wrote in the *Nineteenth Century* in November 1882, is at present in a flaccid state, fancying that because it has thrown off the tyranny of kings, its principles bind it to a Quaker-like quietism, and forbid it to guard the Commonwealth against conspiracy and encroachment: as though it were lawful to defend oneself against a tiger, but not against a tape-worm . . . the forces in favour of Hebrew ascendancy.[145]

For Smith, Jews and Judaism were more than just a modern-day anachronism that liberals would find alien; they were a "conspiracy" and an "encroachment" posing fearsome dangers to be understood and then eliminated. Smith's antisemitism was also more than just a manifestation of his growing pessimism, or what Ramsay Cook has called "a severe case of 'cultural despair'."[146] It was, it seems, a much deeper matter of visceral feeling rather than of cool reason, about the Jewish "danger." To avert this danger, Smith issued to the entire English-speaking world a clarion call to awareness and action.

NOTES

I acknowledge with thanks the helpful comments of Ramsay Cook, Paul Christianson, Jack Granatstein, Klaus Hansen, Phyllis Senese, Marguerite Van Die, Barry Mack and Brian Young on an earlier draft of this essay.

1   Frank Underhill, "Goldwin Smith," *University of Toronto Quarterly* (1933): 285–309, esp. 286.

2   Elizabeth Wallace, *Goldwin Smith: Victorian Liberal* (Toronto: University of Toronto Press, 1957), p. vi.

3   Samuel E. D. Shortt, *The Search for an Ideal: Six Canadian Intellectuals and Their Convictions in an Age of Transition, 1890–1930* (Toronto: University of Toronto Press, 1976), pp. 80, 122–3.

4   Claude T. Bissell, *The Young Vincent Massey* (Toronto: University of Toronto Press, 1981), p. 32.

5   R. MacGregor Dawson, *William Lyon Mackenzie King: A Political Biography, 1874–1923* (Toronto: University of Toronto Press, 1958), p. 70.

6   G. Ramsay Cook, "Goldwin Smith," *Dictionary of Canadian Biography*, vol. 13.

7   See Ian Bradley, *The Optimists: Themes and Personalities in Victorian Liberalism* (London: Faber, 1980), passim.

8   Cook, "Goldwin Smith."

9   Arnold Haultain, *Goldwin Smith, His Life and Opinions* (Toronto: McClelland & Goodchild, 1910), p. 68, 125, 146, 189, 206.

10 See Goldwin Smith, *Essays on the Questions of the Day: Political and Social* (New York: Macmillan, 1893), pp. 183–220, 263–308.

11 Goldwin Smith, *Contemporary Review* 31 (February 1878): 619.

12 Goldwin Smith, "The Jews. A Deferred Rejoinder," *Nineteenth Century* (November 1882): 708–709.

13 Ronald Alexander McEachern, "Goldwin Smith" (Ph.D. thesis, University of Toronto, 1934), pp. 304, 343.

14 Carl Berger, *The Sense of Power: Studies in the Ideas of Canadian Imperialism, 1867–1914* (Toronto: University of Toronto Press, 1970), p. 7.

15 Malcolm Ross, "Goldwin Smith," in Claude T. Bissell, ed., *Our Living Tradition, Seven Canadians* (Toronto: University of Toronto Press, 1957), pp. 29–47, esp. 32, 45.

16 Ramsay Cook, *The Regenerators: Social Criticism in Late Victorian English Canada* (Toronto: University of Toronto Press, 1985), pp. 26–40.

17 Thus Colin Holmes in Britain has noted the incongruity of Smith's "liberalism" and "antisemitism" (Colin Holmes, "Goldwin Smith: A 'Liberal' Antisemite," *Patterns of Prejudice* 6 (September–October 1972: 25–30), while the American Jewish historian, Naomi Cohen, focuses on the sharp reaction of US Jewish communal leaders to Smith's virulent attacks (Naomi Cohen, *Encounter with Emancipation: The German Jews in the United States, 1830–1914* [Philadelphia: Jewish Publication Society, 1984], pp. 278–81).

18 Steven G. Bayme, "Jewish Leadership and Anti-Semitism in Britain, 1898–1918" (Ph.D. thesis, Columbia University, 1977), University Microfilms, no. 48108, pp. 126–27. See also Michael N. Dobkowski, *The Tarnished Dream: The Basis of American Anti-Semitism* (New York: Greenwood Press, 1979), p. 32.

19 See Hector Charlesworth, *Candid Chronicles: Leaves from the Note Book of a Canadian Journalist* (Toronto: Macmillan, 1925), p. 119. I am grateful to Ian McKay for this reference.

20 Benjamin G. Sack, *History of the Jews in Canada* (Montreal: Harvest House, 1965), p. 236.

21 See Jaroslav Petryshyn, *Peasants in the Promised Land: Canada and the Ukrainians, 1891–1914* (Toronto: James Lorimer, 1985), chap. 7.

22 See James S. Woodsworth, *Strangers Within Our Gates: Coming Canadians* (Toronto: F. C. Stephenson, 1909), pp. 111–59.

23 David J. Bercuson, *Confrontation at Winnipeg: Labour, Industrial Relations and the General Strike* (Montreal: McGill–Queen's University Press, 1974), pp. 126–27; Kenneth McNaught, *A Prophet in Politics: A Biography of J. S. Woodsworth* (Toronto: University of Toronto Press, 1959), pp. 119, 135–36; and Henry Trachtenberg, "The Winnipeg Jewish Community and Politics: The Interwar Years, 1919–1939," *Historical and Scientific Society of Manitoba*, Transactions Series 3, nos. 34 and 35 (1977–78; 1978–79), pp. 115–53, esp. 119–20.

24 See Peter Ward, *White Canada Forever* (Montreal: McGill–Queen's University Press, 1978), p. 197, passim.

25 Louis Rosenberg, *Canada's Jews: A Social and Economic Study of the Jews in Canada* (Montreal: Bureau of Social and Economic Research, Canadian Jewish Congress, 1939), p. 10.

26 See Stephen A. Speisman, *The Jews in Toronto: A History to 1937* (Toronto: McClelland & Stewart, 1979), p. 67.

27 Gerald Tulchinsky, "Immigration and Charity in the Montreal Jewish Community to 1890," *Histoire Sociale-Social History* 16, 33 (November): 370–71.

28 See Simon Belkin, *Through Narrow Gates: A Review of Jewish Immigration, Colonization and Immigrant Aid Work in Canada 1840–1940* (Montreal: Eagle Publishing, n.d.), passim.

29 Petryshyn, *Peasants*, passim; John Zucchi, *The Italians in Toronto* (Montreal: McGill–Queen's University Press, 1989), passim; and Anthony W. Rasporich, *For a Better Life: A History of the Croatians in Canada* (Toronto: McClelland & Stewart, 1982), passim.

30 Bernard Figler, *Biography of Sam Jacobs, Member of Parliament* (Ottawa: Published by the author, 1959), and Speisman, *Jews in Toronto*, p. 251.

31 Todd M. Endelman, *The Jews of Georgian England, 1714–1830: Tradition and Change in a Liberal Society* (Philadelphia: Jewish Publications Society, 1979), pp. 86–87.

32 Arnold Haultain, *A Selection from Goldwin Smith's Correspondence* (Toronto: McClelland & Goodchild, n.d.), pp. 2–3.

33 Wallace, *Goldwin Smith*, p. 11.

34 Goldwin Smith, *The Empire: A Series of Letters Published in "The Daily News,"* 1862, 1863 (Oxford: J. Henry and J. Parker, 1863), pp. 255–56.

35 *The Times,* February 27, 1867.

36 Wallace, *Goldwin Smith*, p. 184.

37 See *Appleton's Journal of Popular Literature, Science, and Art* (June 1870): 51–52, and *New York Tribune*, May 16, 1870.

38 Haultain, *Correspondence*, p. 85.

39 Ibid., p. 296.

40 Goldwin Smith, *Reminiscences*, ed. Arnold Haultain (New York: Macmillan, 1910), p. 380, and "England's Abandonment of the Protectorate of Turkey," *Contemporary Review* 31 (February 1878): 603–21.

41 Ibid., p. 619.

42 Colin Holmes, *Anti-Semitism in British Society, 1876–1939* (New York: Holmes & Meier, 1979), p. 11.

43 Goldwin Smith, "Can Jews Be Patriots?" *Nineteenth Century* (May 1878): 877.

44 Ibid., p. 878.

45 Ibid., p. 876.

46 Ibid., p. 882.

47 Ibid., p. 884.

48 Ibid.

49 Jacob Katz, *From Prejudice to Destruction: Anti-Semitism 1870–1933* (Cambridge: Harvard University Press, 1980), pp. 260–72.

50 Ibid. (quoted), p. 261.

51 Moshe Zimmerman, "From Radicalism to Antisemitism," in Shmuel Almog, ed., *Antisemitism Through the Ages*, Vidal Sassoon International Centre for the Study of Antisemitism, The Hebrew University of Jerusalem (Oxford: Pergamon Press, 1989), pp. 251–54.

52 Cf. Fritz Stern, *Gold and Iron: Bismark, Bleichröder and the Building of the German Empire* (New York: Knopf, 1977), p. 512.

53 Ibid., p. 264.

54 Ernest Nolte, *Three Faces of Fascism*, trans. Leila Vennewitz (New York: Mentor Books, 1969), p. 68.

55 Ibid. See also Shmuel Almog, "The Racial Motif in Renan's Attitude to Jews and Judaism," in *Antisemitism Through the Ages*, pp. 255–78.

56 Smith, "The Jews. A Deferred Rejoinder," p. 707.

57 *The Bystander* 3, 1883, pp. 250.52.

58 Queen's University Archives, Goldwin Smith papers, microfilm, Laister to Smith, April 12, 1882; November 17, 1883; January 3, 1884.

59 Laister to Smith, February 12, 1882; "Many thanks for the cheque ... the money is welcome and will help to get me a holiday this year ..."; Laister to Smith, May 19, 1882.

60 Laister to Smith, December 6, 1881; February 27, 1882.

61 Ibid., December 6, 1881.

62 *The Bystander* 3, July 1883, p. 251.

63 Laister to Smith, January 17, February 6, 1882; see also Peter Pulzer, *The Rise of Political Anti-Semitism in Germany and Austria* (New York: John Wiley, 1964), pp. 249–50.

64 Laister to Smith, January 6, 1882.

65 Pulzer, *Rise of Political Anti-Semitism*, p. 94, and *Encyclopedia Judaica (EJ)*, vol. 15, pp. 408–409.

66 Laister to Smith, February 12, 1882.

67 Ibid., January 6, 1882.

68 Ibid., January 22, 1882.

69 Ibid.

70 Ibid., October 15, 1891.

71 *The Bystander* 3, July 1883, p. 251.

72 *Weekly Sun*, July 28, 1897.

73 Ibid., April 29, 1897.

74 Laister to Smith, November 17, 1883.

75 Haultain, *Correspondence*, p. 462.

76 Norman Cohn, *Warrant for Genocide: The Myth of the Jewish World-Conspiracy and the Protocols of the Elders of Zion* (London: Eyre & Spottiswoode, 1967), pp. 53–55; *EJ*, vol. 4, pp. 1287–88; and Smith Papers, Laister to Smith, May 17, 1882.

77 Laister to Smith, January 6, 1882.

78 See *The Bystander* 3, 1883, pp. 250–52.

79 Smith, "The Jew. A Deferred Rejoinder," p. 706.

80 *The Bystander* 3, July 1883, p. 251.

81 See *The Bystander* 3, July 1883, pp. 251–52.

82 See Kenneth Bourne and D. Cameron Watt, gen. eds., *British Documents on Foreign Affairs: Reports and Papers from the Reports of the Foreign Office, Confidential Print, Part I, From the Mid-Nineteenth Century to the First World War, Series A, Russia, 1859–1914,* ed. Dominic Lieven, *Russia, 1881–1905* (Washington: University Publications of America, 1983), pp. 1–65, and Smith, "The Jews. A Deferred Rejoinder," p. 692.

83 *The Bystander* 1, August 1880, pp. 445–46.

84 Ibid., March 1880, p. 156.

85 *Weekly Sun,* July 15, 1897.

86 *The Bystander* 3, July 1883, p. 251.

87 Ibid., February 6, 1882.

88 Ibid., February 17, 20, 1882.

89 Ibid., November 17, 1883.

90 Smith, "The Jews. A Deferred Rejoinder," pp. 688–94, and Goldwin Smith, "New Lights on the Jewish Question," part 2, *North American Review* 153 (August 1891): 129–43, esp. 131.

91 Ibid., p. 133.

92 *Weekly Sun*, March 27, 1907.

93 McEachern, "Goldwin Smith," p. 343; Smith Papers, Laister to Smith, January 17, 1882; and Haultain, *Goldwin Smith*, p. 125.

94 Laister to Smith, March 2, 1882.

95 Ibid., January 6, 1882.

96 Smith, "The Jews. A Deferred Rejoinder," passim.

97 Laister to Smith, February 12, 1882.

98 Ibid.

99 Ibid., February 27, 1882.

100 Ibid., May 21, 1882.

101 Ibid., April 12, 24, 30, 1882.

102 Ibid., February 20, 1882.

103 Ibid., January 22, 1882.

104 Ibid., February 12, 1882.

105 Ibid.

106 Ibid., November 6, 1882.

107 Ibid.

108 Ibid., November 17, 1883.

109 "Altogether they tend to reconcile parties of *all* shades to you, to disabuse them of wrong impressions about you, consequently give what you have to say about Judaism

more weight than it had two or three ago.... If there is a God, He is on our side in this matter, and will rule us aright." (Ibid., April 30, 1882.)

110 Ibid., May 14, 1882.

111 Ibid., May 19, 1882.

112 Ibid., November 17, 1883.

113 "What you tell me about the suppression of your proffered article on the Anti-Semitism movement is most exasperating," Laister wrote in early June 1890. "How long are we to submit to this invidious foe! The worst of it is that so very few people seem to realize the danger. However if the Jews have rope enough they will hang themselves by & by." (Ibid., June 6, 1890.)

114 Ibid., November 17, 1883. See C. C. Aronsfeld, "A German Antisemite in England: Adolph Stöcker's London Visit in 1883," *Jewish Social Studies* 49, 1 (Winter 1987):43–52.

115 Smith Papers, Laister to Smith, November 17, 1883; see Pulzer, *Rise of Political Anti-Semitism,* p. 163.

116 "I like this blood accusation business as little as you; but if they [defenders of Jews?] will have it they must; and I am always glad to give the thoughtless Gentile defenders of the tribe a rap on the knuckles." (Laister to Smith, November 17, 1883.)

117 Goldwin Smith, "Is It Religious Persecution," *The Independent* (New York) 60 (1906): 1474–78.

118 Smith, "Can Jews Be Patriots?" pp. 875–87, esp. 875.

119 Ibid., p. 885.

120 Ibid.

121 Smith, "Is It Religious Persecution," p. 1474

122 Ibid.

123 Ibid.

124 Ibid., pp. 1476–77.

125 *The Bystander* 1, March 1880, p. 156, and 3, July 1883, pp. 251–52.

126 Ibid., 1, August 1880, pp. 444–45.

127 Smith, "The Jews. A Deferred Rejoinder," p. 709.

128 Smith, "Can Jews Be Patriots?" p. 884.

129 *Weekly Sun,* March 27, 1907.

130 *The Bystander* 3, March 1880, p. 155.

131 *Weekly Sun,* July 15, 1897.

132 Smith, "Can Jews Be Patriots?" p. 886.

133 Smith, "England's Abandonment," p. 619.

134 Ibid., p. 620.

135 Smith, "The Jews. A Deferred Rejoinder," p. 687.

136 *North American Review* 153, 2 (August 1891): 129–43.

137 *Weekly Sun,* July 15, 1897.

138 *The Week,* February 24, 1894. If, as Smith suggested, the state should forbid the Jewish rite of circumcision because "it has nothing to do with religious opinion, nor in

repressing it would religious liberty be infringed," then, Grant argued, "the state would have the right to forbid the Christian rite of baptism on the same grounds." However, "the law against it [circumcision] would be a dead letter. Their [the Jews] respect for us would be gone forever, and our self-respect would go at the same time." As for Smith's demand that the Jew forget his allegiance to Zion and Jerusalem, Grant observed: "Why should he be obliged to forget the city that is bound up in his mind with everything that he esteems glorious in the past as well as eternally sacred? The Jew that forgets Jerusalem is not likely to be a better citizen of the country in which he lives." I am grateful to Barry Mack for this reference.

139 *The Week,* February 18, 1897; *Farmer's Sun,* May 1, June 1, September 28, 1904. See John Higham, *Strangers in the Land: Patterns of American Nativism, 1869–1925* (New York: Atheneum, 1975), chap. 4, "The Nationalist Nineties."

140 *Weekly Sun,* July 29, 1897; August 28, 1907.

141 Arthur A. Chiel, *The Jews of Manitoba: A Social History* (Toronto: University of Toronto Press, 1961), pp. 49–50.

142 Cohen, *Encounter with Emancipation,* p. 278.

143 National Archives of Canada (Ottawa), Mackenzie King Diary, February 20, 1946. I am indebted to Jack Granatstein for this reference.

144 See Smith, *Essays on Questions of the Day.*

145 Smith, "The Jews. A Deferred Rejoinder," p. 708.

146 Cook, *The Regenerators,* p. 36.

The Empire's Best Known Jew and Little Known Jewry

Michael Brown

Contemporary historians, wary of the cult of personality, often tend to play down the extent to which individuals can influence human affairs and to forget how much was once expected of "great" men and women. Still, it is the case that individuals often have changed the course of history. Moses Montefiore was one such man. During his lifetime (1784–1885), he was widely admired because of his work as a community leader, largely on behalf of beleaguered co-religionists; because of his loyalty to family, faith, and country; because of his knighthood, then a very rare honour for a Jew; and because of his prodigious longevity. In the contemporaneous Jewish world, Montefiore came to be "regarded . . . [almost] as an institution," serving as an example of what might be achieved through emancipation even when strong Jewish ties were preserved.[1] He was a standard-bearer of British *noblesse oblige* and of genteel Jewish traditionalism. Gradually, however, the memory of Montefiore faded, as historians turned their attention away from the heroes of the past. It is timely to reflect anew on the impact on his own world of the best known unconverted Jew of the Victorian Era, a man who influenced even individuals and communities with whom he had very tenuous connections, often without intending to do so. This *festschrift* in honour of Lavy Becker, one of Canada's most effective and tireless community leaders, provides a most suitable forum for such a re-examination. Canada, a country to which Montefiore did not have a close tie, provides an interesting perspective from which to review some of the less spectacular accomplishments of the eminent Jewish Victorian.

A chronically depressed and politically unsettled outpost of the Empire in the first half of the nineteenth century, British North America excited relatively little interest in Montefiore, either as businessman or as the statesman-philanthropist of Jewry.[2] In all probability, the country's faltering economy and recent political disturbances contributed to Montefiore's feeling in 1838, that Jewish settlers had a "greater certainty of success" in then desolate Palestine than in British North America.[3] Even towards the end of his life, when pogroms and poverty in Russia created an immediate and desperate need for new territories for Jewish settlement, Sir Moses still opposed sending Jews to Canada.[4] The Jews of British North America, no less than the country itself, may well have inspired Montefiore's skepticism. In 1784, when he was born, the community was just a quarter-century old, the settlement of Jews having been forbidden under the previous French regime; and it numbered no more than a few dozen people. When Montefiore died almost 101 years later, Canada's Jewry was still very small, then numbering some 2,500 people. Living in the British Empire, Canada's Jews did not, of course, require Montefiore's intercession with hostile powers on their behalf. In fact, they were granted full civic equality twenty-six years before the Jews in the mother country. Their small number, however, and their consequent political insignificance precluded their being of much assistance in Sir Moses' various endeavours on behalf of oppressed Jews elsewhere in the world.[5] Moreover, in many ways the small Canadian-Jewish community remained dependent upon the larger communities in Great Britain and the United States. Throughout Montefiore's lifetime, Canadian Jews considered their own community an appropriate object of charity, even though some of them had achieved considerable wealth by the mid-nineteenth century and could well have afforded to shoulder the burden of supporting the country's few Jewish institutions. They preferred, however, to seek aid from British Jews well known for their generosity, including Montefiore.

On the whole, Montefiore responded to such requests with restraint: he did send £5 in 1834 towards the building of a new synagogue in Montreal; £20 in 1863 to Montreal's Spanish and Portuguese Synagogue in memory of his wife; £10 to Montreal's Montefiore Social and Dramatic Club, when it was organized in 1880; £5 to the Sabbath School Fund of Bethel Hebrew Congregation of Winnipeg just before his death in 1885.[6] Only rarely, as in 1872, was a large gift forthcoming: £150 on that occasion to Montreal's Spanish and Portuguese congregation to assist them in discharging debts including back taxes.[7] Like some other Britishers, Montefiore was undoubtedly aware of the growing wealth of some Canadian Jews.[8] And, like many of his countrymen, he felt Canada would some day "go the way of all colonies," while in any case not being an ideal place for Jewish settlement.[9]

If Montefiore seemed unenthused about Canada, it cannot be said that Canadians were indifferent towards him. Montefiore's was an age of "adherence to religious tradition (combined) with participation in public life."[10] To Jewish and gentile Canadians, as to others, Sir Moses appeared to be in many ways the epitome of the time, and as such, he was the object of curiosity and admiration. In 1864, when he was awarded the keys to the City of London, Montefiore was hailed by the Montreal *Herald* as symbol and model of British success, toleration, and philanthropy. The paper stated that the honour accorded the octogenarian was:

> an . . . assurance that "the world still moves," and that
> men are daily discovering more and more—that, though
> of diverse creeds and nationalities, they may yet set aside
> minor differences of opinion and dogma, sink the
> odium theologicum, and walk hand in hand together, to
> do the great work, which patriotism and philanthropy
> point out.[11]

Montefiore's interest in the Holy Land sparked by traditional Judaism, attracted the notice of Canadians. In his popular travel book, *A Few Months in the East; or, A Glimpse of the Red, the Dead, and the Black Seas* (Quebec, 1861), Holy Land pilgrim J. Bell Forsyth recounted for Canadian readers Montefiore's "charitable undertakings" there.[12] Henry Wentworth Monk, the Canadian prophet of the British-Israel movement, unsuccessfully appealed to Montefiore to assist him in his work. Monk, who sought a restoration to Palestine of both the Jews and the "lost ten tribes," whom he believed to be the Anglo-Saxons of Britain, Canada, and the United States, hoped that Montefiore's endorsement and financial aid, along with that of other influential Jews, would lend his movement much needed legitimacy.[13]

Not unexpectedly, Canadian Jews were more mindful of Montefiore than non-Jews, and sought to emulate and honour him in a number of ways. An early honour was a very personal one. In 1851, the Abraham Josephs of Quebec, themselves descendants of pioneer Canadian Jews, named their newborn son, Montefiore. Montefiore Joseph became a distinguished resident of Quebec, president of the Board of Trade, the Quebec Snowshoe Club, and the Quebec Skating Rink. He died at the age of 92, having lived almost as long as the man whose name he bore and, albeit on a local scale, with something of his namesake's sense of civic responsibility.[14] In 1863, Montreal's Jewish rhymester, Isidore G. Ascher, eulogized Montefiore in verse as "a true-born, loyal knight,/Loyal of God and holy works of love."[15] In 1870, the Toronto Hebrew Ladies' Sick and Benevolent Society (*Chebre Gemilas Chesed*) was renamed the Ladies' Montefiore Hebrew Benevolent Society.[16] Ten years later, the Montefiore Social and Dramatic Club was formed in Montreal "for the purpose of fostering literary and social intercourse among its members . . . [taking for itself] the revered name of the great and famous philanthropist."[17]

The most intimate and long-term Canadian connection to Montefiore was that of Abraham De Sola, the country's first ordained rabbi, who served in the pulpit of Montreal's Spanish and Portuguese Synagogue from 1847 until his death in 1882, and who may be said to have put Judaism on the Canadian map almost single-handedly. De Sola, who also served as professor of Hebrew and Spanish at McGill, and was a recipient of an honourary doctorate from that institution, was by far the best known Jew in Canada during his lifetime. He was also well known in the United States and Great Britain. In Montreal, he was one of the most respected religious and intellectual figures, although not among French-Canadians, who virtually ignored his presence.[18] Through his family and his youthful association with Montefiore's synagogue in London, De Sola developed a personal tie to Sir Moses, which he maintained and cultivated over the years and miles.

Abraham De Sola's father, David Aaron De Sola, was senior minister of the Bevis Marks Synagogue in London; his maternal grandfather, Raphael Meldola, was the Sephardi *Haham* (that is, chief rabbi) there. It was also the congregation to which Moses Montefiore belonged and in whose affairs he played an important role. Meldola, who appointed Montefiore an executor of his will, was succeeded as presiding minister of Bevis Marks by his son, David, Abraham De Sola's uncle. De Sola's father was succeeded at his death by another son, Samuel. All of them worked closely with Montefiore, although none so much as David Aaron De Sola.[19] The latter became a minister of the congregation in 1818, the same year in which Montefiore assumed its lay leadership. It was David Aaron De Sola who preached the sermon of thanksgiving, "The Providence of God with Israel," in March 1841, welcoming Montefiore home after his triumphant mission to Turkey to rescue the imperiled Jews of Damascus.[20] In various aspects of his work, the senior De Sola was assisted by members of the Montefiore family, most notably Sir Moses' wife, Lady Judith.[21] In publishing the "Cheap Jewish Library" for working people, De Sola collaborated with two nieces of Sir Moses. One of them, Charlotte Montefiore, was especially helpful, contributing among other works of her own authorship, a volume entitled, *The Way to Get Rich,* a subject on which she may be presumed to have had some expertise and of which her readers had undoubted need.[22] Sir Moses himself extended considerable support to the publishing ventures of Hazan De Sola. His first work, *The Blessings* (London, 1829), apparently originated with a suggestion of Montefiore, who is mentioned in the dedication. Later works, including a translation of the Sephardic prayer book, were dedicated to Montefiore and Lady Judith in recognition of friendship and financial support.[23] It was quite fitting, then, that Abraham De Sola dedicated his biography

of his father to Montefiore, who, in turn, felt "obliged . . . for the opportunity
. . . of connecting my name with that of a gentleman for whom I always enter-
tained the sincerest regard and friendship."[24]

In addition to the family ties to Montefiore, Abraham De Sola had early
on formed his own personal ties to the philanthropist. Born in London in 1825,
he grew up in the shadow of Montefiore, apparently fascinated by him. One of
the young De Sola's three surviving copybooks is dedicated entirely to a semi-
fictional account of Montefiore's journey to Turkey in 1840–41.[25] For a time
before his departure for Canada at the age of 22, De Sola was tutored by Louis
Loewe, Montefiore's scholarly secretary cum travelling companion, and later the
principal of the college Montefiore established at Ramsgate.[26] Legend had it
that Sir Moses himself dispatched De Sola to Montreal in answer to a request
from the Canadians for a suitable rabbi.[27] (In fact, the rabbi left London after
losing out in the elections for a new minister at Bevis Marks.)[28] After arriving
in Canada, De Sola assiduously maintained a connection with Montefiore by
soliciting funds for Sir Moses' favourite charities, by reporting to him his own
successes and inquiring about Montefiore's, and in other, more personal ways.

Actually, the record of charitable contributions forwarded by De Sola to
Montefiore is rather sparse, although existing records may be incomplete. (On
the other hand, as noted earlier, Canadian Jews of the period still considered
themselves to be have-nots.) On four occasions between December 1859 and
February 1860, De Sola's synagogue sent a total of £450 to Montefiore for the
relief of Moroccan Jews, and in 1861, a small sum for Persian Jews.[29] On two
occasions during the first half of 1870, De Sola's congregation and "friends" sent
a total of £25 to Montefiore for the relief of "distressed brethren in Jerusalem."[30]
In 1872, Sir Moses received from the Montrealers £3.5.6, again for Persian relief,
and three years later, £20.9.1 "for distribution among the poor in Jerusalem."[31]
Two remittances destined for Moroccan Jews in the Holy Land in 1878, totalling
£25.11 complete the list.[32] For each donation, Montefiore sent a polite letter of
thanks to De Sola. One cannot help but feel, however, that the meager sums
reinforced Montefiore's doubts about Canada, however much they may have
served to maintain contact between the rabbi and the philanthropist. In fact, Sir
Moses himself contributed more to Canadian Jewry during his lifetime, mostly

to Montreal institutions, than De Sola was able to collect for Montefiore's charities from all his friends and congregants, some of whom, as noted above, including his wife's family and the Josephs, were very wealthy.

Rabbi De Sola's reports to Sir Moses of his triumphs in the New World may have created a more favourable impression, except perhaps for the air of self-congratulation about them. (By contrast, Montefiore's reports to De Sola of his 1863 Moroccan mission, of his 1872 mission to Russian, and of his mission to the Holy Land in 1875 strike a rather modest tone and appear to have been sent at De Sola's request.)33 De Sola seemed very eager for Montefiore to know of his achievements, perhaps in part, in order to impress the older man with how well he had done in Canada after his earlier defeat at Bevis Marks. In any case, in 1860, he made sure that Lady Judith received a copy of the Sephardic prayer book, which he translated and published, and that Sir Moses received a "handsomely bound copy" of the sermon he preached in 1864 to commemorate Montefiore's receiving the freedom of the City of London.34 In 1865, De Sola sent Montefiore a report of his successful activities as a member of the McGill faculty, and in 1870, a copy of his remarks "on the occasion of Prince Arthur's presence" at a meeting of the Natural History Society of Montreal, of which De Sola was president.35 The rabbi's proudest hour came in January 1872, when he delivered the invocation at a session of the House of Representatives in Washington. Although the circumstances behind the invitation to De Sola are not clear, everyone at the time understood the appearance to mark the end of the tension that had obtained between Great Britain and the United States since the early days of the Civil War. The rabbi was exceedingly proud to have been the first foreigner to pray before the Congress and publicized his visit widely in Canada, the United States and Great Britain.36 Among those to receive a full description of the event was Moses Montefiore, who congratulated the rabbi on his honour and praised him for having mentioned "the cordial feeling which should subsist between the United States and our own glorious old England."37

Over the years, there existed a private relationship between the two men as well. De Sola invited Montefiore to attend the wedding of his son, Joseph, to Amanda Davis in Montreal in 1881, perhaps as a courtesy, since the journey would have been rather arduous for a 97-year-old man. It was the second time

De Sola had invited Montefiore to Canada, and he assured him of a most enthusiastic reception.[38] The two consoled each other on the death of family members.[39] Montefiore contributed to the testimonial fund collected for De Sola in 1872 on his twenty-fifth anniversary with the Montreal congregation, while De Sola dedicated the 1878 revised edition of his prayer book translation to Sir Moses and his late wife.[40] The rabbi, who as a youth had been fascinated by the statesman-philanthropist, and who as an adult cultivated an association with the hero of his youth, preceded the centenarian in death by more than two years, thus severing Canada's most intimate tie to Moses Montefiore even before the "century of Montefiore" came to its natural end.

If De Sola's was the closest Canadian bond to Sir Moses, it was the centenary of his birth in 1884 that made Montefiore's name a household word to many Canadians. The centenary was celebrated by Jews and gentiles all over the British Empire and by Jews everywhere. Canada was no exception. The Toronto *Globe* marked the occasion with an editorial of considerable length, in which it expressed confidence that "Jew and gentile alike (would) recognize . . . [Montefiore's] virtue and join with equal cordiality in his praise."[41] Other newspapers reacted in a similarly enthusiastic fashion.[42] A group of Montreal Jews sought to honour Sir Moses by establishing in his name the short-lived Montefiore Agricultural Aid Association.[43] On the Sunday closest to Montefiore's birthday, Toronto Jews and their gentile guests gathered at Holy Blossom Synagogue for thanksgiving prayers. The service was graced with a "Hallelujah by the (ladies') choir," something that might not have pleased the very traditional Montefiore.[44] In Winnipeg, the two fledgling congregations held services, followed by a parade from one synagogue to the other, the marchers displaying a large portrait of the centenarian as well as flags.[45] In Montreal, the Montefiore Social and Dramatic Club held "a grand ball," while the Spanish and Portuguese Synagogue, the German and Polish Congregation (today's Shaar Hashomayim), and Temple Emanu-El held separate commemorative services.[46] Unwittingly, Montefiore became embroiled in religious politics in Montreal, when Rabbi Meldola De Sola, the son and successor of Abraham De Sola at the Spanish and Portuguese Synagogue, seized the occasion to flay Reform Jews. The Reformers, he said, "practically opposed the Almighty's design by gradually abolishing every religious observance distinctly Jewish," in contrast to Montefiore, whom he correctly saw as an exemplar of traditionalism. The standing room only service at De Sola's synagogue closed with the singing by the male choir of a Hebrew rendition of "God Save the Queen."[47]

Even after his death, the memory of Sir Moses continued to exercise the imaginations of Canadians. In his *Chronology of Montreal and of Canada from A.D. 1752 to 1893* (Montreal, 1893), Frederick William Terrill paid tribute to Montefiore's wealth and longevity.[48] In 1910, Jewish immigrants to Alberta from the United States adopted Montefiore's name for their new agricultural colony; and a year later, the Montefiore Club of Winnipeg was organized "for the purpose of affording a meeting place for the young business men" of that community. In these and various other ways, the name of Montefiore was kept alive over the years in Canada.[49]

Considering Montefiore's very modest interest in Canada, one may well wonder why Canadians were so interested in him. To a degree, of course, this is no puzzle at all. Abraham De Sola's tie was a natural one. As for other Canadians, the British-Jewish gentleman and amateur statesman caught the attention of people all over the world. In the last quarter of the nineteenth century, moreover, the ties of Canadians to the mother country grew steadily stronger. Nineteenth-century Canadians were conscious of their geographical isolation and nervous about American "manifest destiny," which threatened to destroy their autonomy. This often led to exaggerated pride in being part of an empire "more extended than any over which man has ruled," as Rabbi Meldola De Sola described the British Empire in 1884, the empire that was home to Montefiore and whose sovereign paid him "honour . . . in the most marked manner."[50] Montefiore's "long and noble life" symbolized, to many Canadians, Victorian England at her tolerant and colourful best.[51] They took pride in belonging to Montefiore as they did to other illustrious Britons, and rejoiced in the Montefiore centenary, as they would some years later in the celebration of Queen Victoria's diamond jubilee.[52]

With regard to Canadian Jews, even including Abraham De Sola, one senses an added dimension to their enthusiasm for Montefiore and their eagerness to associate themselves and their institutions with him. With few exceptions, and most of those in the early part of the century, nineteenth-century Canadian Jews failed to achieve the social acceptability and political recognition that their British and American co-religionists of similar wealth and stature were beginning to receive.[53] Although Canadian Jews were granted full civic equality in 1832, they were not elected or appointed to major office until many years later. No Jew would serve in the federal cabinet until 1969. In England, Jews achieved high office much sooner. Moreover, social acceptance to a degree, at least, preceded political advancement there.

In Canada, all through the Victorian Era, Jews remained largely out-siders. Even Montefiore continued to be thought of according to negative stereotypes. The Toronto *Globe*, for example, in congratulating Montefiore on reaching his hundredth birthday, omitted mention of his selfless stewardship of the Jewish people, while dwelling at length on his great wealth, his most "Jewish" characteristic.[54] Among French-Canadians, Jews achieved even less social acceptance than among Anglo-Canadians. French-Canadians, increasing-ly fearful, in the nineteenth century, of losing their religious and cultural dis-tinctiveness, generally opposed immigration into Canada of any sort. They saw it as little more than a ploy to augment British power. They also looked askance generally at urbanization, commerce, and industrialization, which threatened to destroy their traditional rural or small-town way of life. Jews, who were immi-grants and city dwellers, worked in industry and commerce, and belonged to the "deicide race," were, then, undesirable additions to Quebec's population on four counts.[55] The response of French-Canadians to the Montefiore centenary is instructive. Nasty words would have been considered mendacious, perhaps even unpatriotic. Thus French-language papers ignored the event. On the day Canada's English-language press fulsomely reported the birthday festivities around the world, Montreal's *l'Étendard* featured a front-page attack by the bishop of Ottawa on Freemasonry—a movement often coupled in the minds of Roman Catholics of the day with Judaism and socialism, said to be the three main enemies of the Church.[56]

The members of Winnipeg's nascent Jewish community, most of them recent immigrants from eastern Europe, described the sense of isolation felt by many Canadian Jews and their expectations of Montefiore in two memorials composed for the centenary. Canada's Jews were, they wrote to the philanthropist, endeavouring "in a new country to better . . . [their] position in life" but finding the task difficult.[57] As a means of enhancing their inferior position, they hitched their wagon to Montefiore's star. "Your illustrious example," they wrote to him, "has thrown over our whole race a halo of respect which smoothes [*sic*] our paths through the troubles and vexations of life."[58] It is in the context of increasingly unfriendly relations between Jews and French-Canadians that one can understand the attempt of long-settled Jews in Montreal to establish the Montefiore Agricultural Aid Association in 1884, "to make organized efforts to direct the enterprise and industry of our co-religionists into . . . new fields of labour" on the western prairies far from French Canada. The Montrealers felt such a step particularly "desirable at the present stage of our relations with other races and peoples."[59]

In both French and English Canada, Jews hoped for an improved image as a result of their connection with Montefiore. At the centenary service in Montreal's Temple Emanu-El, Rabbi Samuel Marks prayed that Jews and non-Jews would all draw the appropriate "lesson . . . from his life."[60] In Toronto, Rev. Herman Phillips pointedly reminded those gathered in Holy Blossom Synagogue for the centennial service there, that Sir Moses was "beloved by the sovereign of the country."[61] The Toronto *Daily Mail,* unlike the *Globe*, noted on that same occasion that in the liberal atmosphere of Britain, Montefiore's family had "distinguished themselves in science and literature as well as in commerce."[62] Canadian Jews hoped to emulate those achievements and to integrate into Canadian "high society," if that society would become as accepting of Jews as Britain's. Undoubtedly, they hoped that gentiles would note that outside Canada, prominent non-Jews, such as Queen Victoria, the German empress, and Henry Ward Beecher, New York's famous Protestant preacher, were as admiring of Montefiore as his co-religionists.[63] In Montreal and Winnipeg, Jews attached Montefiore's name to elite social clubs, and in Quebec, the wealthy and prominent Abraham Josephs named their son, Montefiore, as a reminder to themselves and to gentiles of the reasonableness of such expectations and of the gains for all to be derived from their fulfillment.

In later years, Montefiore came to symbolize a bygone, heroic era in Canada and the Empire as a whole, and, eventually, to recede from memory. As the Canadian-Jewish community grew and became better rooted in the country, and as Jews began to achieve distinction in their own right and gain a measure of self-confidence, the Montefiore connection, indeed, the British connection in general, declined in importance. In 1902, however, almost two decades after Montefiore's death, Rabbi Bernard M. Kaplan, in his farewell address to the members of Shaar Hashomayim Synagogue in Montreal, reminded his listeners that the day had not yet come when they could stand on their own in Canada without holding onto the coattails of famous and successful co-religionists in the mother country. Kaplan, who was returning to the United States, wished for his congregation and all "Canadian Jews [that they] might produce some day such men as Disraeli and Montefiore," and thereby achieve for themselves the position and self-respect of Jews in the mother country.[64]

The fact that that day was still in the future is illustrated by a footnote to the foregoing. In 1912, almost three decades after Montefiore's death, one of his relatives emigrated to Canada. In that year, William Sebag-Montefiore, grandson of Joseph Sebag-Montefiore, the nephew and heir of the childless Sir Moses, arrived in Montreal, where he lived until his death, except for his British army service during World War I. Sebag-Montefiore married successively two daughters of Horace Joseph, a first cousin of Montefiore Joseph and nephew of Mrs. Abraham De Sola. Thus, the Montefiores became related by marriage, both to Montefiore Joseph and to Rabbi Abraham De Sola.

Sebag-Montefiore joined the Spanish and Portuguese Synagogue in Montreal and served as its secretary while Meldola De Sola, his wife's cousin, was still rabbi. Later, he served as president. It goes without saying that Montreal Jews, especially the wealthy members of the Spanish and Portuguese congregation, were very proud to have a Montefiore in their midst, and that Sebag-Montefiore's name and family connections, as well as his being a British army officer, had much to do with his extraordinarily rapid rise to synagogue office. To be sure, the Spanish and Portuguese was not a large congregation; and, like other congregations, it always needed willing workers. That Sebag-Montefiore was a *bona fide* Sephardi, and that he had married into the Joseph family, would have recommended him for synagogue office in any case. He was, moreover, not without personal merit.[65] Still, it is unlikely that in a hidebound, tradition-conscious institution such as the Spanish and Portuguese Synagogue, anyone less than a Montefiore would have risen so meteorically. Sebag-Montefiore's name provided the synagogue members with an additional claim to the social legitimacy many of them had long been seeking.[66] He naturally became their standard-bearer. Nearly fifty years after his death, then, the name of Moses Montefiore remained in Canada a potent symbol of Jewish achievement and of British toleration; and he continued to serve as an instrument of social advancement for fellow Jews.

In a modest way, then, during his lifetime, Moses Montefiore had directly aided some Canadian Jews, as he did those elsewhere. In addition, he served as a model to Canadian Jews and as an example to non-Jews, of Jewish virtue and accomplishment. Perhaps more important, both during his lifetime and afterwards, association with Montefiore provided a means for Canadian Jews to move closer to full social acceptance by gentiles. If he realized his dual function, Montefiore would undoubtedly have been pleased. His sense of *noblesse oblige* had, after all, led him always to believe it was "the duty of . . . emancipated Jews to work for those yet unemancipated . . . and to use the fact of . . . emancipation as an instrument for striving the more effectively in their behalf."[67] In British North America, he was able to do that without any conscious effort, just by being who he was, the most prominent Jew of his day.

NOTES

1 Cecil Roth, "Moses Montefiore, 1784–1885," in his *Essays and Portraits in Anglo-Jewish History* (Philadelphia, 1962), p. 267.

2 The evidence is largely negative. The two volumes of printed diary extracts, *Diaries of Sir Moses and Lady Montefiore,* ed. L. (Louis) Loewe, 2 vols. (Chicago, 1890), contain only the slightest mention of Canada (1, p. 167) and no mention at all of Canadian Jews. There may, of course, have been some reference in the 85 manuscript diary volumes, which are known to have been destroyed, but it is doubtful that a very different picture would emerge.

3 Montefiore quoted in S. U. Nahon, *Sir Moses Montefiore* (Jerusalem, 1965), p. 67.

4 *Ha-Meliz,* 8 Nisan, 1882.

5 See Louis Rosenberg, *Canada's Jews* (Montreal, 1939), for a brief survey of early Canadian Jewish history and population growth.

6 Minutes of the Spanish and Portuguese Synagogue, Shearith Israel, Montreal (Hereafter, MSP), 16 January 1863; Lawrence H. Lande, comp. and ed., *Montefiore*

Club ([Montreal], 1955), p. 3; Arthur Chiel, *Jewish Experiences in Early Manitoba* (Winnipeg, 1955), p. 26; Benjamin G. Sack, *History of the Jews in Canada,* tr. Ralph Novek (Montreal, 1965), p. 108. See also Esther Blaustein, Rachel Esar, and Evelyn Miller, "Spanish and Portuguese Synagogue (Shearith Israel) Montreal, 1768–1968," in *Miscellanies* of the Jewish Historical Society of England, 8 (1969–70), p. 115.

7   MSP, 3 July 1872, 26 December 1872; personal letter, Moses Montefiore, Ramsgate, to Abraham De Sola, Montreal, 5 December 1872, in McGill University Archives, Montreal, Abraham De Sola Papers (Hereafter, ADSP).

8   See Albert M. Hyamson, *The Sephardim of England* (London, 1951), p. 384.

9   Oscar Douglas Skelton, *Life and Letters of Sir Wilfrid Laurier,* 1 (Toronto, 1965), p. 108. See also Norman MacDonald, *Canada: Immigration and Colonization, 1841–1903* (Toronto, 1966), passim.

10   V. D. Lipman, "The Age of Emancipation, 1815–1880," in *Three Centuries of Anglo-Jewish History,* ed. V. D. Lipman (Cambridge, 1961), p. 69.

11   5 November 1864.

12   p. 10. Although he was not an advocate of Jewish political restoration in the Holy Land, Montefiore was often thought to be so, probably because of his charitable efforts and political intervention on behalf of Palestine Jewry. Compare, for example, "Sir Moses Montefiore," Winnipeg *Daily Times,* 25 October 1884.

13   See Richard S. Lambert, *For the Time Is at Hand* (London, [1947]), pp. 58, 127–28.

14   "Montefiore Joseph, Quebec," in *The Jew in Canada,* ed. Arthur Daniel Hart (Toronto and Montreal, 1926), p. 340. See also E. C. Woodley, *The House of Joseph in the Life of Quebec* (Quebec, 1946), pp. 56–70.

15   "To the Memory of Lady Montefiore," in Isidore G. Ascher, *Voices from the Hearth* (Montreal, 1863), p. 11.

16   Stephen Speisman, *The Jews of Toronto, A History to 1937* (Toronto, 1979), p. 56.

17   "Montefiore Club, Montreal," in Hart, p. 453. See also Lande, *Montefiore Club,* passim.

18   See, for example, London *Jewish Chronicle,* 29 September 1876; Montreal *Gazette,* 7 June 1882; New York *Jewish Messenger,* 9 June 1882; *American Hebrew,* 9 June 5642 [1882]. During his 35 years in Montreal, De Sola became involved in one way or another with most of the city's important English-language cultural and intellectual groups. There is no record of his ever having appeared before a Francophone group, however, a sign of the lack of acceptability of Jews among French-Canadians.

19   Loewe, 1, p. 56.

20   Abraham De Sola, *Biography of David Aaron De Sola* (Philadelphia, 5624 [1864]), pp. 11–13, 33; Loewe, 1, p. 23.

21   De Sola, *Biography,* p. 45.

22   Ibid., p. 28.

23   Ibid., pp. 16, 21, 36, 47–48, and dedication page; Paul Goodman, *Moses Montefiore* (Philadelphia, 1925), p. 218; Richard D. Barnett, "Haham Meldola and Hazan De Sola," *Transactions* of the Jewish Historical Society of England, 21 (1968); pp. 1–39.

24 Moses Montefiore, Ramsgate, personal letter to Abraham De Sola, Montreal, 4 June 1865, in ADSP. See also letter of 9 February 1865.

25 Copybooks in ADSP.

26 Hyamson, p. 304. See also Loewe's note in copybook in ADSP, in which he complains of his pupil's "cramped hand" and advises him to practice his writing more diligently.

27 See letter of Joseph Elijah Bernstein, *Ha-Meliz*, 7 Iyyar, 1984.

28 London *Jewish Chronicle*, 5 September 1845, 16 October 1846; Hyamson, p. 341.

29 MSP, 16, 23, 30 December 1859, 10 February 1860; Moses Montefiore, Ramsgate, personal letter to Abraham De Sola, Montreal, 28 December 5622 [1861], in ADSP.

30 Moses Montefiore, Ramsgate, personal letter to Abraham De Sola, Montreal, 29 April, 16 June 1870, in ADSP.

31 Moses Montefiore, Ramsgate, personal letter to Abraham De Sola, Montreal, 16 January 1872; Moses Montefiore, London, personal letter to Abraham De Sola, Montreal, 2 December 1875, both in ADSP.

32 Moses Montefiore, Ramsgate, personal letter to Abraham De Sola, Montreal, 16 August 5638 [1878], and 30 January 5639 [1879] in ADSP.

33 Moses Montefiore, London, personal letter to Abraham De Sola, Montreal, 17 June 5624 [1864]; Moses Montefiore, Ramsgate, personal letters to Abraham De Sola, Montreal, 10 October 1872, 5 December 1872, 18 November 1875, all in ADSP.

34 Moses Montefiore, Ramsgate, personal letter to Abraham De Sola, Montreal, 9 February 1865; Lady Judith Montefiore, London, personal letter to Abraham De Sola, Montreal, 29 February (1860?), both in ADSP.

35 Moses Montefiore, Ramsgate, personal letters to Abraham De Sola, Montreal, 9 February 1865, 16 June 1870, in ADSP.

36 See among other sources, Congressional *Globe*, 9 January 1872; Montreal *Gazette*, 12 January 1872; New York *Jewish Messenger*, 12 January 1872; London *Jewish Chronicle*, 29 September 1876; Canadian *Jewish Times*, 28 February 1902. In "The 'Learned Hazan' of Montreal: Reverend Abraham De Sola, LL.D.," *American Sephardi* 7–8 (Autumn 1975); pp. 23–44, Evelyn Miller suggests that Montefiore may have had something to do with De Sola's appearance before the Congress. Arthur Cohen, a nephew of Montefiore and a friend of the British De Solas, acted as legal counsellor at the United States-British war claims conference in Geneva in 1871; and, as noted earlier, it is generally assumed that De Sola's prayer was meant to mark the end of Civil War related tensions between the two countries. Miller thinks the invitation to De Sola may have been engineered by Cohen and his uncle. It can only be hoped that hard evidence will emerge to substantiate this fruitful theory.

37 Moses Montefiore, Ramsgate, personal letter to Abraham De Sola, Montreal, February, 1872, in ADSP.

38 Moses Montefiore, Ramsgate, personal letter to Abraham De Sola, Montreal, 30 May 5641 [1881]; Moses Montefiore, Ramsgate, personal letter to Abraham De Sola, London, 8 June 1877, both in ADSP.

39 Moses Montefiore, Ramsgate, personal letter to Abraham De Sola, Montreal, 29 December 5623 [1862]; Moses Montefiore, London, personal letter to Abraham De Sola, Montreal, 22 February 1866, both in ADSP. Sir Moses was also sent a condolence resolution by De Sola's synagogue, which placed Lady Judith's name on the list of people for whom a perpetual memorial prayer was to be recited. MSP, 26 October 1862.

40 Moses Montefiore, Ramsgate, personal letter to Abraham De Sola, Montreal, February, 1872, in ADSP; Abraham De Sola, ed. and rev., *The Form of Prayers According to the Custom of the Spanish and Portuguese Jews*, 6 vols. (Philadelphia, 1878), 1, dedication page.

41 24 October 1884.

42 See, for example, the Toronto *Evening News*, 27 October 1884, 28 October 1884; Toronto *Daily Mail*, 25 October 1884, 27 October 1884; Winnipeg *Daily Times*, 25 October 1884, 27 October 1884; Montreal *Gazette*, 25 October 1884, 27 October 1884; and other papers. See also Toronto *Globe*, 20 October 1884.

43 Sack, pp. 207–10.

44 Toronto *Globe*, 27 October 1884.

45 Manitoba *Daily Free Press*, 27 October 1884; Winnipeg *Daily Times*, 27 October 1884; Chiel, pp. 21–27

46 Montreal *Gazette*, 25 October 1884, 27 October 1884; undated newspaper clippings, Jewish Public Library, Montreal, Bronfman Collection.

47 Meldola De Sola, sermon on the occasion of Moses Montefiore's centenary, quoted in full in the Montreal *Gazette*, 27 October 1884. Although Sir Moses was probably spared knowledge of the fact, his birthday, which in most places served as an occasion for an outpouring of good will, had sparked considerable behind-the-scenes controversy in Montreal. At first, the Spanish and Portuguese and the Polish and German (Shaar HaShomayim) congregations had attempted to get together to honour Montefiore. The effort collapsed, however, when the contentious Rabbi De Sola claimed to have been "grossly insulted" by the president of the German and Polish congregation, John Moss. It is likely that De Sola's sermonic barbs against Reform were directed as much at the German and Polish congregation as they were at Temple Emanu-El. See MSP, 17 March, 20 April, 15 October 1884; New York *Jewish Messenger*, 31 October 1884.

48 pp. 95–96, 367.

49 "The Montefiore Club, Winnipeg," in Hart, p. 454; Simon Belkin, *Through Narrow Gates* (Montreal, 1966), p. 82.

50 De Sola sermon, as quoted in the Montreal *Gazette*, 27 October 1884.

51 Dr. Hermann Adler, chief rabbi of Great Britain, as quoted in Goodman, p. 207. For a contemporary discussion of Montefiore's symbolic value to eastern European Jews, see "The Birthday of Moses, Servant of God," [Hebrew], *Ha-Meliz*, 19 Marheshvan 1884.

52 See Carl Berger, *The Sense of Power* (Toronto and Buffalo, 1971), pp. 87–89.

53 For a discussion of the difficulties of integrating Jews into the Canadian social and political structure in the latter decades of the nineteenth century, see Michael Brown,

"Divergent Paths: Early Zionism in Canada and the United States," *Jewish Social Studies*, 44 (Spring 1982): pp. 159–63.

54   27 October 1884.

55   For a description of Jewish feelings about French-Canadian animosity towards Jews in the year of the Montefiore centennial, see Joseph Elijah Bernstein, letter [Hebrew], *Ha-Meliz*, 11 Iyyar 1884. Among other sources dealing with French-Canadian reactions to Jews, see "Notre Programme," Montreal, *La Vérité*, 14 July 1881; Everett Cherrington Hughes, *French Canada in Transition* (Chicago, 1943), pp. 23–24.

56   27 October 1884. *La Presse* and *La Patrie*, two of French Canada's largest circulation newspapers, failed to mention the event at all.

57   Address of Sons of Israel, Winnipeg, to Montefiore, quoted in Manitoba *Daily Free Press*, 27 October 1884. See also Chiel, p. 26.

58   Address of Bethel Congregation, Winnipeg, to Montefiore, quoted in Manitoba *Daily Free Press*, 25 October 1884.

59   Invitation letter from Mark Samuels, pres., and Lewis A. Hart, sec'y., Montefiore Agricultural Aid Association, Montreal, 8 January 1885, in Jewish Public Library, Montreal, Bronfman Collection of Jewish Canadiana, Scrapbook on Jewish Farming.

60   Quoted in "The Montefiore Anniversary," Montreal *Gazette*, 25 October 1884.

61   Quoted in Toronto *Globe*, 27 October 1884.

62   25 October 1884.

63   See reports in Toronto *Daily Mail*, 27 October 1884; Manitoba *Daily Free Press*, 27 October 1884.

64   Quoted in the Canadian *Jewish Times*, 28 February 1902.

65   On William Sebag-Montefiore, see, among other sources, MSP, 6 May 1914, 8 February and 2 May 1915; Col. J. H. Patterson, Plymouth, personal letter to Vladimir Jabotinsky, London, 23 October 1917, in Jabotinsky Archive, Makhon Jabotinsky, Tel Aviv, 1917 File; *History of the Corporation of Spanish and Portuguese Jews of Montreal* (Montreal, 1918), passim; Mordecai Ben Hillel Ha-Cohen, *Milhemet Ha-'Amim* [*The War of the Nations*], 5 (Jerusalem, 1920), p. 34, entry for 17 Nisan [1918]; Solomon Frank, *Two Centuries in the Life of a Synagogue* (n.p., n.d.), p. 16; Hart, p. 511.

66   In "Our Distant Brethren, the Jews of Canada" [Hebrew], *Ha-Zefirah*, 3 Adar, 1888, Alexander Harkavy, soon to become a noted lexicographer, offers a description of veteran Montreal Jews, most of them members of the Spanish and Portuguese Synagogue, desperately trying to create for themselves an aristocratic lineage. Harkavy, then a teacher in Montreal, reports how Clarence De Sola, son of Abraham and brother of Meldola, admitted to him that he had rewritten Canadian-Jewish history to make it appear that most Jews in the early years had been of Iberian descent, rather than of less "noble" stock, i.e., from central or eastern Europe, their real place of origin. He did this, he acknowledged, in order to give Montreal Jews a better claim to acceptance in "high society."

67   Roth, p. 276.

"And if not now, when?"*: Feminism and Anti-Semitism Beyond Clara Brett Martin

BRENDA COSSMAN & MARLEE KLINE

* *"If I am not for myself who will be? If I am only for myself what am I? And if not now, when?"*

Rabbi Hillel

> Repeatedly, I find that I am preoccupied not with counter-
> ing anti-Semitism, but with trying to prove that anti-
> Semitism exists, that it is serious, and that, as lesbian/fem-
> inists, we should be paying attention to it both inside and
> outside the movement.[1]

The discovery of Clara Brett Martin's anti-Semitism, and the debates that
have ensued as we have struggled to come to terms with its implications, have

launched us into a profoundly difficult process. Difficult because, to this point, anti-Semitism has been very little addressed within the context of feminist legal studies in Canada. And, addressing anti-Semitism means beginning the hard work involved in confronting yet another aspect of difference and power relations among women. The articles by Constance Backhouse and Lita-Rose Betcherman in this volume are important attempts to engage in this process.[2] Our initial reactions to these articles, as referees, were deeply emotional. We each struggled in our own way to find words to express these reactions. We were then provided the opportunity to develop our views more fully through a formal response. As Jewish feminists, the prospect of confronting the topic of anti-Semitism in a public way was daunting.[3] But, through engaging in this process, we have gained important insight into the nature of anti-Semitism and its particular impact on the feminist legal community. We have also struggled with how to confront anti-Semitism in a constructive manner. We offer the following comments in the spirit of continuing the conversation begun courageously by Backhouse and Betcherman, and, of engaging in dialogue to deepen the analysis of anti-Semitism within the context of feminist legal history and feminist engagement with law in general.

Constance Backhouse and Lita-Rose Betcherman have attempted to confront the anti-Semitism manifest in the actions of Clara Brett Martin, the first woman to be admitted to the bar in the then British Empire. In "Clara Brett Martin: Canadian Heroine or Not?" Constance Backhouse re-evaluates Clara Brett Martin's earlier unquestioned status as a feminist heroine in light of the letter written by her in 1915 to the Attorney General of Ontario, which was replete with anti-Semitic accusations and called for legislative action. In the process, Backhouse raises the important question of whether it is appropriate for contemporary feminists to rely on the concept of heroine. She regards this question as being important in relation to current debates in feminism concerning the inclusion of the diverse experiences, concerns, and priorities of women differently located in the web of social relations. The solution advanced by Backhouse is to continue to recognize as heroines, women such as Clara Brett Martin, who challenge and resist the oppression to which they are subject, and to acknowledge the ways in which they have been, at the same time, complicit in, or even active perpetrators of, other forms of oppression. Lita-Rose Betcherman's analysis is directed less to examining the implications of Clara Brett Martin's anti-Semitism for feminists, and more towards examining the nature of Clara Brett Martin's anti-Semitism. Betcherman's historical analysis emphasizes that Clara Brett Martin, in writing to the Attorney General, did not simply reflect the prevailing anti-Semitism of her time. To the contrary, she actively chose to reinforce it in a context where alternative discourses, that went some ways towards resisting and challenging anti-Semitism, were available. Implicit in Betcherman's conclusion is a challenge to those who might attempt to dismiss Clara Brett Martin's anti-Semitism as simply a reflection of the society of which she was a part.

Quite clearly then, Backhouse and Betcherman focus on different implications of Clara Brett Martin's anti-Semitism and come to essentially different conclusions. At the same time, the two authors move from similar premises. Most importantly, the approach they take to the analysis of anti-Semitism tends to focus on individual prejudice and discrimination rather than on systemic and historically rooted dimensions of anti-Semitism. At one level, this is not surprising: the systemic question of anti-Semitism is ancillary, both in these pieces and in current legal feminist discourse, to the more particular question, "What do we do about Clara Brett Martin?" It is our view, however, that the systemic issue of anti-Semitism needs to be addressed in its own right. While the issue has been raised initially in the quite narrow context of Clara Brett Martin, it does not end there. We should move forward with more general and complex analyses of the nature and impact of anti-Semitism in the broader historical context within which anti-Semitism developed in Canada.

The history of the Jewish people, and the history of anti-Semitism, stretching across millennia and around the world, is enormously complex. In disciplines outside of law, the literature analyzing this history is large and rich, and contains many important debates within it.[4] In this response, however, we will attempt only a brief consideration of the nature of anti-Semitism and its historical development.[5] Our intention is a modest one—to highlight some of the central themes in this long history, and to provide a framework within which to consider ways to further develop the analyses of Clara Brett Martin's anti-Semitism offered by Backhouse and Betcherman. We rely on the work of

Backhouse and Betcherman as points of departure to raise more general questions and issues in the analysis of anti-Semitism. In the last part of this comment, we examine another aspect of anti-Semitism, silencing. Silencing has affected and limited the extent to which anti-Semitism has been acknowledged and addressed within the feminist legal community. We conclude by emphasizing the need to confront this silencing and to engage directly in analysis of anti-Semitism beyond the individual context of one person, Clara Brett Martin.

Some Historical Considerations

A nuanced understanding of the wider historical context within which anti-Semitism developed in Canada requires consideration of the political, economic, cultural, and ideological relations that produce and reproduce anti-Semitism. Such an analysis focuses attention on the material relations that contributed to the historical development of anti-Semitic ideas, images, and stereotypes, as well as their manifestation in individuals and institutions, albeit in different ways and to different effect in different periods and places. Ideological analysis is useful in this context because it directs attention to "the connection between ideas, attitudes, and beliefs, on the one hand, and economic and political interests, on the other." It allows for recognition of some continuity of anti-Semitic ideas, images, and stereotypes across place and time, together with recognition of the historical specificity of their reception and manifestation in varying degrees of social and political action and violence.

Distinguishing between anti-Semitic ideas and personal attitudes, on the one hand, and the manifestation of such ideas and attitudes in institutional action, on the other hand, is also fundamental to an analysis of anti-Semitism. Anti-Semitism, at one level, involves personal prejudice. Sometimes, and in some places, it is expressed only in "private acts of contempt and exclusion," without recourse to the state or other institutional forces. In other cases, anti-Semites seek to "harness the coercive power of the state to their hatred and fear of Jews . . . " Anti-Semitism then becomes much more than the product of "personally cruel individuals." It becomes a product, rather, "of actions by privileged sectors of a society attempting to preserve their prerogatives and to deny equality to others." The ways these two forms of anti-Semitism combine in a particular context will be dependent on the particular history of the region or state in question. Even the pattern of how personal prejudice develops cannot be understood without inquiring into the social, political, economic, and ideological context in which such attitudes arise. To focus only on personal prejudice while excluding the context of state involvement, is to miss the ways in which anti-Semitism has structural and systemic aspects as well as individualized aspects.

Central to the ideological development of anti-Semitism is the construction of Jews as "other," as alien. During the Hellenistic and Roman periods, hostility towards Jews was fairly widespread. Their adherence to their own religion and culture was seen as nonconformist, threatening, and hostile towards other religions. To this construction of otherness was later added explicit religious justification in Medieval Europe through the concept of a monotheistic European Christendom, intolerant of any form of deviation. Jews, as a significant minority in Europe at the time, suffered persecution as religious deviants together with pagans, 'witches', and Gypsies (Romanis). The religious focus of anti-Semitic discourses in Medieval Europe did not preclude the relevance of economic factors. The eleventh and twelfth centuries witnessed a significant economic expansion in Western Europe, which resulted in an increased demand for capital. The Church, however, forbade Christian usury: Christians were prohibited from lending money for interest to other Christians. As Robert Chazan has described, the combination of these factors "served to open to the Jews vast new opportunities in banking." The downside to this enhancement of economic opportunities for Jews was the concomitant reinforcement and extension of the construction of Jewish people as hostile "others":

> When Bernard of Clairvaux could, in passing and gratuitous-
> ly, use the verb "to Jew" as a synonym for money lending,
> then surely a dangerous new negative image had developed.

By the thirteenth century, a Christian mercantile class emerged and the economic need for Jews declined. However, the negative stereotypes that had been created during this brief period of prosperity did not. By the end of the century, the Jews began to be expelled from the countries of Western Europe.

With the rise of liberalism in eighteenth century Europe, Jews were, for the first time, granted a measure of legal equality in some regions. This amelioration can be contrasted to the treatment of other peoples who suffered from the contemporaneous rise of European imperialism and the development of the slave trade. However, the late nineteenth century, particularly the 1870s and 1880s, saw a resurgence of anti-Semitism throughout Europe. Numerous factors contributed to this development. There was, at the time, "a general rebellion against the liberalism and modernity that were responsible for emancipating the Jews." This reaction was related to the rise of nationalism and the notion of the organic unity of the state. These developments reinforced the construction of Jews as "other." Economic factors played a related role. Following a period of considerable economic growth, Europe experienced an economic collapse in 1873, which marked the start of a depression that continued until the end of the century.

Jewish economic activity, particularly in banking and finance, was blamed for the collapse. More generally, political elites and intellectuals sought at this time to manipulate public opinion and promote anti-Semitism within a broad social, economic, political, and cultural context. Politicians, journalists, and writers exploited the prevalence of anti-Jewish sentiment, and in so doing, developed a new anti-Semitic discourse, which relied more on racial justifications than on religious ideas. However, the central feature of anti-Semitism remained essentially the same as in the medieval period. Jewish people were constructed as a hostile and evil "other." While the particular historical period of anti-Semitism with which we are concerned is the late nineteenth and early twentieth centuries, an historical discussion of anti-Semitism would not be complete without at least mentioning the rise of its most vicious form in the twentieth century, culminating in the slaughter of six million Jews by the Nazis in the Holocaust.

ANTI-SEMITISM AND CLARA BRETT MARTIN

With this framework for understanding anti-Semitism, we turn to consider Clara Brett Martin. We welcome Constance Backhouse's unequivocal condemnation of anti-Semitism, both past and present. At the same time, however, it is important to discuss some of the limitations of her analysis for understanding anti-Semitism. Anti-Semitism is not just a matter of anti-Jewish acts in the abstract—it has concrete effects that depend on the social power of the actor and how that power is used. Clara Brett Martin was not simply an individual who expressed prejudice against Jews. She was a woman with public recognition and considerable power. She was a member of the Law Society of Upper Canada and an officer of the Court. That she was a woman undoubtedly attenuated her relative social power when compared to her male counterparts. Nonetheless, given her status as a prominent lawyer, her letter to the Attorney General's office would certainly have been treated seriously.[6] The letter was not simply an act of personal, private prejudice or discrimination by Clara Brett Martin. It was a lobbying of the state to take legislative action on anti-Semitic grounds. This institutional dimension relates not so much to Clara Brett Martin's attitudes and feelings about Jews, as to the significance of her social power and the ways she used it. The individualistic focus of Backhouse's analysis only partially captures the nature and impact of the anti-Semitism propagated by Clara Brett Martin.

Backhouse attempts to situate Clara Brett Martin's prejudice within a larger social context when she asks whether that anti-Semitic context could excuse Martin's individual actions.[7] We agree with Backhouse that it does not. Recognizing that an individual has taken anti-Semitic actions consistent with the social and historical context of her time, should not lead us to excuse, minimize, or apologize for those actions. As Backhouse suggests (and Lita-Rose Betcherman confirms), there must have been active resistance to anti-Semitism at the time Clara Brett Martin wrote her letter, and consequently, "[t]here [were] choices to be made, and Canada's first woman lawyer chose to perpetrate some of the abuses, not to fight them."[8]

Unfortunately, this contextual approach is not sustained by Backhouse in her other attempts to situate Clara Brett Martin's anti-Semitism. Her analysis remains individualized when she argues, for example, that Clara Brett Martin must not have been completely prejudiced because, for a short time, she had a Jewish secretary. While Backhouse is careful not to suggest that this fact mitigates the reality that Clara Brett Martin "discriminated with force and clarity" against Jews at other times, for her the employment of Lillian Simon demonstrates that Clara Brett Martin "did not discriminate against all Jews."[9] In other words, Backhouse suggests that a willingness to employ a Jew, and treat her well as an employee, might be tantamount to non-discrimination. This conclusion is somewhat difficult given the inherent inequality of an employment relationship. A further difficulty lies in the fact that Lillian Simon was a Jew who could pass in the gentile world.[10] This capacity raises the concern that Clara Brett Martin's tolerance of Jews may have been limited to those who did not manifest the characteristics of Jewish stereotypes. Tolerance of this sort, however, is of little value. It can serve to reinforce rather than challenge the oppression of those Jews who cannot, or choose not to, conform to the norms of the dominant society.

Yet, even putting these questions aside for the moment, the focus of Backhouse's analysis of Clara Brett Martin's anti-Semitism remains limited to prejudice displayed against individual Jews in individual contexts. The issue is framed as being one of "coming to grips with the complexity of human behaviour and emotion, to recognize that individuals are seldom unequivocally and absolutely bigoted."[11] As we have already discussed, while this kind of psychological account is important, it is important to go beyond it and examine how anti-Semitism develops into, and operates as, dominant ideology.

The individualist focus of Backhouse's analysis leads her in the end to our last problem. She explicitly acknowledges that underlying her concern to retain an "evolving, rehabilitated"[12] notion of heroine within feminism, is an attempt to ensure that we do not lose sight of the lives of individual women in reconstructing feminist historiographies. This is contrasted to the view of those who consider "the very concept of "heroine [as] problematic" in that it serves to deify certain individuals, lionizing their personal deeds artificially and without a full appreciation of the role of the collectivity."[13] The objection to the notion of heroine, however, is an important argument. It is one that we think Backhouse has not taken seriously enough, and has dismissed too quickly. Surely the issue is not that individual women should not be studied, but that they should be more fully considered in their complexity; that the contradictions of their lives must be confronted, not submerged. Whatever Clara Brett Martin accomplished, for example, and whomever's interests she has since been interpreted as advancing, her successes must be recognized as being limited to the range of women to which they must have been meant to apply. It is not clear to us how a concept of heroine helps to reveal this limitation.

In fact, it seems that the notion of heroine, even a rehabilitated one, serves more to submerge, rather than confront the contradictions in women's lives and the political implications that they carry for differently located women. These issues are crucial ones, but it is precisely these issues that we risk losing sight of when we focus on whether individual women should, or should not, be considered heroines. Backhouse's argument for putting Clara Brett Martin back on a heroine's pedestal, albeit a less glorified one, illustrates this point. For example, she makes numerous references to Clara Brett Martin as merely having committed "human error." Clara Brett Martin's anti-Semitism is discussed as a "human failing," a "deficiency";[14] she is a woman who merely "made mistakes."[15] Anti-Semitism, however, is not a mistake about which we should take "an expansive appreciation."[16] It is not something that should be simply dismissed as an individual deficiency. It is, rather, a much more complex and pervasive phenomenon. Characterizing anti-Semitism as merely an individual "error" or "mistake" misses the way it is systemic and ideological. Within Backhouse's individualist framework, it is difficult not to focus on whether Clara Brett Martin, nonetheless, remains a "good" person and feminist "heroine" despite her anti-Semitism, rather than to directly confront the complexity of anti-Semitism and its relationship to feminism.

In contrast to Backhouse, Betcherman attempts to confront much more directly the nature of anti-Semitism in Ontario at the time that Clara Brett Martin wrote her letter. She concludes that Clara Brett Martin did not simply reflect prevailing anti-Semitism. Rather, she reinforced and attempted to institutionalize anti-Semitism at a time when an alternative discourse was available that, to some extent, resisted and challenged anti-Semitism. Betcherman's discussion of the nature of anti-Semitism in Toronto at the turn of the century and the discourse of resistance to it in the press, provides extremely important historical information. Her argument that Clara Brett Martin indeed had a choice to make is well taken.[17]

However, Betcherman's overall analysis of Clara Brett Martin and of anti-Semitism requires development in two important respects. First, while she situates Clara Brett Martin's anti-Semitism within a context of the prevailing discourses of anti-Semitism, we think it is important to deconstruct these discourses by locating them within the more general historical and structural context of anti-Semitism. Secondly, despite her insightful discussion of the broader context of the anti-Semitism of the day, within which we get a glimpse of the impact of these anti-Semitic discourses and policies on Jews, her analysis is also, at times, overly individualistic in focusing on the particular anti-Semitism of a particular woman. A more developed analysis could integrate the long history of anti-Semitism that preceded the events discussed in this article—a history that demonstrates the economic, political, religious, and ideological aspects of anti-Semitism in addition to its manifestation in individuals.

Betcherman describes her motivation in writing the article as being a feminist concern with "discrimination against immigrant and visible-minority women."[18] While this issue is certainly an important one, the long history of anti-Semitism and its vast reservoir of derogatory images suggest that more was going on than general "hostility to immigrants,"[19] when anti-Semitic discourses, policies, and laws were constructed in Canada. Consideration of the particular forms of hostility to which Jews were subjected is important. While Betcherman's analysis introduces some of this history and reveals some of these anti-Semitic images and stereotypes in the prevailing discourse, it is also important to further problematize these derogatory images and stereotypes. For example, in discussing the causes of anti-Semitism, Betcherman observes that "[i]t was not only the number of Jews settling in Toronto that contributed to anti-Semitism. It was also their poverty and different ways."[20] Surely, however, the perception of substantial Jewish immigration and the emphasis on the poverty of those who arrived, and their "different ways," were some of the *forms* in which anti-Semitism was articulated, rather than the actual *sources* of Canadian anti-Semitism. In other words, it is important to analyze the extent to which the discourse used to describe the ostensible causes of anti-Semitism was often itself loaded with anti-Semitism. Rather than simply accepting the alleged attributes of Jewish people, it is important to challenge these constructions. For example, instead of accepting the poverty of Jewish immigrants settling in Toronto as a cause of anti-Semitism, it is important to explore whether Jews were in fact poorer than other immigrants, or whether they were just being singled out as a result of anti-Semitism.[21] Similarly, Betcherman observes that Jews "remained ghettoized" in the Ward in Toronto, but does not fully explore why this was so.[22] Could Jews have obtained housing outside of the area of the Ward, or did landlords discriminate in those to whom they rented? Could Jews afford to live anywhere else? Did Jews tend to live in the same place because of their need for protection and community in an otherwise anti-Semitic environment?[23]

More generally, the suggestion that the failure of Jewish immigrants to assimilate was a cause of anti-Semitism obscures the nature and impact of anti-Semitism on Jews. Assimilation is a response, indeed, a survival strategy, for individuals and communities subjected to societal hostility and hatred. Viewed in this light, the preservation of "old country folkways" by Jews must not be seen as a cause of anti-Semitism. Rather, the reaction of the dominant Canadian society to this failure or refusal to assimilate should be understood as a particular manifestation of historically rooted anti-Semitism. The refusal of Jewish immigrants to assimilate must be seen also as an assertion of agency and resistance in the face of this anti-Semitism.[24]

A second area of Betcherman's analysis that could be taken further is her discussion of the sources of Clara Brett Martin's anti-Semitism. Betcherman presents a number of possible explanations for Clara Brett Martin's anti-Semitism, but these explanations remain individualized. She suggests, for example, that Clara Brett Martin's racial prejudice may have been acquired from "living near a people very different from herself."[25] She also traces particular anti-Semitic individuals to whom Clara Brett Martin was likely exposed, such as Goldwin Smith.[26] It is important to consider, however, the interaction between possible triggers of anti-Semitism such as living near Jews or knowing anti-Semites, and the deeper ideologies of anti-Semitism pervasive in Canadian society and manifest in the thoughts and actions of individuals like Clara Brett Martin. It will be through analysis directed to the ideological nature of anti-Semitism that we will be able to deepen our understanding of the reproduction of anti-Semitism through its individual manifestations.

Another illustration of the problematic nature of Betcherman's individualistic focus lies in the very project undertaken in her article—namely, to "place" Clara Brett Martin on "the spectrum of opinion regarding ethnic minorities [which] ranged from tolerance through all shades of prejudice to outright discrimination."[27] To situate one *individual* on a spectrum of opinion construct-ed on the basis of other *individuals*, risks overlooking the ways that the range of individual opinions converge, sometimes leaving the realm of ideas and erupting into direct discrimination and even state-sanctioned violence. When we remain focused on the particular anti-Semitism of individual anti-Semites, we risk los-ing light of the forest of structural anti-Semitism and its impact on Jews.

To counter this problem, we believe that it is necessary to emphasize the ways Clara Brett Martin did not simply reflect the prevailing anti-Semitism of her time, but served to propagate, reinforce, and institutionalize that anti-Semitism, by calling on the state to take legislative action. We could then increase our understanding of Clara Brett Martin's actions within her own con-text, while taking account of the ways by which she was influenced and, in fact, may have helped reinforce and reproduce ideological forms of anti-Semitism.

CONFRONTING ANTI-SEMITISM AND FEMINISM: BEYOND CLARA BRETT MARTIN

Backhouse and Betcherman have taken an important step to confront anti-Semitism in the history of the Canadian women's movement and women's involvement in the legal profession in Canada. As Backhouse suggests, we can move from the discovery of Clara Brett Martin's anti-Semitism "to produce more research on the history of anti-Semitism, and its current manifestations in our profession and in society."[28] In our brief analysis, we have drawn attention to aspects of anti-Semitism that require further investigation and analysis. We want to conclude with some questions . . . questions for which there are no obvi-ous answers, but questions with which we believe the feminist legal communi-ty, and the women's movement in general, must engage. Why is the feminist legal community so focused on Clara Brett Martin? Why do we feel the need to defend her honour? Why is our first response an attempt to situate and under-stand her anti-Semitism? Why have we not responded to the discovery of Clara Brett Martin's anti-Semitism by interrogating anti-Semitism within the women's movement, past and present, and working towards strategies of transcending this form of hatred and oppression? Why do we never directly confront anti-Semitism? Indeed, why are we so afraid to do so?

The "we" here gets complicated—"We" (the writers) are engaging "we" the women's movement; but "we," the writers, are two Jewish feminists, and the last question is at some level directed more to ourselves and others as Jewish feminists. Though it is imperative that feminists confront anti-Semitism, this is not an easy thing to do, particularly for women who are Jews.[29] Breaking through the silence and daring to confront a form of oppression that has always been denied—coming out as Jews, and confronting the anti-Semitism that pervades our everyday lives and struggles—is a terrifying prospect. It is terrifying for all the reasons that have made us suppress our voice and identity for so long.[30]

It is terrifying because we have no reason to believe that we will not be met with disbelief at best, and hostile negation at worst. We fear that speaking out as Jewish feminists against anti-Semitism will only reinforce the stereotypes of Jewish women as loud and pushy; that having our words published will only reinforce the stereotypes of Jews as powerful. We fear, in other words, that, in speaking out, we will run into a wall of anti-Semitism. The very images that we want to challenge will only be reproduced, as we are recognized as *only* the privileged, the powerful, the oppressors. We do not deny that in our particular situation, as third and fourth generation Canadian Ashkenazi Jewish women, we are now privileged in relation to our skin colour, our economic circumstances, and our education.[31] But this does not mean that we, and other Jewish feminists like us, do not face anti-Semitism in our lives. Nor does it mean that all Jewish feminists share these dimensions of privilege.

We fear, as well, that you will hear what we are *not* saying . . . we are not saying that with respect to our identity as Jews we are *as* oppressed as women of colour, as lesbians, as disabled women; nor are we saying that we, in our identity as Jews, are oppressed in the same way as women of colour, as lesbians, as disabled women.[32] We are claiming neither privilege nor symmetry for the hatred and oppression to which we may be subjected. Indeed, our arguments are based on a rejection of either privileging or analogizing oppressions. Anti-Semitism is not "just like" some other form of hatred or oppression. It is not just like racism, or sexism, or heterosexism. It is a form of hatred and oppression with a very particular history, and a very particular present. It is alive and well in Canadian society, and alive and well in the Canadian women's movement. It is a particular "ism" that will require a lot of hard work on the part of individuals alone, and together within the women's movement, to understand and confront— within ourselves and each other.

With this challenge in mind, we return to the first question asked above: namely, why are we so focused on Clara Brett Martin? The answer is, at a certain level, obvious: Clara Brett Martin was the first woman to be admitted to the legal profession, in the then British Empire. Yet, this very construction of Clara Brett Martin is part of our problem. By universalizing the category of woman, and by privileging gender over race and class and religion, we set ourselves up for difficulty. It is essential that we not lose sight of the fact that Clara Brett Martin was a woman of a particular class, a particular race, and a particular religion. Her class, race, and religion do not diminish her accomplishments, but that does not mean that these aspects of her identity are not equally significant, particularly in terms of the range of women to whom her accomplishments did not extend.

While our obsession with Clara Brett Martin, as the "first woman lawyer," has now forced feminists engaged with law to confront the shocking discovery of her anti-Semitism, it is necessary that we move beyond Clara Brett Martin as our point of departure for feminist discussions on anti-Semitism. Rather than focusing attention on the perspectives of those women who have been complicitious in anti-Semitism, we need to focus on women who have suffered at its hands. We must begin to explore and challenge anti-Semitic ideologies and actions—in particular, those that impact on Jewish women. We cannot continue to focus attention on the question of whether it is anti-Semitic to continue to defend the accomplishments of Clara Brett Martin. This question is not trivial. But it is not the only question that we must ask ourselves as feminists. Rather than continue to frame the issue in terms of the present implications of the past anti-Semitism of an individual woman, we must interrogate the history and present manifestations of anti-Semitism, and investigate its more systemic, institutional, and ideological aspects.

Notes

1   Irene Klepfisz, "Anti-Semitism in the Lesbian/Feminist Movement," in *Nice Jewish Girls: A Lesbian Anthology,* ed. Evelyn Torton Beck (Boston: Beacon Press, 1989), 52.

2   Constance Backhouse, "Clara Brett Martin: Canadian Heroine or Not?," *Canadian Journal of Women and the Law* 5 (1992): 263; Lita-Rose Betcherman, "Clara Brett Martin's Anti-Semitism," *Canadian Journal of Women and the Law* 5 (1992): 280.

3   Indeed, without the groundbreaking courage and insight of other Jewish feminists who have begun to confront and resist anti-Semitism in the public forum, it is unlikely we would have attempted the task. Their words and actions have inspired and encouraged us to add our voice. See Evelyn Torton Beck, ed., *Nice Jewish Girls*, Melanie Kaye Kantrowitz and Irene Klepfisz, eds., *The Tribe of Dina: A Jewish Women's Anthology* (Boston: Beacon Press, 1986); Irene Klepfisz, *Dreams of an Insomniac: Jewish Feminist Essays, Speeches and Diatribes* (Portland, Oregon: Eighth Mountain Press, 1990); Elly Bulkin et al., *Yours in Struggle: Three Feminist Perspectives on Anti-Semitism and Racism* (Ithaca, New York: Firebrand Books, 1984). For a Canadian perspective, see "Jewish Women's Issue," *Fireweed* (1992).

4   Indeed, one of the important historical works analyzing the nature of anti-Semitism in early twentieth century Canada is a book by Lita-Rose Betcherman, *The Swastika and the Maple Leaf: Fascist Movements in Canada in the Thirties* (Toronto: Fitzhenry and Whiteside, 1975).

5   The focus of our discussion is primarily on the history of Ashkenazi Jews and the anti-Semitism experienced by them. rather than on the history of Sephardic and Mizrachi Jews. This is partially a result of our concern with the historical context on anti-Semitism at the time of Clara Brett Martin's actions and partially a result of Ashkenazi hegemony in Jewish history. Ashkenazi Jews are the descendants of German Jews, large communities of whom migrated in the fifteenth and sixteenth centuries to Poland, Lithuania, and Bohemia. Sephardic Jews are the descendants of African and Asian Jews. For a discussion on the history of the Jewish people within Islamic countries, see Jane Gerber, "Anti-Semitism and the Muslim World," in *History and Hate: The Dimensions of Anti-Semitism,* ed. David Berger (Philadelphia: The Jewish Publication Society, 1986).

6   Indeed, this is clear from the response to her letter from the Attorney General's office. See Backhouse, "Heroine or Not?," Appendix, 277; Betcherman, "Clara Brett Martin's Anti-Semitism."

7   Ibid., Backhouse, 268, 270.

8   Ibid., 270.

9   Ibid., 268.

10 Backhouse refers to evidence suggesting that Lillian Simon "could move in both worlds." Ibid., 268, note 13.

11 Ibid., 268.

12 Ibid., 268, 272.

13 Ibid., 271.

14 Ibid., 275.

15 Ibid., 275, 276.

16 Ibid.

17 Betcherman, "Martin's Anti-Semitism."

18 Ibid., 281.

19 Ibid.

20 Ibid., 288.

21 Betcherman does emphasize, at earlier points in her article (282, 287) that Jews were not, in a general sense, singled out for discrimination but, rather, that all eastern European immigrants and indeed, all non-northern European immigrants were subject to the prevailing xenophobia. She observes, at the same time, some factors that contributed to anti-Semitism, and the focus on Jewish immigrants in particular. At 282, she notes that "traditional prejudice pursued them to their new land" and at 287, after observing the racism directed towards other ethnic groups in other parts of Canada, she concludes that in Toronto "Jews" comprised the largest non-British immigrant group, and, as a result, drew the most fire. This analysis of the extent to which Jews were singled out, and the particular nature of the anti-Semitic focus on Jews could be further developed. In terms of the poverty of the Jews in particular, Betcherman tells us only of the media imagery of Jews—that Jews were depicted as the poorest of the immigrants. It thus remains uncertain whether the Jews were singled out in this respect, and the anti-Semitic discourse implicated therein remains uninterrogated. Ibid., 288.

22 Ibid. Betcherman simply observes that there were "external and internal pressures" responsible for such continued ghettoization.

23 Indeed, earlier, Betcherman refers to the practice that Jews "took care of their own." This observation might be connected with the discussion of ghettoization to further reveal the complexity of this phenomenon. It is important to recognize that this practice of community support was likely aided by the fact that many lived in close proximity to one another.

24 Jacob Katz, *From Prejudice to Destruction: Antisemitism 1700–1933* (Cambridge, Harvard University Press, 1980), 322, argues that the central factor in the upsurge of anti-Semitism in the late nineteenth century was "the very presence of the unique Jewish community among the other nations"—that is—the failure of the Jews to assimilate into the broader societies within which they lived. Although recognized as a factor in understanding anti-Semitism, other scholars have argued that this failure to assimilate cannot be seen as the decisive factor. Endelman, "Modern Anti-Semitism," in *History and Hate,* for example, argues,

> . . . if Katz's interpretation were correct, it would follow that in those countries where Jewish solidarity and particularism remained strongest in the post-emancipation era, anti-Semitism would have been at its deadliest. But in fact just the opposite was true. In the years 1870–1939, in the liberal states of the West—Great Britain and the United States—

where Jewish ethnicity and visibility were not radically attenuated, public Anti-Semitism was weaker than it was in Germany, where assimilation had taken a far more extreme course.

It is, at the same time, important to recognize the extent to which Jews themselves have understood anti-Semitism as being caused by their failure to assimilate. As Endelman writes, ibid., 109–110:

> During the late nineteenth and early twentieth centuries, western Jewish leaders often blamed their own people for the resurgence of anti-Jewish feelings. Specifically, they felt that Jewish behaviour that called attention to the existence of the Jews as a distinct group fuelled the fires of prejudice . . . For example, in December 1880, at the peak of an early wave of political anti-Semitism the *Deutsch-Israelitischer Gemeindebund* urged German Jews to avoid displays of arrogance, superiority, aggressiveness, contentiousness, and ostentation; to pursue crafts rather than commerce; to deal honestly with Christians in business; and to forsake socializing exclusively among themselves and instead seek—although not too aggressively—companionship in Christian society.

See also Weinberg, *Because They Were Jews*, xvi–xvii, against blaming Jews for anti-Semitism, and Lynne Pearlman, "Through Jewish Lesbian Eyes," who discusses this as internalized anti-Semitism.

25 Betcherman, "Clara Brett Martin," 290.

26 Ibid., "Possibly his diatribes against the Jewish people took root in her mind," 291.

27 Ibid., 283.

28 Backhouse, "Heroine or Not," 276.

29 It is important to consider Lita-Rose Betcherman's early and groundbreaking work on the history of anti-Semitism in the 1930s in this light: *The Swastika and the Maple Leaf.*

30 As Irene Klepfisz writes in *Nice Jewish Girls*, 53:

> I believe that Jewish lesbians/feminists have internalized much of the subtle anti-Semitism of this society. They have been told that Jews are too pushy, too aggressive; and so they have been silent about their Jewishness, have not protected themselves against what threatens them. They have been told that they control everything and so when they are in the spotlight they have been afraid to draw attention to their Jewishness. For these women, the number of Jews active in the movement is not a source of pride, but rather a source of embarrassment, something to be played down, something to be minimized.

This work is the first we have written as Jewish feminists and, for all these reasons, it is with considerable trepidation that we now do so.

31 The questions of white skin privilege, and of race more generally, is a complicated one in relation to Jews. First, not all Jews are white—many Sephardic and Mizrachi Jews are Jews of colour. Secondly, there is the question of where Jews are located in relation

to white supremacy, and whether Jews constitute a race. Indeed, the understanding of the Jewish people as a race has been a fundamental component of the anti-Semitism of the nineteenth and twentieth centuries. Further, there is the issue of assimilation. The white skin of Ashkenazi Jews, as well as the association of Jewishness with religion has opened up the possibility of assimilation into the dominant culture by repudiating one's religion and downplaying one's Jewish features—a process encouraged, and at different historical moments, enforced by the anti-Semitism of the dominant culture. Many Ashkenazi Jews, including ourselves, can pass as white, or more appropriately as White Anglo-Saxon Protestants, and as such, are afforded the privileges of the hegemonic culture of white supremacy. However, other Jews, including white-skinned Ashkenazi Jews, are not assimilated, and do not pass. Jews with more explicitly "Jewish features" (a product of ethnic differences and anti-Semitic constructions of otherness) are not afforded the same privileges in relation to the hegemonic culture. This is *not* to say that such Jews are located in the same position as people of colour. It is only to say that the relationship of the Jewish people to white supremacy is complicated.

32 Nor are we saying that any of these identities are mutually exclusive; Sephardic and most Mizrachi Jews are Jews of colour. See for example, Rachel Wahba, "Some of Us are Arabic," in Beck, ed. *Nice Jewish Girls.*

Moroccan Jewish Saint Veneration: From the Maghreb to Montreal

JANICE ROSEN

In 1987, a reporter for the organ of Montreal's Sephardic Jewish community, *La Voix Sépharade,* captured the excitement surrounding the "*hilloula* de Rabbi Shimon Bar Yohai" in Laval:

> The *hilloula* has become an annual celebration, organized by the Centre communautaire de Laval. This year the organizers chose to honour Rabbi Shimon Bar Yohai, author of the Zohar.[1] 150 people attended, on a Saturday night in May. The evening featured a dinner accompanied by Oriental music, and an auction. The mystical character of the event produced an emotionally charged ambience that led to exceptional generosity. As concrete proof of the

A montage of Jewish rabbis revered in Morocco. The poster was issued by the Rabbinat Sépharade du Québec (Montreal) in 1987 or 1988, based on paintings by Hazdai Elmoznino and Salomon Benaroch. In the accompanying article, the author discusses how pilgrimages to Jewish "saints" and later hilloulas in honour of these revered figures enhanced religious and ethnic identification. But these events were infrequent. This poster was made available to participants at the hilloula and therefore would reinforce the experience, or could perhaps pique the interest of non-participants who might view it on a friend's wall or posted in a public institution.

Image courtesy of the Canadian Jewish Congress Archives.

bond to the sages, candles and cakes were sold in their names. Paintings and a synagogue vase were also auctioned. One of the paintings of R. Shimon Bar Yohai fetched a bid of $3200. Twenty-five cakes were sold, all of the fifty-two candles were offered, and seven paintings were also sold. A record amount of $22,000 was collected, of which the Centre recouped a profit of $16,000.

The *hilloula*, which fulfils an emotional need, is one of our most rooted traditions, and brings in new followers every year. As the saying goes, 'May the merit of the sages guide forever all those who made the evening a success, and may their wishes be granted!'²

Traditional rabbinical Judaism frowns upon the notion of saints just as vigorously as Orthodox Muslim thought. Nonetheless, saint cults persist in Western North Africa and continue to reappear in countries to which their former inhabitants have migrated.³ Now that the well-established and culturally-integrated Moroccan Jewish community of Montreal is regularly organizing *hilloulas*, the traditional celebrations in honour of a Jewish saint, students of the Canadian Jewish experience are confronted with some interesting questions. The most obvious is: what purpose do these cults serve away from the locales where they were nurtured? In the following pages, we will look at the origin of this phenomenon in Morocco, and will then compare visible expressions of saint veneration in Montreal with similar situations in Morocco, Israel, and the United States. This account is based on fieldwork in both Morocco and Montreal.⁴

The Muslim and Jewish concept referred to in Western accounts as sainthood is actually an imprecise catchall for several native terms. In Arabic, Muslim saints are referred to as *awliyah Allah* or "friends of God," as the saint is seen as an intermediary between God and man. In ethnographic literature more culturally specific to Morocco, one often encounters the Arabic term *mrabit* (tied to God), which was adopted as *marabout* by the French. In Ouezzane, the Moroccan town where I conducted research, residents used *Sidi* as the most common title for saints, or, in the context of the local Taibiyyine brotherhood, spoke of the *sherif* and *shorfa* (pl.), which is a term more specifically associated with descent from the family of the Prophet. Jewish saints are spoken of in Hebrew and Judeo-Arabic as *tsadiq* (righteous) or *qadosh* (holy person). In addition, informal terms such as *Baba* (father) are used, as well as titles borrowed from Arabic such as *Sidi* for male and *Lalla* for female saints.

In the course of his extensive fieldwork on Moroccan Jewish saint veneration, Issachar Ben-Ami documented as many as 656 saints revered by the local population, of which all but twenty-five were males. While the female saint Sol ha-Tsadiqa acquired sainthood through martyrdom as a young girl, the vast majority of male saints gained their holy aura after being rabbis during their lifetime. While many of the saints venerated by Muslims are members of line-ages claiming descent from the prophet Mohammed, several of the most famous Moroccan Jewish saints have their claims to holiness enhanced through their alleged birth in the Land of Israel.

The point of origin of these Jewish saint veneration practices in Morocco is difficult to determine. Early Jewish texts mention both saints and pilgrimages. Norman Stillman notes that reference to Jewish saints can be found as early as the Talmud, as for example, when Rabbi Yohannan, commenting on Isaiah 59:2, says "*Tsadiqqim* are to be considered greater than the administering angels." The act of making pilgrimages to saints' tombs is also a very ancient Jewish custom. Issachar Ben-Ami cites a midrash on Numbers 13:22 that dealt with the famous issue of the spies sent into the Land of Israel by Moses. The rabbis describe vis-its to the grave of the patriarchs in Hebron to pray for help against the evil intentions of the other spies. Moreover, Rashi (c. 1040–1105) said that in Talmudic times Jews already made pilgrimages to saints' tombs, especially on the anniversary of their deaths.

Despite these antecedents, Jewish saint veneration as it is practiced in Morocco exhibits particular characteristics that have much in common with the practices of their Muslim neighbours, and appears to have attained its cultural importance only after similar practices became widespread among Muslims.

By the thirteenth century, Muslim brotherhoods (or groups of saints' fol-lowers) were already found in Morocco, and over the two subsequent centuries, Sufism in Morocco developed its particular "maraboutistic" character. The *marabout*, who is equivalent to a Sufi saint, is perceived as being "bound to God" as well as possessing *baraka* (divine blessing), which can both be inherit-ed and transmitted by contact. As Dale Eikelman explains in his 1976 book *Moroccan Islam: Tradition and Society in a Pilgrimage Center,* believers in *marabouts* assume that these individuals possess "a special relationship toward God which makes them particularly well-placed to serve as intermediaries."[5] These saintly intermediaries in Islamic Morocco often obtained vast political power. Travellers' accounts of the nineteenth and early twentieth centuries abound in references to the influence of the brotherhoods and the saintly line-ages of various families of *shorfa,* or descendants of the Prophet. Contemporary studies of brotherhoods such as those of Gellner and Eickelman also explore the issue of the political power of saintly lineages, although both observe—as did my informants in Ouezzane—that this power has been in decline since Morocco gained its independence in 1956.

Accounts of saint veneration among the Jews of Morocco do not seem to be widely reported before the seventeenth century, although by the eighteenth century, observers were noticing that some of the Jewish saints were attracting pilgrims from among the Muslims as well. Historically, both Jews and Muslims in Morocco have accorded saintly figures an importance undocumented among the popular practices of these two religions anywhere else in the world. Ben-Ami has argued that saint veneration is an important cultural characteristic, present throughout the population of Moroccan Jews.[6] Unlike the situation for many Muslim saints, however, the powers of the Jewish saints did not appear to extend into the political sphere, nor did their shrines have the power to function as legal sanctuaries as did their Muslim equivalents.

Some scholars have suggested that the practices of both Jewish and Muslim Moroccan saint veneration developed as a result of exposure to the saint reverence behaviour observed among Christians during the Moorish period in Spain. This argument, however, ignores the geography of saint worship. Although the majority of Morocco's Jewish population arrived from Spain in the fifteen and sixteenth centuries, Jews first settled in Morocco over two millennia ago, preceding the Arab conquerors who arrived at the end of the seventh and the beginning of the eighth centuries. They lived in the Atlas Mountains alongside the indigenous Berber population, some of whom converted to Judaism. It is this region of the country that is most densely "populated" with the tombs of Jewish saints, and many of them are associated with natural features of the landscape in a manner reminiscent of ancient animist Berber beliefs.

Not surprisingly, Jewish sources tend to downplay these outside influences, and sources on Muslim practices rarely mention equivalent Jewish activities. My own theory is that the impulse for divine intermediaries is a quasi-universal one, and therefore Berber tree and rock worship was already noted by the first Jews in Morocco. This was reinforced by the addition to the mix of Jews from Catholic Spain, where, already during the time Jews lived in Spain, veneration was focused on human beings endowed with saintly characteristics. Muslims, meanwhile, were developing similar beliefs, which influenced the worldview of their Jewish neighbours. The distinctly Jewish aspect of this practice is in the veneration of rabbis and sages more than any other type of holy individual.

Over time, we see a waxing and waning of the influence of the saints of Moroccan Jewry. A characteristic example of a saint's establishment in the Moroccan Jewish "canon" can be seen in the case of one of the country's most famous Jewish saints, Rabbi Amram Ben-Diwan of Asjen.7 Born in the Holy Land and later based in north central Morocco, the Rabbi did not seem to have attracted a following in the period immediately after his death in 1782. By the first half of the twentieth century, however, as many as 100,000 pilgrims were present at the yearly gathering (*hilloula*) at his tomb.8 It seems likely in this case that the increasing power of the Muslim Taibiyyine brotherhood of Ouezzane was an influence on the development of the cult of Rabbi Amram, and therefore that, as in the Atlas mountain region, geographical contiguity and cultural borrowing influenced the development of this shrine. While far fewer pilgrims have been coming to Asjen in recent years, I observed a few hundred in attendance in 1985, and in the early 1990s Moroccan Jewish groups in Montreal were still organizing pilgrimage trips to Morocco, which included visits to his tomb.

Jewish and Muslim motivations and methods for approaching saints for intervention have much in common. The most commonly cited motivations include petitions and expressions of gratitude related to health problems, fertility concerns, and issues involving protection from harm. As the saints are expected to intervene between humans and God, it is not surprising that they are expected to work miracles.

Norman Stillman sees the most significant difference between Muslim and Jewish saint beliefs in the area of miracles, with Jewish saints almost never performing them during their lifetime. Stillman argues that living Jewish saints are known more for mediating disputes. However, recent accounts by Canadian Jewish informants show that the miraculous element is not entirely absent. André Elbaz, in his 1982 collection *Folktales of the Canadian Sephardim,* includes a story of a Moroccan woman visiting a descendant of the saintly Pinto family after a branch of this family had settled in Montreal. She describes an incidence of a narrowly averted disaster involving spilled boiling oil, which she attributes to the powers of the saint, although it is not clear whether it was the living Pinto or the ancestor who was responsible.[9]

In contrast, Muslim saints are said to be able to perform legendary feats, such as changing into animals and flying through the air. The miracles attributed to deceased Jewish saints generally lack this spectacular quality, being confined to those domestic areas also covered by the Muslim saints: the curing of childlessness and many types of (in Stillman's words) "psychosomatic" illnesses. Ben-Ami recounts how Moroccan Jews who have emigrated to Israel frequently recount saintly miracles having to do with safety during army manoeuvres, or in the context of an attack. He concludes that the different types of miracles reported in Morocco and Israel are not significant, as the general focus is on protection from harm, in whatever form it takes. Although the more educated Jews and Muslims are skeptical of the powers of saints, Stillman notes that neither group as a whole tends to reject the notion of miracles.

Petitions to deceased saints are usually made verbally at a tomb, although petitioners have also left letters, or in the case of Rabbi Amram Ben-Diwan, have placed stones over his grave and tied ribbons to a tree associated with him. The most common element in the practices of the two groups is the use of candles. These are lit and left at tombs, purchased and taken away, or, in Jewish cases, used to honour a saint in synagogues bearing a saint's name. They are also used in the home. As late as 1940, according to one observer, "every Jewish family in Morocco"[10] had its own patron saint, with the saint's name written on an inside wall of their home, and votive candles lit all year long.

For both Jews and Muslims, the act of attending a yearly pilgrimage is a source of merit. As reported in the Internet edition of *Maroc Hebdo Internationale* in 1998, seven pilgrimages to select Muslim saints, such as to Moulay Abdessaalam Ben Mchiche, are considered the equivalent of a trip to Mecca. In the words of Alex Weingrod, for Jews to take part in a *hilloula* "is thought to enhance the participants' moral and spiritual qualities."[11] Participating in a *hilloula* is also supposed to bring good luck.

The typical Muslim *moussem* (or pilgrimage gathering) features prayers at the tomb, the bringing of animals for sacrifice, and the sharing of a communal meal. As an experience on the individual level, participants (particularly female ones) tend to see the *moussem* as an opportunity for greater sociability and mingling than is normally possible. This element of holiday atmosphere and freedom at the annual *hilloulas* is mentioned by Ben-Ami and Weingrod's Jewish informants as well. The Montreal participants at local *hilloulas* (as described in the next section) clearly view the occasions as opportunities for social interaction.

As practiced in Morocco and in Israel, the Jewish *hilloula* has many of the features of the Muslim *moussem*. Similar to Muslims who make pilgrimages, both individually and during the annual celebrations, Jews seek to obtain the *baraka (kedusha,* or blessing) of the saint, by placing bottles of drink and scarves close to the tomb. At some sites, as described by Weingrod, devotees even spread a meal over a saint's tombstone and eat it, picnic-style, in the cemetery.

As I observed at Asjen, in the northern part of central Morocco, and at the *hilloulas* described by Ben-Ami, the device of the auction is used as a fundraising technique, instead of having the pilgrims bring tribute directly to the sanctuary. I have been unable to find reference to the origins of this custom in the literature. It is possible that it is of relatively recent vintage, as Semach does not mention it in his otherwise detailed description of Asjen during a *hilloula* in the 1940s. It is a feature that is notably present in the *hilloulas* organized in Montreal and in Washington, D.C., as will be discussed below.

Expatriate Jews have continued to return to Morocco to visit saints' tombs, although numbers are lower than they were twenty years ago. Their visits are encouraged by the local Muslim population as well as by the Moroccan government. Among Muslims, some *moussems* are also reported in the press, although the veneration of saints at these events seems to be minimized. The decreased economic power of the brotherhoods has likely resulted in a decrease in the number of pilgrims and intensity of participation in *moussems*.

The revival of the *hilloula* outside Morocco is a fascinating element of contemporary saint veneration. As late as 1998, Ben-Ami was still able to assert: "The number of saints worshipped [by North African Jews], large as it is, is still growing."[12] And saints continue to be created in Israel. Baba Salé, deceased in 1984 in Netivot, is a well-known example. Moroccan Jews have also transplanted some of their saints, at least on a symbolic level, to their new

Israeli settlements, where they now arrange pilgrimages and *hilloulas* at synagogues bearing the saints' names. Israel's political leaders have been known to use attachments to saints in order to promote candidates in a particular saint's name in Moroccan areas. Even more remarkably, Ben-Ami notes that "thanks to Moroccan Jews or their influence, the number of hagiographic publications produced in Israel during the last ten years considerably exceeds all that was published in the last two centuries."[13] *Hilloulas* have also been noted and studied in the United States. In the 1980s, Ruth Fredman Cernea studied the phenomenon in the suburbs of Washington, D.C. These events, although mostly organized by Jews from Morocco, are attended by Sephardic Jews from a number of countries.

Interpretations of this new phenomenon vary. Ben-Ami sees Israeli manifestations of saint veneration as evidence of cultural continuity with the immigrants' Moroccan past. Weingrod reads them as expressions of ethnic pride and renewal. The *hilloula*, as opposed to conventional synagogue attendance, is an easy way to connect with religious and cultural ties. Its endurance and revival in Israel, therefore, shows not that Moroccan Jews have failed to assimilate, but rather that over time they have become more comfortable in Israel and therefore able to express their distinct identity.

Now that we have looked at the historical background of Moroccan Jewish saint veneration and have considered what the practice means to Moroccan-born Jews in other countries, we can turn our attention to Montreal. Descendants of saintly families have settled in both Montreal and Toronto. In his study, *Folktales of the Canadian Sephardim*, André Elbaz notes that individuals have been known to make pilgrimages bearing gifts to families such as the Pintos of Montreal. These private expressions of saint veneration, however, are seldom visible to the outside observer, and are therefore difficult to document. *Hilloulas*, on the other hand, are public in nature, and are often advertised beyond the boundaries of the organizing group. Among my interviewees is a Moroccan-born Montreal woman whom I interviewed in 1999. For ten years, Miriam had been hosting a *hilloula* for the Israeli saint Baba Salé, and was a devotee of this saint even before his death in 1984. Her initial motivation for organizing the *hilloulas* stemmed from gratitude that her son (born many years earlier thanks to the saint's protection) had recently escaped a serious accident. This home-based *hilloula*, at which her friends contributed dishes of food, once raised $100,000 for the saint's yeshiva in Israel, with a single individual giving $8000.

Most commonly, *hilloulas* are held outside the home. Synagogues are the most frequent site of public *hilloula* events, characteristically organized on an annual basis during the period between Lag B'Omer and early summer.[14] Falling within this period is not a fixed requirement, however, as according to one official at the Otsarenu synagogue and study centre, there is a *hilloula* held there once a month in honour of a historical rabbi or sage, with no admission charge.

In Montreal, the secular *Communauté Sépharade du Québec*—the major representative body for Montreal's largely Moroccan community of twenty thousand Sephardic Jews—has also started to organize *hilloulas*. They held their first event, in honour of Sol ha-Tsadiqa, in June 1999.[15] This event followed a number of other *hilloulas*, so that one community leader later remarked to me that the people "had no money left for *hilloulas*—they had been attending one after the other since April." Nevertheless, the organizers managed to raise a significant amount of money, earmarking the funds for the poor Sephardic children of the city. Each participant was charged a $52.00 admission price (a symbolic number, twice 26, which denotes good luck for Moroccan Jews). The admission price included a lavish dinner, with wine and a wide variety of Moroccan Jewish dishes. In the course of the dinner many individuals purchased auctioned items of ceremonial art ranging in price from two hundred to twelve hundred dollars. Each item for sale was introduced with the name of a saint, many of them in honour of Sol ha-Tsadiqa, while others represented a broad spectrum of popularly-venerated saints. Among the other names were famous Moroccan rabbis such as Rabbi Chaim Berdugo of Meknes, Rabbi Amram Ben Diwan of Asjen, Israel's Baba Salé and Shimon bar Yohai, as well as a few Ashkenazi Hassidic figures such as Rabbi Nachman of Bratslav and, notably, Chabad's Rabbi Menachem Schneerson.

The successful bidders obtained, along with their purchase, a plain white candle to be burned later in the saint's honour. The rabbi present also bestowed upon the purchasers a blessing featuring the holy figure's name. The proceedings were enlivened by a middle eastern orchestra, which played theme music associated with the various religious figures. Most of the musical selections appeared to be easily recognizable to their audience, and according to my informants, the music often bore a relationship to the saint being featured. The then-popular tune *"Moshiach!"* announced the sale of a candle for Rabbi Menachem Schneerson. Meanwhile, on the sidelines, an assembly line of community workers accepted money and pledges, wrote out charitable tax receipts, and wrapped the items to be taken home.

To understand the social significance of events such as the one described above, I questioned participants at the Sol Ha-Tsadiqa *hilloula* about the meaning of the *hilloula* and the Jewish saints for themselves and their families. My most articulate informant, the Baba Salé *hilloula* organizer I refer to here as Miriam, clearly expressed an emotional attachment to what took place that evening. The hopes she associated with this particular *hilloula* were directed, as on many occasions in the past, towards the well-being of her eldest son. This middle-aged woman, who had come to Montreal from Morocco just before the 1967 War in Israel, drew on the power of numerous Jewish saints. She recounted past events when she had asked a saint to intervene on her behalf, such as while a young girl in eastern Morocco, while on visits to Israel, and, more recently, when on a visit to Rabbi Schneerson's tomb in New York. Her motivations for requesting saintly intervention included hope for intercession so that she could find a new home, and so that her son would not follow a Christian girlfriend to Europe. She described how she obtained the *kedusha*, or holy power, of the first member of the Pinto family by touching a Torah scroll handwritten by this saint and later brought to Canada by a Pinto family member. At the *hilloula* she was wearing a red string on her wrist, a gift that a friend had brought her from Baba Salé's tomb in Israel. As was the custom, she had made a wish over it, and was keeping it in place until it wore away.

Her husband, on the other hand, was attending the event largely for its social elements. He enjoyed the dinner and the chance to mingle with old friends. His personal attachment to Jewish saints was most evident in his being named "Amram," a popular choice among women like his mother, who visited this saint in the hopes of becoming pregnant. The couple's children were not present, and indeed the majority of the attendees were middle-aged or older. Miriam said that her daughters helped her when she prepared *hilloulas* in her own home, but she did not expect them to keep up the tradition after she was gone.

Another couple I spoke to was considerably older, the husband being eighty-four years old. He recounted to me the that he had actually spoken to Baba Salé when in Israel, and that the holy man had warned him against using matches, which he claimed contained lard, a prohibition that the man subsequently heeded.

The auctioneer at this and other *hilloulas* that I attended exhorted people to bid and buy items by promising that the "merit of the saints" would attach to the objects purchased. Furthermore, as discussed above, each sale entitled the buyer to receive a spoken blessing as well as a candle associated with the saint in whose name the item had been sold. However, I noted that despite the apparently religious basis for the occasion and the fact that it was being held in a synagogue, several of the men present were not wearing the head-covering (*kippa*) one would expect to see on an observant male at mealtime. One of the women present, when asked about this, suggested to me that many Moroccan Jews had "*la foi*" (belief, or faith) but not "*la religion,*" which she defined as observance. To this I would add that many participants perceived the evening as a social and communal fundraising event rather than a religious occasion, so the staging of the *hilloula* in a synagogue did not enhance its religious significance.

As we have seen, the institution of the *hilloula* is a typically Moroccan event that Canadian Sephardim have imported from the North African milieu. Given its strong association with the community, the *hilloula* can be seen as a marker of Moroccan Jewish identity, but the ethnic origins of the saints who are honoured in the *hilloula* setting do not have to be Moroccan. Upon observing that candles were being sold in the names of Rabbi Nachman of Bratslav and Rabbi Schneerson, I said to one of the organizers, "But they're not Moroccan!" I was emphatically told, "That doesn't matter at all." The Nachman of Bratslav candles got few bids at the Sol ha-Tsadiqa *hilloula*, but those in the name of the *Lubavitcher* Rebbe proved very popular.

What is the nature of this connection between Moroccan traditional saints and the late leader of Chabad? Can one truly speak of Rabbi Menachem Schneerson as a Moroccan saint? From my observations, it appears that one can indeed do so. Building on contacts made in Morocco before the era of emigration to Canada—the head of Montreal's Sephardic branch of Chabad was a rabbi for several years in the large Jewish community of Casablanca—Chabad now has many followers among Montreal's primarily French-speaking Sephardic population. Given that this has occurred in a climate where, since Rabbi Schneerson's death in 1994, many Chabad devotees see their departed Rebbe as the *Moshiach*, or Messiah, it is not that surprising that Moroccan followers of Chabad would use their indigenous concept of "saint" to categorize the Rebbe. To give an example of how this belief is expressed, we can cite again the case of my informant Miriam, who, in addition to her attachment to many Moroccan and Israeli saints, is a member of a Chabad "Sephardic" congregation. She had already made pilgrimages to the Rebbe in New York before his death, and she now periodically travels there to visit his former synagogue and to leave notes at his grave. She recounted to me her success in privately organizing the purchase of a Torah scroll (at a value of $26,000, American funds) in his honour in 1998, with the help and encouragement of her congregation's rabbi. These funds were raised from among her own circle, so her success is another indication of the Rebbe's popularity among Moroccan Jews.

Making a pilgrimage to Chabad headquarters in New York may be a welcome option for Montreal's Moroccan Jews, given New York's proximity to this city as compared to the distance between Montreal and Morocco or Israel. To this practical consideration can be added the high level of devotion to Rabbi Schneerson expressed on many levels in the Montreal Jewish community, home to some of the most ardent promoters of the image of the Rebbe as the *Moshiach*. These factors may help account for the fact that, although neither Moroccan nor Sephardic in origin, in Montreal at least, the Rebbe appears to have joined the ranks of Jewish saints on what seems to be as strong a footing as the new saints created in Israel.

Recognizing the importance of the *hilloula* in Moroccan Jewish culture, Chabad has begun to use the structure of these events as a frame for their fundraisers oriented towards their community. A week after the Sol Ha-Tsadiqa *hilloula* of 1999, Chabad organized an almost identically structured event at a local restaurant to commemorate the anniversary of the Rebbe's death. Treading carefully, however, their signs and publicity for this event avoided direct mention of the words "saint" and "*hilloula*," and characterized the main focus of the event as a "Chinese Auction" for charity.

The Sephardic branch of Chabad has also begun organizing an annual *hilloula* for Baba Salé, and in January 2001 used this occasion as a fundraiser for the Beth Rivka Orthodox girls' school. As a way of reaching out to the Sephardim present, organizers emphasized the Rebbe's ties with Baba Salé and the theme of Sephardic-Ashkenazi cooperation. The admission price to the event was $26.00, again the number Moroccan Jews associate with good luck. When auctioning items, the announcer raised the bids in numerically symbolic increments—260, 320, 770—and made reference to the merit of the sages attaching to the items being sold, as does the auctioneer at a Sephardic-run event. The evening unfolded in a fashion similar to the *hilloula* organized by the *Communauté Sépharade du Québec,* although on a smaller scale.

The *hilloula* has thus adapted to the North American milieu, and has become a modern fundraising event, as well as a public way of reinforcing the Moroccan custom. The Montreal Sephardic community's use of the *hilloula* as a community social event and fundraising device points to the function of the saint cults as ethnic identity markers for Moroccan Jews in this city. For some of the Montreal individuals I interviewed, keeping up the practice of saint veneration evidently fills an emotional and spiritual need, while for others, and perhaps especially for the men, attending events in honour of saintly figures serves primarily a social function.

Expatriate Jews in Canada and Israel have held on to, and even occasionally enhanced, the practice of saint veneration as an expression of their identity within the larger Jewish society. Even when linkages with these larger Jewish societies are courted, it is on the Moroccan Jews' own terms, with Tunisian, ancient Israeli, and even Lubavitch "saints" being re-defined according to traditional Moroccan modes of respect. This custom, with its long history of adaptation, has adapted anew in Canada.

NOTES

1   Tradition ascribes the Zohar to R. Shimon bar Yohai; modern scholarship establishes the date as late thirteenth century.

2   The translation is my own and is slightly abridged.

3   Before the declaration of the State of Israel in 1948, it is estimated that one out of twenty-five Moroccans was Jewish. However, at the present time, following massive emigration after 1948 and again after the 1967 war in Israel, only a few Jews remain, mostly living in the larger cities or as isolated individuals in mountain communities.

4   More specifically, the Jewish ethnographical data that I cite here is drawn from my visits in 1984–1985 to Rabbi Amram Ben-Diwan's tomb at Asjen (a hamlet located seven kilometres northwest of the small city of Ouezzane), and from attendance at *hilloulas* (Jewish saint festivals) in Montreal in June 1999 and January 2001, as well as from recent accounts by Moroccan Jews living in Montreal. My Muslim ethnographic examples were collected between October 1984 and December 1985 in Ouezzane, a town of approximately 40,000 in North-Central Morocco, famous as the home of the Taiyyibine brotherhood founded by Moulay Abdellah Cherif (1597–1678) and named for his son, Moulay Taib (see E. Michaux-Bellaire, "Généalogie des Chorfa de Ouezzane," *Archives Marocaines* 15 (1908): 192.) As Ouezzane is also home to two lodges of the Hamadsha, a Sufi brotherhood, information was obtained from these devotees as well. Additional observations were made at *moussems* (Muslim saint festivals) in 3 other locations.

5   For discussions of Muslim saint veneration in Morocco, see Dale F. Eickelman, *Moroccan Islam-Tradition and Society in a Pilgrimage Center* (Austin, Texas, 1976); also Henry Munson, Jr., "Muslim and Jew in Morocco: Reflections on the Distinction between Belief and Behavior," in *The Social Philosophy of Ernest Gellner, Poznan Studies in the Philosophy of the Sciences and the Humanities* 48 (1996): 357–379.

6   The most comprehensive studies of Moroccan Jewish saint veneration are by Issachar Ben-Ami, whose works I have relied on extensively in researching this essay. In English translation, I recommend in particular his book *Saint Veneration among the Jews in Morocco* (Detroit, Michigan, 1998), and his article "Folk Veneration of Saints Among the Moroccan Jews," in *Studies in Judaism and Islam—presented to Shelomo Dov Goitein,* ed. by Shelomo Morag, I. Ben-Ami and Norman A. Stillman (Jerusalem, 1981), pp. 283–344. Another excellent discussion of the subject is by Norman A. Stillman, "Saddiq and Marabout in Morocco," in *Jews among Muslims—Communities in the Precolonial Middle East,* ed. by Shlomo Deshen and Walter P. Zenner (New York, N.Y., 1996), pp. 121–130. For a detailed account of Moroccan Jewish saint veneration in the 1940s, see Y.D. Semach, "Les Saints Juifs de Maroc. Le Saint de Ouezzane: Rabbi Amran Ben-Diwan," *Bulletin des anciens élèves du l'Alliance Israélite Universelle* 4 (Rabat, Morocco, 1947). For saint veneration as practiced in Israel, some good sources are Alex Weingrod, *The Saint of Beersheba* (Albany, N.Y., 1990), and Yoram Bilu, *Without Bounds—The Life and Death of Rabbi Ya'aqov Wazana* (Detroit, Michigan,

2000), as well as, by the same author, "Oneirobiography and Oneirocommunity in Saint Worship in Israel: A Two-Tier Model for Dream-Inspired Religious Revivals," in *Dreaming* 10–2 (2000): 85–101. For a discussion of the *hilloula* transported to Washington, D.C., see Ruth Fredman Cernea, "Flaming Prayers: Hillula in a New Home," in *Between Two Worlds—Ethnographic Essays on American Jewry*, ed., by Jack Kugelmass (Cornell, N.Y., 1988).

7   The name is variously spelled as "Amram" or "Amran."

8   Issachar Ben-Ami, 1998, p. 103.

9   André Elbaz, *Folktales of the Canadian Sephardim* (Canada, 1992), p. 54.

10 Issachar Ben-Ami, 1998, p. 102.

11 Alex Weingrod, 1990, p. 45.

12 Issachar Ben-Ami, 1998, p. 148.

13 Ibid., pp. 177–178

14 Lag B'Omer is the 33rd day of the Omer, the interval between the festivals of Passover and Shavuot. While the Omer marks a period of mourning for Jews, being associated with a time when many thousands of Rabbi Akiva's students died, tradition has it that the deaths ceased on this day. The state of mourning being thus suspended, festive events are often held then. As Lag B'Omer is the anniversary day of the death of Simon Bar Yohai, long the focus of pilgrimages to the Galilee community of Meron, this day has became generally associated with saintly pilgrimages.

15 In March 2003 a second Sol Ha-Tsadiqa *hilloula* was organized by another mainstream Montreal Jewish organization, the Chai Sépharade committee of the Jewish Federation-affiliated Cummings Centre for Seniors.

A Sense of Time

The essays in this section portray Jewishness as a lived experience, whether through an examination of wedding customs, the role of holy days, or the meaning of rituals of observance.

Important early disagreements between Jews and non-Jews in Canada centred on the question of a national weekly day of rest, which was mandated by the *Lord's Day Act* of 1906. Jewish efforts to amend this law, based on the hardship it placed on their ability to conduct business on *two* holy days—their own Saturday Sabbath as well as Sunday—were not successful. The essays in this section examine evocative discussions concerning the meaning of faith and its daily demands. Ira Robinson explores an early influential Orthodox thinker's response to the relation between secular and religious life. Rebecca Margolis examines the little-known phenomenon—in Montreal and elsewhere—of the radical Yom Kippur Balls. Marlene Bonneau's essay portrays shifting marriage rituals, and makes use of ethnographic study and in-depth interviews.

NR

"A Letter from the Sabbath Queen": Rabbi Yudel Rosenberg Addresses Montreal Jewry

IRA ROBINSON

Those who get their information on the immigrant Jewish communities of North America from movies and television have one certainty: the past belongs to the Hassidim. Whether the film is set in the Lower East Side of New York or Montreal's St. Urbain Street, scenes will feature a number of men in black Hassidic garb, long sidelocks and *streimlekh*—round fur hats. If one's only information derives from cinematographic images, then, a goodly proportion of immigrant Jews in the early part of this century were not only openly religious but were in fact Hassidim.

As is often the case, the image on the screen bears but little connection with reality. In the first place, most of the Jews who emigrated from Europe to North America were not Hassidim. Even those whose religious faith withstood the trauma of emigration nearly all rapidly assimilated in terms of dress. It is not merely that Hassidic dress would brand the wearer as a *griner;* it also subjected him to harassment, ridicule and actual blows at the hand of self-appointed enforcers of North American homogeneity. Those scattered individuals, most of them rabbis, who insisted upon retaining their beards and the clothing they would have worn had they remained in Europe, soon learned that they must avoid walking on the city streets, if possible, to avoid such incidents.[1]

Thus what we are seeing in the media is a gross distortion of what actually went on. That is probably not news to anyone. What is important, however, is that the media, despite the distortion, are using the visual recognition of Hassidic garb to drive home a larger truth—that the majority of Yiddish-speaking Jewish immigrants to North America in this era, whatever their personal compromises with "America" and whatever their level of conscious rebellion against the traditions of rabbinic Judaism, were participants in the traditional Jewish culture of eastern Europe.[2]

When we speak of "Yiddish culture" we tend to refer to secular Yiddish culture. By this we mean the literary and artistic creations of those Jews who, to a greater or lesser extent, had broken with the ethos and lifestyle of eastern European rabbinic Judaism. Though both "orthodox" and "secular" Jews employed Yiddish as a medium of communication and shared much the same cultural heritage, a prevalent assumption on both sides of the *kulturkampf* is that each group utilized separate literary genres in order to express themselves. Thus "orthodox" Jews express themselves by commenting on canonized texts and composing halakhic treatises, sermons, moralistic exhortations and hagiography. "Secular" Jews, on the other hand, use the "Western" literary forms of the poem, play, essay, short story and novel to get their point across. Even when "secular" Jews appear to be utilizing traditional forms, as in I.L. Peretz's appropriation of the Hassidic tale, it is clear that the form is not merely employed—it undergoes a transvaluation. We seem here to have a particular example of "East is East and West is West and never the twain shall meet." Or do we?

One argument of this essay is that the line between "secular" and "religious" with respect to Yiddish/Hebrew literary creativity needs to be reexamined with considerable attention.

First of all, as Yosef Dan has pointed out, the "Hassidic" story, with the major exceptions of the collection of stories entitled *Shivhei ha-Besht* and the *Tales of Nahman of Bratzlav,* both of which were published circa 1815, is a phenomenon of the last third of the nineteenth century. The first major collections of Hassidic stories, with the exceptions mentioned above, were published in the late 1860s. Thus the enterprise of published Hassidic hagiography is not anterior to that of "Modern" Yiddish/Hebrew literature. Therefore, I.L. Peretz was not transvaluing an anterior literary tradition; he was producing literary works based upon a parallel literary genre which had emerged only shortly before and was still developing.[3]

A second point to ponder is that of genre. It is commonly assumed that fiction is not a medium likely to recommend itself to Orthodox Jews. Without going into the problematic area of the extent to which the midrashic literature of rabbinic Judaism was considered "true" by traditional rabbinic Jews, the historiographical literature of the Jews in medieval and early modern times is replete with fictional and fictionalized stories presented in just the same manner as "the facts." One of these chronicles, *Shalshelet ha-Kabbala (The Chain of Tradition)* of the sixteenth century Gedaliah ibn Yahya was widely known as *Shalshelet ha-Shekarim (The Chain of Falsehoods)* for just this reason. Although presented as "fact," it was clear to many that at least some of ibn Yahya's stories were "fiction."[4]

Moreover, there is evidence that Hassidic hagiography itself was often taken by its audience "with a grain of salt." Of the tales of the *Zaddikim* it was said, "He who believes that they are literally true is a fool. He who believes that they cannot be true is an heretic."[5] Thus the presence of "fiction" within traditional literary genres, without even taking into consideration medieval and early modern Jewish adaptations of non-Jewish sagas such as that of King Arthur, is a fact that we must reckon with.[6]

Within Orthodox circles in Poland in the late nineteenth and early twentieth centuries, a genre of fiction undisguised as "fact" began to emerge.[7] However, to an even greater extent, it is apparent that fiction functioned within the Orthodox community in the guise of hagiography. This is so for reasons which, upon reflection, are readily apparent.

Orthodox Judaism in eastern Europe looked upon itself as besieged by modern "secular" ideologies which stemmed from the non-Jewish world.[8] Fiction was a genre that was apparently not indigenous to traditional Judaism and would thus be looked upon by the Orthodox with some suspicion. Given this atmosphere, writers overtly identified with the Orthodox community, such as rabbis, would have considerable incentive to disguise their fiction.

Perhaps the most distinguished practitioner of "disguised" fiction in this sense was the rabbi who is the subject of this essay. His name was Judah Yudel Rosenberg.[9] He was born in 1859 in the town of Skaryszew, near Radom, Poland. His education is typical of nineteenth century eastern European intellectuals. He received a traditional rabbinic and Hassidic education, becoming known as the Skaryszewer *Ilui*. He was also exposed to *Haskala* literature and studied Hebrew grammar, the plays of Moses Hayyim Luzzatto, and such popular scientific works as Pinhas Elihayu Horwitz's *Sefer ha-Berit* and the essays of Hayyim Selig Slonimsky.[10]

Having failed at several business ventures, he began a career as a rabbi in the town of Tarlow. By 1891, he had mastered the Russian language sufficiently to gain a government license to function as an official rabbi. He performed rabbinic functions in Lublin, Warsaw and Lodz. In 1913, he emigrated to Canada where he served as a rabbi in Toronto from 1913 to 1918 and in Montreal from 1919 to his death in 1935.

Rosenberg was a prolific writer. He published over twenty works and left others in manuscript. Though Rosenberg's major work was his multi-volume edition and translation of the *Zohar*,[11] from the point of view of Hebrew/Yiddish literature, his most important contribution was his story of the Maharal of Prague and the Golem. Rosenberg's book, *Sefer Nifla 'ot ha-Maharal im ha-Golem,* published in Warsaw in 1909, purports to be an edition of an old manuscript emanating from a nonexistent "Royal Library of Metz." Critics agree almost unanimously, however, that it is Rosenberg's original work.[12] It gives us the story of the Maharal and the Golem in the form that exercised a profound influence on Jewish and European literature of the twentieth century. Yosef Dan called the Golem story "the best known contribution of twentieth century Hebrew literature to world literature." He further stated that "there is but one source for almost all the stories on this subject—the small book of Rabbi Judah Yudel Rosenberg."[13]

As interesting as the Golem tale, but far less known, is Rosenberg's *Sefer Hoshen ha-Mishpat shel ha-Kohen ha-Gadol* (Piotrkow, 1913), which, in an explicit takeoff on Arthur Conan Doyle's story "The Jew's Breastplate," takes the Maharal from Prague to London to solve the case of the theft of the original breastplate of the high priest from London's "Belmore Street" Museum.

Also supposedly taken from an old manuscript was a series of stories Rosenberg wrote concerning R. Arye Leib of Shpole, *Tif'eret Mhar'el mi-Shpole* (Piotrkow, 1912). Here Rosenberg added to the body of tales concerning the early Hassidic leader with his own imagination. Other works, including collections of legends concerning the prophet Elijah and King Solomon, contain stories that are apparently original with Rosenberg.[14]

Perhaps the most blatant example of Rosenberg's use of fictional narrative "in disguise" is his series of five tales concerning E. Elijah Guttmacher, the "Greiditzer Rebbe" (Lodz, 1912). It was the only one of these works that was written originally in Yiddish and not published in a Hebrew version at all. To realize how far Rosenberg has come "out of his disguise" in these Greiditzer tales, it suffices to note that one of the tales centres on a murder committed in Sao Paulo, Brazil, while yet another turns on whether Moishele, the ex-yeshiva student, will succeed in escaping from a penal colony in French Equatorial Africa. In general in these stories the Greiditzer Rebbe is not only not the centre of attention, he is decidedly peripheral. It seems clear that were it not for Rosenberg's feeling that he needed the hagiographical mantle for his fiction, which the Greiditzer afforded him, the Rebbe would hardly be there at all.

When Rosenberg crossed the Atlantic, he largely gave up writing in this genre. Whether this was because he felt that publishing such works would not reflect well on his position as an Orthodox rabbi in Toronto or Montreal, or simply because he could not maintain contact with his publishers in Warsaw and Lodz, we cannot say with any degree of certainty. It is true, however, that for the most part, his North American writings travelled in the well-worn paths of Orthodox literary genres: responsa, halakhic guides, sermons and commentaries. Nonetheless there were exceptions. He exhibited some of his creative faculties in his bilingual book of tales concerning Rabbi Simeon bar Yohai, supposed author of the *Zohar*, published in 1927 under the title *Sefer Niflous ha-Zohar.*[15]

Another partial exception to this rule is the work we will now examine. It is the one unilingual Yiddish work Rosenberg published in Canada. It appeared in Montreal in 1924 and it demonstrates that the spark of the creative writer was not dead in Rosenberg. When Yudel Rosenberg chose to address Montreal Jewry, he did so indirectly, through a fictional narrator—the Sabbath Queen.

Rosenberg's work is entitled, *A Brivele fun di Zisse Mame Shabbes Malkese zu Ihre Zihn un Tekhter fun Idishn Folk (A Letter from the Sweet Mother Sabbath Queen to Her Sons and Daughters of the Jewish People).* It was published in Montreal at City Printing Co., 712 St. Lawrence Blvd. in 1923–24 (5684). Its price was listed as 25 cents.

As one can gather from the title, Rosenberg has chosen to speak through a "fictional" interlocutor, the Sabbath Queen, the "mother" of the Jewish people, whom Kabbalists like Rosenberg identified with the *Shekhina*, the female aspect of the sefirotic Godhead.[16] He maintained this fiction throughout, asserting on the title page that the letter "appears through (the auspices of) the Montreal rabbi, Yudel Rosenberg." Thus, as in his hagiographical fiction, Rosenberg poses merely as the editor of another's work, though here his conceit is much more transparent.

What did the Sabbath Queen, through Rosenberg, want to tell her children, the Jews? The central theme of the pamphlet was the observance of the Sabbath, or rather the lack thereof within the Jewish community. It is entirely possible, indeed, that the subject of sabbath observance led Rosenberg to the idea of couching his exhortation in the form of a letter, patterned upon Abraham Ibn Ezra's *Iggeret ha-Shabbat,* which begins with an angel delivering a letter to the author from the Sabbath, decrying lapses in Jewish sabbath observance. Furthermore, in one of the classics of Hassidic literature, the sabbath is compared to a love letter from God to the Jew.[17]

The Sabbath Queen tells her "dear beloved children" that she has heard their prayers and their questions as to why the present exile of the Jewish people has lasted so much longer than previous exiles, and why the Jews now suffer more than other peoples. The answer is because so many Jews, in publicly desecrating the sabbath, have abandoned the peace and protection afforded by the *Shekhina*, who is identified with the Sabbath Queen.

The bulk of the Sabbath Queen's letter consists of arguments in favour of the observance of the sabbath. From these we can discern the position of sabbath observance and of Orthodox Judaism as a whole in the Jewish community of Montreal.

The first thing to note is that the Sabbath Queen does not address all Jews, though she longs to reach them all. There are Jews who are materialists and will believe only that which their senses indicate. Such Jews have placed themselves so far away from the Orthodox community that dialogue with them is impossible. The Sabbath Queen can only speak to those in whom the holy soul-spark had not yet been entirely extinguished.[18]

To those willing to listen, the Sabbath Queen spoke of the prevalent notion that sabbath observance was incompatible with modern civilization. On the contrary, she argued, Jews had always had great scientists, philosophers, doctors and astronomers, like Maimonides, who were strict sabbath observers. Men like Maimonides give the lie to the notion that the Torah and civilization were as incompatible as fire and water.[19]

Another thing that annoyed the Sabbath Queen no end was the fact that those who publicly desecrated the sabbath and thus demonstrated their lack of respect for the Creator, nonetheless showed great respect for the memory of their deceased parents, honouring them through the recitation of the *Kaddish* and *Yizkor* prayers. In one of the appendices to this pamphlet, Rosenberg gives this description of public sabbath desecrators going to synagogue for such purposes:

> When they have *yortseit* or on Rosh ha-Shana/Yom Kippur
> they come into a synagogue and buy a "fat" *aliya*. The gab-
> bai together with the president delight in such a fine guest
> and beckon to the *shammes* to seat him in a good place . . .
> is this not a desecration of God's name and a disgrace for
> the Torah?[20]

This seeming discrepancy in the actions of these people gave the Sabbath Queen an argument. Through their observance of their liturgical obligations toward their deceased parents, they demonstrate an awareness that their parents possess souls which live on after death. But how does it appear in heaven, she asked, when a son who publicly desecrates the sabbath and is halakhicly considered on the same level as a gentile, asks her, the *Shekhina*, to give his deceased parents a proper rest under her wings? Having insulted the Sabbath Queen, they now ask her for a favour! The souls of the deceased must be ashamed of this performance while it gives Satan a chance to denounce Israel.[21]

It was not merely from the religious standpoint that sabbath observance was desirable, but also from the point of view of Jewish national pride. The Christians observe their Sunday, Muslims have their day of rest on Friday. There is even a Christian sect, the *subbotniki*, who observe their sabbath on Saturday "as this [work on Saturday] is against the ten commandments of the Bible" (*Vail dos is against [sic] de aseres ha-dibros fun Baybel [sic]*). In contrast to these, the Jews have abandoned their national day of rest and hence their national pride.[22]

Next, the Sabbath Queen examines the economic side of sabbath observance. One of the chief causes of sabbath desecration, according to her, is the lack of employment opportunity for those who would not work on Saturdays and Jewish holidays. In particular, she vented her spleen on Jewish store and factory owners who forced their Jewish employees to work on the sabbath. God would punish them not merely for their own sins, but also for the sins of their employees.[23]

How can the economic situation be improved? The Sabbath Queen pinned her hopes on the five-day, forty-hour week, then being demanded by labour unions. The use of machinery in factories now meant more productivity per work in a forty-hour week than previously in a seventy-two hour week. Moreover, she felt, the forty-hour week would help solve the problem of recurrent recessions caused by excess production. Along with solving the problem of sabbath observance, the forty-hour week would be an economic boon.

With regard to shops remaining closed on Saturday, the Sabbath Queen remarked that, in many places, it was permissible for those who rested on the sabbath to open for business on Sunday. As for those Jewish-owned factories that employed no Jews, the Sabbath Queen reminded her children that it was possible to arrange, under rabbinical supervision, either a "sale" or "partnership" with a non-Jew so that the factory might continue running with no adverse halakhic effect.[24]

At this point, the Sabbath Queen anticipated a question from her loyal children. Why, it might be asked, was it so difficult for those who wished to observe the sabbath to obtain work while those who desecrated the sabbath seemed to prosper? She answered that those who suffered want because of their loyalty to the sabbath were being tested by Heaven, possibly in expiation of transgressions against the sabbath they had committed in previous incarnations. After their sin had been atoned, they would receive a proper livelihood without any necessity of desecrating the sabbath. Seemingly successful people who desecrate the sabbath were merely being recompensed in this life for the good deeds that they had performed. Their fate in the next world, however, would be dire and fearful.[25]

The Sabbath Queen concluded her letter with an exhortation to heed her true children, the Orthodox rabbis, through whom she was sending this letter. Having regard to North American conditions, she further warned:

> Do not listen to the sinful and poisonous speeches of the
> Reform "rabbis" who have the selfsame sinful souls as the
> prophets of Baal in olden times who brought on the
> destruction of the First Temple, or the selfsame sinful souls
> of the Hellenistic leaders who brought upon the Jewish
> people the destruction of the Second Temple![26]

With a final link made between the observance of the sabbath and the messianic redemption, the letter was signed, "From me, your loving true mother, *Shabbes Malkesa.*"[27]

Appended to the letter were two items that Rosenberg published under his own name. Both of them likewise had to do with the state of sabbath observance. The first was a denunciation of Jewish bakers who baked on the sabbath, and of the Jews who bought the sabbath-baked goods. As early as May 1927, Rosenberg had placed the following announcement in the *Keneder Adler:*

> It must be remembered that baked goods from a baker
> who desecrates the sabbath are even more *tref* than gentile
> baked goods which contain lard. Therefore ask for bread
> with a sabbath label which I will give only to sabbath
> observant bakers.[28]

Rosenberg realized that his intervention was unlikely to stop the practice which, like other forms of sabbath desecration, delayed the messianic redemption. He nonetheless felt it his duty to denounce the practice publicly in the hope that at least some customers, who had not realized that, even after the sabbath, Jews were not allowed to derive benefit from such baked goods, would cease sharing in the bakers' sins. He went so far as to say, "He who eats such baked goods does not eat bread, but rather Jewish blood." If there were no customers for the sabbath-baked goods, the bakers might cease their Saturday operations.[29]

The second appendix had to do with another problem of sabbath observance, the use of perambulators (*baby keridzes*) on the sabbath. In the absence of an *eruv*, an halakhic means of allowing carrying on the sabbath, use of perambulators on the sabbath is forbidden. Nonetheless Rosenberg witnessed desecration of this law weekly by women who did not realize it was a sin.

As was the case in both the Sabbath Queen's letter and the warning concerning the sabbath bakers, Rosenberg realized that he was only talking to some Jewish women. As he said:

> I refer here not to the women who go on the sabbath to
> buy bargains in the markets and carry the packages home
> . . . but rather . . . the women who are entitled to the name
> "Jewish daughters" (*Idishe Tekhter*).[30]

To these women, essentially loyal to the Jewish tradition, he offered a solution "according to the Torah." It consisted in modifying the carriages with wood and wire so that the height of the carriages from the ground up should equal at least forty-two inches. Then it could be wheeled on the street.

Rosenberg's halakhic argument, which did not meet with the approbation of any other Orthodox rabbi, was based upon the principle that at a certain height above the ground, the law of "Sabbath boundaries" do not apply. This modification, which Rosenberg said should only cost twenty to thirty cents, would, he hoped, serve to prevent a widespread desecration of the sabbath.[31]

This pamphlet is addressed to those Jews who considered themselves traditional but whose behaviour contradicted in one way or another the laws of the code of Jewish law, *Shulhan Arukh*. This was Rosenberg's constituency. Were he to address his exhortations only to the strictly observant Jews of Montreal, he would have talked differently. But then he would be talking to a practically empty room.

Rosenberg, like many contemporary Orthodox rabbis, saw his generation as living in the immediate pre-messianic era. Seeing Orthodox Judaism collapsing about him, he felt that every effort had to be made to prevent its total collapse. If this meant stretching his literary and halakhic ingenuity to and beyond the limit in order to reach those still within the religious Jewish community at least nominally, he would do so.[32]

What Eliezer Schweid wrote concerning the halakhic enterprise of Rosenberg's contemporary, Rabbi Israel Meir ha-Kohen, the *Hafez Hayyim,* applies to Rosenberg's effort:

> He erected an embankment and wall in order to prevent its collapse, or at least to delay it . . . . Every moment of postponement is precious for at any moment, he was convinced, salvation will arrive from the heavens and the community will be firmly established.[33]

NOTES

1   Cf. Moses Rischin, *The Promised City* (New York: Harper and Row, 1970), p. 91.

2   A good introduction to the ethos of eastern European Jewry is Lucy Davidowicz's introduction to her anthology, *The Golden Tradition* (New York: Holt, Rinehart and Winston, 1967), pp. 5–90.

3   Yosef Dan, *ha-Sippur ha Hasidi* (Jerusalem: Keter, 1975), p. 189ff.

4   Cf. Joseph Heinemann, "The Nature of the Aggadah," *Midrash and Literature*, Geofrey Hartman, ed. (New Haven: Yale, 1986), pp. 41–55. Cf. Also Yosef Haim Yerushalmi, *Zakhor: Jewish History and Jewish Memory* (Seattle and London: University of Washington Press, 1982), p. 57ff.

5   Cited in Abraham Twerski, *Generation to Generation: Personal Recollections of a Hasidic Legacy* (Brooklyn: Traditional Press, 1985), p. 129. Cf. Jiri Langer, *Nine Gates to the Hasidic Mysteries* (New York: David MacKay, 1961), p. 23; Jerome Mintz, *Legends of the Hasidim: An Introduction to Hasidic Culture and Oral Tradition in the New World* (Chicago and London: University of Chicago Press, 1968), p. 6.

6   Cf. Josef Dan, *ha-Sippur ha-Ivri be-Yeme ha-Beynayim* (Jerusalem: Keter, 1974).

7   Dan Miron, "Folklore and Antifolklore in the Yiddish Fiction of the Haskala," Frank Talmage, ed. *Studies in Jewish Folklore* (Cambridge, MA: Association for Jewish Studies, 1980), p. 249, n. 18.

8   An adequate synthesis of the history of eastern European Orthodox Judaism in this era has not been written. For a promising beginning in social and intellectual history, see Shaul Stampfer, *Three Lithuanian Yeshivot in the Nineteenth Century* [Hebrew] (Ph.D. Dissertation, Hebrew University, 1981) and Norman Solomon, *The Analytic Movement in Rabbinic Jurisprudence: A Study in One Aspect of the Counter-Emancipation in Lithuanian and White Russian Jewry from 1873 Onwards* (Ph.D. Dissertation, University of Manchester, 1966), especially part 1.

9   I am presently writing a comprehensive work on Rosenberg's life and times. To the present, the best biographical sketch of Rosenberg is Zvi Cohen, ed. *Sefer ha-Zikkaron le-Hag ha-Yovel ha-Shiv'im shel . . . Rabi Yehuda Rosenberg* (Montreal: Keneder Odler Drukerei, 1931). With some caution, cf. Leah Rosenberg, *The Errand Runner: Reflections of a Rabbi's Daughter* (Toronto: John Wiley, 1981).

10 Cohen, *Sefer ha-Zikkaron*, p. 5.

11 *Sefer Zohar Torah*, Volume 1, on Genesis, was originally published in Warsaw in 1905 under the title *Sha-arei Zohar Torah*. A second edition of Genesis and the rest of the Pentateuch was published in five volumes in Montreal and New York, 1924–1925. Volumes 6 and 7, containing the Zoharic commentary to Psalms, Proverbs, Song of Songs and Ecclesiastes, were published in Bilgoraj, Poland, 1929–1930. On this translation, see my "A Kabbalist in Montreal: Yudel Rosenberg and His Translation of the Zohar," paper presented at the annual meeting of the Canadian Society for the Study of Religion in 1987 and "Kabbala and Orthodoxy: Some Twentieth Century Interpretations," paper presented at the annual meeting of the American Academy of Religion in 1987.

12 This work has been translated into English in Joachim Neugroschel, ed. *Yenne Velt: The Great Works of Jewish Fantasy and Occult* (New York: Stonehill, 1976), Volume 1, pp. 162–225. For interpretations of this work, cf. Gershom Scholem, *On the Kabbalah and Its Symbolism* (New York: Schocken, 1965), p. 189, note 1; Arnold L. Goldsmith, *The Golem Remembered, 1909–1980* (Detroit: Wayne State University Press, 1981), p. 40.

Gershon Winkler attempts to defend the veracity of Rosenberg's account, arguing that a reputable rabbi would not knowingly state such a falsehood. *The Golem of Prague* (New York: Judaica Press, 1980), p. xi.

13   Yosef Dan, "The Beginnings of Hebrew Hagiographical Literature" [Hebrew], *Jerusalem Studies in Jewish Folklore* 1 [1981], p. 85.

14   On the *Hoshen Mishpat* and its source in Arthur Conan Doyle's story "The Jew's Breastplate," cf. Solomon Alter Halpern, *The Prisoner and Other Tales of Faith* (Jerusalem and New York: Feldheim, 1981), pp. 11–12. Cf. Rosenberg, *Sefer Eliyahu ha-Navi* (Piotrkow, Zederboim, 1910); *Sefer Divrei ha-Yamim le-Shlomo ha-Melekh* (Piotrkow, Kleiman, 1914).

15   Rosenberg, *Sefer Nifla'ot ha-Zohar* (Montreal: City Press, 1927).

16   On the *shekhina*, see *Encyclopedia Judaica* (Jerusalem: Keter, 1972) Volume 14, cols. 1349–1354.

17   Ibn Ezra's *Iggeret ha-Shabbat* was published by S. D. Luzzatto in *Kerem Hemed* 4 (1839), pp. 158–160. It is translated in Joseph Jacobs, *The Jews of Angevin England* (London, 1893), pp. 35–38. On the sabbath as a love letter, see Jacob Joseph of Polnoye, *Toledot Yaakov Yosef,* parshat Ki-Tavo, cited in Joseph Dan, *The Teachings of Hasidism* (New York: Berhrman, 1983), p. 135.

18   Rosenberg, *A Brivele*, p. 8.

19   Ibid., p. 4.

20   Ibid., p. 14.

21   Ibid., p. 5.

22   Ibid., p. 6.

23   Ibid.

24   Ibid., p. 7.

25   Ibid., p. 8ff.

26   Ibid., p. 11.

27   Ibid.

28   *Keneder Adler,* May 13 and 15, and June 5, 1921.

29   Rosenberg, *A Brivele*, p. 14.

30   Ibid., p. 15.

31   Ibid., pp. 15–16. In this pamphlet, Rosenberg does not discuss his halakhic reasoning, which would, in any event, be lost on his intended audience of housewives. In his unpublished book of responsa, entitled *Yeheve Da'at,* pp. 26–27, Rosenberg puts his proposal into standard halakhic responsa form.

32   In a tradition preserved among Rosenberg's descendants, he is said to have received rabbinic permission to write the sort of "unorthodox" stories that he did. Whether or not this tradition is accurate, in so doing, Rosenberg demonstrates one of the primary factors influencing his rabbinic career. This is particularly evident in his controversial career as halakhic decisor and communal leader. Cf. Robinson, "I'd Rather Be in Gehenna: The Making of an Halakhic

Accommodationist," paper presented at the meeting of the Association for Jewish Studies, 1987.

33 Eliezer Schweid, *Orthodoxy and Religious Humanism* [Hebrew] (Jerusalem: Van Leer, 1977), p. 14.

The editorial from the Keneder Adler, *"Yom Kippur Sentiments and Yom Kippur Scandals," from October 14, 1908. The editor challenges the anti-religious behaviour of the anarchists and other secularists by responding in Yiddish, what the radicals liked to call "the language of the masses." Under the guidance of the publisher, Hirsh Wolofsky, the newspaper counseled a "consistently traditional and anti-radical stance" in matters of religion.*

A Tempest in Three Teapots: Yom Kippur Balls in London, New York and Montreal

Rebecca E. Margolis

Introduction

Beginning in 1888, Jewish anarchists in London and New York held annual Yom Kippur Balls. These Balls, which took place on the Day of Atonement—the most solemn day on the Jewish calendar, when strict fasting is enforced—featured anti-religious speeches and recitations, music, dancing and refreshments. These widely publicized events served as a mass demonstration against what anarchists perceived as the evils of religion. The Yom Kippur Balls faced wide protest from the established Jewish communities in which they were held, and received extensive coverage in the Jewish and non-Jewish press. Yom Kippur Balls attracted prominent leaders from Jewish socialist circles and enjoyed mass support in the 1890s. They took place annually into the first decade of the twentieth century in London, New York and Montreal, as well as in a host of other centres of eastern European Jewish immigration. Ultimately, these contentious events created visibility and generated support for the anarchist cause. By 1905, waning support and a general decline in the anarchist movement in New York and London marked the decline of the Yom Kippur Ball, reducing them to small local gatherings. However, this was not the case in Montreal. Whereas in other Jewish centres, the anarchist custom of holding an annual Yom Kippur Ball had pretty much come and gone, Montreal freethinkers held their first and only Yom Kippur Ball in 1905.

The first Yom Kippur Balls in London and New York have received attention in widely read historical works such as Moses Rischin's *The Promised City*[1] and Irving Howe's *World of Our Fathers*.[2] These works portray the Yom Kippur Ball as a fleeting phenomenon limited to these two cities. Generally overlooked have been its later and smaller-scale manifestations in other Jewish centres such as Montreal. To better understand these examples and their support, we must address their broader historical context.

JEWISH IMMIGRATION AND ANARCHISM

The mass migration of Jews from eastern Europe, which began in the last quarter of the nineteenth century, created ideal conditions for the dissemination of radicalism. The migration funneled millions of displaced individuals into urban centres and created a mass Jewish proletariat within crowded, squalid quarters. While this was an immigration of families, a large proportion of the new immigrants were young sons and daughters who were receptive to new, radical ideas. London served as a way station for many of these Jewish immigrants on their way to America, and was an ideal percolation and dissemination site for the radical ideas that they brought with them from their native homes. New York, where an enormous newly arrived Jewish population inundated the established Jewish community, was fertile ground for the rise of a radical Jewish left wing. As the largest Jewish centre in Canada, Montreal would also become a hub of Jewish radicalism.

The mass transition of eastern European Jewry to England and America was marked by upheaval. For the new immigrants, who found themselves uprooted from traditional Jewish life and its strong and organized presence, political radicalism served as one means of making sense of the New World. In the eyes of its leadership, the radical left wing represented a viable affiliation for the Jewish immigrant masses, many of whom lacked a strong affiliation to Jewish observance now that they had left *di alte heym*—the Old Country.

A group of agitators, many of whom had exposure to radicalism in eastern Europe, conducted what was in essence a campaign of revolutionary proselytization. The underlying assumption behind these efforts was that Jews, having been freed of the chains of oppression, could cast off the last remnant of the Old World and join the effort to create an ideal society. Although initially these efforts were conducted in Russian, agitators among the largely Yiddish-speaking eastern European Jewish population soon realized that the use of Yiddish would reach the widest audience. While their aspirations were avowedly internationalist, Yiddish served as the dominant language of the Jewish radical movements.

Anarchism represented the most extreme of the radical ideologies. As a movement for a violent and sudden transformation of society, anarchists agitated for the elimination of existing institutions of authority. Rejecting change through the ballot box, anarchists battled government and the existing social order through propaganda, agitation, and, if need be, violence. In the eastern European Jewish immigrant communities of England and North America, anarchism represented an influential force within the left wing, far beyond the actual numbers of adherents. The 1880s and 1890s marked an era of struggle between socialists and anarchists, as factions vied for influence among the immigrant populations. Although the socialist ideal of change through political action ultimately had a greater impact, the writings of anarchist thinkers were widely studied in revolutionary circles.

The Jewish anarchist movement attracted prominent non-Jewish anarchists such as Rudolf Rocker (1873–1958) and Johann Most (1846–1906). By the 1880s, London's East End had become an important socialist and trade union centre, with anarchists particularly active in the forming of Jewish unions. Meanwhile, anarchists on the Lower East Side were gaining visibility among the immigrant population. During the 1880s and 1890s, Jewish anarchists in London and New York organized a network of institutions, including an active press. A group of London social democrats and anarchists founded a Yiddish-language newspaper, the *Arbayter Fraynd (Worker's Friend),* in 1885. Edited by prominent Russian-born radical leader, Philip Krantz (1858–1922), it soon became a locus of anarchist activity, and was widely read in England as well as in America.

Spurred by the events surrounding the Chicago Haymarket Affair,[3] a group of New York anarchists formed the Pioneers of Liberty on Yom Kippur, 1886. The Pioneers of Liberty sponsored mass demonstrations, organized unions, meetings, lectures, concerts and balls, as well as a library, and attracted such radicals as Yiddish poets, David Edelstadt (1866–1892) and Morris Rosenfeld (1862–1922). The group grew rapidly, and clubs were formed in other Jewish urban centres in the United States, including Chicago, Philadelphia, Boston, Baltimore, and New Haven.[4] As the Pioneers of Liberty prepared to publish its own anarchist newspaper, the London *Arbayter Fraynd* served as the main Yiddish organ of socialist and anarchist propaganda among American anarchists. In 1889, the first Yiddish American anarchist newspaper, the *Varhayt (Truth),* was established, appearing for a period of five months before folding. In 1890, the Pioneers of Liberty founded a lasting anarchist newspaper, the Yiddish language *Fraye Arbeter Shtime (Free Voice of Labour).*

Central to the Jewish anarchist program was the battle against religion. Socialists, while supporters of atheism, treated religion as a private concern and thus tended to resist direct confrontation and demonstrative anti-religious agitation. The anarchists, in contrast, understood religion as a fundamental evil rather than a matter of personal conscience, and sought to battle it directly. Anarchists disseminated anti-religious propaganda in the form of leaflets and through the anarchist press, and organized lectures on the subject of religion. The London *Arbayter Fraynd* represented an important organ of anti-religious propaganda on both sides of the ocean, while the New York *Fraye Arbeter Shtime* placed the issue of religion high on its agenda. This anti-religious agitation peaked on Rosh Hashana (the Jewish New Year) and Yom Kippur, the most sacred days of the Jewish year and a time when even the least observant Jews were likely to be found in synagogue. On each Rosh Hashana between 1889 and 1893, the New York Pioneers of Liberty issued a series of anti-religious pamphlets under the title, *Tfilot Zakot: Devotional Prayers on the Days of Awe, Sabbath,*

Holidays, and Every Day of the Year[5], which featured vociferous anti-religious propaganda in the form of articles that attacked religion as well as parodies. Not surprisingly, Yom Kippur, the most solemn day of the Jewish calendar, where complete fasting is required, became the occasion for the most extreme and public expression of anti-religious activism in the form of the Yom Kippur Ball.

YOM KIPPUR BALLS IN LONDON AND NEW YORK

In 1888, a group of London "freethinkers" hosted a Yom Kippur Ball, the first of its kind. The *Arbayter Fraynd* promoted the event:

> We hereby notify all our friends that we are preparing a dinner to be held in our club. This will take place in honour of the great festival of the slaughter of the fowl, Yom Kippur, when all asses and hypocrites beat their breast, repent of the sins they have committed, and fast. For one shilling you can receive a good dinner and spend a most enjoyable day in fine company. The dinner will be followed by singing and dancing. There will also be a number of brief lectures and recitations. . . . We will post bills for those who, sitting in the synagogues and sneaking out now and then for a smoke and a bite to eat, will not read this notice.[6]

The Ball took place from Yom Kippur evening until the early hours of the next day. On Yom Kippur night, a noisy crowd of irate Jews gathered outside the hall and attempted, unsuccessfully, to disrupt the proceedings. By early Yom Kippur morning, despite the angry mob outside, the hall was packed with people and police were stationed in the street. Speeches against religion were held, followed by discussion, joyous singing and recitations. On Yom Kippur afternoon, tables with refreshments were set up. Because of the unexpectedly high attendance, the food was soon depleted and three individuals, including *Arbayter Fraynd* editor Philip Krantz, had to leave the hall, obtain more food from a nearby restaurant and make their way back through a furious crowd.

After the meal, speeches attacking religion were held, followed by discussion, further recitations and more singing. Later that evening, the police arrived to restore order. Several participants in the event were arrested. Despite the disruptions, the *Arbayter Fraynd* reported, "Thus the day, a day which can truly be called historic, passed in a festive manner."7

The first Yom Kippur Ball ended on a victorious note. Attendance at the event had far surpassed the organizers' expectations, and the movement had gained support among the masses. The press coverage had, on the whole, been supportive, backing the organizers' right to hold the event. The Ball did not appear to have faced any organized opposition from the community, and the conservative Anglo-Jewish weekly, the *Jewish Chronicle,* remained silent.

A Yom Kippur Ball was held in New York the following year. An open invitation was published in the 1889 *Tfilot Zakot,* as well as in the London *Arbayter Fraynd* and in the German-language socialist *New Yorker Volks Zeitung.* Thousands of handbills advertising the Ball with the slogan, "Down with fanaticism! Long live free thought!", were circulated on New York's Lower East Side. Members of the "Downtown" Orthodox Jewry and the "Uptown" German-Jewish "*Yahudi*" establishment responded vehemently. Responses to the announcement of the Yom Kippur Ball by the mainstream English and Yiddish Jewish press were immediate and acrimonious; the *American Hebrew* and the Cincinnati-based *American Israelite* strongly condemned the event and its organizers, as did the long-running conservative Yiddish daily, the *Yidishes Tageblatt.* "Uptown" and "Downtown" banded together in an attempt to prevent the Ball from taking place. The Orthodox Jews appealed to the Jewish coroner of the city of New York, Ferdinand Levy, to intercede with the municipal authorities. At the last minute, the Ball was moved to a smaller locale. Despite intervention by the police to impede the event, the hall was packed. The evening's program included recitations, a buffet, and dancing, in addition to speeches by prominent German anarchist Johann Most and others. The chairperson for the evening was "Mr. Hillkovitch," who was none other than future prominent American socialist, Morris Hillquit (1869–1933). The following day, the celebration lasted from morning through evening despite noisy protests by angry synagogue-goers in the streets. The response in the Jewish press ranged from enthusiastic support in the socialist *Folkstsaytung*, to strong opposition in the conservative *Yidishes Tageblatt.*

The uproar evoked by the Yom Kippur Ball ultimately brought with it two unexpected benefits for the Pioneers of Liberty and the anarchist cause. The fracas caused by the Ball provided the cause with increased visibility. The event also endeared the anarchist group to a number of radicals, and brought new supporters and members into the fold of the Pioneers of Liberty. "Perhaps," as anarchist activist Kopeloff later mused, "the Pioneers gained more" from the negative publicity associated with the event, than if it had taken place quietly.[8]

The following year, the New York anarchists organized a Yom Kippur Ball to be held in Brooklyn. With the support of the newly formed newspaper, the *Fraye Arbeter Shtime,* the organizers felt confident that the event would not only take place, but draw unprecedented crowds. The event, however, faced organized opposition from all sectors of the Jewish community, until it was shut down by the police. In the end, despite the disruption, the second New York Yom Kippur Ball ended on an overall note of victory when a protest held at Cooper Union attracted over 2,000 supporters.[9] In the subsequent years, Yom Kippur Balls also took place in Philadelphia, Boston, Chicago, and other American Jewish centres.

The unlikely attention the Yom Kippur Balls attracted can be partly explained by the novelty of the events taking place in a newly developing immigrant community, where traditional power structures were being challenged by new ones. Ultimately, however, the Yom Kippur Ball proved to be as ephemeral as the era of flux that spawned it. The London Yom Kippur Ball movement continued into the first decade of the twentieth century, with the *Arbayter Fraynd* publicizing Yom Kippur Balls on and off through 1906. With an increase in public antipathy and police action, the London Yom Kippur Ball phenomenon waned and finally disappeared. The New York Yom Kippur movement continued off and on for over a decade, with a successful event held in 1900. The Ball announced for the following year was cancelled due to a sudden upsurge in anti-anarchist sentiment.

Labour historian Melech Epstein attributes the decline of anarchist strength to the onset of "normality" among the Jewish population; as Jews acclimatized economically, socially, and politically, they gravitated towards less radical expressions of socialism.[10] Historians such as Elias Tcherikover and Irving Howe present the end of the Yom Kippur Ball movement as an inevitability. Regarding the 1890 Yom Kippur Ball, Howe writes:

> The consequences of such tomfoolery were or should have been predictable. Many immigrants, although no longer Orthodox, still maintained a sense of piety toward religious occasions, and the anarchist assault came to be seen as a threat to their very being [. . .][11]

These remarks oversimplify the end of the Yom Kippur Ball phenomenon. The marginalization of anarchism among the immigrant masses does not adequately account for the demise of the Yom Kippur Ball. In fact, diverse forces simultaneously led to the end of the Yom Kippur Ball in its London and New York centres. Direct anti-anarchist activity represented a significant factor in the decline of Yom Kippur Balls. In the United States, the sudden rise in anti-anarchist sentiment can be directly attributed to one startling event: the assassination of the President of the United States by anarchist Leon Czolgosz; after having been shot at close range on September 6, President William McKinley died from his gunshot wounds on September 14, 1901. The assassination brought with it an upsurge of attacks against anarchists: anarchist headquarters were vandalized, suspected anarchist sympathizers were attacked, and many anarchists were arrested and imprisoned. Several months later, federal legislation was passed to bar anarchists from entering the United States. The effect of these events was extreme and irrevocable. Although public Yom Kippur gatherings did take place in 1903 and 1904, these were the last of their kind held in New York City proper. By 1905, much of the steam had gone out of the anti-religious movement among New York Jews. The previous anti-religious venom was lacking in the pages of the *Fraye Arbeter Shtime,* and the New York Yom Kippur Ball had become a Yom Kippur picnic held in Long Island, far from New York's Lower East Side.

THE MONTREAL YOM KIPPUR BALL

The first and only Montreal Yom Kippur Ball took place in 1905. The event shared similarities with its London and New York counterparts: the Ball featured speeches, refreshments and met opposition from the established Jewish community; it was widely reported in the local Jewish and non-Jewish press. Notable, though, is the late date of the event, and the fact that it was a one-time phenomenon. How did this event come about in Montreal and why, unlike in London, New York and other Jewish centres, did it take place so late and only once? Some background comments are necessary before proceeding to answer these questions.

Montreal absorbed the majority of Jewish immigrants to Canada, and acted as Canada's largest Jewish centre during the peak years of Jewish immigration from 1880 to 1920. Eastern European immigration swelled the Jewish community from 6,500 in 1891 to some 16,000 ten years later, with close to half of the Canadian Jewish population residing in Montreal. By the early years of the twentieth century, Montreal had become a hub of radicalism and served as the Canadian headquarters for Jewish leftist political movements, including the Socialist Zionist Poale Zion, and labour organizations such as the International Ladies' Garment Workers' Union. In many ways, Montreal was the Canadian equivalent to New York or London as far as eastern European Jewish immigrant activity was concerned. And yet, there were marked differences. As historian Eugene Orenstein points out in his essay, "Yiddish Culture in Canada Yesterday and Today,"[12] mass Jewish immigration to Canada, and to Montreal in particular, took place a generation later than in the United States. In the late 1880s, when the anarchist movement was in full swing in London and New York City, Montreal's Jewish population totaled several thousand; only after 1900 did the Jewish population of Montreal number in the tens of thousands.

Many developments within the Montreal Jewish community took place at least a decade later than in the United States. The first Jewish periodical in Canada, an English-language weekly called the *Jewish Times,* was not founded until 1897, decades after the first Anglo-Jewish American periodicals. Canada's first lasting Yiddish language daily, the *Keneder Adler,* was founded in Montreal in 1907, over twenty years after the first lasting New York Yiddish daily, and ten years later than the New York *Forverts (Jewish Daily Forward)*. Organized manifestations of radicalism did not appear until some fifteen years after similar acts occurred in London and New York. The Jewish radicals who did become active in Montreal were, in general, more likely to be nationalist in orientation than the cosmopolitan socialists and anarchists who had been active in New York and London two decades earlier.

Canadian Jewry did not share the sizeable pre-existing Jewish establishment that dominated in England and in the United States before the onset of mass immigration from eastern Europe in the 1880s. In 1900, the eve of large-scale eastern European Jewish immigration to Canada, the English-speaking Canadian Jewish community of Montreal numbered a few thousand and consisted of an anglicized elite, the majority of whom were themselves relatively recent immigrants from eastern Europe by way of England or the United States.[13] Eastern European immigrants to Montreal did not encounter the pre-existing network of Jewish organizations and institutions that were found, for example, in New York City. In contrast to the chasm that separated the established German Jews from the new eastern European immigrants in New York, the split between "Uptown" and "Downtown"[14] in Montreal was, to a certain extent, a question of degree of acculturation within the same stream of eastern European Jewish immigration.[15] While the tiny, anglicized Jewish elite in Montreal shared some of the trepidation and acculturative impulses of its American counterpart in relation to their immigrant brethren, it was soon overwhelmed by a mass of newly arrived Yiddish-speaking eastern European Jews. These newcomers quickly created a vast network of their own organizations and associations.

A number of the Jews who settled after 1900 came to Montreal from London and New York, and had been influenced by radical socialist and anarchist movements. As their numbers grew, so did the radical revolutionary movement in Montreal. Among the skilled textile workers imported from New York to Montreal by the nascent garment industry were a number of active anarchists. Montreal anarchists distributed the *Fraye Arbeter Shtime* and anarchist pamphlets, brought lecturers from New York, and were active in the building of unions. In many ways, the Montreal anarchist movement was a satellite of that in New York. Jewish radical activity began to crystallize in Montreal after 1905, when mass immigration from eastern Europe, spurred by the Russian Revolution, brought with it a tide of radical-minded individuals. The year 1905 marked a number of firsts in the Canadian Jewish radical movement, among them the founding of the first Canadian chapter of Socialist Zionist Poale Zion in Montreal, the first May Day parade and the first Yom Kippur Ball. Two institutions were key in the early development of Jewish radicalism in Montreal: Jewish bookshops and the Poale Zion party.

Canadian historian Israel Medres describes the rudimentary nature of Jewish organizational life in Montreal, at a time when the bookshop served as a cultural centre for Montreal's Yiddish-speaking radical intelligentsia.[16] Several of these bookshops were located along "the Main," or St. Laurent Boulevard, Montreal's equivalent to London's East End or New York's Lower East Side. They stocked Yiddish newspapers from the *Forverts* to the *Fraye Arbeter Shtime*, as well as a selection of books, from sentimental novels or modern Yiddish and Hebrew literature to anarchist propaganda. The first of these bookshops was owned by Hirsh Hershman (1876–1955), a recent immigrant with strong anarchist inclinations, who had been active in the labour movement in New York before settling in Montreal. Opened in 1902, Hershman's bookshop struggled in its early years until 1905, when the wave of immigration brought new customers. According to Medres' account in *Montreal fun nekhtn (Montreal of Yesterday)*, a second bookshop on the Main catered specifically to the more radical elements of the Jewish immigrant community. This bookshop sold anti-religious literature about "the escapades of the most extreme radicals, the anarchists, which in those days included festivities on Yom Kippur."[17] Shops such as Hershman's were gathering sites for Jewish radicals, albeit on a very small scale. The older generation would gather to buy a newspaper and drink seltzer while the younger "more enlightened" and radical-minded immigrants, many of whom had already been exposed to anarchist and socialist ideas, would come to discuss politics. Medres writes:

> Each store had its specialty on the line of "cultural dissemination." In one place, the favourite theme might be anarchism, due no doubt to the prevalence of anarchistic

pamphlets and literature on the shelves. The store-keeper was himself a specialist in this line of literature. . . . When the store-keeper was asked for a glass of soda water or a package of cigarettes by a customer he would take his time and lend an ear to the discussions that were being waged, and would throw in his comment as well. The cigarettes would wait while he championed the teachings of Karl Marx, Peter Kropotkin, Rudolf Rocker, Johann Most, or Emma Goldman.[18]

Many "one time anarchists," writes Medres, would spend hours discussing the pros and cons of anarchism in the bookshops. The bookshop owners would arrange for speakers to come from New York to lecture on socialist and anarchist topics, and on the impending socialist revolution. The Jewish bookshop served as a hub of radical activity during the contentious Jewish holidays. In Medres' view,

The [bookshop] debates were particularly lively when Erev Yom Tov [the eve of the holiday] came around. . . . On Erev Yom Kippur the subject for debate would be whether a true anarchist should stage an anti-religious demonstration by means of a dance, or a feast in the restaurant or ignore the event completely.[19]

The Poale Zion and its socialist Zionist forerunners were likewise significant in the development of Jewish radical activity. Upon its establishment in Montreal in 1905, the Poale Zion soon became a centre of radicalism, and Poale Zion members would attend open lectures organized by already established anarchist and Social Democrat unions. In the rudimentary and fluid state of Jewish radicalism, there was a good deal of overlap between the burgeoning socialist Zionist movement and other radical left-wing movements, and it was not uncommon for members of the Poale Zion to be active anarchists. For example, one of Montreal's most active anarchists, Hayman Lazarus, was a pioneer

Poale Zionist and an active trade unionist.[20] From the onset, Montreal Jewish radicalism tended towards a combination of socialism and Zionism.

Despite the activism of its proponents, anarchism among Montreal Jews represented a marginal phenomenon. As in England and the United States, the majority of Montreal Jewry did not subscribe to the radical extremism of the anarchists. As Medres describes, even the second Jewish bookshop on the Main, with its radical orientation, was soon selling traditional Jewish objects such as prayer shawls for the high holidays; as he writes, "Once more radicalism was forced to retreat under the pressure of traditional Judaism exerted by the immigrant Jews on Main Street."[21] Montreal simply lacked the strong radical base and the sheer numbers of the anarchist movements in London and New York. The rise of anti-religious Jewish radicalism was not welcomed by the "established" Jewish community, however small it was. The voice of this community was represented by the conservative "Uptown" Anglo-Jewish weekly, the *Jewish Times*. The coverage of Jewish holidays in the *Jewish Times* promoted observance and strongly opposed anti-religious behaviour. This stance was particularly marked in its coverage of the High Holidays. A column entitled "The Day of Atonement," which appeared in the *Jewish Times* in October of 1900, glowingly describes the mass observance of Yom Kippur in Montreal, with its overflowing synagogues.[22] An article, which appeared in the *Jewish Times* in September of 1902, entitled "The New Year" states:

> Marvelous must be the hold of Judaism on its votaries when it can compel even the indifferent to pay respect to this season of religious revival. The Jew who does not heed even the call of these days has indeed forfeited his religious birthright; for all practical reasons he ceases to be a member of the Brotherhood of Israel.[23]

During the week of Yom Kippur 1901, several articles critical of anarchism appeared in the *Jewish Times*. In them, anarchism was dismissed as impractical, linked with European anti-Semitism, and blamed for the wider movement away from Judaism. One piece concluded with a strong admonition of Jewish radicals: "for they ceased to be Jews when they became anarchists."[24] Several weeks later, an article appeared praising the violent end resulting from a public infraction of Yom Kippur observance in New York City some years earlier.[25] Until 1905, the *Jewish Times* made no mention of local anarchist activity among Canadian Jewry, nor did it make mention of any Yom Kippur Ball. As can be expected, the *Jewish Times* did not report favourably on the anarchist Yom Kippur Ball that took place in Montreal that October.

Canadian Jewish historian B. G. Sack, in his book, *Canadian Jews—Early in This Century*, provides the following account of Montreal's Yom Kippur Ball:

> In Montreal, for instance, a group of Jewish anarchists, emulating their free-thinking socialist confrères of New York or Chicago, arranged a Yom Kippur dance at St. Joseph's Hall. They distributed circulars inviting the Jewish people to partake of dancing and refreshments on Yom Kippur day. Pious Jews on their way to synagogue were both horrified and infuriated at the distributors of the handbills. This flagrant violation of religious sentiments led to a skirmish, which ended only after the police intervened and the subsequent airing of the incident in court.[26]

Various press accounts provide details of the Montreal Yom Kippur Ball. The event took place on October 9, 1905 in a rented hall located on Ste. Catherine Street and Sanguinet Street in Montreal's east end. The Ball was hosted by a society of socialists and freethinkers that called itself the "Group of Worker's Friends." The event was billed as "a protest against superstition," and the following invitations were distributed in front of local synagogues on Rosh Hashana:

> All free-thinking persons of Montreal are asked to come on the Day of Atonement to St. Joseph's Hall where friend [comrade] Abrahams will lecture on the 'Theme of Religion.' Entertainment the whole day. Admission free.[27]

Some eighty people gathered in the hall on Yom Kippur morning. When the main speaker was late in presenting his lecture, some of those present at the event began to consume the refreshments. At this point, a group in attendance who were not "freethinkers" left the hall to spread the news that "a meeting was being held as an insult to their religion."[28] A crowd soon entered the premises and proceeded to disrupt the event. The protesters broke chairs and looted tobacco, food, and money. By the time the police arrived, the bar had been wrecked, and all the cash from the cash register stolen. The angry mob left the site. Soon after, a second antagonistic group entered the hall and a fight broke out. When the organizers were unable to stop the fighting, they called the police a second time. One man, Harry Rabinovitch, was arrested and brought to the local police station, while the event continued under the guard of a single police officer. Rabinovitch was charged with obstruction and the assault of Benjamin Jauff, one of the speakers at the event, by punching him in the forehead outside of the hall. Upon the arrest of Mr. Rabinovitch, the fighting stopped. The intruders left with lit cigars and cigarettes. The case was heard in court the next day, and the accused was released for lack of evidence.[29]

The Montreal Yom Kippur Ball received coverage in the *Jewish Times*, as well as in Montreal's major English and French press. Much of this coverage was on the disruption of the event, and subsequent arrest and court case. Headlines included: "Row at St. Joseph's Hall" (Montreal *Star,* Oct. 10); "Riot at meeting. . . . One man arrested" (Montreal *Gazette,* Oct. 10); "Une rixe entre juifs" (*La Presse,* Oct. 9); and "Desecration of the Day of Atonement. A Socialist Gathering Broken Up" (*Jewish Times,* Oct. 20). The initial reports in the Montreal press reflected confusion about the nature of the event. The Montreal *Star* and *La Presse* mistakenly attributed the violent breakup of the meeting to the fact that the food served at the event was not kosher:

> In the midst of [the consumption of the food] there appeared
> about thirty people, who were evidently not kindly disposed
> toward their free-thinking brethren, and believing that some
> of the articles of diet were not in accordance with the Jewish
> faith, they proceeded to enter a forcible protest.[30]

The next day, the *Star* reported that the root of the trouble was "what was considered profane treatment of the Day of Atonement by the unorthodox body."[31]

The Montreal Yom Kippur Ball differed in fundamental ways from the first Yom Kippur Balls in London and New York in such areas as organization, scale and dissemination. The various press reports of the event pointed to one main difference between the Montreal Yom Kippur Ball and its counterparts in New York and London: organization, or, more specifically, the lack thereof. The "Group of Worker's Friends" did not seem to represent an established organization within the Montreal Jewish radical scene. The three individuals mentioned in accounts of the Montreal Yom Kippur Ball—Mr. Abrahams, Mr. Jauff and Mr. Rabinovitch—lacked the prominence of the personalities behind the London and New York events. The event was marked by general confusion and pandemonium.

In contrast to the wide efforts to halt the Yom Kippur Balls in London and New York, the Montreal Ball was impeded by spontaneous hooliganism and with no one claiming responsibility. Attempts to suppress the event were limited to haphazard disruptions during the Ball itself; the trouble only began when the event was well underway and attendees actually began to consume food. The crowd that invaded the hall had more than the sanctity of religion in mind; the hall was vandalized and the bar looted.

The event's opponents did not constitute a unified and coordinated force. With the exception of Rabinovitch, no names were mentioned in conjunction with the disruptions, and it seems unlikely that Mr. Rabinovitch represented the leader of any anti-Ball protest. According to the press accounts, he denied any political affiliation, testifying in court that he had not set out to oppose the event; he had unwittingly wound up at the site of the Ball and had found himself suddenly under arrest and accused of striking a man he had never seen before.

In contrast to what transpired in New York, there were apparently no organized efforts or appeals to suppress the event ahead of time. There was also no indication that efforts were made to involve outside legal forces in order to prohibit the Ball from taking place. When the police were summoned, it was by the staff on hand at the event, and not by its opponents. Thus, although the event was effectively sabotaged, one cannot speak of a cohesive anti-Yom Kippur Ball movement. Unlike the expansive and virulent campaign waged by the Jewish community and the press to condemn the New York Yom Kippur Balls, the breakup of the Montreal Ball was roundly condemned. The court, in addition to dismissing Rabinovitch, stated that "the conveners. . . were within their rights in holding [the event]." Even the *Jewish Times,* while generally unsympathetic to the cause, acknowledged the rights of individuals in a free country to air their views and hold gatherings within the law, and reproached those who disrupted the events at the hall.[32]

The Montreal Yom Kippur Ball evoked strong responses from all elements of the Jewish community, with the ensuing court case acting as an intensifier, but on a much smaller scale than the London and New York events. According to *La Presse,* "*Toute la colonie juive de la ville avait envahi la salle du tribunal,*" and much lively discussion ensued. *The Gazette* referred to the aftermath of the event as a "religious war," with "freethinkers" in support of the Ball in one camp and its opponents in the other. The comments of a group of socialists gathered at Hershman's bookstore were quoted in *The Gazette,* the *Star*, and the *Jewish Times:*

> We are freethinkers and Socialists, and we have a right to do as we please, provided we do not disturb others. We did not compel anyone to enter and our gathering could not be an insult to anyone who minded his own business. We have a number of friends here: why there are 3,000 Socialist papers sold every day in this city. We want to educate the people. We are followers of Ingersoll and Tolstoy. We read Spencer. We know something.

In the meantime, a group gathered at the home of Mr. Rabinovitch the evening after the trial were cited as stating: "It was a fight in a good cause [*sic*]. These men had no right to insult us. They are blasphemers and neither Jew nor Gentile would stand for their insults."[33]

The stance of the Jewish establishment can be found in an editorial in the *Jewish Times* entitled "Yom Kippur Outrage." It echoed the response of the *American Israelite* to the first New York Yom Kippur Ball; while the Ball should have been condemned, the writer argued that the best course of action would have been to ignore the celebration of this radical fringe element entirely: "It is to be regretted that any notice was taken of the Yom Kippur desecration meeting. . . . To notice them only magnifies their insignificance."[34] Still, in contrast to the fierce opposition to anti-religious behaviour expressed by the American anglo-Jewish periodicals, the opposition of the *Jewish Times* was mild. The relatively moderate response to the Montreal Ball was likely due, at least in part, to the limited and finite nature of the Ball itself. With eighty attendees, the scope of the Montreal Ball was trivial. With a loosely organized Jewish establishment, it did not cause the same waves as its English or American counterparts.

The issue of dissemination was also key to the disorganized and short-lived quality of the Montreal Yom Kippur Ball. Unlike their counterparts in London and New York, the Montreal anarchists lacked an avowedly radical organ. The *Keneder Adler,* Canada's first lasting Yiddish newspaper, did not come into existence until two years after the event.[35] It largely shared the stance of the *Jewish Times* on anti-religious activity and the Yom Kippur Ball. Founded as a weekly in Montreal in August 1907, the *Keneder Adler* (Canadian Eagle) became a daily in October 1908. In comparison to the radical left-wing newspapers such as the anarchist London *Arbayter Fraynd,* the New York *Fraye Arbeter Shtime,* or the avowedly socialist *Forverts,* the *Adler* was a moderate newspaper that addressed the widest possible readership. Under publisher Hirsh Wolofsky (1878–1949), the *Adler* strove to supply Canadian Jews with an organ to inform, educate, entertain, and represent their general interests, and to strengthen the Yiddish-speaking immigrant community in Montreal and in Canada as a whole. From the onset, the *Adler* maintained a middle ground and tended toward the traditional in matters related to religion. Many of the *Adler's* associates had radical inclinations: bookshop owner Hirsh Hershman was a regular contributor; Eliezer Landau (1877–1942), the paper's editor until 1909, was an active labour Zionist who had begun his literary career at the anarchist *Fraye Arbeter Shtime,* and was active in New York anarchist circles. However, although the *Adler* expressed clear socialist inclinations and was sympathetic to the plight of workers in its coverage of strikes, its stance on religious observance was consistently traditional and anti-radical. Historian David Rome writes:

> Although the *Adler* editors were not religiously observant as a group, they were profoundly steeped in the tradition . . . their poems and articles reminiscent of the holy days as observed in the old home, related to the ideas of the present time, were frequently published in the *Adler* by [contributors] Schneour, Yamploskly, Bercovici and Goldstein, not to mention H. Hirsch, who conducted a veritable political campaign against secularism.[36]

If we look to the *Adler's* columns during the 1908 High Holidays, we find an abundance of nostalgic reminiscences of Yom Kippur in the Old Country and praise for the freedom offered to worship freely in the New Country. These are coupled with an unambiguous lack of sympathy for anti-religious activity. Three years after the fact, it seems, the Yom Kippur Ball still loomed in the consciousness of Montreal Jewry. An editorial entitled "Yom Kippur Sentiments and Yom Kippur Scandals" encapsulated the *Adler's* stance on anti-religious radicalism. Editor Eliezer Landau, who went by the pen name of Wohliner, idealized religious observance in the Old Country and lamented the increase in irreligious and anti-religious behaviour among Jews in America. In Europe, Wohliner wrote that there was an underlying respect for religion, even among the most radical atheists, that was lacking in America; in Europe, a person understood that "Yom Kippur demonstrations, Yom Kippur Balls and public Yom Kippur feasts do not serve to prove anything to anyone. He is *mentsh* (decent human being) enough not to trod on the feelings of others." In America, in contrast, the atheist "lacks education, intelligence and understanding. [The atheist] acts like a hero who equates his Yom Kippur feast with an act of bravery. His Yom Kippur demonstrations often smack of ignorance." Still, the column ended with a criticism of those who attacked these Yom Kippur activities; the attackers were not devout Jews who were too busy observing the holiday to take notice of the non-observance of others; rather, "pogroms against the socialist and anarchist clubs are undertaken by people who themselves spend little time in synagogue and know absolutely nothing about serious religious sentiment."[37]

CONCLUSION

The rise and fall of the Yom Kippur Ball can be attributed to rapidly changing trends within Jewish immigrant life. Like anti-religious agitation in general, the Ball movement can be understood as a fleeting product of upheaval among the Jewish immigrant masses: in a time of displacement and new freedoms, many Jews turned radical; as they adjusted and acculturated, many turned away from the radical left wing in favour of the more mainstream socialist movement. Even the more radical elements understood that extreme anti-religious agitation, through the alienation of a significant proportion of the Jewish masses, ultimately brought more harm than good to the radical agenda.

The Yom Kippur Ball did not fall prey to gradually changing trends. Its demise, particularly in New York, was sudden. This premature death can be attributed directly to an upsurge in anti-anarchist sentiment in the first decade of the century. With anarchist activity suppressed by the authorities, supporters left the movement in droves. Police action and threats of violence drove the movement further underground. Under these conditions, the Yom Kippur Ball, which relied on publicity, could not endure. As we have seen, the Montreal Ball lacked organization and leadership. The movement behind it did not have an anarchist organ to publicize its anarchist agenda. The Ball itself was plagued by disorder, and opposition to it was haphazard and uncoordinated. The event ended in pandemonium, and without any follow-up. Although isolated Yom Kippur Balls did take place at later dates in such disparate places as Havana, Cuba and the Soviet Union, the growth of the Jewish labour movement after 1905 in England, the United States and Canada assured that the anarchist torch would be passed to more mainstream socialists.

NOTES

1   Moses Rischin, *The Promised City: New York Jews 1870–1914* (Cambridge, Mass. and London, England: Harvard UP, 1962, 1977), pp. 154–155.

2   Irving Howe, *World of Our Fathers: The Journey of East European Jews to America and the Life They Found and Made* (New York: Schocken, 1976, 1989), pp. 105–107.

3   In May of 1886, police stormed a demonstration by labour unionists agitating for an eight-hour workday, held near Chicago's Haymarket Square. At a protest meeting, a bomb was thrown and a police officer killed. Four anarchists were convicted.

4   For an overview of the development of the Jewish anarchist movement in New York by one of its activists, including a detailed first-hand account of the Yom Kippur Balls of 1889 and 1890, see Isidore Kopeloff, *A mol in Amerike: zikhroynes fun dem yidishn lebn in Amerike in di yorn 1883–1904* (*Once Upon a Time in America: Memories of Jewish Life in America From 1883–1904*) (Warsaw: [Farlag] Kh. Bjoza, 1928), specifically pp. 230–275. See also Joseph Cohen, *Di anarkhistishe bavegung in Amerike* (*The Anarchist Movement in America*) (Jubilee Issue of the Radical Library, Branch 273, Workman's Circle, Philadelphia, PA, 1905, 1945), specifically pp. 70–79. For an early historical survey of the Jewish anarchist scene, see Elias Tcherikover, ed., *The Early Jewish Labour Movement in the United States.* Trans. Aaron Antonovsky. (New York: YIVO Institute for Jewish Research, 1961), p. 246–271; Herz Burgin, *Di geshikhte fun der idisher arbeter bavegung in Amerike, Rusland un England* (*The History of the Jewish Labour Movement in America, Russia and England*) (New York: Fareynikte idishe geverkshaftn, 1915), pp. 126, 139, 141. See also Melech Epstein, "The Anarchists," *Jewish Labor in U.S.A.* (KTAV, 1969) and Howe, *World of Our Fathers*, pp. 105–107.

5   Israel Davidson, *Parody in Jewish Literature* (New York: Columbia UP, 1907), p. 83, fn. 71.

6   Cited in Tcherikover *The Early Jewish Labour Movement in the United States*, p. 253.

7   This account of the Ball is taken from the *Arbayter Fraynd*, Sept. 21, 1889. Unless indicated otherwise, all translations from the Yiddish are my own.

8   Kopeloff, *A mol in Amerike*, pp. 237–238.

9   New York *Sun*, Sept. 24, 1890, *Fraye Arbeter Shtime*, Sept. 26, 1890, Kopeloff, *A mol in Amerike*, p. 270–271. Cohen, *Di anarkhistishe bavegung in Amerike*, p. 71.

10 Epstein, *Jewish Labor in U.S.A.* , p. 215.

11 Howe, *World of Our Fathers*, p. 106.

12 Eugene Orenstein, "Yiddish Culture in Canada Yesterday and Today," *The Canadian Cultural Mosaic*. Ed. M. Weinfeld, W. Shaffir, I. Cotler (Rexdale, Canada: John Wiley and Sons, 1981).

13 In Montreal, a tiny "old guard" had been adopted into the society of the English Protestant elite, and had enjoyed the rights and freedoms of emancipated members, first of the British Empire, and subsequently as citizens of Canada. For an in-depth analysis, see Michael Brown, "British Roots," *Jew or Juif?* (Philadelphia, New York, Jerusalem: JPS, 1986), pp. 7–67.

14 Much of the historiography of Canadian Jewry, likely under the influence of the works of American Jewish historians, has posited an "Uptown"/"Downtown" divide. For example, in a chapter titled "Immigrants: 'Uptown' and 'Downtown' Montreal," Erna Paris presents a sharp split between the "Uptown" and "Downtown" Jews, with "Uptowners" identifying with assimilation or "Canadianization," and "Downtowners" representing Yiddish and left-wing culture. Erna Paris, *Jews: An Account of Their Experience in Canada* (Toronto: Macmillan, 1980), pp. 30–31.

15 As scholar Keinosuke Oiwa posits, "Uptown" tended to be more of a location on a new immigrant's "Mental Map" than a true divide; the "Uptowner" tended to be the immigrant who had been in the city for a few years and had acculturated somewhat. He still, however, spoke Yiddish and shared many of the values of his "Downtown" counterparts. See Keinosuke Oiwa, "Tradition and Social Change: An Ideological Analysis of the Montreal Jewish Immigrant Ghetto in the Early Twentieth Century" (unpublished dissertation thesis, Cornell University, 1988), specifically pp. 38–45.

16 Israel Medres, "How the Immigrants Found their Intellectual Atmosphere," *The Canadian Jewish Chronicle,* April 3, 1936.

17 Israel Medres "The Second Jewish Bookstore," *Montreal of Yesterday: Jewish Life in Montreal, 1900–1920.* Trans. Vivian Felsen (Montreal: Véhicule Press, 2000), p. 62.

18 Medres, "How the Immigrants Found their Intellectual Atmosphere."

19 Medres, "How the Immigrants Found their Intellectual Atmosphere."

20 Yud Lamed Shapiro, "*Eyner fun unzere rishonim* (One of Our Pioneers)," *Idisher Kemfer,* Jan. 9, 1959.

21 Israel Medres, "The Second Jewish Bookstore," *Montreal of Yesterday: Jewish Life in Montreal, 1900–1920,* p. 62.

22 *Jewish Times,* Oct. 12, 1900.

23 *Jewish Times,* Sept. 26, 1902.

24 *Jewish Times,* Sept. 27, 1901.

25 *Jewish Times,* Oct. 11, 1901.

26 Sack, *Canadian Jews—Early in This Century,* p. 31. This is the only account of the Montreal Yom Kippur Ball of 1905 that I have encountered in a secondary source.

27 Cited in: Montreal *Star,* Oct. 9, 10, 1905; Montreal *Gazette* Oct. 10, 1905; *La Presse,* Oct. 9, 10, 1905; *Jewish Times,* Oct. 20, 1905.

28 Montreal *Star,* Oct. 9, 1905.

29 Account taken from reports in the Montreal *Star,* Oct. 9, 10, 1905; Montreal *Gazette,* Oct. 10, 1905; *La Presse,* Oct. 9, 10, 1905; *Jewish Times,* Oct. 20, 1905.

30 Montreal *Star,* Oct. 9, 1905.

31 Montreal *Star,* Oct. 10, 1905.

32 *Jewish Times,* Oct. 20, 1905.

33 Montreal *Gazette,* Oct. 10, 1905.

34 *Jewish Times,* Oct. 20, 1905.

35 For an overview of the attempts to establish a Yiddish press in Montreal beginning in the 1880s, see: Eli Gottesman, *Canadian Jewish Reference Book and Directory, 1960* (Ottawa: Mortimer Limited, 1963), p. 76; Avraham Rhinewine, *Der id in kanade.* Vol. I–II (Toronto, Canada: Farlag "kanade," 1925–1927), pp. 210–211; David Rome, ed. *The Canadian Story of Reuben Brainin, Part I*, Canadian Jewish Archives, No. 47 (Montreal, Canada: National Archives, Canadian Jewish Congress, 1993), pp. 87–88; Hirsh Wolofsky, "25 *yor 'Keneder Adler,' Yoyvl bukh fun 'Keneder Adler*" (Montreal, Canada, July 8, 1932), p. 23; Benjamin Gutl Sack, *Canadian Jews—Early in This Century*, p. 46; Hirsh Wolofsky, *Journey of My Life.* Trans. A. M. Klein (Montreal, Canada: The Eagle Publishing Co. Ltd., 1945), p. 52.

36 Rome, *Men of the Yiddish Press*, p. 16.

37 *Keneder Adler*, Oct. 4, 1908.

Getting Married In Montreal With Two Wedding Rings

MARLENE BONNEAU

This article is based on a study I conducted of Montreal Jewish weddings, in which all four denominations—Reform, Orthodox, Conservative and Reconstructionist—were represented. The study derived from two main sources of research: 1) Montreal Jewish weddings dating from 1947 to 1964, based on a review of 12,580 photographic negatives; 2) Montreal Jewish weddings dating from 1990 to 2001, based on interviews with 36 rabbis, and 40 brides and grooms.[1] The wedding ring, especially the second ring given by the bride to the groom, became a key element in my research and is critical in understanding how human symbol-making can represent a variety of meanings and mark distinct identities.

One of the main objects featured in Jewish wedding rituals is the wedding ring, a plain metal hoop wrapped around a finger, which represents an individual's identity and the social framework from which it was created. As a concrete symbol needing little explanation, a wedding ring's circular shape points quickly to abstract and concrete meanings of eternal love, commitment, future promises and marital obligations. However, in the case of double-ring ceremonies in contemporary Montreal Jewish weddings, what appears as self-evident to the couples means something quite different to the rabbis. For the couples, their wedding rings are not arbitrary, but natural symbols that link unending shaped metal hoops to promises of eternal love; for the rabbis, the same wedding rings are arbitrary signs of a legal *kinyan*[2], which could be enacted just as easily with a coin or a can of Coca-Cola. The significance of double-ring ceremonies demonstrates that the history of ritual symbols within a religious tradition is often unknown to its religious leadership, even though the practice of using these symbols exists within the tradition. More specifically, the exchange of two wedding rings under the *chuppah*[3] demonstrates how a bride and groom (ordinary community members) shape and influence religious rituals despite the overarching control of specialized rabbinic authorities.

Double-ring wedding ceremonies in Judaism present a conundrum. On the one hand, Jewish law[4] does not acknowledge the bride's giving of a second ring to the groom as a legal *kinyan*, while on the other hand, the practice exists. And because in practice the rings are key ritual objects used during the enactment of the *kiddushin*[5] or legal betrothal, they are, in the words of Victor Turner, "dominant ritual symbols." As dominant ritual symbols, they are, despite rabbinic interpretation, at the core of Jewish wedding rituals. For couples, the second ring does not embody any difficult legal constructs that would render it meaningful. For the rabbis who represent a Jewish legal perspective, the first ring has dominance over the second one, despite its status as an arbitrary sign.

In the case of Montreal Jewish weddings, most of the rabbis interviewed believed that the second ring was a recent phenomenon, which made its appearance in Montreal around the mid-1970s. The rabbis also stated that the reason Jews used two rings was due to the influence of a majority Christian or Catholic population. Going beyond Montreal, the evidence from several historical sources shows that the presence of two rings in Jewish weddings was well known before the 1900s, as early as the 1300s. The explanation for this lack of ritual historical knowledge rests on a number of factors: the non-status of the second ring within the authoritative system of Jewish law, the suppression of symbols that challenge the status quo of traditional gender roles, the importance of maintaining religious differences along Jewish-Christian lines, the need to make clear distinctions between Orthodox and Reform Judaism, and misconceptions about the history of rings in general, including the origins of using one ring in Jewish wedding practices. Moreover, the reason certain symbols become defined as "traditional" or uniquely "Jewish," and why others do not, seems to be related to the way in which these symbols are connected to foundational religious texts from the past and the way these symbols are used.

Despite the sharing of wedding symbols between contemporary Jewish and Christian groups—such as wedding rings, veils, cakes, white gowns and black tuxedos—distinct Jewish identities are communicated in the veiling of the bride, blessings over wine, the ring ceremony, marriage contracts (*ketoubahs*), ritual space (*chuppahs*) and the breaking of a glass. It is a symbol's outward form or the particular way in which it is used during a ritual that determines its religious identification and meaning. Moreover, the communication of particular religious identities through wedding symbols has varied over time and place. For example, Jewish betrothal rings from the seventeenth and nineteenth centuries from such places as Venice and France look very different from Christian wedding rings of the same period. However, contemporary Jewish wedding rings possess few or no qualities distinguishable from those of Christian ones. With the case of present-day wedding rings, one can only demarcate differences between Jewish and Christian ones by observing how the rings are used in the actual wedding rite. By observing how and when the second wedding ring is given within different Jewish denominations, one can demarcate differences within Judaism itself.

Within Montreal Jewish denominations, differences can be identified according to the timing of the giving of the second ring, and the verbal and non-verbal formulae by grooms to brides under the *chuppah*. These denominational markers predominantly concern the rabbis, and not the couples being married. The following excerpts, taken from interviews with rabbis, illustrate this point:

A 1960 wedding shows parents admiring the groom's ring. In contrast to the rabbis' view-point, the second wedding ring has great value for the couple. The groom proudly shows it off to his parents as an egalitarian symbol representing love and commitment.
IMAGE FROM THE DRUMMOND COLLECTION, COURTESY OF THE CANADIAN JEWISH CONGRESS ARCHIVES.

In 1995–1996, I performed 15 to 20 weddings, mostly in the main sanctuary, some in this very office, some at home, some at hotels, as long as the food served was kosher. I never verified if the food in the homes was kosher. Most of the weddings were double-ring cere-monies, about 75%. This has been the practice for the past 25 years. It probably began about 30 years ago. It is rela-tively new. If the bride gives a ring, she can remain silent, compose her own words or say the traditional words from the Song of Songs. I only allow her to give the ring after the *ketoubah*, after the Seven Blessings, just before the breaking of the glass. I would persuade the woman to change her mind if she insisted on saying the same formu-la as the man. If she did not agree, I would not change the traditional ritual. There was once a woman who spoke at length about ecology and the environment. Well it was rather long. As long as there is no political agenda, I do not censor what is said. Change is antithetical to religion. I would think, for example, that the Reform and Conservatives would be more lenient, and more ready for change. To be Orthodox means not to change with every incoming style or fashion. In my congregation, 15% observe, that is observe the Sabbath, do not go to work and do not use their cars; 85% say they are Orthodox and are affiliated with the congregation, but do not observe. I never thought that a woman would want to say the words right after the man. I found it strange that my children [daughters] wanted to circle their grooms seven times. No, I do not perform that circling ritual, nor did I want it performed at my wedding. This circling of the groom by the bride is an example of a tradition going further right, that is more Orthodox.[6]

99.9% of the couples I marry arrive with two rings, and 99.9% give the second ring under the *chuppah*. Most of the couples who come to see me do not know what Jewish law is and don't know what to do at their wedding. They just follow my lead. Both women and men are more independent now, both are more involved with their wedding plans and share the finances more. Today, the couples I marry are more interested in ritual and spiritual matters, more go to the *mikveh*, many couples ask for a special time to go in front of the ark to say their own prayers. This was never done in the '60s, '70s or '80s. Many more couples are circling [bride only] compared to five years ago.[7]

Most of the weddings I have performed have been double-ring ceremonies. The woman does not say the same words as the groom, because this would be negligible, it would be unnecessary since the wedding has already taken place. She is already married after she accepts the first ring. The double-ring ceremony was frowned upon because of its similarity to the Christian wedding ritual. To be ritually too similar to the *goyim* was not desirable.[8]

Traditional Orthodox males do not wear wedding rings. Of course, I do, as many moderns do today. Wearing it is part of the larger cultural custom. I have no problem with the second ring under the *chuppah*, as long as it is given at the very end, just before breaking the glass. I am very aware of not letting the community see the second ring being given too close in time to the first one, so that any confusion as to an exchange rather than an acquisition can be avoided. About the wedding ring, it could be a can of Coca-Cola. It only is a sign of cultural value. But yes, I do see the second ring as being a sign of a more egalitarian value, whereby in the past it was not the case.[9]

I allow the woman to give the second ring immediately after she accepts the ring from the groom. I say the following: 'It is the custom in this country for a woman to give a man a ring.' The second ring is purely a sentimental object—no legal meaning, simply window dressing.[10]

The couples who were interviewed in the study, for the most part, neither remembered the sequencing of events under the *chuppah*, nor identified themselves primarily as denominational Jews. Once more, what remains important for the rabbis—in terms of denominational identity and Jewish law—seems less so for the couples. The following excerpts from interviews with the couples illustrate this point:

Still to this day, some Montreal Orthodox Jews marry outdoors under a portable chuppah, *seen here in the background of this 1953 wedding scene. Stetson hats, fashionable
in Montreal in the 1950s, were worn then in contrast to* kippas.
PHOTO BY BESSER STUDIO, COURTESY THE JEWISH PUBLIC LIBRARY.

Our wedding was very emotional, which I attribute to
the rabbi's words under the *chuppah*. I cried throughout
the ceremony. Yes, my wedding was definitely Jewish,
even though I never converted. We broke two glasses as

an egalitarian gesture. And our rings represent a symbol of our union and, more specifically, our exclusivity to each other. I didn't want to wear a ring but she insisted, and so I do now everyday.[11]

I was not married in a shul. I was married at Chateau Royal because of their kosher kitchen. The rabbi was Orthodox and I did ask for a double-ring ceremony, but the rabbi refused. I did end up giving my husband a ring after the ceremony, but it wasn't the same thing. . . . Well, I do feel bad about not pushing the issue of giving my husband his ring during the ceremony, but the rabbi was a relative.[12]

My wedding was Jewish because I went to the *mikveh* with my mother and my wedding was on a Sunday. We were married by three rabbis, two Sephardic and one Ashkenazi. I had a *ketoubah* and there were witnesses present. I would consider walking down the aisle as being non-Jewish. I know that in Israel it is not done. And I would consider the mixed dancing that we did was not Jewish, although we did start with the Jewish *hora*.[13]

About our rings, well I didn't know, until the rabbi told us, that Mark had no choice in giving me a ring but that I had a choice. It is a contract for him. Yet, we see in the movies two rings given at a wedding and we think 'that's what a wedding is about, giving rings'.[14]

I cannot remember the exact words I said under the *chuppah*, but we both repeated traditional words pledging our devotion and responsibility towards each other, or at least that is the way I felt it happened. I gave her a ring under the *chuppah*, but she didn't. I always wear my wedding ring because I am proud to have entered into the institution of marriage with Rena. For me, the ring is a sign of our bonding and lifelong devotion to each other. My ring has grooves along the edges, but hers is a simple smooth gold ring.[15]

There is no doubt, given the couples' lack of interest or knowledge of denominational ritual differences and Jewish law, that the rabbis play a key role in defining and shaping the wedding ceremonies. Still, the rabbis and couples relate very differently to the same symbols. The rabbis' expertise lies in verbal symbols used in legal and religious texts, while the couples' expertise lies primarily in non-verbal symbols drawn from daily and ritual life. This does not mean that non-verbal symbols are inferior to verbal ones; on the contrary, they demonstrate an ability to communicate complex ideas and feelings about religion, class and gender.

Briefly, non-verbal symbols refer to non-discursive modes of communication, which exclude speaking and writing. Within the context of rituals, non-discursive modes of communication include gestures, objects, clothing, food and organic matter. There is an overwhelming presence of non-verbal symbols in Jewish weddings. Non-verbal symbols show that meanings held in complex discursive legal written texts, like the technical requirements for witnesses to validate a legal marriage, can also be expressed in non-discursive ways. For example, the presence of a wedding cortège (procession) and banquet feast symbolically stand for the public witnessing of a couple's marriage. Yet, differences can arise as to what a non-verbal symbol really means. With the second ring, the rabbis' and couples' perspectives demonstrate that non-verbal symbols can hold opposing and conflicting meanings.

Non-verbal symbols abound at weddings. Wedding canopies, white bridal gowns, black tuxedos, wine, flowers, rings, the breaking of glasses, lavish food, dancing, music, and well-attired guests all have an impact upon our senses, thoughts and feelings. These non-verbal symbols convey impressions of feminine brides, masculine grooms, happy families, joyful couples, financial well-being, Jewishness, marriage, children, and auspicious beginnings. Values and emotions are effectively communicated without sermons or the recitation of complex legal texts. Non-verbal symbols effectively condense ideas and concepts while remaining pleasurable to the mind and senses.

In contrast to written discursive modes of thought, non-verbal modes demonstrate significant, if not deeper, levels of meaning in how individuals and communities communicate amongst themselves. Non-verbal symbols are more familiar to the majority of community members and are handled much more competently than are official written religious texts. Jewish texts are often understood by only an elite religious leadership. It is with non-verbal symbols, appropriated and handled easily by most members of a community, that experiences are most readily remembered and communicated over time.[16]

In order to further understand the role of non-verbal symbols in wedding rituals, three questions need to be addressed: "Who are the principal participants who manipulate these symbols in Jewish weddings?"; "What role do gender issues play in understanding how these symbols are used in these rituals?"; and more generally, "How do symbols create a sense of continuity within a tradition in order to perpetuate certain values and identities?"

The principal participants in a Jewish wedding are the couple. A Jewish wedding is a ritual event that celebrates a couple's commitment and love, which they communicate to each other, members of their family, friends and larger community. They do so primarily through non-verbal symbolic means. Therefore, despite the rabbi's legal expertise, a privileging of his views could conceivably relegate the couple to a secondary position.

Evidence from this study of Montreal Jewish weddings points to the central role of the couple. An entire repertoire of wedding symbols focuses on the couple and not the rabbi, who remains secondary if not absent. Examples of this can be found in the wearing of the white gown and black tuxedo, the reception banquet, the cutting of the wedding cake, dancing, the removal of the bride's garter, the couple's first kiss as husband and wife, and the honeymoon. Privileging the couple over the rabbi is also important when considering the rabbi's values and beliefs about the second ring. For the rabbis, the second ring's status reinforces traditional gender roles whereby the male initiates the only legitimate ring-giving gesture. In the rabbis' eyes, the female's gesture does not count. It is precisely on this point that the couple's desire to exchange rings during the wedding ritual challenges the rabbis' desire to maintain "traditional" gender roles. To say that the second ring does not exist, in the legal language of the rabbis, becomes untenable. The everyday reality of husbands wearing the second wedding ring has become a symbol that couples wish to integrate within religious rituals. The two wedding rings act as dominant symbols that take centre stage and represent the couple's mutual love and commitment to one another.

The couple's interpretation of their wedding rings reinforces the idea that dominant symbols contain opposite meanings, in this case opposite to those of the rabbis. The rings are not arbitrary legal signs but symbols of love, which convey greater meaning and power than do the rabbis' descriptions of them as tools producing legal *kinyans*. The couple's knowledge of ritual symbols, such as wedding rings, does not indicate that as laypersons they are less expert than the rabbis. The couple's expertise simply reflects a different category of knowledge. From the time a couple becomes engaged until the day of their wedding—in handling wedding preparations and wedding symbols from A to Z—they demonstrate a high degree of wedding competence. Expertise concerning the entire lexicon of wedding symbols belongs, quite frequently, to the women in the group (brides, sisters, aunts, mothers and mothers-in-law of the bride). Given the fact that there has been a long history of domestic or secular control of wedding symbols—as early as biblical times, parental blessings dominated religious ones—the relatively narrow roles that rabbis play under the *chuppah* in weddings can be better explained. Yet, even within the exclusive domain of the *chuppah* space, the couples show their expertise by introducing the second ring and confidently handling it despite rabbinic disapproval. As early as 1948 in Montreal, unlike the majority Catholic population, Jewish husbands wore wedding rings. The following excerpt from an interview with a Montrealer who was married in 1948 demonstrates this sense of expertise that couples have with respect to their wedding symbols:

> In 1948, we got married in Montreal at an Orthodox shul on
> Ducharme Street. I had three wedding rings. My mother

lent me hers for the wedding. I bought one with tiny diamonds but the rabbi said we couldn't use it under the *chuppah*. I wore that one for three years until two of the centre diamonds fell out. Just days before I gave birth to my third child, I stopped in at Peoples' Jewellers on Ste. Catherine Street to buy a third wedding ring. I didn't want the people at the hospital to think that I wasn't married when I would give birth. I paid $10 for the ring. Jack always wore a wedding ring until he got hives and took it off one day. I don't know what happened to it. It disappeared.[17]

Although the rabbi plays a significant role as legal expert, his role remains secondary to that of the couple. Likewise, family, friends and invited guests play secondary roles as well. Yet, they all symbolically stand under one canopy or *chuppah* as members of one Jewish community. Hence, Jewish weddings are both personal and communal. Being both personal and communal, couples can face not only rabbinic but parental control. When serious conflicts over wedding styles and plans occur, the stronger identities of those parents or rabbis who refuse to compromise can overpower the wishes of the bride and groom. These conflicts, which usually centre on the couples' wishes to stray from the traditions and identities of their rabbi or parents, point to an important element in contemporary wedding practices: couples want to express their own personal identity and values to a larger community. This is evident even if those needs are frustrated. In one interview, a mother expressed her frustration with her daughter's wedding, one year after the event.

My daughter wanted to add a lot of details that I did not think belonged in a traditional Jewish wedding. I wanted the grandparents to process down the aisle so that people who never met the whole family would know who these people were. My daughter and her future mother-in-law did not want all these relatives to process down the aisle. They wanted friends who were not part of the family to process down the aisle. I did not want outsiders to walk with the family. Also, my daughter suggested that a programme be printed and given out to all who attended the wedding. I absolutely refused for this to happen. For my daughter, she thought that explaining Jewish wedding symbols would be appropriate and it would let people know what was going on. But I told her, 'What is this? Some sort of entertainment? Some kind of event just like Place des Arts, where you need to know what is going on, who the actors or players are?'[18]

The mother, who won the battle, was most concerned with expressing her religious identity to a community whom she believed would frown upon her daughter's choices. Conflicts that arise in planning weddings often become signs for predicting what will happen afterwards. Rituals have the uncanny ability to not only reflect the past and present, but also predict and embody the future.

However, describing a Jewish wedding in ritual terms does not fully capture the meaning of its key players and symbols. The wedding canopy is not only a human artifact representing a community; it is also thought of as a sacred canopy that represents another powerful entity—the heavens above, or in religious language, "God's protective surrounding love." The presence of a rabbi may be interpreted as representing the inner workings of the divine, which appears through the human structures of Jewish law and society. The *chuppah*, combined with the presence of a rabbi, introduces a religious symbol that ultimately defines Jewish weddings as religious, regardless of the denomination practiced. Given such a theological interpretation, then, Jewish weddings would naturally include transformative powers,[19] which work upon the principal participants from both the "outside" (divine forces that transcend human experience) and "inside" (divine forces that are immanent within human experience).

With respect to religious symbols, women have undoubtedly suffered under gendered stereotypes of a male deity represented by a male religious leadership. The notion of a wedding as a transformative rite of passage has long been associated with images of male powers (divine and human) ruling over less empowered females. The disentangling, therefore, of negative "transformative" myths associated with weddings can be accomplished only through the use of a gendered lens when trying to understand these rites of passage. Double-ring ceremonies clearly give evidence that such a move away from negative "transformative" myths (where women become transformed automatically by their male overseers) has been in the making since the early 1960s, when women's rights decidedly affected North American households.[20] Jewish women have definitely given evidence that, much earlier than the 1960s, they have been striving for gender equality through the desire to give their husbands a second ring under the *chuppah*.[21]

Since the 1990s, stronger egalitarian values in terms of a closer sharing of lifestyles, education and career pursuits have been expressed by both brides and grooms. The sharing of two wedding rings symbolizes these values. On the other hand, the single engagement diamond ring symbolizes a challenge to these egalitarian values and still remains fixed by negative stereotypes. The egalitarian exchange of wedding rings flies in the face of images of a bride-to-be waiting passively for Prince Charming to request her "hand in marriage." In an age when chivalry still has its positive romantic image, one might interpret these engagement scenarios as being welcome dramatic performances that a contemporary woman can freely choose to step in or out of.

The engagement ring does not hold the same critical role as that of the second wedding ring because it does not enter into the official religious wedding space of the *chuppah*, where the core religious tradition is legitimately expressed. It is in this unique way that the two wedding rings partake of both the sacred space of the *chuppah* and the secular space of everyday life. This leads us to consider how symbols create a sense of continuity, which places them at the centre of a tradition and enables them to perpetuate certain values and identities. By a "sense of continuity," I mean a perceived or an actual linkage to some time and place in the past that communicates chronology to a religious community. Symbols sometimes appear as if they have little or no history, when in fact they have spanned decades or centuries. So-called "new" symbols, as with the case of the second wedding ring, often meet with resistance within a religious community because they lack this sense of continuity. On the one hand, the second ring occupies an ambiguous ritual place, since it has no legitimate history within the tradition, is associated with Christian usage, and challenges gender boundaries. On the other hand, "old" symbols, such as the *chuppah* and wedding veil, convey an aura of tradition or history that meets with little resistance from all levels of the community, despite the lack of evidence that could substantiate their exclusive ancient biblical roots. When successfully manipulated, the actual or invented repetition of symbols generates a sense of continuity.

When a symbol generates a "sense of continuity," it generates an aura of history, a sense that it has been around for a long time—that it is "traditional." This historical sense usually comes from official canonical written texts rather than from material artifacts or the voices of the community members. A symbol's historical status may loosely connect with a concrete past. Although repeated usage of a symbol over long periods of time can contribute to its "traditional" character, the act of linking history to a ritual symbol often reflects a religious leadership's effort to dig up part of a symbol's past or to recreate its origins so that it can become rooted within its foundational written texts. When trying to connect a present-day Jewish wedding symbol to foundational texts, one is led to argue that it derives from either Torah or rabbinic authorities. A Jewish symbol demonstrates its continuity with the past, therefore, when it can be located in these texts and authorities.

Bridging the gap between the past and present is no easy task. It may be that after two generations, our individual and communal memories fade much faster than we would like to think.[22] If we weren't there, how do we know what really happened? Who do we trust to tell us what happened in the past? And even if we were there, has our memory played tricks on us? Five years after his wedding, one informant explained: "I was the only one who broke the glass at our wedding. That's the way it's done, it's tradition, only the man breaks the glass." But as the wedding photo showed, there were two white napkins on the floor next to both the bride's and groom's shoes, indicating another reality. When I asked this man's wife whether she broke a glass, she said "Yes." The husband, five years after his wedding day, remembered a more "traditional" Jewish ritual where only men broke glasses. His resistance to changes in gender roles, the lack of any experience of a wedding where two glasses were broken, or an

An Orthodox 1950s wedding showing a groom being escorted down the aisle by his parents. Note the sleeveless bridesmaid's dress and top hats, a contrast to today's Montreal Orthodox wedding dress code, in which women cover up and men wear prayer shawls and kippas.

PHOTO FROM THE DRUMMOND COLLECTION, COURTESY OF THE CANADIAN JEWISH CONGRESS ARCHIVES

unconscious desire to keep alive his Orthodox Jewish roots helped to create a fictional account of what really happened. He could have said, "I don't remember" or "I'm not sure." Instead, his memory insisted that two glasses being broken was impossible in a Jewish tradition and implausible in *his* tradition. So, why did he forget that his wife broke the glass? Why would such a unique moment, one which had to stand out as being extraordinarily different from all other Jewish weddings he attended, be erased? This once-in-a-lifetime wedding symbol, two glasses being broken, did not fit with his Orthodox Jewish identity of what Jewish weddings were or "should be." Despite the fact that he was married in a Conservative synagogue by a Conservative rabbi with egalitarian symbols (two glasses were broken, two rings were exchanged, and both he and his bride circled each other), this man's memory of Jewish symbols lay not within a fragmentary real past of his own wedding experience but within a larger mythic past of Orthodox Judaism.

A couple's Jewishness remains bound to particular gestures and symbols, which they understand according to their own world of Jewish experiences. At the level of Jewish law, Montreal Jewish weddings subscribe and adhere to the same formula. At the level of ritual, Montreal Jewish weddings enact more or less the same script of gestures and symbols. At the level of individual performances, Montreal Jewish weddings represent different casts of emotionally, spiritually, intellectually and psychologically unique actors.

What remained in common for the majority of the couples that I interviewed, in stark contrast to the legal focus of the rabbis, was their lack of memory surrounding the ritual gestures that took place under the *chuppah*. Having little memory of ritual events, however, must not be construed as a negative factor. The couples did not fail a "ritual test" by not remembering what they said or did. Their memories, or lack thereof, simply reinforced the dramatic difference between their roles as principal rather than secondary participants in the ritual process. The rabbis, as secondary participants, remembered more because they were directing the ritual.

A sense of tradition is enforced through repetition. Yet, repetition becomes impossible when no marks have been left behind: "without the mark there is no boundary, no point at which to begin the repetition."[23] The continuity of symbols relies on repetition, but the manipulation and handling of this repetition determines whether daughters remember if their fathers wore wedding rings or what their mothers said under the *chuppah*. Ultimately, desired images of women and men filter through symbols that are endorsed and repeated in a community's most valued voices and histories.

NOTES

1 Based on the data from 1947–1964 and 1990–2001, I found that two rings were exchanged by Orthodox and Conservative couples within these two time periods. By the year 2001, double-ring ceremonies were performed more frequently in one Reconstructionist, two Conservative and four Orthodox denominations than in one Reform and two Orthodox congregations.

2 For the rabbis, a marriage in its legal aspect is a meeting of minds between a man and a woman for the purpose of concluding a marriage contract. The rabbis stressed that love and mutual respect between husband and wife are essential for the stability of their life together. At the same time, the sages recognized that without a legal transaction executed with all the requisite formality, the union might be casual and therefore unstable. The man acquires the wife and he must indicate in some tangible way that his intention in acquiring the woman as a wife is legitimate and serious. The woman, on the other hand, has to consent to her being acquired as a wife of her own free will and is not to be coerced into marriage. Accordingly, the Talmud (Kiddushin 2a) states that a wife can be acquired in one of three ways: through her acceptance of an object of monetary value, such as a coin or ring; through a written document in which the man declares his intention to marry her; through cohabitation. This act of acquisition is called *kinyan*. (Summarized from Abraham Chill's *The Minhagim*, 275–277.)

3 The act of *chuppah*, "enveloping," is generally symbolized by a canopy representing the house that the newly wed couple set out to build together.

4 The data from the interviews in the study showed that Reform and Reconstructionist denominations did express different views on the meaning of Jewish law, *halacha*, and the role that *halacha* played in their respective denominations. Only Reform stood out as allowing both groom and bride to utter the same *halachic* verbal formulae. However, this was not a consistent practice. More importantly, Reform performed more single-ring ceremonies than did one Reconstructionist, four Orthodox, and four Conservative congregations.

5 The basic meaning of *kiddushin* or betrothal is "separation," since through the act of betrothal the groom separates his bride from everyone else. It also means "consecration": far from being a mundane act, matrimony in Judaism is the mutual consecration of husband and wife for the purpose of fusing their lives into one holy union.

6 Interview with an Orthodox rabbi: August 16, 2001.

7 Interview with an Orthodox rabbi: June 15, 2001. The *mikveh* is a ritual bath.

8 Interview with an Orthodox rabbi: February 20, 1996.

9 Interview with an Orthodox rabbi: April 24, 2001.

10 Interview with a Conservative rabbi: June 9, 1997.

11 Interview with a husband married by a Reform rabbi: July 4, 2001.

12 Interview with a wife married by an Orthodox rabbi: February 9, 1996.

13 Interview with a wife married by an Orthodox rabbi: August 6, 2001.

14 Interview with a wife married by an Orthodox rabbi: August 6, 2001.

15 Interview with a husband married by a Conservative rabbi: July 31, 2001.

16 In his book, *Marrying and Burying* (1995), Ronald Grimes highlights the power that non-verbal modes of thought have over language proper, both spoken and written, within the ritual context. He writes: "Action is the primary form of engagement: talk is secondary. Posture, gesture, and placement take priority over verbal interpretation. Cultures, societies and groups do not merely surround bodies. Bodies incarnate but also transform, and even undermine cultural values. Religious competence in many traditions is fundamentally choreographic, not verbal. Everything depends on the quality of the sitting." (225, 249).

17 Interview: May 24, 2001.

18 Interview: May 1, 2001.

19 Within the context of Montreal Jewry and based on the interviews that I conducted, the couples understood "transformative powers" or transformational experiences as being transformative passages that they navigated at various stages of their relationship. They expressed that leaving their parental home, falling in love, sharing sexual intimacies and buying their first house together were examples of transformative passages even before they got married. However, parenthood was universally understood in the Montreal Jewish population as belonging exclusively to the married state.

20 See Jaclyn Geller's *Here Comes the Bride: Women, Weddings, and the Marriage Mystique* (2001).

21 Jewish wedding rings that date from 1690 (including the famous Wertheimer ring) and the nineteenth century raise important questions about when two rings were used. In an 1871 Reform Responsum from Augsburg, the second ring was officially recorded as being used under the *chuppah* primarily because of the demand of the women in the congregation. At that critical time, Orthodox Judaism may have distanced itself from the second ring as a reaction against the Reformers. In doing so, the second ring was repressed, either consciously or unconsciously, from Jewish historical memory. By the late twentieth century, the history of the second ring in Montreal was understood by the rabbis (Orthodox, Conservative, Reconstructionist and, to some extent, Reform) as being "Christian," without their knowing that this may have really meant Reform Judaism.

22 See Maurice Halbwachs' *On Collective Memory* (1992).

23 Susan Stewart, *On Longing: Narratives of the Miniature, the Gigantic, the Souvenir, the Collection* (1993:31).

PRIMARY SOURCES

Interviews. Transcripts of 109 interviews conducted from January 1996 to 2002.

Photographic negatives. 12,580 photographic negatives, Drummond Photo Collection,

Montreal (Canadian Jewish Congress National Archives, Montreal, Quebec).

Photographs. 50 photographs of Montreal Jewish weddings, 1900–1953 (40 photos from the Allan Raymond Collection, Jewish Public Library Archives, Montreal, Quebec).

Rings. 18 Jewish betrothal rings,17th–20th century, (Jewish Museum of New York, Judaica Archives). Catalogued as JM 90–52, F4867, F5365, F845, F846, F5408, JM 79–47, F4713, F2012, F5508, F5509, F2010, F5017, F2011, JM 126–47, F2889, F2110, JM 47.

_____. 10 Jewish betrothal rings, 14th–20th century. Private collection.

_____. 1 Jewish betrothal ring (provenance unknown). *Petit Musée*, Montreal, Quebec.

Talmud. Translated by J. Neusner. [Kiddushin.]

Secondary Sources

Biale, Rachel. *Women and Jewish Law*. New York: Schocken Books, 1984.

Chadour, Beatriz. *Ringe: The Louis and Alice Koch Collection*. Vols. I & II. London: Maney Publishers, 1994.

Chenon, Emile. *Recherches historiques sur quelques rites nuptiaux*. Bar-le-Duc: Contant-Laguerre, 1912.

Chill, Abraham. *The Minhagim: The Customs and Ceremonies of Judaism, Their Origins and Rationale*. New York: Sepher-Hermon Press, 1979.

Elon, Menachem. *The Principles of Jewish Law*. Jerusalem: Keter Publishing House, 1975, p. 353–377.

Federation of Jewish Community Services of Montreal, Census Series (1991). "Issues of Jewish Identity" (Part 2). Montreal: December 1994.

_____."The Sephardic Community" (Part 6). Montreal: 1995.

_____. "The Jewish Family in Montreal: Living Arrangements, Fertility, Poverty and the Family" (Part 4). Montreal: May 1995.

_____. "A Survey of Jewish Life in Montreal" (Part II). Montreal: May 1997.

Geller, Jaclyn. *Here Comes the Bride: Women, Weddings, and the Marriage Mystique*. New York & London: Four Walls Eight Windows, 2001.

Grimes, Ronald. *Beginnings in ritual studies*. Washington, D.C.: University Press of America, 1982.

_____.*Research in ritual studies: a programmatic essay and bibliography*. American Theological Library Association, Metuchen, N.J. : Scarecrow Press, 1985.

_____. *Ritual Criticism: case studies in its practice, essays on its theory*. Columbia, S.C.: University of South Carolina Press, 1990.

_____. *Reading, writing and ritualizing: ritual in fictive, liturgical, and public places.*Washington, D.C.: Pastoral Press, 1993.

_____. *Marrying & Burying: rites of passage in a man's life*. Boulder: Westview Press, 1995.

_____. *Deeply into the bone: re-inventing rites of passage*. Berkeley: University of California Press, 2000.

Halbwachs, Maurice. *On Collective Memory*. Chicago: The University of Chicago Press, 1992. Edited and translated by Lewis A. Coser from *Les cadres sociaux de la mémoire* by

Presses Universitaires de France, Paris 1952 and from *La topographie légendaire des évangiles en terre sainte: Etude de mémoire collective,* published by Presses Universitaires de France, Paris, 1941.

Handelman, Don. *Models and mirrors: towards an anthropology of public events.* Cambridge: Cambridge University Press, 1990.

Kaplan, Aryeh Rabbi. *Made in Heaven: A Jewish Wedding Guide.* New York: Moznaim Publishing Corporation, 1983.

Kelman, Naamah, Rabbi. "New Forms of Wedding Ceremonies in Israel: How Young Couples Construct Jewish Meaning." Unpublished paper presented in New York, May 10, 2001 at Ma'yan, Jewish Feminist Research Group.

Kunz, George Frederick. *The Curious Lore of Precious Stones.* New York: Dover Publications Inc., 1913.

_____. *Rings for the Finger.* New York: Dover Publications, 1917.

Lamm, Maurice. *The Jewish Way in Love and Marriage.* New York: Jonathan David Publishers, 1980.

Mutembe, Protais et Jean-Baptiste Molin. *Le rituel du mariage en France du XIIe au XVIe siècle.* Paris: Beauchesne, 1974.

Ostriker, Alicia Suskin. *Feminist Revision and the Bible.* Cambridge, Massachusetts: Blackwell, 1993.

Plaut, Gunther W. *The Rise of Reform Judaism.* New York: World Union for Progressive Judaism, 1963.

Plaskow, Judith. *Standing Again at Sinai: Judaism from a Feminist Perspective.* New York: Harper & Row, 1990.

Stauben, Daniel. *Scènes de la vie juive en Alsace.* Paris: Michel Lévy Frères, Librairies-Éditeurs, 1860.

Stewart, Susan. *On Longing: Narratives of the Miniature, the Gigantic, the Souvenir, the Collection.* Durham: Duke University Press, 1993.

Turner, Victor. *The Forest of Symbols: Aspects of Ndembu Ritual.* Ithaca, New York: Cornell University Press, 1967.

Van Gennep, Arnold. *Manuel de folklore français contemporain.* Tome Premier, volume II: *Du berceau à la tombe* . Paris: A. et J. Picard et cie, 1946, p. 373–694.

_____. *Rites of Passage.* (First published, 1903.) Chicago: University of Chicago Press, 1960.

Yalom, Marilyn. *A History of the Wife.* New York: HarperCollins Publishers, 2001.

Jewish Spaces

Just as regionalism has become a key issue for understanding aspects of Canadian cultural and political life, so specific landscapes—both at home and abroad—have come to play a role in the development of Canadian Jewish identity. The essays in this section examine how a suburban community, a literary salon, the State of Israel, and a far-flung Soviet province helped Jews formulate a sense of who they were. In Miriam Waddington's memoir of Ida Maza's salon, the Yiddish language itself is portrayed as a region of the imagination.

NR

Sanctifying Suburban Space
from *And I Will Dwell in Their Midst: Orthodox Jews in Suburbia*

ETAN DIAMOND

In 1960, a columnist in the Toronto-based *Canadian Jewish News* reacted with some surprise to the increased "Hebrewization" of Bathurst Street, the central street on which many Jewish establishments had opened in suburban Toronto. Stores such as the Matana (Gift) Gift Shop and the Kol Toov (All That Is Good) Delicatessen testified that it had suddenly become "no novelty to see Jewish names and kosher insignia on rows of storefronts" on Bathurst.[1] Four decades later, Bathurst Street's Jewishness surprises few people in or out of the Jewish community. As one Toronto resident explained in 1995, Bathurst Street is to Toronto Jewry "what the Nile is to Egypt: a narrow strip of life with desert on both sides."[2] If anything is surprising about Bathurst Street, it is that the street's dense Jewish infrastructure is found not in an urban setting but in the sprawling geography of post-World War II suburbia. Since the early 1950s, Toronto's Jews have settled Bathurst Street in successive waves, continually pushing the Jewish frontier northward. But unlike Jewish relocation from urban to suburban areas that occurred in other North American cities during this period, the Jewish settlement of Bathurst Street in suburban North York did not follow the settlement-expansion-relocation-abandonment cycle so prevalent in other cities. That is, the development of newer Jewish areas of Bathurst Street did not come at the expense of older areas, but rather extended the existing areas of settlement northward. By the end of the twentieth century, Jewish neighbourhoods strung out along Bathurst Street like pearls on a necklace, stretched for over eight miles in a progression from 1950s neighbourhoods at the southern end to still uncompleted subdivisions in the middle of cornfields at the northern end.

How can one understand the evolution of this Jewish space in suburban Toronto? How did undistinguished suburban neighbourhoods become transformed into vibrant landscapes of Jewish religion and culture? Or, to borrow a phrase from the geography of religion, how did these Jewish "sacred spaces" develop in the heart of post-war suburbia? Such questions are particularly appropriate to begin an inquiry into Orthodox Jewish suburbanization. Through an examination of the post-World War II creation of Bathurst Street as an Orthodox Jewish corridor, this chapter stresses the theme that Orthodox Jewish suburbanization blended traditionalist religion with modern suburbia. Orthodox Jews clustered in middle-class neighbourhoods adjacent to Bathurst Street, and created an active and visible religious landscape along the street itself, thus defining a new sacred space in an otherwise mundane and secular environment.

In its traditional usage, "sacred space" refers to places with explicit religious sanctity, such as a shrine or a holy city.[3] But there are other ways to understand sacred space. For example, the social spaces in which religious communities live also have a sacredness that, although not explicitly holy, is nevertheless essential to those communities.[4] Put differently, sacred space can include those socially and culturally constructed environments that are not necessarily associated with explicitly holy or religious events or objects.[5] Bathurst Street in postwar suburban Toronto, and places like Cedar Lane in Teaneck, New Jersey, and

Harvard Street in Brookline, Massachusetts, are such socially constructed sacred spaces.[6] Bathurst Street, after all, was never and still is not holy or religiously important to Orthodox Jews or any other religious group; it is a suburban traffic artery like that found in any North American city. Nevertheless, in the four-decade period following World War II, Orthodox Jewish residential concentration in the neighbourhoods adjacent to Bathurst, together with the emergence of a visible Jewish landscape of synagogues, schools, and kosher food stores on the street itself, created an environment pervaded by religion and religious activities. Both inside and outside the Orthodox Jewish community, Bathurst Street became known as a Jewish space. In this process, the mundane suburban space of Bathurst was transformed into something that had symbolic meaning—a suburban sacred space. Moreover, the story of Bathurst Street makes it clear that for Orthodox Jews, suburbanization did not mean spatial dispersal and abandonment of religious practice. Rather, the creation of a new suburban sacred space consciously articulated an identity that combined adherence to tradition with a pattern of suburban mobility.

A Jewish presence in Toronto existed as early as the middle of the nineteenth century, when various Jewish individuals settled in what was then known as Upper Canada.[7] In 1832, governing British authorities granted full political and civil rights to the small community of Jews in the Canadian territories. By 1856, a Jewish community of mostly British origin had established itself in Toronto by forming a Hebrew cemetery and a synagogue, the forerunner to the present-day Holy Blossom Temple. Over the rest of the nineteenth century, the Jewish community grew slowly but steadily, although it remained a relatively marginal ethnic and religious group in an overwhelmingly Anglo-Protestant city. The community's small size precluded the development of any identifiable Jewish neighbourhood, such as would emerge half a century later.

As in other cities across North America, rapidly increasing rates of Jewish immigration in the early twentieth century changed the spatial dynamics of Toronto's Jewish community. The city's Jewish population increased sixfold between 1901 and 1911, and then doubled in the next ten years.[8] Despite this rapid population growth, Toronto's Jews maintained compact residential patterns. In the initial wave of immigration at the beginning of the century, Jews settled in the "Ward," a few-square-block area between Yonge Street and University Avenue, just west of downtown and north of Lake Ontario. As the Jewish population grew, however, the neighbourhood expanded westward, along Dundas and College Streets, across Spadina Avenue toward Bathurst Street. By the second decade of this century, the neighbourhood known as Kensington had surpassed the Ward as the centre of Jewish life.

Life in the Jewish district, as in many urban immigrant neighbourhoods, was dense and compact and resembled classic "walking city" neighbourhoods, where homes, businesses, shops, and institutions were in close proximity. No single area or street dominated the neighbourhood, although certain specialized districts emerged. Kensington Market, a collection of streets just north of Dundas and Spadina, developed into the commercial centre. The jumble of butchers, bakeries, dry goods stores, and other establishments made Kensington Market a vibrant Jewish street economy, similar to New York's Hester Street or Chicago's Maxwell Street.[9] Although, by 1931, Jews still constituted less than six per cent of Toronto's population, Kensington's residential, economic, and commercial concentration gave the Jewish community a much higher profile than this proportion would suggest.[10]

Kensington's dense Jewish life created an environment that the Orthodox Jewish community in particular considered a sacred space. All the religious, cultural, and social necessities an Orthodox Jew required could be found in Kensington. Here were the synagogues and religious schools, the kosher butchers and bakeries, the Jewish bookstores and the *mikvaoth* (ritual baths used by women following their monthly menstrual period; singular is *mikveh*). For Orthodox Jews whose lives were immersed in Kensington's religious infrastructure, any place north of Bloor Street—less than half a mile from the neighbourhood's symbolic centre at the intersection of College and Spadina—was "the end of the Jewish population."

The Orthodox Jews to whom the proximity of religious institutions mattered represented only a small percentage of Toronto's overall Jewish population. The majority of the city's Jews used Kensington's religious institutions on a less regular basis than did the Orthodox Jews. As such, they could religiously afford to separate themselves from the urban neighbourhood and, in fact, it was the non-Orthodox Jewish population who first moved to suburbia in the late 1920s and early 1930s. In those years, demographic pressures spurred a movement away from Kensington. Continued immigration and natural population increases had made the Jewish neighbourhood a "congested mass," and College Street was filled with an "almost impassable mass of human beings" on many Saturday nights.[11] In time, this bulging neighbourhood began to spill northward, beyond Bloor Street and St. Clair Avenue into the newly developing municipalities of York Township and the village of Forest Hill.[12] The main traffic artery linking these new and old neighbourhoods was Bathurst Street.

Between 1931 and 1951, the Jewish population in York Township and Forest Hill increased from twelve hundred to over eighteen thousand people, or almost one-third of the entire Jewish community.[13] This rapid relocation to neighbourhoods around the Bathurst-Eglinton intersection occurred, however, without any significant Orthodox Jewish participation. Most Jewish institutions also remained in Kensington. By 1954, only five of the city's forty-eight synagogues lay north of St. Clair Avenue; the rest remained in the older downtown areas. Similarly, five of six social service agencies still maintained downtown addresses, as did six of eleven schools.[14] Although one cannot make an exact count, the majority of kosher food establishments were also located in the older neighbourhoods.[15] The first wave of suburbanization in the 1940s, then, did little to restructure the geography of Toronto's Orthodox Jewish community, which remained rooted in the sacred space of Kensington.

Beginning in the early 1950s, a second wave of suburbanization to neighbourhoods farther north did succeed in transforming Toronto's Orthodox Jewish religious geography. In this phase of religious suburbanization, the Orthodox Jewish community moved not only its residences but its entire religious infrastructure to the new suburban environment. In so doing, the Orthodox Jewish community created a new sacred space along suburban Bathurst Street that replaced the declining, and ultimately disappearing, urban Kensington district.

In the years before World War II, few observers would have expected the township of North York to become home to a geographically and socio-economically mobile Orthodox Jewish community. Through the mid-1940s, North

York survived as a quiet, undeveloped, generally rural township a few miles north of Toronto. The community's roots as a farming centre stretched back into the nineteenth century, when the area was part of the larger York Township. In 1922, a contingent of rural residents voted in a plebiscite to separate from York and to incorporate as its own township.[16] Despite the incorporation, the town of North York remained relatively rural, with most of the twenty-three thousand residents concentrated in the central southern edge of the city, abutting York Township and the village of Forest Hill and along the central strip of land on either side of Yonge Street. The township's population concentration was matched by its homogeneity. Like much of the Toronto area (and Canada in general), British Protestant ethnic groups dominated.[17] Religiously, this translated into a heavy weighting toward Anglican and United Church affiliation, with a smaller presence of Presbyterians and Baptists. Other religious groups, including Jews and Catholics, were little represented through the 1940s.[18]

North York's settlement patterns derived largely from a combination of economic factors and natural geography.[19] In the late 1700s, land surveyors had created a vast checkerboard system of roads and landholdings. They spaced major north-south and east-west roads at one-and-a-quarter-mile intervals each. The grid system worked well for an agricultural economy because it granted each landholder access to at least one major transportation artery. Underneath this imposed geography, lay the natural terrain, which, as might be expected, was far less rigid about its shape and format. In particular, the west and east branches of the Don River wound their way through the northern sections of North York, cutting deep ravines through the relatively flat landscape. Although streets were technically laid out across the ravines, the steep valleys often limited expansion in the spaces beyond and meant that North York's development did not occur evenly. Until the 1940s, only Yonge Street, the township's physical and economic central thoroughfare, experienced much suburban development. Streetcar and bus service on Yonge Street facilitated residential development in neighbourhoods just east and west of Yonge. In contrast, most other areas of the township remained rural farmland well into the 1940s.

North York's quietude came to an end as it emerged from the Depression and World War II. The township found itself with a large stock of vacant land that had been seized during the many fiscal crises of the previous decade. Township leaders recognized that this land could provide a desperately needed outlet for the growing housing shortage in Toronto and began to sell the lots to developers.[20] By 1947, North York was experiencing an unprecedented building boom, setting annual records for building permits and property assessments, which rose from $11 million in 1947 to over $40 million two years later.[21]

The building boom quickly caught up to Bathurst Street. Before the war, Bathurst had served as a secondary access road to dairy and produce farms that stretched across the northern part of North York Township. Only minimal suburban development occurred on the east side of Bathurst, but these neighbourhoods were generally extensions of Yonge Street neighbourhoods rather than originating from Bathurst. The rapid transformation of Bathurst Street began in 1950, when plans for the corridor's first major planned subdivision were unveiled. That spring, a consortium of the Canadian Mortgage and Housing Corporation, the Great West Life Assurance Company, and the Investor's Syndicate of Canada announced plans to build a $20 million, seventeen-hundred-unit housing complex on two farms at the northwest corner of the Bathurst–Lawrence intersection. The land, previously owned by the Mulholland family, was bought and subdivided by the CMHC and was serviced by the two insurance companies. The forty-five-foot-wide lots were then sold off to individual home builders, usually in blocks of ten. Although not as large as suburban projects elsewhere in Toronto, such as E. P. Taylor's Don Mills, Lawrence Manor showed the new direction of suburban development in the post-war era.[22] The incorporation of a twelve-acre shopping plaza into the residential project was a relatively new feature in suburban development. The neighbourhood also featured other designs now commonly associated with suburbia: winding roads, a central neighbourhood park, and limited external traffic access.[23]

The construction of Lawrence Manor set off a chain reaction of development up Bathurst Street. Aerial photographs, taken at yearly intervals over the metropolitan Toronto region, clearly showed the rapid progress in North York's development. For example, pictures in 1950 show the predominance of farmland along Bathurst, except for streets in Lawrence Manor that had been bulldozed and graded and awaited construction. By 1953, Lawrence Manor was completely built, and most of the lands between Lawrence and Sheppard Avenues showed signs of subdivision activity. Three years later, the Bathurst Manor subdivision north of Sheppard was well under way.[24] Within a decade and a half, virtually no large areas of undeveloped land remained in the entire Bathurst corridor, between Dufferin Street on the west and Yonge Street on the east, and from Eglinton Avenue to the northern North York boundary at Steeles Avenue.[25] In thirty years, this slice of North York had been transformed from a rural community of 3,400 people into a bustling metropolitan corridor of 93,000 people.[26]

The rapid growth on both sides of Bathurst Street seemed to overwhelm the street. The increase in residents brought an increase in traffic problems. Only after several accidents—one of them a hit-and-run killing of two schoolgirls—did the township install proper sidewalks along Bathurst.[27] By 1957, the street had become the third busiest traffic artery in metropolitan Toronto, with approximately thirty thousand vehicles traveling daily on only four paved lanes.[28] The newly built Toronto bypass highway (now known as Highway 401) added to the congestion with an interchange at Bathurst Street. The increased flow of traffic also magnified a major parking shortage on Bathurst. Curbside parking was simply not an option. Compounding the parking problem south of Wilson Avenue, many of the existing commercial properties fronting the street were built without any parking facilities, either in front of or behind the structures. Zoning regulators sought to encourage developers to build new strip mall-type properties with small parking areas, although such regulations concerned some Bathurst Street businessmen who thought that a "strung-out corridor" of stores would prevent the street from becoming a central business centre.[29] Their fears were largely realized but not only because of the ribbon-like development. Uncoordinated zoning bylaws created an unregulated patchwork of storefronts, apartment houses, and mostly vacant lots. Hasty development forced zoning regulators to make quick decisions permitting a variety of uses with little regard for the street as a whole.[30] Such a mishmash of growth meant that, in the 1950s at least, a pre-suburban transportation route was being overrun by new forms of suburban commercial and residential development.

Into this reluctant and somewhat unprepared suburb, Toronto's Orthodox Jews, together with their non-Orthodox co-religionists, moved in the

1950s. To be sure, some Jewish settlement had occurred along the southern edges of the township's border with Forest Hill and York Township in the 1940s. The 1951 census reported, for example, that the two southernmost census tracts along Bathurst Street contained two-thirds of the township's four thousand Jews.[31] But although they formally lived in North York, Jews in these areas formed no new religious institutions, and remained tied to neighbourhoods in Forest Hill and York Township and further south.

A more accurate starting point for the development of the Bathurst corridor is 1951, when Orthodox Jews formed the first suburban Jewish institution in North York. That year, a group of Jewish residents who had recently moved to the Lawrence Manor subdivision organized a small *minyan* for prayer services. Two of the congregation's founding members had canvassed the area to assemble enough men for services, which were initially held in the home of one of the members. As the congregation grew, it moved to a rented storefront, and by the late 1950s, Shaarei Tefillah Synagogue had hired a rabbi and had undertaken plans to construct a permanent synagogue building.[32] Shaarei Tefillah's success was followed in the next two decades by the formation of at least eight other built-from-scratch synagogues—Orthodox, Conservative, and Reform—in the neighbourhoods adjacent to Bathurst. The success of these new congregations spurred many of the older synagogues located downtown to join the suburbanizing Jewish population up north, some merging with another congregation and others moving to their own location in the corridor.[33]

That North York's first Jewish congregation was Orthodox immediately highlights some of the differences between this wave of suburbanization and earlier migrations into York Township and Forest Hill, when Orthodox Jews did not actively relocate out of Kensington. Several factors accounted for the Orthodox presence in this second generation of suburbanizing Jews. In the four decades preceding World War II, Toronto's Orthodox Jewish community displayed a tendency to remain spatially tied to the established religious institutions in Kensington. They had little incentive or desire to recreate a new religious infrastructure in new suburban neighbourhoods. In the years immediately before and after World War II, however, Toronto received a large influx of European refugees. This group had neither sentimental ties to particular neighbourhoods nor any preconceived notions about the community's religious geography. Moreover, as a socio-economic group, they moved into the middle class soon after they arrived. Although this pattern contrasts with the stereotype of immigrants, one should not be surprised at this group's rapid upward mobility. Many of the Hungarian Jewish refugees had been highly successful businessmen and professionals before the war. Although many were stripped of their possessions by the tragedies of Europe, they came to Toronto with business acumen and a familiarity with financial success. Their relatively quick movement into the middle and upper-middle class, then, should be seen more as a return to an earlier way of life than as any drastic shift in socio-economic status.[34] The prominent Reichmann family might be the best example of this experience, as they used business and family connections from Europe to build a global real estate empire based in Toronto.[35]

Presented with the opportunity to obtain new suburban housing, this group had no qualms about leaving their temporary residences in downtown neighbourhoods for the fresh suburbs of North York, and, in fact, these non-native Torontonians made up many of the early Orthodox Jewish suburbanites of the 1950s. For example, the founders of Clanton Park Synagogue included a large contingent of Hungarian and German Jews who came to Toronto immediately after the war, quickly established themselves in businesses or professions, and bought homes in the new neighbourhoods along Bathurst Street. Several of them also facilitated Jewish suburbanization by entering the construction and development business. Many of the houses in the neighbourhood were built by synagogue members. A survey of Clanton Park Synagogue shows that about one-quarter of members in the 1950s and 1960s were involved in the construction industry, including the Hofstedter and Rubinstein families, two Hungarian Jewish families who later built their firm into one of Toronto's leading real estate development companies.[36]

Toronto's native Orthodox Jews (those who had been in the city for at least a couple of decades) saw the recent immigrants' settlement and realized that movement away from the Jewish core was religiously possible. They recognized this at a time when other pressures, such as rising rents and an aging housing stock, were pushing Jews of all types out of Kensington. The suburban periphery offered a spacious environment and affordable housing; only the most stalwart of urbanites would have been able to resist the lure of the new neighbourhoods. But moving to newly constructed subdivisions was a double-edged sword for Orthodox Jewish families because Jewish *halakhah* forbids any form of vehicular travel on the Sabbath and permits only travel by foot. Leaving the downtown neighbourhoods meant that Orthodox Jewish families would move beyond walking distance of their former congregations. Still, needing to attend services on the Sabbath, they had no choice but to create new congregations as soon as they settled in their new environment. By contrast, Conservative and Reform Jews, whose Sabbath observances permitted vehicular driving, could travel to their former neighbourhoods to attend synagogue services. Thus, throughout the post-war period, non-Orthodox Jewish congregations generally formed only after suburban neighbourhoods had been established, rather than as part of the initial settlement process.

By 1961, after only ten years of Jewish suburbanization, the overwhelming Jewishness—both Orthodox and non-Orthodox—of the Bathurst corridor had already become evident. That year, the census reported that the eleven census tracts abutting Bathurst Street contained forty-two thousand Jews, an increase of over 800 per cent from a decade before. On the west side of Bathurst, four of the five tracts were more than fifty per cent Jewish, and one of these tracts registered as more than three-quarters Jewish.[37] Despite their residential domination, Jews were not evenly scattered throughout the neighbourhoods. A review of property assessment records from the 1950s shows that Jews tended to concentrate on certain streets in specific neighbourhoods. For example, in the Clanton Park neighbourhood on the west side of Bathurst between Wilson and Sheppard Avenues, Jewish families lived in 124 of 127 houses on Palm Drive and its adjacent side streets. Only two blocks to the north, however, Jewish households were entirely absent. In general, Jewish families tended to move to newly built streets and avoided moving onto blocks of existing homes. Between Finch and Steeles Avenues, for example, far more Jews moved into the newly constructed subdivisions on the west side of Bathurst than moved into the slightly older streets on the east side.[38]

By 1971, Jews had staked for themselves an even more clearly defined corridor along Bathurst Street, where they constituted the single largest ethnic or religious group in the Bathurst corridor.[39] Their dominance continued through the 1970s and into the 1980s, when Jews filled new Bathurst neighbourhoods in Thornhill, the suburban municipality to the immediate north of the North York boundary at Steeles Avenue. Thornhill was home to the first subdivision conceived from the start to be a Jewish space. The Spring Farm community, built by developer Joseph Tannenbaum beginning in 1981, included a large Orthodox Jewish synagogue-cum-community centre, a shopping plaza with kosher food stores, and a Jewish book and gift store.[40] By the late 1980s, forty-five Orthodox Jewish congregations were located on or adjacent to Bathurst Street.[41] In fact, in the five decades since World War II, only three new Orthodox Jewish congregations have been located outside the Bathurst corridor. Of these three, two failed to develop into major congregations, while the third was formed as an Orthodox Jewish outreach congregation targeted at non-Orthodox Jewish families.

Orthodox Jewish residential settlement in neighbourhoods adjacent to Bathurst and the formation of local congregations were a first step in creating a sacred space along Bathurst Street. But homes and congregations alone did not create sacred space. For that to occur, other religious institutions were needed, institutions that would add to the visible religious activity of the district and to the sense that *this* was a Jewish neighbourhood. This second stage of sacred space creation began in 1954, when the Jewish Old Folks Home (now Baycrest Centre) moved to its present location at Bathurst and Baycrest Avenue. A year later, a branch of the Associated Hebrew Day School opened a block away at Bathurst and Neptune Drive. In time, other institutions joined these pioneers, including the Viewmount Street branch of Eitz Chaim Day School, which began operations in 1958; the community *mikveh* on Sheppard just west of Bathurst; and the city's first kosher restaurant, which opened just south of Baycrest and the Associated school that same year. As would be expected, these and other institutions increased the level of visible Jewish activity on Bathurst Street. A passerby on Bathurst could not help but see Jews of all types—and particularly Orthodox Jews—going to school, doing their shopping, or, on the Sabbath, walking to synagogue.

The visibility of this developing Jewish landscape was aided by a pattern of clustering among Jewish commercial establishments. Clustering was particularly important on a street such as Bathurst, which was generally inhospitable to the automobile. Because of parking difficulties on Bathurst itself, customers had to park on side streets and walk from store to store. By clustering, stores enabled shoppers to run their errands without having to return to their cars between stops.[42] The importance of store clusters, however, ran deeper than merely providing an easier shopping environment. Life in Kensington had bred a Jewish community geographically and culturally accustomed to a dense and compact religious infrastructure; the typical suburban pattern of dispersed commercial activity was foreign to many former urban residents. The commercial clusters along Bathurst, then, worked to integrate urban and suburban patterns of communal activity. After driving to the cluster and parking on a side street—a suburban pattern—Jewish shoppers could stop and chat with store owners or other shoppers in a manner common to urban environments. Moreover, because many of the stores had been previously located downtown, shoppers were already familiar with the shopkeepers and felt a continuity between Kensington and the new centres along Bathurst. By transplanting some stores, opening new ones, and mixing them with schools and synagogues, Toronto's Orthodox Jewish community recreated an infrastructure that serviced its religious and cultural needs, all in a geographic pattern commonly absent from main suburban roads. The result was a suburban-oriented road with urban-like pedestrian activity, a religious landscape filled with "the business types in the pinstripes, the *chassid* with his *streimel* [large, black hat] and *capote* [black coat], the Orthodox matrons with their fashionable *sheitels* [wigs], the bicycle-riding yeshiva students with earlocks flapping in the wind—and the majority, the ordinary Jewish man and woman, shopping, conversing, going about their daily tasks."[43]

Given the large Jewish population in Kensington, it is surprising that the massive relocation of people and institutions northward to Toronto's suburbs provoked as little reaction as it did. In reviewing the *Canadian Jewish News* and the *Jewish Standard*, the two local Jewish newspapers, one finds very little critical analysis of what the personal and institutional abandonment of Kensington would do to the neighbourhood. A rare comment was made by the editor of the

Canadian Jewish News in 1961, in an editorial that focused on Toronto's suburbanization as a whole (not just that of the Jews.) The most recent census reported that the city of Toronto's population was only forty per cent British in heritage, down from seventy per cent in 1951. The Jewish community had a dual
role in this shift. As part of the "old guard" of ethnic groups with a long history in the city, second- and third-generation Jews were part of the northward
migration into suburbia. At the same time, more recent European immigration
from Hungary made Jews a large part of the "new guard" that moved downtown, at least initially. Because of this continual turnover of population in
Kensington, the "Jewish community has much to gain by maintaining its identity with the 'historic' part of Toronto." Furthermore, the editorial continued,
Toronto's Jews should avoid as much as possible becoming "linked exclusively
with the outer ring of suburbs." In this last point, the editorial contrasted
Toronto Jewry's connection to Kensington with Cleveland, where black migration into the inner city had made those neighbourhoods "virtually *Judenrein*
[free of Jews]."44

This comment was the exception. Synagogue records and newsletters and
newspaper articles betrayed little feeling of hesitation or regret at suburbanization. Oral interviews with participants in the suburbanization process expressed
similar feelings. Bathurst Street represented space, newness, and modernity,
three characteristics lacking in the immigrant neighbourhoods of Kensington.
Perhaps it was the seeming inevitability of suburbanization, or perhaps it was
the absence of conflict pushing Jews out of Kensington. As the editorial alluded
to, Toronto had no influxes of African-Americans to push Jews out of inner-city
neighbourhoods, as happened in New York, Boston, Cleveland, Indianapolis,
and almost every other American city.45 Moreover, unlike Protestant and
Catholic communities undergoing suburbanization in the same period, the
Jewish community lacked any institutional ties to the urban neighbourhood.46
Absent the perceived threats from immigrating African-Americans and any
sense of "mission" to the neighbourhood, there was little reason to express concern for those being "left behind." It was unstated, but likely felt, that eventually everyone in the Jewish community would come "up north," simply because
that was where everyone was going.

Of course, not all Jews who left Kensington went to Bathurst Street. For some of Toronto's Jews, Bathurst was too Jewish. They interpreted the clustering of synagogues, schools and stores, and the extent to which Jews' daily lives overlapped with one another, as insularity and cliquishness rather than cohesion and community. In an open letter to the rest of the Jewish community, one Jewish housewife proudly described her family's decision not "to live in a self-made ghetto" such as Bathurst, but rather in a non-Jewish environment in Toronto's western suburbs. The advantages were many. For example, her children could be exposed to other cultural groups; her daughter attended Christmas parties and hosted non-Jewish friends at her Hanukkah parties. Moreover, when her Jewish friends got together, they did not fill their conversations with "daily trivia." "Perhaps we have to work a little harder to preserve our Jewish identity," she explained, "but we feel we have made the proper choice." Despite the letter's defiant tone, other comments hint at a yearning for Bathurst that the author may not have even realized. She noted the lack of good Jewish delicatessen and the need to chauffeur children to Jewish activities. Although the few Jewish families in the area formed a three-day-a-week Jewish education program, she recognized that Jewish education "could be another problem." Finally, she had few Jewish companions in her circle of friends. Such comments suggest the extent to which Bathurst had become embedded in the minds of Toronto's Jews. Even when portraying the neighbourhood negatively, such critics could not help but recognize the community-building qualities of Bathurst Street.[47]

Bathurst's Jewishness did not go unnoticed in the non-Jewish world. Various sociological and demographic studies of Toronto's ethnic population noted the Jewish community's tendency to concentrate along the Bathurst Street corridor.[48] Bathurst's Jewishness was even mentioned in official North York planning documents. A 1985 study of the development needs of Bathurst described the corridor as one of the few "street-oriented" commercial strips behind which, both east and west, lay low-density, stable residential neighbourhoods. The study noted that most of these street-oriented commercial uses "cater to the particular needs of the area's and the city's Jewish community. Jewish bookstores, kosher markets and delis are visible on virtually every block."[49]

One might have thought that in a predominantly Anglo-Protestant community, as North York was in the 1950s and 1960s, the rapid influx of Jews and the construction of a visible Jewish infrastructure along Bathurst Street would have raised anti-Jewish issues. In general, however, religious and political relations with other groups remained positive. At least nothing happened in Toronto that resembled the anti-suburban synagogue lawsuits or zoning board controversies that occurred in suburban Cleveland in the 1950s or in Rockland County, New York, in the 1990s.[50] Instead, one finds examples of cooperation between Jews and non-Jews. For example, when it was initially founded, the Reform Temple Sinai rented space from the Asbury and West United Church on Bathurst Street. Later, after it moved into its own building, the synagogue occasionally joined with the church for combined ecumenical services.[51] When the Wilson Heights United Church closed in 1968, it transferred its building to Congregation Beth Meyer, a small Conservative Jewish synagogue in the area.[52] Jews integrated into North York's political world as well. Within a decade of their settlement in North York, Jews were being elected to the township's political bodies, and in 1972, voters chose the brash Mel Lastman as mayor, a job he held continuously for more than two decades.

Still, cordial and even friendly relations between Jews and Christians did not preclude occasional problems. One Friday night in November 1966, for example, a group of youths in North York beat up an Orthodox Jewish teenager who was walking home from a friend's house.[53] More prominent was the "Leiner Affair" four years earlier. One Friday night in January 1962, Rabbi Norbert Leiner, a teacher at the Orthodox Jewish Ner Israel Yeshiva, was stopped by police in the Bathurst–St. Clair neighbourhood in York Township. The police in the area had been put on alert for a suspicious person whom neighbourhood residents claimed was stalking the area. Although Rabbi Leiner looked nothing like the suspected stalker, the police nevertheless confronted him, used abusive language, and demanded that he enter their automobile. Rabbi Leiner refused, citing the Jewish Sabbath's prohibitions against riding in a vehicle. The officers pushed the rabbi into their car, drove him to the police station, and held him overnight. At the station, officers slapped Rabbi Leiner after he again refused to cooperate with fingerprinting and other procedures because of his Sabbath observances. Rabbi Leiner was released the next day when authorities admitted that he had been mistakenly apprehended.[54] Both the Jewish and non-Jewish press attacked the police for their actions, and a specially convened royal commission condemned the authorities for the incident. Although the arrest was not deemed anti-Semitic, the commission admonished the police for failing to understand or be sensitive to Rabbi Leiner's religious observances. At the same time, the commission did not spare Rabbi Leiner, criticizing him for not cooperating to the extent that he might have.[55] The "Leiner Affair," and other occasional assaults, reminded Jews that, though they might have dominated Bathurst Street, they were still a minority in an Anglo-Protestant environment.

Although many inside and outside the Orthodox Jewish community saw Bathurst as distinctly Jewish, it must be made clear that Bathurst's "sacredness" was neither universal nor universally relevant. The clusters of Orthodox Jewish neighbourhoods, synagogues, schools, and stores created a sacred space that was meaningful only to those whose lives were connected to those neighbourhoods, synagogues, schools, and stores. Throughout the entire post-war period, thousands of individuals—both non-Orthodox Jews and non-Jews—lived along Bathurst and remained generally unaffected by the Orthodox Jewish subculture. In fact, throughout the entire post-war period, only a small proportion of all stores, businesses, and other institutions on the street were Jewish. Even the dense clusters of Jewish bakeries, butchers, and restaurants shared their street frontages with non-Jewish entreprises. The street's many synagogues were joined by several churches situated on or immediately adjacent to Bathurst. For those who frequented these stores and institutions, Bathurst was a suburban traffic artery and little more; the Orthodox Jewish infrastructure had little real or symbolic value. The same was true for Orthodox Jewish centres in other metropolitan areas. For example, in Rockland County, New York, which developed in the 1970s, 1980s, and 1990s into one of the largest concentrations of suburban Orthodox Jews, Jews accounted for less than one-quarter of the county's population. Even in dense urban neighbourhoods, such as Brooklyn's Crown Heights, Jews were a minority. In fact, as late as 1990, only one county in the United States even had a plurality of Jews, that being Palm Beach County in

South Florida.⁵⁶ The point, then, is that sacred space is neither exclusive nor all-encompassing. The same spaces that some people—usually insiders—recognize as "Jewish" might have absolutely no relevance to someone else. As Vivian Klaff noted in 1987, "We need to be careful not to confuse the concentration of Jews in an area with the Jewishness of an area. In fact, in most areas for which the data point to a concentration of Jewish population, the population is generally a minority in the area."⁵⁷ But the presence and even predominance of non-Jews and non-Jewish institutions on Bathurst, and in the many other centres of suburban Orthodox Jewry, does not negate the concentration of Orthodox Jews and Orthodox Jewish institutions in those same places. The fact remained that, in all of Toronto, Bathurst Street was where Orthodox Jews lived and practiced their religion. For the hundreds of families who moved into houses in the neighbourhoods adjacent to Bathurst Street and for the dozens of store owners who located their businesses on the street itself, the sacredness was obvious even though it was not universal.

But the clustering of Orthodox Jewish families and businesses along Bathurst Street is not the only evidence that Bathurst Street held special significance for the Orthodox Jewish community. Another source can be found in the ways urban synagogues undertook the process of relocation to suburbia. When it was founded in the early 1930s, Shaarei Shomayim Synagogue was located at the northwestern edges of Jewish settlement on St. Clair Avenue, between Bathurst and Dufferin Streets. After some financial delays, the congregation built an imposing edifice on Winona Avenue in the mid-1940s and established itself as the dominant Orthodox Jewish synagogue in Toronto. Its prominence was helped by the membership of many of the Jewish community's elite and by its location near upper-middle-class neighbourhoods just north of the synagogue. Unfortunately for Shaarei Shomayim, the Jewish exodus to suburbia began only a few years after the congregation had dedicated its sanctuary. The newer suburban neighbourhoods in North York and the new Orthodox Jewish congregations in the Bathurst corridor attracted many young, religiously observant families, who years before might have moved into the Shaarei Shomayim area.

For the most part, Shaarei Shomayim weathered this initial northward push through the 1950s. By the end of that decade, however, it had become clear to the synagogue's leadership that because of its location on St. Clair, Shaarei Shomayim was losing its viability as a Jewish centre. The congregation, through its executive board, actively began to debate the question of congregational relocation. The possibility of relocating was first broached at an April 1957 board meeting. Some at the meeting questioned the need for moving, especially when most members had not moved northward yet. In addition, the membership had a "vested interest" in the present St. Clair location, where, as one board member trumpeted, the synagogue had given "inestimable service and value to the general Jewish community and to its own members." On the other side, those favouring a move pointed to the success of the Orthodox Jewish synagogues that had emerged north of Wilson Avenue. In particular, this faction saw the Bathurst–Sheppard area as "fertile ground" for the "expansion of Orthodox ideology" through a "progressive, modern Orthodox synagogue." Unstated but implicit in this argument was the inevitability of northward migration along Bathurst Street; the congregation simply *had* to move.[58]

Over the next four years, the issue of relocation arose several more times. Board members repeatedly stressed that a "prestigious" congregation like Shaarei Shomayim needed to move northward to ensure access to a "middle class" and "relatively well-to-do" membership, and to maintain its place as the community's "leading" Orthodox Jewish synagogue.[59] By the fall of 1962, however, the board's discussion had clearly changed from a matter of "if and why" to "where and when." The answers to both questions came quickly, when the synagogue obtained a large lot on Glencairn Avenue, just east of Bathurst, about three miles north of the existing St. Clair building. After a dispute with a local neighbourhood group over the presence of a synagogue was resolved, construction began in September 1964. The first Shabbat services were held on 10 September 1966, and within a year, the St. Clair branch closed, and all synagogue activities relocated to the Glencairn and Bathurst site.[60]

Shaarei Shomayim's relocation experience reflected the extent to which Bathurst Street had become the core space for Toronto's Orthodox Jewish community. From the start, Shaarei Shomayim's leaders recognized that if they had to relocate, there was only one place to do so: suburban Bathurst Street. The presence of other successful Orthodox Jewish congregations and of other Jewish institutions, such as schools and kosher food stores, convinced Shaarei Shomayim's leaders that the future of the Orthodox Jewish community was rooted in Bathurst Street. There was no discussion of Shaarei Shomayim moving elsewhere in suburban Toronto and hoping then to attract Orthodox Jews. Instead, the congregation looked to the growing numbers of young, middle-class, religiously observant families who had settled in the Bathurst corridor and knew that that space would be the backbone of the Orthodox Jewish community for decades to come.

Just as Shaarei Shomayim's relocation to Bathurst Street highlighted the Orthodox Jewish community's sacred space, the experiences of other Orthodox Jews who moved away from Bathurst told the same story. In the early 1970s, when the Bathurst Street corridor was fully built to the North York border at Steeles Avenue, the Orthodox Jewish community faced a bit of a problem. The disappearance of available land meant that housing costs began to increase.[61] Now, many young families, who had been the Orthodox Jewish community's backbone of settlement along Bathurst Street, had to look elsewhere for affordable housing. A small portion of them looked eastward to the northeast part of North York, where non-Orthodox Jewish settlement had been occurring for some time. Although removed from the sacred space of Bathurst Street, these families assumed that despite their divergence from the corridor, they could create a new religious infrastructure that would extend the sacred space eastward. As their story showed, they were wrong.

In September 1971, a group of Jewish families, who had moved to neighbourhoods along Leslie Street between Finch and Steeles Avenues, began to hold Orthodox services in the home of one of the group. Two years later, the now-named Shaare Zion Congregation moved to a portable trailer that sat on the lawn of one of the members. Expecting continued growth, the group began to look for a more permanent home, and in March 1975, received permission from the local residential association to erect a building. Neither the growth nor the building ever came. In 1981, the congregation had expanded to only forty-four members and still met in the trailer. Even the hiring of a rabbi in 1980 and the affiliation with the National Council of Young Israel, a North American Orthodox synagogue organization, failed to spur growth. By the mid-1980s, the congregation moved into space in a new building of the Associated Hebrew Day School on Leslie Street, but despite the efforts of a small but dedicated core of membership, the congregation remained far smaller than its founders had originally anticipated.[62]

One major street closer to Bathurst on Bayview Avenue, a second Orthodox Jewish congregation developed with a marginally better outcome. In the mid-1970s, a small contingent of South African Jews moved to Toronto and settled, not in the Bathurst corridor but east of Bathurst around the intersection of Bayview and Sheppard Avenues. Wanting to preserve the traditions of the community left behind, this group organized a regular Friday evening Shabbat service that soon became known as the "South African *minyan*." By the fall of 1979, the congregation held High Holiday services in one of the apartment complexes where some members lived. One year later, the Kehillat Shaarei Torah, as the South African *minyan* became known, hired a full-time rabbi.[63] As had Shaare Zion, the congregation worked to find a permanent building so they would not have to meet in a nearby junior high school. Despite disagreements with local neighbourhood groups over the noise and traffic a synagogue building was expected to generate, the congregation completed a new sanctuary by 1986.[64] Despite its building, however, Shaarei Torah never attracted a large enough membership to make it a major force in the Orthodox Jewish community.

There would seem to be nothing out of the ordinary in the history of these congregations that precluded their success. Most new synagogues in the suburban environment were built-from-scratch congregations that started with a small group and grew into more complete institutions, a model that fit both of these synagogues. Yet neither synagogue made that step from small congregation to mature institution. Moreover, a broader religious infrastructure never developed in North York's northeast neighbourhoods; not a single kosher butcher, bakery, grocery store, or restaurant opened in the area, and the only day school to be built attracted a largely non-Orthodox Jewish student population. In contrast, the other stages of Toronto's Orthodox Jewish suburbanization brought with them new stores and schools to serve the expanding population.

The explanation for this failure was, to quote many a real estate agent, location. Simply put, the northeast neighbourhoods were not in the Bathurst corridor. All of the earlier waves of Orthodox Jewish suburbanization had occurred along Bathurst Street. The string of neighbourhoods that developed along this corridor was seen as a single entity. One might have lived further north or south but at least one lived *on* Bathurst. In the terminology of the urbanist Kevin Lynch, Bathurst Street acted like a "path" that connected various "districts" or neighbourhoods into a single community.[65] The northeast congregations, located parallel to Bathurst on Bayview Avenue and Leslie Street, lacked this geographical connection to the central community space. Even though the northeast neighbourhoods were physically closer to the religious infrastructure on Bathurst Street than the original Orthodox Jewish suburbanites had been to Kensington downtown, the distances were perceived as being much greater. Living parallel to Bathurst meant that one had to travel in an east-west plane to reach the religious infrastructure, a psychologically difficult prospect in a city where a north-south mentality had long dominated growth. In Lynch's terms, the north-south streets between Bathurst and the northeast neighbourhoods acted as "edges" dividing neighbourhoods rather than as "paths" joining them. To live in northeast Toronto and to drive to Bathurst meant to leave one neighbourhood and go to another; one felt no sense of continuity between the two places. To a degree, the Orthodox Jews who moved to the northeast anticipated some of these problems. In September 1981, for example, Rabbi Eliot Feldman of Shaarei Torah admitted that his Orthodox congregation "is itself a great wonder, for the area of Leslie and Sheppard is not known for being a place for observant Jews."[66] As it happened, it did not become one either; the attraction of Bathurst Street proved too strong.

A final example of the Orthodox Jewish community's relationship to Bathurst Street is found in the history of Toronto's *eruv*. According to Jewish religious law, an observant Jew is forbidden to carry any object in public property on the Sabbath. Carrying is permitted only in private space. This restriction can be circumvented, however, with the construction of an *eruv*, a fence or enclosure that encircles the public space and, in religious legal terms, transforms that space into private property. A proper *eruv* permits a range of activities on the Sabbath that would otherwise be prohibited, such as carrying food and pushing baby strollers. While to those not familiar with the Sabbath prohibitions, being able to carry a tissue to synagogue might seem trivial, for others the presence of an *eruv* is more serious. For example, an Orthodox Jewish woman in Twin Rivers, New Jersey, explained, "I have a 17-year-old son who has to be pushed in a wheelchair. To go to synagogue (without the *eruv*) I have to hire a nurse at $30 an hour with a four-hour minimum. That's $120 if I want to go to the synagogue."[67]

Although an *eruv* is entirely irrelevant to those outside the Orthodox Jewish community (excepting the small numbers of non-Orthodox Jews who observe the Sabbath prohibitions against carrying), the presence of an *eruv*, or proposals to build one, can spark controversies. Opponents often reject an *eruv* for practical reasons, such as lower property values or aesthetic reasons. But other feelings have simmered close to the surface and occasionally have bubbled over. For example, a historic preservationist in London, England, claimed that a proposed *eruv* in the Golder's Green neighbourhood "affronted every other sect by insisting on imposing a series of poles and wires" on the area. But, perhaps betraying his true feelings, the same man wondered whether a "totem pole" would be next. In Twin Rivers, New Jersey in 1997, one protester explained his opposition to the *eruv* quite rationally: "You might have a legal right to put it up but not a moral right," he said. But he quickly lost credibility when he asked, "What happens when the black community wants to put Kwanzaa around the community? What do we do then?" Opposition came not only from outside the Jewish community. Sometimes non-Orthodox Jews expressed concern that the *eruv* would result in too many "visible Jews" moving to the area. One Holocaust survivor feared that the *eruv* would create another "Williamsburg," referring to the Hasidic Jewish neighbourhood in Brooklyn. Another likened the *eruv*'s posts and wires to those in the Auschwitz concentration camp.[68]

This last reaction, a rejection of an *eruv* because of the presence of unsightly wires and poles, is not uncommon. Many people who hear about a proposed *eruv* fear that it will "fence them in." One woman in London was horrified by the thought that a post would go "right next to" her neighbour's house. Were these opponents to know how an *eruv* is actually constructed, they would realize how laughable their fears were. In reality, an *eruv* is a rather mundane and unexciting technology. Often, the *eruv* is "built" with existing utility wires around the perimeter of an area. In some cases, religious authorities have allowed major highways or train tracks to be considered part of an *eruv*, since they can act as enclosures of a particular space.[69] Where existing wires or other natural boundaries are absent, new wires and poles have to be erected, usually in consultation with utility companies, which permit wires to be attached to their poles. However the construction, an *eruv*'s structure is almost always unnoticeable except to those who know the locations of the particular poles and wires.

But even if most Orthodox Jews do not know the exact dimensions and location of their local *eruv*, they recognize that its very existence is an essential part of Orthodox Jewish community life. Because an *eruv* delineates the area where carrying is permissible on the Sabbath, its boundaries will generally parallel the boundaries of Orthodox Jewish settlement. Orthodox Jewish families will usually seek to live only within an *eruv* because doing so makes Sabbath observances easier than they would be outside the *eruv*. Furthermore, if enough Orthodox Jewish families live outside an existing *eruv*, the *eruv* is often expanded to include this contingent. The erection of an *eruv*, then, involves the literal creation of sacred space, since it demarcates the area within which—and outside of which—certain religious behaviours are permissible or prohibited.[70]

In Toronto, the *eruv*, as initially set up by Rabbi Abraham Price before World War II, extended only as far north as Bloor Street. This boundary sufficed because an overwhelming majority of the observant community lived south of Bloor and would have had no reason to carry objects on the Sabbath north of the *eruv*. Throughout the post-war period, however, the *eruv* was extended as necessary to encompass the areas of Orthodox Jewish settlement. For example, in 1951, the *eruv* was extended to Wilson Avenue, at that point the northern limit of Jewish settlement. Over the next decade, Orthodox Jews moved further north, and in 1966, another adjustment brought the boundaries all the way north to Steeles Avenue, the outer edge of North York. Later, when Orthodox Jews began to move into neighbourhoods in northeast North York and in Thornhill directly north of North York, the *eruv* was extended again.[71] With each extension, the *eruv* eased certain Sabbath difficulties for Orthodox Jewish families. More important, each extension repeated the process of spatial sanctification; each new area became integrated into a single "religious space." Not coincidentally, at the core of this space stood Bathurst Street, with its blend of middle-class subdivisions full of Orthodox Jews and their synagogues and strip malls full of kosher food stores and restaurants.

As much as it organized the sacred space of Toronto's Orthodox Jewish community along Bathurst Street, the *eruv* also became a point of conflict within that community in the 1980s. Although most of Toronto's Orthodox Jews abided by Rabbi Price's *eruv*, those within the *haredi* community tended not to, both out of a specific concern for the correctness of Rabbi Price's *eruv* and a more general practice of not relying on any *eruv* to permit carrying on the Sabbath. Through the 1980s, this division remained generally unarticulated and simmered below the surface of intra-Orthodox Jewish community relationships. The status quo changed, however, when Rabbi Jacob Sofer, a rabbi brought in by the Reichmann family to lead one of the synagogues that they supported, publicly announced that Rabbi Price's *eruv* was faulty and to carry on the Sabbath within his *eruv* would violate Sabbath law. Immediately, Rabbi Price's defenders, and Rabbi Price himself, published defenses demonstrating the *halakhic* reliability of the *eruv*. Most of Toronto's Orthodox Jews did not stop carrying on the Sabbath because of Rabbi Sofer's pronouncement, but the damage was already done. Although not declaring Rabbi Price's *eruv* invalid, the *Va'ad HaRabbonim,* one of Toronto's Orthodox Jewish rabbinical councils, ruled that Rabbi Sofer could erect his own *eruv*.[72] By the early 1990s, soon after Rabbi Price died, a new *eruv* was constructed with the backing of the *haredi* community. The irony of the entire episode was that the differences between the two *eruvim* were minor and mostly concerned the outer boundaries where few Orthodox Jews lived. In both cases, the central Bathurst Street corridor and the adjacent neighbourhoods were squarely inside. But if it articulated the cleavages between the *haredi* and centrist Orthodox Jewish communities in Toronto, it also pointed to their spatial similarities. Both groups lived along that same narrow suburban corridor and, despite the differing interpretations of the margins of the community's sacred space, neither showed any hint of loosening those spatial ties.

The debates within the Orthodox Jewish community over the definition of sacred space, as well as Bathurst Street's invisibleness, or at least its irrelevance, to a large proportion of Toronto's population suggest the extent to which the

Orthodox Jewish community has blended into the broader suburban society. Although they had built a thriving religiously traditional subculture, they had done so in the context of the secular host culture. The post-war Orthodox Jews in suburban Toronto chose not to isolate themselves in an insulated enclave, away from the city or in some way independent from the city. Instead, they built their religious infrastructure right in the heart of post-war suburbia, in neighbourhoods that were never exclusively composed of Orthodox Jews and on a street that was never exclusively populated by religious institutions and businesses. Their lives were suburban as much as they were Orthodox Jewish, and the space of Bathurst Street was both suburban *and* sacred.

Ultimately, the sacredness of Bathurst Street derived not from any intrinsic holiness but from the institutions and activities of Toronto's suburbanizing Orthodox Jewish community. The new congregations that formed, the schools that were built, the kosher food stores and Jewish bookstores all contributed to Bathurst's Jewish identity. In each of these areas—the formation of congregations, the development of institutions of religious socialization, and the creation of a religious consumer infrastructure—Orthodox Jews combined an adherence to traditionalism with an acceptance of modern secular styles, although each developed at its own pace with its own historical peculiarities.

NOTES

1   *Canadian Jewish News (CJN)*, 18 March 1960.

2   Jakobovits interview.

3   Eliade, *The Sacred and the Profane*. See also a discussion of sacred space in Park, *Sacred Worlds*, 245–85. See also Scott and Simpson-Housley, *Sacred Places and Profane Spaces*.

4   For a similar analysis of the religious landscape of suburban Los Angeles, see Weightman, "Changing Religious Landscapes in Los Angeles."

5   Geographers R. H. Jackson and R. Henrie describe sacred space as any "portion of the earth's surface which is recognized by individuals or groups as worthy of devotion, loyalty, or esteem. Sacred space does not exist naturally, but is assigned sanctity as man defines, limits, and characterizes it through his culture, experience, and goals" ("Perception of Sacred Space").

6   For a brief description of Teaneck, see Korn, "Modern Orthodox Community." For a discussion of Orthodox Jewish suburbanization in Boston, see Gamm, "In Search of Suburbs."

7   For a complete history of Jewish Toronto in the prewar period, see Speisman, *Jews of Toronto*. See also Hayman, *Toronto Jewry.*

8   Rosenberg, *Canada's Jews*, 308.

9   For a history of Toronto's garment industry, see Frager, *Sweatshop Strife,* and Hiebert, "Jewish Immigrants and the Garment Industry of Toronto."

10 Rosenberg, *Canada's Jews*, 308.

11 *JS*, June 1949.

12 Forest Hill became famous as the fictionalized community in the 1956 sociological study of Crestwood Heights. See Seeley, Sim, and Loosley, *Crestwood Heights*. For a more recent review of this still important study, see Schoenfeld, "Re-reading an American Classic."

13 Rosenberg, *Study of the Changes in the Geographic Distribution of the Jewish Population.*

14 DBS, *Ninth Census of Canada*, Table 1.

15 The story of Toronto's kosher food industry is complicated. Not until 1958 did a central supervisory organization for kosher food emerge out of the Canadian Jewish Congress's Orthodox Division. Before that, the community had a disorganized system of individual rabbinical supervision. Personality conflicts and economic competition drove the market, and, more often than not, it was easier for a butcher simply to post a sign claiming his meat or poultry was "kosher" rather than to submit to rabbinical supervision that would actually certify the food's kosher status. The community's attempt to form a *kehillah* (central communal organization) in the 1920s included a try at kosher food regulation. This failed miserably when the various butchers and slaughterers protested the costs of supervision. Even after the 1958 supervisory system was in place, deceit in advertising and selling continued into the early 1970s. For a concise history of the legal controversies over kosher supervision in North America, see Stern, "Kosher Food and the Law."

16 Hart, *Pioneering in North York*. See also Reitman, "North York."

17 There is virtually no historiographical work on twentieth-century religion in Toronto or Ontario. Nevertheless, the common perception (and most likely the accurate one as well) is that the religious patterns set in the nineteenth century held true for the first half of the twentieth century also. Only with the postwar immigration from Europe, the Caribbean, Asia, and the Middle East did the Anglo-Protestant hegemony decline. See Westfall, *Two Worlds*, and Grant, *Profusion of Spires.*

18 DBS, *Eighth Census of Canada*, Table 38.

19 Much of the information in this section is from Hart, *Pioneering in North York.*

20 For a contemporary discussion of the housing shortage in Toronto and Canada, see Carver, *Houses for Canadians.*

21 *Enterprise*, 6 January 1949, 12 January 1950.

22 For a brief history of Don Mills, see *Globe and Mail*, 29 May 1993.

23 *Enterprise*, 2 March 1950; *Asbury and West. United Church Herald*, 12 October 1950, UCC/VUA, LCFHC, Toronto, Ontario Asbury and West United Church.

24 Northways, Metro Toronto Aerial Photographs.

25 The North York–York-Township boundary is actually a few blocks north of Eglinton along Hillhurst Boulevard. But because there is little qualitative difference between the neighborhoods on either side of the border and because Eglinton is a major east-west road, I have used Eglinton as the boundary of the corridor rather than Hillhurst.

26 The population figures are only estimates from the 1940 and 1970s population census- es, derived from the sum of the population of those census tracts that abutted Bathurst Street In larger tracts that extended beyond the immediate vicinity of Bathurst, I included only a percentage of the tract population in the estimate. DBS, *Eighth Census of Canada*, Table 38; and Statistics Canada, *1971 Census of Canada*, Table 1.

27 *Enterprise*, 6 April, 16 November 1950, 15 March 1951.

28 Deacon, Arnett, and Murray, *Bathurst Street, Forest Hill to Don River.*

29 *Enterprise*, 28 February 1952.

30 Deacon, Arnett, and Murray, *Bathurst Street, Forest Hill to Don River.*

31 DBS, *Ninth Census of Canada*, Table 1.

32 *CJN*, 4 December 1964; Grossman interview.

33 The following chapter provides a more detailed history of Toronto's suburban Orthodox Jewish congregations.

34 Rubinstein interview. For a personal history of one Hungarian immigrant family who achieved much success in Toronto, see Mandelbaum, ed., *Family Chronicles.*

35 Bianco, *Reichmanns.*

36 Data taken from Clanton Park Synagogue, Membership Lists (1957–58, 1960–61), SEPP; and City of North York, Property Assessment Rolls (1957–60).

37 DBS, *Ninth Census of Canada*, Table 1; DBS, *1961 Census of Canada,* Table 1.

38 City of North York, Property Assessment Rolls (1955–65).

39 Statistics Canada, 1971 *Census of Canada*, Table 1.

40 *CJN*, 3 September 1981, 13 August 1987.

41 Lipsitz, ed., *Ontario Jewish Resource Directory.*

42 The journalist Joel Garreau, in his analysis of contemporary suburban "edge cities," makes the same point regarding the design of shopping malls. He explains that a rule of thumb among mall developers is to keep shoppers from seeing how far it really is between stores. If shoppers realized the distances they actually walked in a mall, they would get in their cars and drive to the other end of the mall rather than walk. The developers' fear, of course, is that once in their car, shoppers might leave the mall alto- gether. See Garreau, *Edge City.*

43 *CJN*, 4 October 1979.

44 *CJN*, 22 June 1961.

45 Levine and Harmon, *Death of an American Jewish Community;* Diamond, "Urban Ministry and Changing Perceptions of the Metropolis." For an Orthodox Jewish perspec- tive on white flight and black-Jewish relations, see Cohen, "Changing Neighborhoods" and "The Orthodox Synagogue," and Goldstein, "Exploitation in the Ghetto."

46 See Gamm, *Urban Exodus*.

47 *CJN*, 20 January 1961.

48 See Gad, Peddie, and Punter, "Ethnic Difference in the Residential Search Process";
Richmond, *Ethnic Residential Segregation in Metropolitan Toronto*; Breton, Isajiw,
Kalbach, and Reitz, *Ethnic Identity and Equality*.

49 North York Planning Department, *South Bathurst Street Study*.

50 In the town of Beachwood, Ohio, a suburb of Cleveland, a proposal to build a new
synagogue was met with harsh opposition. See Schack, "Zoning Boards, Synagogues,
and Bias." These anti-Jewish opinions did not ever dissipate, and in the 1990s, several
zoning battles still simmered in the Cleveland suburbs. In Airmont, New York, in the
early 1990s, the United States government filed a lawsuit against the town for passing
zoning laws that made it all but impossible to establish local synagogues. See *CJN*, 27
February 1992.

51 *Asbury and West United Church Herald*, 12 April 1958; *Toronto Telegram*, n.d. (prob. early
1960s), UCC/VUA, LCFHC, Toronto, Ontario–Asbury and West United Church.

52 *Toronto Telegram*, 10 August 1968, UCC/VUA, LCHFC, Toronto, Ontario Wilson
Heights United Church.

53 *CJN*, 18 November 1966.

54 Wells, *Report of the Royal Commission*.

55 Ibid.

56 See Bradley et al., *Churches and Church Membership in the United States, 1990*.

57 Klaff, "Urban Ecology of Jewish Populations," 61.

58 Shaarei Shomayim Synagogue, Board of Governors Minutes, 7 April 1957, OJA.

59 Ibid., 30 January 1958.

60 *JS*, 1 May 1963; *CJN*, 26 April 1963, 11 September 1964, 9 September 1966.

61 For a fuller discussion on the reasons for the inflated costs of suburban housing
throughout Canada in the mid-1970s, see Lorimer, *Developers*.

62 Zaionz interview; *CJN*, 27 August, 24 September 1971, 5 October 1973, 7 March 1975,
28 August 1980, 15 January 1981, 28 October 1982.

63 *CJN*, 5 February, 17 September 1981.

64 Kehillat Shaarei Torah, *A Tribute to Dr. Joel David Cooper* (ca. 1985), OJA; Gerry
Urbach to congregational membership, ca. 1986, OJA.

65 Lynch, *Image of the City*.

66 Kehillat Shaarei Torah, *Nachas of the North East Hebrew Congregation* (September 1981),
OJA.

67 *Windsor-Heights Herald*, 21 November 1997.

68 Ibid.; *New York Times*, 22 February 1993. See also Trillin, "Drawing the Line."

69 In an entirely different context, this halakhic reasoning echoes the complaints often
voiced about urban expressways. So often over the past half-century, an urban express-
way would be bulldozed through an inner city neighborhood, leaving one area cut off
from another and generally destroying the fabric of neighbor hood life. Even when

transportation officials built bridges over the highway, the road clearly acted as a barrier and impediment to neighborhood interaction. As if to confirm this situation, the halakhic perspective similarly interprets a highway as a "fence" and permits it as an *eruv*.

70 See Weiss, "Eruv."

71 *CJN*, 4 March 1966, 22 November 1974, 8 October 1981.

72 Bianco, *Reichmanns*, 475–76. See also *CJN*, 27 August 1987.

Mrs Maza's Salon

MIRIAM WADDINGTON

In the fall of 1930, when I was twelve, my family moved to Ottawa from Winnipeg. The reason was this: my father had lost his small sausage-making and meat-curing factory to a partner in a lawsuit. The world was then in the grip of the great Depression, and the west had been especially hard hit. My father had the idea of starting a small sausage factory in Ottawa, and since there seemed nothing else to do, my parents rented out our Winnipeg house, sold the piano, packed us children into the car, and set out.

The whole family was unhappy about the move. My parents had come to Canada before the First World War. They had met and married in Winnipeg and once there, became firmly integrated in a circle of secular Jews who had founded a Yiddish day school and named it after the famous Yiddish writer I.L. Peretz. They had many close friends and led a busy social life of meetings, lectures, and family-friend dinners in winter, and picnics or camping with other families in summer.

In Ottawa, it was a different story. There were very few non-observant Jews and even fewer Jews who had, like my parents, made Yiddish language and culture their home and community. It took them some months to find congenial friends, especially since their energies were absorbed by the task of finding a place to live and settling us four children—all under the age of fourteen—into a new school environment.

Their problems in adjusting to this strange and unfamiliar Ottawa community must have affected us children. I know that I mourned the loss of my two best friends until I found a new one with whom I could walk to school, go to the movies, and share my innermost thoughts and feelings. Also, Ottawa in 1930 was still a small city, which with its population of 80,000 seemed like a village compared to Winnipeg. There was some compensation in the fact that Montreal was so close—only 120 miles away, with frequent two-dollar weekend train excursions. After a year or so, my parents discovered the Jewish community in Montreal, and we came to know a number of families whom we could visit.

Among them was a Yiddish poet, Ida Maza. She had published several volumes of poetry and knew all the Yiddish writers and painters in Montreal and New York. Her husband was an agent who represented several manufacturers of men's haberdashery—mostly shirts and ties. His route took him through the small towns between Ottawa and Montreal, and also past Lachute up into the Laurentians. Whenever he was in Ottawa he stayed with us, and he often took me back with him at times when I had no school.

It is hard to describe Mrs Maza and what I have come to think of as her salon without placing her in the social context that I remember from my childhood. For example, my parents and their friends spoke Yiddish among themselves and regularly addressed one another by their surnames. If it was a man, he would be addressed simply as 'Maza', and if it was a woman, it would be 'Mrs Maza'. First names were rare and reserved for close relatives. Similarly, when speaking Yiddish—which is an inflected language—they used the polite form of 'you', never the intimate 'thou'.

Mrs Maza was what is called a *jolie laide*. She looked Japanese and emphasized her oriental exoticism with her carriage, her way of walking and dressing, and her hairdo. She had thick black hair, which she piled up around her face in interesting twists and turns like doughnuts and buns. Her colouring was that of the native girls in Gauguin's paintings, and like theirs, her cheekbones were wide apart and prominent. Her eyes were large and dark and Mongolian in feeling. She was short in stature and slight in build, and always wore long kimono-like dresses with sashes and wide sleeves into which she would tuck her hands. Her shoes were simple low-heeled slipper affairs, and she walked with small shuffling steps, for all the world as if her feet had been bound. She had a beautiful low voice, full of dark rich tones, and a chanting, trance-like way of talking. Most of the time she was serious and melancholy in mood, but every now and again she would break into short little bursts of soft chuckling laughter. This was usually when she was with her husband, whom she always treated with tender affection. She liked to tease and jolly him because he took everything to heart with a childlike seriousness.

Looking back I realize she was not only a very intelligent woman, but full of cleverness and wisdom. She had been born in a village in White Russia and been brought to Montreal while she was still a child. Since she had lived most of her life in Montreal, she spoke English with only a slight accent.

I met Mrs Maza when I was fourteen. I had been writing poetry for about four years, and my mother must have mentioned it, because Mrs Maza at once offered to read my work. I showed it to her hesitatingly, and with fear, because she was not just a teacher but a real writer. She praised it and at once took charge of my reading, urging me to Emily Dickinson, Edna St. Vincent Millay, Sara Teasdale, Vachel Lindsay, Conrad Aiken, and Yeats. Occasionally she would read me one of her own Yiddish poems. I listened but I confess that I didn't give her poems my fullest attention. Most of them were children's poems, playful and tender; or else they dealt with the relationship between mothers and children, not a subject of great to interest to an adolescent girl. I have since gone back to read Ida Maza's poems with an adult eye, and find them full of warmth and a lyrical charm that manages to shine through even a rough translation.

In the next two or three years, I often stayed with the Mazas during my Christmas and Easter holidays. They lived in a third-floor walk-up on Esplanade. The building was old and resembled a tenement. It contained a buzzing hive of small apartments that you entered through an enclosed courtyard. It faced east and looked across a small park to the Jewish Old People's Home, and just down the street, also on Esplanade, was the Jewish People's Library, which served as a lively community centre for lectures and educational programs.

The staircase leading up to the Maza apartment was narrow and dark. Once inside, however, the front room was bright and colourful, the walls covered with paintings and the furniture draped in Eastern European embroideries and weavings. The furniture consisted of a small sofa and two mission-style oak chairs sternly upholstered in brown leather. There was a matching oak library table loaded with books, and more books were encased in glass on the shelves of an oak bookcase. A long skinny hallway led from the front room to the kitchen past two bedrooms that branched off to one side. On the way to the kitchen, and before you reached it, there was a dining room with a round table in the middle, surrounded by chairs. There was also a sideboard, and what was probably the most important and most used piece of furniture in the house, something called a Winnipeg couch—but by Mrs Maza and her friends it was referred to as a lounge, and pronounced *lontch*. On this couch her husband took his Sunday afternoon naps, and in the evenings visiting poets and painters sat on it two or three abreast, listening to poetry being read out loud by one of them or, on occasion, trying out new ideas for publishing a magazine or a manifesto. Or else they discussed new books and gossiped. The reason they sat in the dining room instead of the front sitting room, I now realize, was that it was close to the kitchen, that universal, nonpareil source of food.

To these artists, most of them middle-aged and impecunious, and all of them immigrants, Mrs Maza was the eternal mother—the foodgiver and nourisher, the listener and solacer, the mediator between them and the world. There she would sit with hands folded into her sleeves, her face brooding and meditative, listening intently with all her body. As she listened she rocked back and forth, and, as it then seemed to me, she did so in time to the rhythm of the poem being read.

She gave herself entirely and attentively to the poem; she fed the spiritual hunger and yearning of these oddly assorted Yiddish writers whenever they needed her; but not only that. She also fed them real food, and not just once a week, but every day. She served endless cups of tea with lemon, jam, and sugar lumps, plates of fresh fruit, Jewish egg-cookies, home-made walnut strudel, and delicately veined marble cake. And for the really hungry there were bowls of barley soup, slices of rye bread thickly buttered, and eggs—countless eggs—boiled, omeletted, and scrambled. I never knew her to serve anyone, including her family, a conventional meal from beginning to end; but she was always making someone an egg or opening a can of salmon or slicing a tomato to go with a plate of pickled herring.

Who were these Yiddish writers and painters? Some were occasional visitors brought from New York or Israel to give a lecture in Montreal. If I ever knew their names I have forgotten most of them, but there is one writer I remember well. She was Kadya Molodovsky, a Yiddish poet from Warsaw living in New York. One of her poems, *Der Mantel* (*The Coat*) was read and loved by Jewish children everywhere. She had a mild European face that shone with blessedness.

One occasion I remember is Louis Muhlstock's coming to Mrs Maza's apartment to draw Kadya's portrait. He was very tall and thin with a mop of dark hair and an animated rosy face. He was a well-known painter even then, although he couldn't have been more than twenty-three or -four. He set up his easel in the front room, unrolled his paper, tacked it up, and in the most relaxed way began to draw and talk, talk and draw. Kadya talked too, and laughed, and told funny stories—and neither of them minded the awkward fifteen-year-old girl who sat there watching.

Of the poets who lived in Montreal and frequented Mrs Maza's salon, J.I. Segal was the most outstanding. He was a prolific writer, well known in the Yiddish literary world, and had already published many books. At the time I stayed with the Mazas, Segal was on the staff of the Yiddish newspaper *Der Keneder Adler* (*The Canadian Eagle*) and was also giving Yiddish lessons to children. A number of other poets also frequented Mrs Maza's. Moshe Shaffir, Shabsi Perl, Esther Segal—the sister of J.I. Segal—N.J. Gottlieb, Yudika (Judith Tzik), and one or two other women poets. Some of the writers worked in factories and lived lonely lives in rooming houses. One of them wrote a poem with an image that has stayed with me to this day. He likened his heart to the jumbled untidiness of an unmade bed. At the time I thought the metaphor with its image of the unmade bed was so weird that I remembered it for its absurdity.

But since it has stayed in my mind for more than fifty years it can't really have been so absurd. The more I think about it, the more it seems to epitomize and sum up the essence of poverty with all its disorder and loneliness.

The image must have also touched a sensitive spot in my own unconscious, and that was my ambivalence about my parents' generation of immigrant Jews. At that time I bitterly resented my difference from my Canadian friends whose parents had been born in Canada of English background, and who spoke without an accent. How could it have been otherwise? Canadian society during the twenties and thirties brainwashed every schoolchild with British Empire slogans, and promoted a negative stereotype of all eastern European immigrants, but especially of Jews. Moreover, during all my primary-school years, the phrase 'dirty Jew' had regularly been hurled at me from the street corners and back alleys of North Winnipeg. Later, when I attended Lisgar Collegiate in Ottawa, I also sensed a certain disdain directed towards Jews, a disdain equalled only by that felt for French-Canadians in those days. Perhaps it was no accident that the girl who became my bosom friend was French. She was also from a minority within her social group because her parents were that rare thing, French-speaking Protestants. Her mother came from an old clerical Huguenot family in France and her father was the son of a well-to-do converted Catholic who had quarrelled with the priest in his small Quebec village.

I was not very conscious in those adolescent years of the nature and source of my ambivalences and conflicts—but they manifested themselves in vague feelings of uneasiness and guilt and an awkward sense of always being a stranger in both worlds and not belonging fully to either. Ambivalence, I now realize, also tinged my admiration and fondness for Mrs Maza and her circle. I often felt uneasy at what I thought of as their exaggerated feelings, or at any rate, their exaggerated expression of those feelings.

I didn't see Mrs Maza only when I visited Montreal on school holidays. For several years our families spent part of each summer together near St. Sauveur in the Laurentians. The Mazas would rent an old farmhouse, and my parents would camp somewhere not far away. Mrs Maza loved the gentle contours of the mountains and the way the changing light continually moved up and down their slopes. And there was always a little river—hardly more than a creek—in the neighbourhood of her house. It was good for wading in the shallows, but we children wanted to be near a lake where we could swim. Failing that, we had to amuse ourselves by hunting for mushroom puffballs in the farmer's pasture or climbing up the mountain to pick raspberries.

Sometimes I would wander over to the Mazas' house at four o'clock when the humming heat hung over the afternoon, and would find Mrs Maza sitting alone on the veranda, her hands folded into her sleeves—she always wore long sleeves, even in summer—rocking back and forth and looking sad. I remember asking her once why she was so sad. She answered in her slow, musical voice, making every word count, that today was the anniversary of Jacob Wasserman's death. Thanks to her I already knew who he was, and under her tutelage had read *The Maurizius Case, The Goose Girl*, and *Dr. Kerkhoven's Third Existence*. There wasn't much I could say, so I sat there dumb as a stone, watching the bees alight on the blue chicory flowers beside the veranda, listening to her as she dramatized Wasserman's unhappy life and mourned for him in sad funereal tones.

And he wasn't the only writer whose anniversary of death she observed; there was Edna St. Vincent Millay, Elinor Wylie, Sara Teasdale, and a long roll call of dead Yiddish writers. She mourned them all, and recounted their tragic lives as well as their artistic triumphs in spite of adversity. She would often read me passages from their work, and sometimes she would ask to see my poems and read them back to me, analyzing and praising and prophesying a good future.

When I think back to those summer afternoons on her veranda—actually it was a low open balcony in the French-Canadian style—I can still picture her rocking and keening. She radiated a sibylline and mystical quality, and possibly that was the secret of the magnetism that drew so many artists to her Esplanade apartment.

My parents, in spite of their unquestionable identification with Jewishness, were not observant of rituals and never went to synagogue. When it came time for the high holidays, Rosh Hashanah and Yom Kippur, my parents, the Mazas, and two or three other families all converged upon a farmer's house near St. Sauveur—the Lamoureux place. There we stayed for a week or ten days enjoying continual harvest pleasures. Mme Lamoureux set a long table with huge bowls of food: soup, chicken, beef, vegetables—raw and cooked—apple and blueberry pies, and homegrown Lamoureux pears, apples, and plums. Everyone heaped his or her own plate at these country feasts. And I have no doubt that the grownups, as they strolled along the gravel roads, gave thought in their own way to the year past and the year still to come.

The Lamoureux are long dead and their farm is no longer a landmark. It was long ago absorbed by modernism and the autoroute to the Laurentians. And Mrs Maza is no longer alive to mark and mourn the anniversaries of the death of her favourite writers or the loss of the Lamoureux farm with its harvest bounties that were so happily shared by a group of friends. But they are still alive and present in my mind, and they keep me company whenever I watch the light change on mountains or pick wild raspberries in some overgrown ditch. Somewhere Mrs Maza is still urging hungry poets to have a bite to eat, and turning on the light in her dining room to illuminate a crowd of displaced Yiddish writers. And behind them stretches a larger crowd, the long procession of every writer who ever wrote in whatever language. No matter. Each one paid his individual tribute to the love of language and to its inexhaustible resources. And their traces still linger, marking out the path for all writers still to come.

Learning to be a Diaspora Jew through the Israel Experience

FAYDRA L. SHAPIRO

I definitely notice a change [in how I feel about Israel] because I love it here . . . The land here is beautiful. The views, the sunsets . . . I used to feel, like Israel, whatever. Israel, Florida, Mexico, whatever. Definitely nothing special. Nothing special would happen when I talked about Israel, and now there is . . . a connection to Israel. (A 23-year-old participant of an Israel Experience Program)

In scholarly theorizing about diaspora, the Jewish experience of displacement from the land of Israel and the dispersal of the community to multiple locations tend to be held up as the paradigmatic examples. According to William Safran (1991), the Jewish diaspora experience is the "ideal type" against which other diasporic claims should be measured. At first glance, an attachment to Israel appears to be a cornerstone of North American Jewish life, while an analysis of public American Jewish life gives the impression that Israel plays a central role in contemporary Jewish identity. However, Steven Cohen (1991) asserts that, contrary to this public impression, Israel remains largely peripheral in the private religious sphere for most American Jews. Cohen argues that while support for Israel is a focal point of public Jewish life in America and, though pro-Israelism is part of the American Jewish understanding of what it means to be a Jew, that relationship to Israel is often very superficial, particularly among Jews with moderate to low levels of affiliation with the Jewish community. Israel, a country whose existence is perceived to be of vital importance and whose image is hotly defended publicly in the Jewish community, does not function as a sacred centre for many North American Jews. Equally, most American Jews know nothing of the centrality of the land of Israel in the Jewish religious tradition. The tie that binds most American Jews to Israel is neither emotional nor religious, but is based on a practical, political concern for the security of world Jewry (Eisen 1986b; Liebman and Cohen 1990).

In contemporary usage, the term "diaspora Jewry" commonly refers to Jews living in communities outside the state of Israel, the largest of which is in the United States. Technically, this might be a correct appellation. But does the mainstream of North American Jewry really possess the double consciousness of diaspora life, the profound attachment to a prior home, the serious ambivalence about life outside of Israel that one expects from the term "diaspora"? To address these issues, we need to move beyond objective categorizations of what constitutes diaspora and pay attention to the nuance of subjective, lived experience. Such attention permits us the possibility of assessing the depth of diasporic consciousness among North American Jews, as well as its development and maintenance. James Clifford notes that "[t]he language of diaspora is increasingly invoked by displaced people who feel (maintain, revive, invent) a connection with a prior home. This sense of connection must be strong enough to resist erasure through the normalizing processes of forgetting, assimilating and distancing" (1997: 255). This article illustrates the process of creating/remembering that emotional and religious connection to the land of Israel among young North American Jews who take part in an Israel Experience Program.

The invention of the modern Jewish attachment to Palestine has relied on a variety of techniques. Modern Jewish historiography focused, until recently, on the intellectual appeal of the various Zionist thinkers, such as Theodor Herzl and Ahad Ha'am. More recent historical writing has emphasized the emotional connections that can be fostered by rituals (e.g. modern pilgrimages and tourism) as well as by images of Palestine. Here, Mr. Leib Goldsmith of Edmonton has bought a piece of the dream of Palestine as the new pastoral reality for Jewish men, women and children, as depicted in the image of this certificate of the Jewish National Fund, dated 1914. The Jewish National Fund raised money from diaspora Jews to buy and develop lands for Jews in Palestine.
IMAGE COURTESY OF THE JEWISH ARCHIVES AND HISTORICAL SOCIETY OF EDMONTON AND NORTHERN ALBERTA.

Israel Experience Programs have emerged as a popular rite of passage for thousands of young North American Jews. The organized Jewish community has poured money and resources into these programs, hopeful that such programs will help to stem the tide of assimilation and culture loss perceived to be assailing Jewish youth. One of the most established of these programs has been showing Israel to young Jews from North America for twenty years. *Livnot U'Lehibanot* (to build and to be built) is a three-month, work-study program designed for Jews in their 20s who possess "weak" Jewish backgrounds and education.[1] The program combines Jewish studies, hiking and manual labour, to teach participants about what the religiously observant staff call "traditional" Judaism. This article is particularly concerned with the presentation of the land of Israel to participants who arrive with little connection to Israel or knowledge about it, and the effects of creating that attachment to Israel as the Jewish homeland for the study of diasporas and diaspora consciousness.

In ethnographic terms, I wanted to make sense of a disconcerting fieldwork situation. What did it mean to be standing in Israel with a group of young North American Jews who possessed little knowledge about, identification or involvement with Israel or Judaism, singing: "My place is the land of Israel"? How could Israel have become such an important place for them?

The findings in this article are grounded in fieldwork that took place in several places and over several periods. In Israel, I engaged in participant-observation at *Livnot* and interviewed participants during the summer program of 1996 and the fall of 1997. I also interviewed past participants in Israel, Toronto, New York and San Francisco. The length of time that had passed since they took part in *Livnot* varied with individual alumni with whom I spoke. A total of sixty-eight *Livnot* participants, past participants and staff members were interviewed. Except for Barb, who was at *Livnot* in 1995, all the people quoted below were in the program in 1997.

As will be demonstrated, it is through the process of *Livnot* that Judaism becomes (re-)territorialized for participants, and, correspondingly, participants as residents of North America, become (re-)diasporized. While it is possible that the biological ancestors of *Livnot* participants were among those who left Palestine almost 2,000 years ago, the idea of diaspora expresses more than simply displacement. Rather then just a neutral term of location, "diaspora" is a loaded label that suggests periphery, and necessarily implies an organic, original, more authentic sense of rootedness in a centre elsewhere. Without a deep sense of attachment to another place, diaspora is simply an empty technical term that connotes nothing more than the physical location of a community in a place other than where it had been previously. Diaspora necessarily suggests a doubled relationship or dual loyalty toward places, that assumes some connection to the location currently inhabited, alongside a continued involvement with and relationship to "back home" (Clifford 1997; Lavie and Swedenburg 1996). Through

learning about and experiencing the territorialization of Judaism and its grounding in the land of Israel, *Livnot* participants as North American Jews, become
"diasporized." Through this (re-)centring of Israel from vague space to holy
place, participants are transformed not only from tourists to potential pilgrims,
but, paradoxically, into diaspora Jews.

One might wonder why these young North American Jews choose to go
to Israel rather than somewhere else, if they feel no particular attachment to the
country. In fact, participants travel to Israel to take part in this work-study program for all kinds of mundane reasons, none of which suggest any deep emotional connection to an alternative homeland or religious attachment to an historical sacred centre. It is a relatively inexpensive, structured, family-supported
distraction from their regular lives. Many *Livnot*ers come to Israel seeking little more than a change from the routine at home; they are often between jobs,
dissatisfied in temporary jobs, taking a year off from school, unemployed
recent graduates or college students on summer holidays. *Livnot* also appeals to
participants' desire to travel in a way that they perceive to be authentic and not
"touristy," allowing them (as they see it) to live in another culture rather than
simply tour a country.

In the case of one participant, Barb, Israel was a second choice. Her original plan was on go to India, but her parents encouraged her to go to Israel
instead. Barb herself had never really considered Israel as a possible destination
before going to *Livnot*.

> I was going to go to India when I graduated from universi-
> ty. I was taking a year and nobody wanted to travel at that
> point or had the money to go for a whole year, so I decid-
> ed fine I'm going on my own. What the hell, everybody
> goes to India. And my parents were like "You've never been
> to Israel." . . . I never had a desire to go to Israel; I guess
> until I was ready to do it. So I contemplated their sugges-
> tion. It took me a couple of months and I thought, "Why
> not? Let's give it a shot." So I decided to go to Israel.

Like Barb, and many other *Livnot* participants, Laura had no active urge to visit Israel. Rather, she wanted a temporary change from her life, which she felt had stalled. She thought that the *Livnot* program offered a good chance to try something different and exciting by going to Israel.

> I figured this was a good point in my life. I was at a stand-still as far as work and school and where I wanted to be in the future, and I'm not too settled in my ways. So I thought it would be a good time to come here and do a program like this.

While Israel was perhaps perceived by participants as somehow different from other countries by virtue of its Jewish character, for most participants in my research sample, Israel was neither a particularly meaningful nor symbolic destination prior to their involvement with *Livnot*. More distant space than holy place, Israel represented a country toward which participants tended to feel more abstract pride than religious reverence before the program. However, during the program, participants experienced an Israel seen through the lens offered by *Livnot U'Lehibanot* and came to assign the religious meaning and personal relevance to the country that transform it from vague space into holy place, any land into homeland.

The main campus of *Livnot* is located in the old city of Tzfat, a small town in northern Israel. For three months, participants enjoy living in a pictur-esque mountaintop location. Tzfat's winding alleys, restricted motor traffic, reli-giosity and isolation from urban Israel envelop the old city in a distinctly quaint, other-worldly aura that is in keeping with the town's role in the historical devel-opment of Jewish mysticism. Thus, most of regular program life transpires in an environment that is distinctly out of the ordinary for Israel, but one that partic-ipants come to view as the norm.

Among the most popular features of the program are the weekly day-long nature hikes (*tiyulim*) that take participants to see another non-urban side of Israel. There is also a three-day "sea to sea" (Galilee to the Mediterranean) hike across the country. Hiking has always played an important role in Zionist education. It is encouraged as a way of strengthening one's love for the land (*ahavat ha'aretz*) through the development of an experiential knowledge of the land (*yediat ha'aretz*) (Katriel 1995: 6). The Zionist practice of hiking the land has its roots in German youth movement culture, and in groups such as the *Wandervögel* and the German Jewish youth association, *Blau Weiss,* which encouraged rambling as a way to experience nature and as an expression of their high respect for physical activity.

These weekly *tiyulim* at *Livnot* offer participants an opportunity to learn about the land of Israel through intensive immersion in it—walking the land, eating from its vegetation and swimming in its rivers. These hikes focus on learning about nature and on experiencing Israel through its trees, birds and animals, themes that resonate deeply among environmentally conscious North American youth. Through hiking in scenic, isolated nature reserves or remote parts of the Galilee and the Golan Heights, *Livnot* constructs a picture of Israel that is characterized by rugged rural landscapes and endowed with tremendous natural beauty. Just as extensive time in Tzfat offers a romantic, small-town portrait of Israel, hiking offers an Israel whose essence and meaning can be located in its physical landscape. Together, they manage to create an experience that avoids the many elements of contemporary urban Israeli life that would not appeal to participants.

It is particularly through the weekly hikes that participants are extended a mythical view of the land, as they learn about the relationships between nature and Judaism, between Israel's agricultural cycle and the holiday cycle or between carob trees and creation. Participants come to develop a strong sense that compared to other countries there is something inherently different about the physical land of Israel. Another young woman, Fern, expressed a similar sentiment, echoed by many participants:

> It's really weird thinking about going back to the States and going out to some random mountain. The land [of Israel] is different. It's just different. There are beautiful places in the world. There are beautiful places in the States. I feel like saying that there's something that does truly feel holy about

it [Israel], but it seems too cliché. The land here is so deep, it's just so deep . . . The trees are deep . . . It's so connected. I just don't see the United States like that. I don't see Canada like that. I don't see anywhere else in the world like that. Nowhere. It's so deep, it's so symbolic. And the reason why it's so powerful, that whole feeling is that it's who I am. It's not just that I'm an American [and] therefore I connect with Montana. It's different and I understand that now. Whereas before I thought I could connect as much with Montana, or should connect, as much with Montana as an American, as with the land of Israel.

Livnot participants are encouraged to understand their walking the land as developing for themselves a sense of belonging and connection to Israel, through marking territory and signifying ownership. In the classroom, they learn about the talmudic teaching that "if one walks the length and breadth of a parcel of land which he has purchased, he thereby takes formal possession of it" (*Bava Batra* 100a). Through participants' extensive hiking of Israel, the land becomes perceived as "theirs." No longer simply an abstract concept, nor just another location far from home, Israel is transformed into a place that belongs to participants by virtue of their Jewishness and the impression of their footsteps. Equally, Israel is presented as a country that has been marked with the presence of Jews throughout history, and is ready to be similarly marked by the presence of *Livnot* participants. In a discussion of another talmudic text that states "anyone who walks four cubits in the land of Israel is assured a portion in the World to Come" (*Ketubot* 111a), it was explained to participants by one of the program's education directors that

Rabbi Yochanan said that when you walk four cubits in the land of Israel, you have basically marked off your personal space. You have, in some kind of abstract sense, written with your feet "Kilroy was here." You know, that famous ancient graffiti? "Kilroy was here in the land of Israel." You

can't read it. You look at the stones, and you can't see that
it says "Kilroy was here" on the stones. But it does . . .
Jewishly speaking, by walking the land, one establishes
one's presence in the land.

Through *Livnot*, Israel is also presented to participants as the land of
Jewish history and ancestors. The biblical patriarchs Abraham, Isaac and
Jacob, the prophetess Devorah, the first-century martyrs at Gamla and the sec-
ond-century revolutionary Bar Kochba are all figures that populate the Israel
of *Livnot* hikes. *Livnot* offers participants the land of the Bible and historic
legends, the setting for the dramatic heroes and tragic defeats of the Jewish
past. This creation of a link between Israel and participants' ancestors is regularly reinforced on hikes that stop at sites deemed to possess historical
significance. This portrait of the nation is one that studiously ignores the
Israel of urban blight, development town poverty and materialist longings for
American consumer products.

As the symbolically potent "land of our ancestors," rather than a modern
nation-state, the physical land of Israel, together with its plants and animals, is
rendered uniquely meaningful to participants. This construction of Israel
prompted Tamara to note:

I'm intrigued by learning about the trees and realizing they
supported my ancestors and how they can support me too,
with life, with fruit, with shade, with animals. Knowing
that every footstep I took, is a footstep that Abraham, Isaac
or Jacob might have taken, makes hiking in Israel a more
intense experience than anywhere else in the world.

The portrait of Israel that is painted by *Livnot* is clearly one that is highly selective, owing to both active constructions and features that are absent.
Contemporary Israel as a modern state is encountered only abstractly in the
classroom or through brief discussions of the daily news. Participants are not led
to experience modern Israel anywhere near the degree to which they experience

the historical and mythical aspects of the land. *Livnot* avoids dealing with the modern state of Israel (*medinat Yisrael*), with its modern problems and dilemmas, in favour of the mythical, trans-historical, biblically based *eretz Yisrael* (land of Israel).

For participants of *Livnot*, contemporary Israel is either obscured or it is idealized as a unified and homogeneous Jewish country. The Israel constructed by *Livnot* is one that is significantly unmarked by secular-religious divisions and violence. Through *Livnot's* construction, participants come to understand Israel primarily as a Jewish country that offers a unique freedom to express one's Jewishness in public. This perception of Israel as offering an exceptionally free place to be Jewish can both result from and lead to a deeply romantic view of Jewishness in Israel, ignoring, as it does, the concerns of secular Israelis about religious coercion. Many participants, none of them sabbath-observant, expressed their joy at being in a place where "everything" shuts down on *shabbat,* from stores and restaurants to public buses, a situation that is more true of Tzfat than other places in the country. Of course, *Livnot* is not itself responsible for creating these diverse ways of being Jewish in Israeli society. But by completely avoiding the issue of secular Jews and their concerns about religious coercion in Israel, *Livnot* can help to foster the misleading notion that *shabbat* closures are uncontested. A number of participants were enthusiastic about the idea of being Jewish in what they perceive to be a society in which Judaism is a shared, common feature of life. Steven's suggestion that "everybody's on the same page" when it comes to Judaism in Israel is undeniably romantic.

> It's just the strangest feeling. I take it for granted now. That everyone's Jewish. No one really questions anyone about what they're doing . . . Everybody's on the same page and everybody understands what's going on. Everything shuts down on Saturday. It just shuts down. Everybody deals with it, they understand it.

Similarly, *Livnot* offers a radically depoliticized Israel. In each three-month *Livnot* program, participants spend one *shabbat* in a Jewish settlement on the

West Bank. Although this event is optional, participants are given no information about why some people might choose not to participate. According to one staff member, the aim of the settlement *shabbat* is to counter what he sees as a "vilification, or even demonization in the American Jewish public's eyes" of settlements in the Occupied Territories. Participants are sent to carefully chosen settlements that are both physically and politically safe, most often located close to Jerusalem. In this way, *Livnot* fosters the impression that Jewish settlements, whose presence in the West Bank is a hotly contested national and international issue, are really just misunderstood suburbs. The settlement *shabbat* serves to "declaw" the settlement issue and to turn it into a non-issue. To avoid ideological tensions for participants, *Livnot* deliberately places them for *shabbat* with families that are not political extremists. This decision also contributes to presenting the settlement movement as a group of people who simply want to escape big-city Israel, with little in the way of ideological motivation or moral and political consequences. For *Livnot* participants, settlers are often viewed as just regular families living in small communities. Some participants are simply bored by the settlements, finding the experience banal, and conclude that the experience was the same as celebrating *shabbat* anywhere in Israel. Others view the settlements simply as a safe, community-oriented escape from big-city life. The notion, however, that the settlements are nothing out of the ordinary, that the West Bank is just like any other part of Israel and that the settlements are not political, is clearly a highly political conclusion and one that carries significant implications.

Regardless of the picture of Israel painted by *Livnot*, there are various aspects of the "other" Israel outside *Livnot* that participants do encounter on their three free weekends during the program. The disjuncture between the Israel participants' experience at *Livnot* and the one they discover during their travels often leads to surprise, dislike and confusion. Nonetheless, even by the end of the program, many participants know nothing about secular Jews in Israel and their often acrimonious relationships with religious Jews. Hannah's visit to a secular *kibbutz* was an unpleasant experience for her, awakening her to the fact that not all Israeli Jews are as positively inclined toward Judaism as she had expected. Hannah's surprise was coupled with extreme disapproval, which included the suggestion that secular Jews should not live in Israel.

> I have very negative issues about the secular society and
> how they're just, to me, I just perceive it as anti-religion.
> *Don't be here if that's how you are.* That's my personal feel-
> ing on it. I didn't know it was like that I knew that every-
> one wasn't religious, but I didn't know that there were peo-
> ple who would actually refuse to do Jewish things. That
> people would go out of their way to be as un-Jewish as pos-
> sible in a Jewish country . . . The main place I saw it was
> when I saw my brother at his *kibbutz.* Someone said that
> the bar was open on Friday night and I said, "Really? On
> *shabbat?*" And she was like "Oh, we don't do that here." . . .
> It was really disturbing.

The *Livnot U'Lehibanot* experience does not tend to make ardent political Zionists out of uncommitted North American Jews. This lack of basic
engagement with Israeli or Zionist history made it possible for a participant at
the end of a program to ask a teacher who David Ben-Gurion was. His question, posed most seriously, was supported by group murmurings of equal confusion. As the first prime minister of Israel and a figure instrumental in the creation of the state, awareness of his identity constitutes extremely fundamental
knowledge about the contemporary political entity of Israel. Marni was per-
plexed by feeling a lack of any emotional attachment to contemporary Zionism
and the state, which she contrasted to her strong sense of connection to biblical, ancient Israel.

> I feel an intense connection with Tzfat and this place and
> *Livnot* and the land that I walked over. But Israel as an
> entity and what it stands for, I still have a lot of issues
> clouding my mind about it. The whole aspect of Zionism.
> So feeling connected in that sense, I don't get it. I get the
> biblical connection, I really do. I get that and I feel it and
> I'm so amazed with it. It's a really beautiful thing to me . . .

Certainly the hikes and the hike to Gamla really affected me. Touching the flint. Walking across the land in three days. Being in the desert affected me profoundly. That was a whole unique, amazing, wordless experience unto itself. Being in the desert I really did connect with the biblical sense out there and felt its power. It was more through the *tiyuls* than anything that I got that. As far as Zionism and the State of Israel, that was more in class, but I didn't get the connectedness. I didn't get it. I still don't get it.

As illustrated, it is particularly through their weekly hikes and, to a lesser degree, in the classroom, that participants at *Livnot* experience an Israel that is deeply meaningful, marked with the presence of ancestors, inherently Jewish in nature and society, apolitical and rural-Israel becomes a "homeland" that belongs to them as Jews. The *Livnot* construction of Israel is a portrait that tends to ignore both contemporary and troubling aspects of the state, focussing rather on romantic, heroic or tragic events that possess a strong emotional appeal. *Livnot*'s construction is grounded in the concept of *eretz Yisrael,* the land of Israel, instead of developing a relationship with or understanding of *medinat Yisrael,* the state of Israel. *Livnot* encourages the development of a personal, religious, symbolic relationship between participants and "their ancestral land," rather than a nationalist connection to the political entity of the contemporary Israeli state.

This construction of Israel is highly selective, idealistic and deeply romantic. In many ways, it is precisely the selectivity of the portrait that makes it compelling to a young North American audience that is imbued with particular ecological sensitivities. In contemporary North America, the sense of being indigenous or otherwise rooted in one's "native" soil is "powerfully heroized" (Malkki 1997: 59), a phenomenon that Lowenthal labels the "mystique of native antiquity" (1996: 183). Equally, the "new strands of 'green politics' that literally sacralize the fusion of people, culture and soil on 'Mother Earth'" (Malkki 1997: 60) serve to romanticize and valorize the grounding of people and cultures in what is conceived of as their natural place. *Livnot* participants are often environmentally aware, sensitive to the land claims of indigenous groups in North America and deeply interested in nature. An Israel that appeals to participants' own desires to be indigenous, and that does so in a way that is natural, rural and spiritually significant, is powerfully attractive to them.

For many North American Jews, the complicated relationships between historical and political factors such as immigration, Anglo-conformity, the demands for allegiance by the modern nation-state, Western education and assimilation, have caused their sense of personal or religious connection to Israel as a "homeland" to become "erased and forgotten" (Clifford 1997: 255). At the same time, the perception that North America provides an equality of opportunity and religious freedom unheard of in other diasporic communities ensures that there are few factors inspiring Jews in North America to dream of a utopian, safer, more complete Jewish life in the land of Israel.

Even though "echoes of Israel" might still be heard in common Jewish rituals, such as the breaking of a glass at the wedding ceremony to recall the destruction of the Temple, that meaning, Cohen asserts, "is probably lost on most members of the wedding party" (1991: 124). I would argue that even if the members of the wedding party shared an intellectual understanding of the traditional rationale behind the practice of shattering the glass, most contemporary North American Jews would not possess the emotional connection, the deep attachment to the land of Israel, that would imbue such a gesture with meaning. It is precisely the feeling of a spiritual, emotional bond to the land of Israel that most moderately affiliated North American Jews lack, and which *Livnot* encourages participants to develop. *Livnot* allows North American Jews to feel that Israel possesses some inherent, religious meaning, value and significance beyond simply its political importance as a modern nation-state.

Jewish understandings of the land of Israel, its role, importance, requirements and implications have changed significantly according to period, place and historical circumstances. Nonetheless, for almost 2,000 years, until the creation of the contemporary state of Israel, the idea of the *land* of Israel functioned as an integral part of Judaism (Elazar 1986: 215). Much-yearned for in religious imagination, Israel was an abstract, spiritualized, mythologized construct that possessed little grounding in earthly reality or in the actual situation of Palestine of the time (Eisen 1986a: 52–53; Liebman and Cohen 1990: 68). In traditional Jewish thought, *eretz Yisrael* functions at least as much as a moral, spiritual destination as it is a topographic entity (Malkki 1997: 66). Religious tradition suggests that the physical city of Jerusalem is an imperfect, lower or earthly expression of an ideal, heavenly or upper Jerusalem (see *Ta'anit* 5a; *Hagigah* 12b). The goal of return to the idealized land of Israel, regardless of how spiritualized and future-oriented, has formed a central part of the Jewish experience until the modern era. It is easy—and some might say desirable—to imagine a Judaism without the modern nation-state of Israel. But it is impossible to imagine Judaism without the love of the mythic, ancestral land of Israel. It is in this sense, then, that the symbolic, romanticized, religious Israel displayed by *Livnot* is extremely powerful, allowing these disaffiliated, alienated or poorly educated Jews to tap into a powerful historical sense of longing for a utopic Israel that can never be fully realized.

As one might imagine, this emotional attachment to Israel, based on a selective, idealistic portrait of the country, also creates serious problems for participants. A systematic discussion of the lasting effects of *Livnot*'s construction of Israel is beyond the scope of this article. On the one hand, *Livnot* transforms participants into "diaspora Jews" who are consciously, acutely aware of living outside Israel upon their return to North America. But the program can also function to alienate participants from contemporary Israel. Participants told me many painful, conflicted stories about encountering the "real" Israel.

Yet fantasy and idealism are the life-blood of diaspora. It is often easier to dream of a lost homeland that one does not actually have to live in. Diaspora is a rich concept that resonates with the loss and yearning that requires an emotional attachment to an elsewhere, however real or imagined. It is a condition that can fuel prayer, political activism and poetry, and it is an idea that can become only impoverished if used to indicate little more than where one is or is not geographically located. To label unaffiliated, alienated North American Jews with little information about or attachment to Israel "diaspora Jews" illustrates only a superficial fraction of diaspora realities. However, the experience of Israel through *Livnot U'Lehibanot* transforms participants' spiritual and emotional relationships to "the homeland" and deepens their diaspora on return to North America. Rather than simply creating future immigrants or philanthropic supporters of Israel, *Livnot* achieves something far more subtle. The program makes the "traditional," religiously meaningful concept of Israel and the longing for it a palpable, plausible possibility for participants. In so doing, *Livnot*'s construction of Israel allows its audience to participate in a mainstay of Jewish tradition: the yearning for an idealized land of Israel, a romantic attachment to "the land of our ancestors" and an Israel that has profound emotional, and even religious significance.

NOTE

1   The three-month *Livnot* program in Tzfat is the "classic" *Livnot* experience. Several years ago, a campus was opened in Jerusalem where condensed, three-week programs were offered. Because of recent funding from a program called "Birthright Israel," shorter programs are now encouraged and offered.

REFERENCES

Clifford, James

   1997 "Diasporas." In James Clifford, *Routes: Travel and Translation in the Late Twentieth Century*, 244–77. Cambridge, MA: Harvard University Press.

Cohen, Steven

   1991 "Israel in the Jewish identity of American Jews: A study in dualities and contrasts." In David Gordis and Yoav Ben-Horin (eds.), *Jewish Identity in America*, 119–36. Los Angeles: Wilstein Institute.

Eisen, Arnold

   1986a *Galut: Modern Jewish Reflection on Homelessness and Homecoming*. Bloomington: Indiana University Press.

   1986b "Off center: The concept of the land of Israel in modern Jewish thought." In Lawrence Hoffman (ed.), *The Land of Israel: Jewish Perspectives*, 263–97. Notre Dame: University of Notre Dame Press.

Elazar, Daniel

   1986 "The Jewish people as the classic diaspora: A political analysis." In Gabriel Sheffer (ed.), *Modern Diasporas in International Politics*. London: Croom Helm.

Katriel, Tamar

   1995 "Touring the land: Trips and hiking as secular pilgrimages in Israeli culture." *Jewish Folklore and Ethnology Review* 17, 1–2: 6–13.

Lavie, Smadar and Ted Swedenburg, eds.

   1996 *Displacement, Diaspora, and Geographies of Identity*. Durham, NC: Duke University Press.

Liebman, Charles and Steven Cohen

    1990 *Two Worlds of Judaism: The Israeli and American Experiences.* New Haven: Yale University Press.

Lowenthal, David

    1996 *The Heritage Crusade and the Spoils of History.* London: Viking.

Malkki, Liisa

    1997 "National geographic: The rooting of peoples and the territorialization of national identity among scholars and refugees." In A. Gupta and J. Ferguson (eds.), *Culture, Power, Place: Explorations in Critical Anthropology,* 52–74. Durham, NC: Duke University Press.

Safran, William

    1991 "Diasporas in modern societies." *Diaspora* 1: 83–99.

Red Star Over Birobidzhan: Canadian Jewish Communists and the "Jewish Autonomous Region" in the Soviet Union

Henry Srebrnik

The Jewish Communist movement, active within the Canadian Jewish community for some three decades, included various groups whose main aim was to
provide support for the Soviet project to establish a Jewish socialist republic in
the Birobidzhan region in the eastern USSR. One of these groups, the
Organization for Jewish Colonization in Russia (*Yidishe Kolonizatsye
Organizatsye in Rusland*), known by its transliterated acronym as the ICOR, was
founded in the United States in 1924, and was also active within the Canadian
immigrant working-class milieu; its members were mainly first and second generation Yiddish-speaking Jews of east European origin.

Little has been published about the ICOR in the US, and even less is
known about its Canadian counterpart. Erna Paris, who devotes three chapters

to the Canadian Jewish Communist movement in her book *Jews: An Account of Their Experience in Canada,* has one passing reference to the ICOR, though Gerald Tulchinsky, in his *Branching Out: The Transformation of the Canadian Jewish Community,* does devote over two pages to it.[1] Other histories of the Communist movement or the Canadian Jewish community ignore it altogether. This research note is therefore very much a preliminary undertaking; there remains much "digging" still to be done.

In the years following the Bolshevik Revolution, the Soviet regime decided to set aside specific territory for those Jews who wished to build a collective Jewish socialist life. Two agencies were created to settle Jews on the land: the Commission for the Settlement of Jewish Toilers on the Land (KOMZET in Russian, KOMERD in Yiddish), a government body; and the Association for the Settlement of Jewish Toilers on the Land (OZET in Russian, GEZERO in Yiddish). On 28 March 1928, the Soviet government approved the choice of Birobidzhan, a sparsely populated area of 14,000 square miles in the Soviet far east, as a national Jewish unit. On 7 May 1934, in an effort to make the project more attractive to Soviet Jews, Moscow declared Birobidzhan a Jewish Autonomous Region (Oblast), with the promise that when Jews would number at least 100,000, or form a majority of the total population, it would become a Soviet republic.[2]

Many Jews in Canada during this period gave support to the Soviet Union, and became involved, either as members or sympathizers, with the Communist Party of Canada (CPC). Founded in 1921, the CPC by 1927 had formed a Jewish section, with members in Montreal, Toronto, and Winnipeg.[3] Historian David Rome asserted that the Jewish group was the most vital faction in the Canadian Communist movement: "It was a total society with its own political and cultural institutes."[4] The Jewish Communists, in particular, felt duty-bound to "counteract the nationalist, imperialist Zionist movement" by demonstrating that the Soviet Union had "the only true and sensible solution" to the "national question."[5]

The Comintern had directed Communists to create mass organizations that would unite people who were not necessarily Communists "in activities connected to the defense of the Soviet Union and the popularization of its achievements—particularly people who were pro-Soviet but not yet ready to join a Communist party."[6] Communists found such so-called front groups an effective means of attracting supporters for their causes; some who joined would eventually become full-fledged members. Less centralized and hierarchical than the CPC, fronts enabled the party to gain access to the broader community to further its goals. Although "nominally independent," they were "organized around single-issue or special-interest concerns, in which the Communists exercised effective organizational control."[7]

Hence, Communists active in the Jewish community encouraged the formation of mass organizations which would appeal to Jews interested in preserving their Jewish culture in non-Zionist ways and combat ethnic nationalism while harnessing feelings of Jewish identity with the class struggle. Canadian supporters of Birobidzhan were soon enough involved in the work of the ICOR, which by 1933, claimed a North American membership of 10,000, spread out over 165 branches in twenty-five states—and in ten cities in four Canadian provinces.[8]

Given the close proximity, geographic and cultural, of Canadian Jews to American Jews, the Canadian ICOR at first functioned as a section of the U.S.-based ICOR. Sam Lapides of Toronto, chair of the Jewish Bureau of the Communist Party of Canada, spoke at the March 1932 plenum of the ICOR national executive in New York. He told delegates that the ICOR in Canada had recently gathered much strength, despite the reactionary politics instituted in Canada—a reaction, he added, that benefitted Zionism.[9] The March 1934 plenum again noted the reactionary character of the Canadian Conservative government of R. B. Bennett; ICOR literature and speakers from the United States, considered Communists by Canadian authorities whether or not members of the party itself, were often denied entry to the country.[10] The sixth national ICOR convention, which gathered in New York 8–10 February, 1935, celebrated ten years of the ICOR. Included among the 565 delegates was a large contingent from the Canadian ICOR, headed by, among others, Harry Guralnick, editor of the Canadian Communist Yiddish newspaper, *Der Kampf,* and Toronto activist Abraham Nisnevitz, both members of the CPC. Guralnick promised that despite the political difficulties in Canada, the ICOR would gain hundreds of new members.[11]

Following two small conferences held by eastern Canadian branches in Montreal in 1932, the third conference of the Canadian section of the ICOR, in Toronto 10–11 March 1934, had brought together 56 delegates from 5 eastern Canadian cities. Abe Victor noted that the ICOR was still technically banned in Canada. Literature sent from the New York office was returned by the postal authorities and ICOR speakers from the U.S. were prevented from entering Canada at the border; sometimes ICOR gatherings were disrupted. When the Canadian Communist leader Rev. A. E. Smith, general secretary of the Canadian Labour Defence League, recently freed from jail, addressed the conference, it spontaneously broke out singing the "Internationale." Delegates vowed to make the ICOR a mass organization, one that could take action in defence of the Soviet Union and the battles against fascism and misleading Zionism.[12]

The conference decided that ICOR ought to begin publishing a periodical, and *Kanader "Icor,"* with Guralnick undertaking the editing duties, appeared in June 1934: the first issue, not surprisingly, carried as its lead story the decision made by the Soviet government the month before to transform Birobidzhan into a Jewish Autonomous Region.[13] An editorial entitled "An Important Step Forward" called the launching of the journal a sign of the ICOR's increasing relevance to the Jewish working class in Canada. It demonstrated that the organization was becoming strong enough to operate autonomously of the American ICOR and would be able to address the specific issues facing the pro-Soviet, anti-fascist, and anti-war Jewish masses in Canada. The ICOR would be more than just a "collection agency" or fund-raising organization.[14] Lapides asserted that the ICOR provided a home for those who had realized that the Soviet Union had abolished racial hatred and pogroms, and was now a country where hundreds of thousands of Jews worked alongside other nationalities in socialist industries and agricultural production. The ICOR served as an antidote to the "divide and conquer" tactics of the ruling class.[15]

According to an undated teller (probably written in the summer of 1934) from the executive of the Canadian section of the ICOR, the Canadian movement, headquartered at 414 Markham St., in Toronto, the home of the Labour League, claimed chapters in Toronto, Montreal, Winnipeg, Vancouver, Windsor, Hamilton, Cornwall, Ontario, Ottawa, the farming community of

Edenbridge, Saskatchewan, and the Niagara region of Ontario. There were also affiliates in Calgary, Edmonton, Regina, Saskatoon, London, Ontario, Kitchener, and Halifax.[16] The October 1934 issue of *Kanader "Icor"* announced that there were 5,000 ICOR members in Canada, with thousands more supporting socialist construction in Birobidzhan.[17]

Local ICOR committees were active across Canada that year and worked hard to raise money for goods and supplies; the Canadian section of the ICOR, in its first national campaign, was collecting money for two tractors for Birobidzhan on behalf of two activists who had recently died.[18] Abraham Shek, secretary of the Canadian section, noted that the 7 May 1934 declaration of Birobidzhan's Jewish status had resulted in celebrations in its honour throughout the entire country—though, he added, the ICOR had not done enough to publicize this incredibly important decision among others in the community. In Toronto, the establishment of Birobidzhan as an autonomous region had been celebrated at a concert and mass meeting on 27 May at the Labour Lyceum; 2,000 special leaflets were printed for the occasion.

Shek commended Montreal's ICOR committee for its excellent observance of the 7 May declaration. Hamilton celebrated the announcement of Birobidzhan autonomy with a concert on 20 May, featuring the *Frayhayt gezang farayn un mandolin orkester* from the Toronto Cultural Centre. There was a large turnout, despite calls for a boycott on the part of various rabbis and businessmen. The Winnipeg branch had been spearheading an anti-fascist campaign among the various Jewish organizations. When news of the Soviet decision making Birobidzhan a Jewish autonomous region was heard, it decided to immediately hold a celebration on 9 June and make it part of its anti-fascist work. Vancouver, too, had done exemplary work, especially on behalf of the tractor campaign. The branch members also greeted a Soviet ship when it docked in Vancouver harbour.[19]

The struggle against Zionism remained a major component of the ICOR's work: a "declaration of chairs of revolutionary mass organizations" reminded the "Jewish masses in Canada" that the "historic decision" to create a Jewish entity in Birobidzhan was "entirely different" from the "hot air" "*belfer-dekleratsye*" about "a 'Jewish homeland' in Palestine," which had been nothing but a wartime manoeuvre on the part of the British imperialist government.[20] The Zionist movement, wrote Moishe Feldman, was fascist and a tool of the Jewish bourgeoisie, maintained the ICOR, and had preceded even Hitler in its use of ultra-nationalist discourse. Zionist fascism was no better than any other; indeed it was the most dangerous enemy of the Jewish masses. Birobidzhan, on the other hand, remained the "great shining hope of the Jewish masses world-wide."[21] The time had come, contended Y. Trachimofsky, secretary of the Montreal ICOR, to carry forward the battle against Zionism: in Palestine, the Zionists were "appropriating the land and appropriating the work" of the Arabs. While the Zionists had become servants of British imperialism, the Arab mass-es were carrying on the struggle against it.[22] The creation of Birobidzhan was a "catastrophe" for the Zionists. It would serve as a "death blow" to their "adven-ture" in the so-called "Jewish homeland."[23] Readers of the *Kanader "Icor"* were reminded in 1936 that the Birobidzhan settlement "was no 'rival' to Palestine but rather a symbol and a message for the Jewish masses throughout the world, including Palestine."[24]

Nor did the Canadian Jewish Congress (CJC), re-established in 1934, escape the ICOR' s wrath. In its inaugural issue, the *Kanader "Icor"* castigated the Congress as the creation of the Jewish bourgeoisie, a means to control the masses and divert them from the path of revolution. The notion of "one Jewish people" was a fantasy that had been exposed by the realities of class conflict. Fortunately, the workers and impoverished masses of Jews would not allow themselves to be swayed by the "bigwigs" *("karpen-kep")* of the Congress, whose aim was to perpetuate the hegemony of the wealthy bosses and the religious "parasites" in the community, whose only aim was to keep the poor hungry and in darkness.[25]

For that reason, the ICOR in November 1934 sent speakers to western Canada to counter the anti-Soviet propaganda of the Zionists and the CJC.[26] On 29 January 1935, Professor Charles Kuntz, president of the ICOR in the United States, one of the speakers on the western tour, addressed a public meet-ing in the Peretz Hall in Winnipeg. It was such a success that hundreds of peo-ple had to be turned away for lack of accommodation. Kuntz described the eco-nomic progress being made in Birobidzhan and the increasing prosperity of the settlement. He also contended that Jews there "have lost their national clannish-ness and have welcomed into their midst people of other racial origin with whom they live like brothers."[27]

In 1935, the Canadian ICOR became a separate organization and held its first national convention in Toronto 24–25 March. The American ICOR activist and *Morgn Frayhayt* correspondent Gina Medem, widow of the Bundist Vladimir, and Joshua (Joe) Gershman of the CPC, were among the guest speak-ers. War and fascism were condemned and the delegates called for the "Jewish masses" in Canada to mobilize for the defence of the Soviet Union, which had "eliminated the bleak lack of rights which the Jews had experienced in tsarist Russia, abolished pogroms, anti-Semitism and in general every form of national oppression." The Soviet solution of the national question had justified the perse-verance of the ICOR'S members and had confirmed their position in defending the correct line of the Soviet Union. The convention also resolved to initiate a campaign for a "people's delegation" to visit the Soviet Union, an idea that would gain wide currency in American pro-Soviet Jewish movements a year later.[28]

Should the ICOR concern itself with domestic political concerns? Some members felt that as a "non-partisan" organization the ICOR ought not to get mixed up in political campaigns. But they were wrong, contended Sam Lipshitz, a member of the national executive. "We here in Canada wish to deliver the strongest death-blow against international fascism" and "we want to halt the spread of the fascist blaze in this country. To do this we must fight against every manifestation of fascist tendency, in whatever form it appears," he declared.

"Does the ICOR have its own interests in the [upcoming] election cam-paign? Of course! The Bennett government carries on a consistently anti-Soviet, imperialist, warmongering policy . . . . Our government carries on a policy in the country which leads to blatant fascism." Clearly, therefore, the ICOR had to take a stand and endorse the Communist candidates.[29] None of these won seats in the October 1935 federal election, but the victorious Liberals did rescind Section 98 of the Criminal Code, which had effectively made illegal the Communist Party and groups such as the ICOR.

The Canadian ICOR was second to none in its praise of the USSR. Calling on Jews to ready themselves to celebrate the anniversary of the Bolshevik revolution, *Kanader "Icor,"* in October 1935, noted that during the past 18 years Soviet Jews had been economically, politically, and culturally liberated and had been elevated by the Soviet state to equal membership in the Soviet family of nations. "Today we meet the Soviet Jewish masses as a self-governing nationality with its own autonomous nation governed in the Yiddish language . . . . The Soviet Jew was building a happy life, without fear of pogroms, anti-Semitism or worries about tomorrow. All this would have been impossible without the October Revolution, without the direct co-operation of the Soviet state." The journal contrasted this state of affairs with that of Jews in the fascist countries, where life had become arbitrary and the future one of uncertainty. The ICOR called upon its members to organize celebrations in Jewish communities throughout the country and to defend the "only homeland of all the oppressed and the exploited, the country that had liberated all national minorities, including the Jewish masses—the Soviet Union!"[30] Herman Abramovitch, another member of the national executive, recalled a time when tsarist Russia had been the "prison house of nations." Today, he wrote, "The Soviet Union is a family of peoples collectively building a happy, worry-free life. Is it any wonder that on the seventh of November—the day that they forever defeated not only tsarism but also capitalism—the Soviet masses dress up in their finest clothes and remonstrate their joy in front of the entire world?" For Jews, in particular, the anniversary was an occasion for celebration; Abramovitch compared their current lives to those of Jews in neighbouring Romania and Poland, where destitution and anti-Semitism still prevailed. "Two worlds: the first a world of despair, hunger and need—those are the capitalist countries! The second—a world of good fortune and happiness—that is the Soviet Union, being built under the leadership of the workers and peasants."[31]

Even better, this regeneration of Jewish life in the Soviet Union was taking place through the medium of the Yiddish language, which was the "mirror reflecting their battles and their hardships." Yiddish had been denigrated as a "jargon" by "the capitalist class as a way of expressing their hatred of the masses and their language." They had preferred either Hebrew or Russian; "the language of the masses was excommunicated." But just as "the Jewish masses in the Soviet Union have prospered, so has their language—Yiddish." It was now gaining prestige, with the development of Yiddish-language technical institutes, universities, courts, literature and theatre. The government of Birobidzhan now functioned entirely in Yiddish, "further proof that under Soviet role the autonomous cultural life of the masses was developing and that the Soviet government was quickly and with practicality fulfilling its promises." However, such progress was not accomplished without its own difficulties. One of the things that the Birobidzhan government lacked due to this transition to Yiddish were typewriters. The ICOR had received an assignment from GEZERD to provide five Yiddish typewriters to the Birobidzhan government and the national executive undertook this task with enthusiasm. "On our typewriters will be written the decrees, orders, proclamations, and other government documents that will improve, enhance, and make more joyful the life of the Jewish masses in Birobidzhan . . . . One typewriter from each branch—in the name of each branch—this should be our decision!"[32] GEZERD would later send a letter thanking the Canadian ICOR for its gift of Yiddish typewriters and for undertaking a campaign to send a linotype machine. This was especially appreciated as a number of Jewish writers, such as David Bergelson, had now settled in Birobidzhan, wrote GEZERD.[33]

In the fall of 1935, to boost the ICOR's fortunes in the west, Harry Guralnick undertook a tour with stops in Winnipeg, Moose Jaw, Saskatoon, Regina, Edenbridge, Calgary, Edmonton, and Vancouver. He was, reported the *Kanader "Icor,"* received with great enthusiasm, and it helped the ICOR branches strengthen their organizational work. While in Edmonton, Guralnick was interviewed by the *Edmonton Journal* about the Soviet solution to the "Jewish question" and the building of Birobidzhan. The journalist described Guralnick as a Rumanian Jew educated in Russia and a Canadian citizen for the past fifteen years. He was "the fellow with the sensitive face, wide brows, piercing grey-blue eyes and heavy dark brows" and a "voice that is soft but impregnated by a guttural accent." Guralnick told the newspaper that the situations in Germany and the USSR were exactly opposite: "Fascism endeavors to solve national problems by exterminating national minorities both physically and culturally . . . . The Soviet solution of national problems means full freedom of cultural, economic and political development." The *Journal* reporter noted that "it is with Biro-Bidjan . . . that he deals most lovingly." Guralnick assured the paper that "by the end of 1937 Biro-Bidjan will be a Jewish Soviet republic . . . . My people have all the symptoms of a nation." He also made no secret that he had no sympathy with the Zionist movement, because the ICOR's aims were "entirely different" from those of the Zionists.

"Such an interview with a capitalist newspaper is especially fortunate," observed the *Kanader "Icor,"* "because it reaches a set of people which we are still unable to reach with our own declarations." In Saskatoon, Guralnick was asked by the chair of the ladies auxiliary of the Talmud Torah to speak to them. He also addressed, in English, a general meeting celebrating the anniversary of the October Revolution on 7 November on behalf of the ICOR; the *Saskatoon Star* ran an excerpt of Guralnick's speech.34

The ICOR's view of Nazism reflected the standard Soviet line of the period. Herman Abramovitch provided a typically simplistic analysis in an article published in October 1935, arguing that the worsening condition for Jews in Nazi Germany was a function of the weakness of the Hitler regime. "The economic situation in the country grows increasingly worse," he wrote. Unemployment was on the rise, prices of essential goods were going up, and the unhappiness of the workers was manifesting itself in strikes and demonstrations. Hitler's promise to end class conflict "had come hack to haunt him like a spectre." Even many rank-and-file Nazis were beginning to realize that Hitler, who had promised them jobs, "had duped them." Hence his use of the "race card" (*"rasn-mitl"*). Anti-Semitism and pogroms "are always used by capitalist countries as a device to cover up the class character of their power." No wonder Hitler had made the Jew "the scapegoat (*"kaporeh hindl"*) for his setbacks." Abramovitch concluded by pointing to the strong wave of protests and the united anti-Hitler campaigns now underway. "The progressive forces are demonstrating an impressive determination to vanquish Hitler fascism."35

In February 1936, Abramovitch reminded ICOR activists of the growing strength of anti-Semitic and fascists movements in Canada itself. Quebec, in particular, had become a province where anti-Semitism had spread "like wildfire." There had been some anti-Semitic rallies staged there by fascists such as Adrien Arcand "that would not be put to shame even by Hitler's bandits." Yet the government shut its eyes to these anti-Semitic activities.³⁶ The Jewish mass-es in Canada, he wrote in another piece, were beginning to realize that it had been an illusion to assume that under the "British flag" anti-Semitism and racial discrimination were impossible. Only in one country did Jews live in harmony with other peoples, without fear of pogroms or economic discrimination. It was a country without capitalism, "out of which racial hatred develops," a country under the rule of workers and peasants, whose solution to national problems "stands as an example to the whole world." Thus the creation of a Jewish region in Birobidzhan was "a slap in the face to all the capitalist countries which foment animosity between peoples apart from hatred of Jews, in order to pre-serve their shaky control."³⁷ Anti-Semitism in Quebec would remain a matter of concern for the ICOR. "The whole province of Quebec is seething with the poison of fascism," it stated in the summer of 1939, commenting on the infa-mous anti-Jewish signs posted in the Laurentian resort of St. Agathe. "The French-Canadian part of Canada has obviously been chosen by the Nazis as a springboard for an attack upon Canadian democracy and as a probable base for an attack upon the United States as well."³⁸

Given the increased awareness that Hitler posed a terrible threat to European Jewry, and that the USSR might serve as a bulwark against the spread of Nazism, many Canadian Jews became more receptive to the propaganda of pro-Soviet groups such as the ICOR. The Winnipeg branch was doing so well early in 1936 that it would soon move into larger quarters in the city's new Talmud Torah. As well, a youth branch had been organized in the city. It also organized a conference on Birobidzhan in April, which attracted fifty-six dele-gates representing twenty-three Jewish organizations. Dr. B. A. Victor, an ICOR activist who had just returned from a trip to the USSR, including Birobidzhan, delivered a lecture about the Jewish Autonomous Region—its location, land area, population, and natural resources. All this progress was made possible due to the leadership of the Soviet Communist Party, contended Victor, "done not out of pity for the Jews but because of national duty." His lecture "was a slap in the face to those who minimize or completely discount the significance and development potential of the Jewish Autonomous Region," said Abe Zeilig, treasurer of the Winnipeg ICOR.

"Even in cold, far-off Edmonton hearts are beating with love for the Soviet Union, for the revival of Jewish culture in one-sixth of the world," wrote Sam Wine, secretary of that ICOR branch. The new Toronto youth club, reported Adolph Epstein, had improved the overall tenor of ICOR activity in the city—and he hoped that a women's group could be organized as well. Hamilton's branches—which already included a women's group—had begun holding frequently scheduled open forums. More people were gravitating to the ICOR than to any other Jewish organization in the city, wrote protocol secretary Harry Price. "Our active members are progressive intelligent people, politically astute comrades . . . they are idealists, for whom the Icor is the organization helping to rebuild Jewish life on a healthy basis." The Hamilton chapters had organized large protest demonstrations against Nazi Germany in the spring of 1936 and had persuaded the local CCF and the Trades and Labour Council to join in a boycott of German goods.

Montreal was the site of the second national convention of the Canadian ICOR, held 8–10 May 1936 to coincide with the second anniversary of the Birobidzhan autonomy declaration. It was attended by seventy-six delegates, who were asked to think of ways to broaden and strengthen the organization. Abraham Shek, the secretary, reported on the campaign on behalf of Birobidzhan, which had made "great strides" in the two years since the territory had been declared a Jewish Autonomous Region. "We are also taking note today with great pride another fact, that GEZERD at its last plenum reported that in 1935 not a single settler abandoned Birobidzhan." Shek provided statistics regarding the increase in the number of kindergartens, elementary and secondary schools, scientific and technical institutes, evening university courses, clubs, reading rooms and libraries, and sporting groups. The Jewish Autonomous Region was now home to many fine Jewish writers; he mentioned David Bergelson by name. On the other hand, bloody pogroms, racial discrimination, and economic destitution were the lot of Jews in the capitalist countries. "Here in Canada, too," noted Shek, "capitalism tries to divert the wrath of the masses by inciting them against the foreign-born and the unemployed." He singled out Quebec and Manitoba as particularly egregious examples of places where anti-Semitic baiting had become particularly severe.

Shek then turned his attention to the Middle East where the Arab revolt in Mandate Palestine was underway. "The current events in Palestine, which have already cost tens of victims dead and hundreds wounded, and the destruction of hundreds of homes, is the result of the bloody politics of British imperialist rule in the colonial world, the politics of divide and rule, and also the chauvinistic racial politics carried on by the leadership of the Zionist movement and on the part of some Arab landowners, against the interests of the impoverished Arab and Jewish masses.

"The ICOR believes that the only solution to the national question is the Soviet one. Every other solution is a diversion and weakens the struggle of the Jewish masses in the capitalist countries." Today, Shek warned, the world stood on the threshold of a war which the fascist powers planned to unleash against "the country that has liberated nations, that sustains culture and civilization, freedom and happiness for all of oppressed humanity . . . . It was more than ever necessary to mobilize the widest strata of the Jewish people for the defence of the Soviet Union."

The convention passed a resolution supporting the sending of a "people's delegation" to Birobidzhan; it instructed the national executive to select five to ten members who would travel to the region in April 1937. It noted that pro-Birobidzhan support groups had taken similar steps in the United States, Argentina, and Uruguay.[39]

Why had the "people's delegation" become so central an issue? The notion that Birobidzhan might serve as a place of political refuge as well as a centre of Jewish economic and cultural regeneration became more pronounced following Hitler's rise to power in Germany, and the ICOR saw its chance to recruit potential members among Jews who hoped that Birobidzhan would prove a potential haven from racial persecution for their European co-religionists. In August 1934, a front-page article in *Kanader "Icor"* datelined Moscow had announced that "Birobidzhan will accept Jewish Workers from abroad."[40] Moishe Katz published a long piece in the June 1935 issue describing the proposal in detail.[41] "Birobidzhan will become the base for a mass migration not just of Jews from the Soviet Union but from countries beyond its borders," another article in late 1935 assured ICOR supporters.[42] Louis Koldoff, national chair of the ICOR, described the ongoing preparations by the American ICOR to send a delegation from the United States, and explained its importance. It would put to rest the lies that had been spread about the Soviet Union ever since the revolution. "The Jewish masses in America instinctively realize that something significant is taking place in the land of the Soviets . . . . Let the people's delegation travel [to Birobidzhan] and see for themselves how the Jewish question should and *can* be solved."[43]

But the American and Canadian Jewish Communists were not apprised of the real situation in the Soviet Union. A rising tide of xenophobia had begun to engulf the country and Stalin's great purges, which would also decimate the Jewish leadership in Birobidzhan, prevented the "people's delegation" from visiting Birobidzhan, thus placing the entire program in a political limbo. The whole matter remained an embarrassing incident, one that the ICOR's enemies would not let them forget.[44]

By 1937, the Spanish Civil War had taken centre stage in the Communist movement. In January, Herman Abramovitch embarked on a six-week tour of western Canada to once again shore up the ICOR branches there. In Montreal, the ICOR had already taken the initiative in organizing a committee for Dr. Norman Bethune's medical unit in Spain; it raised over $1,000 in May and June. A Toronto conference later that year decided to mount a special campaign to help the Mackenzie-Papineau Battalion, formed in July 1937 as a unit of the International Brigades. This culminated in a mass meeting and concert on 6 February 1938 in the Strand Theatre. Despite all these efforts, the Mac-Paps came home and the Loyalists went down to defeat a year later.[45]

The ICOR continued to defend the Soviet Union through the crisis precipitated by the signing of the Hitler-Stalin Pact of August 1939. By checkmating Hitler and occupying eastern Poland, and later Bessarabia, Bukhovina, and the Baltic states, declared the ICOR, the Soviets had liberated some three and one half million Jews who had been living in "enslaved and dejected" conditions under the rules of fascist regimes. Stalin had kept them safe from Nazi persecution, so that they had become "secure and happy as part of the Soviet family of nations and as a part of the fortunate Soviet Jewry."[46] There seemed to be, at least in official statements, little concern with the fate of Jews in occupied

Europe nor any sense of danger that Germany might sooner or later turn on the Soviet Union itself. But that is another story.

The ICOR's backers included people of some note in Jewish circles. Probably the best-known was Reuben Brainin, the Russian-born *maskil* (Enlightenment scholar) well known in Zionist circles before World War I. He had come to North America in 1912, settling first in Montreal, where he edited the Yiddish newspaper *Keneder Adler* and was involved in trade union and Poale Zionist activities. Brainin helped found the Canadian Jewish People's Alliance (*Folks Farband fun Kanader Yidn*), which would become the nucleus of the first Canadian Jewish Congress held in 1919. When he moved to New York in 1916, he was instrumental in working on behalf of the American Jewish Congress and for the Jewish Legion, which fought in Palestine in 1918. During the 1920s, he moved further left and abandoned Zionism, which he had begun to criticize as being elitist and having lost its "Jewish spirit."[47] He was favourably impressed by Soviet plans for Jewish rehabilitation during a visit to the USSR in 1930 at the age of 68, and upon his return to America he joined the ICOR and became a well-known figure at gatherings on behalf of Birobidzhan until his death in November 1939. Former Zionist confreres such as Chaim Nachman Bialik, shocked, denounced him as a traitor and falsifier worthy only of rejection and contempt.[48]

On 7 May 1934, when Mikhail Kalinin officially declared Birobidzhan the Jewish Autonomous Region, Brainin recalled that the ICOR was the first organization outside the USSR to provide aid. "Long live the Leninist national policy of the Soviet Union!" proclaimed rapturous ICOR members. Brainin related an encounter with former friends, still anti-Soviet, who were dumbstruck by the news. For them, he said, it was "*Tisha B'av,*" and they could only denigrate the wonderful news and try to make of little worth (*"ash und bloteh"*) the "great gift which the Soviet government has granted the Jews in the far east." But for the ICOR, which had helped build Birobidzhan by contributing modern machinery and techniques, it was a great "*yontev.*"[49] At a rally held on 2 June in Madison Square Garden, New York, which included among its speakers Earl Browder, general secretary of the American Communist Party, Brainin called it a world event of the greatest historical significance. For the first time, a great power had of its own volition given Jews an area to call their own; the fact that it had been effected by a Communist state was no coincidence. "It is the logic of the whole construction of the Soviet Union, in which every nation has the right to its own territory, to its own language and culture." And, he added, Birobidzhan "now becomes the first fortress against the growing hordes of fascism, which infest the neighboring countries." Brainin called upon every Jew to help in the task of building Birobidzhan, so that "hopefully not too much time will elapse" before it would become a Jewish socialist republic. The ICOR deserved to be congratulated for its material and moral help, "which was the result of the sympathy of the Jewish workers of America with the workers' republic in the Soviet Union."[50] Leninist ideology allowed those Jews who wished to pursue a collective destiny to create a socialist state of their own. Birobidzhan, declared Brainin, provided "a shining example to the whole world [which] will show what Jews can create when they are set free. It must work, when one thinks of the new pioneering spirit of the Jewish youth in the Soviet Union."[51] Brainin noted that "the just treatment of nationalities under the Bolshevik regime is the highest joy for the Jews in the Soviet Union."[52]

On 14 April 1936, Brainin wrote a letter to the newly-formed English-language ICOR branch in Montreal, which had been named in his honour.

> The task of building Birobidzhan should be strengthened and aided by all who want to contribute. Those who have carried the burden of the Birobidzhan concept in the face of narrow-minded opposition, in the face of fanatical ideologies and in the face of the wildest calumnies—they need new strength if Birobidzhan is to truly become a Jewish republic.
>
> I have no doubt that history will validate the correctness of those who, despite opposition and hardships, became the shock-brigades of the Jewish settlement of Birobidzhan. You, as a new group, will encounter many difficulties. You will have a most arduous task in overcoming the obstacles placed in your way. It is a well-known fact that the Soviet Union stands for social justice and for eliminating all the

evils that destructive capitalism has spread throughout the world. Because we are Jews, who believe in the true words of Jewish tradition and culture, we should be grateful and proud to become part of a country that carries the weight of a new and better world for all people.[53]

Interviewed on his 75th birthday in 1937 by *Nailebn-New Life,* Brainin, a member of the national committee of the ICOR, remained "firmly convinced that our pioneers in Biro-Bidjan will create new cultural values that will be altogether different from what is regarded in Jewish ghetto life as Jewish culture." The "Grand Old Man of Hebrew Literature," as the article referred to him, told interviewer Morton Deutsch that although he had never totally turned his back on Hebrew, "Yiddish, which is spoken by the majority of our people, must be regarded by any realist as the language of Jewry." He also stated that one could support both Palestine, "provided it is based on social justice," and Birobidzhan, since Palestine by itself "cannot effect a normalization of Jewish life in the Diaspora." He criticized those Jewish leaders who were "rejecting the generous hand extended to them by the Soviet Government. I have a feeling that in the not distant future many world Jewish, and Zionist leaders will have a lot of repenting to do."[54] Brainin, declared the magazine, had become "the symbol" of "the struggle of the Jewish masses for a revolutionary solution of the national question."[55] Brainin continued to defend the ICOR even after the Hitler-Stalin Pact was signed, in 1939, stating by phone from his summer residence in Val Morin, Quebec, on 31 August that his belief in the organization remained unshaken. "In this sacred work I stand shoulder to shoulder with you, and I reject every attack hurled at you."[56]

Brainin died in New York on 30 November 1939, after a lengthy illness, which caused him to be paralysed for the last three years of his life. *Nailebn-New Life* eulogized him as a "fighter for truth, a leader of the Jewish people towards a brighter future and a devoted friend of the Soviet Union." His commitment "remained unshaken and did not waver in these dark times."[57] Brainin's body was brought back to Montreal for burial, and, in the words of one writer, "to his funeral there came tens of thousands of people, to pay last respects to their beloved spiritual leader."[58] A memorial to Brainin was held at the Hotel Diplomat in New York on 31 January 1940. Shloime Ahnazov, national secretary of the American ICOR, recalled Brainin's presence at many ICOR events and also read out Brainin's "historic statement" reiterating his faith in the Soviet Union despite the Hitler-Stalin pact. Brainin had been one of the Jewish world's foremost Hebraists and Zionists, and was never a Communist or even socialist but a Jewish nationalist, declared Jacob Milch, a member of the national executive. But all that changed "when Birobidzhan appeared on the scene." Although well advanced in years, he then became a champion of the Birobidzhan project, the Soviet Union, and the ICOR, "although he knew full well the price he would have to pay." Even after August 1939, he continued to support the Soviet Union when many others had "scattered like frightened mice." Concluded Milch, "coming generations will include [Brainin] among the greatest of Jews" (*"gedolim Yisrael"*). Benjamin Schecter of Montreal, Brainin's grandson, described "the great crowds that thronged about the Talmud Torah Building in Montreal to get inside the hall where the funeral service was being held." Canadian Jews were proud, stated Schecter, "that for over a quarter of a century Reuben Brainin was connected with Montreal by close ties, that he spent at least a portion of each year in Canada, and that finally he lies buried in their midst." Schecter, too, said that when he had spoken to Brainin in Montreal the previous fall, "his faith in the morality and integrity of the Russian people was unshaken and . . . his optimism regarding the destiny of millions of Russian Jews was undiminished."[59]

Today we know that the Birobidzhan project was largely fraudulent and a complete failure. When these facts, which have now been documented by numerous historians, were revealed after 1956, along with the crimes of Stalin, nowhere was the crisis of faith more profound than among the Jewish Communists.[60] Sam Lipshitz has acknowledged that in the ICOR "the political line was dominated by the Communist Party." By virtue of his position as a high-ranking CPC official, he said, "I was involved in the ICOR. I made it my business to in some way supervise their activities. At one point in the early 1930s, during the very deep economic crisis, when a lot of people were leaning towards the left-wing movement, and out of sympathy for the Soviet Union, the ICOR had a good following." As Arab-Jewish conflict in Palestine intensified in the 1930s, he explained, the idea of a Jewish state in the Middle East began to seem more problematic, "so Birobidzhan was presented as an alternative. A lot of Jews who were not left-wing but nationalist, for them the idea of a Jewish state even under the Soviet regime, was very attractive. But later on it just disintegrated."[61] In 1940, Ahnazov, in defending the Soviet agreement with the Nazis, made reference to a phrase used by Brainin, who had died a few months earlier: "to trample upon the truth is no lesser a crime than murder."[62] Unfortunately, the Jewish Communists, in engaging in the former, had ended up supporting those in the Soviet Union guilty of the latter.

NOTES

1   Erna Paris, Jews: *An Account of Their Experience in Canada* (Toronto 1980), 185; Gerald Tulchinsky, *Branching Out: The Transformation of the Canadian Jewish Community* (Toronto 1998), 123–25.

2   Much has been written about the Birobidzhan project. See Robert Weinberg, *Stalin's Forgotten Zion: Birobidzhan and the Making of a Soviet Jewish Homeland. An Illustrated History, 1928–1996* (Berkeley 1998).

3   Norman Penner, *Canadian Communism: The Stalin Years and Beyond* (Toronto 1988), 273.

4   Quoted in Lewis Levendel, *A Century of the Canadian Jewish Press: 1880s–1980s* (Ottawa 1989), 151.

5   Quoted in Lita-Rose Betcherman, *The Little Band: The Clashes Between the Communists and the Political and Legal Establishment in Canada, 1928–1932* (Ottawa 1982), 98.

6   Sylvia R. Margulies, *The Pilgrimage to Russia: The Soviet Union and the Treatment of Foreigners, 1924–1937* (Madison 1968), 41.

7   Maurice Isserman, *Which Side Were You On? The American Communist Party During the Second World War* (Middletown 1982), 20.

8   "*Barikht fun General-sekretar tsum 'Icor' Plenum, Gehalten in New York 25tn Marts, 1934,*" ICOR, 4 (April 1934) 19 [Yiddish]; ICOR, 5 (May 1934), 23.

9   "*Protokol fun Plenum,*" ICOR, 5 (May 1932), 8–9 [Yiddish].

10   "*Barikht fun Icor Plenum, Gehalten Gevoren in New York, dem 25tn Marts, 1934,*" ICOR, 5 (May 1934), 21 [Yiddish].

11   S. Almazov, "*Di 'Icor'-Konvenshon un vos hot zi uns Gelernt,*" ICOR, 3 (March 1935), 5–6 [Yiddish]; "*Baricht fun der Natsyonaler Ekzekutiv fun 'Icor' tsu der 6–ter Konvenshon,*" ICOR, 3 (March 1935), 12, 16–18, 24–26 [Yiddish]; "No. 746: Weekly

Summary Report on Revolutionary Organizations and Agitators in Canada, 27th February, 1935," in Gregory S. Kealey and Reg Whitaker, eds. *R.C.M.P. Security Bulletins: The Depression Years, Part II*, 1935 (St. John's, Nfld. 1995), 129–130.

12   "*In der Icor Bavegung*," ICOR, 5 (May 1932): 17 [Yiddish]; Abe Victor, "*Oyfn 3tn Tsuzamenkumpft fun Alkanader Icor Sektsye in Toronto 10tn un 11tn Marts, 1934*," ICOR *Biro-Bidzhan Souvenir-Zhurnal* (New York June 1934), 40 [Yiddish].

13   "*Bido-bidzhan Farvandlt in Yidisher Autonomer Sovyetisher Teritorye*," Kanader "*Icor*," 1 (June 1934), 1 [Yiddish].

14   "*Editoryals: A Vikhtiker Shrit Foroys*," Kanader "*Icor*," 1 (June 1934), 2 [Yiddish].

15   S. Lapides, "*Di Sovyetishe Layzung iz di Eyntsike*," Kanader "*Icor*," 1 (June 1934), 9, 15.

16   The letter is deposited among the papers of the Toronto political activist, Moray Nesbitt (Abraham Nisnevitz). See Multicultural History Society of Ontario, Series 85, Jewish Canadian papers, F1405, File 085–015, MU 9003.02, at the Archives of Ontario, Toronto.

17   "*An Icor-nik*," "*Unzer Rol-kol*," Kanader "*Icor*," 3 (October 1934) 8 [Yiddish].

18   "*Barikht fun General-sekretar tsum 'Icor' Plenum, Gehalten in New York 25tn Marts, 1934*," ICOR, 4 (April 1934), 16 [Yiddish]; "*Dem Dritn Yuni vert Oyfgedekt der Monument nokh Khaver Philip Halpern*," Kanader "*Icor*," 1 (June 1934), 4 [Yiddish]; undated letter, Moray Nesbitt papers.

19   Minutes of Hamilton ICOR meetings of 19 November 1933; 5 February, 18 April, 17 June, and 11 November 1934; 14 February 1935, "Minute Book of Hamilton Chapter of Icor," Goldie Vine papers, 1930–1948, Multicultural History Society of Ontario, Series 85, Jewish Canadian papers, F1405, File 085–015, MU 90042.01, deposited in the Archives of Ontario, Toronto; "*ICOR-Taytikayt Iber Kanada*," Kanader "*Icor*," 1 (June 1934), 13–14 [Yiddish]; Y. Trachimofsky, "'*Icor'-Arbet in Montreal*," Kanader "*Icor*," 2 (August 1934), 10 [Yiddish]; A. Shek, "'*ICOR'-Taytikayt Ibern Land*," Kanader "*Icor*," 2 (August 1934), 12 [Yiddish]; F. Kudin, "*Di Arbet fun Vinipeger 'Icor'*," Kanader "*Icor*," 2 (August 1934), 13 [Yiddish]; "No. 727: Weekly Summary Report on Revolutionary Organizations and Agitators in Canada, 10 October, 1934," in Gregory S. Kealey and Reg Whitaker, eds., *R.C.M.P. Security Bulletins: The Depression Years, Part I, 1933–1934* (St. John's, Nfld. 1993), 325–326.

20   "*Der Historisher Bashlus fun der Sovyetn-regirung vegn Biro-Bidzhaner Teritorye*," Kanader "*Icor*," 1 (June 1934), 5, 10 [Yiddish].

21   M. Feldman, "*Der Yidisher Fashizm un Bido-bidzhan*," Kanader "*Icor*," 1 (June 1934), 8, 15 [Yiddish].

22   Y. Trachimofsky, "*Di Oyfgabn un Oyszikhten fun Unzer Arbet*," Kanader "*Icor*," 1 (June 1934), 10 [Yiddish].

23   A. Hamer, "*Biro-bidzhan-An Umglik far di Tsyionistn*," Kanader "*Icor*," 1 June (1934) 11 [Yiddish].

24   A Minsker, "*Nisht Kayn 'Konkurents' nor an Onzog*," Kanader "*Icor*," 1 (May 1936), 15 [Yiddish].

25   S. Lapides, *"Di Sovyetishe Layzung iz di Eyntsike,"* Kanader *"Icor,"* 1 (June 1934), 9, 15 [Yiddish]. Lapides also accused the Jewish garment manufacturers of colluding with the Roman Catholic Church in Quebec to keep French-Canadian women workers backward and exploited, thus driving many into prostitution.

26   S. Lipshitz, *"Der Maariv-Kanader Tur furn 'Icor',"* Kanader *"Icor,"* 4 (November 1934), 10 [Yiddish].

27   "No. 744: Weekly Summary Report on Revolutionary Organizations and Agitators in Canada, 13th February, 1935," in Gregory S. Kealey and Reg Whitaker, eds., R.C.M.P. *Summary Bulletins: The Depression Years, Part II, 1935*, 105.

28   *"Deklaratsye fun dem Ershtn Natsyonaln Tsuzamenfor fun dem 'Icor' in Kanada,"* ICOR, 4 (April 1935), 10–11 [Yiddish]; "No. 752: Weekly Summary Report on Revolutionary Organizations and Agitators in Canada, 10th April, 1935," in Gregory S. Kealey and Reg Whitaker, eds., *R.C.M.P. Security Bulletins: The Depression Years, Part II, 1935*, 226–227. For a brief biography of Joshua Gershman, see Irving Abella, "Portrait of a Jewish Professional Revolutionary: The Recollections of Joshua Gershman," *Labour/Le Travailleur*, 2 (1977), 185–213; and Sol Shek, "A Lifetime in the Labour Movement: Interview with Joshua Gershman," *Canadian Jewish Outlook*, 9–10 (September-October 1987), 7–8, 10, 37. Gina Medem was a frequent contributor to Canadian ICOR publications as well. See, for instance, her report on the 1934 GEZERD convention, *"Rirndike Redes oif der Fayerlicher zitsung fun 'Gezerd' in Moskve,"* Kanader *"Icor,"* 2 (August 1934), 9 [Yiddish].

29   S. Lipshitz, *"Darft der "Icor" zikh Batayliken in Kumende Federale Valn?"* Kanader *"Icor,"* 8 (June 1935), 2, 7 [Yiddish].

30   *"Editoryals: Grayt zikh tsu di November-fayerung!,"* Kanader *"Icor,"* 9 (October 1935), 1 [Yiddish]. See also the reprint of an article from the *Frayhayt* in New York, *"Yidn Hobn Buzundere Grintn tsu Frayen Zikh mit dem Oktober-Yubili,"* Kanader *"Icor,"* 10 (November-December 1935) 7 [Yiddish].

31   H. Abramovitch, *"Tsvay Veltn,"* Kanader *"Icor,"* 10 (October-November 1935), 8–9 [Yiddish].

32   *"Editoryals: Biro-bidzhan vert Regirt in Yidish...,"* Kanader *"Icor,"* 9 (October 1935), 1 [Yiddish]; *"An Icor-nik,"* *"'Zhargon' iz gevorn a melikhe shprakh,"* Kanader *"Icor]"* 10 (November-December 1935), 5 [Yiddish].

33   *"Mir Shiken Akht Shrayb-mashinkes Anshtot Finf,"* Kanader *"Icor,"* 1 (May 1936), 3 [Yiddish]; Yosef Blitshtein, *"In Kanader 'Icor',"* Nailebn-New Life, 4 (April 1937), 20 [Yiddish].

34   *"Editoryals: Der Tur fun Khaver Guralnick,"* Kanader *"Icor,"* 9 (October 1935), 1, 14 [Yiddish]; *"Editoryals: Der 'Icor' in Kanada vert Farshtarkt,"* Kanader *"Icor,"* 10 (November-December 1935), 1 [Yiddish]; *" 'Icor'-Taytikayt iber Kanada,"* Kanader *"Icor,"* 10 (November-December 1935), 10–11 [Yiddish]; *Edmonton Journal*, 31 October 1935, Section 2, 13, 15; "No. 744: Weekly Summary Report on Revolutionary Organizations and Agitators in Canada, 25th September, 1935," in Gregory S. Kealey and Reg Whitaker, eds., *R.C.M.P. Security Bulletins: The Depression Years, Part II, 1935*, 500.

35 H. Abramovitch, "*In Kamf Kegn Fashizm in Antisemitism,*" *Kanader "Icor,"* 9 (October 1935), 7, 14 [Yiddish].

36 H. Abramovitch, "*Antisemitism in Kanada,*" *Kanader "Icor,"* 11 (February 1936), 6–7 [Yiddish].

37 H. Abramovitch, "*Vos Toronter Yidish Klal-tuer Zogn vegn Birobidzhan,*" *Kanader "Icor,"* 1 (May 1936), 11, 14 [Yiddish].

38 "Anti-Semitism in Canada," *Nailebn-New Life,* 8 (August-September 1939), 3 [English]. The name of the American ICOR's English-Yiddish monthly magazine was changed from *ICOR* to *Nailebn-New Life* in May 1935.

39 Minutes of Hamilton ICOR meetings of 2 February, 1 March, and 19 April, 1936, "Minute Book of Hamilton Chapter of ICOR"; "*Editoryale Notitzn,*" *Kanader "Icor,"* 11 (February 1939), 3–4 [Yiddish]; A. Shek, "*Mit di Icor-Brenches iber Kanada,*" *Kanader "Icor,"* 11 (February 1936), 10–11 [Yiddish]; Front cover, *Kanader "Icor,"* 1 (May 1936); Harry Price, "*Der 'Icor' in Hamilton Gayt Foroys,*" *Kanader "Icor,"* 1 (May 1936), 2 [Yiddish]; A. Shek, "*Foroys, tsu a Brayter Folks-Organizatsye fun dem 'Icor' in Kanada!,*" *Kanader "Icor,"* 1 (May 1936), 5–7 [Yiddish] (emphasis on original); A. Zeilig, "*Der Icor in Winnipeg Fartsaykhent Groyse Dergraykhungen,*" *Kanader "Icor,"* 1 (May 1936), 8 [Yiddish]; A. Trachimofsky, "*Nor Nisht Kayn Falshe Oystaytshungen!,*" *Kanader "Icor,"* 1 (May 1936), 9–10 [Yiddish]; S. Wine, "*Oykn in Edmonton Shlogn Hertser mit Libe far Birobidzhan,*" *Kanader "Icor,"* 1 (May 1936), 10 [Yiddish]; M. Speisman, "*Unzer Idea Vortsit zikh ayn Tsvishn di Yidishe Masn,*" *Kanader "Icor,"* 1 (May 1936) 10 [Yiddish]; A. Epstein, "*'Icor'-Arbet in Toronto,*" *Kanader "Icor,"* 1 (May 1936), 14 [Yiddish]; Toronto ICOR Youth Club ad in *Nailebn-New Life* 11, 11 (November 1937): 90 [Yiddish]; "No. 808: Weekly Summary Report on Revolutionary Organizations and Agitators in Canada, 27th May, 1936," in Gregory S. Kealey and Reg Whitaker, eds., R.C.M.P. *Security Bulletins: The Depression Years, Part III,* 1936 (St. John's, Nfld. 1996), 221. For more on Victor's Russian excursion, see B. A. Victor, "The Soviet Union Takes Great Care of the Health of its People," *Nailebn-New Life,* 11 (November 1937), 8–9 [English].

40 "*Der Gantser Sovyetn-Farband Boyt Di Yid. Autonomye Gegnt in Biro-bidzhan,*" *Kanader "Icor,"* 2 (August 1934), 1.

41 Moishe Katz, "*Sheftum iber Biro-bidzhan Oyslandishe Aynvanderung,*" *Kanader "Icor,"* (June 1935) 8–9 [Yiddish].

42 "*An Icor-nik,*" "'*Zhargon' iz Gevorn a Melikhe Shprakh,*" *Kanader "Icor,"* 10 (November-December 1935), 5 [Yiddish].

43 L. Koldoff, "*Farvos a Folks-Delegatsye?*" *Kanader "Icor,"* 1 (May 1936), 4 [Yiddish].

44 Melech Epstein, *The Jew and Communism: The Story of Early Communist Victories and Ultimate Defeats in the Jewish Community, U.S.A. 1919–1941* (New York 1959), 313–317.

45 Yosef Blitshtein, "*In Kanader 'Icor',*" *Nailebn-New Life,* 4 (April 1937), 20 [Yiddish]; "*In Kanader 'Icor',*" *Nailebn-New Life,* 2 (February 1938), 35–36 [Yiddish]; "*In Kanader 'Icor',*" *Nailebn-New Life,* 3 (March 1938), 35 [Yiddish]; F. Golfman, "*Montreal 'Icor'-Taytikayt in 1937,*" *Nailebn-New Life,* 3 (March 1938), 36.

46 S. Almazov, *"Di Oyfgabe fun 'Icor' in der Itstikn Moment,"* *Nailebn-New Life*, 10 (December 1940), 13–14 [Yiddish].

47 Nakhman Meisel, *"Reuben Brainin un Dr. Khaim Zhitlovsky,"* in Nakhman Meisel, ed., *Tsum Hundertstn Geborintog fun Reuben Brainin* (New York 1962), 147–148 [Yiddish].

48 David Rome et al., eds., *Canadian Jewish Archives: The Canadian Story of Reuben Brainin Part 2*, New Series, 48 (Montreal 1996), 113–115.

49 *"Der Historisher Bashlus fun der Sovyetn Regirung tsu Farvandlen Biro-bidzhan in a Yidisher Autonomye Teritorye,"* *ICOR Biro-bidzhan Souvenir-Zhurnal* (New York 1934), 9–10 [Yiddish]; Reuben Brainin, *"Der Yontev fun Biro-bidzhan,"* *ICOR Biro-bidzhan Souvenir-Zhurnal* (New York 1934), 15–16 [Yiddish].

50 Reuben Brainin, *Umshterblekhe Reyd vegn Birobidzhan un vegn der Sotsyalishtishe Layzung fun der Natsyonaler Frage* (New York 1940), 3–4, 10 [Yiddish]. The celebration was covered by the *New York Times*, 3 June 1934, 26.

51 Reuben Brainin, *"Yidishe Pyonern in Bido-bidzhan Boyen far Zikh a Gliklekhe Tsukunft,"* in Brainin, *Umshterblekhe Reyd*, 12 [Yiddish].

52 Reuben Brainin, *"Hot der Natsyonaler Yid a Tsukunft a Sovyetn-Farband?,"* in Brainin, *Umshterblekhe Reyd* , 26 [Yiddish].

53 *"Reuven Brainin Shraybt Tsum Kanader 'Icor',"* *Kanader "Icor,"* 1 (May 1936), 2 [Yiddish]; "We Should be Happy and Proud to Become Part of a Country Which Stands as the Torchbearer of a New and Better World for all Men-Reuben Brainin," *Kanader "Icor,"* 1 (May 1936), 24 [English].

54 Morton, Deutsch, "Reuben Brainin at 75 Looks to Biro-Bidjan for the Future of Jewish Culture," *Nailebn-New Life*, 4 (April 1937), 6–7 [English].

55 *"Mir Grisn Khaver Reuben Brainin Tsu Zayn 75tn Geburts-Tog,"* *Nailebn-New Life*, 4 (April 1937), 3 [Yiddish].

56 *"A Historishe Erklerung fun Reuben Brainin Tsum 'Icor',"* *Nailebn-New Life*, 9 (October 1939), 26–27 [Yiddish]. Brainin was by now paralysed and very near death; his son Joseph, a member of the Communist Party U.S.A., may have had a part in releasing this statement.

57 *"Reuben Brainin-Toyt,"* *Nailebn-New Life*, 11 (December 1939), 4–5 [Yiddish].

58 I. L. Becker, *"Reuben Brainin in Montreal,"* in Nakhman Meisel, ed., *Tsum Hundertstn Geborintog fun Reuben Brainin*, 106 [Yiddish].

59 Yacov Milch, *"Der Umfargeslekher Reuben Brainin,"* *Nailebn-New Life*, 3 (April 1940), 15–17 [Yiddish] (emphasis in original); Benjamin Schecter, "Reuben Brainin was a Truly Great Man," *Nailebn-New Life*, 3 (April 1940), 6–7 [English]. After Brainin's death, the ICOR printed 100,000 postcards of the "historic statement" alongside his portrait. *"In Der Icor Bavegung,"* *Nailebn-New Life*, 3 (April 1940), 27 [Yiddish].

60 For more on this period, see Merrily Weisbord, *The Strangest Dream: Canadian Communists, the Spy Trials, and the Cold War* (Montreal 1994).

61 Interview, Sam Lipshitz, Toronto, 9 June 1998.

62 S. Almazov, "Why Did Rabbi Theodore N. Lewis Slander Biro-Bijan?," *Nailebn-New Life*, 3 (April 1940), 9 [English] (emphasis in original).

Sites of Memory

The pace of change in Canada, as well as the gap between an Old World past and New World realities, have contributed to the sense, among Jews, that memory is central to the development of a local identity. When things like homeland, language, and modes of daily life are suddenly changed for newer replacements, the issue of what to make of the past can present difficult challenges. In this section, Franklin Bialystok's work on the reception of the Holocaust in Canada examines the circuitous route by which Canadian Jewish identity linked itself with the events of the war. Barb Schober's essay presents an early example of the complexities of this phenomenon, as it played out in Vancouver. Norman Ravvin's essay on Eli Mandel and the Jewish Prairie farming colonies argues for the particularities of memory, as they relate to place.

NR

Eli Mandel's Family Architecture: Building A House of Words on the Prairies

NORMAN RAVVIN

It's difficult to be a "memory-tourist" on the Prairies, to return to relics and ruins and examine our own lives in light of the absence and brokenness of our forbears' world.[1] The cities are new, built and rebuilt so a minimum of history remains visible. As early as the 1940s Canadian architects bemoaned the "dead hulks" western cities and towns inherited from earlier generations and began the transformation of their main streets, stripping them of the venerable structures they saw as "dull monuments" to "ignorance and sentimentality."[2] What can the avid memory-tourist find of interest on the Prairie? What places remain that are evocative of the past, and which objects resonate so richly with the lives of the dead that they have the power to shape our understanding of the present? Poet and critic Eli Mandel made his way back to the ruins of Saskatchewan and wrote what are arguably his finest poems about the Jewish ghost towns of Hirsch and Hoffer, the battered landscape called badlands by the locals, around Weyburn and Estevan, where he encountered not only physical ruins but the ruins of memory—in his words, "the endless treachery / that is remembering."[3] In a collection called *Out of Place* (1977), Mandel depicts the visit he made with his wife Ann to the abandoned homesteads and one-street towns of his Saskatchewan youth, to the relics of an era separated from ours not so much by the passing of many years, as by the brute change of our society from one that was largely rural to one that is increasingly urban. In a landscape that would read for most of us like a blank page, a sheet of brown dusty scrub, Mandel conjured the "ghostly jews / of estevan,"[4] and stranger still, the absent Jews of the Europe that Hitler made.

Western Canada is often characterized as having a "short [and] exclusively 'modern'"[5] history, but such appraisals tend to gloss over the distinct stages of transformation the landscape and built environment of the Prairies have undergone. More than thirty years ago, in an article entitled "Time and Place in the Western Interior," John Warkentin noted how farming practices had obliterated native systems of land use, and went on to describe how the gradual decline of many agricultural communities had brought about another "remaking of the face of the land in the prairies":

> The pace of change is increasing. Examples of ordinary-seeming buildings, the ones which were most common and hence all the more important, are those we are apt to lose . . . . Many kinds of rural buildings are disappearing rapidly. Churches, schools and halls, essential facilities for community activities in any farm district, were scattered through the countryside in pioneer days. Numerous structures of this type are abandoned and have fallen to ruin, because of the consolidation of social activities in villages and towns.[6]

Among the once common structures that are now largely preserved through photographs are the round barn, designed to shed snow and withstand wind; storefronts marked "Saloon"; the wooden onion-domed churches of

Ukrainian farmers; and washed-out billboards that advertised Bull Durham, Chinook Beer, and Stanislaus Flour from the sides of barns.7

Mandel, interestingly enough, does not include any of these vanishing melancholy sites in the Saskatchewan poems that appear in his early collections, in increasing number in *Stony Plain* (1973), and as the focus of interest in *Out of Place*. Instead, he returns repeatedly in his writing to Estevan, the city of his youth on the edge of the Souris River Valley in Southeastern Saskatchewan, near to which the Jewish pioneering settlements of Hirsch and Hoffer struggled and eventually sank. The colonists Mandel encountered as a boy at Hirsch and Hoffer came from Russia, Poland and Romania—most of them were shopkeepers and tradespeople in their native towns—to pursue the promise of a life free of persecution and the opportunity to work their own land. During the late nineteenth century the Canadian government was eager to settle its western territories, and 160 acres of Prairie could be had for ten dollars.

As Mandel offers almost no explanation of what brought such settlements into existence, and only obliquely describes the kind of lives that were lived there between the 1880s and the outbreak of the Second World War, the reader might mistake the poems in *Out of Place* for surrealist experiments, wild impositions of Chagall's Vitebsk onto the glyph-marked banks of the Souris River. In "near Hirsch a Jewish cemetery:" Mandel writes: "the Hebrew puzzles me / the wind moving the grass / over the still houses of the dead."8 In "slaughterhouse:"

> grandfather leading me back to the kitchen
> the farm unpainted weathered grandmother
> milking guts of shit for skins and kishke
> it's not a place for boys she says
> her face redder than strawberries
> her hands like cream9

Mandel's juxtaposition of worlds must read like a fantasy, a daydream, to anyone without memories of such scenes, to anyone who has not stumbled onto their ruins. And in fact, Mandel does not hide his urge to play with this unusual juxtaposition of Prairie landscape and Jewish culture, to come up with his own fiction using the facts at hand. Included in *Out of Place* is a letter he received from a citizen of Weyburn, a town near to Hirsch and Estevan, which takes him to task for his reliance on poetic licence. The letter reads:

> Dear Professor Mandel,
>
> Heard you on "This Country in the Morning" and was more than surprised when you mentioned that your new book on Poetry and Prose will be about the ghost Jewish Colony of Hoffer (or Sonnenfeld Colony which is the correct name).
>
> Whereas my husband and I were both born in the colony and are still carrying on farming operations there and have a great interest in that area we were wondering where you got your information.
>
> It was interesting to hear you say that your wife has been out taking pictures. Would it be possible to know of this, and when and where do you plan to have your book published. We would like to buy it when it becomes available.
>
> Thank you.
>
> Yours Truly.
>
> Mrs. N. Feldman[10]

It is difficult to judge if the tone of these three neat paragraphs is sarcastic, a dismissal of Mandel's version of history as a sloppy fiction, or if it is simply searching, open to all possibilities. In his poetic response to Mrs. Feldman's letter Mandel admits that his own imagined sense of the landscape had "disappeared" those still living on it:

> Mrs. Feldman
> I say to myself softly
> I can't see you in the picture
> there is no one there.[11]

Mrs. Feldman is, in a sense, one of the survivors who didn't fit into the fiction Mandel derived from the absence and total abandonment he found on the Saskatchewan Prairie.

In an essay discussing his poem, "On the 25th Anniversary of the Liberation of Auschwitz," Mandel makes a striking connection between his struggle to develop a "Poetics" appropriate to writing about his Prairie past and the challenge of writing about the Holocaust:

> The place of death, Europe and the Jews, I had identified as tradition, fathers, all that named me, connected me with the past, the prophetic, Hebraic, Judaic sense—in its alien and tragic sense not in its ethical and legalistic aspects. If the camps recorded death, it was that death I had to record, an attempt too horrible to contemplate. But the possibility of re-enacting that death began at the same time to occupy me. Its substitution, the graves of the war dead, in Europe, for example, the place of the Jewish dead on the prairies . . . .[12]

Without making any explicit reference to this "substitution" in *Out of Place,* Mandel intimates that there is an uncanny doubleness between the alien European deaths "too horrible to contemplate" and those of his forbears on the Prairies: the unlikelihood of a Jewish pioneer by the Souris River mirrors the unlikelihood of meeting a Jew today in Krakow or in Munich; European towns and countrysides, emptied of Jews, are the tragic double of the abandoned town sites at Hirsch and Hoffer. The "town lives," Mandel writes of Estevan, and "in its syntax we are ghosts."[13] Just as memory-tourists visit the sites of death camps to view the ruins of an architecture of death, Mandel finds at Hirsch and Hoffer far more benign but equally moldering ruins.

In his earlier collection, *Stony Plain,* Mandel points to the similarity in identity and world view between those who perished in Europe and his own forebears on the Prairies. But he does so to evoke the vast difference between their respective fates:

and father knew father
mothering the last of the jews
who in the Hirsch land
put in new seed
and new codes
and new aunts

so we survived
but had become
being as
we were

solutions

the seed

the new seed

final solution[14]

The Holocaust exists as an after-image of the Mandels' survival on the Prairies, the two experiences like opposite ends of an hourglass, flaring away from each other but still inextricably connected. This doubleness that exists between two vastly different vanished Jewish worlds lends Mandel's ruminations on the ruins of Saskatchewan a deeper resonance.

In his effort to tell the stories of the Jews of Hirsch and Hoffer—stories he calls "heroic"[15]—Mandel must return to the ruins of these places as well as to the ruins of his own memories. At the town sites themselves he finds relics: seed catalogues, "machinery bills" and "clapboard buildings," "quebec heaters," iron bedsteads,[16] recollections of "wild strawberries cocoa-butter"—what he refers to as the "taste of Hirsch."[17] In *Out of Place,* Mandel's poems are juxtaposed with Ann Mandel's photographs of the southern Saskatchewan landscape. In black-

and-white the storefronts and Prairie roads of Bienfait and Hirsch look like vacant film sets, peopleless under a sky so clear and vast the galaxy seems to have been emptied of all its heavenly bodies. Abandoned frame buildings are shot through with sun and the brilliant still air. But Mandel himself undercuts any sense that these stills provide proof that Ann Mandel's vision of the landscape, her account of relics and recollection, reveals the truth. The photographs are anything but sure representations, he says: "we take the photographs to be the reality. But they're not, they're only photographs. They're interpretations . . . ."[18] So how much less reliable memory must be. In "lines for an imaginary cenotaph:" Mandel erects a monument that serves as his own interpretation of the landscape:

> george hollingdale
> bruce carey
> george chapman
> jacob barney mandel
>
> William Tell Mandel: sd
> Capt A.W. (ab) Hardy
>
> Isaac Berner
>   Annie's
> son
>
> all the kinds of war
> we say our kaddish for
>
> chief Dan Kennedy
> singing
> beneath the petroglyphs
> hoodoos we sd
> at Roch Percée
>
> Assiniboine songs[19]

But the poet is quick to point out the blind spots in his own interpretation. With the rush of years, and his inability to confidently read the landscape and its ruins, he admits that he must inevitably lose contact with the past. Standing before the glyphs in the badlands left by the Assiniboine, Mandel asks, "do they mean anything?"[20] In the same way, disinterested travelers fly by on the highway beside the Jewish cemetery at Hirsch; "no one there," Mandel writes, "casts a glance at the stone trees / the unliving forest of Hebrew graves."[21] What you don't know, quite simply, isn't there, in or out of place.

Architecture in the city means hope; it means home-building. Its practitioners build structures evocative of the stories of progress and prosperity every community needs to hear to believe in its own strength and good sense. In Canada, Calgary and Toronto have most wholeheartedly embraced the tower. Our skyscraping needles strive to counter the legendary fiasco at the Tower of Babel; with their tops in the clouds they are unfettered by heavenly decree, much less by concerns over usefulness or expense. These buildings assert a narrative at once archetypal and modern, with all relics of the past and the stories they might convey removed from sight. But on the Prairies, in the wild places abandoned by their short-lived communities, the human art of architecture is reversed by the weather. Windows turn in on themselves, roofs furrow and fall, fence posts and corner beams bed down, softened to termite dust and mulch. Buildings are slowly unmade as the world reverts to form, or formlessness.

One might assume then, that Mandel returned to Hirsch and Hoffer to undo this process of transformation and obliteration, that he wrote with the reassuring hope that his poems would "reconstruct the original artifact . . . by returning to the scene of it,"[22] and that through his poems he would erect a monument to all the dead Mandels and Berners of Saskatchewan, a "version of history calling itself permanent and everlasting . . . ."[23] But the outcome of *Out of Place* could not be more contrary to this urge. Mandel goes to great lengths to leave documented history out of his poems. He fashions instead an almost purely personal and imaginative meditation on Prairie ruins. Left out of *Out of Place* is any background information on the colonies themselves. The development of Jewish farm settlements at Hirsch, Hoffer, Moosomin, Wapella and

Lipton, as well as at sites scattered across Manitoba and Alberta, has been documented by Jewish community leaders, historians, and parliamentarians alike. John A. Macdonald and his High Commissioner in London, Alexander Galt, had low expectations of the Jewish newcomers who applied through their co-religionists in Montreal for land titles in the West. They will "at once go in for peddling and politics," Macdonald wrote to Galt in 1882.[24] Galt, however, believed that by taking an interest in the Jews willing to homestead in the wilds of the Prairies he might instill greater interest in Canada in the famous Jewish philanthropists of Europe.[25] Galt had, in fact, tried to interest the German-born Baron Maurice de Hirsch in investing in the Canadian Pacific Railroad, having heard of Hirsch's success at developing and running the Oriental railway linking Constantinople and Europe.[26] Nothing came of this, but it was the philanthropic efforts of Baron de Hirsch that allowed the first Jewish settlers to go west in numbers, and through his support of the Montreal office of the Jewish Colonization Association, families continued to join established colonies. Settlements like those founded in Canada sprung up, with the baron's support, in Palestine, Brazil, Argentina, Oregon, South Dakota and New Jersey. In 1929, the *Encyclopedia Britannica* referred to Hirsch's Jewish Colonization Association as "probably the greatest charitable trust in the world."[27]

Although Mandel conjures his relatives' life on the Prairies in *Out of Place,* he does not claim for his forbears the central role they played in the history of the Hirsch settlement. His grandfather, Rabbi Marcus Berner, was the rabbi and *shochet* at Hirsch for thirty-two years, marrying and burying two generations of pioneers. The synagogue in which he taught and led services was the first synagogue building erected in Saskatchewan.[28] Berner was also an established farmer, a chairman of the school board and a municipal councillor.[29] Among the intermediaries who connected the colonists at Hirsch with their often snobbish benefactors at the Baron de Hirsch Institute in Montreal, was Lazarus Cohen, the grandfather of Leonard Cohen, a literary peer whose career Mandel followed with great interest. Lazarus Cohen, a lumber and coal merchant in Montreal, spent five weeks at the colony, working and studying with the settlers.[30]

Mandel positions the poems in *Out of Place* almost entirely outside this rich history, recounting none of it. Rather than turn to communal history he includes, almost perversely, a footnote more relevant to literary than Jewish historical archives. Instead of mining the rich stories concerning Israel Hoffer, the patriarch who gave his name to the colony he led, Mandel notes that Hoffer's son Abraham is mentioned in Aldous Huxley's *The Doors of Perception* and *Heaven and Hell:*

> A psychiatrist, Abraham Hoffer has done pioneer work in
> the uses of lysergic acid as a means of exploring the nature
> and causes of schizophrenia and alcoholism. His father was
> a wheat farmer.[31]

This urge to avoid recounting documented events, to present instead a portrait of personal encounter with the memories conjured by a visit to the Hirsch area, accounts for the treatment in *Out of Place* of the old Hoffer community "vault." There is no precise description in the book of what it is Eli and Ann Mandel discover in a vault they visit on what was the Hoffer family farm near Estevan. It is said to contain documents and artifacts of the history of the Jewish Prairie settlements. The vault's floor is "littered with prairie," and Mandel recounts how he began "to feel gloomy" as soon as the discourse of "family lines," of the "census" and "newspapers" began to intrude on his own recollections and vision of the landscape.[32] One critic has written that "Writing, the subject and matter of *Out of Place,* finds its first configuration in the image of the vault."[33] Yet surprisingly little is read out of this configuration. The archive is a mess, a disappointment that brings on the poet's gloomy mood. In Ann Mandel's preface to *Out of Place,* she describes herself and Eli Mandel as two memory-tourists who used pages

> for mattresses, sheets, and head rests. When we decided
> a page was insignificant for our purposes or saw it was
> blank we placed it in a pile to use for wiping ourselves
> or for after love. Others became serviettes, sunshades,
> etc.[34]

This extravagant image of the archivists actually making use of history, bringing it up to date by including it in their daily lives, offers the most explicit condemnation in *Out of Place* of the urge to represent "any version of history calling itself permanent and everlasting," the kind that is presented through a monument or museum exhibit.[35] To quote James Young, whose book *The Texture of Memory* examines Holocaust memorials, Mandel would have us see that sites of historical importance and communal experience need not assume the "polished, finished veneer of a death mask, unreflective of current memory, unresponsive to contemporary issues."[36] Ann and Eli Mandel live in the vault, eat and make love on top of what it contains. For them, the Prairie ruins are ripe with history, bearing the traces of the "ghostly jews / of estevan."[37]

By forcing us to meditate on the absence and brokenness of the vanished lives of Hirsch and Hoffer, the poems and photographs in *Out of Place* enliven the landscape and re-people the empty Prairie. The "magic of ruins persists," Young tells us, in

> a near mystical fascination with sites seemingly charged
> with the aura of past events, as if the molecules of the sites
> still vibrated with the memory of their history.[38]

Such sites of memory "begin to assume lives of their own . . . ."[39] And so it is with the landscape surrounding Estevan. In "the return:" Mandel writes,

> my father appears
> my mother appears
> saying no words
> troubled[40]

And for Mandel, absence provides as sure a marking on the landscape as presence:

> I read the land for records now

wild strawberries cocoa-butter

taste of Hirsch

    bags of curdling

warm spent streams

tested on the hair of berner's beard

the ritual slaughter knife

even the blood has disappeared[41]

Within the gates of the cemetery at Hirsch, where the dead were brought from the surrounding communities, Mandel describes himself standing "arms outstretched / as if waiting for someone."[42] Even in a dead graveyard the past threatens to send an emissary.

Hirsch, in southern Saskatchewan, was one of the longest-lived Jewish Prairie farming colonies. Now it is part of what might be called Hidden Canada—an aspect of the past that has been largely forgotten, yet still leaves marks on the landscape. The cemetery at Hirsch is all that remains, marked by a Government of Canada plaque, noting the history of Jewish farming in the area. Once a kind of shtetl *on the Prairies, the site now offers little to a well-meaning memory-tourist.*
Photo by Norman Ravvin.

Gurevitch, Ben, Rumsey; right shoulder

Hanen, Sam, Rumsey; left shoulder

Sengaus, Elias, Rumsey; right shoulder

Aisenstat, Sam, 2718 - 17 St. S.W., Calgary; right hip

Belkin, Harry, 1711 - 12 St. W., Calgary; left ribs

Belzberg, A., 327 - 8 Ave. E., Calgary; left ribs

Bikman, L., Milk River; left shoulder (1920)

Cohen, Hyman, Calgary; left shoulder (1924)

Cohen, Hyman, 1610 - 6th Ave. S., Lethbridge; left hip

Davids, Abie, 718 - 9 St. S., Lethbridge; right ribs

Davids & Cooper, 718 - 9 St. S., Lethbridge; left hip

Dvorkin, David L., 840 - 18 Ave. W., Calgary; left hip

Dvorkin, Harry, Calgary Stockyards, Calgary; left shoulder

Dvorkin, L., 408 - 3 Ave. W., Calgary; left hip

Dvorkin, Morton, 237 - 11 Ave. N.E., Calgary; right hip

Dvorkin, Tony, 2328 - 24 Ave. S.W., Calgary; right shoulder

Dvorkin, Yale, 727 - 3 Ave. W., Calgary; left hip

Estrin, Harry, 206 Devenish Apts., Calgary; right hip

Fefferman, Morris, & Davids, Abraham L., Lethbridge; right hip

Gediger, Harry, 1414 - 2 St. E., Calgary; left hip

Geffen Co. Ltd., 228 - 15 Ave. E., Calgary; left hip

Gorasht, Sam, 611 - 3rd St. E., Calgary; left shoulder

Gurevitch, Raphael, Rumsey; right shoulder

Hanson, Mrs. A., c/o Union Milk Co., Calgary; left hip

Hashman, Harry, 229 - 4 Ave. E., Calgary; right hip

Katchen, L.B., Alberta Stock Yards, Calgary; left ribs

Kline, I., 1240 - 15 Ave. W., Calgary; left ribs

Kline, Sam, Lethbridge; left hip

Kline, Samuel, 130 Scarborough Ave., Calgary; left hip

Levitt, Hyman & Jack, Hubalta; left ribs

Levitt, John, Hubalta; left hip

Manolson, M.F., 1403 - 12 St. W., Calgary; right hip

Morris, A., Calgary; right hip

Sanderson, J., & Dvorkin, H., 115 - 11 Ave. E., Calgary; right shoulder

Sengaus, E., Rumsey; right hip

Sheftel, Harry, Stock Yards, Calgary; left ribs

Switzer, Abraham, 409 - 12 Ave. E., Calgary; right thigh

Switzer, Max, 334 - 7 Ave. E., Calgary; right hip

Veiner, Harry, 634 - 3 St., Medicine Hat; left ribs

Cattle Brands of Jewish dealers, farmers and ranchers.

While Eli Mandel's poems call for a necessary confrontation with absence at the abandoned farm colonies of Saskatchewan, the Jewish Historical Society of Southern Alberta insists on the importance of remembering a Jewish "rangeland culture." The cattle brands gathered here were presented by the Society in order to evoke a sense of a deeply-rooted presence of the Jews in the west.

The illustration shows a large number of brands registered to Jewish dealers, farmers and ranchers. They were found in Alberta Brand Books dated between 1937 and 1954. A few brands from the 1920s have been so noted. The Journal of the Jewish Historical Society of Southern Alberta *offered the brands as evidence that for several decades, Jews were an important part of the livestock industry and Canada's western heritage.*

COURTESY OF JACK SWITZER, FROM THE WINTER 1997 EDITION OF *DISCOVERY* [WITH SOURCES OF THE GLENBOW ALBERTA INSTITUTE AND MORRIS HANSON], THE JOURNAL OF THE JEWISH HISTORICAL SOCIETY OF SOUTHERN ALBERTA.

Mandel's approach to history and forms of memory fits nicely with what might be termed a postmodern suspicion of any effort at freezing the past like a death mask, at preserving an official record of events.[43] It is this suspicion that has led contemporary architects to reject what they judge to be the exhausted forms of their predecessors: nineteenth-century historical facades bearing tableaux of national and mythic heroes; the neo-classicism exemplified by public buildings whose style, borrowed from Revolutionary France and ancient Greece, promotes "the ideal of universal laws . . . science, art, government and justice . . . ."[44] After the shock of this century's killing fields these public myths no longer thrill us, and architects have begun to find inspiration for their buildings in "narratives which resonate with the history of a specific place,"[45] and which derive their inspiration from "personal stories grounded in life."[46] In the words of Vancouver architect Richard Henriquez, such work situates

> the individual in a perceived historical continuum . . .
> which includes both the built and the natural world, real
> and fictional pasts, and allows members of the community
> to project their lives into the future.[47]

Within this historical continuum, ruins and relics can be built into a new building, as a structure is made to take into account its site, the buildings that preceded it there, as well as its relationship to geology and native culture. In *Out of Place,* Eli Mandel finds inspiration in a similar historical continuum. He reads the landscape for the leavings of the Jews, of the Assiniboine, even of the identityless parade of travellers who roar by in their cars, and he devises from all this a portrait of intricate depth and particularity, a scaffolding of story and image supported by ruins.

For Mandel, it would seem, the richest site for the memory-tourist is an accidental one rather than a deliberately cared for monument; it is one that is overgrown and infested rather than one that politely offers an officially sanctioned commemoration. There is no rhetoric in *Out of Place* pronouncing on the absence of official signs marking the history of Jewish settlement in the Hirsch area. Mandel makes no rancorous request that his ancestors' first home in Canada be better preserved.[48] In what appears at first to be an enigmatic utterance—"no one has the right to memories"[49]—Mandel affirms the rightness of ruin, the need to let the land sweep back over failure and abandonment, to let it take back its ghosts.

NOTES

1 James E. Young, *The Texture of Memory: Holocaust Memorials and Meaning* (New Haven, 1993), p. 70.

2 W. Bernstein and R. Cawker, *Building With Words: Canadian Architects on Architecture* (Toronto, 1981), p. 12. In Calgary, the architects working during the city's boom years chose modernism's mirrored facades to replace the brick and sandstone blocks that had been discredited as old world monuments with little relationship to local mythologies. Glass towers, the eventual replacement for these monuments, were thought to "reveal the truth of the modern world to those who lived in it." And in Calgary, the truth of the modern world might be traced back to the oil find at Leduc No. 1 that initiated the area's unprecedented growth in the postwar years. H. Muschamp, "How Buildings Remember," *New Republic* (28 Aug. 1989), p. 27. The icons of industry, of progress and technological development became so close to the heart of Canadian architects that one devoted a 1937 article, published in the *Royal Architectural Institute Journal*, to a celebration of "Gasoline Stations," praising the automobile, and going on to enthuse about the "romantic" qualities of certain Canadian Tire "pit stops." Bernstein, *Building With Words*, p. 11.

3 Eli Mandel, *Out of Place* (Erin 1977), p. 19.

4 Ibid., p. 13.

5 A. Pérez-Gómez, "The Architecture of Richard Henriquez: A Praxis of Personal Memory," in Howard Shubert, ed., *Richard Henriquez et le Théâtre de la mémoire/ Richard Henriquez: Memory Theatre* (Vancouver, 1993), p. 13.

6 John Warkentin, "Time and Place in the Western Interior," *artscanada* 22 (1972): 20–35.

7 See photos numbered 51–63, and 232 in R. Woodall, *Taken By the Wind: Vanishing Architecture of the West* (Don Mills, 1977).

8 Mandel, *Out of Place*, p. 20.

9 Ibid., p. 22.

10 Ibid., p. 36.

11 Ibid., p. 37.

12 Eli Mandel, "Auschwitz: Poetry of Alienation," *Canadian Literature* 100 (1984): 213–218.

13 Mandel, *Out of Place,* p. 14.

14 Eli Mandel, "Earthworms Eat Earthworms and Learn," in *Stony Plain* (Erin, 1973), pp. 54–55.

15 Mandel, *Out of Place*, p. 75.

16 Ibid., p. 38.

17 Ibid., p. 23.

18 David Arnason, " Interview with Eli Mandel, March 16/78," *Essays on Canadian Writing* 118/119 (1980): 70–90.

19 Mandel, *Out of Place*, p. 30.

20 Ibid., p. 34.

21 Ibid., p. 20.

22 Robert Harbison, *The Built, the Unbuilt and the Unbuildable: In Pursuit of Architectural Meaning* (London, 1991): p. 108.

23 Young, *Texture of Memory*, p. 4.

24 A. J. Arnold, "Jewish Immigration to Western Canada in the 1880's," *Canadian Jewish Historical Society Journal* 1 (1977): 82–96.

25 Ibid., p. 93.

26 "Hirsch, Baron Maurice de," in *Encyclopedia Judaica* (1971).

27 *A Worldwide Philanthropic Empire: The Life Work of Baron Maurice de Hirsch* (Tel Aviv, 1982), p. 3.

28 Louis Rosenberg, *Canada's Jews: A Social and Economic Study of Jews in Canada* (Montreal, 1993), p. 218.

29 Cyril Leonoff, *Jewish Farmers of Western Canada* (Winnipeg, 1984), p. 34.

30 After Lazarus Cohen left Hirsch, the settlers wrote to him in Yiddish: "You know what we have—or to put it better—what we don't have. You know everything and we have nothing more to say. All we want to say and plead is: Do not forget in Montreal your brothers in Hirsch! Do not forget that more than forty families are praying daily for you and we call your name as our saviour and protector." A. J. Arnold, "The Life and Times of Jewish Pioneers in Western Canada," *The Jewish Historical Society of Western Canada Second Annual Publication: A Selection of Papers Presented in 1969–1970*, pp. 51–77.

31 Mandel, Out of Place, p. 15n.

32 On a recent visit to the Hoffer vault, I discovered the Mandels' portrait of it to be a fiction, another imagined monument to the ephemerality of history. I was told by Usher Berger, on whose property the vault stands, that when the Mandels came to visit the structure—which once acted as a safe for the profits from local businesses but never as an archive—it looked as it did when I found it, full of nothing but loose board, twig and newspaper scraps, its concrete walls stripped of their wooden panelling. Mandel, *Out of Place,* p. 38.

33 Smaro Kamboureli, "Locality as Writing: A Preface to the 'Preface' of *Out of Place,"* *Open Letter* 6.2/3 (1985): 267–277.

34 Mandel, *Out of Place*, p. i.

35 Young, *Texture of Memory*, p. 4.

36 Ibid., p. 14.

37 Mandel, *Out of Place*, p. 13.

38 Meditation upon motifs of brokenness and loss plays an important role in Jewish traditions of mourning: "The rent garment and broken artifacts of daily life have long served as communal signs of mourning . . . . Tombstone reliefs of broken candle-sticks, or a splintered tree, or a bridge half torn away, are among several images recalling life interrupted by death." Young, *Texture of Memory*, p. 119 and p. 186.

39 Ibid., p. 120.

40 Mandel, *Out of Place*, p. 13.

41 Ibid., p. 23.

42 Ibid., p. 20.

43 Definitions of postmodernism proliferate like the leaves in spring. Umberto Eco, however, offers one that is relevant to the context of this essay: "The postmodern reply to the modern consists of recognizing that the past, since it cannot really be destroyed, because its destruction leads to silence, must be revisited: but with irony, not innocently." Umberto Eco, *Postscript to the Name of the Rose* (New York, 1984), p. 67.

44 Muschamp, "How Buildings Remember," p. 44.

45 Shubert, *Richard Henriquez*, p. 44.

46 Pérez-Gómez, "The Architecture of Richard Henriquez," p. 14.

47 In the plans for a condominium to be built on Vancouver's English Bay, Henriquez includes the footprint of the apartment building that stood on the site, the houses that preceded it, and the first-growth forest that preceded the beach houses is referred to by concrete cast stumps set into the yard. Shubert, *Richard Henriquez*, pp. 32, 44.

48 Without commenting on it in poem or note, Mandel includes at the end of *Out of Place* a letter from a representative of the Jewish Colonization Association in London to a Canadian Member of Parliament who suggested the site of the cemetery at Hirsch be marked. Beside the letter is Ann Mandel's photograph of the cemetery gates. Mandel, *Out of Place*, p. 69. A plaque is in place at the cemetery today, which reads: "Hirsch Colony 1892–1942. Erected in Commemoration of the Baron de Hirsch Jewish Agricultural Colony. Jewish Immigrants who mostly came from Czarist Russia, Roumania, Austria and Poland were assisted by the Baron de Hirsch Colonization Association. These Colonists were motivated by a keen desire to escape religious persecution and racial discrimination, with the rights to own and farm their land and freely adhere to their orthodox faith."

49 Mandel, *Out of Place*, p. 27.

"Were things that bad?" The Holocaust Enters Community Memory from *Delayed Impact: The Holocaust and the Canadian Jewish Community*

Franklin Bialystok

On 17 April 1978, when I was in my seventh year of teaching history, I was walking down a hall at North Toronto Collegiate Institute to teach a grade twelve class on the rise of the Nazis. I was joined by two students, who asked if I had watched the NBC miniseries *Holocaust* on television the previous evening. I replied that I had not. They were surprised, given my background and my vocation. They remarked on the horrible scenes that had been shown and asked, in complete innocence, "Were things that bad?" I was stunned. I had read previews of the program that had dismissed it as a trivial, sugarcoated project designed to sell products for its advertisers. It had not dawned on me that children born in

1960 who had no familial connection with World War II had little or no idea of what had happened to European Jews. As we entered the classroom, the rest of the students joined in the discussion. I had rarely seen such keen interest in a historical event. Students asked what they could read and requested that more class time be devoted to the subject. When I went to the school library, I was surprised to find that there was little information available. Certainly the course text mandated by the Ontario Ministry of Education was of no value. In time, the other teacher of the course and I put together some materials, and the following summer we worked on developing a few lessons for the coming year.

My students' experience was not unique. Thousands of high school students in Ontario and elsewhere first learned of the Holocaust that week. The miniseries was a catalyst in the raising of awareness about the catastrophe, a process that had been building for several years. There were three factors that contributed to this development. The first was a commitment by the Jewish community to Holocaust education and commemoration. By 1975 the community had, with some reluctance, acceded to the demands of Holocaust survivors that the legacy of the tragedy be part of the community agenda. The National Holocaust Remembrance Committee, established by Congress, begun its activities in 1973. Local HRCs quickly sprang up in a number of Canadian cities. Through a process of trial and error, and despite some opposition from local federations, these committees succeeded in developing programs, most significantly in education. It was largely through the efforts of the survivors, some of whom had been in the forefront in confronting the established community in the 1960s over its apparent inaction regarding neo-Nazism and antisemitism, that these endeavours took place. In time, many survivors who had been silent about their experiences or unwilling to become involved in community affairs took the courageous step of speaking publicly.

When they first told their stories in an open setting, they were astounded at the reception they received. Most survivors had shut their experiences inside the closet of their memories. They had not been asked about their lives for thirty years, and they had been unwilling to speak out. According to Gerda Steinitz-Frieberg, "the main reason survivors didn't speak is that they had a real problem with recalling the terrible memories. They tried to push it [sic] out of their lives, They tried to live their normal lives, not realizing that speaking about it made it easier to cope with. They knew they were third-class citizens; *they* didn't have the courage to speak up, so *they* withdrew into survivor communities."[1]

By the mid-1970s, this attitude was changing. Survivors had shed their immigrant mentality and now considered themselves Canadians, and some were no longer embarrassed about discussing their past. As well, after more than a decade of witnessing the revival of antisemitism, they were no longer willing to remain silent. This was especially so in the late 1970s, when Holocaust denial began to attain notoriety. Their most receptive audience was students. Philip Weiss of Winnipeg began talking because he felt the responsibility to speak "for those here and those who perished. [I was accepted by the students] with open arms. They listen, they want to know, they are passionate." Leo Lowy of Vancouver first spoke at the first Holocaust seminar for secondary school students in Canada in 1976. He recalled: "The inner feeling was that I had a story to tell, and for one reason or another, I never told my children. They knew that I survived the camps. We never discussed it . . . I relived my life to the point that I didn't realize the impact that it had on my psyche . . . I just had to go back to describe to these kids the emotions, the feelings, the behaviour that I had at that age." Nathan Leipciger of Toronto broke down the first time he was interviewed on a local television program, but in time he developed a strategy to overcome his emotions. "I could talk about it and detach myself from the story, almost as an observer. It helped me isolate that period and put it as a separate part of my life. While I still felt it emotionally, I could express it without becoming emotional. I really appreciated the interaction and the satisfaction n. This became the means of me dealing with my own feelings, reliving my own experience, being able to vocalize things . . . I always have nightmares before I'm going to talk, not after I talk."[2]

The second factor was the explosion of research and media coverage about the event. In the 1960s a monumental study, *The Destruction of European Jewry*, by Raul Hilberg, constituted the acme of scholarship on the subject. The scope and language of the work, however, made it inaccessible to most readers.[3] More readable were the novels of Elie Wiesel, based on his experiences and reflections,[4] and a Canadian work, *Child of the Holocaust*, by Jack Kuper, a fictionalized account of the author's life during the war. The most widely read book was, and remains, *Anne Frank: The Diary of a Young Girl.* Meanwhile, scholars were carrying out research in archives in Washington and Germany and at Yad Vashem, the memorial institute in Jerusalem. The collective outpouring of scholarly works, fiction, and memoirs aroused growing public interest. This focus was accentuated in the 1970s with such works as Lucy Dawidowicz's readable, though flawed, account *The War against the Jews.*[5] By 1980, a field of research had been firmly established that encompassed history, literary analysis, and the social sciences. Concurrently, university courses on the Holocaust, scholarly conferences, and professional development programs for educators were underway.

Of greater import was the depiction of the Holocaust in the popular media. One example was the attention devoted by Hollywood. Between 1962 and 1978, there had been few films that had Holocaust related themes. But in the next decade at least twenty-three feature films and thirty-four documentaries on the topic were made in the United States.[6] Together with novels, plays, memoirs, and collections of stories, poems, and articles, a veritable library of Holocaust literature was becoming available and accessible to a wide readership.

In Canada, with the publication of *None Is Too Many* in 1982, the revelation of this country's shameful immigration policies created a national response. Its authors, Irving Abella and Harold Troper, appeared on national news programs and spoke at universities, commemoration services, and book fairs across the country. The book was a wake-up call for the Canadian Jewish community. It made them mindful of the fragility of their position by documenting Canadian antisemitism for a new generation. For the wider community, *None is Too Many* questioned the Canadian myth of tolerance and acceptance contributed to the new examination of immigration policies and ethnicity.[7] The publication of the book coincided with the second decade of official multiculturalism. Whereas the first decade had stressed the accomplishments and contributions of ethnic and racial groups to the Canadian mosaic, the emphasis in the early 1980s was changing to the empowerment of ethnic communities.[8] This development had ramifications in a number of areas, most notably education. As the Jewish community was instrumental in developing materials and methodologies for teaching the Holocaust, educators found that the event could be used as a vehicle for anti-racist awareness.

The third factor in the growing awareness about the Holocaust in the 1970s arose as a generation of young Canadian Jews, born during and after the war, found themselves disengaged from their roots in the Jewish community. Unlike their parents and grandparents, they had no traditional neighbourhoods, secular organizations, or Yiddish to tie them to each other and to their past. Many of them felt rootless. For some, re-establishing the connection lay in a return to religious observance. For others, it meant becoming involved in Jewish causes. In the post-1967 period, these causes included support for Israel, opposition to anti-Jewish policies in the Soviet bloc, and combatting antisemitism. In combination, they created the perception, whether real or imagined, that Jews were vulnerable. It was not a long stretch to reach back three decades in order to understand that vulnerability might lead to extinction. In the 1970s, a small but influential group of young Canadian Jews seized on the legacy of the Holocaust as a defining element of their identity. They transformed this appreciation of the tragedy into practical ends. Working together with survivors and their children, they were instrumental in pushing the established community to adopt Holocaust programs and erect memorials to the event. As a result, the institutionalization of the Holocaust was an unmistakeable aspect of Jewish ethnic identity by 1985.

HOLOCAUST REMEMBRANCE IN MONTREAL

In the 1970s, Lou Zablow, a founder of the Association of Former Concentration Camp Inmates/Survivors of Nazi Oppression and the first survivor on the Congress executive, occasionally met Saul Hayes for lunch. Hayes had not been particularly receptive to the survivors' concerns in previous years. When asked later why the two men got together, Zablow responded that, although they had not agreed on Congress's response to the antisemitic incidents of the 1960s, there was no personal animosity between them. On the question of why Congress had acceded to the resolution at the 1971 plenary that had led first to the creation of the HRC Quebec Region and then to the national committee, Zablow commented: "It was strictly a practical political decision. It was better to have a Lou Zablow in than out."[9]

While pragmatism may have been the guiding principle underlying the inclusion of the survivors in the established community, within a decade this expedient had outgrown its original purpose. The reality was that commemoration and education about the Holocaust had become institutionalized in Montreal's Jewish community. This was a logical development given that in the 1970s the city had the largest Jewish community and the largest survivor community in Canada, proportionately the largest survivor community of any city in North America, and the headquarters of the Congress. The process of making Holocaust remembrance an integral part of the community's agenda, however, was not assured. Some community leaders were reluctant to carry out the construction of a Holocaust centre within the federation building, concerns about costs and design may have masked a greater reluctance to yield territory to survivors, who wanted their story told. But the mood of the community was in contrast to the hesitancy shown by the establishment. The commitment of survivors, their children, and young Canadian Jews was more persuasive than the reluctance of some leaders in the community.

In the early 1970s, Holocaust programming in Montreal was neither systematic nor centralized. The Hillel Student Society (an organization of Jewish students on university campuses) at McGill University, under the sponsorship of the Eastern Region of Congress, hosted a three-day teach-in on the Holocaust in 1970. Invited speakers included Raul Hilberg, Irving Greenberg, and Richard Rubenstein, three pioneers of American scholarship on the subject.[10] In May 1972, the HRC of the Eastern Region was established. Its mandate was restricted to Holocaust education in the community, including at summer camps. Commemoration services were still sponsored by the Warsaw Ghetto Committee. But in 1975, the latter committee merged with the HRC, and from that point, Yom Hashoah services came under the HRCS purview.[11]

The first education seminar organized by the HRC was held in that year. It was designed for academics, students, and community professionals and featured workshops for CEGEPs and universities, high schools, elementary Jewish day and afternoon schools, and camps. Several recommendations emerged from the seminar, including the establishment of a speakers' bureau and an education resource centre to collect materials.[12] These recommendations mirrored the initiatives of the NHRC. Indeed, at this early organizational stage there seems to have been little difference between the aims, structure, and leadership of the national committee and those of the regional committee in Montreal. Education, however, was not restricted to the HRC. The Hillel Student Society held another conference on the Holocaust in 1975, sponsored by Hadassah-Wizo Canada, a Jewish women's organization.[13]

The stiffest challenge facing the promoters of Holocaust education was in initiating programs in the French-language schools in Quebec. An article by Gerard H. Hoffman, a professor at Vanier College, notes that most textbooks in history and the social studies completely ignore the Holocaust. At best, one writer mentioned the event in discussing the "horrors of Vietnam, Biafra, etc." Hoffman felt that part of the problem was that younger teachers were sympathetic with the anti-Zionist rhetoric of the New Left (which viewed Zionism as imperialism) and that the erosion of the education department's inspectorate meant that teachers were free to teach what they wanted.[14] Given this distance from the majority of Quebec's students, the regional committee limited itself to educational programs designed for Jewish and post-secondary students.

To commemorate the Holocaust, the HRC of the Eastern Region distributed the kits prepared by the national committee, conducted a teach-in, and held a memorial observance at which Emil Fackenheim gave the keynote address. Other activities included a weekend retreat, camp programs, sending women survivors to speak to students, an essay contest for students, and intensive seminars for students at Vanier College and Sir George Williams University (now Concordia) in 1976.[15]

In 1971, the local Allied Jewish Community Services (AICS) established a committee to look into the creation of a Holocaust memorial. The committee floundered for seven years. Its efforts were obstructed by the Jewish Public Library (JPL), in whose basement the memorial was to be housed, and by conflicting initiatives articulated by the NHRC and the HRC Quebec Region. One officer of the Jewish Public Library reportedly exclaimed, "I don't want horror chambers."[16] At the AJCS there was concern about funding the capital costs of the project and finding money for its operation. There were also questions about the design and purpose of the memorial. Was it to be a shrine to victims? Was it to be a place for research and study? Was it to be an exhibition hall? The NHRC had presented a resolution at the 1974 CJC plenary that a permanent memorial be erected. Was the memorial at the JPL a duplication of this project or a replacement for it? If the memorial was to have an educational function, would it supplant the mandate assumed by the regional HRC to promote educational materials and seminars? These questions hobbled the committee. Yet the memorial was opened as the Montreal Holocaust Memorial Centre in October 1979. In a period of less than two years, some of the obstacles that had beset the project were overcome, funds were raised, a design was accepted, construction proceeded quickly, and the first Holocaust centre in Canada was established.[17] Most of the credit for this achievement is owing to a small group of individuals, whose personal background was far removed from the horrors of wartime Europe.

Stephen Cummings was the driving force behind the creation of the centre. At first glance he was a most unlikely candidate for the job. In 1976 he was in his mid-twenties, the son of an influential and well-established Westmount family. He had been raised in affluence, without much contact with survivors or knowledge of the Holocaust. His first exposure to the tragedy occurred during the Eichmann trial in 1961. "I was just stunned . . . all of a sudden this was not a tragedy that happened somewhere else in the world. It became very personal . . . From that point I became more tribal." As an undergraduate student in the United States, Cummings became disillusioned with the civil rights movement because of the increasing alienation between Jews and Blacks. In 1976, shortly after the birth of his first child, he went to Israel. Cummings remembered that while visiting Yad Vashem, "[I] was overwhelmed by power and powerlessness and the sense of being a parent and not being able to protect your children . . . I came back to Montreal thinking, 'I've got to talk about this, got to teach people.' As a Jew I have that responsibility to myself and as a human being. The Holocaust is the worst example . . . There is something unique about a cultured Europeanized civilization having manifested so much evil . . . There's something that really resonates here. This is something we should have in Montreal."[18] Stephen Cummings was a notable example of his generation among Canadian Jews. Estranged from their European roots and unable to find meaning, as Jews, in other causes, they looked to the recent past. In many ways, the legacy of the

Holocaust fulfilled several needs: the link with their forebears, the imperative of Jewish survival, counteracting dehumanization and racism, and the necessity to commemorate and to educate themselves and their children.

In the fall of 1976, Cummings and approximately twenty other young Montrealers approached Michael Greenblatt, chair of the AJCS Holocaust Committee. Greenblatt recorded: "This group asked me and other members of the committee if they could be given the authority to implement and carry out such a project to completion. In view of the foregoing, the fact that these young men and women were so vitally concerned, interested, and might have funding potential, the group was given the authority to move ahead with the suggestion that the original committee be kept informed."[19] Cummings and his group knew that they had not only to keep the committee informed but also to include it in their plans. The committee was made up largely of survivors who for fifteen years had been through the battles with the established community. For Cummings, the problem was immediate. "The Holocaust Committee was not accomplishing its goals . . . I said, 'Look, we'll do it together' with a group of younger people, most of them born here, mostly in their 20s and 30s. [We] combined that group with survivors, most from the Association of Survivors . . . we essentially told the powers that be in Federation that they had to let us run the committee . . . not to be snotty; [we didn't want] the survivors to think that we were this month's fad, and we were able to come together as a group."[20]

The reconstructed committee first met in Lou Zablow's den. He remembers that it was "the young people working with us" that ended the deadlock with the federation. At the time, it was an uncommon alliance—the children of established Jews, who had largely disregarded the survivors and felt that the Holocaust was a tragedy that did not affect them directly, and survivors, a generation or more older than their fellow committee members. But the reality, as Cummings remembers, was that the committee was effective because "our common denominators were much stronger than our differences. Credibility began to develop. We were able to gain their trust which was not an easy thing. Sometimes it was a pain in the ass for us and for them. It was a passionate issue, and many times people said unfortunate things."[21]

The committee settled on the mandate, design, and budget for the centre in 1978. It was to have a dual function. First, it was to be a memorial with a place for contemplation, and second, it was to house two kinds of exhibits, one permanent and the other consisting of special projects. A capital fundraising campaign was established to meet the projected cost of construction, which was $215,000, and an operating budget of $39,900 in the first year, with a 10 per cent increment for the second year.[22] The "Resolution of Principles" stated: "The goal of the Centre is to become the focus of Holocaust awareness and programming in the community by co-ordinating and implementing educational activities; by maintaining an archival repository for exhibits and research; and by establishing resources that encourage current and future Holocaust scholarship. The Montreal Holocaust Memorial Centre fervently believes that by actively remembering the past we can ensure the future. In the words of George Santayana, 'those who do not learn from history are condemned to repeat it.'"[23]

The centre opened on 15 October 1979. Subcommittees dealing with finance, community liaison, volunteers, and program were established. As a result, the centre received widespread publicity. A comprehensive article in the *Montreal Gazette* described the layout and permanent exhibit. The first two special exhibitions were *The Jewish Child before the War,* which opened on 31 May 1980, and *Spiritual Resistance,* beginning on 5 October that year.[24] Yet in a short time, problems regarding the centre's status became apparent. There was no written commitment from the AJCS to support the centre on a long-term basis. The committee was relatively powerless within the federation and had no written regulations and procedures guaranteeing its perpetuity. A special Task Force Committee recommended to the larger committee that the centre become affiliated with the JPL, and this recommendation was approved.[25] Negotiations with the JPL for affiliated status hit roadblocks, however. The centre continued to be part of the AJCS and received most of its operating budget from this source, the remainder came from fundraising. Affiliation with the JPL would not end this relationship. The merger between the centre and the JPL was formalized on 31 August 1982. On the surface, the centre now appeared to have a permanent home. A full-time director was to be hired, and an evaluation of the agreement would take place on an annual basis for the first two years.[26]

While the centre was being built, the regional HRC continued its programming. It produced an educational kit to accompany the Holocaust miniseries in 1978, a seminar and materials on Janusz Korczak the following year, and another seminar for high school teachers on moral issues in 1982.²⁷ As with their earlier initiatives, these programs were either duplications or offshoots of projects developed by the national committee. The committee also continued with earlier programs, including the Yom Hashoah commemoration, essay contests, resource acquisitions, and teachers' seminars. It managed to carry out these projects on a minuscule budget. In 1981, for example, its expenditures totalled $15,500.²⁸ When the centre opened, its programming mandate was limited because of the latitude allowed the regional committee. Meanwhile, an independent organization in Toronto, the Canadian Centre for Studies in Holocaust and Genocide, which had existed with minimal impact for several years, provided a seed grant of $75,000 for the production of *Dark Lullabies,* a documentary about a survivor's return to Germany, by Montreal filmmaker Irene Lilienheim Angelico.²⁹

The merger between the centre and the JPL lasted for only two years, from 1982 to 1984. While the centre was responsible for presenting a budget and program, all decisions during that time were subject to approval by the JPL officers. The centre's first full-time director, Krisha Starker, was hired in 1983. She described those first two years: "The library wanted to swallow the centre, so it was fight, fight, fight. There was division [as well]. Yom Hashoah belonged to the CJC *HRC Quebec Region*, education belonged to the CJC, survivor testimony as well. Here was the centre. What the hell do you do? For me it was a responsibility to do a job. I had to protect the centre so that it would not become a subcommittee of the programming committee of the library." When asked why the JPL insisted on this imbalance in the relationship, Starker cites the fact that the centre had not been able to deliver its services adequately in the first few years because of inefficient resources, fundraising problems, and the wide mandate given to the HRC.³⁰ In the first three and a half years of operation, there was little outreach, no educational plan, and no systematic recording of subcommittee minutes. Further, only 2,500 students visited the centre during that period, a single exhibit was launched in 1981, and none was organized the following year.³¹ The centre was reinvigorated in 1983, with

Starker at the helm. But it was not until the affiliation with the JPL ended in the early fall the following year that the centre was given a wider scope. It entered in a new arrangement with the AJCS, which proved to be more amicable and equitable. In 1984, the centre hosted a special exhibit on the Lodz Ghetto, which was eventually displayed at the Gathering of Holocaust Survivors and Their Children the following year in Ottawa.[32] A few months later the HRC yielded its control over education, and an education subcommittee chaired by Professor Frank Chalk, a historian of comparative genocide at Concordia University, was established.[33]

In the early 1980s, according to one estimate, there were 30,000 survivors and their descendants in Montreal, or almost one-third of the Jewish community. In the late 1970s, the children of survivors became active participants in community affairs. One important issue for them was continuing the memorialization and knowledge about their families, who had perished in the Holocaust. Second Generation groups were established across North America, and their first conference was held in New York in 1982. The Montreal group published a newsletter, *Montreal Second Generation.* Its third issue articulated the legacy taken up by the children at the gathering of survivors in Jerusalem in 1981. It read in part: "WE TAKE THIS OATH! Vision becomes word, to be handed down from father to son, from mother to daughter, from generation to generation." The "acceptance," stated in part: "WE PLEDGE to remember."[34] Morton Weinfeld, a sociologist at McGill University and a student of the Montreal survivor community, put it this way: "I only made peace with the Holocaust at a deeper level when my daughter was born. In this way the generation process was being carried on and in some sense I was 'undoing Hitler.' I felt a certain self-confidence about the future that I had not felt prior."[35] Stephen Cummings, whose family background was far removed from Weinfeld's, expressed a similar view. "When I look into a survivor's eyes, I see these are the eyes that have seen more than me. I felt that these were my people . . . I just felt I could unabashedly embrace them. I felt respected. The adults [his parents' generation] reacted differently [to the survivors] than Jews would react today. . . It was a more hostile environment . . . 'Don't rock my boat.' If Jews truly understand Auschwitz they would have spoken because it was so overwhelming. I became involved because this was one of my ways of expressing myself as a Jew . . . It was important to make a difference as a Jew."[36]

CONTROVERSY AND DIVISION IN TORONTO

By 1980, Toronto's Jewish community was larger than that in Montreal. It was relatively wealthy and close-knit with a high proportion of synagogue members and community volunteers, and was renowned in the Jewish diaspora as, per capita, one of the greatest contributors to Israel. Toronto had become one of the primary magnets for Jewish immigrants to North America. It had a burgeoning population of newcomers from the Soviet Union, Israel, and South Africa and was the destination for most of the Montreal Jews who were leaving Quebec in the wake of the Parti Québécois's electoral victory in 1976.[37] Yet, as was the case in Montreal, when it came to imprinting the Holocaust on the collective memory of the community, some leaders were reluctant to take the initiative. It was the wider community, led by survivors and the generation born in the 1940s and 1950s, whether the children of survivors or not, and non-Jews, that provided the impetus for the project. These efforts, however, did not come without controversy. Two major splits in the community, one concerned directly with the politicization of Holocaust memory and the other with organizational primacy, meant that by the mid-1980s there were several organizations articulating the need to remember and learn about the tragedy.

After several incarnations, the Holocaust Remembrance Committee in Toronto was finally established as a standing committee of Toronto Jewish Congress (TJC), the federation of local agencies, in 1972. Its place within the organizational structure remained clouded however. Despite its name, TJC'S sole affiliation with Congress was that it was one of the myriad organizations under the umbrella of, but in no sense subservient to, the CJC. But the HRC of TJC was also connected to the Central Region of Congress. When its first director was appointed in 1976, she was employed by the region and not by TJC. The region determined the parameters of the HRC, and TJC enforced them. This confusing situation reduced the efficacy of the HRC. For example, as a committee of the local federation, it could not conduct programs outside Metropolitan Toronto. Yet it was a provincial body, the executive of the Central

Region (formerly the Ontario Region) of Congress, to which the chair of the HRC reported. Given this confusing state of affairs, it is not surprising that in its first five years the HRCs activities were restricted. The committee was not entirely ineffectual however. Its focus was on three areas: commemoration, responding to neo-Nazi groups, and education.

The annual Yom Hashoah commemoration had become an important event in the community calendar by the 1970s. Until late in the decade most of the HRC's programming and expenses were devoted to the event. Held in the city's largest synagogues, the commemoration featured prominent Jewish scholars and non-Jewish political leaders. In 1977, for example, Professor Howard Roiter of McGill University, an early advocate of Holocaust studies, was the keynote speaker.[38] The next year Emil Fackenheim was featured, together with Roy McMurtry, a member of the provincial legislature.[39] The committee was also instrumental in establishing ties with the non-Jewish community. In 1976 it sponsored a lecture by Dr Douglas Young entitled "A Christian View of the Holocaust" and a presentation by Giorgio Bassani on the movie *The Garden of the Finzi-Continis.*[40]

In the 1976–77 fiscal year, the HRC was granted a half-time staff person. Ruth Resnick, a long-time employee of the local federation, was given the position. Her kind-heartedness and determination were central to the success of the committee for the next decade. The operating budget of the committee was $15,900 in 1976–77, but this was reduced to $13,687 the following year. In 1978–79, the committee was disbanded and then reconstituted; it undertook a wider range of programming, and the budget was raised to $29,462.[41]

With the demise of John Beattie and the Canadian Nazi Party in the late 1960s, the perceived threat of right-wing extremist groups in Toronto had diminished but was not extinguished. In February 1967, Donald Andrews founded the misnamed Edmund Burke Society. While not outwardly antisemitic or proto-Nazi, its program was influenced by the John Birch Society, the largest extremist group in the United States. Andrews was joined by Paul Fromm, an articulate university student who remains active in extremist groups. Fromm formed the Western Guard, Toronto's most prominent radical right-wing organization in the 1970s,[42] Andrews and Fromm in those years were expounding racist but not overtly antisemitic views. The community had difficulty countering this problem. The hate-propaganda legislation did not offer much promise as a deterrent to racist activities. The first person charged under the legislation was Armand Siksna, who was accused of posting "white power" placards in 1974. He was acquitted because of insufficient evidence. Jewish leaders were frustrated by this development, fearing that the provincial attorney general would be unwilling to test the legislation again.[43]

For the first few years of its existence, the HRC did not respond to extremists since doing so was not part of the committee's mandate. This situation changed in 1977 when its chair, Harry Wolle, resigned and was replaced by Helen Smolack. A Canadian Jew, she was part of a more vocal group within the HRC, made up of survivors and Canadian Jews, who wanted the committee to venture into anti-Nazi endeavours. Its attempt to expand its mandate was obstructed by the JCRC, however. On 20 January 1978, the parent body resurrected the Anti-Nazi Committee (formerly CANC), which had ceased operation in 1969. Its task was to respond to extremist groups. The Nationalist Party of Canada was the newest radical right-wing organization to gain prominence, as a result of its recruitment of students and its attempt to gain tax-exempt status by declaring itself a political party in Ontario.[44] The Anti-Nazi Committee met with Arthur Wishart, attorney general of Ontario, to discuss the party's activities, and Wishart turned down the party's application because of irregularities. The committee took credit for this decision.[45] The Anti-Nazi Committee's focus, however, was soon diverted by events in Skokie, Illinois.

For months the American Nazi Party had been seeking permission to hold a march in Skokie, a suburb of Chicago in which many survivors had established homes and businesses. The publicity given to the town was widespread, especially following a showing of a docudrama on network television starring Danny Kaye. The HRC, seeing the controversy as an opportunity to become actively involved, planned to send a large delegation to Skokie to join American Jews in a counter-demonstration. In preparation, it held a protest at Nathan Phillips Square in front of the Toronto City Hall, in conjunction with the thirty-fifth anniversary of the Warsaw Ghetto Uprising. Franklin Littell, a theologian from Philadelphia, pledged that Christians would stand with Jews in

Skokie. Congress president Rabbi Gunther Plaut stated that he expected Canadians to go to the Illinois community. Other speakers at the protest included John Roberts, the federal secretary of state, Larry Grossman, Ontario's minister of consumer and commercial relations, and David Crombie, the mayor of Toronto. The HRC launched a petition to the federal government urging that "Nazi War Criminals still among us be brought to justice and the Nationalist Party of Canada be denied legitimization." This petition subsequently gathered 30,000 signatures.[46]

The Anti-Nazi Committee regarded the HRC activities as an intrusion on its mandate. To mollify the HRC, the ANC sponsored a rally at Earl Bales Park in North York on 25 June 1978, the same time as the Skokie march was held, at which Rabbi Plaut was the main speaker. The rally attracted 3,000 people, according to the *Toronto Star*.[47] It was judged by the committee to be a successful compromise between sending a large delegation to Skokie and doing nothing. Yet within the Anti-Nazi Committee the divisions between proponents of action and milder voices, led by committee chair Harry Simon, returned. Jacob Egit declared that "survivors will not stand back and will fight them [neo-Nazis] whenever and wherever." Simon replied that the Chicago organizers had told him that the march was to take place on 25 June, but that there were no facilities in Skokie for outside protestors, and if a delegation was to come, it could be there for only half an hour. The committee, lukewarm to pressure from the HRC to sponsor a large contingent, used this information as a pretext for sending a symbolic delegation instead.[48] Simon, still upset, responded that "we were not responsible for the Skokie decision. It was made by their [the HRC] community. We were reacting to it in a moderate way."[49]

For the HRC, moderation was a code word for passivity. The new guard in the HRC, led by Helen Smolack, Rose Ehrenworth, and Sabina Citron, had been frustrated for years by Congress's apparent unwillingness to counteract the neo-Nazis. In addition, it was outraged that the CJC had not been adamant in pressing the federal government to bring suspected war criminals to trial.[50] According to Citron, the only survivor among the three women, "they [Congress] never touched the issue of war criminals, and when they did it was too late. It wasn't a question of acceptance [of survivors]; it was a question of not doing anything."[51]

TJC was not about to tolerate the HRC's excursion into uncharted waters. Congress had been quietly lobbying the government for decades about war criminals, and the Anti-Nazi Committee was countering the racist propaganda of the neo-Nazis. At first, TJC, under the leadership of Rose Wolfe, tried to accommodate the frustrations of the HRC. At an officers' meeting on 6 July 1978, with Smolack present, she stated, "It was necessary for any responsible community organization to work in a disciplined manner." She then read a resolution which concluded, "The Holocaust Remembrance Committee is advised that it issue no public statements in respect to social and political action and it conduct its activities and affairs within the purview of the defined purposes."[52]

The resolution was adopted by TJC on 17 July, but Smolack refused to accept it. At a meeting of the HRC on 9 August, she read a telegram from committee member Celia Airst which condemned the actions of the officers of TJC. A recommendation that representatives be selected from the HRC to patch up relations with TJC was rejected. The division between Smolack and her supporters and a group urging reconciliation was growing. In a report on the meeting to Irwin Gold, the director of TJC, E.Y. Lipsitz, the executive director of Congress's Central Region, wrote, "Mrs. Smolack is biased and hostile which makes her unfit to chair this Committee."[53] She was asked to resign, but she refused.[54] Finally, the executive committee of TJC dissolved the HRC.[55]

A front-page article in the 23 November issue of the *Canadian Jewish News* stated, "Toronto Jewish Congress Vote Oust Anti-Nazi Group in Controversy." Letters to the editor opposed the TJC decision. One reader wrote: "It may well be that some group in the Toronto Jewish Congress is doing some work to combat our enemies, however, the effect seems [*sic*] to be minimal if any." Rose Ehrenworth stated: "The words 'never again' embedded in the hearts and minds and on the lips of Jews everywhere, have no meaning whatsoever unless they are translated into action." In a letter to the *Jewish Standard* entitled "PROgress or CONgress," Arnold Friedman, another member of the HRC, wrote: "The action of the Toronto Jewish Congress in disbanding the Holocaust Committee . . . is tantamount to 'Shooting the Messenger' if you don't like the message."[56]

TJC reconstituted the HRC in the winter of 1979. Some of the old members decided to remain, but the leaders on the new committee were mostly younger Canadian and second-generation people. Meanwhile, Smolack, Citron, and a number of their supporters created their own organization, the Holocaust Remembrance Association (HRA). For many years, it was affiliated with the Toronto Zionist Council. Smolack became the association's first chairperson.[57] Although the HRA and Congress have locked horns on a number of issues, the feeling in the community is that they have worked toward common goals. Since 1980, the most prominent leaders in the HRC in Toronto have been Nathan Leipciger and Gerda Steinitz-Frieberg. Leipciger served as chair of the local HRC from 1981 to 1988 and since then as chair and co-chair of the NHRC. Steinitz-Frieberg was chair of Congress's Ontario Region in the early 1990s. Yet they demonstrate no rancour toward the Smolack-Citron group. Leipciger commented: "I always supported Sabina Citron. Although I was in Congress, I became a member of the HRA. I believe that Sabina should act on her own. She was a free agent. She didn't have to go to the president. She could act independently and quickly. . . So officially she was not supported, [but] personally many survivors supported her." Steinitz-Frieberg said that the ouster of the committee was unique in the history of TJC. It showed, she said, "the insensitivity of the community." Citron responded, "I really have no animosity with respect to anyone, but I feel bitter that nothing was being done about war criminals. I can't say that I hate anyone. People were misguided and they acted on what they believed."[58]

The dissolution of the HRC and the creation of the HRA were indicative of the divisions that still existed in Toronto between the established "old guard" of Canadian Jews and the survivors and their supporters. It would be fair to state that while not all survivors who were becoming politically active in these years took as strident a stance as the nascent HRA, most were supportive of their criticisms of the traditional leadership. The split was unfortunate in that the various positions held by community leaders regarding the mandate of a local Holocaust committee could not be accommodated within one body. The splintering of the community over the ownership of Holocaust memory became a feature of ethnic politics in the early 1980s.

Another manifestation of the split in the Jewish community took place at this time. Since 1947, B'nai Brith Canada (BB) and Congress, together with the Canadian Zionist Federation, constituted the NJCRC and the regional

JCRC. But in the mid 1960s the relationship between BB and the CJC began to be strained.[59] Ultimately, in 1981 the CJC decided to restructure the NJCRC without BB. The events leading to the rupture were complex and controversial. What follows is a short history of those events to explain how BB became involved in Holocaust remembrance and education under its own aegis.

With 15,000 members in 1964, BB was the largest Jewish service organization in Canada. Its role in community affairs was overseen by a special committee, the Anti-Defamation League (ADL) of District 22, modelled on its American counterpart. On 21 June 1971, BB replaced the ADL by creating the League for Human Rights (the League) of B'nai Brith Canada. This change was approved by the JCRC Central Region.[60] Problems arose later that year, however, when BB refused to send delegates to the CJC plenary. The organization stated that its lodges were prevented by the Supreme Lodge from being members of other organizations. In fact, in many instances, especially in smaller communities, the same individuals served on both organizations. In response, Sydney Harris, the outgoing chair of CJC Central Region and the incoming president of Congress, accused BB of "isolationism" and "parochialism."[61]

Throughout the 1970s, tensions between the two organizations increased. Congress viewed BB's entry into anti-Nazi activities and its comments about Israeli affairs, Soviet Jewry, and war criminals as an attempt to stake out territory outside the NJCRC. BB, for its part, felt increasingly shut out of the decision-making process on the joint committee, and it saw the committee as impotent, since final decisions were made by the CJC.[62] Harvey Crestohl, president of BB, in a letter to Frank Diamant, the executive vice-president, wrote: "I am sure that I am not alone in believing that as it presently exists, the JCRC is a mere shadow of what it was intended to be, and of what is [*sic*] once was, and of what it should be again."[63]

On 13 September 1981, the officers and executive of CJC passed a motion to "reconstitute and expand the JCRC," code words that effectively expelled BB from the committee. This decision was made executory in a letter from Congress to BB four days later, which gave notice of the former's termination of the partnership.[64] In essence, the position of BB and the decision by the CJC indicated that each organization was asserting its claim to speak on behalf of

Canadian Jews. The struggle came at a price. As the editor of the *Jewish Standard* put it: "Now the partnership is coming to an end and the Jewish community looks on at the disruption with dismay. Cooperation must yield to competition and competition to confrontation."[65] By the early 1980s, this unfortunate development had created fissures in the Toronto Jewish community over organizational primacy. One of these was a power struggle over how best to respond to expressions of antisemitism and the legacy of the Holocaust. The principal players were the HRC of TJC, the HRA, and the League.

TEACHING THE HOLOCAUST IN ONTARIO

When the Toronto HRC was formed in 1972, it had identified three areas of primary importance: remembrance, combatting antisemitism, and education. Commemoration of the victims of the tragedy had begun even before the Holocaust ended. Commemorative services were relatively easy to organize. They required a venue and a program, and the audience was ready-made. Combatting antisemitism was much more difficult from a strategic and organizational perspective. The traditional approach of backroom diplomacy employed by the established community had been challenged by survivors and their supporters since the 1960s. Conflicts between these two groups over exerting pressure on the government to legislate against war criminals and deniers of the Holocaust was a constant in the Toronto community until 1985. When it came to education, however, a different set of obstacles had to be overcome. There was little division in the Jewish community over the necessity to teach about its recent past. Essentially, the problems were pragmatic rather than philosophical. How could the Jewish community convince educational authorities that the curriculum should include the Holocaust? How could the event be taught without adequate resources or teacher training? Who should be the primary target—students in Jewish schools, students in public schools, Jewish adults, or the community in general? Where would the funding come from? Would learning about the Holocaust not reinforce the feeling that Jews were a people forever slated for exclusion? How could learning about the tragedy not cause trauma?

These practical problems meant that education was the last frontier to be conquered. In the mid-1960s the frontier seemed impassable. The problems were manifold: insufficient public awareness and consciousness; a Jewish community preoccupied with responding to antisemitism; and, most important, an antiquated, Anglocentric education system. A decade later, the frontier was being explored. Interest in and knowledge of the Holocaust was rapidly increasing; the Jewish community was better organized; tentative programs for students and teachers had been inaugurated; and educators had been freed from the constrictive teaching model of decades past. By the mid-1980s, the frontier had been crossed. In Ontario the Holocaust was on the provincial curriculum; two curricula had been written for the two largest school boards in the province; student and teacher training was growing; a Holocaust education and memorial centre had opened in Toronto; and adult education programs were proliferating. The impetus for Holocaust education in Ontario emanated from the HRC of TJC, but the League for Human Rights also played an important role, as did groups outside the mainstream organizations. It was this interest and involvement that most clearly illustrated the appropriation of the Holocaust as a defining point of ethnic identity by the Jewish community in Ontario.

The Modern Age, first published in 1963, was the sole textbook for the compulsory history course in grade twelve in Ontario. Its author was an outstanding professor of education who had trained a generation of teachers. Yet in more than five hundred pages, the only remarks made about the destruction of European Jewry were as follows: "[Hitler] blamed the Jews for many of Germany's troubles . . . [in Germany] most of them [the Jews] were slaughtered. They numbered about half a million but they had incurred the hatred of many peoples for their success in business and the professions, and the Nazis delighted in destroying them."[66] A new work, *The Modern Age: Ideas in Western Civilization,* was published in 1987 and became one of the approved texts for an optional course on modern history. A book of readings accompanying the text contains sixteen pages of selected readings on the Holocaust, including excerpts from *Anne Frank: The Diary of a Young Girl,* Elie Wiesel's *Night,* Yevgeny Yevtushenko's poem "Babi Yar," Paul Tillich's *The Courage to Be,* and Dietrich Bonhoeffer's *Letters and Papers from Prison.*[67]

The evolution from *The Modern Age* of the 1960s to the similarly titled work a generation later is indicative of the delayed impact of the Holocaust on public education. While the earlier text provided little and erroneous information, the later one utilized carefully chosen primary materials. That all senior students in Ontario in the first case did not learn about the Holocaust, and that some students who elected to study modern history a generation later may have learnt a fair amount, symbolizes the extent to which the Holocaust entered the public discourse.

Ben Kayfetz, the executive director of the JCRC, undertook a one-person campaign for the inclusion of the Holocaust in public education. In 1966, he persuaded a reluctant JCRC to submit a brief to the Hall-Dennis Commission, which was reviewing the provincial education system. He pointed to *The Modern Age* as a prime example of the poor quality of resources available to teachers.[68] The commission did not even send a letter of acknowledgment to the committee. On reflection, Kayfetz, who had been a high school teacher before entering the service during World War II, remarked, "This is a perfect example of the indifference that applied in the sixties to the [teaching of the] Holocaust. I was disturbed by this."[69] Yet the commission made sweeping recommendations in its 1968 report, many of which were adopted by the government. Three years later, spurred by these changes and the release of the federal government's report on official multiculturalism, the Ontario Human Rights Commission funded a survey on bias in Ontario textbooks. The result was *Teaching Prejudice,* by Garnet McDiarmid and David Pratt, two professors at the Ontario Institute for Studies in Education (OISE). With respect to the Holocaust and the treatment of minorities in World War II, they reported that the lack of information was "astonishing." In general, Jews were stereotyped more than other minorities. From my perspective as a teacher, the survey had a major impact on pedagogy in the 1970s. The Anglo-Celtic bias in the curriculum that had dominated Ontario schools since their inception was rapidly giving way to a more universal paradigm.

In the early 1970s, the Toronto HRC was captive to the same impediments regarding education as its counterpart in Montreal. It lacked both a systematic approach and knowledge of the workings of the educational bureaucracy and the needs of students and teachers. Initially, the committee approached the Board of Jewish Education (BJE) of Metropolitan Toronto to inquire about the state of Holocaust studies in its schools; it was not a promising start.

Between 1967 and the late 1970s, the only mention of the Holocaust, the Nazi period, or antisemitism recorded in the minutes of the BJE was to an exhibit on the Holocaust on loan from the United States in 1973.[70] Three years later Harry Wolle, chair of the HRC, wrote to Rabbi Irwin Witty, the director of the BJE, requesting that it and the HRC co-sponsor a conference on teaching the Holocaust. Witty surveyed the teachers as to their willingness to devote seminar sessions to the topic in August. They were not interested and stated that teaching the Holocaust was "a low order of priority." Witty maintained, however, that they were not uninterested. Only one school in eighteen did not teach the topic, he said, but there was room for professional development. Yet he rejected the HRCs involvement in such a conference since it "belongs strictly within the prerogative of the Board of Jewish Education."[71] In 1979 the HRC requested that the BJE provide a summary of programs on the Holocaust. There is no indication in the HRC or BJE files of any response to this request.[72]

Jacob Egit was the committee member most concerned with education in the mid-1970s. He had had a long and distinguished career in public service. Born in Poland, he had been a journalist before the war and had survived the Holocaust in the Soviet Union. After returning to Poland, he served as a member of the Central Committee of Jews in Poland and as its organizer in Lower Silesia, where he planned to create a new Jewish presence. This dream was shattered by events in Poland, and in 1958 Egit immigrated to Canada, where he became the assistant director of the Histadrut, an Israeli-based labour organization.[73] In 1975, he put together a proposal for a program "of ongoing activity and education in our community to further the knowledge of the Holocaust and resistance." The proposal had thirteen recommendations, including three involving the BJE. Egit estimated that an annual budget of $15,000 to $20,000 would be needed to carry out the program. The proposal was summarized in the 1976 HRC report to the TJC executive, but without any recommendation that it be considered. This response was hardly surprising. The BJE was not well disposed to the interference of the HRC in the training of its teachers, and TJC had little appetite for spending a large sum on a project that was clearly not a priority for its own Holocaust committee. Egit's proposal, though well intentioned, did not recognize that the frontier lay in the public schools.[74]

Some progress in Holocaust education in the late 1970s occurred at the post-secondary level, partially as a result of the efforts of the HRC, but more significantly because of the rise of interest in the topic in academe. Yehuda Bauer, the noted Israeli historian of the Holocaust, spoke to the Canadian Friends of the Hebrew University at the homes of patrons of the university in 1975. A series of lectures at the University of Toronto sponsored by the Joseph and Gertie Schwartz Foundation featured Bauer, Raul Hilberg, and Emil Fackenheim. York University started the first course on the Holocaust in Canada in 1975, and the University of Toronto followed suit three years later. York's Jewish Student Federation sponsored a Holocaust Remembrance Week in 1977. Henry Feingold, a historian who had written about the American role in the Holocaust, was the keynote speaker. Films and a mobile exhibit were provided by the NHRC; the use of these resources was facilitated by the local HRC. Two months later the HRC co-sponsored "The Second Encounter," a one-day seminar, with OISE."[75] The HRCS involvement in these programs was mainly due to the efforts of its part-time director, Ruth Resnick, rather than to the efforts of committee members themselves.

Until 1978, the various initiatives taken by the NHRC and the local organization in the field of education were limited in their impact. There was still no systematic framework or policy for dealing with school boards or ministries of education. This was also true of adult education. Despite the continuous outpouring of scholarship, including the publication of some of the documents that had been used in *None Is Too Many*,[76] there was no single catalyst that generated widespread interest. This situation changed over the four nights in 1978 when NBC aired the docudrama *Holocaust*. This presentation, a prototypical Hollywood miniseries based on the *Roots* model, was banal and was excoriated by serious scholars. Historian Henry Feingold commented: "The 'Holocaust' was sold much like toothpaste. . . [Gerald Green, the producer and screenwriter] was not interested in finding some meaning or lesson in Auschwitz . . . Thus, while it may be true that the individual incidents are based on fact, the story in its entirety is the most improbable fiction . . . I suspect that in a few weeks we will hear very little about 'Holocaust.' The public will be anxiously awaiting the next TV happening."[77] Feingold's review was valid, but his predic-

tion of the program's short-term impact was not. The miniseries was enormously popular and the subject of numerous articles. It did more to spur interest in
the Holocaust in Canada, the United States, and western Europe than any other
event since the Eichmann trial.[78] For the post-war generation, which had been
either shielded from the horror or told that the Nazi era was an aberration, the
glossy images of well-fed actors parading as concentration camp inmates had
much less impact than the fact that the program opened old wounds. This was
especially the case when it was broadcast in West Germany the next year. The
historian and journalist Joachim Fest, writing in the influential *Frankfurter
Allegemeine Zeitung,* stated: "What has been said about the triviality of the film
remains undeniable; the sensationalism, the sentimentality, the bad taste whereby the gruesome is made entertaining. Despite all this, in the end one is inclined
to concur with the undertaking."[79]

Before the miniseries was shown, Congress president Gunther Plaut had
contacted the CBC about broadcasting it. The corporation did not do so, but
CBC radio devoted a special to the program.[80] Meanwhile, Ruth Resnick enlisted the aid of Professor Roger Simon of OISE to produce classroom materials for
Ontario schools. An announcement about the series and the availability of these
materials was sent to heads of history departments in Ontario secondary
schools. More than one month prior to the screening, over one hundred pack-
ages had been sent. In total, almost two hundred were mailed.[81] The response
by teachers was overwhelming. John Baker's letter to Ruth Resnick typified the
reaction. "The NBC production, your literature and CBC's *Cross Country
Check-Up* have certainly struck a raw nerve! . . . I would like more information
about the Holocaust Remembrance Committee . . . I would be willing to attend
workshops in Toronto or Kingston, speak to people in my community, donate
money, add my name to a membership list, and anything else you think might
be useful . . . I will strive to include Holocaust in the county curriculum for
Contemporary Canadian and World Concerns."[82]

Baker's interest and that of scores of other teachers in the province in
learning more about teaching the Holocaust could not be accommodated by the
HRC in Toronto until 1979, because of the dissolution of the existing committee the previous September. After the HRC was reconstituted, it embarked on a

policy of meeting the needs of Ontario's teachers and students. In the meantime, the League initiated its own foray into Holocaust education and creation of awareness about antisemitism.

The divisions between BB and Congress were so strong in 1979 that the League was unwilling to send a representative to the new HRC. Sandra Wolfe, educational coordinator of the League, in a letter to Resnick, explained that it had been working with schools and school boards "for many years." She went on to say, "Very shortly, the League for Human Rights and B'nai Brith will be integrating and it is my understanding that a more major emphasis will be given to the specific area of Holocaust Programs."[83] In 1980, the League announced that a bibliography for teachers had been produced, with a section on the Holocaust. Of greater significance, BB hired Yaacov Glickman, a sociologist, to prepare a profile of Ontario history textbooks, with an analysis of the information devoted to the Holocaust.[84] When Glickman's proposal was accepted, he teamed up with Alan Bardikoff, a doctoral student in psychology at OISE, to conduct the research and write the report. Bardikoff was the chair of the Holocaust Education Sub-Committee of the HRC. Despite the rivalry between Congress and BB, Alan Shelman, the director of field services of the League, accepted Bardikoff without hesitation.[85]

The Glickman-Bardikoff study was published by BB as a book rather than as a report. The study found that of seventy-two history textbooks dealing with the modern world that were in use in Canada, half had nothing or less than one paragraph on the Holocaust. Only three books did a "good" job on the topic. Further, of 208 high school students attending a seminar on the Holocaust organized by the HRC in 1981, only 28 per cent had a "good" knowledge of the subject according to their self-evaluation after the seminar.[86] Clearly, the legacy of *The Modern Age* was still alive in Ontario schools. Nevertheless, the commitment by BB to fund the study, and by the HRC to inaugurate an annual student seminar indicate that changes were underway.

The League was active in other areas regarding Holocaust education in the early 1980s. Under Shelman's guidance, it produced a series of materials on different aspects of the event, including antisemitism, Nazi war criminals in Canada, and Holocaust denial.[87] In 1982 the League announced that it would publish an annual review of antisemitism in Canada "within the larger context of racism in Canada." The review relied upon antisemitic incidents reported to the League and an analysis of media coverage of events that might impact on the growth of antisemitism.[88] In 1985, Shefman proposed that fifteen educators from Canadian secondary schools engage in a two-and-half-week study tour of Germany, Poland, and Israel every two years. The first tour took place in 1986, and regular visits have been organized since then.[89] Shefman was not averse to co-operating with Congress on education projects. For instance, the two organizations were among a number of sponsors of the first symposium on teaching the Holocaust in high schools in Toronto, held in 1980. The keynote speakers included Gideon Hausner, the chief prosecutor at the Eichmann trial, Irving Greenberg of the U.S. Holocaust Memorial Council, Professor Irwin Cotler of McGill University, president-elect of the CJC, and Professor Deborah Lipstadt, who would go on to become a noted scholar of the American response to the Holocaust. The conference attracted over two hundred high school teachers from across the province.[90]

Three months after TJC dissolved the HRC, a new committee was established. Its chair was Rabbi Mark Dov Shapiro, a young assistant rabbi at Holy Blossom Temple. He immediately asked Alan Bardikoff to chair an education subcommittee. Bardikoff was only twenty-three. He had been born in Toronto and had no familial connection to the Holocaust. As a teenager, he had read poetry at Yom Hashoah services, where it was "an honour to meet with some of the survivors." He spent a year as an undergraduate at the Hebrew University, where he studied the Holocaust under the historian and educator Ze'ev Mankowitz. Returning to Toronto, Bardikoff became the director of education at Temple Har Zion, where the Holocaust was integrated into the curriculum. When he joined his friend Shapiro, a new spirit imbued the HRC. Unlike earlier leaders of the committee, the two men were young, with no direct link to the event and no political bones to pick with established Jews or with survivors, and they were educators. Bardikoff remembered that "there was a feeling that there was mistrust among the survivor community about the HRC" because of the ouster of the Smolack-Citron group. At the time, "it was clear the Congress [i.e., both TJC and the Ontario Region of CJC, who each had a hand in directing

HRC activities] didn't know what to do with us; it was gun-shy. [TJC thought,] 'Would this also become more political than it wanted it to be, more vociferous than it wanted to be?' So there was this element of never really being confident that Congress was really behind the committee."[91]

Bardikoff invited a few teachers in the public boards, including Harold Lass of the Toronto Board of Education, to join the subcommittee. At its first meeting, the new subcommittee limited its mandate to the following: "(1) organizing annually a communal observance of Yom Hashoah; (2) encouraging and promoting educational programs relating to the Holocaust."[92] Its first program was a seminar for teachers in public high schools, held on 28 October 1979. In the interim, Bardikoff and Lass began meeting with bureaucrats in the social studies and English curriculum offices of the Metropolitan Toronto boards of education and spoke at teachers' subject conferences.[93]

Bardikoff's subcommittee was unique in the TJC/CJC superstructure. Its members were all teachers from the public school boards. (I was invited to join the subcommittee in 1980.) Most were not the children of survivors, and several were not Jewish. (At present, about half the members are gentiles, as is the director of the Holocaust Education Memorial, Dr. Carole Ann Reed.) Non-Jews were not automatically ineligible for membership on Congress committees. They could be members if they contributed to the United Jewish Appeal, but this fact was not revealed by the committee leaders. Of greater significance, there was no opposition from Congress because, according to Bardikoff, "the committee [i.e., the education subcommittee] had success."[94] Its members, however, were all experienced classroom teachers who had been early proponents and practitioners of Holocaust education. Individually, they conducted professional development workshops for their own school boards and spoke to subject councils, notably in English and history.[95] The subcommittee launched two initiatives. The first was an annual one-day seminar for high school students from southern Ontario. Beginning in 1981, the seminar, held at OISE, presented a morning program of a film and a keynote speaker and an afternoon program of small workshops with speakers on a specific subject and a meeting with a Holocaust survivor.[96] This structure necessitated the participation of more than thirty teachers as speakers and facilitators, and about twenty survivors.

Thus the subcommittee enlisted the support of teachers themselves, creating a network of educators and survivors, many of whom had never spoken publicly about their experiences before. Some six hundred students (the capacity of the OISE auditorium) attended the seminar. By the mid-1980s, demand was so great that strict limits had to be placed on the students and schools participating.[97]

The second initiative was an annual one-day seminar for high school teachers. The subcommittee planned the program, and arranged with York University's Faculty of Education to co-sponsor this event, beginning in October 1982. In the morning, faculty members from York, and a keynote speaker delivered papers. In the afternoon there were content sessions, chaired by York faculty and committee members, which dealt with pedagogical approaches. Initially, seventy teachers participated, and by the mid-1980s almost one hundred were attending.[98]

While the education subcommittee was planning these seminars, boards of education in southern Ontario, most notably the two largest boards in the province—Toronto and North York—were being won over to the merits of teaching about the Holocaust. By the 1970s, the Hall-Dennis report and the federal government's policy of official multiculturalism, had changed the direction of education. Among the Metropolitan Toronto boards there was a distinct shift from the decades-old Eurocentric approach to history and literature. Now, under the guidance of the provincial Ministry of Education, they were promoting materials dealing with multiculturalism to their teachers.[99] Bardikoff and some members of his subcommittee who were teachers in Toronto and North York seized on this new direction. They held numerous meetings with board officials about developing materials on the Holocaust. As a result, each board in the spring of 1982 decided to commission its own curriculum on the Holocaust. The North York version was written by Bardikoff and Jane Griesdorf, a teacher for the board. It was designed for the language arts in grades nine and ten. Toronto determined that an interdisciplinary approach for all secondary students was preferable. It hired two of its teachers, Barbara Walther and me, to write the curriculum. All four authors were members of the education subcommittee. Drafts were prepared in 1982, but because of bureaucratic snags, the curricula were not published until three years later.[100] As word of the curricula spread to other boards in the province, requests for copies and for in-service training proliferated. Between 1982 and 1987, I conducted a number of workshops for teachers in southern Ontario as part of their professional development. For this work, I was relieved of my teaching duties, and the sponsoring board paid the Toronto board for my replacement. Similar arrangements were made to allow other members of the subcommittee to conduct seminars.[101]

Both Toronto-area boards also undertook a systematic in-service training procedure. North York held workshops for its teachers led by experienced teachers and representatives from Facing History and Ourselves, an educational foundation in Brookline, Massachusetts.[102] The Toronto board established its own Holocaust Advisory Committee, made up of board teachers, including some from the subcommittee, as part of its race relations program. Until the amalgamation of Metropolitan Toronto's school boards in 1998, this committee conducted several workshops annually. It was the only committee devoted to Holocaust education in a school board in North America.[103]

Buoyed by its success at the board level, the HRC undertook a campaign to convince the Ontario Ministry of Education to include the Holocaust in its revision of the secondary school curriculum in history and social studies. Bardikoff met with Dr Bette Stephenson, the minister of education, late in 1983. A letter was then sent out to those on the HRC's mailing list, which included hundreds of teachers. It read in part: "We believe that in a multi-cultural society like ours it is important for students to understand that extreme acts of racism and genocide have their origins in common behaviours like stereotyping and prejudice. Our endeavours have also been prompted by the generally inadequate treatment the Holocaust has received in public education. While improvements appear to have been made, we feel further effort is necessary to make this event part of our public sector's current curriculum . . . We ask that you convey your endorsement for our proposal to Dr. Stephenson."[104] Stephenson responded in a form letter. She wrote: "A review of senior division history is currently underway. As a result of these findings, I anticipate a revision of all history curricula from grade 7 to the completion of secondary school. I am referring your letter to the Ministry official responsible for this revision."[105]

The "ministry official" may have been swayed by the letters sent to Stephenson. He or she may also have been influenced by a resolution passed by the Association of Large School Boards in Ontario in May 1984 that the "provincial and territorial ministers of education incorporate studies of the Holocaust in the History, English and Social Studies curriculum" in order to "foster greater understanding of cultural relations in our schools . . . to combat racism . . . and to stem the seeming growth of intolerance towards immigrant and ethnic groups." The HRC and the League acted in an advisory capacity to the task force that wrote a report based on this resolution.[106] Ultimately, the ministry, in its revision of the curriculum in 1987, stated that students "should develop an understanding of the background to and scope of the Holocaust" in the course on twentieth-century world history. In another course on modern Western civilization, it declared that a "sample teaching strategy" on democracy should employ "the background, the progress, and the horrors of the Holocaust."[107]

A measure of credit for this development should have been given to the HRC. Congress leaders, however, were ignorant of the efforts made by the committee regarding Holocaust education until after the fact. According to Bardikoff, "the leadership was following the committee rather than leading the committee. This didn't come from the leadership. Regarding education, we went to the Ministry. Congress didn't and didn't know . . . that we would have an impact. So they would have to catch up and be pulled along . . . The survivor committee made sure that their agenda became part of the Congress agenda.[108]

By the mid-1980s, the Holocaust was being widely taught in Ontario's secondary schools. The impetus had come from the HRC and to a lesser degree from the League. They understood that the practical problems of teaching the subject in Ontario schools could only be overcome if teachers saw that the Holocaust could be used as a vehicle for anti-racist education. As Bardikoff related, "from the outset [teaching the Holocaust] was directed toward multi-culturalism and anti-racism . . . [this was] the key to success, rather than as a part of Jewish history, or for Jewish students . . . Hence the emphasis on racism, prejudice, and stereotypes."[109]

The determination by teachers to undertake the teaching of a difficult topic, however, did not stem solely from this impetus. Rather, the seminars and resources supplemented a more widespread demand by teachers that the curriculum be more meaningful. They had found that students wanted to learn about the Holocaust because of the universal questions it posed. Students asked: How could an advanced society undertake such barbarism? How and why did individuals respond in abnormal situations? What did the Holocaust reveal about intolerance and prejudice in their own society? And students struggled with the question, What was the true nature of humanity? These issues were central in the minds of my students on that day in 1978 when I was asked, "Were things that bad?" In the subsequent decade, in my classroom and in the in-service training that I and other members of the subcommittee provided, the questions had less to do with teaching about the events from 1933 to 1945 than with dealing with universal themes. In seeking answers to these questions, teachers were eager to avail themselves of the services provided by the Jewish community. As the community came to understand the workings of the educational structure by inviting teachers to be part of its work, it was better able to provide these services. Thus not only did the Jewish community become committed to Holocaust education, but its relations with the wider community were strengthened.

There are numerous examples of this process. In 1989, a survey was conducted in the history departments of the public and separate school (Roman Catholic) boards in Waterloo County regarding the teaching of the Holocaust. It revealed that thirteen of the fifteen public schools and four of the five separate schools taught the subject in the only compulsory history course.[110] In 1991, ten years after the first student seminar, the HRC education subcommittee conducted a survey of teachers who had used the resources of the committee. The vast majority responded that their motivation to teach this difficult material was the response by students to questions of human behaviour.[111]

Community outreach became a significant part of Holocaust education in the early 1980s, not only in Ontario but throughout the country. In Toronto the HRC created a Christian Outreach Subcommittee in 1981. The timing could not have been more propitious. For several years some Protestant and Catholic theologians had been reinterpreting the history of Christian antisemitism and the role of the churches, both in occupied Europe and in the West, during the Holocaust.[112] The first program in Toronto was a conference on the Holocaust and Christian education at Holy Blossom Temple, arranged by several Protestant and Catholic organizations, and the Canadian Council of Christians and Jews. Also, the subcommittee helped to program ecumenical services at several Toronto churches to commemorate Yom Hashoah, beginning in 1981.[113]

In order to further community outreach, the HRC established the Holocaust Education Week Subcommittee in 1981. Its mandate was to promote interest in the subject by having community organizations, such as libraries, community centres, synagogues, and churches, sponsor programs for adults on specific topics relating to the Holocaust. The programs were held in early November in conjunction with the anniversary of Kristallnacht. This endeavour was unique in North America. Within two years some thirty sessions had been held. By 1999 there were more than one hundred programs, attended by some ten thousand people.[114]

Rabbi Mark Dov Shapiro had accepted a pulpit in the United States in 1981. The new chair of the HRC was Nathan Leipciger, a survivor who had not been active in Holocaust-related developments until he was drafted by Shapiro to chair the subcommittee on the Yom Hashoah service. Leipciger's lack of involvement in earlier committees was an advantage, given the divisions among community organizations in the early 1980s. As he put it, "I was completely apolitical, I didn't have any baggage. I wasn't even a member of Congress, My entry card was my ignorance."[115] As chair, Leipciger became embroiled in a campaign for which he was not prepared. A new centre to house the main communal organizations, next to the Jewish Community Centre in North York, was being planned. Two benefactors had donated half a million dollars to erect a Holocaust remembrance centre within the new building, but TJC was reluctant to give its consent to the plan. It was concerned that there would be insufficient funds to pay for the interior design and to maintain the memorial. It was also worried that the memorial would be grotesque.[116]

Leipciger met with a design coordinator and a few members of the education subcommittee. This ad hoc group decided that the emphasis should be on education rather than commemoration, and a fundraising campaign, headed by Gerda Steinitz-Frieberg, was launched.[117] She raised half a million dollars to complete the interior design. TJC, however, would still not give its consent, fearing a shortfall. But when a capital grant of $243,000 was received from the Ontario government and another $50,000 came from the West German government following a meeting between Steinitz-Frieberg and Helmut Kohl during a Group of Seven summit in Toronto, TJC relented.[118] The Holocaust Education and Memorial Centre was opened in the Lipa Green Building for Jewish Community Services in 1985. During its first decade, over 100,000 people visited the centre. The vast majority were students who came with their teachers. Each group toured the centre and met with a survivor speaker.[119]

The battle between the building committee and TJC was more than a matter of funds, according to Leipciger and Steinitz-Frieberg. At issue was leadership, focus, and power. Survivors claimed, "We have the funds; we have the plans; the need is immediate." The response was "There is a process that needs to be followed." Would the established community yield some of its space at the top to survivors? Would it allow them to dictate the design and operation of a centre devoted to the victims of the Holocaust—but more importantly, to educating the public—within the new confines of the federation building? To the leaders, the issue may have been more with the autonomy of any one interest group than a disinclination to embark upon the project. In the end the established leaders were outmanoeuvred. The survivors' agenda had become the community agenda as well. As in the Montreal scenario, the Holocaust had become a pillar of ethnic identification for the Jewish community. The proof lay in the memorial tiles, exhibits, and visitors at the Holocaust centre. According to Bardikoff: "With the construction of the centre . . . Holocaust issues were no longer second place."[120]

HOLOCAUST REMEMBRANCE IN OTHER CANADIAN CITIES

After Montreal and Toronto, the Jewish community in Vancouver has been the most active in promoting Holocaust education and commemoration. Beginning in 1953, Holocaust remembrance in that city had been under the auspices of the Warsaw Ghetto Committee. By the early 1960s, the commemoration had become an important event in the community calendar. Other aspects of Holocaust commemoration and education, however, did not begin until 1975.

On 9 September of that year a meeting of three survivors and Murray Saltzman, executive director of CJC Pacific Region, concluded that a Holocaust committee of Congress, in conjunction with the Warsaw Ghetto Committee and the Jewish Historical Society, be established, with education as its priority. Shortly after, Saltzman met with Graham Forst, a professor at Capilano College, the Reverend Bob Gallacher of the University of British Columbia, and Dr. Robert Krell, a professor of psychiatry at UBC, who had been hidden as a child during the war. They were interested in planning a symposium on the Holocaust for secondary school students. Because Gallacher, Forst, and Bill Nichols, a professor of religion at UBC, were not Jewish and therefore nominally outside the scope of Congress, the group decided to call itself the Standing Committee on the Holocaust. It was independent with respect to fundraising, participation, and programming. Forst became chair of the committee. In point of fact, the HRC of the Pacific Region and the Standing Committee acted jointly, and each had members in the other organization.[121]

The first symposium for secondary students on the Holocaust in Canada was held at the Oakridge Auditorium in Vancouver on 27 April 1976. Speakers included Forst, Nichols, Gallacher, and Professor Rudolf Vrba, who had escaped from Auschwitz and written a report on the camp that found its way to the World Jewish Congress in Switzerland. The following year, the symposium was held at UBC, where it continues.[122] The event in 1980 was covered by the *Vancouver Sun,* which related the stories of several survivors who spoke to students on that occasion.[123] Within a few years, two one-day symposia were held, attracting one thousand students from the lower mainland. The Standing Committee and the HRC undertook other projects as well. An outreach program sent a large core of survivor speakers and materials to schools in the lower mainland, and conducted professional development sessions.[124] An essay contest on the Holocaust began in 1978,[125] and five years later the Standing Committee offered its resources to the Vancouver School Board. The board responded positively and acceded to the request that meetings between representatives of the committee and the board take place.[126] The Vancouver seminar was a model for the one established by the Toronto committee five years later. According to Bardikoff, "We learned from them, and tried to do it better."[127]

Despite this promising start, neither the board nor the British Columbia Ministry of Education recommended that the official curriculum include a study of the Holocaust. This did not sit well with the British Columbia Teachers' Federation. Referring to the Glickman-Bardikoff study and the gaps in the new curriculum designed for the province's schools, the federation commented in its newsletter: "The new social study curriculum bombards students with a wild collection of topics . . . What they need is a coherent set of historical perspectives that will enable them to draw lessons from the past. And that can only be achieved if the curriculum faces the record of the past squarely. The stuff of history, after all, is humanity with all its warts, embarrassments, contradictions and wrinkles. When one looks over the bloody record of mankind and the challenges before us, should such a study be any less?"[128]

The HRC Pacific Region had its own programs as well. Its main focus was to conduct the Yom Hashoah memorial. But it expanded its activities into other areas, sponsoring an annual lecture on the anniversary of Kristallnacht, with speakers such as Elie Wiesel. It sent representatives to the gatherings of survivors; videotaped more than seventy witnesses; established an institute of Jewish studies; and provided resources and funds to the Community Hebrew Foundation Council of Greater Vancouver and the "Alternatives to Racism" guide for British Columbia schools.[129]

In 1984, Robert Krell decided that a permanent memorial to the victims of the Holocaust, incorporating an archive and a place for exhibits, should be erected. In a letter to CJC Pacific Region, he cited the success of the Standing Committee and the increasing interest by educators. His primary goal, however, was that the centre should "prove to be an important and lasting legacy of the survivor community of British Columbia to the future generations of its citizens."[130] As a result, the Vancouver Holocaust Centre Society for Education and Remembrance was established. However, survivors first wanted a memorial at the Jewish cemetery before they would commit to building a centre. After the memorial was unveiled in 1987, the community centre was expanded to become the home of the Vancouver Holocaust Education and Remembrance Centre, which opened in 1994. Leo Lowy, a member of the centre society, remarked that there was no resistance from the established community towards these endeavours.

Survivors had gained standing in the community through their work in raising funds and speaking to the public. This view was corroborated by Professor Moe Steinberg, who was chair of CJC Pacific Region in the late 1970s. Ultimately, the HRC Pacific Region merged with the centre society, while the Standing Committee remained as an autonomous body with links to the centre.[131]

On the Prairies, commemoration and education emanated from Winnipeg. One feature of the Jewish community there was that, although there were several separate organizations, it was sometimes difficult to determine which one was responsible for a particular event. In many cases, the same people belonged to the Winnipeg Jewish Community Council (WJCC, the local federation), the Jewish Historical Society of Western Canada, and CJC Western Region, which was later renamed the Manitoba-Saskatchewan Region. Until 1975, Holocaust commemoration was carried out by the Shaareth Hapleita Committee of the WJCC, which that year was described as "the most active group in Winnipeg at the present time."[132] The committee then became the Holocaust Memorial Committee of CJC.

An early example of the community's willingness to mark the Holocaust was an exhibit, *Journey into Our Heritage,* created by the Jewish Historical Society of Western Canada. It premiered at the Museum of Man and Nature in Winnipeg in 1970 and then travelled throughout western Canada for two years. The exhibit included interviews with survivors, including Rabbi Peretz Weizmann, theatre director John Hirsch, and community leader Paul Berger. A CBC documentary, *An Hour of Lifetimes,* based on these interviews, was aired.[133] This exhibit resulted more from the efforts of the established community than of the survivors. The survivor community of four hundred families was not yet active, aside from the Shaareth Hapleita Committee. As Philip Weiss related, "The voice of survivors was shut out in most cases either because of lack of education, language skills, and the authority rested with those who could break the barriers of the Jewish community and the legitimate authority of the country [on issues such as war criminals]."[134] But by the mid-1970s, with the formation of the Holocaust Memorial Committee, the survivors' voice was mute no longer.

Two ongoing events were the highlight of the community's observance of the Holocaust. The first was Holocaust Awareness Week, held in conjunction with the Yom Hashoah service. This practice, begun at the instigation of CJC Western Region in the 1960s, was amplified in the next decade. As we have seen, the mayor of Winnipeg proclaimed the week and changed the name of a block on a city street to the Avenue of the Warsaw Ghetto Heroes.[135] In 1975, the proclamation read in part: "I call upon all citizens to participate in this memorial observance and to work together to combat racism and eradicate discrimination wherever it is manifested. In light of continuing harassment, and in many cases imprisonment of Jewish people wishing to leave the Soviet Union, it is urged that those citizens be accorded the rights proclaimed for all people in the Universal Declaration of Human Rights, including the right to emigrate. Steven Juba, Mayor."[136]

The second event was an education program. This program was sometimes designed for students in Jewish schools, as when the first seminar took place in 1975.[137] The next year there was a three-day seminar for the community on recent scholarship. Entitled "I Never Saw Another Butterfly," it included lectures based on the works of the historian Lucy Dawidowicz and the literary critic Lawrence Langer. Its purpose, according to the *Jewish Post,* was "to assure unflagging interest and continued understanding of the Holocaust for what it was, the central, shattering experience of modern history, the releasing of those demonic forces that we assumed forever subdued by the triumph of modernism." In 1980 another three-day session, "Encounter with the Holocaust," was taught by Evita Smordin, a local teacher.[138] Four years later Manuel Prutschi, director of the JCRC Western Region, held a series of meetings with the minister of education, school superintendents, and school trustees about providing resources for teaching the Holocaust. One outcome was that education workshops for public school teachers were inaugurated in Winnipeg on a division (board) basis."[139]

The culmination of the efforts of the Holocaust Memorial Committee and the symbolic recognition of acceptance of the Holocaust in the public consciousness occurred on the grounds of the Manitoba legislature on 16 September 1990. A granite memorial in the shape of a broken star of David, inscribed with the names of 3,200 victims of the Holocaust whose families had migrated to Winnipeg, was erected. The memorial had taken five years from conception to completion.[140]

Elsewhere in western Canada, Holocaust remembrance programs were centred in Edmonton. The local HRC constructed a memorial on the grounds of the Jewish cemetery and conducted an annual Yom Hashoah service. A plaque recognizing and commemorating the contributions made by Jewish communities in Alberta was presented to the community by the provincial government.[141] In remembrance of the plight of Jewish refugees denied sanctuary in Canada, the community sponsored twenty refugee families from Vietnam.[142]

Throughout Canada in the period from 1975 to 1985, activities related to the Holocaust proliferated in smaller Jewish communities as well. Some resulted from outreach programs of the national committee or HRCS in the largest cities or from initiatives launched by the League. Most, however, were conducted by local committees.

The most active of the smaller communities was Ottawa. Although its Jewish population grew at a faster rate than in any other city in Canada in this period, it had a small core of survivors. From their first days in the city, the survivors had become integrated into the wider Jewish community, especially in the old neighbourhood in the market area. The local federation, the Va'ad (Hebrew for community), willingly embraced the survivors, but did not understand their experience or appreciate their suffering.[143] Only after 1973, when the local HRC was formed, did the Holocaust became part of the community's agenda. Even then it took several years and some arm-twisting for the established community to yield to the HRC's requests. At issue was its determination to erect a memorial to the victims at the local cemetery. The Va'ad would only agree to place a plaque in the community centre. Mendel Good, the chair of the HRC, remembered: "[I said that] it was an insult to the memory of the six million. I went to the mayor [Laurie Greenberg, a Jew], who was not supportive. I went to the cemetery committee and they relented." He said that the negotiations were difficult because "you were dealing with nice people. They could not understand . . . we could not talk about it [the pain] then." The monument was completed in the spring of 1978 and was unveiled at a ceremony at which Chief Justice Bora Laskin was the guest speaker.[144]

The memorial provided the spark for further activities. An exhibit of artifacts from the Holocaust was held at the Canadian War Museum. Student groups were brought to the exhibit, and with their teachers as a base, an education committee was established. Its first initiative was a seminar for educators. An attempt to convince the Ottawa Board of Education to adopt a curriculum on the Holocaust, however, was not successful. Upon hearing of the request by the HRC and the League, Arab Canadians voiced their disapproval, and the project was shelved. Nevertheless, a small but committed contingent of survivors was regularly invited to speak to students by individual schools. The committee conducted an oral documentation project of witnesses. It was revealed that an immigrant from the Netherlands who had been honoured as a righteous gentile among the nations for having saved Jews was resident in Ottawa. This flurry of activity in Ottawa in the early 1980s illustrated that the community had embraced the memory of the Holocaust as part of its self-definition. It helped the community to gain credibility when it lobbied for permission to host the first Gathering of Holocaust Survivors and Their Families in 1985.

NOTES

1   Interview with Steinitz-Frieberg.

2   Interviews with Weiss, Lowy, and Leipciger.

3   Another perspective was presented by Nora Levin in *The Holocaust: The Destruction of European Jewry, 1933–1945*. Other notable early works included Arendt, *Eichmann in Jerusalem: A Report on the Banality of Evil;* Feingold, *The Politics of Rescue: The Roosevelt Administration and the Holocaust, 1938–1945;* and Poliakov, *Harvest of Hate.*

4   Wiesel, *Night,* and *The Town beyond the Wall.* Other important works in this genre in the 1960s included Kosinski, *The Painted Bird;* Levi, *Survival in Auschwitz;* and Schwartz-Bart, *The Last of the Just.*

5   Dawidowicz adopted an extremely intentionalist analysis which has been challenged by many scholars. She also did not understand the nuances of Jewish complicity and resistance. She maintained her views with steely obstinacy until her death in 1991.

6   Doneson, *The Holocaust in American Film;* Insdorf, *Indelible Shadows,* 267–76. The figure is from Insdorf, who cautions that her list is "by no means complete."

7   See the historiographical articles by Perin, "Writing about Ethnicity," and Palmer, "Canadian Immigration and Ethnic History in the 1970s and 1980s."

8   Dahlia and Fernando, *Ethnicity, Power and Politics in Canada;* Troper, "As Canadian as Multiculturalism."

9   Interview with Zablow, 28 August 1995.

10 The teach-in was held on 17–19 February 1970 (JCC, File: Institutions-National Holocaust Committee, JPLA).

11 Minutes of the Meeting of the HRC, Eastern Region, 7 October 1975, Quebec Region Papers, db06, *r*16, CJCA. The CJC Eastern Region thru approved a bylaw making the Holocaust Memorial Committee a standing committee of the region, with subcommittees dealing with education and commemoration (Minutes of the CJC Eastern Region, 21 October 1975, unclassified, file: HRC, MHMCA).

12 *Program on the Seminar on the Holocaust,* Samuel Bronfman House, Montreal, 16 February 1975; Report on the Seminar, 18 March 1975, box 31, unclassified, JHS/BC.

13 "Symposium on The Holocaust—The Jewish Experience in World War II," McGill University, 20–23 October 1975, HRC of TJC Papers, 1976, unclassified, OJA.

14 Gerard H. Hoffman, "Holocaust Teaching in the French Schools of Quebec," *Canadian Zionist,* March-April, 1976, Plaut Papers, file: HRC, 1976–77, na.

15 Report of the Holocaust Committee, Eastern Region, CJC, 1975–76, Quebec Region Papers, DB04, file 24, CJCA;

16 Interview with Zablow, 28 August 1995.

17 Report of the Holocaust Memorial Project, 20 October 1978, Alan Rose Papers, da 5, file 28, CJCA; Michael Greenblatt, chair of the AJCS Holocaust Committee, Memorandum to Committee Members, 17 January 1978, unclassified, file: MHMC History, MHMCA interviews with Isaac Piasetsky, Aba Beer, and Lou Zablow (28 August 1995).

18 Interview with Stephen Cummings, Montreal, 31 August 1995.

19 Greenblatt, Memorandum to Committee Members, 17 January 1978, MHMCA.

20 Interview with Cummings.

21 Interviews with Zablow (August 28, 1995) and Cummings. The importance of the young Montrealers in the establishment of the group is confirmed in interviews with Aba Beer and Isaac Piasetski, members of the committee and influential in their own right since Beer was the chair of the NHRC and Piasetski the chair of the HRC Quebec Region. Confirmation is also provided by Krisha Starker, who, while not in Montreal at the time, was director of the centre from 1983 to 1994 (Starker interview).

22 Budget Memo, 10 September 1979; Report to Officers of the AJCS, 20 October 1978; Proposal, 19 December, 1978, unclassified, file: MHMC; History, MHMCA; interview with Cummings.

23 Draft Resolution of Principles, 27 September 1978, unclassified, file: MHMC History, MHMCA.

24 Lawrence Sabbath, "Centre is 'a Warning to the Living'" *Gazette,* 4 December 1981; information on exhibits, unclassified, box: Exhibit Archives, 1979–83, MHMCA. Other press coverage was given in the *Canadian Jewish News, La Presse, Suburban, Monitor,* and the *Westmount Examiner* (Minutes of the Centre Committee, 13 November 1980, file: MHMC History, MHMCA).

25 Report on Status (n.d., February 1980); Minutes, Centre Committee, March 3, ibid.

26 *Memorandum* on the Holocaust Memorial Centre/Jewish Public Library Merger, 15 June 1982, ibid.; interview with Cummings, Starker, and Zablow.

27 JCC, file: Institutions - NHRC, JPLA.

28 Quebec Region Papers, da 6, 7/16, cjca.

29 DA 5, 14/31, ibid. The Canadian Centre for Studies in Holocaust and Genocide was an independent organization, based in Toronto that existed for several years in the 1980s.

30 Interview with Starker, and a follow-up telephone conversation, 8 November 1996. Starker's views about the relationship with the JPL were echoed in the interviews with Zablow.

31 Unclassified, binder: Education—Minutes and Agenda, MHMCA; box: Exhibit Archives, 1979–83, ibid.

32 "Working Agreement between the AJCS and MHMC," 6 June 1985, binder: Board of Management—Agenda and Minutes—Affiliation with AJCS, ibid. This partnership ended in 1989 when the centre became fully independent.

33 "Dear Educator," Letter from Starker to educators about the centre, 19 November 1984; Minutes, Centre Committee, 14 February 1985, binder: Steering Committee—Agenda and Minutes, ibid. In 1993 Yom Hashoah programs were taken over by the centre, effectively ending the HRC Quebec Region's activities.

34 *Montreal Second Generation—Seconde Generation,* December 1984, Quebec Region Officers Papers, Ki, 6/9, CJCA.

35 Weinfeld quoted in Janice Arnold, "Survivors' Children Try to Keep Memory of Holocaust alive," *Canadian Jewish News,* 22 April 1982, HRC of TJC Papers, unclassified, OJA.

36 Interview with Cummings.

37 Abella, *A Coat of Many Colours,* 232–5. According to the 1981 census, approximately 95,000 Jews lived in Quebec and 146,000 in Ontario. According to the 1986 mini-census, there were 98,000 in Quebec and 166,000 in Ontario (Statistics Canada, as cited in Robert J. Brym, "The Rise and Decline of Canadian Jewry? A Socio-Demographic Profile," in Brym et al., *The Jews in Canada,* 25). In 1981, approximately 83 per cent of Ontario's Jews lived in Toronto, and 98 per cent of Quebec's Jews lived in Montreal (adapted from Elazar and Waller, *Maintaining Consensus,* 7–6, 167–70). On wealth distribution, synagogue attendance, support for community organizations and for Israel, by Toronto's Jews, see Jay Brodbar-Nemzer et al., "An Overview of the Canadian Jewish Community," in Brym et al., *The Jews in Canada* 57–66.

38 HRC Report to the Executive Committee of TJC, 24 June 1976; 17 March 1977, TJC Executive Committee. Papers, RG i/A, OJA; *Canadian Jewish News,* 22 April 1977, 1, HRC of TJC Papers, unclassified, OJA.

39 HRC of TJC Files, file: Correspondence, 1978, OJA.

40 Report, 17 March 1977, ibid.

41 Budget, TJC to HRC, Social Planning Papers of TJC, box 5, OJA.

42 BB Papers, vol. 98, file: Edmund Burke Society, NA.

43 JCRC Papers, 1974, 58/43, CJCA.

44 Minutes, JCRC Central Region, 20 January 1978, 22 February 1978, 31 May 1978, 27 September 1978, JCRC Papers, 1978, 67/2, OJA.

45 Harry Simon, chairman of the Anti-Nazi Committee, letter to the editor, *Jewish Standard,* 27 December 1978, 1978, 67/6, ibid.

46 Report of the Holocaust Remembrance Association to the CJC Plenary, 1980, Plenary Sessions Files, CJCA; interview with Sabina Citron, 18 September 1996; interview with Frieberg.

47 Resolution of the HRC, 17 May 1978, JCRC Papers, 69/43 A, OJA; Plaut Papers, vol. 133, file: HRC Correspondence, 1978, part 1, NA; Simon to the *Jewish Standard,* 27 December 1978, JCRC Papers, 67/6, OJA.

48 Report of the Anti-Nazi Committee to the JCRC Central Region, 31 May 1978, OJA.

49 Minutes of the JCRC Central Region, 28 June 1978, JCRC Papers, 1978, 67/2, OJA.

50 Smolack to Milton Harris, president of CJC, Ontario Region, on a resolution of the HRC requesting information on the documentation of Naziwar criminals, 31 January 1978, HRC of TJC Papers, File: Correspondence, 1978, unclassified, OJA.

51 Interview with Citron.

52 Minutes of Meeting of TJC Officers, 6 July 1978, TJC Officers Papers, RG I/C, OJA.

53 Lipsitz to Gold, Confidential Memo, "Summary and Assessment of the Holocaust Remembrance Meeting held on Wednesday, 9 August 1978, at the Sharei Shomayim Synagogue," 14 September 1978, ibid.

54 Minutes of JCRC Central Region Meeting, 27 September 1978, JCRC Papers, 1978, 67/2, OJA.

55 Minutes of the TJC Executive Committee, 28 September 1978, 16 November 1978, TJC Executive Papers, OJA.

56 Correspondence, 1978, HRC of TJC Papers, unclassified, OJA; JCRC Papers, 1978, 67/6, file: Anti-Nazi Committee, OJA; interview with Citron.

57 Interview with Citron; HRA Report to the CJC Plenary, 1980, Plenary Sessions Files, CJCA; HRA Letter, "Dear Friend" (n.d., 1986), HRC of TJC Papers, unclassified, OJA.

58 Interviews with Leipciger, Steinitz-Frieberg, and Citron.

59 "Brief on Recommendations and Comments concerning B'nai Brith Participation in Community Relations Work in Canada—By the ADL Chairman for District 22," 14 July 1964, BB Papers, 36/8, NA; "Declaration Pursuant to a meeting of officers of CJC and District 22 B'nai Brith," 25 March 1965, ibid.

60 Minutes, ADL Meeting, 4 March 1970, file 1970/6, ibid.; Minutes, JCRC Central Region Meeting, 19 May 1971, 23 June 1971, file 1971/37, ibid.

61 "Congress accuses B'nai Brith of Isolationism," *Canadian Jewish News,* 12 November 1971, ibid.

62 Minutes of Meeting of BB Delegation to Confer with CJC, 20 June 1972, BB Papers, 37/1972, Part 2, ibid.; "Congress, B'nai Brith Study Joint Body on Human Rights," *Canadian Jewish News,* 23 April 1976, 37/1975–78, ibid.

63 Crestohl to Diamant, 18 December 1979, 37/1979, ibid.

64 Alan Rose, executive vice-president, Canadian Jewish Congress to Frank Diamant, executive vice-president, B'nai Brith Canada, 17 September 1981, Morley Wolfe Papers. The author thanks Morley Wolfe for providing this document, and for explaining the controversy during informal conversations in October 1998. For further information on the split, see the following correspondence: Morley Wolfe, chairperson, JCRC Central Region, to Phil Leon, president of B'nai Brith Canada, 5 October 1981, BB Papers, 37/1981, NA; Irwin Cotler, president of Canadian Jewish Congress, to Leon, 4 February 1982, Quebec Region Papers, da 6, 7/5, cjca; Leon to BB membership, 19 January 1982, BB Papers, 37/1981, NA.

65 Julius Hayman, "Canadian Jewish Congress and B'nai Brith," *Jewish Standard*, 1–14 February 1982, BB Papers, 37/1982, NA.

66 Cruickshank, *The Modern Age*, 468, 470. Professor Cruickshank was my instructor at the Faculty of Education at the University of Toronto in 1971–72 and recommended me for my first teaching position.

67 Berman, *The Modern Age: Selected Readings*, 417–21, 431–9, 487–8.

68 Minutes of JCRC Central Region Meetings, 23 June 1971, 22 September 1971, 22 December 1971, JCRC Papers, 1971, 45/2.

69 Interview with Kayfetz, 13 November 1995.

70 Minutes, BJE Meeting 30 April 1973, BJE Papers, RG 41/B, 1/50, OJA.

71 Witty to Wolle, 3 June 1976; 2/30, ibid; Report of the HRC, 24 June 1976, TJC Executive Committee Papers, OJA.

72 Harold R. Malitsky, associate director of BJE to all principals, 21 December 1979, HRC of TJC Papers, file: Holocaust Remembrance, 1979, unclassified, OJA.

73 Jacob Egit also served on the JCRC, where he was an outspoken critic of the Jewish establishment in the 1960s. He remained active in community affairs until his death in 1996. ("Egit, Jacob," in Gottesman, *Who's Who in Canadian Jewry*, 409; Egit, *Grand Illusion*; Lipshitz interview).

74 Egit, "Proposal for a Program of Ongoing Activity and Education in Our Community to Further the Knowledge of the Holocaust and Resistance—and Its Meaning for the Present and Future Generations," Egit to the HRC, CJC, Central Region, 25 October 1975, HRC of TJC Papers, file: 1976, unclassified, OJA. Note that there was no such committee; the reference was to the HRC of TJC. See also the Report of the HRC to the TJC Executive Committee, 24 June 1976, ibid.

75 Regarding the Bauer lecture and the University of Toronto series, see Report of the HRC to the TJC Executive Committee, 24 June 1976, ibid. Regarding university courses, see HRC of TJC Papers, file: Correspondence, 1978, unclassified, ibid. Regarding the Holocaust Remembrance Week at York University, see HRC Report to the TJC Executive Committee, 17 March 1977; Avraham Weiss, Director of the NHRC to Lydia Toledano and Andrew Kohn, Jewish Student Federation, 26 November and the program 1976, ibid. Regarding Second Encounter, see unclassified, ibid.

76 Sheldon Kirshner, "Immigration Policy 'Racially Motivated'," *Canadian Jewish News,* February 3, 1978, unclassified, ibid. Kirshner's full-page article quoted a number of documents given to him by Harold Troper in the early stage of research for *None Is Too Many.*

77 Henry Feingold, "Four Days in April: A Review of NBC's Dramatization of the Holocaust," *Shoah,* 1:1:15–17, JCRC Papers, 1978, 69/43A, OJA.

78 For the response in the United States, West Germany, and the Netherlands, see the relevant chapters in Wyman, *The World Reacts to the Holocaust.* See also Novick, *The Holocaust in American Life,* especially 209–14.

79 The Fest review is found in the CJC Papers, 3½/27, JHS/BC.

80 Plaut to A.W. Johnson, president, Canadian Broadcasting Corporation, 21 February 1978, HRC of TJC Papers, unclassified, OJA.

81 Ruth Resnick, Announcement to Heads of History Departments, Ontario Secondary Schools, 28 February 1978, JCRC Papers, 1978, 69/43A, OJA; Resnick to Heads, 15 March 1978, HRC of TJC Papers, 1978, unclassified, OJA; Minutes of JCRC Central Region meeting, 2 May 1978, JCRC Papers, 1978, 67/2, OJA; interview with Dr Alan Bardikoff, chair of Holocaust Education Subcommittee, 1978–88, 27 September 1996, Toronto.

82 John Baker, teacher of history, Napanee District Secondary School, to Ruth Resnick, 24 April 1978, HRC of TJC Papers, 1978, unclassified, OJA. The course referred to by Baker was the only mandatory history course, as set out by the Ontario Ministry of Education. It was taught in either grade nine or grade ten.

83 Wolfe to Resnick, 12 February 1979, 1979, unclassified, ibid.

84 Frank Diamant, executive vice-president of B'nai Brith Canada, to Glickman, on the agreement on behalf on the League of Human Rights on "The Treatment of the Holocaust in Canadian History Textbooks," 7 March 1980, BB Papers, vol. 79, file: LHR 1980–82; 6 March 1980, file: LHR News Releases, 1980–82; file: Y. Glickman Research Proposal for LHR, 1979–82, NA.

85 Interview with Bardikoff, 27 September 1996; informal conversations with Shelman in the early 1980s.

86 Glickman and Bardikoff, *The Treatment of the Holocaust in Canadian History and Social Science Textbooks,* 12–13, appendix C. B'nai Brith took the responsibility for advertising the book and selling it. Glickman was upset about the apparent lack of commitment to the project. Although the manuscript was ready in late 1981, it was not released until August 1982. Two months later he wrote to Diamant: "[I] express my disappointment, indeed my frustration, concerning the promotion of our monograph." Diamant replied: "Your letter was highly disappointing. You will recall that during the study, which lasted two years longer than initially contracted for." Two years later Shelman wrote to Diamant that between January 1984 and June 1985, eighty-four copies of the book had been sold. This underwhelming statistic indicates that the study was one of the best-kept secrets in the educational network in Canada. See Glickman to Diamant, 18 October 1982; Diamant to Glickman, 28 October 1982; Shelman to Diamant, 10 July 1985, BB Papers, vol. 107, file: Glickman Research Proposal, NA.

87 Alan Shelman, Annual Report, LHR, vol. 76, file: Annual Report 1981–82, ibid.; Shelman, "The League for Human Rights and Holocaust Education," vol. 107, file:LHR Resource Materials Guides on the Holocaust, 1980–84, ibid.

88 B'nai Brith Announcement, Annual Review of Antisemitism (n.d., approximately 12 October 1982), vol. 80, file: LHR Review of Anti-semitism in Canada, 1982, ibid.

89 Files: League for Human Rights Guides; League for Human Rights Correspondence; Holocaust and Hope Tour, 1986, Bialystok Papers.

90 Bar Ilan University Institute of Holocaust Studies International Symposium on "Teaching the Holocaust in High Schools," Toronto, 26–28 August 1980, Cotler Papers, box 3, file: World Gathering of Jewish Holocaust Survivors, CJCA; [Zachor,] January 1981, DB 07, 1/1, ibid.

91 Interview with Bardikoff, 27 September 1996. Bardikoff eventually obtained his doctorate in clinical psychology, and in his practice he counsels survivors and their descendants.

92 "Congress Names New Committee on Holocaust," *Canadian Jewish News*, 8 February 1979, HRC of TJC Papers, 1979, unclassified, OJA; Minutes of HRC Meeting, 24 January 1979, ibid.

93 Memo: To the President's Commission on the Holocaust, 11 July 1979, ibid.; Report of the HRC of TJC to the CJC Plenary Session, 1980, 47–8, Plenary Sessions Files, CJCA; Report of the HRC, 1979–86, to the TJC Executive Committee, 15 May 1980, TJC Executive Committee Papers, OJA; interview with Bardikoff (2 October 1996) and Leipciger (25 January 1996).

94 Interview with Bardikoff, September 27, 1996.

95 *Zachor*, January 1981.

96 Report of the HRC to the TJC Executive Committee, 18 February 1982, TJC Executive Committee Papers, OJA; HRC, "Student Seminar," file: Yom Hashoah, 1982, ibid.

97 HRC to "Dear Friend," 1 February 1983, HRC of TJC Papers, file: Student Seminar, 1983, unclassified, OJA; file: Student Seminar, 1981–86, Bialystok Papers; Report of the HRC to the CJC Plenary, 1986, 18–19, Plenary Sessions Files, CJCA.

98 File: Educators' Seminar, 1982–86, Bialystok Papers.

99 Task Force, *Multiculturalism, Ethnicity and Race Relations Policy; Sub-Committee on Race and Ethnic Relations* and *Multicultural Policy, Race and Ethnic Relations and Multicultural Policy; Final Report of Sub-Committee on Race Relations; Race, Religion and Culture in Ontario School Materials*.

100 Griesdorf and Bardikoff, *The Holocaust;* Bialystok and Walther, *The Holocaust and Its Contemporary Implications;* interview with Bardikoff, 27 September 1996.

101 Files: Draft Proposal of tbe Curriculum; tbe Correspondence; In service, 1982–87, Bialystok Papers.

102 HRC to "Dear Friend," 1 February 1983, HRC of TJC Papers, OJA.

103 File: the Holocaust Advisory Committee, Bialystok Papers; Holocaust Studies Advisory Committee, Office Files, Equity Studies Centre, Toronto Board of Education, courtesy of Myra Novogrodsky, director.

104 Bardikoff and Leipciger to "Dear Friend," January 1984, HRC of TJC Papers, file: Bette Stephenson's Reply, unclassified, OJA.

105 Stephenson to Irwin Diamond, principal, Cambridge International College of Canada, 2 April 1984, ibid.

106 Minutes of the ALSBO Curriculum Committee, May 1984; Report of the ALSBO Curriculum Committee, 14 September 1985; file: ALSBO, "The League for Human Rights and Holocaust Education, ALSBO," Bialystok Papers; BB Papers, file: LHR Resource Materials, Guides on the Holocaust, 1981–84, NA.

107 *Curriculum Guideline, History and Contemporary Studies, Senior Division,* 49; *Curriculum Guideline, History and Contemporary Studies, Ontario Academic Courses,* 26.

108 Interview with Bardikoff. This view was also expressed by Leipciger and Steinitz-Frieberg.

109 Interview with Bardikoff.

110 W.D. McClelland, superintendent of curriculum and progam development, to Barry Preson, history consultant, Waterloo County Board of Education, 11 May 1989, file: Waterloo County, Bialystok Papers.

111 HRC Questionnaire on Teaching the Holocaust, 1991, file: Questionnaire, Bialystok Papers, HRC Education members were also active in pedagogical research. Some of their findings appeared in Alan Bardikoff, guest editor, "Teaching the Holocaust," *History and Social Science Teacher* 21 (Summer 1986), which includes articles by Bardikoff, Harold Lass, Frank Bialystok, Jane Griesdorf, and Mary Samulewski. Nine years later another special issue on the topic, edited by Michael Charles, appeared in the renamed *Canadian Social Studies* 29 (Summer 1995), with articles from members of the HRC and the League's Holocaust Committee.

112 Some of the important studies in this genre in the 1970s include Flannery, *The Anguish of the Jews;* Fleishner, *Auschwitz: Beginning of a New Era?* Littell, *The Crucifixion of the Jews;* and Reuther, *Faith and Fratricide.*

113 On the conference held on 10 March 1980, see HRC of TJC Papers, box 4, file: Christian-Jewish Dialogue, unclassified, OJA. For the first service, see Graham Hall, "Christians Remember the Holocaust," *Catholic New Times,* 10 May 1981, file: Christian Commemoration, 1981, ibid. For subsequent services, see separate files for each year, ibid.

114 File: Holocaust Education Week, Bialystok Papers.

115 Interview with Leipciger.

116 The projected cost of the memorial was approximately $400,000. TJC officers informed the design committee that there were no funds available, and that it would have to raise the entire amount (Minutes of TJC Officers Meeting, 19 August 1982, TJC Officers Papers, OJA; interview with Leipciger).

117 Minutes of TJC Executive Committee meeting, 1 January 1982; Leipciger to A.J. Green, of the Lipa Green Building for Community Jewish Services, 27 January 1982, Office Files of the Jewish Federation of Greater Toronto, TJC Executive Papers.

118 Interviews with Leipciger (25 January 1996), Steinitz-Frieberg, and Bardikoff (2 October 1996).

119 Author's correspondence with Pnina Zylberman, director of the Holocaust Education and Memorial Centre, 1996.

120 Interview with Bardikoff, 2 October 1996.

121 Minutes of a meeting to discuss the formation of a Holocaust committee, 9 September 1975, CJC Papers, 31/18, JHS/BC; interviews with Krell and Waldman.

122 "Symposium on the Holocaust," 27 April 1976, box 31, unclassified, JHS/BC; interviews with Krell, Steinberg and Waldman; Minutes of Meeting of Standing Committee, 10 May 1979, CJC Papers, 31/13, JHS/BC.

123 Report of the HRC, Pacific Region, to the CJC Plenary, 1980, 48–9, Plenary Sessions Files, CJCA; Stewart McNeill, "Survivors Tell Tales of Holocaust Horror," *Vancouver Sun,* 11 April, 1980.

124 *Tenth Annual Symposium,* 1985, outreach programs, Mark Silverberg Papers, box 96, unclassified, JHS/BC.

125 "Essay Prizes," 1983, Standing Committee on the Holocaust, CJC Papers, 31/14, JHS/BC.

126 Standing Committee to the Vancouver School Board, 20 September 1983; Jean Gerber for the Standing Committee to J. Wormsbecker, Vancouver School Board, 17 June 1983; Wormsbecker to Gerber, 28 June 1983, 31/13, ibid.

127 Interview with Bardikoff, 2 October 1996.

128 George Major, "The Holocaust Is Totally Ignored," BCTF [BC Teachers' Federation] 23 November 1983, CJC Papers, 31/14, JHS/BC.

129 Report of the HRC, Pacific Region, to the CJC Plenary, 1986, 45–6, Plenary Sessions Files, CJCA.

130 Robert Krell, "Proposal for the Vancouver Holocaust Centre for Remembrance and Education," 20 September 1984, Silverberg Papers, unclassified, JHS/BC.

131 File: CJC Pacific Region, Bialystok Papers; interviews with Krell, Waldman, Lowy, and Steinberg.

132 *Jewish Post,* 22 May 1975, 17, JHS/WC.

133 Interviews with Gutkin and Arnold. The brochure and program for the exhibit was graciously provided to the author by Abraham Arnold from his personal papers.

134 Interview with Weiss.

135 For 1972 see the *Jewish Post,* 23 March 1972, 11, JHS/WC. For 1980 see the *Jewish Post,* 27 March 1980, 6, ibid. For 1981, 1982, and 1984 see WJCC Papers, P4641/20, PAM. For 1981 see the *Jewish Post,* 19 November 1981, 6.

136 Proclamation, 8 April 1975, WJCC Papers, P3542/33, PAM.

137 "Seminar on Holocaust Education," 9 November 1975, ibid.

138 Editorial, *Jewish Post,* 22 April 1976, 2, JHS/WC. "Encounter with the Holocaust," *Jewish Post,* 21 February 1980, 3, ibid.

139 Manuel Prutschi, "Monitoring of and Outreach to Educational Institutions" (n.d., approximately January 1984), WJEE Papers, P4641/18, PAM; Prutschi to Israel Ludwig

et al., regarding Holocaust Education Kit Outline distributed to ministry and board officials, 20 February 1984, ibid; interview with Manuel Prutschi, 30 August 1996, Toronto.

140 Interview with Weiss; *Jewish Post*, 13 September 1989, A3,29 August 1990,3,19 September 1990,1,3, JHS/WC; Author's visit, 20 November 1995.

141 "Edmonton," *Zachor* January 1981; Report of the HRC, Alberta Region, to the CJC Plenary Session, 1980, 4, 388–9, Plenary Sessions Files, CJCA.

142 Mark Silverberg, chairperson, CJC, Jewish Community Council of Edmonton, "Lest We Forget," editorial in *Your Community News*, January 1980, Arnold Papers, file 90.3, PAM.

143 Interview with Good.

144 Interview with Good; Harry Hecht, president of the Va'ad, Report of the Holocaust Committee of the Ottawa Jewish Community Council (n.d.), WJEE Papers, P4641/19, PAM.

The Vancouver Holocaust Monument that Wasn't: Arnold Belkin's "Warsaw Ghetto Uprising" Mural

BARB SCHOBER

When Canadian-born artist Arnold Belkin died in 1992, he lay in state at the Modern Art Museum in Mexico City.[1] Many of his works remain highly lauded in the Spanish-speaking world; in fact, it is not uncommon to see his name mentioned in conjunction with such icons of Mexican muralism as Diego Rivera, Jose Clemente Orozco, and David Alfaro Siqueiros. Some critics even insist that Belkin's international reputation exceeds that of any other Canadian artist.[2] Yet within Canada, Arnold Belkin is hardly known. "Warsaw Ghetto Uprising", the only Belkin mural ever displayed in his native country and the city where he grew up, is currently in storage at Vancouver's Jewish Community

This photograph of the Belkin mural was taken in April 1964, at the piece's official unveiling in the lobby of Vancouver's Jewish Community Centre. A broad level of community participation in the ceremony is suggested by the presence of numerous members of the left-wing Peretz Institute, as well as a local rabbi. There would, however, be more rancour than agreement in the subsequent history of the mural. The artist himself can be seen in profile at the far right of the crowd.

PHOTO BY SEARLE R. FRIEDMAN.

PHOTO COURTESY OF SYLVIA FRIEDMAN.

Centre, a status it has suffered more than once since it was donated by the artist in 1964.

Considering Belkin's reputation abroad, this particular mural's fate is even more difficult to account for in that the April 1943 Warsaw Ghetto uprising, which it depicts, made a significant impression in Vancouver when it occurred. News of the desperate resistance mounted by Warsaw's Jews as German troops "liquidated" the ghetto generated extensive tributes and front page headlines in the city's Jewish and non-Jewish press alike.[3] Newspaper coverage from the period surrounding the uprising likewise reveals a growing awareness of the fate of European Jewry, and as regular commemoration of the Holocaust emerged in the postwar period among different segments of Vancouver Jewry, the Warsaw Ghetto revolt remained the central motif around which various forms of remembrance developed.

Vancouver rabbis began sermonizing about the uprising and the death of six million Jews in annual Passover programs by the 1950s, emphasizing the dual themes of resistance and martyrdom. Like the city's numerous Zionist groups, they maintained that the spirit of the ghetto fighters had been fundamental to the preservation of Judaism and the establishment of the State of Israel in 1948. This view was also advanced in the Vancouver Jewish community's weekly newspaper, the *Jewish Western Bulletin*. The approach of Passover each year was hailed with regular *Bulletin* editorials pointing to connections between the Warsaw Ghetto uprising's anniversary and Israeli Independence Day. The proximity of these events on the Jewish calendar tended to further strengthen these parallels in the community's tributes and public discourse.

Vancouver's small left-wing and secular Jewish groups also began commemorating the anniversary of the ghetto revolt in the late 1940s. A local Peretz Institute was established in 1945 with the explicit purpose of providing progressive, activist education to fill the tremendous void left by the mass murder of most of eastern Europe's Yiddish-speaking population. The school established an annual Warsaw Ghetto evening in 1948, often joined by members of the Vancouver branch of the United Jewish People's Order (UJPO), a left-wing cultural and political organization based in Toronto. These memorial evenings were marked by a theme of "Never to forgive, never to forget", and program features included dramatized readings and speeches against fascism. In light of Cold War tensions, however, both the Peretz School and certainly the UJPO were fairly marginalized within the wider Vancouver Jewish community, and their commemorative activities tended to be insular.4

Nonetheless, a forum for community-wide commemoration of the uprising did emerge in 1956, when a small group of Polish Jews who had come to Vancouver during the war formed a Warsaw Ghetto Memorial Committee under the sponsorship of the Jewish Community Council and the Pacific Region of the Canadian Jewish Congress. Soon after, numerous UJPO members joined the Memorial Committee in organizing commemorative programs at the Jewish Community Centre (JCC) on each anniversary of the event. The revolt's legacy thus provided a shared reference point for various groups and individuals concerned with perpetuating the memory of the Holocaust through an annual ceremony and promoting the message of tolerance, Jewish pride, and vigilance against oppression. By the early 1960s, community leaders were hailing the Warsaw Ghetto Memorial evenings as "one of the most successful annual events of our community."[5]

One might think, then, that a large mural depicting the uprising would be generally welcomed, particularly as it was painted by an up and coming Jewish artist from Vanrouver.[6] Born in 1930, Belkin's early roots lay in the highly activist tradition of the Peretz Institute, where his parents were longtime members. Emerging from this unapologetically left-wing environment, it appears that a broad sense of political concern and a passion for art blended early for Belkin. He won a B.C. Labour Guild art competition at the age of fifteen with a drawing of workers on a street car, allowing him to study for a time in Banff with artist A. Y. Jackson of Canada's famed Group of Seven. Landscape painting, however, was not in his future.

Attracted by the proletarian and revolutionary murals being painted by artists like Diego Rivera, in 1947 a teenage Belkin moved to Mexico. The great Mexican muralists appealed to him, he later said, "because their paintings dealt with people, politics, and with social/historical events."[7] Between the 1930s and 1960s muralism was the dominant form of artistic expression in Mexico, where, unlike in Canada, the integration of art and politics was pronounced and artists played an important social role.[8] The muralist movement as a whole was distinctly extroverted and humanistic, providing the most significant means by which socially aware artists could convey collective human suffering and make art accessible to a largely illiterate people.[9]

In Mexico, Belkin initially trained with one of the masters of Mexican muralism, D.A. Siqueiros, a Spanish Civil War veteran who was later jailed for organizing student protests. Siqueiros had a lasting impact on Belkin, who asserted that, "For me, he was a model, the artist as hero, the artist as public orator, the artist as political activist."[10] Belkin himself often spoke about the role of artists in society, including a 1955 lecture in Vancouver to the literary groups of the National Council of Jewish Women. [11] In the early 1960s he and fellow artist Francisco Icaza founded "Nueve Presencia", an aesthetic movement which, according to its manifesto, condemned middle-class taste and complacency and championed art that was "real, raw and eloquent" [12] In a further description of his motives as an artist, he stated, "to express the human condition is and always has been my aim and preoccupation in art. Especially the heroism inherent in man."[13]

A great deal of Belkin's work also dealt with Jewish themes and figures, for instance, his largest mural "Kehila," an immense depiction of the Jewish holidays commissioned by Mexico City's Jewish Community Centre in 1965.[14] His frequent letters home to his parents in Vancouver often mentioned smaller pieces including etchings from the Bible or paintings entitled "Jews in a Synagogue" and "Tzaddik", while his set design work sometimes involved such classics of the Yiddish theatre as "The Dybbuk." Belkin's imagination was captured by many episodes of the Jewish past and their parallels to the present, with Job in particular striking him as a symbol of eternal injustice and eternal rebellion.[15] According to his longtime friend Dr. (Rabbi) William Kramer, with whom he often discussed these matters, Belkin was deeply interested in Jewish spirituality and history; his politics and humanism were inseparable from his Jewish concerns.[16]

Many of these preoccupations and elements can be discerned in his "Warsaw Ghetto Uprising." The three-paneled, darkly-coloured oil painting measures approximately eight feet by sixteen feet, covering a total area of over one-hundred square feet. Like in many of Belkin's murals, the piece conveys a distinct narrative flow from left to right. The left-most panel of the mural features images of patriarchs, looking skyward, just above pyramid-shaped rows of doomed, gaunt figures staring outward, at the viewer. The pyramid, with its blackened visages towards the top, also invokes a pyre in flames. The flames follow the mural's largest figures, the ghetto fighters, into the centre panel, where they reach out, not skyward exactly but forward, ostensibly to the future, but also toward a just barely-visible menorah. Below them lies a tumult of twisted and emaciated bodies that evoke images of the documentary footage taken when Allied troops overran some of the Nazi camps. These destroyed figures overlap into the third panel of the mural, where they merge into the long lines of adults and children looking outward and forward again, symbols of regeneration.

In Belkin's own words, in painting the mural he had attempted to depict:

an historic moment of great drama which I wished to
express in a spirit of struggle, of resistance, the fight to
preserve human dignity. I did not want to use obvious
symbols such as guns, flags and grenades. Instead, I used
gestures and faces of people . . . of children who are the
hope of the future generation, those that live and are a
remembrance of the thousands of children killed—the
broken stem. [17]

Belkin's description of the mural's motifs is of particular interest considering a drawing he had done for the cover of the *Jewish Western Bulletin's* 1953
Passover issue. Although both works portray the Warsaw Ghetto uprising, the
1953 depiction is quite unlike the later mural. Guns and weapons are a central
element of the Passover cover, lending it an almost military tone. Children and
other victims are absent. There is also a marked difference in the facial expressions and gestures of the fighters, who are palpably animated by revolt and defi-
ance. While the later mural also conveys a sense of outrage, its representation is
more subtle. Even the bodies and faces of the resisters are slightly contorted,
their less defined countenance varying from despair to anger to almost no
expression. Unlike the Passover cover, the presence of children is a key element
of the mural, both those who perished and those who survived. Belkin's own
children were born in 1953 and 1957, which perhaps influenced this more complex rendering. Heroism does not disappear as a theme in the mural, but it is
somewhat muted.

At any rate, judging by his correspondence, Belkin began painting
"Warsaw Ghetto Uprising" sometime in early 1959. By the end of that year he
was already pondering appropriate locations for the piece, including a Jerusalem
museum or the new Jewish Community Centre planned for Vancouver.[18] In the
meantime the mural was displayed at the Jewish Sports Centre in Mexico City,
under the Spanish title "El levantamiento del Ghetto de Varsovia."[19] At some
point in 1962, Belkin offered the work to the Vancouver Peretz School, where,
as mentioned, his parents were active. It is quite likely that his father's October

1962 death played a role in this decision. The members of the Peretz Institute, for their part, were duly honoured by Belkin's offer, but they felt that such a piece needed to be seen by the entire community, which they believed was still not doing enough to remember the events and lessons of the Holocaust.[20]

While Belkin was in Vancouver for his father's funeral, he was also approached by Sam Heller, a highly respected community member and Chairman of the Warsaw Ghetto Memorial Committee. Having heard from others about the mural and Belkin's indecision as to where to donate it, Heller added his voice to those in favour of the Community Centre, and upon Belkin's return to Mexico, he received a letter from Heller reconfirming these views. The letter reads in part:

> [I]t is my sincere and unbiased opinion that a mural of such high artistic value (especially now that I have seen a reproduction of it) would be lost in the Peretz School. It would be there in view of the children who are too young to appreciate its beauty—maybe it would be viewed from time to time by a few parents who might come to a P.T.A. meeting, but that is all. If you were to decide on the new Community Centre, it would be hung on the light wall to the right of the main entrance; it would be in full view of anyone in the vestibule, and it would be seen day in and day out by hundreds of people entering the Centre—be it Jewish or, as is often the case, non-Jews.
>
> It is my feeling that this mural would add very much to the appearance of the Centre. It would give the finishing touch as right now, it is nothing but a modern concrete box, designed by the architects. The mural would bear a bronze plaque at the bottom, with a proper inscription to be designated by you. . . .[21]

This letter, as it turned out, tipped the scales for Belkin, who wrote back agreeing to donate the mural to the Centre.[22] Soon after receiving Belkin's approval, Sam Heller brought the proposal to the Executive Committee of the Jewish Community Centre. A photo of the mural was circulated, followed by a long discussion as to the appropriateness of a depiction of so somber a topic in a location like the Centre. Nonetheless, it was agreed to recommend to the Centre's Executive Board that they accept Belkin's offer.[23] The minutes of the ensuing Board meeting in mid November 1962 likewise indicate that there had already been "considerable controversy concerning the suitability of the painting for placing in the Centre due to the theme that it represented."[24]

Although the exact nature of this "controversy" is not elaborated in the minutes, some of the individuals involved recall that the main objections of those against accepting the mural lay not so much in having a work dedicated to the uprising but that Belkin's painting would be too graphic, morbid, and unpleasant for those entering the building, and that it might somehow emotionally damage the children who played in that area. [25] It also appears that some may have worried that the mural would invite anti-Semitism rather than stand as a monument against it.[26] Those arguing in favour of the work, several of whom were themselves artists, asserted that it was a tremendous piece of art by an important artist portraying a crucial historic event and that the Centre was an ideal location for it, indeed, that it should consider the gift an honour.[27] As for the contention that it was better not to expose children to such things, these individuals argued that it was nonsensical to try and shield young people, particularly Jewish young people, from the world's realities.

In the end, after another long discussion and some "interpretation by Mr. Heller," the Board agreed to accept the mural on the condition that they could hang it where they thought most suitable.[28] This stipulation proved unacceptable to Arnold Belkin, and on that note the matter seemed closed. Not having heard back from the Centre by February 1963, Belkin all but gave up and contemplated re-approaching the Peretz School until he was reassured a month later that the Centre was still "in discussion" over the matter.[29] That spring the Board had received a petition signed by seventy-five community members requesting that they re-open negotiations with Belkin about the painting.[30] Although they agreed to do so, for reasons which are not clear, this debate was not taken up again until a September meeting.

In the interim, reverberations of some of the issues raised by the prospect of hanging the mural in the Community Centre lobby were in evidence at the 1963 Warsaw Ghetto Memorial Evening. As part of his opening address on this occasion, Sam Heller made the following statements, decrying

> the voices in our community who would like to forget and not be reminded; who object to our bringing back memories, gruesome memories of days past; who are afraid that this gruesomeness of our past, our history and heritage will affect their children. Those are the people who will die in submissiveness if such a day should ever happen again. They bury their heads in the proverbial sand hoping that if they forget, it will ease their existence in the Gentile world.[31]

Needless to say, the subject was highly charged, and from some accounts, emotions also ran high at the September 1963 JCC Board meeting when the matter of the mural was once again raised.[32] Sam Heller and two other Warsaw Ghetto Committee members, including Dr. Ludmilla Zeldowicz who was a psychiatrist, appeared at this meeting to ask that the question of the painting be reconsidered. The small party presented coloured slides of the mural and its various aspects, followed by yet another long discussion about whether it should be mounted in the lobby or whether alternate arrangements could be made. Both Dr. Zeldowicz and a University of British Columbia child psychologist who was present made statements opposing the view that children could or should be protected from such images.[33] Finally, a motion to hang the mural in the lobby, as desired by the artist, was passed by a vote of fifteen to nine with four abstentions.[34]

As part of this agreement, it was also arranged that the painting would be unveiled during the Warsaw Ghetto Memorial Evening for 1964. Even aspects of this process proved troublesome. To begin with, the Centre's insurance company refused to insure the mural against "malicious damage" unless a three foot fence was built around it at a distance of three feet, or, alternatively, if the work was hung in the far corner of the lounge area above the staircase.[35] Perhaps preferring not to revisit the issue, the JCC's president Albert Kaplan agreed to leave the mural in the lounge uninsured. Chrome stands linked by a cord were installed in front of the piece as a compromise. One related item that remained permanently unresolved however, was the Warsaw Ghetto Committee's suggestion that some sort of mimeographed "interpretation" of the mural's symbolism be mounted close to the painting so that teachers or youth leaders could discuss it with their classes or groups.[36] It does not appear that this measure was ever taken; the only text accompanying the mural was a plaque dedicating the work to Belkin's father. Any other impressions were left wholly to the viewer.

In spite of this sequence of events, the unveiling itself was quite successful. Publicity preceding the event was enthusiastic, quoting reviews such as "the artist has created a mural which has a message for everyone, a message for all humanity. The distinctively Jewish and the universal, are blended together into a great work of art."[37] The memorial and unveiling ceremony were attended by over five hundred people, including Arnold Belkin, who introduced his work. Subsequent *Bulletin* coverage announced that Belkin was "well-known in Vancouver as an artist" and that his work was part of collections around the world.[38] While he was in the city for the unveiling, Belkin was also invited to the Community Centre to speak about the role of artists, giving several interviews on various radio programs as well.

In the ensuing years, Belkin's prominence as a muralist and painter only increased, particularly in Latin America, but also in Israel and the United States. He also continued to be an outspoken critic of popular art, which avoided the controversial and painful elements of human experience.[39] Some of his later commissions included a large mural for a disabled children's home, which was covered over after being deemed "too depressing," as well as works depicting the student shootings at Kent State University and the massacre of Vietnamese civilians in the village of My Lai. In addition to his voluminous writing about the social role of art, Belkin's lifetime body of work includes twenty-eight large scale murals and many smaller pieces. Shortly before his death, the Mexican government honoured him with a major retrospective of his work at the Palace of Fine Arts.

Back in Vancouver, by contrast, Belkin's "Warsaw Ghetto Uprising" did not fare nearly so well. Despite the high hopes of the Memorial Committee, it did not become a focal point for remembrance. Aside from the occasional photo opportunity that it provided for visiting community notables, the mural seems to have more or less faded into the background of the hustle and bustle of the Community Centre. A series of renovations resulted in its being taken down or temporarily covered over many times, until it was removed from sight altogether.[40] It was only re-hung in the Centre in the mid 1990s, this time high at the back of the building's Wosk Auditorium, where it continued to stir the passions of only the relatively few people who noticed it, either because they still believed it was a most significant artistic contribution and deserved far greater prominence, or because they felt it was bad art, disturbing and out of place, or simply ugly. At the time of writing, the mural has been once again placed in storage, with no immediate plans to re-hang it.

In retrospect, there are several possible reasons why "Warsaw Ghetto Uprising" failed to find an enduring space in either the Centre or the community's ongoing Holocaust commemoration. Leaving aside for a moment all debate regarding the piece's aesthetic merits, the Belkin mural was absent from the rhythms of the community calendar; with the exception of its 1964 unveiling it was not a feature of the annual Warsaw Ghetto Memorial evenings or any other type of community remembrance. The latter continued to be largely ritual in form, with each annual ceremony beginning with the lighting of six memorial candles and the chanting of the *El male rachamim* (God is full of compassion) prayer for the repose of the dead, followed by guest speakers and dramatic works or music. The ceremony itself was eventually relocated from the Community Centre altogether in favour of the larger Vancouver synagogues. Over time, emphasis on the Warsaw Ghetto revolt also faded as the yearly event was renamed Yom HaShoah in keeping with Israeli practice, while the wider survivor experience came to the fore of commemorative evenings.

For that matter, the community's Holocaust survivors clearly did not see the Belkin mural as a memorial site. Whether or not individuals liked the piece or supported its installation in the JCC, shortly thereafter discussions were initiated for a more traditional monument where local survivors could hold Yizkor services and say Kaddish for their murdered loved ones.[41] The permanent memorial eventually erected by Vancouver's Holocaust survivors is much more symbolic in design than Belkin's stark images of the uprising, consisting of a black granite obelisk rent apart down the centre but connected by three white doves. Located in the community's largest cemetery, the monument is the regular gathering place for well-attended memorial services on Yom HaShoah and Yom Kippur. By contrast, Belkin's "Warsaw Ghetto Uprising" simply lacked any similar role or fixedness in the community's rituals of remembrance, most of which were eventually conducted outside of the Community Centre.

Clearly though, the mural's eventual descent into obscurity can be mainly attributed to matters squarely within the JCC. It seems that at least some of the community administrators who gave the Warsaw Ghetto Memorial Committee their solid support and praise were far more ambivalent when it came to Belkin's piece. This sentiment is perhaps best expressed in a late 1964 letter by Lou Zimmerman, then Executive Director of the Centre, who answered an inquiry about Vancouver's Warsaw Ghetto commemorations by first describing the activities and success of the Memorial Committee. As for fixed structures, he wrote:

> It was never our intention to create a permanent memorial to those who died at the hands of the Nazis. *However, we do have one.* This is a mural in the lounge of the Jewish Community Centre, painted by Arnold Belkin, and donated to the Jewish Community Centre of Vancouver in memory of his father who lived here. The mural depicts the horrors of the concentration camp, the glory of the battle of the Warsaw Ghetto. *I do believe it is generally considered to have merit as a work of art.*[42]

Hardly a ringing endorsement, one can only suspect that many day-to-day users of the Centre were even less enthusiastic about the mural's "merit as a work of art." Although Holocaust discourse was steadily increasing by the early 1960s, particularly after the Eichmann trial, certain depictions of the Jewish wartime experience were still an extremely sensitive matter. The yearly memorial programs organized by the Warsaw Ghetto Committee were indeed generally a success, but they roused angry opposition if the presentation was seen by some as too morbid or shocking. For instance, the 1962 showing of the documentary film "Night and Fog" by Alain Resnais, which involved extensive scenes of piles of starved bodies and other Nazi atrocities, prompted numerous members of the audience to write in to the *Jewish Western Bulletin* calling for more "uplifting" and "fitting" tributes.[43] Considering that Belkin's "Warsaw Ghetto Uprising" depicted many of the very same disturbing images and that Belkin was himself an admirer of Resnais' work in general, his mural would assumedly have raised similar objections among many JCC users, even more so in light of its prominent placement in the Centre's lobby and the above-mentioned "controversy" over exposing children to the world's horrors.

In this regard, there is little doubt that Belkin's "Warsaw Ghetto Uprising" would have found a more receptive viewership had it been donated to Vancouver's small Peretz Institute as he originally intended. Not only were the staff, executive, and P.T.A. of the school more highly versed in left-wing activism, but they also held the philosophy that Jewish youth should be familiar with the events of the war, no matter how gruesome, precisely because this history was too stark and terrible to be complacently forgotten. A corresponding level of enthusiastic support from the administration was certainly not forthcoming at the Community Centre. Although this caused many members of the Peretz Institute to view the subsequent neglect of Belkin's gift as yet another slight, it seems unlikely that most JCC directors or users were aware that the mural had ever had any connection to the school. Nor does it seem likely that the piece's adverse reception was in any large part due to Belkin's personal politics and artistic activities in Mexico, as neither appear to have even registered in Vancouver.

The inescapable difficulty encountered by Belkin's "Warsaw Ghetto Uprising" was that the widespread use of muralism to convey tragic events and to confront suffering and injustice in public spaces was more or less alien to the Canadian cultural landscape. Within both the Jewish and non-Jewish communities, the past was more typically evoked through literature and other print and mass media, monuments, and ritual, while the appreciation and critique of art remained mostly the private pursuit of a relative minority of collectors and gallery visitors. One might venture the observation that this situation has not much changed. In any case, Belkin's mural has never been fully accepted in the JCC either as a work of art or a permanent memorial, despite the fact that variations on the theme of the Warsaw Ghetto revolt were otherwise embraced by much of Vancouver's Jewish community as the central motif of Holocaust remembrance well into the 1970s. Today's even greater prominence of Holocaust discourse notwithstanding, Belkin's mural has been all but forgotten.

NOTES

1   Belkin's biographical details are provided in: William M. Kramer. "Sr. Arnold Belkin: The Mexican Jewish Artist from Calgary, Canada, A Memoir of the Artist," *Western States Jewish History,* 26 (1994), pp. 233–250, 365–77; Heather Pringle. "Stealing Fire," *Equinox,* March–April 1992, pp.51–61; Bob Carty. "Arnold Belkin, The Canadian Son of Mexican Muralism," CBC Radio Archives, 1998, <http://radio.cbc.calprograms/thismorningarchiveshib_trllls.htmp

2   Bob Carty. "Arnold Belkin: The Canadian Son of Mexican Muralism," CBC Radio.

3   "Hun Tanks Wipe Out 40,000 Warsaw Jews," *Vancouver Sun,* May 14, 1943, p.1; "Hun Division Quells Bloody Polish Revolt (Warsaw Jews Rebel)," *Vancouver Province,* May 29, 1943, p.1; "Warsaw Jews Kill 300 Nazi Elite Troops (Ghetto Cost Huns 2300 Casualties)," *Vancouver Sun,* June 4, 1943, p.1; "Memorial Services for Martyred Polish Jews This Sunday Evening at Schara Tzedeck Synagogue,"*Jewish Western Bulletin,* July 23, 1943, pp.1–2; "City Requiem for Jews who Died in Poland," *Vancouver Sun,* July 26, 1943, p.8.

4   The UJPO was in fact permanently expelled from Vancouver's Jewish Administrative Council in 1953. See Faith Jones, "Between Suspicion and Censure: Attitudes towards the Jewish Left in Postwar Vancouver." *Canadian Jewish Studies* 6 (1998): 1–24.

5   "Report of the Pacific Region to the Plenary Session," 1962 CJC Pacific Region files, Box39\File738.

6   Although he was actually born in Calgary, Belkin's family moved to Vancouver when he was six years old.

7   Transcript, Arnold Belkin Interview, 1972 Smithsonian Oral History Archive.

8   Shifra M. Goldman. *Contemporary Mexican Painting in a Time of Change.* Austin: University of Texas Press, 1981, pp. xix–xxvi

9   Heather Pringle. "Stealing Fire," p.53.

10 Ibid, p.55.

11 "Arnold Belkin Speaks On Role of Artists," *Jewish Western Bulletin,* December 12, 1955, p.1.

12 Heather Pringle. "Stealing Fire," p.56.

13 William Kramer. "Sr. Arnold Belkin," p.247.

14 Arnold Belkin to parents, November 1965. Belkin's personal correspondences are the property of his widow, Patricia Quijano Belkin. Copies of these letters were generously provided to me by David Pettigrew, a local writer-filmmaker who researched Belkin's life for an as yet unproduced documentary film.

15 Shifra Goldman. *Contemporary MEXICAN Painting*, p.78.

16 Personal conversation with Dr. William Kramer, March 2001.

17 "Unveil Belkin Mural at Warsaw Ghetto Night," *Jewish Western Bulletin*, April 3, 1964, p.5.

18 Arnold Belkin to parents, December 7, 1959.

19 William Kramer. "Sr. Arnold Belkin," p.244. One of the Mexican reviews from this showing later quoted in the *Jewish Western Bulletin*, April 3, 1964, p.5, said of Belkin: "Jewish artist and artist of humanity, possesses the greatness of combined profundity and superb mastery of techniques."

20 Personal conversation with Sylvia Friedman, a very active longtime member of the Peretz Institute.

21 Sam Heller to Arnold Belkin, quoted in a letter from Arnold Belkin to his sister, November 5, 1962.

22 Ibid.

23 JCC Executive Committee Minutes, November 19, 1962.

24 JCC Executive Board Minutes, November 28, 1962.

25 Personal conversations with Gertie Zack, then Vice-President of the JCC, and Paul Heller, Sam Heller's brother and an active member of the Warsaw Ghetto Memorial Committee.

26 Personal conversation with Dr. William Kramer.

27 Personal conversation with Gertie Zack.

28 JCC Executive Board Minutes, November 28, 1962

29 Arnold Belkin to parents, February 14, 1963, and March 4, 1963.

30 JCC Executive Board Minutes, May 13, 1963.

31 "Many Pay Silent Tribute to the Memory of Six Million," *Jewish Western Bulletin*, April 26, 1963, pp.5, 12.

32 Personal conversation with Gertie Zack.

33 Personal interview with Paul Heller.

34 JCC Executive Board Minutes, September 24, 1964.

35 Warsaw Ghetto Memorial Committee Minutes, April 7, 1964. CJC Pacific Region Files, Box I 5\ File 505.

36 Ibid. The matter of an "interpretive" plaque for the mural was raised again at the January 27, 1965 Committee meeting and perhaps several times thereafter. For whatever reason, the idea was eventually abandoned.

37 "Unveil Belkin Mural at Warsaw Ghetto Night," *Jewish Western Bulletin*, April 3, 1964, p.5.

38 *Jewish Western Bulletin*, April 17, 1964, p.3.

39 William Kramer, "Sr. Arnold Belkin," p.245. Dr. Kramer speculates that the overtly political nature of Belkin's work is the reason he was never given an exhibition in Canada.

40 Statements as to the whereabouts of the mural over the last 25 years tend to vary. By some accounts it was covered over on a regular basis until finally it was simply left that way. Others have mentioned an obscure hallway or storage. This uncertainty itself suggests the degree to which the mural was eventually ignored.

41 These discussions began in late 1966, but the outbreak of the Six Day War in 1967 and subsequent Middle East tensions greatly delayed the construction of a monument. My sincere thanks to Dr. Robert Krell, Kim Baylis, and Jack Kowarski for providing me with copies of letters from their personal files and the Schara Tzedeck Cemetery Board Minutes pertaining to this subject.

42 Lou Zimmerman to Morris Stein, January 6, 1965. CJC Pacific Region Files, Box 13a\ File 366. The emphasis is mine.

43 *Jewish Western Bulletin,* May 4, 1962, p.2.

Multicultural Encounters

Although this *Reader* focuses on Jewish identity, as it is expressed through creative, religious, political, and commemorative acts, it also aims to convey the changing relationship between Canadian Jews and the rest of Canada. The essays in this section present narratives within which this entanglement is put in particularly sharp relief. Pierre Anctil's essay aims to account for the poet A.M. Klein's relationship with Québécois culture; Harold Troper and Morton Weinfeld tell a fascinating story of ethnic rivalry in the postwar years; and Howard Adelman maps a recent Toronto-based dialogue between Blacks and Jews over the mounting of a well-known American play. Norman Ravvin's essay on Matt Cohen raises questions about the role of Jewish literature in mainstream Canadian culture at the turn of the twenty-first century.

NR

A. M. Klein: The Poet and His Relations with French Quebec

PIERRE ANCTIL

The life and work of the Montreal poet A. M. Klein abounds in antinomies. From the diligent study of the law to the outpouring of poetic emotion, Klein was able to swing easily from one literary genre to another, from a critical analysis of Ulysses to the autobiographical novel, from polemics and pamphlets to the inspirational Hebrew psalm. Thirsting for all sources of inspiration and searching out in himself all the potentialities of his art, Klein ended up by making a series of clean breaks—some dramatic, such as his departure from McGill University, others, minor, numerous, and simultaneous—without affecting the quality of his art. Finally, the poet, perhaps overly affected by the events of the turbulent era of the 1940s, produced a work, *The Rocking Chair and Other Poems,* which is difficult to understand in its entirety, for it has its literary roots entwined in several millennia of biblical and talmudic tradition. To fully appreciate Klein's work, the reader must be well versed in Judaic studies and in several languages, know how to appreciate all literary genres and be an expert on the subject of the immigration of the Ashkenazi Jews from eastern Europe—a formidable assignment indeed.

Before becoming too discouraged by such an agenda, let us look at the social milieu, which Klein wholeheartedly embraced, and to which he remained faithful throughout his life. Although he was not born in Montreal, he spent nearly his whole life in the Jewish community of that city. If the poet felt the heritage of the *shtetl* intensely within him and pulsated to the call of Jewish Palestine, it was above all in the Québécois community that he lived his life in its various phases—at McGill University, the Faculty of Law at l'Université de Montréal, in the Montreal Jewish Public Library, with his neighbours in Cartier riding, and his successive homes in the Mount Royal district. At every moment of his life, Klein was both Québécois and Jewish, deeply concerned with his personal well-being and the well-being of the Jewish people, yet living in the midst of a great metropolitan society impregnated with an incipient Quebecitude. Even though he was Yiddish-speaking, how could he have escaped the multicultural milieu that still distinguishes Montreal today, a milieu in which he ended up feeling so much at ease?

Quebec also was the home of a Francophone people who, in the thirties and forties, had not as yet discovered the term "Québécois" to describe themselves. Living in the country since the beginning of the seventeenth century, a rural and Catholic minority people since the English conquest, the French-Canadians made up almost 60 per cent of the population of Montreal at the time of Klein's arrival, and possessed the political and institutional power that made them one of two dominant groups, along with the Anglos. They were ever present in the poet's social world, and although he could not help but perceive them through the lens of his Jewishness, we cannot draw from this any conclusion regarding his understanding of the Québécois. Perhaps he had an intuition that these two peoples shared a difficult experience in common in their recent history, and that they had acquired little in a world where neither force of arms nor strength of numbers belonged to them.

In Klein's work, support for the Franco-Québécois cause constitutes one of the turning points. In a sense, the publication of *The Rocking Chair and Other*

Poems in 1948 marked the abandonment of the theme that had been dear to him until then: the poetic exploitation of his Jewish identity. After *The Rocking Chair*, Klein almost abandoned poetry to devote himself to literary analysis, and later, to writing his only novel, *The Second Scroll*. Furthermore, the period immediately following World War II saw a profound transformation of the relations between the Jewish community and the intellectual and political elite of Francophone Quebec. The world of the habitant and the snowshoe burst into the poet's work precisely at this point following the tensions of the thirties, when Jews and Francophones learned to coexist on a new basis. One can therefore assume that Klein did not write *The Rocking Chair* in a void, on a mere impulse, but that he responded specifically to a sympathetic undercurrent or at least to the lack of hostility that began to develop between the two longstanding Montreal neighbours—the Jews who had emigrated from the distant Polish or Russian plains, and the Québécois who had emigrated from the countryside of the St. Lawrence valley.

Indeed, there is nothing especially Québécois in *Hath Not a Jew* (1940), nor even in *The Hitleriad* (1944), which remains a book almost exclusively preoccupied with the death pangs of the Holocaust and the anguish of genocide. Until then, Klein relished using archaisms and terms that were learned or specifically Jewish, which made his poetry obscure or, at best, difficult to follow. It seemed as if Klein, having come to English late, attempted, by great display of scholarship, to make up for lost time and to invest his poetry with all the historic depth of the language of Shakespeare. Once he had completed this task, there would have been few persons within the Montreal Jewish community who could claim to have a better knowledge of Elizabethan English than Klein. The poem "The Rocking Chair" upsets this mode of writing and introduces into Klein's poetry a gentle contemplation of daily life, which he describes as a kind of lingering, perpetual experience:

> It seconds the crickets of the province. Heard
> in the clean lamplit farmhouses of Quebec,—
> wooden,—it is no less a national bird;

and rivals, in its cage, the mere stuttering clock.
To its time, the evenings are rolled away;
and in its peace the pensive mother knits
contentment to be worn by her family,
grown-up, but still cradled by the chair in which she sits.

(The Rocking Chair, p. 1)

Certainly, some of the poetic erudition of the first volumes remains in this new work, but this time it serves to mark the cultural distance between the Jewish poet and the object of his interest: French-Canadian civilization. Without a trace of animosity, Klein shows in *The Rocking Chair* that he is no longer discussing himself or his ancestors, but, the unexpected other. In this book, the expression "*fleur-de-lys*" or "*autre temps,*" by their strangeness, correspond to such erudite references as "White Levites at your altar'd ovens," or such biblical allusions as "Our own gomorrah house, the sodom that merely to look at makes one salt?" Furthermore, one poem in particular of this period, "Parade of St. Jean Baptiste," is studded with an especially scholarly and obscure vocabulary, for the simple reason that in the writing of this poem, Klein wanted to use only words common to both French and English: "This is one of a series of experimental poems making trial of what I flatter myself to believe is a 'bilingual language' since the vocabulary of the poem is mainly of Norman and latin origin." Without doubt, he thus made sure that his reader would perceive the distance separating him from the Québécois theme, to which the poem was dedicated, without ever having to depart from the historical fastness of the English language.

Of course, Klein remains Jewish in his *Rocking Chair* and more especially as he approaches a subject where the mystical and daily life perpetually coexist, as in his famous poem, "The Cripples." And then, after all, this taste for word games, this desire to merge the vocabularies of different languages, had already been practised by Jewish writers in the Italian peninsula and in the Arab world several centuries before Klein's birth. Above all, the poet had direct access, through his own experience, to a feeling that gave him empathy with his Francophone compatriots; like them, he belonged to a culture in which family values had an enormous importance and formed an anchor of protection against the siren call of the outside world.

Notwithstanding, Klein had a completely external knowledge of French-Canadians, and of their ways and customs. Completely at ease in the language of Molière, thanks principally to his studies in law undertaken in 1930 at l'Université de Montréal, an institution that was, at the time, exclusively Francophone and Catholic, and also because of a short stay in Abitibi in 1937–1938, Klein nevertheless had few French-Canadian friends, and he certainly had no close friends in that community. Furthermore, his vision of Francophone Quebec in *The Rocking Chair* remains oriented toward outdated and folkloric aspects of the culture. All the same, Klein had frequented Francophone circles often enough to be capable of conveying superb portraits of French-Canadians, such as M. Bertrand, the dandy yearning for Parisian culture, or Hormidas Arcand, the anti-Semite. Klein was also capable of composing, as in "Sire Alexandre Grandmaison" and in "Annual Banquet: Chambre de Commerce," complete descriptions of a distinctive world of the forties. In "Librairie Delorme," the poet succeeds admirably in portraying the atmosphere of Montreal's famous Ducharme (antique) bookstore. When reading the poem, one could almost see prospective customers filing into the small shop:

> . . . an *abbé*, perhaps, beatified with sight
> of green Laurentia, kneeling to church-bell.
>
> (*The Rocking Chair*, p. 44)

However, the most successful evocation of the Francophone milieu of Montreal in this volume is found in the poem "Political Meeting." Accustomed as he was to political debates and a fervent follower of partisan rhetoric since his student days at McGill, Klein had followed the flamboyant career of Camillien Houde with a certain amount of interest and apprehension, especially because this man symbolized, more than anyone else at the beginning of the forties, the very idea of the Francophone—an idea that commanded attention through the power of Houde's speeches. The populist mayor, born in a poor neighbourhood in the east end of Montreal, campaigned at the time against conscription and the involvement of French-Canadians in a war that was being waged in Europe. Klein was quick to grasp the possible anti-Semitic implications of such a position, and he denounced it on several occasions in his editorials, written for the *Canadian Jewish Chronicle*. Taking this ideological reservation into account, one feels in "Political Meeting" that the character of Houde has succeeded, up to a certain point, in casting a spell on the poet, who feels, perhaps vaguely, that the orator also wishes to defend his people in the face of the agony of the war, which was close at hand:

> praises the virtue of being "*Canadien*"
> of being at peace, of faith, of family,
> and suddenly his other voice: "Where are your sons?"
>
> He is tearful, choking tears; but not he
> would blame the clever English; in their place
> he'd do the same: maybe.
>
> Where are your sons?
>
> The whole street wears one face,
> shadowed and grim; and in the darkness rises
> the body-odour of race.
>
> (*The Rocking Chair*, p. 16)

Several critics of Jewish origin were inclined to recognize, in *The Rocking Chair*, the mark of the Jewish education Klein had received early in his life, even if this collection of poetry, unlike the first collections, did not bring an especially Jewish theme to the fore:

> because the parallels are so great between the Jews and the French-Canadians. The French-Canadians saw themselves as almost a biblical people with a language and religion that separated them from the majority around them.

> Quebec was a kind of Palestine, a French ghetto in North
> America.
>
> Like the Jews, French-Canadians are also concerned,
> almost preoccupied, with survival. It is a constant theme
> for the poets of both peoples.[1]

However, I do not believe that this parallelism between the two peoples,
although it was very real, was the author's only motivation when he began the
composition of his Québécois poems. I would maintain, rather, that at the end
of World War II, Klein was looking for a new channel for rapprochement with
his Francophone compatriots, and that the writing of *The Rocking Chair* was in
this sense a catharsis for him. This motivation, closely linked to the circumstances of the time, is revealed when one studies the history of the collection
itself, and when one examines the situation in which the Jewish leadership of
Montreal found itself following the peace of 1945. This does not diminish the
quality of Klein's poetic inspiration in any way, but it places his actions in a
social context to which the author was very sensitive, and which could not fail
to affect him in his writing.

In July 1947, Klein published seven of his Québécois poems in the journal *Poetry*, of Chicago.[2] When one considers how little attention the author
received in Quebec, even within his own community, one could certainly
assume that all of the poems would have ultimately gone unnoticed in
Montreal. Shortly afterwards, Klein was offered the Edward Bland Memorial
Fellowship, a prize awarded by a black American organization to a collection of
poems of high literary quality, whose contents have had an impact on social relations. In its October 1947 edition, the *Congress Bulletin*, the official mouthpiece
of the Canadian Jewish Congress, announced Klein's award and republished the
prize-winning poems under the new title *Poems of French Canada*.[3] Not content
with having published the seven poems in this form, the directors of the
Congress published the poems again, at the end of the year, in a pamphlet, with
yet a different title: *Seven Poems*. In an internal memo dated November 25, 1947,
David Rome, editor of the *Bulletin*, wrote to Saul Hayes, the executive director
of the Congress:

I wish to report to you that our release of Mr. Klein's poems has met with a response which, frankly, I had not anticipated. *La Presse* made even more of the story than I had expected. We are receiving a number of requests for copies from Jewish, French-Canadian and English members of the public. We are sending some of them the *Congress Bulletin* which contains these poems.

It is also suggested that the pamphlet should be sent to our list of priests and to doctors, government officials, etc., in Quebec and among those who read French. In order to do this, we would have to reprint the poems.[4]

All evidence suggests that Klein had struck a responsive note with his Québécois poems, to the point where the leadership of the Congress had been touched by it, and perhaps it had also affected those people who worked at maintaining and developing positive institutional ties with the Jewish community and the general public.

The work of the public relations people of the Canadian Jewish Congress to publicize these poems bore fruit very soon. In November 1947, David Rome wrote, probably in a letter of introduction to the poems themselves:

You may agree with me that it is significant that poems which so exactly and understandingly reflect the French-Canadian scene should be written by a Jewish writer who is acknowledged by his community as its literary spokesman. The appearance of these poems is indicative of a very desirable development in Canadian group relations.[5]

The Congress was quickly overwhelmed with praise for Klein's work, which seemed to indicate that the publicity campaign had been well managed and that Klein's poems were well received in all circles, including the clergy, as the text of this letter, signed by Claude Sumner, a Francophone Jesuit of the Collège Jean-de-Brébeuf, indicates:

> It is indeed very significant that these poems, which reflect
> so accurately the French-Canadian life, should have been
> written by a Jewish author. They reveal, not only a careful
> observation, keenly intent upon the facts and details of the
> French-Canadian scene, but a remarkable insight which
> enables the writer to reach and even penetrate the [soul] of
> the men and women he describes. Such accurateness
> implies on his part a sensitiveness in perfect consonance
> with his subject, a great sympathy, a comprehension wide
> open to all things of beauty.[6]

The Congress published Klein's poems a fourth time in 1948, in a pamphlet entitled *Huit poèmes canadiens,* this time adding a preface in French and the text of the laudatory book review that had appeared in *La Presse* the previous year, written by Jean-Marie Poirier. In addition to the seven poems already published, an eighth poem, "Parade of St. Jean Baptiste" was added, which had appeared first in the February 1948 edition of *Canadian Forum,* and which developed the same theme in a more detailed manner. The distribution of these small brochures must have been very efficient, for in January 1948, a journal as clerical in nature as *Les carnets viatoriens* took note of their publication: "Here is a song of exceptional value. Its moderate and touching tone, tender and yet virile, humbly interested in the vision of every object in its surroundings, its sense of poetic appearance and of the words which express it; all of this touches the soul and delights the mind."[7]

Even the very serious *Action universitaire* of Montreal complimented Klein, praising his dual role of a poet and a man sympathetic to French Canada:

> French Canadian life has obviously attracted him, there he
> has found a stamp of humanity capable of nourishing his
> inspiration. It is not that everything appears idyllic and

admirable to him; we do not ask so much of him, good heavens! In Klein's writing, there is a certain tendency to view things in both an ironic and amused manner at the same time, which allows him to recreate charming cameos, in which individual characterizations approach caricature, without ever displaying a trace of bitterness or mockery.[8]

Between 1947 and 1949, David Rome probably did more to make Klein known in Quebec than did Klein's publisher in Toronto, the Ryerson Press, which published the collection of Québécois poems under the title of *The Rocking Chair and Other Poems,* in the summer of 1948. One can appreciate the magnitude of Rome's efforts among the Québécois public when one remembers that in 1952 Klein earned the literary prize of the province of Quebec for *The Rocking Chair and Other Poems,*[9] an honour that never would have been conferred on him if his work had not reached the Francophone literary milieu of the time. Left to himself, the poet, a man of solitary and modest temperament, would have undoubtedly been unable to obtain the same results in such a short time.

Nevertheless, Klein had not always harboured such feelings of openness towards the Francophone community, which he rediscovered at the end of the forties. During the thirties and even earlier, he had felt an iciness in the relations between the two neighbouring communities, and like other people among the Jewish community, he was troubled by it. Even if a great deal has been written on the subject of Canadian anti-Semitism during these last years, in certain circles the specific character and extent of this phenomenon is still poorly appreciated, particularly with regard to Quebec.[10] Klein's personal experience and the testimony of his work appear to be symptomatic of the general state of intercultural relations that had existed for more than a century between Jews and Francophone Québécois. A polemicist and writer for the *Canadian Jewish Chronicle* since the beginning of the thirties, Klein wrote scathing articles attacking Francophones who had been stricken with the virus of anti-Semitism. In one of these articles, an editorial of 8 July 1932 entitled "The Twin Racketeers of Journalism," which surely was directed at Adrien Arcand and Joseph Ménard, he writes:

To give it a touch of modernity, however, the editors brought their defamations up to date by reiterations of the notorious *Protocols of the Elders of Zion*. They filled their papers with slanders as headline, garbled quotation as foot-note, and forgery as space-filler. The contents of their pages, moreover, when analysed, proved that what its pub-lishers could not invent or copy, was supplied to them by a syndicate of anti-Semitic propaganda, trafficking in syn-thetic venom and co-operative hate. Its headquarters seemed to be Germany: when Hitler sneezed, they caught cold. Thus the pest of Jew-hatred, like the bubonic plague, was being brought from continent to continent, through the medium of rats.[11]

It is interesting to note in the anthology published by M. W. Steinberg and Usher Caplan, that the poet put an end to his violent attacks on Quebec anti-Semitism precisely at the end of World War II, after he had denounced a whole series of anti-Jewish incidents, including riots against conscription and the partial burning of the Quebec City synagogue in 1943. Of the twelve edito-rials concerning Quebec chosen by the editors of *Beyond Sambation,* eight were written about anti-Semitism in Quebec, and they were all written before 1946. On 29 December 1944, in "The Tactics of Race-Hatred," Klein warned the read-ers of the *Canadian Jewish Chronicle* to distrust people who apply the term "anti-Semitic" to French Quebec as a whole: "Either the pious defence of a discrimi-nated minority is being used as an instrument of denigration against the French-Canadian minority; or the crusader, adopting the tactic of 'Stop thief,' is point-ing to Quebec anti-Semitism only to draw attention off his own."[12]

After 1945, Klein thus adopted a new attitude towards the Quebec Francophone community. Was this simply an isolated gesture, a whim on the part of the poet, who could have been affected by his own intuitions? Several factors seem to indicate that Klein joined a movement of rapprochement after the war that was still tentative but well under way, one which he did not lead or anticipate. In its edition of 30 May 1947, the *Congress Bulletin,* in an important article, gave voice to the new perception that was developing among the Jewish leadership concerning the general nature of its relations with the Franco-Québécois:

> Since the last Plenary Session, in January 1945, there have been a series of developments whose import cannot be exaggerated. This is not to say that racial or religious prejudice has disappeared from this part of Canada (Quebec) any more than from any other part. Nor is it implied that there has been a *volte-face* or a change of policy or of doctrine among this section of the Canadian people (the French Québécois). Rather might it be said that the friends whom we have always had among them have become more active in the presentation of their views. It might also be that the Jewish community of Canada has learned with the passage of time and with experience the means of presenting its case more effectively before French Canada and of winning its support.
>
> The change has been very great although its symptoms are intangible.[13]

In an article entitled "The State of Anti-Semitism in French Canada," David Rome presented the readers of the *Bulletin* with some new facts on this issue, and advanced an interpretation of the dynamics between the two communities, which heretofore had been undisclosed. Rome noted, among other things, that the large majority of the Francophone press condemned anti-Semitism from then on, and that they granted the Jewish community the space it was entitled to for the printing of press communiqués sent out by the Canadian Jewish Congress on this subject, and that the Catholic Church of Quebec encouraged the Francophone press in these activities. Above all, Rome noted that *Le Goglu*, a particularly anti-Semitic periodical that had resurfaced after 1945 and invoked Christian justice as its authority, had been publicly condemned by influential Catholics, including some priests. Elsewhere in his article,

Rome described several minor but significant developments in the attitudes of Francophone Catholics, which led him to conclude, with a great deal of enthusiasm, that "it is not too much to say that the pro-Jewish statements which have appeared in the press of this country have no parallel in the entire literature of Catholicism in two thousand years."[14]

A short time earlier, on 5 May 1947, Louis M. Benjamin had discussed the same theme in the *Congress Bulletin,* and he had treated the subject in the same way, proceeding from the same information gleaned here and there from current events: "A change in the relationship of the French and the Jews of Quebec is coming about. There are now definite signs of a rapprochement between our people and the Gallic population of this province. This is evidenced in many ways."[15]

Although these articles appeared anonymously in this type of publication, somewhat like the editorials in the Anglophone newspapers of Canada, they were perceived as being the official position of the mother institution—in this case, the Canadian Jewish Congress. The new language used by the *Congress Bulletin* around 1947 with regard to the Francophones of Quebec went well beyond the simple level of personal opinion, in importance and in subject matter; in fact, it involved the entire community and indicated new priorities of concern among the traditional Jewish leadership. In October 1949, in the official report of the eighth plenary session of the Canadian Jewish Congress, one chapter reiterated the same views developed two or three years earlier on the subject of French Canada, and granted them the endorsement of a biennial general assembly.

Whatever the relative weight of such opinions on the part of any Jewish organization may have been, it was still up to the Canadian Jewish Congress to invest a great deal of time and energy in the attempt to bring the two communities closer together in those decisive years. At the time, the Congress was the most respected Canadian Jewish institution, and it was also the institution that was most closely listened to outside of the Jewish community. It actively undertook the building of the friendship between the two peoples on a renewed basis. Klein must have been acquainted rather early on with this new spirit, since the items on the agenda of the Congress had to be freely circulated among the collaborators and staff of the Congress. Indeed, the poet was very close to the Congress through his privileged relationship with the philanthropist, Samuel Bronfman, who had been the president of the organization since 1939 and was a dominant figure in the Montreal Jewish leadership in the post-war period. In addition, Klein maintained close ties with David Rome and Saul Hayes through his para-professional activities linked to his writing and his responsibilities as a lecturer at the Jewish Public Library and other Jewish organizations.

However, this openness on the part of the Jewish community was not accomplished without due consideration, and without sufficient evidence of good faith on the part of both parties. Certain attitudes of the Quebec Francophones had thus paved the way for a mutual understanding. Without such efforts, the good intentions of the Jewish community would have been in vain, due to a lack of reciprocity. David Rome was not mistaken when he asserted in 1947 that the Jews had Catholic and Francophone friends, whose importance and influence began to be felt. In order to judge the contrast in attitudes between the thirties and the end of the forties, it may be useful to cite a little-known text of M.Ceslas Forest, a Dominican priest who taught a course on social ethics at *l'École des sciences sociales, économiques et politiques de l'Université de Montréal*.[16] Published in 1935, *"La Question juive au Canada"* perfectly summarizes the opinion held by educated and informed Francophones of the time, and this was in line with the doctrine and Catholic ethics practised since the mid-nineteenth century and earlier. The author's opinion remains explicit and it lays the foundation of an entire school of thought, which was very widespread at that time: Quebec is a Christian state in its law and in its institutions, and this character must be protected against all attacks: "By becoming Canadian citizens, the Jews have accepted to live in a Christian country. There, the promised freedom finds its limit. Their demands, however legitimate they may be, must never interfere with the character of our institutions and our laws."[17]

This way of thinking had been applied in Quebec to the question of Jewish schools, a problem that had been debated practically since the period of mass immigration in the 1880s. On this basis alone, the Catholic clergy had insisted in 1930, and even earlier, on the exclusion of Jewish people from *le Conseil de l'instruction publique* (Public Education Council), which would have placed Jews on equal footing with Christians in the area of education. As Forest recalls, "All the same, one cannot require a Christian state to provide religious education for non-Christians in their non-Christian faith."[18]

This attitude, adopted by the Catholic hierarchy of Quebec, engendered a social climate that rapidly became awkward during the thirties, when one takes the presence of a small number of notorious anti-Semitic agitators among the Francophone population into account, including Adrien Arcand and Joseph Ménard, to mention only the most well known. During this period, however, the Catholic clergy did not undertake any anti-Jewish campaigns in Quebec, for it was restrained by its own adherence to the principle of Christian charity, which remains universal in its application: "There are not two sets of morals: one which governs our relations with the Jews and the other which governs our relations with the rest of humanity. There is only one set of morals, and its regulations are clear: one is never permitted to wrong others by unjust means."[19]

Nevertheless, the Catholic Church and its adherents did nothing to bring an end to the racist banter of the anti-Semites, who declared themselves to be fervent Catholics and claimed to be defending their religion and their nationality by their actions. During the thirties, not one official representative of the Catholic Church of Quebec openly opposed anti-Semitism, in whatever form it appeared. Yet, another obstacle blocked the way to a better understanding between Jews and Francophone Québécois: it was felt that people of Mosaic religious persuasion had no national allegiance "in exile," and that they mocked the country where they had settled, or the customs that were practised there: "We do not see why we should upset the management of our educational system just for this group of immigrants who has never sincerely adopted its new country."[20]

Poised in a position of national withdrawal and cultural survival on one hand, and imprisoned in the narrowest interpretation possible of the duties of Christian ethics on the other hand, the vast majority of Quebec Francophones had witnessed, with a growing indifference, the deterioration of their relations with the Jewish community. This is precisely the situation that would undergo a change after the war, without, of course, an official or public announcement of this change, or the majority of the population being immediately aware of it.

In May 1945, in a clerical journal called *Relations*, which had exhibited anti-Semitic tendencies some years earlier, a young Québécois Jesuit published an article on the Jewish minority and education, "*La minorité juive au Québec*," which is still of interest. In this brief study, Stéphane Valiquette merely noted some known facts and statistics. The reader would not have been able to find the slightest evidence of hostility, or the smallest reservation concerning the presence of these immigrants and descendants of non-Christian immigrants in Quebec, where there were approximately seventy thousand such people at the time. Even better, Valiquette had gone to the very source to obtain his information, to the offices of the Canadian Jewish Congress, where he had enjoyed warm contacts with the leadership for a long time.

In fact, the biography of Father Valiquette compresses in itself almost all the direct ties the Catholic clergy had maintained with the Quebec Jewish community. Born in 1912 at the corner of Rachel and Saint-Dominique Streets, in the heart of Montreal's traditional Jewish ghetto, Valiquette lived in an Orthodox Jewish milieu during his entire childhood, even acting as a "*shabbes goy*" for several years at a corner synagogue.[21] This early experience must have profoundly affected the young Valiquette, who never forgot his Jewish brothers once he entered the Jesuit novitiate in 1931, and who wanted to maintain his contacts with them. In 1937, through his own superior and with the permission of other authorities, he obtained an interview with H. M. Caiserman, who was the secretary general of the Canadian Jewish Congress. This act was in itself remarkable for the time, even more so because Valiquette, by acting in this way, was fighting the inclinations of the vast majority of Francophone clergymen, who were indifferent if not hostile to any organized form of rapprochement, and who were readers of the often anti-Jewish Catholic press. In the entire Jewish community of Montreal, only the Reform Rabbi Harry Joshua Stern had had any contact with a Catholic priest: the Jesuit Joseph Paré of the Collège Sainte-Marie; and this meeting occurred by chance during an Atlantic voyage in 1929. Stern and Paré developed an admiration for one another over the years, and together they organized meetings between Christians and Jews on several different occasions during the thirties—meetings that, however, did not involve institutional or superior Catholic authorities. Valiquette would go much further than this; as of 1939, he began to speak before members of the seminary of the diocese of Montreal, to inform them about the Jewish community of Montreal and to discuss what their attitude towards this community should be. In 1944, the same year in which he was ordained as a priest, Valiquette completed a thesis on liberal Judaism, with the help of Rabbi Stern.[22]

Valiquette and a small group of clergymen committed to his cause came to the fore in the months following the end of the war. In 1945, the well-known Canadian fascists who had been imprisoned by the federal government for the duration of the war, regained their freedom, and some of them soon started their outcry against the Jews. Around 1946, *Le Goglu* was published again, under the direction of Joseph Ménard, reproducing the same anti-Jewish slander and attempting to regain its audience of the thirties. This time, however, the social climate had changed. But what interests us here is the fact that the Catholic Church of Montreal had in the meantime created a commission to serve the needs of the non-Catholic citizens of Montreal. Founded at the end of 1940 by Mgr. Charbonneau, *la Commission des oeuvres d'apastolat auprès des non-catholiques* (the Commission of the Works of the Apostolate for non-Catholics) even included a sub-section devoted to the Jewish cause: *le Comité St-Paul* (the St. Paul Committee). The priests who were active in this committee, including Valiquette, published a brochure in 1946 entitled "Why Work Towards the Conversion of Israel" ("*Pourquoi travailler à la conversion d'Israël*") and urged Christians to be more understanding towards the Jews.[23] In such a context, Ménard's anti-Semitic literature struck a sour note, and the committee wrote to the members of *Le Goglu* in February 1947, to ask them to retract their statements. This was the first time in the modem history of Quebec that clergymen publicly opposed the spreading of hate literature against the Jews:

> In its last meeting, the St. Paul Committee examined a few
> issues of *Le Goglu* and thought it should warn you (Joseph
> Ménard) that the paper, of which you are the director, is
> proving to be an obstacle in the path of the Committee's
> apostolic work. We are attempting to make Christianity
> known and loved in Jewish circles, in order to make them

"see the light" by means of this display of kindness. We
believe that the general tone of your publication and some
of its remarks do not conform to the courtesy which is cus-
tomary on the part of journalists, and do not uphold the
requirements of evangelical charity of which Christians,
above all, should be the example.[24]

By protesting against the reappearance of anti-Jewish literature in
Quebec, the St. Paul Committee took everyone by surprise. Ménard responded
to the attack by publishing a pamphlet entitled "The Clergy and the Jews" ("*Le
clergé et les Juifs*"), which was directed against the priests who ran the St. Paul
Committee. At first, the editor of *Le Goglu* believed that Valiquette and his colleagues were acting in isolation, and that it would be easy to ignore them.
However, Mgr. Charbonneau and the high clergy of the diocese of Montreal had
not created the Commission of the Works of the Apostolate for non-Catholics
as a mere formality. The new atmosphere that the episcopate was seeking to
establish with the other churches and religions of the city was able to withstand
the indignity of this anti-Semitic propaganda: *Le Goglu* disappeared from circulation in mid-1947 and Ménard had to cease all public activity directed against
the Jews. As for the Jewish leadership of Montreal, it was quick to grasp the
meaning of this incident, and through it, began to perceive the new dynamics
of the relations that were already developing in Montreal between the Catholic
Church and the Jews. In his article concerning the state of anti-Semitism in
Quebec, published in May 1947, David Rome referred to the *Goglu* affair: "If
this cessation is due to this pressure (of the Roman Catholic committee which
deals with Jewish affairs) it represents one of the few cases where public opinion
in Canada was able to stop the publication of an undesirable periodical without
the instrumentality of governmental agencies."[25]

After the war, the Catholic clergymen were not the only people in
Quebec to feel the need to draw closer to their Jewish compatriots. The surge
of liberalism and sympathy also reached lay people, one of whom, Jean
Lemoyne, left a detailed account of his efforts to shatter the iron grip of mutual ignorance that embraced the two communities. In 1948, Lemoyne visited

Israel and brought back some strong impressions of his voyage, which he described in an article entitled "The Return from Israel" (*"Le retour d'Israël"*). This is undoubtedly one of the first texts in Québécois literature that allowed the appearance, in lyrical terms, of a thorough knowledge of Jewish history, the Judaic religion and contemporary Zionism. Indeed, in "The Return from Israel," a contradiction to the slanderous writings that had circulated in Quebec during the period between the two wars, the author almost succeeds in identifying himself with the Jewish condition, and even aspires, like the Jewish people, to freedom in the face of long centuries of obstacles: "A people made for apocalypse, those violent meetings of the eternal and the contingent, Israel only stirs by rousing the swirling waters of eternity around it."[26] Lemoyne, who could be considered a mystic Zionist, linked his preoccupation with Israel with the ideal of his Christian faith: "Zionism is an expression of the will of being; it appeals to the right of being, the most urgent and respectable of all rights. Here the exercising of this right corresponds to a providential design, in accordance with our faith."[27]

In his opinion, Catholicism arose directly from the Judaic religion, and he did not know how to detach himself from his roots, without running the risk of drying up and becoming paralyzed. It is unnecessary to add that faced with such historical perspectives and the depth of the link he had rediscovered between Christianity and Judaism, any manifestation of anti-Semitism could only arouse Lemoyne's disgust, even more so when the Catholic Church became the accomplice of anti-Semitism through its silence and impotence: "Anti-Semitism, a product of those base, disgraceful and inferior consciences and which knows no other justification than that of the scapegoat, which is in demand, not only symbolically, but literally, presently, in the thick of humanity."[28]

As for Klein, he never participated directly in the post-war efforts of rapprochement undertaken between the Québécois Jews and the Franco-Catholics. His temperament and his lifestyle predisposed him to assume a completely different role, less direct but more lasting and, above all, more intangible: the writing of the collection, *The Rocking Chair and Other Poems*. The poet had always been sensitive to current world events as they affected various Jewish communities, particularly his own. One has only to recall, for example, *The Hitleriad*, written in 1942–1943, which was a long pamphlet in poetic form and represented Klein's entire "war effort." There is also *The Second Scroll*, which finds its dramatic conclusion in Israel after its independence: these two works reveal the depth of the author's historical consciousness. A poet of a certain type of militant Judaism, Klein was also the intimate witness of his Montreal surroundings, of two complementary divisions in his mind, without which his works could never be read and appreciated in their entirety. In such a contradiction in terms lay the foundations of a good part of the dynamics of Klein's writing, which culminate in *The Rocking Chair*. For this reason, undoubtedly, the collection became associated with the profound social and ideological changes that affected all of French Quebec and would lead to a complete redefinition of its relations with the Montreal Jewish minority.

The Jewish-Catholic rapprochement, which took shape at the end of the forties in Quebec, was rooted in a combination of socio-economic changes that were unprecedented, and whose effects were beginning to be felt by the end of World War II. The Francophone Québécois, like many other peoples, took far too much time to apprehend the impact of the Holocaust upon the Jews of the world for this unimaginable disaster to have influenced their relations with the Montreal Jewish community during the forties. Neither this catastrophe, nor the proclamation of the State of Israel, played any role in the proclivity of Francophone Québécois for rapprochement with the Jews living in Canada. In fact, the opening up of all of Quebec to secular and liberal North American influences, the evident prosperity of the new Francophone middle classes and their access to a certain occupational mobility, began to shatter the visceral mistrust that traditional Québécois society had of everything that did not conform to its cultural and religious ideas. This radically new social climate, largely the result of external influences, led directly to the political events of the sixties and to the ideological ferment known as the Silent Revolution. During the fifteen years from 1945 to 1960, when Quebec society underwent institutional change, such forms of pathological behaviour as the xenophobic rejection of the contemporary world and a withdrawal to the comforting hearth of the past diminished among the Francophones, whose anti-Semitism Klein had decried so frequently during the thirties.

Thus, the virulent anti-Semitism of such people as Ménard and Arcand had principally been a particular form of social pathology, produced by a society whose horizons were walled in by a double alienation, born of the economic effects of the Depression and a certain national sclerosis. The fact that a person so highly sensitive to his surroundings as Klein had recognized the dawning of a new day in the relations between Francophones and Jews, and that he made himself its hearty propagandist, raises the deeper question of the history of the relations between the two communities since the 1880s. Unfortunately, researchers and historians are more inclined to remember dramatic events, such as the strike of 1934 at the Notre-Dame Hospital in Montreal, or the Plamondon affair of 1910, than to dwell on the nature of the daily exchanges that took place between the two communities for more than a century. As for Klein himself, who had so brilliantly depicted the traditional identity of Quebec Francophones in poetic tones, a long descent into silence awaited him shortly after, and as of the mid-fifties, his pen became silent. Such a dénouement snatched one of its most magnificent poets away from the Jewish community, and one of its best ambassadors of peace to the Francophones of the city.[29]

NOTES

This article was originally published as "*A. M. Klein: Du poète et de ses rapports avec le Québec français*" in the *Journal of Canadian Studies/Revue d'études canadiennes* 19 (Summer 1984), pp. 114–131, and this translation by Barbara Havercraft is used here by permission.

1   M.W. Steinberg and Seymour Mayne, "A Dialogue on A. M. Klein," *Jewish Dialog* (Passover 1973), p. 16.

2   These poems were "Grain Elevator," "The Cripples," "For Sisters of the Hotel Dieu," "Air-Map," "The Break-up," "M. Bertrand" and "Frigidaire."

3   At this time, David Rome was editor of the *Congress Bulletin*. I do not believe that Klein's pamphlets were first published to counter the anti-Semitic influences and opinions in Quebec, but because the social climate had freed itself from this question. I believe that these poems were expected to receive a favourable welcome in Francophone circles.

4   This document is kept in the archives of the Canadian Jewish Congress.

5   Ibid.

6   Ibid.

7   Le Scrutateur (pseud.), "Poems of French Canada," *Les carnets viatoriens* 8, no. 1 (1948): 62–63.

8   Roger Duhamel, "Courrier des lettres," *L'Action universitaire* 15 (April 1949), pp. 82–83.

9   The Governor General's Award had already been bestowed on Klein in 1949 for the same work.

10 On the subject of anti-Semitism in Quebec, consult Lita-Rose Betcherman's excellent study, *The Swastika and the Maple Leaf* (1975) and *None Is Too Many* by Abella and Troper (1982).

11 M. W. Steinberg and Usher Caplan, eds., *Beyond Sambation: Selected Essays and Editorials, 1928–1955* (Toronto, 1982).

12 Ibid., p.230.

13 Although this article is not signed, like many others of similar content, one can assume that they were written by David Rome, because he was the editor of the *Congress Bulletin* at that time.

14 Anon., "The State of Anti-Semitism in French Canada," *Congress Bulletin* 4 (May 1947), pp. 24–25.

15 Louis Benjamin, "The Jews and the French Canadians," *Congress Bulletin* 4 (May 1947), pp. 8, 10.

16 An officially Catholic institution until the sixties, l'Université de Montréal required Catholic students in all disciplines to take courses in Christian ethics that would be suited to their profession.

17 M.-Ceslas Forest, "La Question juive au Canada," *La Revue Dominicaine* 41 (November 1935), pp. 246–277.

18 Ibid., p. 268.

19 M.-Ceslas Forest, "La Question juive chez nous," *La Revue Dominicaine* 41 (December 1935), pp. 329–349.

20 Ibid., p. 268.

21 This is a Yiddish term of Hebrew origin that designates a non-Jewish person who is responsible for certain tasks in a Jewish household or religious establishment. Jews were forbidden by Mosaic law to carry out such tasks. In this case, the young Valiquette's duties probably consisted of extinguishing the candles and turning off the lights after the beginning of the Sabbath.

22 Stéphane Valiquette, "Chronologie autobiographique," 1981.

23 The reader should note that there is a problem of semantics here, which is difficult to avoid. Before Vatican II, the Roman Catholic Church was in the habit of maintaining a certain reservation in its relations with representatives of non-Christian religions, including the Jews. At this time, the only path open to a Catholic clergyman eager to associate with believers of other religions was proselytism. The early writings of Valiquette and the St. Paul Committee thus borrowed this language of "the conversion of Israel." However, it should be stated clearly that the number of Québécois Jews who were converted to Catholicism remained extremely low and that Valiquette and his

associates did not make apostasy their principal goal in their relations with the Jews. Until the sixties, the regulations of the Catholic Church simply required that the language used in the dialogue with the Jews had to call for their conversion to Catholicism.

24 Joseph Ménard, "Le clergé et les Juifs," *Le Goglu* (1947), p. 6.

25 Anon., "State of Antisemitism," pp. 24–25.

26 Jean Lemoyne, "Le retour d'Israël," in *Convergences* (Collection Constantes), no. 1 (Montreal, 1961).

27 Ibid., p. 182.

28 Ibid., p. 174.

29 Even today, Klein remains almost totally unknown among Québécois critics, despite the obvious legitimacy of his Montreal roots, and he does not appear in any of the numerous histories or anthologies of Québécois literature that have been published in French.

Two Solitudes: The Legacy of the War from *Old Wounds: Jews, Ukrainians and the Hunt for Nazi War Criminals in Canada*

Harold Troper *&* Morton Weinfeld

As hundreds of thousands of DPs waited in camps across Europe, ethnic communities across Canada began to lobby for the admission of their brethren to the country—and Ukrainians and Jews were no exception. In many ways, their lobbying efforts paralleled each other. Both Jewish and Ukrainian campaigns swung into action shortly following the war and both were at first ignored by Mackenzie King's Liberal government.[1]

Tough anti-immigration restrictions imposed during the Depression remained intact. Moreover, government planners, fearing that the end of massive wartime spending would derail a fragile post-war Canadian economy, showed no sympathy whatever for the admission of job-hungry immigrants from Europe. Jobs for demobilized Canadian servicemen would come first. If immigrant labour was needed, most would agree, it should be met by admitting immigrants in a descending order of ethnic preference. Most desirable were those from Britain and the United States, followed by northern and western Europeans, central and eastern Europeans and finally Jews, Asians and blacks.

But if Canadian Ukrainian and Jewish communities had suffered this sort of racial humiliation in the pre-war years, they were unwilling to endure it in the post-war. Both communities had sent large numbers of their children off to fight for Canada. Both communities harboured a deep sense of the suffering endured by their brethren in wartime Europe, and both had relatives languishing in the DP camps of Europe. Both communities galvanized in an effort to relieve their suffering and to lobby for their admission into Canada.

There was little or no contact between the two community campaigns. Nevertheless, their collective input began to be felt as fears of post-war economic backslide into depression subsided in the face of sustained economic strength. The buoyancy of the Canadian economy, a surprise to many economic planners, was so strong that by late 1946, little more than a year after the war's end, labour-intensive Canadian industries joined ethnic leaders in clamouring for immigration reform. The DP camps of Europe promised labour in abundance.

Ukrainians, popularly pictured as simple farm folk, non-disruptive, non-competitive, ever docile and prepared to do rural labour, seemed ideal for those manpower-short sectors of the Canadian economy in need of manual labour. Strangely enough, this stereotype, which today must be seen as negative, actually gave them an advantage over Jews in winning admission to Canada.

Jews were identified as urban in the popular mind of a country that still felt the proper place of immigrants was in rural areas; they were seen as cosmopolitan, perhaps tainted by leftist ideologies, in a country secure in its narrow parochialism; they were seen as aggressively competitive by a community that would truck no "foreign" challenge to its artisans or small-business entrepreneurs. Added to all this were the smouldering embers of ancient religious prejudice and perhaps even suggestions among some that the Jews of Europe must have been guilty of something to make Germans single them out for genocide. The result was to make the Jewish DP as undesirable in the public mind as the

Jewish refugee had been in pre-war and war years. In an October 1946 Gallup Poll, Jews were chosen as the least desirable of potential European immigrant groups seeking admission to Canada.²

Among Ukrainian-Canadians, there grew a fear that Ukrainians in Displaced Persons camps would be forcibly repatriated to the Soviet Union. Canada, like its western allies, originally felt the post-war refugee crisis would be short-lived. If refugees could simply be shuffled back to their countries of origin, the refugee problem would soon resolve itself. But almost a million persons from the Soviet Union and Soviet-controlled territory refused to go home in spite of allied encouragement and Soviet insistence. This clouded post-war Soviet-Western relations and complicated social, economic and political stability in Europe. Canada continued to favour voluntary repatriation but rejected compulsion. However, opposition to forced repatriation was one thing, readiness to take these recalcitrant DPs into Canada was quite another.

In time, however, continuing labour shortages in Canada, a shortfall in immigration from Britain and western Europe and growing domestic sympathy for the anti-Soviet stance of many DPs offered the Ukrainian-Canadian lobby the opening it needed. When removal of DPs to Canada was finally authorized in late 1947, Ukrainians immediately joined the stream of those moving to new homes in Canada.³

But why did Ukrainian DPs want to come to Canada? Nobody wanted to stay in the camps, and return to a now-Soviet Ukraine was out of the question. Other options were limited. Canada opened its doors. It has been argued that migration to Canada was encouraged by Ukrainian nationalist leaders in the politically charged DP camps of Europe. Perhaps they saw resettlement in Canada as an opportunity to regroup and recoup strength for the protracted struggle for a national homeland, which still lay ahead.⁴

The Ukrainian DPs allowed into Canada before 1950 did not include members of the Galicia Division. The first official word Ottawa received about the Division probably did not come from the Ukrainian-Canadian lobby. It may have come in early 1947 from a Canadian attached to the Allied Refugee Screening Commission in Europe, charged with judging the eligibility of applicants for official refugee status. He visited a Division camp in Italy supervised by the British. With the aid of a translator appointed from among the few English-speaking Ukrainian personnel, he interviewed a selection of officers and enlisted men in an effort to determine the Division's history, organization and post-war disposition. His impression was favourable. "They strike us," he reported to Ottawa "all as being a decent, simple minded sort of people."

> The national emblem of the Ukraine, in the form of a tri-
> dent, is freely displayed all over camp, and the inmates
> clearly regard themselves as a homogeneous unit, uncon-
> nected either with Russia or Poland, and do not seem con-
> scious of having done anything wrong.

The camp, he continued, had been security screened by both the British and the Soviets. The Russians had also tried to encourage the wholesale repatriation of the Division to the Soviet Union. They failed. The Division, he concluded, was unfortunately ineligible for DP status. Those who had volunteered their services or given aid and comfort to the enemy were expressly prohibited refugee status.

Nevertheless, dismissing the Division as simple quislings was unjust. He argued for taking "into account their motives for having volunteered their services to the enemy." These, he said, included helping family stave off the deteriorating social and economic conditions in Ukraine and a desire "to have a smack at the Russians, whom they always refer to as 'Bolsheviks.' They probably were not, and certainly do not now seem to be at heart pro-German, and the fact they did give aid and comfort to Germans can fairly be considered to have been incidental and not fundamental."

If official DP status, with its assumed protection against forced repatriation to the Soviet Union, proved out of the question, then the Canadian officer hoped the British would "have them removed lock stock and barrel from Italy" to someplace where the Soviets could not get at them. This is exactly what the British did. They moved most of the Division to England.

Efforts by the Ukrainian-Canadian community to bring the Division to Canada began in October, 1947. Gordon Bohdan Panchuk, director of

Ukrainian-Canadian post-war relief efforts, informed Ottawa that at the request of the British his organization, the Central Ukrainian Relief Bureau, was accepting responsibility for the day-to-day needs of the Division members in Britain. But Panchuk did more than just care for the Division's needs in Britain. He requested they be allowed to settle in Canada. He explained that they had cleared British security checks; Division members had joined the German war effort only to defend their homeland against the Russians.[5]

The request was refused. Members of the German armed forces were specifically prohibited entry into Canada under subsection (b) of the security prohibitions which expressly demanded "Not Clear for Security" be stamped on immigration applications from all "members of SS or German Wehrmacht found to bear mark of SS Blood Group (Non German)."[6]

For three years the government stood fast in the face of lobbying efforts involving several MPs representing heavily Ukrainian ridings.[7] In the spring of 1950, however, the Liberal cabinet, now under the leadership of Louis St. Laurent, again expanded admissible immigration categories by removing existing prohibitions against *Volksdeutche*, non-German citizens of ethnic German origin, and those who had acquired German citizenship after the war began. Although Division members did not qualify under either of these changes, it was further agreed in Cabinet that subsection (b) be waived to permit Division members in Britain to resettle in Canada.[8]

In June 1950, two weeks after Cabinet approval, John Decore, Liberal member of parliament for Vegreville, Alberta, rose in the House with a question for Immigration Minister Walter Harris. "I was wondering," the prominent backbencher began, "whether the minister was in a position to make a statement with reference to the possible admission of a certain Ukrainian group now in the United Kingdom and who formerly went under the name of 'division Halychina' [*sic*]?"

With the House listening in unusual silence, Decore gave members a thumbnail sketch of the group's history, much of it, as it turned out, incorrect. The Division, Decore explained, was organized "on Soviet territory" during the war as a core group around which "other military units" could coalesce to battle for an independent Ukraine. Without mentioning that the Division was a

Waffen SS unit organized by the Nazis from plentiful Ukrainian volunteers, Decore noted, almost in passing, "In the turmoil this military division found itself under German jurisdiction." Lest this be seen as a problem, he reassured the House that Division members "detested the Nazis as they hated the communists . . ." With Canadian combat units then under fire in Korea and memories of World War II still fresh, Decore pictured the Division, then assembled in England, as hapless victims of tyranny. He concluded, "A lot of them are anxious to reach the shores of Canada and to settle here. I am sure they would make desirable citizens if they come into this country."

As Decore took his seat, Harris rose in reply. It was likely that Decore's question was prearranged. The minister promptly announced a policy departure for which Decore could assume partial credit in his heavily Ukrainian home riding. The minister assured the House the Division had the history outlined. "We have investigated not individuals but the group as a whole, and we are quite prepared to accept them provided they come within the ordinary rules with respect to immigrants; that is, they might be agricultural workers, settlers, and the like."[9]

If the minister hoped his announcement would slip by without controversy, he was sadly mistaken. The Montreal *Gazette* jumped on it as "Easily the most sensational immigration change announced by the minister." However much the government might want to overlook the past, the *Gazette* pointed out, the Division had been not only an active Nazi military formation but an SS unit at that.[10]

Jewish leaders were also shocked. Louis Rosenberg, Polish-born demographer and research director of the Canadian Jewish Congress, sounded the alarm. In an angry memorandum to Saul Hayes, Congress's executive director, Rosenberg attacked the admission of the SS Division as an outrage. He stated, incorrectly, that charges of "massacre and torture" had been laid against the Division. He was correct, however, in noting the "'Halychyna Division' were not conscripted by the Germans or taken into forced labour by them but volunteered to serve in the German Armed Forces against Russia which was a member of the Allied Forces fighting Germany." For Canadian Jewry, still mourning the loss of millions of their brethren; the admission to Canada of any who served the Nazis was bad enough. That the Galicia Division was an SS Division, which had seen active duty, made matters even worse.

But did any of the Division members to be admitted to Canada have blood on their hands? The minister's reassurance to Parliament that his authorities had "investigated not individuals but the group as a whole" was not good enough. Rosenberg protested that any investigation should be public and allow for presentation of evidence against the Division or specific members of it.[11]

Anticipating the need for hard evidence, Rosenberg, a scholar in his own right, appealed to Jewish research centres in the United States and Europe for data which might allow Congress to "make strong representations to the Canadian government against the admission of such elements to Canada."[12] But gathering evidence was going to be time consuming. Some Jews berated the Canadian Jewish leaders for their seeming caution. "How," demanded a Toronto Jewish druggist, "can Canadian Jewry remain silent . . . Not one Nazi or Nazi collaborator should be allowed into Canada. Immediate action is needed."[13]

The same cry came from the far left. The *Canadian Jewish Weekly,* a pro-Soviet paper in Toronto, published a front-page editorial entitled, "Keep Out Nazi Thugs, Admit Their Victims!"[14] The same call was echoed by the Ukrainian-Canadian left, only too pleased to attack the Division, its anti-Soviet Ukrainian supporters in Canada and the Canadian government as soft on "Fascists." The Association of United Ukrainian-Canadians protested to the Minister of Immigration. "All of them [Division members] were volunteers who responded to the call of the 'Fuehrer' to come and defend the 'Greater Germany' and the 'New Order' when Germany was on its last legs."[15]

Although pressure on Congress to mount public demonstrations grew, Canadian Jewish Congress leaders remained convinced that hard evidence of wrongdoing, not heated protest by the Jewish community, was the best weapon to forestall the Division's entry to Canada. On the last day of June, the Canadian Jewish Congress received what information the World Jewish Congress could muster on the Galicia Division. It was not much. The World Jewish Congress research office conceded they "could find no documentary evidence concerning their participation in anti-Jewish action in Galicia or elsewhere." Nevertheless, it notified Congress "the Nuremberg Military Tribunal declared the SS a criminal organization." This included the Waffen SS of which the Galicia Division was a part. "Since the Halychyna [Galicia] Division was a voluntary organization," the World Jewish Congress continued, "all members must be considered members of a criminal organization."[16]

Although the World Jewish Congress had not delivered the smoking gun, evidence of actual Division participation in war crimes, few doubted the evidence was out there. But, Rosenberg counselled Hayes, even without hard evidence, the World Jewish Congress had given Congress grounds for demanding that Division members be excluded from Canada.[17]

Early in July 1950, three weeks after ministerial permission for admission of the Division was announced, the Canadian Jewish Congress dispatched a formal protest to Ottawa. A telegram over the signature of Samuel Bronfman, National President of the Canadian Jewish Congress, expressed "deep concern" at any welcome accorded recognized Criminals who, according to a Jewish Telegraphic Agency report, "participated in the Nazi extermination of Jews in German occupied territories."[18] Bronfman especially decried any entry of SS volunteers into Canada without individual screening. If the government would not immediately reverse its decision to admit the unit's members into Canada, then at least it could grant time, time to gather evidence of the Division's complicity in war crimes and, if possible, the hands-on role of individual Division members in Nazi atrocities.[19]

In an effort to still controversy, the Minister of immigration was conciliatory. He agreed that individual visa approval would be delayed "for a reasonable time." This would allow Congress a period of grace to gather and present evidence. In the meantime, administrative arrangements for the Division's processing by Canadian immigration authorities would continue.[20]

Congress gave the government's reply wide circulation, perhaps in part to reassure Canadian Jewry that their leaders were on top of the issue and, in part, to keep the government from reneging on its promised delay.[21] But if the government's reply was conciliatory, it was also disappointing. It made the Canadian Jewish Congress responsible for gathering evidence. It did not volunteer government resources to further investigate the Division's record. The Canadian Jewish Congress was on its own.

All agreed it would have been easier to stop the admission decision before it was made; reversing it was far more difficult. The government's move had taken

Congress leaders by surprise. They had been so preoccupied by problems of Jewish refugee resettlement in Canada and the uncertain survival of the fledgling Jewish state, they had paid little or no attention to Ukrainian political lobbying on behalf of the admission of Ukrainian Displaced Persons or Division members.

Nevertheless, the government's readiness to withhold visas to Division members following Congress's protest gave Jewish leaders one "opportunity to furnish [the authorities] with pertinent materials sustaining the allegations . . ."[22] The scramble to find incriminating evidence was on again. Requests for information went out to a series of Jewish organizations in the United States and Europe and, through the Jewish Telegraphic Agency, to American Jewish newspapers.[23] Many Jewish papers picked up on the story and ran articles attacking the Canadian government's admission decision. The widely read and influential New York Yiddish daily, *The Forward,* exploded in hysteria. "As part of the Nazi army," *The Forward* charged, "the Galician Division of Ukrainians marched with Gestapo units from town to town through Nazi-occupied Ukraine and drove thousands of Jews to their destruction."

> In many cities they compelled Jews to march to the outskirts of the town and dig their own mass graves. In other towns they participated in the mass murder of Jews in horrible ways. . . The Jews in Canada are naturally uneasy. Everybody knows that the members of this Hitler Division were Hitlerites. Everyone knows that this Ukrainian Division was a part of the Gestapo army. Everyone knows the text of the oath which each member took, under which he obligated himself to destroy Jews. What further evidence is necessary?[24]

Unfortunately for Congress, it was not emotionally charged rhetoric the government wanted. It was evidence—evidence of hands-on Division participation in war crimes and, equally important, the names of Division members who had personally committed crimes. Rosenberg, charged with gathering the needed documentation, found the going rough. He hoped to assemble a massive convincing dossier. He was forced instead to piece together a case from small scraps of material that came his way. A press reference to the SS oath taken by Division members to "fight Jews" set off a search for a photostatic copy of the original wording.[25] The American Jewish Committee came up with a memorandum listing key individuals known to have collaborated with the Nazis in Poland and Ukraine and the text of a published "apologia" for the Division prepared by the Ukrainian Congress Committee of America, itself described as an ultra-nationalist organization. The text put the best possible face on the Division's inception and record, but it allowed that Division members were volunteers. In addition, it identified the Division as an integral part of the Nazi SS organization. These two points—that the Division was both a volunteer and an SS unit—were key elements in the Jewish case for exclusion.[26]

Rosenberg also unsuccessfully plodded through the index to the twenty-two-volume proceedings of the Nuremberg Trials, hoping for a reference to the Division.[27] He found none. But if he could not tie the Division to the Nuremberg Trials, perhaps he could tie the Nuremberg Trials to the Division. Efforts were made to contact both Justice Jackson, chief American judge at the trials, and the American prosecutor, Brigadier General Telford Taylor, in hopes of eliciting from each a statement that the Tribunal's declaration as criminal all "those persons who were officially accepted as members of the SS," extended to members of the Division. Although neither replied personally, Rosenberg did establish that the Tribunal and the Allied Control Council for Germany worked under the principle "that knowledge of these criminal activities was sufficiently general to justify declaring that the SS was a criminal organization." On this basis all members of the Waffen SS, including the Galicia Division, would be denied admission to the United States.[28]

Rosenberg pulled together what he could find for consideration by Canadian immigration authorities. Adding to bits and pieces relating directly to the SS or the Division, he included several affidavits taken from Holocaust survivors recently arrived in Montreal who accused Ukrainians of participating in Nazi atrocities. Rosenberg also forwarded assessments of Ukrainian complicity drawn from the Jewish press, two articles from Ukrainian sources which, although firm in their declaration of the Division's innocence of war crimes, affirmed the Galicia Division's integration within the SS and the unit's voluntary membership. He also included several Allied documents attaching criminality to the entire SS. Only too aware that he had failed to find evidence linking the Division or any of its members to specific war crimes, Rosenberg sent the package to Ottawa in early August 1950. He hoped it would be enough to further delay the visa process if not derail it entirely.[29]

The government was not impressed. After six weeks, the Minister of Immigration informed Congress leaders that the government's own "further" but unspecified investigation left him confident "screening facilities are adequate" to assure that the Division members admitted to Canada would be free of any war-crimes association. Accordingly he saw no reasons for further delay. The minister reminded Congress officials that he had originally agreed "to delay approval of applications for a reasonable time and this has been done." While he would entertain any additional information on specific individuals that Congress might supply, the minister intended "to give approval to applications on hand and to continue the screening process of any applications received in the future."[30]

Congress had failed. Its argument for exclusion was predicated on the assumption that as part of the SS, an organization declared criminal by Allied authorities, and composed entirely of members who voluntarily joined the unit, the Galicia Division and all its members should be denied entry to Canada. The government dismissed these arguments. Cabinet had already short-circuited the Congress argument by lifting its subsection (b) security prohibition against SS members in this instance. In the absence of specific information linking individual immigration applicants to specific crimes, the government was determined to press on with admissions. The Jewish community could do nothing beyond lodging protest and hoping that incriminating evidence might still turn up.[31]

In one last-ditch effort to uncover the kind of evidence against specific individuals the government demanded, Congress again turned to its sister agencies in the United States and abroad.[32] From Simon Wiesenthal's newly formed Documentation Center in Vienna came an analysis of Ukrainian complicity in the Nazi destruction of eastern European Jewry and warnings that Ukrainian DP camps were infested with war criminals.[33] But Wiesenthal included no names—no incontrovertible evidence. An American Jewish Congress report was also received. It reviewed the history of Ukraine during the war but did not link the Division to specific criminal acts, let alone offer up the names of individuals who could be tied to such acts.

> Strictly speaking, this information does not pertain to the Galician Division which was organized, as most reports indicate, in 1943, at a time when the mass extermination of Jews in Poland and Galicia was substantially complete. But there are reasons to believe that the division might have been recruited mostly among these militia men and guards [who participated in the genocide]. A general survey of the background and activities of the Ukrainian extremist movement, its collaboration with the Germans, and of the activities of the militia is in order.[34]

The assessments from Wiesenthal and the American Jewish Congress yielded no names and no evidence. From here and there a few names were pulled together. Several names were gleaned from a pamphlet published by the left-wing Association of United Ukrainian-Canadians, then waging its own separate campaign against the Division's admission. An American Jewish Committee list of Ukrainian Nazi collaborators was culled for more names. It wasn't much, but the names were sent to Ottawa.[35]

The Minister of Immigration agreed to forward the names to Canadian officials abroad "for their information," but he underscored the fact that with two possible exceptions, those listed were not linked to the Division.[36] In a personal letter to Samuel Bronfman, a long-time Liberal Party supporter, the minister again politely dismissed the Congress argument for the wholesale rejection of Division members. Simple membership in the SS, the minister explained, was no longer sufficient reason in and of itself to exclude any individuals from Canada, nor would Canada abide any blanket condemnation of all SS members as criminals. In defence of the Galicia Division the minister pointed out that non-Germans were not permitted into the regular army. They were shuffled into special SS Divisions. "You will understand," he reassured Bronfman, "that these troops were not necessarily of the training or mentality we usually associate with Hitler's personal SS formation."³⁷

Bronfman and Congress officials were not reassured. Failing to persuade immigration authorities that SS membership was cause for rejection, they tried an end run around the Immigration Minister. A hurried meeting was arranged with the Minister of Justice in hopes of persuading him "of the dangers of ordinary routine screening if applied to . . . Germans and Ukrainians." The Minister of Justice listened but gave little. He would not "for jurisdictional reasons" interfere in immigration affairs. The decision to admit the Division members was not his to reverse. He would, however, "insist that the security net be made very tight to prevent politically undesirable elements from passing through." Congress Executive Director Saul Hayes came away from the meeting almost empty-handed, but he put the best possible light on the meeting. "It showed the Minister that we were prepared to fight through an unpopular cause because of the principles involved."³⁸

But, Hayes wondered, was there still a small opening left by the Minister of Justice—screening to prevent the admission of "political undesirables"?³⁹ In the past, Congress had not been pleased with political screening. This type of action was, as often as not, used to reject the immigration of individual Jews on the political left. But could it now apply to the Division? In its efforts to gather information on the Division and its members, Congress officials had become marginally acquainted with the political infighting both between various factions of the Ukrainian nationalist camp in Europe and between these nationalists and the Ukrainian left in Canada. There was finger pointing by one Ukrainian nationalist faction against the other that efforts to transplant members in Canada were merely a ploy to use Canada as a staging ground for further political activities. There were also warnings from the Ukrainian left of further political turmoil if the right-wing nationalists tried to regroup in Canada. Could Congress build a case that the Division was a political threat to Canadian stability? In the end Congress did not know enough about the matter and, again, the Ukrainian infighting did not deal specifically with members of the Galicia Division. The idea was dropped.⁴⁰

The Jewish campaign against the Division had failed. In early January 1951, Hayes sent a confidential memorandum to his national executive.

> There is a good deal of derivative material and oblique references all of which have been submitted to Government and several dossiers have been sent to the Ministry involved. In the main, however, it has to be conceded that most of the allegations against the Halychyna [Galicia] Division membership is of the hearsay variety and all our attempts to obtain statements from the Nuremberg Crime Commission or other officials thereof have proved abortive . . . . To reiterate, unless and until more evidence is forthcoming from sources which we don't know of since we have exhausted all known sources, the matter will have to be considered as closed.[41]

Congress's surrender bespoke not only the Jewish community's inability to dent the government's determination to admit Division members but also signalled the emergence of Ukrainian-Canadian lobbying strength, in this case on behalf of the Division. Of course, not all Ukrainian-Canadians were united in support of the Division's entry. As we have seen, the left-wing Association of United Ukrainian-Canadians mounted its own anti-Division campaign. The AUUC offered "to work with Congress on this matter and supply [Congress] with all the information we have on this problem."[42] Congress rejected the offer. It had only just gone through a process of expelling the Jewish equivalent of the AUUC, the United Jewish People's Order, from the Canadian Jewish Congress. Given the anti-Communist temper of the time, any working relationship with the AUUC would have been problematic at best.

Indeed, Congress officials were concerned lest the AUUC's campaign undermine the legitimacy of their own. If the AUUC staked out a claim to this issue "as proof that the Canadian Government was favouring pro-Fascist and anti-Semitic elements" it was feared the Canadian Jewish Congress's arguments would be tarred by association. As a result Congress took pains to carefully and publicly dissociate itself from any AUUC initiative.[43] But as they scrambled for incriminating evidence against the Division and its members, Congress staff quietly monitored AUUC statements, reports and publications, hoping to pick up leads to reliable data.

If the Canadian Jewish Congress rejected overtures of co-operation from the AUUC, it also had almost no contact with the Ukrainian-Canadian Committee (UCC), then still lobbying for the Division's entry into Canada. The UCC was stung by Congress's effort to undermine their campaign. In a letter to Congress's Winnipeg office the UCC president dismissed any and all allegations against the Division. Several investigations, he protested, had "completely exonerated the said Division from the accusations levelled against them." Even more, he continued, the "authorities found that the accusations were merely a communist propaganda that was indiscriminately circulated at the time by the communists against anyone who disagrees with them." As far as he was concerned, authorities had "given this division a clean slate."

> To be able to make an accusation of the nature you have made, you must be in possession of some documentary evidence that was not available to the above-mentioned Allied Military Authorities or to the Nuremberg Court. We, therefore, would appreciate if you would be kind enough to submit the said evidence to us for our perusal.
>
> May we assure you that we are no less anxious than you are to maintain harmony among the various ethnic groups in Canada and trust that you will cooperate with us in solving the difficult problem created by the action taken in this connection both by your press and the Canadian Jewish Congress.[44]

Congress was conciliatory. Hayes offered a UCC-designated representative both access to copies of Congress representations to government and full and free access to files covering Congress's Galicia Division investigation. The UCC accepted.[45]

The civility of this tentative UCC-Congress contact was not long sustained. Just as the Jewish press excoriated Ukrainians for their alleged participation in the genocidal war on the Jews, *Nasha Meta,* voice of the Ukrainian Catholic community in Toronto, editorialized:

> international communism and Jewry for some reason choose to condemn only Ukrainians and their "philo-Germans" although they offered the very smallest number to the German army and they choose to shut their eyes to the many volunteers who were offered by other nationalities. And this communist-Jewish propaganda besmirches [the] entire Ukrainian nation and blames her for crimes she never committed and was in no position to commit. At Moscow's order these Ukrainian soldiers are smeared by this propaganda because the Ukrainian soldier is the most dangerous one for communist Moscow and her tyranny.[46]

By early 1952, members of the Division began arriving in Canada, but their arrival did not end the matter. The episode left a legacy of bad feeling between the organized leadership of the Ukrainian and Jewish communities, a legacy sustained by mutual mistrust informed by a sense of historical wrong that each community laid at the doorstep of the other. While individual Jews and Ukrainians might live and work side by side as friends, community organizational life was separate, all too often punctuated by conflict.

This proved the case in the spring of 1957. The Ukrainian National Federation of Canada, a nationalist organization with roots in pre-war Europe, announced a Music Festival Jubilee to celebrate the movement's twenty-fifth anniversary. As part of the festival the federation planned to bring Andrii Melnyk, the movement's international leader, to Canada.

Melnyk's name set off an alarm for the editor of the *Jewish Post* in Winnipeg. In a *Post* editorial, he denounced Melnyk as "famous in Poland as a ruthless antisemite" and an active Nazi agent involved in the murder of Ukrainian Jews.[47]

The Federation was incensed. They were accustomed to attacks of this type from the Ukrainian extreme left; they almost welcomed them as a sign of their movement's vibrancy. But an attack in the Jewish press was different. After all, the Jewish community was seen by the larger Canadian community to have public respectability, economic strength and political influence. If the editor's charges were not dealt with quickly and firmly, the Nazi label could spread and besmirch the whole Ukrainian community.

Thus, it was not just the Federation that felt itself under attack—it was the entire nationalist core within the Ukrainian community. Putting aside the internal wrangling that often marked its deliberations, the UCC united in the face of the *Jewish Post* challenge. The editorial was denounced and a public apology demanded.[48]

It was too late to defuse the tensions. The *Post*'s accusations had already spilled into the national and international press. Some Canadian Jews, angered that any alleged Nazi would be allowed into the country, demanded Congress act. Congress, pressed by its rank and file but uneasy lest it get caught again without a strong case, needed reliable information on Melnyk. Independently of one another, the *Post*'s editor and Congress put out a call for data on Melnyk's wartime record.[49] If damning evidence could not be found, the Congress director in Winnipeg suggested, the *Jewish Post*'s accusations must be publicly recanted. The Jewish community might harbour suspicions, "But publishing them in the *Jewish Post* before we are sure of our facts and starting a big controversy with the Ukrainian community, certainly does not look like a practical way of handling the case."[50]

A search of available historical records proved disturbing but inconclusive. "It is obvious from what has been published," wrote Saul Hayes, "that Melnyk must have had something to do with anti-Jewish activities."

> But from our point of view, the evidence is by no means
> enough to warrant a formal submission to Ottawa. The
> books, for example, contain statements like "Ribbentrop
> incited Melnyk to take action against the Jews," but there
> is no evidence anywhere that he took such action.

Secondly, the excellent treatment of the major war crimi- .
nals which appeared in the "Black Book" published by the
World Jewish Congress a number of years ago, does not
mention Melnyk. It is obvious to the layman that he was
somewhere about and unfriendly. From our point of view
we need more evidence.[51]

If none of Congress's information or respondents could exonerate
Melnyk or his movement from pro-Fascist sympathies or Nazi contacts, they
were unanimous in agreeing no form of evidence was then available linking
Melnyk to actual atrocities against Jews.[52]

As the controversy dragged on, the Ukrainian National Federation began
to have second thoughts. The adverse publicity surrounding the *Jewish Post* editorial continued to embarrass those planning the twenty-fifth anniversary celebrations drawing near. A banquet in Toronto with Melnyk as honoured guest
was scheduled. Among those who originally accepted invitations were the
Ontario Premier, Mayor Nathan Phillips (Toronto's first Jewish mayor), federal
senators, elected politicians and cabinet ministers, including the Minister of
Immigration.[53] The Federation leaders feared prolonged controversy or Jewish
pressure might force these prominent personalities to stay away or, even worse,
lead to Melnyk's visa being revoked by the very Minister of Immigration who
planned to attend the banquet. Pressed to the wall, the Federation requested a
meeting with Congress officials in Toronto.[54]

A three-man Ukrainian delegation led by the secretary of the Ukrainian
National Federation arrived at Congress offices in Toronto, probably unclear
just how forceful they should or could be. Although convinced they were the
aggrieved parties in the affair, the Ukrainians still needed to defuse a confrontation that might ruin their planned festivities. With Congress officials listening
quietly, Melnyk's record was defended.

"Melnyk," the delegation spokesman reportedly began, "was known as a
respected national hero to all Ukrainians, a man of deep religious conviction, a
leader of Catholic youth who would never stoop to any kind of pogrom action."

Ukrainians in general felt hurt when from time to time their whole nation is identified as Jew haters on the basis of the action of individuals. [The Secretary] cited the case of Germany. Many Jews and Israelis feel the time is now ready to forget the experience with Germany, this only 12 years after the gravest Jewish experience in history. But Ukrainians do not enjoy such good fortune as Germans.[55]

Could not the two communities put the *Post* editorial behind them? It would be the first step towards a larger and overdue reconciliation. In a follow-up letter to Congress, the Federation secretary appealed to "traditional Jewish justice." He requested Congress "issue a public statement disassociating itself from the article published in the '*Jewish Post.*'" The statement, it was further suggested, might "condemn the use of unprovoked and unverified allegations against persons or peoples . . ."[56]

Congress refused. It denied responsibility for the original *Jewish Post* editorial and saw no need to apologize for it or repudiate its content. On the other hand, Congress leaders privately recognized the editorial had generated needless bad feelings between Jews and Ukrainians, especially in Winnipeg, all without any substantiating evidence. An apology, they realized, was in order but it had to come from the *Jewish Post.*

The *Post*'s editor was "invited" to a meeting with Congress officials in Winnipeg. A heated discussion ensued. It was made clear to him "that freedom of the press notwithstanding, an editor of a Jewish newspaper should use some self-imposed restraint when the interests of the entire Jewish community is at stake." In spite of objections to Congress censorship of his newspaper, he agreed to publish an editorial retraction as well as "lengthy letters of apology" sent to four prominent Ukrainian newspapers and similar letters mailed to major Ukrainian organizations.[57]

In the end, the Federation and the UCC were pleased to put this round of accusations and recriminations behind them. The apology was officially accepted "recognizing the fact that [the *Jewish Post*] fell victim to unreliable information."[58]

The Melnyk banquet went ahead on schedule but not without incident. Just as the prominent guests at the fifty-dollar-a-plate dinner were finishing their strawberry shortcake, police rushed in to clear the packed hall. According to press reports, an anonymous woman caller had telephoned police and the press with a bomb threat. As the crowd of notables milled about on the street in front of the Ukrainian Federation Hall, a federal minister scheduled to deliver his government's official greetings to the gathering made light of the bomb threat. "Some people," he joked, "will go to any length to stop us [politicians] talking." A spokesman for the Federation was not nearly so amused. Melnyk, he told the assembled press, was a leading anti-Communist crusader. The Communists would not be above using bombs to silence him. No bomb was found, and at the time, no suggestion was made that Jews were behind the bomb scare.[59]

It cannot be denied, however, that throughout the post-war period there were those within the Ukrainian nationalist camp who saw Communists and Jews in league to destroy the Ukrainian nationalist movement. Jews, some Ukrainian nationalists were ready to point out, played a leading role in the 1917 Revolution and the Soviet consolidation of power that followed. Those links, they believed, remained strong still. For example, in 1960 *Life* magazine printed a feature on anti-Semitism in the Soviet Union, making special reference to the history of anti-Semitism in Ukraine. The article, quoting a representative of the World Jewish Congress, drew considerable fire from the Toronto Ukrainian-language press. *Novy Shliakh* (Toronto), the voice of the Federation, dismissed talk of Ukrainian anti-Semitism as an insulting hoax. There were anti-Semitic outbursts in Ukraine, the paper allowed, but since oppressed Ukrainians did not control their own territory, anti-Jewish acts could only be the product of Russian, Polish or most recently, Communist initiative. As for anti-Semitism under the Soviet regime, it could be little more than a "cuff on the ear" to the Jewish people who had loyally served in building Communism.

The privately owned *Vilne Slovo* (Toronto) did not deny that anti-Semitism existed in Ukraine but observed that anti-Semitism existed everywhere and that the issue was not whether Jews were disliked, but why. "If the Jews are such angels," *Vilne Slovo* asked, "why is anti-semitism so universal?" *Homin Ukrainy* (Toronto), often the voice of the Banderite League for the Liberation of

Ukraine, also blamed Jews for any anti-Semitism exhibited by Ukrainians. On balance, it claimed Jews were responsible for more violence done against Ukrainians than Ukrainians ever inflicted on Jews. According to the paper, Jews had most recently allied themselves with the Communists who occupied western Ukraine in 1939; co-operating with the Soviet Militia, the NKVD, and eagerly informing on their Ukrainian neighbours. Therefore, "who if not the Jews is responsible for the thousands of prisoners murdered in Soviet prisons and for other thousands sent to Siberia?" As for Jews in Canada, the paper was quoted as saying, "We should all take this into account even in our commercial relations with Jews until we can get some kind of assurance from their leaders that their hostility toward Ukrainians will be terminated."[60]

These three themes—that the scale of Ukrainian anti-Semitism was exaggerated; that anti-Semitic acts in Ukraine were orchestrated by non-Ukrainians who controlled Ukrainian territory; that any native Ukrainian anti-Semitism was largely a response to anti-Ukrainian acts by Jews—would recur again and again.

Through much of the 1950s and 1960s, formal relations between the two communities were cool. It took only a small spark to ignite underlying suspicion and mistrust. A case in point was the televising in 1960 by the French-language network of the Canadian Broadcasting Corporation of a less than flattering documentary on Symon Petlura and the trial of his Jewish assassin. According to *Press Digest,* the federal government's analysis of the ethnic press, *Vilne Slovo* declared the film yet another incident of Soviet disinformation designed to undermine the Ukrainian national cause. The paper noted that since Congress had made no public comment on the film, this must mean the Jewish umbrella organization gave tacit approval to those intent on smearing the good name of the Ukrainian people. For others, simple Jewish condemnation of the program would not have been enough. Jews could have prevented it. *Moloda Ukraina* (Toronto) felt Jewish statesmen should have used their influence to halt this and other attacks, but didn't.

The Ukrainian press uproar was reported in the *Canadian Jewish News,* which explained to its readers, many of whom had likely never heard of Petlura, why the Ukrainian leader was seen as a patriot and idealist by Ukrainian nationalists. The article outlined the role Jews played in Petlura's short-lived government, the historical controversy surrounding his role during the pogroms and his assassination. The *CJN* conceded that much about Petlura and his death was still shrouded in mystery, but one fact was crystal clear—the death of 100,000 Jews at the hands of Petlura's men. "Either Petlura's [anti-pogrom] orders were found easy to ignore," the *CJN* declared, "or Petlura himself, much as he found such bloodshed distasteful, found it useful for political reasons and did not pursue his prohibition of pogroms too strenuously."[61]

The *CJN* article was a red flag to the Ukrainian press. In retaliation, *Homin Ukrainy* decried the *CJN* story. Ukrainians, it pointed out, had suffered at the hands of "Jewish commissars," like Trotsky and Kaganovich. *Vilne Slovo* dismissed the CJN piece as baseless, and *Postup* (Edmonton), voice of western Ukrainian Catholics, feared there was a deliberate effort afoot to undermine relations between the two Canadian ethnic communities, and stir up animosity towards Ukrainians. "There is a hidden Communist hand behind this action," *Postup* warned, "and for this reason the Ukrainian Community in Canada will not allow itself to be provoked."[62]

The *CJN* took up the challenge. While the Jewish paper declared itself in favour of Jewish-Ukrainian "rapprochement on this continent," this could not be "based on the falsification of history." In a broadside sure to set off yet another Ukrainian salvo, the *CJN* observed that Jewish-German reconciliation could never have moved forward if the "present leaders of West Germany insisted on keeping Hitler on a hero's pedestal."

As expected, the Ukrainian press roundly condemned the comparison of Petlura and Hitler as "Ukrainian baiting." The *Ukrainian Echo* (Toronto), weekly English-language supplement of the *Homin Ukrainy,* went further. Ukrainians, it declared, were the victims of Jews, not vice versa. The Bolshevik revolution in Ukraine was spearheaded by Jews and led by a Jew, Rakovsky. As for Jewish suffering during World War II, the *Ukrainian Echo* placed that at the door of Jewish police who worked hand in hand with the Germans.

The *Ukrainian Voice* (Winnipeg) protested that Jews made honest discussion and inter-group dialogue impossible. Any critical comment about Jews, however intended, "and they [Jews] will immediately raise a hue and cry that you are anti-Semitic, an enemy of Jewry and thus alert public opinion against you." As to the *CJN* demand that Ukrainians renounce Petlura, the *Voice* felt this was as absurd as Ukrainians demanding Jews renounce then Israeli Prime Minister David Ben Gurion because, as the *Voice* explained, several years earlier Israeli border guards had killed Arab men, women and children working their fields near the border. In perhaps the final word in this particular inter-press skirmish, the *Voice* declared no good purpose served by the attacks. "We do not consider it in Canada's interest."[63] The *CJN* did not respond.[64]

This type of press jousting was rare not because the attitudes reflected were not widely held in the two communities but because communication of any kind, even so negative, was rare. Through the 1960s, the leadership and institutional relations between the two groups were distant, formal contacts few. In 1963, the UCC invited Congress representation at a conference to commemorate the thirtieth anniversary of the Ukrainian famine, "the cruelest disaster in the history of mankind." Active participation by representatives of the Jewish community at any Ukrainian community function would have raised the ire of Holocaust survivors. Congress was saved the problem of how to respond to the invitation. The conference, as it turned out, was in the midst of the Jewish High Holidays. The invitation was graciously declined.[65]

In the 1970s, some movement, albeit one-sided, developed for rapprochement. Tentative efforts to bridge the gulf of historical suspicion and mistrust separating Jewish and Ukrainian communities in Canada began, largely, at Ukrainian initiative. In part, this initiative proved a reflection of demographic shifts in the two communities. A new generation of Canadian-born, urban, educated Ukrainian and Jewish professionals were gradually making their weight felt within their respective community councils. This is not to argue the younger leaders were immune to Old World antipathies. They were not. Nor is it to argue that the older generation of leaders readily stepped aside in favour of the new. This was also not the case. But in both communities, especially the Ukrainian community, there were voices raised in favour of better relations.

Perhaps Ukrainian moves towards bettering relations also grew out of a fear that their shared heritage was now casting Ukrainians as historical villains. Ukrainian historical self-definition painted their people as an oppressed, dispossessed and victimized people. But it was also running headlong into the western world's understanding of the Holocaust and the history of European anti-Semitism that preceded it. Increasingly, Ukrainian historical truth was trampled under the weight of the larger accepted historical view that seemed transfixed on the Jewish historical drama. Not only did many Ukrainian-Canadians see the Ukrainian national struggle ignored, their litany of suffering overlooked, but they also feared Ukrainians were being made the villains of Jewish and western historical narrative. The more the Holocaust captured the public and scholarly historical imagination, the more these Ukrainians felt their every spark of hard-won and short-lived national self-assertion was being dismissed, as a pogromist's licence to murder Jewish men, women and children. Ukrainian heroes were vilified as collaborators and murderers in someone else's historical epic. To a Ukrainian community struggling to keep group identity alive, to retain community pride and commitment, to encourage continuity from generation to generation, this challenge to its historical sense of self was a heavy weight to bear. Perhaps if common cause could be made with the Jewish community in areas of mutual interest—the future of multicultural policy in Canada, the Soviet question, positive inter-group relations—the heat would be turned down.

For Ukrainian-Canadians increasingly active in community institutional affairs there was much to learn from the Jews. Jews had blazed a path through North American urban business and professional life for others to follow. By the 1970s, as more Ukrainians were travelling this path, one-to-one contacts with Jews increased, as did appreciation of the model of Jewish mobility in America.

What was more, Jews seemed to have succeeded in carving a place for themselves in urban North America without sacrificing commitment to Jewish community. On the contrary, as individual Jews built a socially, economically and politically secure place for themselves in North American society, Jewish communal life thrived. The Jewish polity was active and took pride in both community fulfillment in North America and the growth of a Jewish national homeland in Israel. Israel's electrifying victory in the 1967 Six Day War served to further energize Jewish communal life in the diaspora. All this was not lost on the Ukrainian community. The very idea that after two thousand years of statelessness diaspora Jewry celebrated the rebirth of its homeland stood as a beacon of hope to a Ukrainian diaspora dispossessed of an independent homeland. Thus, on the individual and communal level there was much to learn from the Jews.

The time seemed appropriate. There was a precedent. If Israelis and Jews could make post-war accommodation with Germany and Germans, why not with Ukrainians? What is more, some Ukrainians believed they could offer Jews reciprocity in forgiveness. Ukrainians, after all, believed they had much to forgive the Jews.

Nothing could have been further from the Canadian Jewish consciousness than the notion that Ukrainians had historical grievances against Jews. The very idea would have been greeted with disbelief in Jewish circles. And Jews knew little or nothing of the agony of the Ukrainian diaspora experience, of the famine or the loss of Ukrainian lives during the war. If anything, Jewish leaders believed the Ukrainian community was now among the more politically powerful ethnic community voices in Canada—if, not through its organizational strength, then by sheer weight of numbers.

Jewish leaders felt repeatedly frustrated in their dealings with government. They could not make headway on such basic Jewish issues as anti-boycott legislation to prohibit foreign firms or governments from demanding discrimination against Canadian Jews or other Canadian citizens as a precondition of a business contract.[66] At the same time Ukrainian political will seemed to be growing in strength. Was it not Ukrainian pressure that led to the federal government's 1971 policy of multiculturalism promising financial and political support to ethnic continuity in Canada? That was an achievement the Jewish polity, for all its supposed influence, could not match.

If Jewish communal leaders needed any more proof of the surging strength of the Ukrainian polity, it came on October 9, 1971. The very day after the government's formal announcement of its multiculturalism policy in the House of Commons, Prime Minister Pierre Trudeau flew off to Winnipeg to address the Tenth Tri-Annual Congress of the Ukrainian-Canadian Committee. In his banquet address, he personally congratulated the Ukrainian-Canadian community for its key contribution in reshaping Canadian social policy. Multiculturalism was a Ukrainian victory. But the content of Trudeau's keynote address, full of the platitudes such an occasion demands, was obviously less important than the fact of his presence. By seemingly "reporting in" to the

UCC, he lent credence to the notion that a new era of ethnic political influence, most importantly Ukrainian influence, was dawning.[67]

But the flexing of Ukrainian political muscle in Canada did not mean an easing of Jewish-Ukrainian relations. In Israel a small group, composed largely of recent Jewish immigrants from Ukraine, attempted to forge links to the Ukrainian diaspora while hoping to educate world Jewry to the need for inter-ethnic co-operation if Jews in the Soviet Union were to be helped. A spokesman for the fledgling group visited Canada in 1971 at the invitation of the Ukrainian Community. While in Canada he met with Jewish leaders, who greeted him more as a curiosity than a prophet of co-operation.[68] Indeed, when it came to efforts on behalf of Soviet Jewry, Canadian Jewish leaders proved exceedingly shy of working with Ukrainians or others—Estonians, Latvians, Lithuanians—now dispossessed of a national state.

But in the summer of 1971, when the state visit of Soviet Premier Alexei Kosygin was in the offing, just such co-operative efforts were considered by Jewish leaders. A major joint protest was suggested as a possibility,[69] but in the end, the idea was rejected. In this instance the burden of historical grievances proved secondary to political strategy. It was argued that the Ukrainians and their allies had very different goals from those of the Jewish community. Many among the Ukrainians and their supporters were fundamentally hostile to the Soviet system *per se*. They looked forward to the destruction of the Soviet polit-ical structure and a rupture of the federated Soviet state. The main goal of Jews, on the other hand, was to enable Soviet Jews to leave the USSR or, at least, pub-licly identify as Jews without fear. Thus it was concluded that to combine the Jewish protest for human rights with that of Ukrainians or other eastern Europeans for political change would blur the critical distinction between the Jewish agenda and that of other protesters.

Across Canada, Jewish leaders organized their anti-Kosygin demonstra-tions separately from those of others. In Toronto, this proved fortuitous. The Jewish protest incorporated a twenty-four-hour candlelight vigil followed by a mass evening demonstration, all in a park across from the Soviet premier's hotel, about half a mile from the Ontario Science Centre where an official state din-ner was in progress.

Ukrainian and other eastern European protesters, joined by a swelling throng of sympathizers, filled the streets in front of the Science Centre. As the night wore on, the crowd grew and tension increased. Demonstration marshals never had full control of the crowd, and a spark ignited violence. The police, mounted on horseback, waded into the crowd swinging billy clubs. A near riot erupted. Ambulances and paddy wagons took away the injured and arrested.[70]

Even though hopes of a joint protest did not materialize, Jewish and Ukrainian participation in federal advisory councils such as that on multiculturalism enlarged the circle of Ukrainian-Jewish leadership contacts and opened the door to further discussions—if only a crack. Building on these contacts, prominent Ukrainian community leaders made several overtures in the hope of engaging in further dialogue with Jewish leaders.

In Winnipeg, with its long history of inter-ethnic mixing, this was easier than in Toronto where distance was a fact, if not the rule. But even in Toronto several efforts at bridge-building were begun. In the autumn of 1974, for example, Robert (Bohdan) Onyschuk, a young lawyer and head of the UCC in Ontario, approached fellow lawyer Sidney Harris of the Congress executive in Toronto and Ben Kayfetz of the Congress staff. In what would soon become a ritualized pattern of knife and fork contacts, the three went out to dinner. "Our discussion," Kayfetz observed about the evening, "ranged across the whole spectrum of Jewish-Ukrainian concerns. We touched, of course, on the animosity and suspicion that persists in certain quarters on both sides. It was felt this might be to some extent a form of generation gap which may diminish in the course of time." In the meantime, it was agreed, informal contacts like their dinner should continue in spite of the negative feelings such contacts might generate among militant factions in both communities.[71]

And such hostility was not hard to generate. The Jewish community's official position on the Soviet Union called for Soviet adherence to the freedom of religion and freedom to migrate, as set down in the Soviet Constitution. In 1974, Congress officials felt it quite in keeping with this position to publicly support those demanding the release of imprisoned Ukrainian activist Valentyn Moroz. But even this symbolic gesture of solidarity with one whose imprisonment touched the conscience of humanity raised the ire of some in the Jewish community, predominantly Holocaust survivors, for whom negative memories of the Jewish experience in Ukraine remained fresh.[72] Whatever one might say about Moroz, his personal or political views, or his incarceration was irrelevant. It was enough that a Jewish statement of support for Moroz's human rights bonded them with Ukrainian-Canadian nationalist organizations, which some Jews regarded as little more than a collection of unreconstructed Nazi sympathizers.[73]

Ironically, the Moroz statement was credited with stilling some of the more strident anti-Jewish voices in the Ukrainian community. Alex Epstein, a Toronto Jewish lawyer with professional contacts in the Ukrainian community, repeatedly tried to find common ground for the two ethnic polities. Forever pressing Congress officials to open avenues of dialogue with Ukrainians, he welcomed the Moroz statement as a good first step by a Jewish community leadership that had previously avoided anything but cautious distance from the Ukrainian community. Ukrainians, Epstein wrote Congress, "were deeply moved by this expression of sympathy and support from the Jewish community." It was a gesture which could not but help "young and liberal" leadership then coming to the fore "in stifling anti-Semitic remarks and statements made by other Ukrainians."[74]

As a follow-up to Congress's Moroz initiative, Epstein arranged a dinner hosted by several Toronto Congress leaders with Walter Tarnopolsky, a law professor and Moroz activist. Although Tarnopolsky held no formal position in the Ukrainian community structure, he was "well regarded by them. They seek his advice on political and communal questions, as one of their leading intellectuals."[75] Tarnopolsky was not unknown to Toronto Jewish leaders. His long prominence in the Canadian Civil Liberties Association cemented his friendship with several like-minded Jewish civil liberties activists also important in Canadian Jewish Congress affairs.

The dinner meeting was held at an upscale Russian restaurant in downtown Toronto. Discussion was light, cordial yet frank. There was no agenda, and except for agreeing on a second meeting to be hosted by Ukrainian leaders nothing concrete was accomplished.[76]

The follow-up dinner, three months later, in an equally elegant restaurant, this time Chinese, brought out a large Ukrainian contingent. Again nobody had any fixed agenda for the eggroll diplomacy. As heaping dishes of Chinese food were passed around the table, informal but guarded conversation ranged over topics as varied as immigration, the International Women's Year Congress in Mexico City, CBC overseas broadcasts, third-language broadcasting in Canada, reunification with family from the Soviet Union and racial tensions in Canada.[77] Dinner ended with no suggestions made as to joint actions or programs, but all agreed such meetings were useful in breaking the ice. Unspoken was a disquieting awareness that there were vocal constituents in both camps who would attack any co-operative effort, no matter how tentative, as tantamount to consorting with the devil.

Nevertheless, new lines of contact had been opened. If the mood was not one of mutual trust, at least Ukrainian participants believed a useful foundation now existed on which to build. In the summer of 1975, for example, a Congress representative was invited and attended a public demonstration on behalf of Valentyn Moroz. Congress official Ben Kayfetz was seated prominently between two local Ukrainian-Canadian politicians on a raised platform in Toronto's City Hall Square. The following year the rally fell on the Jewish New Year, Rosh Hashana.[78] No official representative of the Jewish community was able to attend, but a letter of support was sent. When, two years later, Moroz was released from Soviet prison, Congress immediately sent Moroz a telegram of congratulations through the World Congress of Free Ukrainians head office in Toronto. The telegram, honouring "a fearless champion of human rights, cultural and national freedom," was, in turn, greeted as a gesture on behalf of all those "suffering religious and political persecution in the Soviet Union."[79]

These preliminary contacts were reinforced when Rabbi Gunther Plaut, President of Congress and newly appointed to the Ontario Human Rights Commission, accepted an invitation to address the influential Ukrainian Professional and Business Club of Toronto. This association, an important and temperate voice within the UCC, was judged by Kayfetz as "an excellent forum at which to present a representative Jewish speaker . . . at this juncture in Ukrainian-Jewish relations." Rather than a bastion of the Ukrainian right wing, he saw the association as representing "an intellectual, younger group" of Canadian-born professionals. Plaut was asked to address "The Challenge of

Human Rights in the USSR and the Western World"; but at his request the topic was revised simply to "Human Rights," although he promised to comment on the Soviet situation.[80]

Plaut appreciated the sense of occasion attending the event. It was, he noted, "the first occasion on which a representative of the Jewish community addresses a Ukrainian-Canadian association." Nor, he resolved, would he avoid the past which "divided us."

Plaut's audience of two hundred was identified as "the elite of the Ukrainian community of our city." As they listened somewhat uneasily, Plaut spoke of psychic associations some Jews held of Ukrainians. He explained how many Jews identified the infamous Babi Yar massacre with Ukrainian collaborators and linked Khmelnytsky and Petlura, Ukrainian national heroes, with "memories of persecution, and of widespread participation of the population in these crimes." Ukrainian-Canadians must understand, he demanded, "why Jews will continue to insist that those who offended against human rights must be brought to justice—here or wherever they live at present."[81]

During the question period that followed, Plaut was struck by what he sensed was pain caused by what Ukrainians felt was the "stereotype of Ukrainian antisemite [sic]" portrayed in the *Holocaust* mini-series shown on television that very week. Few, however, confronted the issue head on. Although one questioner called upon all Ukrainians to come to grips with the anti-Semitism in both their history and community, others queried what they saw as Jewish exclusivity in its Soviet Jewry campaign, refusing to unite with others in similar straits. Surely, they urged, anti-Soviet co-operation could help overcome any legacy of mutual mistrust. By and large pleased by the evening, Plaut reported a "desire for rapprochement was sincere; though it was apparent (and perhaps natural) that [he] met a good deal of defensiveness about Ukrainian history even that of 300 years ago."[82]

Plaut was right. History could not easily be set aside. Only a month after Plaut's Toronto speech, at the invitation of Ukrainian community leaders, a number of prominent Winnipeg Jews attended a luncheon honouring Petro Mirchuk, a Ukrainian Auschwitz survivor living in Winnipeg, whose wartime memoirs had just been published. Following a Kosher meal, Mirchuk addressed the small gathering. One representative of the Winnipeg Jewish Community Council reported that Jewish participants were taken aback when Mirchuk saw "nothing wrong in comparing Chmelnitsky [Khmelnytsky] *vs* the Jews to Bar Kochba *vs* the Romans." The very suggestion enraged the Jewish guests, who considered any attempt to parallel the Jewish position in seventeenth-century Ukraine with the might of occupying Imperial Roman legions in first-century Palestine to be nothing short of obscene. An attempt by the hosts to generate a Ukrainian-Jewish dialogue fell flat. Ukrainian speakers urged that the past be set aside. Both communities had suffered; now was the time for reconciliation, co-operation and efforts to find grounds for joint action. Most Jews sat in silence. Not even a Ukrainian survivor of Auschwitz could bridge the historical antipathies still alive in the room.[83]

Bridge-building would be difficult. Most Jewish leaders felt no urgency to make common cause with Ukrainians. They could not comprehend the Ukrainian desire to transcend the past, the need to move beyond historical grievances. But any suggestion that Jews could set aside their shared historical understanding, especially that of the Holocaust, which increasingly bonded them one to the other, was not only wrong minded, it was impossible.

If Jewish leaders remained hesitant, one must note that the desire to reach out to Jews was far from universal among Ukrainians. Some, especially among the extreme nationalists and immigrant groups, still harboured anti-Jewish feelings and had deep misgivings about any dealings with the Jewish community. Those who made overtures to the Jewish community leaders did so with some trepidation at how their initiatives would be received within community circles. When they were not responded to in kind by the Jewish community, there was some bitterness. Ukrainians had taken the first step; it went unreciprocated. In a letter to Alex Epstein, Yuri Shymko, then President of the nationalist World Congress of Free Ukrainians, lamented the lack of a positive Jewish response. Recent Jewish and Ukrainian history was marked by so much pain that these two groups, perhaps more than others, should be able to find common ground for co-operation and understanding.[84]

Epstein, still pressing Canadian Jewish Congress leaders on the value of better relations with Ukrainian organizations, again challenged Jewish leaders to respond. With "our common interest for human rights for our people in the USSR, our acute concern and fear of Soviet global policy, our desire and need for Canadian unity," co-operation was essential. As a first step, Epstein urged, it was necessary to build "links of communication with all groups, on an open and friendly basis whenever it is opportune . . . If we are to be a light to the nations, we must first get out of the darkness ourselves."[85]

Epstein's plea did not strike a responsive chord. Few Jewish leaders could object to better relations with any other group, including Ukrainian-Canadians. But to the degree that Jews gave any thought to the problems of Ukrainian-Canadians, which was neither much nor often, they were seen as separate and distinct from those of the Jewish community. Khmelnytsky cast a long shadow. So did war criminals.

Tentative and guarded contact between leaders of the Jewish and Ukrainian communities continued. Discussion of historical grievances remained part of almost every dialogue. Rarely, however, did discussion turn to war criminals in Canada. Perhaps it was unnecessary. Most Canadians, including Jews, might instinctively identify Nazi war criminals with Germans, but some Jewish leaders had not forgotten the Division episode of 1950 and some still doubted the innocence of the Division's wartime record. For their part, Ukrainian leaders were growing increasingly restive at a rash of investigations of Ukrainian and other eastern Europeans then under investigation in the United States for Nazi-related activities. The United States was not Canada, but could the Nazi hunt spread northward?

In the spring of 1977, several Congress officials in Toronto lunched with leaders of the Toronto-based Banderite World Congress of Free Ukrainians, again at the instigation of Alex Epstein. The mood was positive. Informal discussion again ranged over a broad series of topics but eventually and for the first time focused on the Jewish community's efforts to force the government's hand on Nazi war criminals. Yuri Shymko assured his Jewish luncheon partners "that his organization would not knowingly harbour war criminals and he was interested in seeing a positive policy on this question enacted."[86] The pledge seemed unequivocal.

It took very little, however, to test the pledge. Several months after the pleasant luncheon, an anonymous flyer was mailed to Ukrainian organizations across Canada. It requested information on one Ivan Solhan (Sovhan) said to have been a ranking Ukrainian police official accused in the death of several hundred Jews. Solhan was thought to be living in Canada. "It is hoped," the flyer stated, "people in Ukrainian circles will be able to find Solhan." The flyer requested that any information be sent to Wiesenthal's documentation centre in Vienna. It was signed "a concerned Canadian."[87]

Perhaps smarting at the suggestion that Ukrainian organizations could snap their fingers and deliver up Nazi war criminals, Shymko wrote to Ben Kayfetz who had attended the recent lunch meeting. Shymko affirmed the "bond of friendship between the two communities" and the co-operation of his organization "in bringing to justice any individual who has been responsible for premeditated murder whatever his racial or national origin, whatever his political or ideological motives." But the assurance was not without an accompanying caution. There had been, Shymko noted, "a number of mistaken" accusations against innocent individuals which were legally challenged and withdrawn." The flyer, he suggested, smacked of the same slander; but this time the victim of the accusation could not defend himself. The accuser remained nameless. Shymko urged that henceforth Jewish officials communicate directly and openly with "the numerous central organizations of our communities in the world, rather than by anonymous channels."[88]

Kayfetz was concerned at any suggestion that Congress was linked with the anonymous flyer, and he was equally amazed anyone could believe the Jewish community was so tightly organized that a word from Congress could rein in those circulating the flyer. This monolithic vision was as far from true of the Jewish community as it was of the Ukrainian community. In a memo to Congress leaders, Kayfetz noted that the offending flyer was clumsily produced but it was not an accusation of guilt. It was a request for information necessary to avoid the very kind of false accusations Shymko protested. As to Shymko's declaration of support for bringing war criminals to justice—Kayfetz was now somewhat skeptical. "On close reading of the letter, I see it is something less than that."[89]

For jurists, the terms "war criminal," "war crimes," "collaborator" and "crimes against humanity" have very specific legal meaning. But legal and semantic niceties aside, the sense of Jewish community pain that persons who knowingly aided and abetted in the Holocaust might be alive and well, living peacefully in Canada, remained real. If the term "war criminals" as used by many in the Jewish community and larger civic culture lacked legal precision, it was still a term fraught with meaning.[90] And for decades Jews had tried to get the Canadian government to act.

Official Jewish concern in this matter, of course, stretched back to the Galicia Division episode. In the years immediately following, few doubted that the mass immigration of Displaced Persons and others had included war criminals. But it was one thing for Canadian Jews to feel incensed that war criminals had secreted themselves in Canada, perhaps with the connivance of the Canadian government, church officials or ethnic political leaders; it was another thing that year after year the government and larger civic culture had refused to do anything about it. Pressed on the subject, Canadian authorities had always had one answer—they lacked an evidential or legislative basis for action.[91] Most Jews suspected that they did not care. Throughout the fifties, the Holocaust had remained a Jewish memory and war criminals a Jewish concern.

In May 1960, however, Israeli Prime Minister David Ben-Gurion announced the apprehension of Holocaust mastermind Adolph Eichmann. Ben-Gurion proclaimed that Eichmann would stand trial in Israel for war crimes, crimes against humanity and, under Israeli law, crimes against the Jewish people. Eichmann's kidnapping and lengthy trial, front-page news around the world, captured the public imagination. It sensitized Jews and non-Jews alike to the reality of the Holocaust as no previous event had done. The trial helped turn the Holocaust from a private Jewish agony into part of the western historical legacy—an event of monumental proportions destined to plague historians, moral philosophers and the conscience of the world. After the Eichmann trial, thoughtful people could no longer dismiss the Holocaust as the momentary excess of a few Nazi extremists run amok; it was now revealed as the centrepiece of a political and racial ideology with deep historical roots, an ideology that commanded the loyalty of millions.[92]

Nor did the Eichmann trial close the book on Jewish efforts to apprehend and bring war criminals to face justice. It intensified it. In 1964, world

Jewry was galvanized by the realization that the German twenty-year statute of limitations on war crimes would soon take effect. If this was allowed, many Nazi war criminals would escape accountability. Some feared they could emerge from the shadows in which they were hiding to again proclaim dedication to Nazi ideals, perhaps to rebuild for the future. The Canadian Jewish Congress joined Jewish organizations around the world to protest the German statute of limitations. They pressured the Canadian government to endorse the protest.[93]

The statute of limitations issue was put high on the agenda when a Congress delegation gathered in the office of Prime Minister Lester Pearson in October 1964. Pearson was asked to intercede personally with the West German government. Canada, he was reminded, had "no statute of limitations whatever for crimes involving murder or, for that matter, other homicidal crimes."[94] Surely Canada should not sit by and let those who murdered millions go free. Pearson agreed. In part because of the world Jewish protest and the diplomatic representations by friendly governments like Canada, West Germany proclaimed a ten-year delay in the implementation of its statute of limitations in the case of war crimes.

But even as the Eichmann trial and the statute of limitations controversy were still fresh, events in Canada brought the threat of a Nazi revival home to Canadian Jewry. In 1965 a small band of self-styled Canadian Nazis, trying to ape the American Nazi party of George Lincoln Rockwell, organized a series of public meetings. Nazi regalia and swastika-emblazoned flags were unfurled in a Toronto park. The popular press splashed stories of these home-grown Nazis across the front page, and television brought their provocations into every home. The reaction of the Jewish community was instant. Congress and its constituent organizations immediately demanded appropriate police action and received the support of responsible civic, media and church leaders. But for some Jews this was not enough. Younger more militant Jewish groups, reinforced by Holocaust survivors, organized counter-demonstrations that occasionally spilled over into violence. As exaggerated rumours of a growing national neo-Nazi movement percolated through the Jewish community, Jewish self-defence groups sprang up and Holocaust survivors set up their organizational infrastructure, dedicating themselves to combating any manifestation of

Nazism, commemorating the Holocaust and promoting a public program of Holocaust education.[95]

One other event that reinforced Jewish sensitivity to the Holocaust was the Israel-Arab War of 1967. The weeks preceding the outbreak of fighting in June were traumatic ones for diaspora Jewry. What they saw were Arab armies massing on all sides, threats being issued, United Nations troops pulled out of dangerous zones, and the straits of Tiran blocked to Israeli shipping. Many feared an imminent replay of the Holocaust; and again the non-Jewish world seemed ready with eulogies but no help.

Israel's lightning victory was seen as miraculous. It also served as a symbolic corrective to those who pointed fingers at the alleged passivity of Jews during the Holocaust. Understandably, the spectre of a second Holocaust also served to reinforce commitments to sanctify the memory of the first and seek justice against Nazi war criminals. The problem now was not community commitment to the issue. It was tactics.

Given the Canadian government's dismal record of inaction in following up any information on alleged Nazi war criminals passed along by Congress, simply appealing to the government's sense of justice seemed pointless. But no other strategy seemed effective. One approach again brought to the fore was "naming" alleged war criminals and exposing them to the court of public opinion. Perhaps public reaction to revelations about specifically named war criminals living freely in Canada might just force politicians, police and immigration authorities to act.

But this plan had its pitfalls. Hasty allegations made without incontrovertible evidence could leave the accuser and the Jewish community open to charges of harassment if not libel or slander. The embarrassment of the Melnyk episode was not forgotten. Moreover, naming could undermine the moral authority of the Canadian Jewish community and make any campaign to bring Nazi war criminals to justice seem more like an indiscriminate witch-hunt.[96]

As we have seen, naming and trial by press or in the court of public opinion were dangerous. They could, and did, backfire on both the press and the Jewish community when evidence proved less than solid. But trial by press was troubling on another count. Why must it be left to victims or the press to indict a murderer in the name of justice? In a society based on the rule of law, prosecution is the duty of the state through its legal system. What can be done, however, when the state refuses to act or claims it does not have the legal authority to act? And even as knowledge of the Holocaust grew, the problem of war criminals in Canada remained too distant a problem for most Canadians—including old allies of Jews in the post-war human-rights crusade. As a result, war criminals remained, for the most part, a parochial Jewish concern easily dismissed by government.

The Liberal Party of Pierre Trudeau, with the lion's share of Jewish voter support and prominent Jews, both active in Jewish communal organizations as well as Liberal organization and fundraising, yielded few dividends. Why then was the Liberal government so unbending? Several factors suggest themselves.

Trudeau, a firm believer in meritocracy, surrounded himself with the most able men and women he could find, including Jews. But if Trudeau harboured no ethnic intolerance or would not tolerate it in others, he felt little or no sympathy for the politics of ethnic particularities. The Trudeau who in 1971 approved multiculturalism as an instrument of domestic cultural policy still believed Old World antipathies should be discarded when immigrants entered Canada. Accordingly he had little sympathy with Japanese-Canadian demands for reparations associated with their World War II internment, with Chinese calls for repayment of their head tax and the Ukrainian call for an apology for internment of community members during World War I. It was his view that recycling the past might serve the needs of ethnic communities but not the needs of Canada. The road to ethnic harmony, he held, lay more in ensuring future equality than in resurrecting the injustices of the past. It is likely he placed Jewish community pressure on war criminals in the same class. Certainly his ministers knew the Prime Minister was less than enthusiastic about any initiative in this area, and they took their cue from him.[97]

Long in power, old Liberal political hands must also have sensed that the Nazi war-criminals problem posed a potential minefield of inter-ethnic tension. Most Canadians might equate Nazis with Germany, but key Liberal strategists likely understood the sensitivity eastern Europeans felt on this issue. Almost forty years of experience in government had taught them something. The

Liberal Party may have had limited voter support in eastern European communities where the party was often identified as too soft on Communism, but party strategists, aware of domestic reaction to American initiatives against war criminals, felt such action could exacerbate inter-ethnic tensions in Canada. With the Jewish vote already in the Liberal bag and nothing political to gain, it was better to avoid the issue.

The failure to engage government interest in war criminals as a matter of human rights is clear in the case of Harold Puntulis. A post-war Latvian immigrant and naturalized Canadian citizen, Puntulis was accused and tried in absentia for war crimes by the Soviet Union. Although Canadian Jewry had ample reason to mistrust the workings of the Soviet legal system, the evidence of Puntulis's participation in mass murder of Jews seemed irrefutable to them. A Soviet request to Canada for Puntulis's extradition was rejected. Congress acquired, translated and forwarded a copy of the Soviet trial transcript to the federal government in hope of changing the government's position. It claimed that Canadian respect for justice, human rights and dignity demanded it. Congress failed.[98]

For more than ten years, Congress badgered the federal government on Puntulis and other cases, which periodically came to the attention of Jewish authorities. Nothing was accomplished. To every appeal the government's answer was the same. Desirable though it might be, action against Puntulis or others was legally impossible. In the Puntulis case, for example, the government claimed extradition was out of the question; Canada had no extradition treaty with the Soviet Union. But with or without a treaty it was not Canadian policy to submit individuals to foreign courts where different rules of evidence apply (and especially to a Communist court). Puntulis was also a naturalized Canadian citizen. He had spent five years of peaceful domicile in Canada, as required by Canadian law, before being granted Canadian citizenship. He had committed no crimes in Canada. While government officials agreed it was unfortunate such a person should have the protection of Canadian citizenship, they warned denaturalization procedures were, at best, a dubious legal procedure.

Puntulis was not alone. In 1974, for instance, David Geldiaschvilli was tried in the Soviet Union and sentenced to death for the murder of 4,000 innocent people, 3,000 of them Jews. Geldiaschvilli was a naturalized Canadian citizen arrested on a visit to his native Soviet Georgia. It was claimed at his trial that in 1968 the Soviet Union had requested Geldiaschvilli's extradition from Canada to stand trial for his crimes. Canada had refused, even though the government had information that Geldiaschvilli was a suspected mass murderer. Three years later, "Geldiaschvilli applied for and received Canadian citizenship."[99] Eminent Canadian jurist and McGill law professor Maxwell Cohen dismissed the government's legal gymnastics. Yes, there were legal problems, Cohen argued, but they could all be overcome if the government had the political will to do so.[100]

Old hands in the campaign shrugged their shoulders. The government already knew there were war criminals in Canada and didn't seem to care. The public didn't seem to care. Nobody cared except Jews, who could and would not let the matter pass. Increasingly outraged by seeming public indifference, they repeatedly broached the issue with politicians and public servants alike, even though they already knew the government's answer. Time after time the government offered sympathy but claimed their hands were tied by the lack of a remedy in Canadian law.

As Canadians vacillated, Americans confronted Nazi war criminals in their backyard. Unlike Canada, the United States acted. The Americans prepared to strip Hermine Braunsteiner Ryan of her naturalized American citizenship in 1971. Braunsteiner Ryan, a former concentration camp guard, was known as the mare of Majdanek for allegedly stomping an innocent victim to death with her boots. American authorities claimed that as a Nazi, Braunsteiner Ryan had never been eligible for entry into the United States or for American citizenship. The government was ready to argue in court that she could only have achieved both by fraud. In the end, Ryan surrendered her citizenship and was extradited to Germany to stand trial. It is worth noting that Braunsteiner Ryan entered the United States from Canada, where she immigrated after the war.[101]

In the winter of 1975, a Jewish delegation that included several Holocaust survivors visited Ottawa. They asked the minister responsible for Canadian citizenship if Canada could not do the same. Once again the answer was not one of right or wrong, but of legal barriers. Canadian and American law and legal systems, it was explained, were not parallel in the area of immigration and citizenship. What was legally possible in the United States was not necessarily possible here. Indeed, even if stripping away immigration and citizenship status were possible, there seemed some doubt whether fraud in applying for immigration could be proved in Canadian cases. Unlike the United States, it was unclear whether prospective post-war immigrants to Canada were asked about "past Nazi associations . . . although questions were put on Communist association." Could an immigrant be held guilty of withholding information about a Nazi past if he or she was never asked about it?

The Immigration Minister, as always, was sympathetic but promised little. "His departmental aides," he allowed, "would carry out a detailed investigation to determine if any loopholes could be found in the records" to see if the American model might work in Canada. But his words had a hollow ring. The Jewish delegation left as they had come—empty-handed.[102]

As Canadian authorities waffled, the Americans took another step. In 1977, the US Congress passed the Holtzman Amendment enabling immigration officials to investigate alleged Nazi war criminals who might have entered the United States by falsifying their past. Two years later the Office of Special Investigations, the OSI, was organized within the Justice Department to take over these investigations. More denaturalizations and deportations seemed likely.[103] These American moves inflated expectations in Canada, especially among survivor groups and their children, the second generation.

On the heels of the American initiatives came the impact of television's *Holocaust* mini-series. The Canadian public, some argued, might now be ready to support rooting Nazis out of their Canadian sanctuary. Some survivors advocated a dramatic protest to dramatize their anguish at the Canadian government's inaction on war criminals. One group was dissuaded only with difficulty from undertaking a mass demonstration or a hunger strike to bring this to the attention of the public. Survivors were told that the problem was not that the public did not know, it was that the government steadfastly refused to act.

In Toronto, frustrated Congress leaders met yet again to assess their campaign against war criminals. While they agreed that the program of public information—reaching out to other groups and keeping the war criminals issue present in every official government contact—must continue, they were only too aware of the weakness of their approach. The Jewish community had for years discussed human rights. The government responded with the law. It was time, it was suggested, to respond in kind, to see what legal arguments could be mustered to counter those of the government. The war criminals problem was referred to the Legal Committee, a committee of Congress in Toronto made up of lawyers.[104]

The lawyers quickly settled on several possible avenues of legal argument to be explored and committee members were assigned to do the legal spade work on each. They were aided by Kenneth Narvey, a former law student from Winnipeg, who offered himself as legal consultant to Congress. Narvey proved self-motivated and single-minded, with a crusader's zeal for rooting out war criminals. After ten months as a volunteer he was given a small stipend. Nobody thought that more than thirty years of government inaction could be ended without a struggle, but at least among Congress insiders, there was now a new sense of momentum.[105]

NOTES

1   For an examination of the Canadian Jewish post-war campaigns for admission of Jews from Europe, see Irving Abella and Harold Troper, *None Is Too Many: Canada and the Jews of Europe, 1933–1948* (Toronto, 1982), 190–279. On Ukrainians, see Lubomyr Luciuk, "Searching for Place: Ukrainian Refugee Migration to Canada after World War II" (unpublished Ph.D. thesis, University of Alberta, 1984).

2   Canadian Institute of Public Opinion, Public Opinion News Release, October 30, 1946; Harold Troper, "Canadian Resettlement Policies" (unpublished paper, November 1983).

3   Myron Momryk, "Ukrainian Displaced Persons and the Canadian Government 1946–1952" (unpublished paper, September 1983), 5–6.

4   Luciuk, "Searching for Place," 318–23.

5   PAC, Department of Labour Records, Refugee Screening Commission, Vol. 147, File 3–43–1; D. Haldane Porter, "Report on Ukrainians in SEP Camp No. 374 Italy," February 21, 1947; Alti Rodal, "Nazi War Criminals in Canada: The Historical and Political Setting from the 1940s to the Present," prepared for the Commission of Inquiry on War Criminals (Ottawa, 1986), 366–408; For a discussion of Panchuk's key role, see Lubomyr Luciuk (ed.), *Heroes of Their Day: The Reminiscences of Bohdan Panchuk* (Toronto,1983).

6   For an example of the process by which restrictive immigration regulations were chipped away, see CIWC, Unclassified Public Exhibit, "An Outline of Recent Orders-in-Council. Broadening Canadian Immigration Holdings," in *Evolution of Policy and Procedures Security Screenings, 1945–1957.*

7   CIWC, Unclassified public Exhibit, Memorandum Fortier to Jolliffe (Commissioner of Immigration), February 7, 1949.

8   Momryk, "Ukrainian Displaced Persons," 15–21.

9   House of Commons *Debates*, June 15, 1950, 3696. The Halychyna Division is the name commonly used for the military unit among Ukrainians. It is also commonly referred to by its German designation, Galicia Division, the term also used in this book.

10 *The Gazette* (Montreal), June 16, 1950.

11 CJC, CJCP, Ukrainian Galician Division, 1950–1951 Files, "Immigration," Memorandum Rosenberg to Hayes, June 19, 1950.

12 CJC, CJCP, Ukrainian Galician Division, 1950–1951 Files, Rosenberg to Segal, June 20, 1950; Rosenberg to Robinson; June 20, 1950.

13 CJC, CJCP, Ukrainian Galician Division, 1950–1951 Files, Segal to editor, *Daily Hebrew Journal,* June 30, 1950.

14 *Canadian Jewish Weekly*, June 29, 1950.

15 CJC, CJCP, Ukrainian Galician Division, 1950–1951 Files, Prokop to Harris, June 21, 1950.

16 CJC, CJCP, Ukrainian Galician Division, 1950–1951 Files, Robinson to Rosenberg, June 27, 1950.

17 CJC, CJCP, Ukrainian Galician Division, 1950–1951 Files, Memorandum Rosenberg to Hayes, June 30, 1950.

18 *JTA News*, July 7, 1950, 6.

19 CJC, CJCP, Ukrainian Galician Division, 1950–1951 Files, Telegram Bronfman to Harris, July 4, 1950.

20 CJC, CJCP, Ukrainian Galician Division, 1950–1951 Files, Harris to Bronfman, July 5, 1950.

21 CJC, CJCP, Ukrainian Galician Division, 1950–1951 Files, Telegram Hayes to *Israelite Post* (Winnipeg), *Daily Hebrew Journal* (Toronto), *Jewish Post* (Winnipeg), July 7, 1950; Hayes to Crestohl, July 10,1950.

22 CJC, CJCP, Ukrainian Galician Division, 1950–1951 Files, Bronfman to Harris, July 12, 1950.

23 CJC, CJCP, Ukrainian Galician Division, 1950–1951 Files, Rosenberg to Easterman, July 14, 1950; Rosenberg to Robinson, July 14, 1950.

24 *The Forward* (New York), July 23, 1950. Translation in CJC, CJCP, Ukrainian Galician Division, 1950–1951 Files.

25 CJC, CJCP, Ukrainian Galician Division, 1950–1951 Files, Levine to JTA, July 10, 1950.

26 AJC, Foreign Affairs Department: Canada/Émigré Groups, FAD-1, Joseph Kellman to Rosenberg, July 13, 1950; CJC, CJCP, Ukrainian Galician Division, 1950–1951 Files, Kellman to Rosenberg, July 14, 1950; *Ukrainian Resistance: The Story of the Ukrainian National Liberation Movement in Modem Times* (New York, 1949), 98–103.

27 CJC, CJCP, Ukrainian Galician Division, 1950–1951 Files, Memorandum Rosenberg to Hayes, "Halychyna Division" July 26, 1950.

28 CJC, CJCP, Ukrainian Galician Division, 1950–1951 Files, Robinson to Rosenberg, August 1950; Hayes to Kellman, September 6, 1950; Kellman to Hayes, September 29, 1950; Hayes, to Kellman, October 5, 1950; Rosenberg to Robinson, October 10, 1950; Robinson to Rosenberg, October 18, 1950; Memorandum of Rosenberg to Hayes, "Halychyna Division," October 23, 1950.

29 CJC, CJCP, Ukrainian Galician Division, 1950–1951 Files, Hayes to Harris, August 2, 1950; "Control Council Law No. 10," December 20, 1945 (a); Hayes to Harris, October 25, 1950, "Index of Materials Submitted to Honourable Walter Harris, Minister of Citizenship and Immigration," August 2, 1950; Affidavit, Bernard Berglas, Montreal, July 31, 1950; Affidavit, Jonas Freiman, Montreal, July 28, 1950.

30 CJC, CJCP, Ukrainian Galician Division, 1950–1951 Files, Harris to Bronfman, September 15, 1950. It has been argued that Canadian officials were not just under pressure from the Ukrainian community to proceed with the admissions. British authorities were also concerned to move the Division to Canada. Rodal, "Nazi War Criminals in Canada," 389–90.

31 CJC, CJCP, Ukrainian Galician Division, 1950–1951 Files, Hayes to Harris, October 5, 1950; Bronfman to Harris, September 25, 1950.

32 CJC, CJCP, Ukrainian Galician Division, 1950–1951 Files, Hayes to Bernstein, October 10, 1950.

33 CJC, CJCP, Ukrainian Galician Division, 1950–1951 Files, Wiesenthal to CJC, October 7, 1950.

34 AJC, Foreign Affairs Department: Canada/Émigré Groups, FAD-1, "The Galician Ukrainian Division (Preliminary Report)," December 1, 1950.

35 CJC, CJCP, Ukrainian Galician Division, 1950–1951 Files, Rosenberg to Hayes, October 23, 1950; Extract from pamphlet entitled "Trail of Terror."

36 CJC, CJCP, Ukrainian Galician Division, 1950–1951 Files, Harris to Hayes, November 6,1950.

37 CJC, CJCP, Ukrainian Galician Division, 1950–1951 Files, Harris to Bronfman, November 7,1950.

38 CJC, CJCP, Ukrainian Galician Division, 1950–1951 Files, Hayes, Memorandum, "Hour Meeting with Honourable Stewart Garson, Minister of Justice, on November 17, 1950."

39 CJC, CJCP, Ukrainian Galidan Division, 1950–1951 Files, Rosenberg to Robinson, November 20, 1950; Rosenberg to Weiner, November 20, 1950, Rosenberg to Kellman, November 20, 1950; ACJ, Foreign Affairs Department: Canada/Émigré Groups, FAD-1, Edelman to Hexter, Segal, Faire and Cohen, November 30, 1950.

40 CJC, CJCP, Ukrainian Galician Division, 1950–1951 Files, Aronsfeld to Rosenberg, November 27, 1950; Aronsfeld to Rosenberg, December 10, 1950; Robinson to Rosenberg, December 27, 1950; Memorandum Rosenberg to Hayes re: "Halychyna Division," January 15, 1951; Rosenberg to Aronsfeld, January 26, 1951; *Chaz* as quoted in Rosenberg to Robinson, January 26, 1951.

41 CJC, CJCP, Ukrainian Galician Division, 1950–1951 Files, Memorandum of Hayes to National Executive, January 10, 1951.

42 CJC, CJCP, Ukrainian Galician Division, 1950–1951 Files, Karol to Hayes, July 25, 1950. The AUCC, incorporated in 1946, was the newest incarnation of the Ukrainian left, previously known as the Ukrainian Farmer Temple Association.

43 CJC, CJCP, Ukrainian Galician Division, 1950–1951 Files, Memorandum Rosenberg to Hayes re: "Immigration," June19,1950.

44 CJC, CJCP, Ukrainian Galician Divison, 1950–1951 Files, Kushnir and Syrnick to *The Israelite Press* and CJC/Winnipeg, August 26, 1950; Frank to Hayes, August 28, 1950.

45 CJC, CJCP, Ukrainian Galician Division, 1950–1951 Files, Hayes to Kushnir and Syrnick September 6, 1950; Hayes to Frank, September 6, 1950; Zaharychuk to Hayes, September 15,1950.

46 *Nasha Meta*, June 23, 1951, as quoted in translation in CJC, CJCP, Ukrainian-Canadian Committee, 1963 File, Kayfetz to Hayes, June 29, 1951 (enclosure two).

47 *Jewish Post*, May 2, 1957.

48 CJC, CJCP, Melnyk, Andrii (Alleged War Criminals) File, British United Press dispatch, May 4, 1957.

49 CJC, CJCP, Melnyk, Andrii (Alleged War Criminals) File, Telegram Fenson to Hayes, May 8, 1957; Hayes to Fenson, May 9, 1957, Hayes to Wiesenthal, May 9, 1957; Hayes to Yad Vashem, May 9, 1957; Hayes to Kibbutz Mordei Haggettaot, May 9, 1957; (M) Fenson to Tennenbaum, May 4, 1957.

50 CJC, CJCP, Melnyk, Andrii (Alleged War Criminals) File, Frank to Hayes, May 8,1957.

51 CJC-T, Catzman Papers, Hayes to Kayfetz, May 9, 1957; Among the secondary volumes examined were Joseph Tannenbaum, *Underground: Story of a People* (New York, 1952); CJC, CJCP, Melnyk, Andrii. (Alleged War Criminals) File, Memorandum Kayfetz to Hayes, May 17, 1957.

52 CJC-T, Catzman Papers, Jacobs to Hayes, May 9, 1957; Wiesenthal to Hayes, May 13, 1957.

53 *Toronto Telegram*, May 9, 1957.

54 CJC-T, Catzman Papers. Ben Kayfetz, "Items for Administrative Committee," May 10, 1957; CJC, CJCP, Melnyk, Andrii (Alleged War Criminals) File, Memorandum Kayfetz to Hayes, re: "Melnyk" May 10, 1957.

55 CJC-T Catzman Papers. Memorandum Kayfetz to Harris, re: "Meeting with officers of Ukrainian National Federation," May 14, 1957.

56 CJC, CJCP, Melnyk, Andrii (Alleged War Criminals) File, Bilak to Kayfetz, May 14, 1957.

57 CJC, CJCP, Melnyk, Andrii (Alleged War Criminals) File, Frank to Hayes, May 16, 1957; Frank to Hayes, May 22, 1957; *Jewish Post,* May 23, 1957.

58 CJC, CJCP, Melnyk, Andrii (Alleged War Criminals) File, Kochan to Fenson, May 31, 1957; Hayes to Jacobs, June 3, 1957; CJC-T, Catzman Papers, Frank to Hayes, June 4, 1957.

59 *Toronto Telegram*, May 29, 1957; For reactions to an earlier bombing in Toronto, see TCA, Mayor's Office Records, RG7A1 Box 59, File IIIB Skorokhid to McCallum, October 11, 1950; *The Toronto Star*, October 9, 1950; *The Globe and Mail*, October 9, 1950; *The Toronto Telegram*, October 9, 1950.

60 Much of the following discussion of the press is culled from *Press Digest,* the federal government's monthly review of the ethnic press. We quote their translations of non-English-language material. *Press Digest,* Vol. 16, no. 2, January 1960, 5–7.

61 *Press Digest,* Vol. 16, no. 6, May 1960, 4.

62 *Press Digest,* Vol. 16, no. 7, June 1960, 3–5.

63 *Press Digest,* Vol. 16, no. 8, July 1960, 6–8. For a public airing of Ukrainian-Jewish relations during the 1960s see, for example, "Ukrainians and Jews: Must They Be Enemies, *Canadian Jewish News*, May 22, 1964; Zaharkevich to editor, Montreal *Gazette*, May 27, 1960. The discussion of Ukrainian-Jewish relations within the respective heritage press of both groups was often strident in its hostility. The *Kanadiysky Farmer* (Winnipeg) ran an eight-part series entitled "Ukrainians and Jews" by M. Trykhrest between August 22 and October 10, 1970. It seemingly blamed Jews for every evil that had befallen Christendom, and Ukrainians in particular, from the crucifixion of Christ to the subjugation of Ukraine by the Soviets. At one point the article simply listed the names of more than 400 prominent Jews claimed to have been at the "centre" of the Bolshevik Revolution. The author summed up the Jewish role in history:

> History supplies us with no evidence that the Jews, being the spiritual captives of aggressive materialism, have ever stood in defence of any enslaved nations, or have ever taken a neutral position. On the contrary, the Jews have always stood on the side of the stronger, the oppressor, so that they themselves could benefit.

M. Trykhrest, "Ukrainians and Jews" *Canadian Farmer*, August 22–October 10, 1970, as translated by Department of Secretary of State, Translation Bureau, November 3, 1970, 18.

64 *Press Digest,* Vol. 16, no. 8, July 1960, 6–8.

65 CJC, CJCP, Ukrainian Canadian Committee, 1963 File, Kushnir to CJC, September 16, 1963; Commemorative Committee, "The Western Free World in the Shadow of the Cruelty of Russian Imperialism over the Ukraine and Other Nations in the USSR," September 1963; Hayes to Kushnir, September 30, 1963.

66 Howard Stanislawski, "Canadian Jews and Foreign Policy in the Middle East," in *The Canadian Jewish Mosaic*, M. Weinfeld, et al., eds. (Rexdale, 1981), 397–483.

67 R. Louis Ronson Papers: NJCRC, Ukrainian-Jewish Relations 1971–1975, Vol. 4, File 20, "Note for Remarks by the Prime Minister to the Ukrainian-Canadian Congress, Winnipeg, Manitoba, October 9, 1971," October 9, 1971.

68 Peter Worthington, "A Jew Who Helps Ukrainians," *The Toronto Sun*, November 29, 1972; PAC, R. Louis Ronson Papers: NJCRC, Ukrainian-Jewish Relations 1971–1975, Vol.4, File 20, Kayfetz to Pearlson, et al., November 30, 1972.

69 Peter Worthington, "A New Dialogue Against Soviet Oppression," *Toronto Telegram*, July 23, 1971; PAC, R. Louis Ronson Papers: NJCRC, Ukrainian-Jewish Relations 1971–1975, Vol. 4, File 20, Memorandum Levy to Korey, July 28, 1971; Memorandum Korey to Levy, August 2, 1971.

70 Harold Troper and Lee Palmer, *Issues in Cultural Diversity* (Toronto, 1976), 87–101; *Report of the Royal Commission of Inquiry in Relation to the Conduct of the Public and the Metropolitan Toronto Police* (Toronto, 1972).

71 PAC, R. Louis Ronson Papers: NJCRC, Ukrainian-Jewish Memorandum Levy to Ronson, "Ukrainian Contacts with JCRC," August 5, 1971.

72 Similar sentiment abounded in the American Jewish community. See Abraham Brumberg, "Poland and the Jews," *Tikkun* (July/August 1987), 15–20, 85–90.

73 CJC-T, J.C. Hurwitz Papers: File 1, File July-December, 1974, Memorandum Kayfetz to Horwitz re: Relations with Ukrainian Canadians, September 9, 1974; Minutes, JCRC, Toronto, September 11, 1974, 6–8.

74 CJC-T, J.C. Hurwitz Papers: File 1, File July-December 1974, Epstein to Kayfetz, November 5, 1974.

75 CJC-T, J.C. Hurwitz Papers: File 1, File January-June 1975, Memorandum Kayfetz to Pearlson and Hurwitz re: "Ukrainian-Canadians," February 4, 1975.

76 PAC, R. Louis Ronson Papers: NJCRC, Ukrainian-Jewish Relations 1971–1975, Vol. 4, File 20, Memorandum Kayfetz to Harris, et al., March 25, 1975.

77 CJC-T, J.C. Hurwitz Papers: File 1, File January-June 1975, Memorandum Kayfetz to Harris, et al., re: "Continuing Conversations with Ukrainian Leadership," April 15, 1975; Report of Ben Kayfetz, re: "Meeting with Ukrainians," June 3, 1975.

78 CJC-T, J.C. Hurwitz Papers: File 1. File July-December 1976, Kayfetz to Pearlson, October 17, 1976; Telegram of Pearlson to UCC, October 15, 1976. The 1977 invitation to Rabbi Gunther Plaut, President of Congress, to attend the CJC 12th National Congress in Winnipeg was delivered although representatives from the CJC in Winnipeg attended. PAC, Gunther Plaut Papers: CJC Ukrainian-Jewish Dialogue, 1977–78. Bardyn to Plaut, September 12, 1977; Plaut to Bardyn, September 28, 1977.

79 PAC, R. Louis Ronson Papers: NJCRC, Ukrainian-Jewish Relations 1971–1975, Vol. 4, File 20, Telegram Pearlson to Bezchlibnyk reported in *Ukrainian Echo*, June 20, 1979; Sokolsky to Kayfetz, May 11, 1979; Memorandum Kayfetz to Pearlson, July 16, 1974 re: Ukrainians/Moroz.

80 PAC, Gunther Plaut Papers: CJC Ukrainian-Jewish Dialogue, 1977–78, Bardyn to Plaut, January 31, 1978; Kayfetz to Plaut, February 15, 1978; Plaut to Bardyn, February 17, 1978; Plaut to Bardyn, March 7, 1978.

81 *Canadian Jewish News*, April 28, 1970; PAC, Gunther Plaut Papers: CJC Ukrainian-Jewish Dialogue, 1977–78, Summary of an address to Ukrainian Professional and Business Club of Toronto, April 20, 1978; *The Globe and Mail*, April 22, 1978.

82 PAC, Gunther Plaut Papers: CJC Ukrainian-Jewish Dialogue, 1977–78, Memorandum of Plaut re: "Visit of Rabbi Plaut and Address to Ukrainian Professional and Business

Club of Toronto, April 26, 1978," April 24, 1978.

83 PAC, R. Louis Ronson Papers: NJCRC, Ukrainian Jewish Relations 1971–1975, Vol. 4, File 20, Memorandum Schachter to Kayfetz, May 30, 1978; Report by Schachter, "Meeting Between Representatives of W.J.C.C. and Ukrainian-Canadian Committee," May 29, 1978.

84 PAC, R. Louis Ronson Papers: NJCRC, Ukrainian-Jewish Relations 1971–1975, Vol. 4, File 20, Shymko to Epstein, December 2, 1977.

85 PAC, R. Louis Ronson Papers: NJCRC, Ukrainian-Jewish Relations 1971–1975, Vol. 4, File 20, Epstein to Ronson, December 16, 1977.

86 PAC, Gunther Plaut Papers: CJC, NJCRC, Memoranda (Pt.1), 1977, Memorandum Kayfetz to Plaut et al. re: "Ukrainians," August 18, 1977.

87 PAC, R. Louis Ronson Papers: NJCRC, Ukrainian-Jewish Relations 1971–1975, Vol. 4, File 20, Relations 1971–1975, Vol. 4, File 20, Flyer entitled "Nazi Crimes in Przemysl (Poland)," n.d.

88 PAC, Gunther Plaut Papers: CJC, NJCRC, Memoranda (Pt.1), 1977, Shymko to Kayfetz, August 8, 1977.

89 PAC, Gunther Plaut Papers: CJC, NJCRC, Memoranda (Pt.1), 1977, Memorandum Kayfetz to Plaut et al. re: "Ukrainians," August 18, 1977.

90 For a comprehensive analysis of the concept of "war criminals" in the Canadian legal context, see Commission of Inquiry on War Criminals, *Report, Part I: Public* (Ottawa, 1986), 37–44.

91 See for example CJC-T, Catzman Papers, Memorandum Kayfetz to Catzman, et al., September 5, 1958; Kayfetz to Finestone, September 23, 1958.

Beyond passing on chance information on alleged war criminals in Canada to authorities and making repeated representations, there seemed little the Canadian Jewish Congress or Jews could do to arouse government or public. The case of Alexander Laak is a case in point. At a 1960 Congress National Executive meeting, discussion of federal immigration policy turned to the recent suicide of Alexander Laak, a naturalized Canadian citizen. Before coming to Canada Laak was accused of being the commandant of a Nazi concentration camp in Estonia. How, it was asked, could immigration authorities who reportedly knew of the accusations have allowed Laak and his sort into Canada unless the government decided to "intentionally allow these people in"?

But, if the position of the federal authorities was troubling, several Jewish leaders felt the view of some in the press was even worse. They were shocked when a *Globe and Mail* editorial, rather than demanding to know how an accused war criminal like Laak could gain Canadian entry and citizenship in Canada, seemed to condemn those who denounced Laak and might have pushed him to suicide. Reflecting the temper of the time, the paper suggested it was time for the victims to put bitter memories behind them even if forgiveness in this case meant that mass murderers would never face justice.

Did the federal government and Canadian people quietly endorse the *Globe and Mail*'s position? Perhaps so. The government "had whitewashed the whole affair," a Congress executive member lamented, "and the public was left with the impression that the man had been persecuted." It was obvious that fifteen years after the Holocaust ended most Canadians knew next to nothing of the genocidal crimes of the Nazis and cared less. CJC-T, Catzman Papers, Minutes of CJC National Executive Meeting, Montreal, September 11, 1960.

92 Hanna Arendt, *Eichmann in Jerusalem: A Report on the Banality of Evil* (New York, 1964) and Gideon Hausner, *Justice in Jerusalem* (London, 1967).

93 CJC, CJCP, Submissions to L.B. Pearson file, Memorandum Saalheimer to Garber, March 27, 1964; Prinz to Rusk, March 2, 1964; Garber to Martin, April 13, 1964.

94 CJC, CJCP, Submissions to L.B. Pearson file, Hayes to Courts, October 1, 1964; Bronfman to Pearson, October 14, 1964.

95 Interview with Ben Kayfetz, August 9, 1986, Toronto; Stanley R. Barrett, *Is God A Racist: The Right Wing in Canada* (Toronto, 1987).

It was not long before these survivor groups were welcomed under Congress's umbrella. Survivor spokesmen were appointed to Congress committees, their voices increasingly heard, their priorities given special attention. Few questioned their moral authority.

But not all newly organized Jewish groups fit neatly into the Congress structure. In Toronto and Montreal the most important self-defence group remained for a time outside Congress. After first battling the neo-Nazis in the parks, N-3, named for Newton's Third Law—for every action there is an equal and opposite reaction—formalized their structure. They began self-defence training for members and eventually often provided security service at Jewish community meetings and gatherings. As the 1965 neo-Nazi scare subsided, N-3 turned its attention to unmasking war criminals living in Canada. Rumour had it that the group was gathering material for the Wiesenthal Documentation Center in Vienna.

Eventually absorbed into Congress, the N-3 spokesmen joined the survivors in pressuring Congress for a more militant and, at times, more confrontational response to any and all manifestations of anti-Semitism in Canadian society. They also demanded active lobbying of government to take legal action against alleged Nazi war criminals in Canada. Interview with Max Chirofsky, May 21, 1986, Toronto.

96 Past experience with naming had been none too successful. In 1962, for example, the editor of the then privately owned *Canadian Jewish News* made allegations about the wartime record of a central European newspaper editor in Canada. It was widely accepted within the Jewish community that the editor had been a Nazi activist and party organizer in his homeland. When the Nazis took power, he is alleged to have surfaced as a senior official in the Nazi puppet government and actively supported the implementation of the anti-Semitic Nuremberg-type laws against Jews in the new political jurisdiction. But the paper went further. It accused the editor of collaborating in Eichmann's wartime deportation of Jews to death in concentration camps.

The editor sued for libel. The case dragged on until the *CJN*, unable to produce solid evidence of its more damning charges, surrendered. The *CJN* was forced to recant and offer up a public apology. The lawsuit was dropped. Interview with Ben Kayfetz, August 9, 1986, Toronto; PAC, Imri Rosenberg Papers, Rosenberg to "Sir," August 3, 1962; Gasner to Rosenberg, August 8, 1962; Kayfetz to Rosenberg, August 20, 1962; Rosenberg to Gasner, August 13, 1962; Rosenberg to Kayfetz, August 21, 1962; Kayfetz to Rosenberg, October 27, 1962.

Nor was the larger public press immune to dangers inherent in naming. Almost ten years after the *CJN* incident, in the spring of 1971, *The London Free Press* ran a follow-up story about a Galicia Division member and previous resident of London then working as a janitor in Vancouver. He was reportedly accused of war crimes by Simon Wiesenthal. The story was picked up by the Vancouver *Sun*. In several articles over three days, the janitor was identified as having been chief of a Ukrainian Auxiliary Police unit which, Wiesenthal was said to have explained, took part in the murder of 10,000 Jews. A letter from Wiesenthal listing charges and containing the Nazi-hunter's evidence was allegedly on the way to Ottawa with a demand for legal action.

The janitor denied all and sued the Vancouver *Sun*. Under investigation, the Wiesenthal story began to crumble for lack of hard evidence. In a telephone interview with the *Sun*, Wiesenthal reportedly named several witnesses who, he claimed, would corroborate his charges. They failed to do so. The janitor's counter-story held up.

With a lawsuit pending the *Sun* argued that the public's right to know, its right to place detailed information about the Wiesenthal accusation before the public, was paramount. The case never went to court. The paper had not, it claimed, intended to defame the janitor. The *Sun*, perhaps concluding its case was weak and the publicity from a lawsuit unwelcome, offered an out-of-court settlement. The janitor, content to avoid a costly trial and wishing only to be exonerated, dropped his suit. In addition to compensation, he received a letter from the *Sun*'s solicitor stating "the allegations that were made . . . were untrue."

The end of the janitor affair did not pass without comment from the UCC in London, Ontario, where the episode began. In a sharp rebuke to Wiesenthal, copied to local Jewish organizations and the Ukrainian press, a UCC spokesman attacked the Nazi-hunter. The letter allowed that the Nazis had indeed made use of Ukrainian collaborators. But, it claimed, Nazis also found willing Jews ready to serve their ends, just as the Soviets have since found both Ukrainians and Jews willing to serve their cause in Ukraine. Collaborators, both Ukrainian and Jewish, both pro-Nazi and pro-Soviet, had "committed heinous crimes against our people and against humanity in general ... We feel therefore that every effort should be made to bring them to trial." But the letter warned against making a war criminal a case study in mass ethnic collaboration. "Since Nazi collaborators were in no way representative of either the Ukrainian or the Jewish people, but because members of the Auxiliary Police acted as individuals and served the interests of a foreign power, you will readily understand that Ukrainians are sensitive about being linked with activities of these criminals." Vancouver *Sun*, March 9, 10, 11, 12, 1971; Legal documentation and other materials pertaining to the incident are assembled as a package in CLC. Subject files: Legal Matters File. The package has been widely circulated through the Ukrainian community as an example of the false accusations of war criminality made periodically against Ukrainians; CIUS, UCC Civil Liberties Commission, 1985 File, Butler to Chrabatyn, May 10, 1972; UCC/Winnipeg Papers, Roslycky to Wiesenthal, April 5, 1971; PAC, R. Louis Ronson Papers: NJCRC, Ukrainian-Jewish Relations 1971–1975, Vol. 4, File 20, Roslychy to Kayfetz, April 5, 1971.

97 Interview with Monique Bégin, January 23, 1986, Montreal; commenting on her study for the Deschênes Commission, Alti Rodal noted that Pierre Trudeau's negative attitude towards action against war criminals in Canada was "politically motivated" and widely understood as such in Cabinet. the *Globe and Mail*, August 8, 1987; the *Gazette* (Montreal), August 12, 1987; the *Gazette* (Montreal), August 13, 1987; the *Gazette* (Montreal), August 19, 1987. In a luncheon talk at a conference in Montreal marking the fortieth anniversary of the Nuremberg trials, Trudeau spoke of his reluctance while prime minister to address the issue. It was, he said, just not a priority of his government. It was a problem "of previous times." He mused that the opening of the war-crimes issue could dredge up war-crimes allegations against the Allies and wondered where one could draw the line in trying to redress the past. Author's notes on Trudeau lecture, November 4, 1987, Montreal; the *Globe and Mail*, November 9, 1987.

98 PAC, Gunther Plaut Papers: CJC, JCRC 1966–67 (Pt. 1), Minutes of the National JCRC, Toronto, June 8, 1966.

99 PAC, Gunther Plaut Papers: CJC; War Criminals, Correspondence, 1977–80, Confidential Memorandum Rose to National Officers, October 7, 1974.

100 PAC, Gunther Plaut Papers: CJC, JCRC 1965–66, Minutes of National JCRC, Montreal, January 16, 1974.

101 See Allan A. Ryan, Jr., *Quiet Neighbors: Prosecuting Nazi War Criminals in America* (New York, 1984), 46–52.

102 CJC-T, J.C. Hurwitz Papers: File 1, File Jan.-June, 1975, Members of JCRC/Toronto, January 29, 1975; PAC, Gunther Plaut Papers: CJC Executive Committee Meetings, 1975–78, Memorandum Rose to National Executive, January 12, 1975; Memorandum Rose to National Executive, February 24, 1975; CJC-T, J.C. Hurwitz Papers: File 1, File Jan.-June, 1977, Minutes of JRCI7T March 30, 1977.

103 Ryan, *Quiet Neighbors*, 60–62, 66.

104 CJC-T, J.C. Hurwitz Papers: File 1, File Jan.-June 1977, Minutes of JCRC/T, March 30, 1977; Memorandum Cooper to Legal Committee, May, 26, 1977; Memorandum Cooper to Legal Committee re: Geneva Convention," June 1, 1977.

105 CJC-T, J.C. Hurwitz Papers: File 1, File July-Dec. 1977, Memorandum Kayfetz to Rose re: "War Crimes," July 19, 1977; interview with Kenneth Narvey, February 23, 1988, Montreal.

Blacks and Jews:
Racism, Anti-Semitism, and *Show Boat*

HOWARD ADELMAN

This essay examines a conflict that emerged in Toronto during 1993. Some Blacks[1] protested against opening the new North York[2] Centre for the Performing Arts (now the Ford Centre) with a production of *Show Boat*. They claimed that this 1927 American musical was racist, demeaned and stereotyped Blacks, misrepresented history, and represented them in secondary roles. Though the controversy began as one pitting the protesting Blacks against the producers of the show and the political authorities in North York, it was extended to the general community when efforts were made to enlist the support of community and charity groups by having them cancel their respective fundraising events. These events entailed a commitment to pre-purchase a block of tickets to the show, which could then be sold to individuals or groups at a premium. This "sponsorship" of an evening production had been arranged to raise funds for the charities "sponsoring" the evening's performance. In the development of the protest, a very specific Jewish dimension emerged.[3]

This essay focuses on the Black-Jewish aspect of the conflict. Though I make many references to the Black community, the emphasis is on the character of the Canadian Jewish identity. I discuss the Black community only enough to allow us to understand the various Jewish responses to the protest. Any assessment of the Black community offered here is highly tentative and speculative.

There are three levels of analysis and an implicit fourth level (which I touch on only briefly). On a basic level, the essay probes how some Jews and Blacks see each other and themselves, and how they deal with each other within the Canadian cultural mosaic. On a second level, it probes Canadian identity-formation by comparing and contrasting the way Jews and Blacks in Canada, and their U.S. counterparts, deal with each other in the context of the meaning and consequences of the multicultural policies of the two countries.

On a third level, this essay depicts brokerage politics within civil society and among ethnic groups. It is a tale of success for one group and, in this particular case, failure for the other. This analysis also suggests norms that can guide successful brokerage in Canada at least (in contrast with the breakdown of brokerage politics that has occurred between English and French Canada). If the first level is about the micro-sociology of ethnic groups in Canada, and the second is about the socio-politics of Canadian identity-formation, the third involves the micro-politics of ethnicity in Canada.

The fourth level has to do with post-modernism, modernism, and pre-modernism. The post-modernist motif is obvious, since the clash was about how one is represented; in post-modernism, the essential ingredient of identity is representation. The debate was also about truth claims and historical consciousness—there was an argument that *Show Boat* inaccurately and inadequately depicted the history of Blacks; accurate and adequate historical representation is the hallmark of modernism. Finally, there was also a debate over fundamental moral principles—what I claim to be the core characteristic of all premodern societies. The conflicts over freedom of artistic expression versus social responsibility toward deprived minorities, and the mode and appropriate language for conducting debates over these moral issues, had an impact on the concern for both historical truth and group description.

If one argued for cultural pluralism indifferent to any historical or truth claims (in the extreme, insisting that cultural pluralism itself made any moral claims about representation irrelevant), one could be identified as a post-modernist. If one argued that historical accuracy was the domain of history, and artistic expression was the domain of the imaginative arts, and that facts and values were separate realms of discourse, one could be identified as a modernist; as such, only artistic representations that disrupt the public order should be subject to social control.

In the controversy over *Show Boat,* the arguments made by most parties on both sides presumed that moral convictions are fundamental to resolving conflicts in a society committed to cultural pluralism. In this Black-led protest, moral convictions seemed to dictate the choice and strategy governing the protest.[4] Neither side in the debate presumed that moral convictions dictated cultural homogeneity. Rather, the debate was over which moral principles should adjudicate issues of appropriate modes of representation in culturally pluralistic societies.

A British conference at Cambridge University in 1993 ("Canada: The First Post-Modern State") had as its premise the idea that Canada was based on diversity without any unity—a country caught up with the question of its own image of itself and its self-representation because it lacked an essence, a defining core of values. Accordingly, Canada was a country that showed the victory of diversity per se; the preoccupation with the imaginative construction of its own identity was precisely the characteristic of the post-modern world.[5]

I use this case study to imply the reverse. Through an examination of a conflict over representation (a post-modernist preoccupation) of one group in Canada, namely Blacks, I try to reveal the modernist and pre-modernist values of Canada, and the core of the emerging Canadian identity. In the process, I seek also to explain why Canadian Jews behaved as they did in response to the protest and the anti-Semitic elements that shadowed that protest.

I first sketch in the context—*Show Boat,* the position of the protesters, and one of their targets, the United Way. Second, I look at the protest itself—

the Jewish role in and response to the protest, a misuse of John Stuart Mill by an apologist for the protest as an example of the misunderstanding of basic concepts of liberal freedom, the anti-Semitic element in the protest, the impact of the protest on both communities, and rationales offered for the protest. Third, I consider the implications of the analysis for understanding the identity of Blacks and Jews in Canada in the context of Canadian multiculturalism.

I have two apologies to make—one for providing too little detail and one for providing as much as I do. Because of space restrictions, what I present is still only a sketch of the controversy and of the background details. However, I devote most of this essay to describing details of the issue. As Professor Avishai Margolit of Hebrew University reminded me, the devil is in the details.

THE CONTEXT

The Toronto Production

In 1993, *Show Boat*[6] was honoured in the United States with a commemorative stamp. *Show Boat* is a venerable 1927 American musical written and composed by Jerome Kern and Oscar Hammerstein II,[7] both Jews. It is memorable for its famous songs, especially "Ol' Man River." The musical was controversial when it first opened, but for the very opposite reason it became a centre of controversy in Toronto in 1993. The musical introduced serious social commentary into what had previously been a light form of entertainment with virtually no real plot. *Show Boat* was the musical that served as the progenitor of both Rodgers and Hammerstein's *South Pacific* in 1949, which attacked colour prejudice even more forcefully than *Show Boat,* and the all-Black musical *Carmen Jones,* the American adaptation of Bizet's opera *Carmen.* It was overtly and intentionally a statement against racism.

The plot is a teary romantic melodrama covering four decades from 1887 in Natchez, Mississippi, to the roaring twenties in Chicago. The show boat of the title is the *Cotton Blossom,* a vessel towed from place to place on U.S. rivers and used as a portable theatre. The theme of racism emerges in two parts. There is the backdrop of Black labour on the Mississippi in the post-reconstruction period, which began c. 1877. And there is the sub-plot: Julie Laverne, star of the on-board show and emotional "mother" of Magnolia (the female romantic lead and daughter of the owner of the *Cotton Blossom)* is denounced by the villain, Pete, a spurned suitor of Julie, for being a Black posing as a white and, more significant, given the laws against miscegenation in Mississippi at the time, for being married to a white. Julie and her husband are forced to leave the show. Magnolia takes Julie's place.

Julie is replaced by Magnolia a second time. The way it happens relies on the sort of coincidence characteristic of operas and musicals. Magnolia had married Gaylord, an itinerant gambler, who, after many ups and downs, eventually deserts Magnolia and their child. Magnolia attempts to return to the stage in Chicago. Julie, who has by then become an alcoholic, sees Magnolia audition. She leaves the same nightclub show without Magnolia's even knowing that Julie had watched her audition or even that Julie had been in the nightclub act. The producer hires Magnolia to take Julie's place. The Black sub-lead in the plot is used as a doormat for the romantic realization and fulfillment of the white female lead.

Garth Drabinsky, a prominent Jewish impresario and entrepreneur from Toronto, the producer of *Phantom of the Opera* and *Kiss of the Spider Woman* in both Toronto and New York, obtained the rights to run the new City of North York Arts Centre. Mel Lastman, also Jewish, was the mayor of North York. Drabinsky decided that his opening production would be *Show Boat,* directed by the Broadway veteran Hal Prince. The show, originally written and composed by Jews and adapted from a 1926 novel by Edna Ferber, a Jew,[8] was produced by a Jew under the auspices of the Jewish mayor of North York, one of the most culturally diverse municipalities in Canada, where the largest portion of the Jewish population of Greater Toronto live. North York has as well a significant portion of the region's Black population. Greater Toronto now has more Blacks than Jews.

In a time when issues of cultural proprietorship, political correctness, and cultural sensitivity are so alive, an American musical dealing with Blacks and racism in the deep South was produced to open a municipally financed performing arts centre in Canada.

THE PROTEST

The announcement of *Show Boat*'s opening for October 1993 led to a protest movement by Toronto's Blacks, beginning in the spring of 1993.[9] In September 1993, just before the scheduled opening on 5 October, the Coalition to Stop *Show Boat* made an official complaint to the Metro Toronto Police that *Show Boat* was "racist, anti-African propaganda" and asked that it be investigated as hate literature under a federal law against hate crimes. The group claimed that Ferber's novel portrayed Blacks through "demeaning and derogatory stereo-types"[10] as "somewhat savage . . . simple souls . . . Since the play is based on the book, the play has to be racist . . . Such a hateful portrayal of African people sends the message to the audience that slavery couldn't have been so bad."[11]

This assertion was the culmination of a six-month campaign. Stephnie Payne, a member of the North York Board of Education, had claimed, "*Show Boat* portrays blacks as 'subhuman savages, dim-witted, childlike, lazy, drunk, irresponsible and devoid of any human characteristics.'"[12] M. Nourbese Philip stated: "*Show Boat* was racist when it was written in 1927, and in all its subsequent incarnations. It is still racist in 1993."[13] Angela Lee, general manager of the Canadian Artists Network: Black Artists in Action, summarized the opposition to the musical in a more moderate way, conceding that *Show Boat*'s original intention may have been honourable; however, "black people remain nothing but a backdrop, a background. They're caricatures; they're cartoons . . . What could be more insidious than being portrayed as subservient background characters and happy to be so."[14]

In the most moderate position of all, but still one opposed to the production, Jeff Henry, a colleague of mine who is a professor of drama at York University, argued that *Show Boat* was created by white people for white people. While Black writers such as Langston Hughes of the Harlem Renaissance were trying to define Black dreams, hopes, and ambitions, this musical portrayed Blacks as "civil and accommodating" when, in fact, during the 40–odd years covered by the story there were protests and uprisings. As Arun Mukherjee summed up the opposition to what was termed cultural racism, "Although a non-white living in North America must face several types of blatant and not so blatant racism, it is the cultural racism of the subtle kind that hurts the worst."

Referring to the film *Out of Africa,* Mukherjee continued, "The non-white viewer can only react with anger . . . after seeing the marginalization and caricature of African people."[15]

In cultural racism so understood, racism is indirect. It places Blacks in backdrop roles, assigns them menial positions, and stereotypes them. Racism is built into the fabric of the text rather than arising from the explicit intent: "Racism is not simply a phenomenon which afflicts the minds of individuals and causes these individuals to perform discriminatory acts. Racism is something which affects an entire society. It is ingrained and reinforced in all the major and minor institutions of the society." As *The Colour of Democracy* depicts it, "Cultural racism . . . consists of the tacit network of beliefs and values that encourage and justify discriminatory practices."[16]

Note, conventional racism in its mildest form was not just stereotyping, but stereotyping done in a way that attributed specific traits and tendencies, regarded as despicable, to members of a group or race. Such racism was institutionalized when organizations practised discrimination against individuals—for example, by denying them opportunities for employment or for advancement because they were presumed to have those unworthy characteristics. Conventional racism, at its worst, simply considered a whole group inherently inferior and undesirable. Cultural racist analysis claims to probe deeper into the roots underlying behavioural and institutionalized racism.

I have distilled ten specific critical contentions of those who protest against cultural racism:

1 When racism itself is portrayed, the portrayal can be characterized as culturally racist.

2 When there is insensitivity to the effects of any representation on an oppressed group, whatever the intentions of the author or the producer, the representation can be characterized as culturally racist.

3 An aesthetic representation that detracts from the understanding and appreciation of minority cultures, or even fails to increase the understanding and

appreciation of a minority culture, can be characterized as culturally racist.

4 When there is ignorance of the historical context of the
situation represented and that context is not corrected
by the mode of representation, cultural racism makes
us "think about representational practices in terms of
history, culture and society."17

5 Any time-worn and archaic representation of a group
that does not correspond to current realities can be
characterized as culturally racist.

6 Cultural racism occurs when history is mis-depicted as
entertainment, when it is the history of an oppressed
group that is still fighting against oppression and for
reconstruction of its "authentic" history.

7 The unfavourable portrayal, even if it is unique or
insightful, of any traditionally oppressed minority
invites a characterization of racism.

8 The stereotypical portrayal, even if favourable, of any traditionally oppressed minority is racist.

9 When a work of art succeeds in imprinting or reinforcing images of minority caricatures, whatever its intent,
the art is racist.

10 When members of one culture appropriate the symbols
and representations of another culture for their own
purposes, their actions are racist; a more extreme view
claims that cultural representations are the sole propri-
etary right of the group represented, and it is racist for
any individual of another group to appropriate those
representations.18

Cultural racism is considered dangerous because it perpetuates negative
images of a group through stereotyping. Ophelia Averitt, who runs a health and
soul food store in Akron, Ohio, would not see *Show Boat:* "We do not need to

be reminded of things that are unpleasant."[19] In the same article, her grandson Fenner, a communications graduate of Kent State University, was more critical of the production and generalized about the value of resurrecting the musical. "People are tired of seeing negative images."

As Robert Alton wrote, "We live in a racist society, in which images of Black people and others of colour in the mainstream media are consistently narrow and negative. Plays and musicals that perpetuate those images do nothing but help perpetuate racism: I make the same assertion about *Miss Saigon,* which perpetuates the stereotype of Asian women as exotic prostitutes. Until we live in an equitable society, images such as those in *Show Boat* can only serve to perpetuate the evil of racism."[20] Another commentator, Arnold Minors, wrote, "*Show Boat* is not a harmless piece of 1920s fluff. The original intention was to shock or 'wake up' audiences to the reality of racism. Although the show may have succeeded in doing that in 1927, it also succeeded in perpetuating the same myths it sought to debunk. Its intention to shock audiences today is a failure; it merely perpetuates myths about blacks in North America."[21]

Fundamentally, in the view of those who levy charges of cultural racism, art has primarily a moral, educational function. With respect to previously victimized groups, art should serve to present historically accurate images of those portrayed; historically comprehensive portraits of the various social and political roles of members in the group portrayed—what Kobena Mercer calls the reflectionist argument;[22] and uplifting images of both the individuals and the groups portrayed—what Mercer terms the social engineering argument.[23] (The third function directly conflicts with the goals of the first two.) In this view of art, racism is not about behaviour.[24] It is primarily about the construction of an identity.

The correlative of this theory of "identity politics" seems to be a postmodernist view of racism. *Show Boat* creates the wrong image of Blacks: "This theatrical production is unsuitable learning material, is historically inaccurate, and depicts Blacks in a stereotypical role, as 'back drop'. . . Members of the BEWG [Black Educators' Working Group] are unanimously opposed to the inclusion of *Show Boat* in the school curriculum, since it is contrary to the policies of the North York Board [of Education] and Ontario's Ministry of Education, both of which are seeking to eliminate materials based on stereotypes from our schools."[25] Blacks are portrayed as secondary, and this reinforces a stereotypical image of Black inadequacy and impotence, even if in the musical Blacks play critical roles in the running of the show boat and in publicizing the productions on the *Cotton Blossom* to other Blacks, and even if they are portrayed as possessed of superior artistry, kindness, and consideration.

Note also the characterization of historical inaccuracy. After all, *Show Boat* does not imply that Blacks were not victims; in fact, the musical portrays Blacks as subject to unjust laws about miscegenation. The complaint focuses on the musical's failure to portray Blacks rebelling against their victimization. This aspect of the Black experience is missing from the story, say the protesters—as if any artistic representation could ever hope to include or should aim to include all aspects of the Black experience. Nor do the protesters take into consideration the fact that this is a piece of art with only stock character types, where the women are even more typecast than the Blacks.

But the position of the protesters was even stronger: "We need learning media that accurately portrays [*sic*] the experiences of African-Canadians, including slavery in a true context. The rich culture of African civilization, and the positive contributions of Blacks for example, in art, medicine, science, early Canadian history, and the military needs [*sic*] to be included in school curricula. *Show Boat* does not facilitate this process . . . Our children's heritage is an integral part of their personality and socialization. Making them feel ashamed of their culture, or by denying them the opportunity to learn about their legacy is tantamount to violence against the young."[26]

The protesters claimed that *Show Boat* is historically inaccurate and misleading in its portrayal of Blacks, that it caricatures Blacks and portrays them only in the role of backdrops, and, in the most extreme criticism of all, that the caricatures are definitively negative and inhuman. These were the reasons given for the protest. But there was an affective dimension as well that seemed to have little to do with accuracy, caricaturing Blacks, assigning them backdrop roles, or portraying them negatively. Though some Blacks in Toronto viewed *Show Boat* as racist and others considered it at least insensitive, the issue was not just a conceptual and critical one. Individuals were truly pained by the treatment of Blacks in the musical.[27]

Key Target: The United Way

One major target of the political protest against *Show Boat* was the United Way of Greater Toronto,[28] and its sponsorship of an evening performance (purchasing a block of tickets as a fundraising event). The United Way, a coalition of social agencies, runs an annual campaign to collect funds for redistribution to its member agencies. It raises almost $50 million per year. The United Way had made large strides in overcoming what just fifteen years earlier had been a white- and gentile-dominated major Toronto charity. Not only does the board of trustees now include Jews, Asians, and Blacks, but it has an overt policy to ensure that its member agencies are sensitive to the diverse, multicultural character of Toronto in the way they choose governing boards and staff, as well as in programming.

The immediate past chair of the board of the United Way, during the period when the protest first developed, was ethnic Chinese. Dr. Joseph Wong, who had been born and raised in Hong Kong, is a leader both within his own community as well as in the larger Canadian society. He is also a well-known advocate of both civil and group rights. Because of his prestige in the wider community and his eminent leadership on issues of discrimination, Dr. Wong was asked to play a leading role with Ruth Grant, chair of the United Way during the protest. The president and chief professional officer of the United Way, Anne Golden, is Jewish. At the time of the controversy, the proportion of Jews on the board was greater than their proportion of the population.

Leaders in the Black community organizing the protest against *Show Boat* requested that the United Way withdraw its sponsorship of its evening. After several debates, and several votes, the board affirmed its participation in the sponsorship.[29]

The Protest

The Jewish Dimension

As mentioned above, Jews were involved in the production of the show and as members of the United Way supporting or opposing continuing sponsorship. The Jewish role also can be discerned through two specific Jewish organizations, one—the Canadian Council for Reform Judaism—took a political stand in support of the Black protest, and one—the Canadian Friends of the Hebrew

University in Jerusalem—withdrew its sponsorship of a charitable fundraising event involving *Show Boat*. As well, individual Jews in the media supported the boycott of *Show Boat*.

The Canadian Council for Reform Judaism was one of the very few organizations, and the only major non-Black one, to support the call for a boycott of the show. The author of the Reform Jewish position, Carol Tator, chair of the National Social Action Committee of the Canadian Council for Reform Judaism and a former director of the Urban Alliance on Race Relations, identified with the middle position in the range of rationales for the protest—*Show Boat* portrayed Blacks as stereotypes. She noted: "racial stereotyping of blacks in *Show Boat* is so serious that Jews should be among the first to protest."[30]

In a talk that Tator gave on 8 September 1993, sponsored by the Social Action Committee of Holy Blossom Temple—Toronto's largest Reform Jewish congregation, with 6,000 families—she argued that Jews should support and join the boycott because Jews could and should identify with the pain that Blacks feel, both in society and in watching *Show Boat*. In that presentation, she based her case primarily on an appeal to feeling, not on a critical analysis of *Show Boat* that revealed negative stereotyping, let alone stereotyping of Blacks as inherently possessing despicable traits. In the book that she co-wrote published following the controversy (*The Colour of Democracy*), the good-natured passivity of Blacks who "never challenged their repression" in the musical was found to be offensive. The play "romanticized and trivialized one of the most oppressive periods of Western civilization and misrepresented the deep emotions, conditions, and experiences of Blacks in those horrific times."[31]

Gunther Plaut, Holy Blossom's well-known rabbi emeritus and a leading civil rights advocate, supported Tator's position in print in an article in the *Canadian Jewish News*. Rabbi Dow Marmur, Holy Blossom's senior rabbi, offered the congregation's board of trustees an ethical, religious, and social justification for the Reform Council's support of the protest.

Marmur began by retelling the Exodus story from the perspective of the Egyptians in order to make the point that the Bible does not intend to be objective but only claims to have right on its side because it takes the side of the slaves and dispossessed. "Reform Judaism has, since its inception, identified this championship [of the dispossessed] as the essence of Prophetic Judaism." He concluded: "The road to truth goes through empathy," echoing Tator's thesis that the essence of the Judaic ethic is compassion. Note, the stress is on compassion, not justice. We should, and do, "understand the pain of Blacks when their degradation is paraded on stage."

Marmur conceded that the opposition to *Show Boat* might be unjustified but claimed that "we should recognize that hurt and refrain from supporting the show in order to help that healing"—a refrain picked up by journalists who seemed to see support of the boycott as a means of obtaining social peace and harmony. This seemed to be a statement of the type of rectificatory psychology propounded in the United States by Michael Lerner, editor of *Tikkun*, who, in his editorials, invited each community not simply to celebrate its own experience of hardship and achievements but also "to empathize with the other communities in the name of the universality of suffering and of a common desire to heal."[32] To remain silent on this issue, Marmur asserted, would be a betrayal of the "traditional Jewish position" and identifying with the status quo. In other words, if Jews do not protest, they are identifying with the power elite, which some of the Blacks had accused Jews of doing, rather than with the downtrodden and dispossessed.

Gary Lewis echoed those sentiments in a letter to the editor:

> I was moved by their eloquent outpouring of pain and anguish over the issue. As a Jew I could only identify with the feeling of isolation, injustice and impotence felt when dealing with institutionalized racism . . . Many people are offended by its contents and historical inaccuracy . . . The reality is that some works, such as this one, are so deeply offensive that in the present climate of racial inequality they should simply be bypassed and laid to rest . . . What have we done to support the African Canadian community in their anguish over this production? Our own outpouring of rage has deflected attention from what should be a common fight against institutionalized racism.[33]

Steve Shulman, associate director of community relations for the Canadian Jewish Congress, told the Brotherhood of Beth David B'nai Israel Beth Am Synagogue in Toronto, "It is not for Jews to tell another community what should offend them."[34] Empathy, not a specific political project or object of reform, was to be the basis of an alliance with the downtrodden. Empathy, in this case, did not entail identifying with the experience of that pain and even less with understanding it, but meant merely responding to the claim of Blacks that they experienced such pain and complying with their demand that its alleged source be terminated.

The only cancellation of a charitable evening at *Show Boat* that I know of was by the Canadian Friends of the Hebrew University in Jerusalem. The organization was celebrating fifty years of work on behalf of the university.[35] As it turns out, the board's vote was split. The older members, who may have experienced discrimination and could identify somewhat with the discrimination and the pain of Blacks subjected to racism,[36] were largely resistant to withdrawing sponsorship. The younger members of the new leadership who grew up in a privileged environment and were unlikely to have ever experienced anti-Semitism supported withdrawal, largely on two grounds: the Friends of Hebrew University should not involve itself in sensitive political questions, and Jews should not be involved in something that Blacks claimed caused them pain. The new leadership had attempted to reach out and create dialogue with the Black community. During the previous two years, it had invited eminent American Black leaders to address it and members of the Black community in joint sessions. Jeff Henry and Roger Rowe spoke to the board and made the case for withdrawing.

Steve Diamond, then president of the Toronto chapter, who supported withdrawal from sponsorship, indicated that though Jews had empathy for the hurt of the Blacks, they in fact did not understand the hurt. "Because we felt people were hurt by this play . . . we felt that for us to go and raise money, when this was clearly causing hurt to people, would not be the right thing for us to do . . . [We] were not taking a stand either for or against the musical, but understood the 'genuine concern' being expressed in the Black community."[37]

In the debate over whether to withdraw sponsorship, the new leadership, brought onto the Board to introduce young blood, won. The Friends withdrew sponsorship. Toronto's main Black newspaper, *Share*, carried the withdrawal as a front-page headline: "Major Jewish group scraps *Show Boat* fundraiser." The story claimed that the Jewish group understood "the hurt being felt in the Black community over the proposed staging of the musical in October."[38] The Jews in question, in fact, had specifically declared that they made no claims to understand Black pain. Other Blacks had declared that any claim to understand that pain would be regarded as presumptuous. "Harold Cruse once remarked that what really roused his 'enmity toward Jews' was hearing people who are Jewish say, 'I know how you feel because I, too, am discriminated against.' What concerned him, clearly, was an attempt to proclaim not only fellow feeling, but a bond of experience. To Cruse and many others, this attempt to establish parity insults the ordeals black Americans have undergone since they were first put on slave ships."[39]

The doctrine justifying cancelling sponsorship was not that wounds recognize wounds. The doctrine was not about the universal understanding that the experience of suffering brought, but that each history of suffering was unique, that only the Blacks could feel or understand their own suffering, and that the other that recognized that suffering should engage in actions that minimized the pain. Empathy and fellow feeling, but not identification and certainly not understanding, were to be the foundation for action. As I try to demonstrate below, there is an enormous contrast between this posture, which advocates helping a group because of empathy for the pain of its members, and a very different position—assisting someone out of respect for the group's sense of and claim for justice.

Even though Friends specifically stated that it was not taking a stand on the controversy, the cancellation was treated as a victory and endorsation of the Black protest. Roger Rowe, a Toronto lawyer and co-chair of the Coalition to Stop *Show Boat,* told a protest rally outside the show's ticket office that the members of Friends had taken the "moral high road." For the protesters, this symbolic act from those (including me) whom I label the "do-gooders" had been even more important than that received from those (again including me) whom I call the "bleeding hearts."

The professional journalists, however, seemed to be neither bleeding hearts nor do-gooders willing to take action and not just provide moral support. They appointed themselves experts on how to maintain civil societies. David Lewis Stein, a prominent journalist and columnist, and a member of a modern orthodox synagogue,[40] was one such "social pacifier." He advocated boycotting the show not because he expressed an empathy with Black pain or because he wanted to make a symbolic gesture of support. In an open letter, he urged producer Garth Drabinsky to cancel the show for the benefit of community relations.

Thus, Jews supporting the boycott variously offered three rationales: the bleeding hearts posited empathy with Black victimization, the do-gooders expressed a willingness to take symbolic actions to second Black claims that *Show Boat* was racist simply because some Blacks declared it to be so, and the social pacifiers advocated pragmatic politics to foster improved community relations with Blacks. Some Jews acted out of all three motives. One, Carol Tator, was the only Jew who attempted to justify the protest ideologically but the justification, as I will try to show, was not based on objective principles or universal values.

AN ASIDE "ON LIBERTY"

Richard Gwyn implied that Jews, and others, should support the boycott based on another motive. In his *Toronto Star* column on 28 April 1993, he compared the *Show Boat* case to producing a musical version of *The Merchant of Venice*. Imagine, he argued, that such a show were put on by a pair as equally and grossly insensitive as Mayor Mel Lastman and Garth Drabinsky. Imagine a sympathetic but stereotypical portrayal of Shylock. Gwyn suggested that it would risk alienating the Jewish community in the same way that the "dis" and "dem" portrayal of Blacks in *Show Boat* had already alienated many Blacks.[41] Paradoxically, at the same time as Gwyn portrayed the producer and political patron in terms of traditional, negative stereotypical formulas applied to Jews, he advised Jews and others to join in boycotting Blacks because of stereotyping.

Not only were those who opposed the boycott and supported the show personally maligned by such defenders of the protest as Gwyn, but those who would have explicitly condemned the boycott were cited as intellectual supporters of it by advocates of the protest such as Carol Tator. In her presentation at Holy Blossom Temple (referred to above), she quoted John Stuart Mill in support of her stance. In spite of suggestions (by me) that she check her sources she repeated the sort of misuse of John Stuart Mill that occurred in *The Colour of Democracy* (221):

> The tension between the competing principles of an individual's right to freedom of expression and the right of communities to be protected from forms of expression that do harm was recognized by the most revered of libertarians. John Stuart Mill (1984), who suggested that "as soon as any part of a person's conduct affects prejudicially the interests of others, society has jurisdiction over it, and the question whether the general welfare will or will not be promoted by interfering with it becomes open to discussion. (41) . . . Whenever, in short, there is a definite damage or a definite risk of damage either to an individual or to the public, the case is taken out of the province of liberty and placed in that of moral or law." (49)

Mill does assert that actions that harm others must be restricted by society: "Acts, of whatever kind, which without justifiable cause do harm to others may be, and in the most important cases absolutely require to be, controlled by the unfavourable sentiments, and, when needful, by the active interference of mankind."[42] But he makes it abundantly clear that such actions may be undertaken only in very restricted circumstances: "Even opinions lose their immunity when the circumstances in which they are expressed are such as to constitute their expression a positive instigation to some mischievous act. An opinion that corn dealers are starvers of the poor, or that private property is robbery, ought to be unmolested when simply circulated through the press, but may justly incur punishment when delivered orally to an excited mob assembled before the house of a corn dealer" (67–8).

Mill was concerned with limiting, not expanding, encroachments on free expression: "There is a limit to the legitimate interference of collective opinion with individual independence; and to find that limit, and maintain it against encroachment, is as indispensable to a good condition of human affairs as protection against political despotism" (7). Mill wanted individuals to be exposed to as wide a set of interpretations as possible without prejudging their truth: "But it is the privilege and proper condition of a human being, arrived at the maturity of his faculties, to use and interpret experience in his own way. It is for him to find out what part of recorded experience is properly applicable to his own circumstances and character" (70). More specifically—and this relates to those who supported the protest—Mill adamantly opposed those advocating public interference with the right of free expression based on feeling: "No one, indeed, acknowledges to himself that his own standard of judgement is his own liking; but an opinion on a point of conduct, not supported by reasons, can only count as one person's preference; and if the reasons when given, are a mere appeal to a similar preference felt by other people, it is still only many people's liking instead of one" (8–9).

Tator's turning of Mill on his head seems unworthy of someone protesting misrepresentation. Mill explicitly and clearly defends open discussion in the public realm, not censorship of such discussion or presentation of a point of view.

A second misuse of Mill is even more insidious and dishonest. Mill was concerned about the nature and limits of the power that can be legitimately exercised by society over the individual; there is a limit to the legitimate interference of collective opinion with individual independence. His book, *On Liberty*, aims at restricting collective power as much as is reasonable in a democratic society. It is an explicit, clarion call for freedom of conscience, freedom of expressing and publishing different opinions, and freedom of association. When there is a risk of damage to an individual or the public, restrictions on speech and association are warranted. But Mill was referring to someone screaming "Fire!" in a crowded theatre when there is no fire. Mill would defend the rights of the protesters to misrepresent those they criticized, or even to misuse himself as a supporter, even as they protested against the misrepresentation of Black history.

Mill rejects restricting freedom of speech because a group claims that its feelings are hurt by that speech or that the speech does not represent their character or their history adequately or fairly. Thus, in *Utilitarianism*, which deals more with the common good than with individual liberty, Mill says explicitly that personal (or group) hurts, however painful, are to be considered only if they are pains in which society as a whole has an interest. He was interested in objective standards and the interests of humanity collectively. He believed that particular pains should not be the basis for determining public morality.

Mill is explicit and unequivocal in claiming that discussion or public presentations, whether correct or incorrect, are not to be suppressed on grounds of causing personal pain or pain in a particular group. One may agree or disagree with him, but to claim as a supporter one such as Mill who is so opposed to one's position is dishonest—and even more so when the perpetrator is seemingly so anxious about historical misrepresentation.

Characteristically, protesters dubbed those who opposed the boycott as lackeys of the rich and the powerful. For example, Lorrie Goldstein is a journalist with a reputation for supporting underdog causes. He did not support the boycott. Consequently, Arnold Auguste, editor of *Share*, the leading Black newspaper and a strong supporter and leader of the boycott, alleged: "Garth's support is in the corridors of power," and hence Lorrie Goldstein must be walking in those passages. In other words, anyone not supporting the Black protest had to be in league with those in power, if not in their actual pay.[43]

The issue became whether one supported the powerless or sold out to the powerful. It was the language of Third Worldism imported into the domestic arena. Anyone who disagreed with the protest was not regarded as having any valid position whatsoever.[44] Instead of considering the issue as something to be debated, protesters immediately branded their opponents as in the pay of those with power. Integrity of heart and respect for human beings who differ were lacking among many of the leaders of the *Show Boat* protest. They tended to use a rhetoric that was provocative and highly charged rather than language that was fair-minded and accurate.[45] This tendency became self-destructive when it extended to accusing all those opposed to their position of being aligned with the rich and powerful and to claiming that Jews controlled the outcome because they were rich and powerful.

THE PROTEST AND ANTI-SEMITISM

Jews were involved in the controversy in yet another and very different way—not as advocates on its behalf, but as victims of the protest. This was critical in determining the failure of the boycott. It was not a role that Jews chose but one in which they were cast. Though Jews dominated creation and production of the show, helped decide whether the major charitable fundraiser—the central symbolic focus of the protest—should continue sponsorship, and became the major non-Black supporters of the protest by urging withdrawal, with one Jewish organization actually cancelling its sponsorship, their main role was passive. The portrayal of Jews and the symbolism of that portrayal became crucial to the controversy in both the non-Jewish and the Black communities. Ironically, though Black protesters were focused on criticizing the portrayal of Blacks by non-Blacks, some of their members' portrayal of Jews became, I believe, the turning point in determining the effectiveness of the protest.

On 9 July 1993, Arnold Auguste published an open letter in *Share* addressed to "Garth," in which he accused the Canadian Jewish Congress of "rank hypocrisy" for refusing to "turn against the rich, although somewhat arrogant, powerful, well-connected, rising star" rather than supporting "a bunch of Black folks." Auguste apparently never learned the lesson that bell hooks[46] taught—that Blacks should resist passively consuming images constructed by Black folks just as steadfastly as images created in the white imagination. Unfortunately, Auguste neglected the complementary part of the core dictum of cultural racist analysis—the duty to be self-critical about one's own representations.[47] He accused the United Way of choosing "to support power and privilege over people." As he summarized his view in the same issue: *Show Boat* "will continue to represent, for us, the tyranny of money and power over the helplessness of the powerless."

Certainly, proponents of the boycott continued to accuse their opponents of being in the pay of those with power and money. Stephnie Payne, for example, queried Mr. Doldrom, a 43-year-old Black high school teacher opposing the boycott, by asking him how much he was being paid for taking his stand. In a more universal version of this individual libel, Auguste asserted: "One can only be a racist if one has power."[48] Those who identified themselves as the powerless were evidently free to engage in negative stereotyping of other groups.

Since the controversy was largely about the representation of Blacks in a theatrical production, it is ironic that it was the image of Jews projected by Blacks in the political drama that became a turning point in the effort of the Black protesters and their supporters to enlist backing for the boycott. The same people who associated opponents of the boycott with being in power or in the pay of those in power were also the ones who easily slipped into anti-Semitic remarks.[49] Marc Grushcow summarized a variety of these slips—"Stephnie Payne's comment that Jewish writers are responsible for the negative portrayal of blacks; Dudley Law's references to Shylock at a North York Board of Education meeting; and articles and editorials in the black community newspaper, *Share*, which equate the Holocaust with Wounded Knee and claim that Jews receive a disproportionate share of United Way funding."[50]

Furthermore, instances of anti-Semitism were not rare and isolated, as I first believed. The Payne supporter who said of her accusers that they were asking for a "pound of flesh" perhaps did not recognize that this was the accusation hurled at Shylock, which evoked both the false charges against Jews of "Christ killer" in the past, going back to the Christian gospels, and the charge of ritual cannibalism used against Jews in European pogroms. But Arnold Auguste, publisher of *Share*, cannot claim the same historical innocence. He began an editorial with his own testimony that he had always admired Jews and defended them. He was the only one in his community to support Israel in the Six Day War. He wrote: "I felt a greater kinship with them. I felt both races had a common bond." As Shelby Steele wrote in "Breaking Our Bond of Shame": "There is an underlying kinship that blacks and Jews in America have always shared. And though it once inspired a fruitful cooperation, I believe it is now the source of much bitterness between us."[51]

There was also a failure by some protesters to recognize that identifying Jews as a race is racist, even if one accepts the dubious proposition that the Blacks can be identified as a single race.[52] Whatever it is to be Jewish, race is not the common factor that creates that community—note the 50,000 Black Ethiopian Jews airlifted to Israel, the Chinese Jews, and the Jews of India.

The leaders of the protest identified Jews with power. Certainly, Jews are now disproportionately represented among those with power and privilege in Toronto, but Jews are not a dominant group and are not even significantly represented in the higher reaches of finance in Canadian banks, insurance companies, and many industries. Nevertheless, many Blacks involved in the protest identified Jews, and no others, as a group with power and privilege. Sidelining this phenomenon and characterizing it as simply "a ripple effect" of the alleged cultural racism itself[53] understates the significance of this expression of anti-Semitism both for the outcome of the controversy and for what it says about those who used the expression and those who did or did not respond to anti-Semitic references.

In the United States, the Anti-Defamation League's *Survey on Anti-Semitism and Prejudice in America* (1992) found that a much larger proportion of Blacks than whites believed that Jews had "too much power in the business world." In the "Highlights" of the survey results, the report claimed that, though "the Jewish community, especially in the United States, has gained a lot of respect—even if it is sometimes grudgingly given," that respect is rendered "not because of the principles for which it [the Jewish community] stands or because of the causes it fights or for its intellectual and cultural contributions, but because of its wealth and power."[54] I do not know of an equivalent survey of Blacks in Canada indicating a disproportionate and large number of Blacks who accuse the Jews of controlling the media, wielding too much power, and so on, but among the Black boycott leaders in Toronto, a vocal few used a similar type of anti-Semitic rhetoric.

The emergence of Black anti-Semitism and the way in which it was articulated indicated that the controversy over *Show Boat* was not just about racism, but about perceived power and privilege and the negative, anti-Semitic association of Jews with that power and privilege. Perhaps, as Rabbi Hertzberg suggests,[55] a fundamental cause of both perceived racism and anti-Semitism is a discrepancy in privilege and power: "Almost everywhere in the West, anti-Semitism can be found among two groups: poor people who feel dispossessed, or are afraid of being dispossessed, and a variety of ideologues for whom anti-Semitism is a useful weapon in what they believe is a political struggle." The evidence that

Hertzberg cites certainly seems to find a parallel in the *Show Boat* protest. "All of the surveys made during the last few decades have shown that black Americans are markedly more anti-Semitic than whites . . . Among better educated and more progressive blacks one in four has anti-Semitic views such as 'Jews have too much power in business' (compared with two in five reported in a general survey [of Blacks])." Certainly, Martin Knelman, in a study of the Toronto controversy, concluded, "The *Show Boat* furore is less about a venerable old musical than it is about empowerment, control, and censorship."[56]

But if it was a fight over power, the Black leadership organizing the protest took a path that doomed its effort. Further, Blacks in Canada are not powerless. Nor is there any parallel in the statistics about Blacks in the United States, where seventy-five per cent of Black infants are born to unwed mothers, half of whom are teenagers, where the largest causes of death for Black men are either murder or suicide, where "Blacks comprise twelve percent of the population but account for forty-five percent of all deaths by fire," and where "forty-seven percent of all black seventeen-year-olds are functionally illiterate."[57] In Canada, there is no comparison to the hopelessness and despair that haunt the Black ghettos of U.S. inner cities, except perhaps among some Native reserves, though Blacks and Portuguese are evidently disproportionately directed away from pursuing a college education.

Anti-Semitism is not invoked in an effort, akin to that of American radical Blacks, to drive a wedge between previous allies and thereby foster a separatist movement opposed to integration. The anti-Semitism may not have been intended to destroy a historical alliance but may have been "the result of higher expectations black folk have of Jews. This perspective holds Jews to a moral standard different from that extended to other white ethnic groups, principally owing to the ugly history of anti-Semitism in the world, especially in Europe and the Middle East. Such double standards assume that Jews and blacks are 'natural' allies, since both groups have suffered chronic degradation and oppression at the hands of racial and ethnic majorities."[58]

If the protest and the anti-Semitism that seeped from it were not the expression of the desperate against the perceived powerful, what were they about? And why did the Black leadership allow the protest to be infected with anti-Semitism? Certainly, it was the use of anti-Semitism that turned many non-Jews and Jews away from supporting the Black protest. Just before the meeting at which the United Way first voted on continuing its involvement in the charitable evening, I had the impression that non-Jewish businesses and a number of important non-Jewish business leaders would cancel their financial support for the United Way if the charity surrendered to the demands of the protesters, but this possibility did not seem to influence the debate or the vote. In fact, it looked to me as if a majority might support cancellation because they believed that the United Way should not be involved in controversy; or thought that if the Blacks felt they were hurt, the United Way should support them; or did not want the Black community to withdraw from participation in the United Way after the great progress that had been made in obtaining their inclusion.

No one seemed to support the protest because they agreed with the protesters' analysis of *Show Boat* or because they thought that the protest was just. However, in the period between the conducting of an informal survey of board members and the meeting at which the first vote was held—in fact, just three days before that critical meeting—an issue of *Share* came out with the strongest and clearest anti-Semitic statements up to that time, including false accusations that Jews controlled the United Way and obtained a disproportionate amount of its funds for Jewish charities.

At that meeting, the only support that the protesters obtained on the board came from two members who claimed that if the Blacks felt victimized by the production of *Show Boat* that should be enough to justify withdrawal of the United Way's sponsorship of the charitable evening. There were, of course, other factors that resulted in the defeat, but I believe that anger at anti-Semitism was the most significant. I now want to analyze all the factors more systematically, examining the role of the Jews and the Blacks, and use that analysis to say something about the respective identities and roles of the two groups.

IMPACT ON BLACKS AND JEWS

The Black leaders of the protest initially brought enormous energy and organizational skills to their efforts. The energy was focused, sustained, and applied on a number of fronts. Though some of the leaders' methods involved verbal intimidation and verbal abuse, which sometimes included threats of physical violence to silence Blacks who opposed the protest, there is no evidence whatsoever of any real physical threat being made to anyone. Opponents were accused of being in the pay of the establishment. There were threats, explicit and implicit, to use violence or to spare no method that might achieve the goal; Auguste wrote: "I will do whatever I have to do to make my stand perfectly clear."[59] The Black leaders demonstrated energy but also a rhetorical readiness to use coercive power. In reality, except for one minor incident between Stephnie Payne and another individual who was Black, all the protests were totally peaceful.

Those Blacks who supported the protest lacked significant material or intellectual influence in the wider political arena. There were no major Black contributors to the United Way who threatened to withdraw support, so any boycott that resulted would not significantly have reduced the money raised each year. (In fact, the United Way, in spite of a severe recession, raised more than ever before in the fall of 1993.) By contrast, the threat posed by the withdrawal of corporate support, if the United Way gave into the protest and withdrew its sponsorship, was seen to be real. Jews, though sizeable contributors, never made any formal threat to withdraw support, despite a great deal of speculation among some board members of the United Way that there might be a loss of such support if the organization gave in to the protesters. Many Jews on the board had material influence but did not threaten to use it either way. Given the overwhelming material forces on one side and the slight ones on the other, if the protesters' analysis—that this was a struggle between the powerful and the powerless—had been correct, the protest could not have developed any inroads in the United Way at all, let alone almost win the support of the board effectively to join the boycott because overwhelmingly, with some high-profile exceptions, the most vocal Black voices from the community supported the boycott. (Some Black leaders who occupied positions of prominence—specifically, the former lieutenant-governor of the province—supported the production of *Show Boat*.)

The intellectual critique of the boycott in the United Way was led by two women, one Jewish and the other a WASP, and two men, one Jewish and the other Chinese, all of whom had agonized over and studied the issue as well as consulting reasonably widely over a relatively long period. Various Jews were very active and very vocal in trying to influence the outcome in opposite directions. There was almost as much influence by prominent and respected Jews on the side of the Blacks as in opposition to them. The Jews on both sides, however, did not resort to threats to use coercive power.

Though the protesters cast the conflict in terms of power, it was really a fight over ideas. Both Blacks and Jews were split. Overwhelmingly, the majority of the Black voices that were heard seemed to support the boycott. The Black leadership of the protest cast the battle in terms of the powerless against the powerful in a battle over the representation of its group. Those Black leaders who overcame the efforts to delegitimize their views and spoke out against the protest did so in the name of freedom of expression as well as castigating the protesters for misrepresenting *Show Boat*. The Jews, even though slurred with anti-Semitic comments, were divided between those who viewed the protest as an unfair attempt at censorship and an illegitimate use of the threat of a boycott, and those who did not want to antagonize the Black community and were willing to allow the protesters' pain to determine public policy. The majority of Jews who were heard seemed to oppose the boycott, but it is not clear how large that majority was.

The most evident difference between the Black protesters and the Jews who both opposed and supported them was in the rhetoric associated with the various positions. None of the rhetoric of the Canadian Black protesters could be compared with the ravings of the spokesmen for the Nation of Islam in the United States[60] or Bal Thackeray, leader of Shiva Sen in India, who reportedly said of the Muslims that, if they "behaved like Jews in Nazi Germany," there would be "nothing wrong if they were treated as Jews were in Germany."[61] The rhetoric never got as bad as that used by Professor Leonard Jeffries, who teaches at the City College of New York, who attacked the Jews "as the historical enemies and exploiters of blacks."[62]

Yet the language appeared extreme by Canadian standards, even in describing the representation of Blacks in *Show Boat*. Payne, as I noted above, described the Blacks portrayed in *Show Boat* as "subhuman savages, dim-witted, childlike, lazy, drunk, irresponsible and devoid of any human characteristics"— a description so inaccurate as to be ludicrous. In fact, if *Show Boat* could be faulted for cultural racism, it would be for portraying Blacks as possessing a surfeit of "human sympathy, moral sacrifice, service to others, intelligence and beauty"—a portrayal based on an assimilationist and a homogenizing impulse, or what Cornell West called a "false universalism."[63]

Associated with this misuse of descriptive terminology was misuse of logic as well. For example, Dr. Odida T. Quamina, in the article in *Share* quoted above, leapt from the statement "I feel insulted," to "I am insulted," to "Someone is deliberately insulting me and my group," to "there is an organized group who, to defend their power and privilege, are out to insult me and my group."

The extremist rhetoric employed by radical Blacks was most pointedly directed at Jews. But the explanation for such rhetoric given for some American Black's use of anti-Semitic language—as a deliberate effort to "convert a relation of friendship, alliance, and uplift into one of enmity, distrust, and hatred"[64]—seems inappropriate in the Canadian context, since the Blacks sought out and welcomed Jewish support. Their strategy looked to building strength by seeking allies. However, the Black leaders of the protest adopted a rhetoric of alienation rather than one of inclusion and alliance, even though their goal was integration. The Black protesters were not isolationists or separatists like the American radical Blacks of the Nation of Islam, from whom some of the Black Canadians borrowed their rhetoric.

The power struggle among Blacks in Canada was between post-modernists, who saw at the centre of the debate issues of representation and were prepared to misrepresent in order to further their protest, and Blacks who defended the traditional system of coalition building in fighting against overt rather than cultural racism. Possibly the majority of Blacks were intimidated into silence by a style of rhetoric that had not been an integral part of the traditional Canadian idiom. None of the Black leaders seemed to advocate isolationism and separatism. However, they, in public at least, gave no evidence of any critical self-consciousness and failed to recognize that a protest movement cannot be built on a claim of respecting history and the sensitivities of the victimized, while at the same time either tolerate historical deformations or actually contribute to those distortions and indulge in racist remarks in the heated language of the protest.

The integrationist strategy, so much at odds with the language of some protesters, may have resulted from the Black experience in Canada. Despite Canada's endemic racism, that experience has not been equivalent to the suffering of Black Americans. "Unlike Canadian blacks, most of whom chose (or choose) Canada, American blacks have to deal with the ongoing legacy of slavery."[65] Thus, though the strategic goals of all the Black protesters seemed to be the same as the traditional integrationist goals of most Canadians, the tactics differed, as indicated by their failure to analyze the show itself in detail in order to demonstrate the moral, social, and ethical issues at stake. Their tactics relied on accusation rather than analysis. Their Jewish allies—as bleeding hearts or do-gooders—relied on empathy with the pain of the Blacks without making any claim to understanding that pain or making any effort to ascertain whether the pain felt merited the actions proposed.

In contrast, the opposition rested its case on freedom of artistic expression, sensitivity to Black feelings, clear recognition of a history of social deprivation, an accumulation of historical facts, and recognition that fundamental moral issues were at stake. The text of *Show Boat* was examined to ascertain the accuracy of the protesters' claims. But, in the end, the debate concerned not the authenticity of the claims but the validity of criteria of cultural racism, which condemned the show without any detailed analysis.[66]

JEWISH AND BLACK IDENTITY

Let me suggest briefly what all of this says first about Canadian Jewish and then about Canadian Black identity. There is no evidence that, in Canada, Jews are paranoid about Blacks, as sometimes seems to be the case in the United States.[67] Nor do the two groups feel the close kinship that American Jews and Blacks seem to possess, arising out of their twentieth-century collaboration in seeking justice. For those Jews in Toronto who allied themselves with the Black cause, the basis was empathy with the pain of Blacks responding to projected images rather than identification with the historical victimization of Blacks.[68] The Jews who opposed the Black position were also traditional allies of the Blacks. They grounded their case on critical analysis rather than on either fear of or, alternatively, identification with Blacks. Though they recognized the Black reaction to the show, and did not dismiss it or disregard it, they did not claim an emotional empathy with Black pain in viewing the show. More important, they did not believe that the felt pain justified a boycott. The Jewish opposition worked within an alliance with other Canadians, including some Blacks, to forge a position opposing the boycott.

The Black protesters, in contrast, appeared to be led by a coalition of Caribbean and African Blacks, and seemed to lack extensive and demonstrable support from Canadian-born Blacks, let alone from other communities. They seemed to be following a very mild version of American Black organizing, based on exploiting grievances and on public protests, without making reference to and seemingly ignorant of the Canadian history and pattern of Black protests and in spite of their own emphasis on the importance of knowing that history.[69] Their costliest error was a resort by a few leaders to a relatively mild version of the anti-Semitic sloganeering of some of the extremist U.S. Black leaders, whose pillorying of the Jewish community rested on an erroneous charge of the allegedly prominent role of Jews in the slave trade.[70] Further, the Canadian Black protesters did not follow the example of Chinese Canadians in the early 1980s who organized the community across Canada, used alliances with other established groups to create legitimacy, and put forth a clear case of abuse or racism as a target (a W5 show on CTV with camera shots of Chinese Canadians studying medicine while the narrator asserted that Chinese immigrants were taking the place of Canadians in Canadian medical schools) that required a united community to oppose it. Finally, they did not base their protests against wrongs by appealing to the dominant morality of society and, sometimes, the laws of that society—that is, in terms of universal standards aimed at the protection of all peoples. The Black protesters referred to particularistic feelings of hurt as the basis of their protest. They neglected to forge strong alliances either with other ethnic communities or with people or groups in positions of power; instead, they appealed to a dichotomy that identified them as the powerless and everyone else opposed as satraps of those in power. Further, the protest leaders learned nothing from their own failure. "*Show Boat* is a clear example of how the cultural power and racist ideology of individuals and institutions converge to further marginalize, exclude, and silence people of colour."[71] The events merely confirmed their prior, dogmatic convictions.

In reality, despite their accusing those who opposed the protest of being beholden to the powerful, in spite of some use of verbal intimidation, they still had a chance of winning. That opportunity began to dissipate, however, when a few leaders—beginning with Stephnie Payne's making a charge, in front of a CTV camera, that Jews were always the ones responsible for racist plays that denigrate Black people—started resorting to anti-Semitic rhetoric. Even worse, the other leaders did not dissociate themselves from such people and remarks.

The result of the protest was not simply failure of the protest but what I believe has been widespread discrediting among the wider Canadian community of those Black leaders involved in the protest. Such a response may have also occurred among the Black community. On the first night that I went to see *Show Boat*, over 15 per cent of the audience was Black. Further, the protest had effectively died once the show opened. Critics universally concluded that the show was both sensitive to Blacks and clearly not racist. The assessment that the protest was misdirected was reinforced one year later when Garth Drabinsky opened *Show Boat* on Broadway to rave reviews in African-American newspapers, one of which praised director Harold Prince for developing the musical's Black characters[72] and another (*Afro-American*) complimented him for erasing the "negative image of shiftless black Americans." I gained the impression that many segments of the Black community in Toronto became more fragmented and more disillusioned, both with their leadership and with themselves, as a result of this defeat.[73]

RATIONALIZING THE PROTEST

Those who defended the protest continue to accuse the United Way of Greater Toronto of being insincere in its anti-racist policies. They not only ignore any evidence to the contrary but fail to come to terms with the failure of the protest or the harm done to the Black community by it. Further, they continue to offer a rationale for their ideology of cultural racism.

One major theme of Henry and her colleagues' *The Colour of Democracy* is cultural racism, referred to as "democratic racism." It is characterized as a hegemonic ideology with an array of defences that support entrenched racial inequalities, which create a climate hostile to race-equity initiatives and redistribution of power. The focus of this critique is not racists per se, or "closet" racists, who avoid people of colour while advocating anti-discriminatory practices, or symbolic racists, who present abstract characterizations of Blacks as a group. Rather, its concern is with cultural racism and those who support institutions and practices that reinforce the values, attitudes, and beliefs of racists.

It is one thing to argue that, within a democracy, half or slightly more than half the population may harbour racist attitudes that affect public policy decisions; it is another to posit that those who take stands against policy proposals that are said to be intended to counter racist conditioning are then, by implication, either closet racists or unwitting fellow travellers. This is a primary error of the book's discussion of the *Show Boat* controversy. While railing against "intellectual sloppiness, dishonesty, fabrication, smear, and innuendo" (28) in the discussion of the *Show Boat* case, the book is intellectually sloppy and dishonest both in quoting Mill to interpret him to mean precisely the opposite of what he meant and in using innuendo to identify those who opposed the boycott's advocates as, in effect, closet racists or fellow travellers. Most important, the volume's analysis never adequately sets forth the position of those who opposed the boycott while shunting aside the anti-Semitic element as itself a preoccupation and distortion of closet racists or supporters of racists. In other words, instead of trying to explicate the anti-Semitic remarks, the book faults those who focused on those remarks for diverting the debate from the real issues and for manifesting insensitivity to the deep cultural racism aimed at people of colour. Those who zeroed in on the anti-Semitism were but part of the ripple effect of the closet racism that the boycotters were attacking.

By this reasoning, it is not the boycotters who created the controversy but the United Way's decision to sponsor the fundraiser that did. Further, according to these analysts, the refusal to comply with the boycotters' demands led many in the Black community to question the validity of the United Way's anti-racist policies. The authors never analyze whether those who questioned the anti-racist credentials of the United Way were right to do so. Instead, they imply that the United Way was guilty simply because some Blacks questioned the authenticity of its commitment to anti-racism. The authors seem ignorant of the implications of making charges by association—of condemning individuals, groups, and institutions not for what they do or don't do but for their failure to bow to those who criticize them because the critics happen to be charging them with abetting racism; those accused are a priori deemed to be guilty of fostering racism and to be insincere in their anti-racism. Though lacking the coercive power or methods, the mode of argument is identical to those used in Soviet or U.S. show trials when individuals had to prove their true communist or American credentials, since they were presumed to be guilty simply because they had been accused of failing a test of their true loyalties; in this case, the issue is whether they were true anti-racists.

The worst part of this ideology as ideology is not simply its inability to resolve inconsistencies in its position, or even the accusations that it levels against those who refuse to bow to its prejudgments, but its illogic. It has a propensity to make fundamental logical leaps and errors. For example, one illogical line proceeds as follows: since a network of values and ideas underwrites behavioural and institutionalized racism, anything that might possibly reinforce such values and ideas, and thereby contribute to cultural racism, should be prevented from occurring—a leap in judgment that lacks justifying arguments. This stance is akin to arguing that since evolutionary Darwinism underwrites social Darwinism, which in turn is sometimes used to justify the rule of the strongest, evolutionary Darwinism should be eliminated from our repertoire of ideas. The next and even larger jump is to suggest that all those who oppose elimination of representations considered demeaning are supporters of those who hold racist attitudes, if not closet racists themselves.

In the twentieth century, Jews have been leaders of moral crusades, including the very justifiable attack on racism. Some of them also end up in the vanguard of those making such irrational charges in the name of the pursuit of what is right and good. Carol Tator, one of the authors of the book, is a Jew and has been devoted to leading the movement against racism. She has been an exemplary leader in that role. However, there is no necessary connection between taking a moral position and ensuring that the position always has a rational foundation. Nor are all the targets of a moral crusade necessarily well chosen. As a result, Jews have also been a main target of such irrational attacks. Anne Golden, the president of the United Way, led the resistance to the demands of the protesters. The *Show Boat* controversy was not unusual in having Jews play leading roles on both sides of the controversy.

We now have to see where such rationales fit in the panoply of ideas about how various cultures can and should live together in the same society.

IMPLICATIONS

Varieties of Multiculturalism

I now want to explore the role of multiculturalism in this controversy and the implications for the Canadian identity. There are three types of multicultural cohabitation—"intolerant," "empowering," and "tolerant" or "cosmopolitan."

Intolerant cohabitation reflects the sum of the feelings of intolerance expressed by different communities. Behind this conception is the view that enjoyment of the arts should be limited to areas that do not offend another group's sensibilities. India tried to build multiculturalism, not on rules of civility and dialogue to which all the groups in society would adhere, but on the basis of groups' sensibilities as determined by each specific group: "One of the problems with secularism as it is practised in India is that it reflects the sum of the collective feelings of intolerance of the different communities and is not based on combining their respective capacities for tolerance. Any statement or action that causes the wrath of any of the major communities in India tends to be seen as something that should be banned. This trigger-happiness in the use of censorship sits uncomfortably with India's otherwise good record of tolerating freedom of expression."[74]

The affects and sensitivities of each community determine what should be tolerated. This type of multiculturalism does not seek to combine the respective capacities of each community for tolerance.

If intolerant multiculturalism is based on feelings and the heart, the empowering type is based on will and guts, and its essence is power. It is the central characteristic of American multiculturalism. "Multiculturalism [is] to empower, to give authority to students as members of certain preferred groups: blacks, Latinos, homosexuals, Asians."[75] Multiculturalism, when applied to U.S. Blacks, has been identified not only with Black empowerment but with anti-Semitism. "There is still no clear recognition of the extent to which it [Black anti-Semitism] is the imposition of an agenda of multiculturalism and 'diversity' that is responsible for making open, poisonous, anti-Jewish bigotry into a veritable fixture of campus political life."[76]

Though all forms of multiculturalism value diversity, the empowering variant expresses that diversity in a particular way: "Diversity gurus reject the very notion of universal values which unite Americans as Americans, and they are using multiculturalism as a siege weapon aimed at what turns out to be America's most vulnerable institution, the university. On the ground, where the battles are fought, the diversity agenda works not to bridge differences, but to stimulate a sense of minority grievance and to enable racial minorities, homosexuals and feminists to acquire and protect turf, secure jobs and resources, dilute standards, and reshape curriculum."[77]

So multiculturalism in general, rather than its specific U.S. form, gets blamed for the ills of division and power fights over money and positions that have infected U.S. civil society: "The diversity program, which grows stronger even as the list of atrocity stories grows longer, has become the single most virulent source of anti-Semitism in America today. . . The root cause, to borrow a once-popular term, is multiculturalism itself."[78]

The sort of multiculturalism that Puddington is attacking advances group interests and often reinforces anti-integrationist strategies of those groups in the quest for establishing the integrity of Black culture in opposition to interracial mixes and exchanges: "[American] Multiculturalism's blind spot does not lie in its understanding of liberalism, which the advocates of identity politics explicitly reject, but in its repression—in a Freudian sense—of cosmopolitanism, which represents a perspective that is erroneously associated with the liberal position. Liberalism calls for transcending racial and sexual difference in the name of the universal rights of human beings. Cosmopolitanism, on the other hand, entertains curiosity about these differences. It is 'color curious' rather than color-blind or color-bound."[79]

Cosmopolitan multiculturalism is built "On Tolerance," to quote the title of John Locke's famous treatise, written at a time when religious groups in Britain were trying to build a society based on a form of cohabitation while lacking any principles of tolerance to unite them. According to Locke, the only thing that we must be intolerant of is intolerance itself and that which leads to and produces it. We must be intolerant not of that which disturbs this or that particular community, but of that which offends the principles of tolerance of our entire community. We must be intolerant of that which threatens the norms that unite our communities—a positive sense of toleration. We must respect and attempt to understand the various and particular sensibilities that constitute our society, but we must never elevate any one group of sensibilities into a dictatorial role.[80]

Intolerant multiculturalism sees groups cohabiting by ostensibly attending to the particular sensibilities of each group; but instead of building and reinforcing the principles of tolerance, it exaggerates and undermines the sensibilities of each group, thereby reducing the space for mutual cooperation. In empowering multiculturalism, groups cohabit in terms of alliances of interests rather than any curiosity about differences. It is the collective version of liberal individualism, but one that emphasizes group rather than individual interests.

Tolerant multiculturalism, of which Canada offers a prime example, grounds itself in universal norms of tolerance, applicable to all parts of society. Canadian multiculturalism has shifted over the last two decades in the priority of one or other of its three foundations—full participation, intercultural communication, and heritage preservation. But it has been fairly constant in basing all of these on universal norms and standards and not catering to the pains and sensibilities of particular groups or an emphasis on empowering specific groups. In fact, I would suggest, the perception has become widespread that policies on the French-English issue have been determined by power politics and sensitivities rather than by universal norms, and this is why we have seen the fragmenting of the political consensus on which Canadian identity has been built. What may have been partially lost in the area of English-French relations has been incorporated into inter-ethnic politics. Inter-ethnic brokerage politics on the micro-scale has largely maintained the domination of rational and moral modes in opposition to appeals to either empowerment or group sensibilities.

All three forms of multiculturalism are opposed to individualistic liberalism, which assumes that humans are primarily and overwhelmingly individuals in pursuit of their own interests and willing to combine with other interests to advance their own. The basic unit in the liberal idea is the individual person, and groups are relevant only in so far as they promote the interests of individuals. Ethnic and racial differences are ultimately transcended in terms of the individual rights of human beings, which remove any significant meaning from group identity and relegate the group to a strictly instrumental role.

BLACK PERCEPTIONS OF SELF AND JEW

Most Blacks and Jews in Canada identify themselves with a Canadian multiculturalism based on pride in their own identity and history and in Canada's values, which respect diversity constructed on universal principles of individual rights and tolerance. Using epithets and historical distortions to victimize others, whether they make up a materially wealthy group or a relatively deprived group, does not enjoy widespread support. At the same time, artistic productions in Canada are not required to provide a comprehensive and all-encompassing representation of a group's history, nor necessarily to portray its members in a positive light. As well, in inter-group communication, civil behaviour, including refraining from branding and stereotyping the motives of others with whom one disagrees, is a requisite and a condition of building inter-ethnic alliances.

Nevertheless, there has emerged within the Black community a small cadre of leaders who do not support these norms and have adopted a purely "post-modern" method to construct a Black sense of self-identity and history, based on a collective memory of victimization and a construction of the Other as the Powerful Other, with Jews pre-eminent in that scenario. In this process, the popular arts play a prominent part. Art is seen by this cadre primarily as a tool in creating positive role models. When the models deviate, the art may be subjected to censorship.

I have no conclusive explanations for such self-defeating behaviour. But let me conjecture a bit (if only to contrast these speculations with the greater confidence that I feel in the explanation of the behaviour of the Jewish community). Let me deal with a number of questions that may produce a plausible explanation. Why *Show Boat*? Why was this musical chosen as an object of protest? Why did anti-Semitism insert itself into the rhetoric of opposition, without being paired, as in the United States, with isolationism as a goal? The integrationist objectives of virtually all Canadian and most American Blacks were retained. In other words, what do the subject matter and the style of the protest reveal about the character of the Black leaders who chose to launch the boycott?

Note that a central moral theme of *Show Boat* was a diatribe against anti-miscegenation laws, which made it illegal for races to intermarry. Since the strongest and most loyal and sacrificial love in the show is that between Julie, a Black person who looks white, and Magnolia, the white star of the show, the clear moral message is that colour is inconsequential in human relations. This is the overt message. But the covert one is another matter. Julie is lost in history. Unlike Magnolia's marriage, hers is not resurrected in the romantic happy ending. Even Julie's love for Magnolia must be felt at a distance, as she departs unknown and unmissed in a despairing slide downward into alcoholism.

So there appears to be a double message—an explicit one about racial harmony and human equality, and an implicit one, suggesting that an individual cannot escape her colour even if that person appears white, perhaps only because others will not let her. On the one hand: "I found no escape from the trap I was describing except the wholesale merging of the two races." On the other hand: "I was wrong to think that miscegenation could ever result in the elimination of color 'as a fact of consciousness,' if for no other reason than that (as Ralph Ellison bitingly remarked to me) the babies born of such marriages would still be considered black."[81]

Black is an accidental attribute of a person, no different in that respect than eye colour. Black is an inescapable, integral attribute of a person, if only because others insist that this be the case. The musical projects two very opposite messages, explicit and implicit. The Black protesters were equally ambivalent. Their objectives were integrationist and liberal. Their style was borrowed from American Blacks who were isolationist and racist. They had a vision of integration into the power structure and a style that ensured that they would be isolated and left out. But the fact that the rhetoric was borrowed seemed evident in its lack of venom. None of the protesters seemed to hold the conviction that "hatred is an element of dignity, that a proper respect for oneself and one's own is well expressed by a proper disrespect for others."[82]

There was none of the passionate hatred of Jews that is found in the rhetoric of radical, separatist, educated American Blacks. Phrases of hatred were used, but few if any protesters thought that the phrases arose out of either deeply felt convictions or a deeply ingrained pathology. They seemed more like temporary garments rented from a store recycling used clothing. At the same time, there was also none of the toughness and irreverence of the anti-Semitism of American street Blacks and rappers, who prize mean talk and give the impression that they are indomitable and do not give a damn for anyone or anything.[83]

In other words, the Canadian Black protesters' rhetoric of hatred and opposition suggested that they were ersatz American radicals without either a popular base or deep convictions. They chose *Show Boat* as a vehicle of protest not because it merited condemnation but because it so closely reflected their own ambivalences. The protest was weak and paradoxical just as the position of the Black leaders was weak and paradoxical—not because of their position in any power structure but because they felt neither physically tough nor morally strong. Like Julie, their protest and self-sacrifice end up in self-destruction, in an intellectual as well as moral decline, as they hold to their position without wrestling with its weaknesses or even recognizing the positions of those opposed to their stand.

Why did they evince this ambivalence and target a show that so ill-fitted their claims about cultural racism but so superbly mirrored their own state of mind? I speculate that it was because they were Canadian Blacks who had immigrated to Canada but were neither like other immigrants nor yet shared a collective narrative with Canadian-born Blacks. They had little of the history of oppression of American Blacks, so their pain did not go very deep. Further, theirs was much more the pain of colonialism, which had its own particular form of racism and oppression. However, because of Canada's proximity to the United States and its own history of racism,[84] they were not merely Blacks who originated in Jamaica or Guyana or Ghana—ethnics with a national home elsewhere. They were Blacks, made into and identified as Blacks by the racism of others. However, as a collectivity, Canadian Blacks lacked a common story, a narrative of their affliction that belonged to them, was widely known, and with which they could readily identify.

American Blacks and American Jews shared a narrative originating in slavery. Both groups had been subjected in their histories to discrimination and segregation. Both were forcefully expelled from their homeland. But American Blacks had no known homeland to which to return. They lacked a common language. Their narrative and experience, though remarkably similar to the Jewish tale of oppression, was fundamentally different. They had been subjected to heinous violence, not in the homelands that they left and that were now forgotten, but in the process of being transported and settled in the United States. The experience of Canadian Blacks was vastly different again and so diverse, given the variety of backgrounds. Further, unlike the vast majority of American Blacks, who lacked a common narrative because the country of origin was missing from the story,[85] Blacks in Canada had no shared narrative because they came from many countries. The story for most Canadian Blacks was much more akin to that of other immigrant groups who retained ties to their home countries. A protest against the representation of American Blacks in the later nineteenth century could not launch and develop a common narrative for Blacks in Canada. It is doubtful if any experience, other than an overt act of racism by the media or a major institution directed at Blacks, could have done the job.

Why then was *Show Boat* chosen by the protesters and so directly connected by them with its Jewish artistic creators, producers, and political patrons? Some Canadian Blacks wanted to create a community, not a separatist one, but a sense of a community that was Black. To do that, they needed to offer a common narrative of the Blacks in Canada. If such a tale were to be told, they wanted to be its tellers. They did not want a recurrence of the U.S. experience, in which Jews initially served as minstrels of Blacks in communicating to the white world. "I'll be honest. I hate them sometimes. Because they were minstrels. Al Jolson was a Jew and the Beastie Boys are Jews . . . It's the Jews making the money. They act like your friend but they're the number one pimps of niggas . . . Jews have done a majority of thieving from us."[86]

This perception of the role of Jews in the arts extended into the area of social policy: "During the 1930s and 1940s, Jews spearheaded the national campaign for anti-discrimination legislation . . . 'many of these laws were actually written in the offices of Jewish agencies, by Jewish staff people, introduced by Jewish legislators and pressured into being by Jewish voters. In addition, literally hundreds of court actions were taken by Jewish attorneys on behalf of Negro plaintiffs.'"[87] As West put it, in more historical terms and in the language of cultural deconstruction, "This Jewish entrée into the anti-Semitic and patriarchal critical discourse of the exclusivist institutions of American culture initiated the slow but sure undoing of the male WASP cultural hegemony and homogeneity."[88]

The fact is that Canadian Blacks have neither a need for Canadian Jews to play the role of minstrel nor any history of their doing so, except in the most general sense of Jews helping to create human rights legislation in Canada. In putting together a sophisticated and artistically brilliant show, Jews serve in effect as minstrels for American Blacks; their show was of course an import into Canada. Canadian Jewish politicians and producers became minstrels of the new continentalism, rather than defenders of Black rights. Black protesters responded by becoming ersatz American Blacks, a role that even Black Americans disdained.

Protesters' uncivil treatment of those who differed with them, borrowed from radical American Black separatists, intimidated and created fear of taking a stand among many Blacks who did not support the boycott. In such an atmosphere, Blacks opposed to the boycott found it difficult to take an open stand against it. When uncivil methods of typing all those in opposition as sell-outs to the interests of white or even Jewish power were employed, uncivil discourse became the norm. Further, there was a failure to separate a need for uplifting narratives of one's own people from the equally important principle of respect for artistic expression. Finally, Black protesters tolerated or indulged in gross distortions in representing both the musical *Show Boat* and history, all in the name of righting historical injustices.

The effort to build a Canadian Black identity in a post-modernist mould, built on the historical memory of victimization and the construction of the Other in terms of power and participation in that victimization, is doomed to failure in Canada and should fail anywhere. The paradigm of this construction has been developed by a minority of radical U.S. Blacks. One of the ironies is that a Canadian group of largely foreign-born Blacks sought to construct a community identity using a paradigm of the Other borrowed from radical

American Blacks and a concept of multiculturalism borrowed from ex-colonial countries. Further, some Black leaders chose to do so by targeting Jews as the core of the evil power behind this history of oppression, homogenizing and reifying Jews as a "race" in the process, including in those charges egregious distortions of fact and history. They boycotted *Show Boat* not for objective reasons but because this construction of themselves as victims and the Other as powers led by a Jewish core made such a selection inevitable, despite its inappropriateness for mobilizing Canadian Blacks.

Garth Drabinsky may well have been insensitive in choosing the great musical to open the North York Performing Arts Centre. But a small group of Canadian Blacks borrowed even more heavily from American Black radicals, who attempted to define their sense of victimization on a fragile and, I believe, erroneous platform of cultural racism, combined with a view of an oppressive Other that controls the levers of power. Fortunately, the effort failed, and the majority of Canadian Blacks and Jews did not fall into the trap of this effort at self-construction.

What I am suggesting is that the Black-led protest is better conceived of as performance art than as a significant act of political protest, an occasion that allowed those involved to act out their inconsistencies. It was not a coherent and well-targeted protest carried out with a means and a rhetoric to achieve political goals.

Imported "Jewish" Rhetoric

If this was the case, why was the protest treated so seriously by the Jewish community, whether in support or in opposition, while it was effectively ignored or dismissed by most of the establishment? Why did Jews on both sides base their response largely on an expression of empathy with the pain that Blacks allegedly experienced in watching *Show Boat?* These Jews may or may not choose to attend a performance of *The Merchant of Venice,* but they would all have been the first to protest censoring or boycotting of a performance. Why did a small group of prominent Jewish leaders deviate from the mainstream model of inter-ethnic alliances by basing their coalition building on what others felt rather than on any objective analysis of a claim or on opposition to clear breaches against shared, objective principles of justice?

Rather than using rational analysis, many Jews based their stance on empathy (the "bleeding hearts"), or negative stereotyping of themselves as incapable of identifying with the pain of the Other (the "do-gooders"), or a positive definition of themselves as prophets of peaceful inter-ethnic relations (the "social pacifiers"). Further, the ideology of cultural racism gave them a rationale for giving art primarily a moral role and thereby allowing a form of private artistic censorship to enter into political action. Just as the parallel group of Blacks has identified Jews with power, this group of Jewish leaders based its political position on stereotypical images of Blacks in terms of victimization.

One part of the reason for their ignoring rational analysis and "buying into" the ideology of cultural racism lies in the relationship, or absence thereof, between Blacks and Jews in Canada. In contrast to the U.S. situation, some Black protesters in Canada expressed their identification and commonality with the history of Jewish oppression and victimization, a version of Black-Jewish relations opposed by many American Blacks. They appealed to Jewish moral leadership on race relations. Reciprocally, many Jews identified with Black pain and victimization in the abstract.

Blacks and Jews in Canada are not half-brothers and -sisters who share a love-hate relationship. Canadian Jews share none of the closeness with Blacks and history of common political struggles that characterize the U.S. experience. Canadian Jews did not commit the "original sin" (in the pathological unconscious of the Nation of Islam) of American Jews in their inordinate and tremendously disproportionate involvement in the front ranks of the civil rights movement. Further, in that struggle, American Jews were acting not as Jews but as Americans and liberals. "The men and women who fought for school integration and black voter registration didn't see themselves in terms of their ethnic or religious identity but rather as driven by a shared aversion of all forms of inequality based on race, religion, or nationality."[89]

In contrast, Rabbi Dow Marmur indicated that it was a Jewish commandment, not a liberal one, that demanded identification with and support for the pain that the Blacks claimed was inflicted on them by the Toronto production of *Show Boat*. Further, those Jews who supported, acquiesced in, or opposed the boycott had no phallic anxiety or fear of Blacks. The Blacks whom they knew were mostly very well-educated professionals, and they had only passing acquaintance with sales clerks, real estate agents, bank tellers, civil servants, hard-working skilled people who repaired appliances or fixed pipes, and dedicated domestic servants. Canadian Jews lacked the experience of encounters with undereducated, unemployed, irreverent, and tough-talking Black youth from the ghettos on whom they could project their anxieties and fears. Further, though the educated Black leaders of the protest used a rhetoric that spoke of isolation, their goal was to forge an alliance and not intentionally to sow seeds of enmity, distrust, and hatred, though the rhetoric used around the *Show Boat* incident by a few Black protesters did alienate others by characterizing the Jews as having obtained disproportionate benefits and control over the United Way and, by implication, other institutions in society.

If we examine the positions of Jews (including me) who opposed the protesters, our criticism was articulated before anti-Semitism became so closely identified with the protest. Further, the rationale for the opposition was based on Canadian, and not specifically Jewish, values. Nor was there any self-interested pleading on behalf of Jews when the anti-Semitism was articulated. It may be the case that an impetus for American Black anti-Semitic rhetoric arises from an awareness of Jewish sensitivity, hence ensuring at least some public response to a protest, but if the Canadian Black protesters were consciously or unconsciously playing copycat, it did not work. In Canada, Jewish hypersensitivity seemed absent. The Jewish response was cool on all sides. Attention was very concentrated before the protest became identified with the anti-Semitic rhetoric. The only effect of the association with anti-Semitism was to turn potential supporters away. If the use of anti-Semitism by Black protesters was an effort at demagoguery intended to enhance their political power, following the American pattern, it was a distinct failure.

At the same time, if Jews and others displayed any hesitation and carefulness in taking a position opposed to the protest, they did so not because they feared playing into the hands of white racists but because they wanted to understand the basis and grounds of the protesters' position and not alienate them from the alliance already forged between Blacks and other groups through such institutions as the United Way.

In sum, the absence of a hysterical Jewish response to the employment of anti-Semitic rhetoric by some leaders of the protest can be attributed to three factors: the security that Jews feel about their place in Canada; the protest leaders' poor strategy of choosing *Show Boat* as a trigger for anti-Semitic remarks, combined with the lack of venom and power in their employment of that rhetoric; and, most important, the relative strength of the institutional arrangements introduced in Canada in the last twenty-five years that protect all Canadians against racist attacks.[90]

However, the existence of Jewish support for the protest, in spite of its weak foundation, can be explained by the numbers of bleeding hearts, do-gooders, and social pacifiers in the Jewish community. Their (and my) attitudes are very valuable except when isolated from the ethical norm required to unite all three—a clear identification with universal norms of social justice.

Despite the complementarity between the minority of Black leaders who organized the protest and a smaller but prominent minority of Jewish leaders who supported or acquiesced in it, the process of identity formation differed enormously in the two communities. Both groups favouring the boycott, minorities within their respective communities, borrowed from their American counterparts; both were very different from the Canadian mainstream. The dominant strain of Canadian leadership has organized Canadian society on the basis of liaisons between communities, based on universal principles applicable to all communities, not on empathy for the victimization of another community or compacts of mutual interest. Canadian multiculturalism is premised on respect for rights and freedom of artistic expression, predominant values in the Canadian Jewish organized ethos. However, I speculate that the prominent Blacks in Canada who hold such views were not able to lead their community because they saw themselves not primarily as leaders of the Black community, but as community leaders who happened to be Black.

In contrast, the Jewish-Canadian community has been thoroughly Canadianized but remains a community, even though a prominent minority in the leadership identified with the Black leadership of the protest movement. In all aspects of the controversy within the Canadian Jewish community, civility and respect for the views of others remained guiding principles, even if Black protesters linked, in the abstract, those who did not support the boycott with the powerful Other. There were no attacks on the other Jews as sell-outs to powerful interests. Respect for freedom of artistic expression was maintained, along with respect for freedom to decide which commercial artistic productions of support or not support. There was no endorsement of the historical or contemporary validity of the claims of the Black leadership of the protest by most Jews who supported the boycott. However, that same small core of Canadian Jews (who cross religious affiliations with respect to Orthodox, Conservative, and Reform, but whose leadership is largely Reform) also seemed willing to ignore their own victimization in terms of historical misrepresentation by the very group with which they identified as victims. They identified with the self-sacrificing Julie who viewed Magnolia's victimization by her mother as more important than her own. Julie so loved the other that she overlooked the other's easy willingness to accept Julie's sacrifice without any protest.

CONCLUSION

In conclusion, contrary to those who see Canada as the first post-modern society, this essay argues that Canada is a very strongly pre-modern society, holding solidly to a core set of basic values. However, it is also a modern society, insisting on historical truth, but not at the cost of censoring artistic expression. Also and paradoxically, Canada is post-modern in the sense of building a pluralistic mosaic of a specific form of tolerance on a pre-modern moral foundation and modern respect for both historical truth and freedom of artistic expression. Most Jews in Canada and, I believe, the majority of Black Canadians base their identity on these premises.

NOTES

1   "Blacks" as a term of reference is capitalized in this essay, contrary to the custom in most publications.

2   North York is one of the cities that make up the federated municipality of Metropolitan Toronto.

3   Discussions on Black-Jewish relations in Canada are rare, reflecting the negligible connection of the two groups. Even in Henry et al., *The Colour of Democracy*, which

discusses the *Show Boat* controversy, there is only a glancing reference to the anti-Semitic elements of the protest and none to Black-Jewish relations.

4   This seems to characterize the initial stages of many protest movements. "The initial black diasporan response was a mode of resistance that was [moralistic in content and communal in character]." Cornel West, *Keeping Faith: Philosophy and Race in America* (New York: Routledge, 1993), 17.

5   Richard Gwyn, a *Toronto Star* columnist, in his D.G. Willmot Distinguished Lecture at Brock University, St. Catherines, Ontario, on 23 November 1994 (reprinted in the *Toronto Star*, 26 Nov. 1994, section B), argued that Canada was a pioneer in forging the first post-modern state, based on "multiple loyalties among their citizens, of individuals possessing multiple identities, and of an ever-shifting balance between the opposed virtues of unity and divisions, of solidarity and segregation . . . (in) the curious, fractured, radically decentralized nation-state of Canada" (B5).

6   Three film versions have been made of the musical *Show Boat*, the most famous being the 1937 film with Irene Dunne, Allan Jones, and Paul Robeson.

7   Jerome Kern (1885–1945) was an American Jewish composer and wrote over 1,000 songs for more than 100 stages shows and films, *Show Boat* being his greatest success. Oscar Hammerstein II was the librettist who pioneered in developing light musical comedy into an integrated dramatic form. He is best known for his collaboration with Richard Rodgers in *Oklahoma* (1943), *Carousel* (1945), *South Pacific* (1949), *The King and I* (1951), and *The Sound of Music* (1959). Both Kern and Hammerstein won Academy Awards for their film songs.

8   Edna Ferber was an American Jewish journalist, novelist, and playwright, originally from Kalamazoo, Michigan. She wrote such best-selling novels as *Cimarron* and *Giant*, both adapted into Academy Award-winning films, and, with George S. Kauffman, well-known plays such as *Dinner at Eight* and *Stage Door*, both also filmed.

9   Garth Drabinsky, through his company Live Entertainment in Canada, filed a $20.5 million suit in Ontario Court General Division, against the Ontario government, alleging that the Anti-Racism Secretariat in the province's Ministry of Citizenship had funded the coalition and other groups that had protested against the musical.

10   Henry et al., *The Colour of Democracy*, 219.

11   *Toronto Star*, 23 Sept. 1993, A12.

12   *Toronto Life*, June 1993, 36.

13   *Toronto Star*, 6 May 1993, 8.

14   Henry Mietkiewicz, "*Show Boat* Sails On," ibid., 27 March 1993, K3.

15   Arun Mukherjee, "The Third World in the Dominant Western Cinema: Responses of a Third World Viewer," in Ormand McKague, ed., *Racism in Canada* (Saskatoon: Fifth House, 1991), 151–8. Cf. Mukherjee, *Toward an Aesthetic of Opposition: Essays on Literature, Criticism and Cultural Imperialism* (Stratford, Ont.: William Wallace Publishers, 1988).

16   Adrienne Shadd, "Institutionalized Racism and Canadian History: Notes of a Black Canadian" (appendix, no page numbers) in Carl E. James, ed., *Seeing Ourselves:*

Exploring Race, Ethnicity and Culture (Oakville, Ont.: Sheridan College of Applied Arts and Technology, 1989), reprinted in McKague, ed., *Racism in Canada*, 4.

17 West, *Keeping Faith*, 5.

18 "*Show Boat* is seen as an example of both misrepresentation and cultural appropriation;" Henry et al., *The Colour of Democracy*, 220.

19 *Toronto Star*, 14 April 1993, A13.

20 *Globe and Mail*, 12 March 1993, A21.

21 *Share*, 13 May 1993.

22 The rejectionist argument uses an essentialist rhetoric to argue "that the fight for black representation and recognition must reflect or mirror the real black community, not simply the negative and depressing representations of it." West, *Keeping Faith*, 18.

23 The social-engineering argument "claims that since any form of representation is constructed—that is selective in light of broader aims—black representation (especially given the difficulty of blacks gaining access to positions of power to produce any black imagery) should offer positive images of themselves in order to inspire achievements among young black people." Ibid., 18.

24 Behavioural racism need not be only about behaviour, but if it includes beliefs, it does so because those beliefs can be connected with action.

25 *Akili Newsletter*, 1 no. 2 (Aug. 1993), 4. The *Akili Newsletter: Knowledge through Time* is published by the Centre for African-Canadian Studies, North York.

26 Ibid., 5.

27 "The foreigner is hypersensitive beneath his armor as activist or tireless 'immigrant worker.' He bleeds body and soul, humiliated ... who embodies the enemy, the traitor, the victim." Julia Kristeva, *Strangers to Ourselves*, trans. Leon S. Roudiez (New York: Columbia University, 1991), 6.

28 The block of tickets was actually co-purchased by the Canadian National Institute for the Blind (CNIB), but the CNIB let the United Way decide whether or not to withdraw from the fundraising event.

29 My involvement became intimate when Joseph Wong asked me, given my past connection with other ethnic groups and Black African refugee communities, to look into the issue. Some of the material in this essay is taken from that analysis. As a board member, I took part in the initial debates and voting.

30 *Toronto Star*, 6 May 1993, 8.

31 Quotes from Henry et al., *The Colour of Democracy*, 219 and 220.

32 Michel Feher identifies this claim as a doctrine of recovery psychology. Cf. "The Schisms of '67: On Certain Restructurings of the American Left, from the Civil Rights Movement to the Multiculturalist Constellation," in Berman, ed., *Blacks and Jews*, 285 note.

33 *Canadian Jewish News*, 22 July 1993, letter to the editor.

34 Ibid., 22 Dec. 1994, 7.

35 Though willing to involve themselves passively in collective support of a boycott as a form of censorship, individually they did not participate in a boycott. Members of the

board bought the tickets to which the organization had committed itself; they sold the tickets to their friends in order that the Friends of Hebrew University not lose its deposit and the university suffer because they cancelled the sponsorship of the evening.

36 Cf. S.A. Speisman, *The Jews of Toronto: A History to 1937* (Toronto: McClelland and Stewart, 1979).

37 *Share*, 16 no. 14, 22 July 1993, 1.

38 *Share*, 16 no. 14, 22 July 1993.

39 Cf. Andrew Hacker, "Jewish Racism, Black Anti-Semitism," in Berman, ed., *Blacks and Jews*, 161.

40 I note Stein's synagogue affiliation to indicate that, though Reform Jews appeared prominent in support of the Blacks, significant support also came from members of Conservative and Orthodox synagogues.

41 Sympathetic but negative versions of Shylock have been produced frequently, with no organized boycotts emerging from the Jewish community, though there have been protests about specific portrayals.

42 John Stuart Mill, *On Liberty,* (Indianapolis, Ind.: Bobbs-Merrill Company, 1975), 68. All my quotes are taken from this edition.

43 The three major Toronto newspapers were accused of supporting the production because they were recipients of large ads.

44 What is most notable, even in retrospective accounts such as Henry et al., *The Colour of Democracy*, is the failure to present the position of opponents with any degree of adequacy or accuracy, while remonstrating with the larger community for insensitivity to accurate representation in fiction of the past history of Blacks.

45 Cf. André Alexis' book review in the *Globe and Mail*, 8 Jan. 1994, which accuses Dionne Brand of committing these same excesses in her essays in *Bread out of Stone* (Toronto: Coach House Press, 1994).

46 Bell hooks, also known as Gloria Watkins, Distinguished Professor of English at City College in New York, is the author of *Black Looks: Race and Representation and Outlaw Culture: Resisting Representations* (Boston: South End Press, 1992).

47 "I call demystificatory criticism 'prophetic criticism'—the approach appropriate for the new cultural politics of difference—because while it begins with social structural analysis it also makes explicit its moral and political aims. It is partisan, partial, engaged and crisis-centred, yet always keeps open a skeptical eye to avoid dogmatic traps, premature closures, formulaic formulations or rigid conclusions." West, *Keeping Faith,* 23.

48 *Share*, 6 May 1993.

49 Jeff Henry described the identifying of some of the protesters with anti-Semitism as an attempt to paint the whole protest as anti-Semitic, and that, in turn, he charged was a deliberate effort to divide Jews and Blacks. Cf. the report in *Share*, 16 no. 31 (16 Nov. 1993), of Henry's remarks in a forum on lessons from the *Show Boat* controversy.

50 *Canadian Jewish News*, 18 July 1993, 14.

51 In Berman, ed., *Blacks and Jews*, 179.

52 As Ellen Willis noted in "The Myth of the Powerful Jew," in Berman, ed., *Blacks and Jews*, 188: "Jewishness in not a racial category—since, on the contrary, the definition of Jews as one people is an offense to the very idea of pure races—to identify fully as Jews is to refuse to define ourselves in racial terms, to repudiate race as a way of categorizing people, and to oppose all institutions and practices that perpetuate racial hierarchies."

53 Cf. Henry et al., *The Colour of Democracy*, 222.

54 The quotes from the *Highlights from an Anti-Defamation League Survey on Anti-Semitism and Prejudice in America* (Nov. 1992) are taken from Arthur Hertzberg's article, "Is Anti-Semitism Dying Out?" *New York Review of Books*, II no. 12 (24 June 1993), 51–7.

55 Hertzberg, "Anti-Semitism Dying Out?" 51.

56 *Toronto Life*, (June 1993), 36.

57 Cf. Julius Lester, "The Lives People Live," in Berman, ed., *Blacks and Jews*, 171–4.

58 Cornel West, "On Black-Jewish Relations," in Berman, ed., *Blacks and Jews*, 150–1. As Dinnerstein put it, "both Jews and blacks wanted civil rights legislation and frequently their interests meshed." *Anti-Semitism*, 208.

59 *Share*, 6 May 1993, 8.

60 The bible of the new anti-Semitism is *The Secret Relationship between Blacks and Jews*, an official publication of the Nation of Islam that boasts 1,275 footnotes in the course of 334 pages.

61 Cf. *Economist* (13–19 November 1993), 38–40.

62 Cf. Jim Sleeper, "The Battle for Enlightenment at City College," in Berman, ed., *Blacks and Jews*, 239–63.

63 West, *Keeping Faith*, 17.

64 Gates, "The Uses of Anti-Semitism," 221.

65 André Alexis, "Taking a Swipe at Canada," *Globe and Mail*, 8 Jan. 1994.

66 The requirement of disinterested, dispassionate, and objective inquiry is associated by some scholars of cultural racism with the nineteenth-century social critic Matthew Arnold (*Culture and Anarchy*) and his alleged effort to cement a stable and *secular* civil culture based on universal principles. West, *Keeping Faith*, 7. In specifically linking culture with safety, Arnold (Matthew, not Auguste) explicitly viewed Blacks as a source of threat.

67 Cf. Norman Podhoretz's classic essay, "My Negro Problem—and Ours," which first appeared in *Commentary* in 1963 and is reprinted in Berman, ed., *Blacks and Jews*, 76–96.

68 "Jews are convinced that they have much in common with blacks, because the two groups share histories of oppression and suffering." Julius Lester, "The Lives People Live," in Berman, ed., *Blacks and Jews*, 165.

69 Cf. Robin Winks, *The Blacks in Canada: A History* (Montreal: McGill-Queen's University Press; New Haven: Yale University Press, 1971), and James Walker, *Racial Discrimination in Canada: The Black Experience*, Historical Booklet No. 41 (Ottawa: Canadian Historical Association, 1985).

70 This accusation, even though irrelevant and taken totally out of context, has been supported by scholarship indicating Jewish involvement in the Atlantic slave trade. "Jewish

students of Jewish history . . . have produced a significant body of scholarship detailing the involvement of our ancestors in the Atlantic slave trade and Pan-American slavery." Ralph A. Austen, "The Uncomfortable Relationship: African Enslavement in the Common History of Blacks and Jews," *Tikkun* (March/April 1994), 66.

However, that involvement was minuscule. David Brion Davis, Sterling Professor of History at Yale and author of *The Problem of Slavery in Western Culture and Slavery and Human Progress*, writes in "The Slave Trade and the Jews," *New York Review of Books*, 41 no. 21 (22 Dec. 1994), 15: "Jews had no important role in the British Royal African Company or in the British slave trade of the eighteenth century, which transported by far the largest share of Africans to the New World . . . Between 1658 and 1674 the Jewish investment in the slave-trading West India Company seems to have risen to 6 or even 10 percent. Keeping in mind that the Dutch share of the trade accounted for only 16 percent of the total, one sees how small the involvement was, and it is as close as Jews ever came to 'dominating' the nefarious Atlantic traffic."

71 Henry et al., *The Colour of Democracy*, 223.

72 *Amsterdam News.* Ironically, one of the few Black criticisms against *Show Boat* when it first opened was by a correspondent of the *Amsterdam News*, who complained of its "lazy, good-natured, lolling darkey" stereotypes and charged that it "constituted 'anti-Negro' propaganda."

73 The leaders were even prone to make exaggerated claims about their success and largely ignored the defeat and failed to learn any lessons from it that could benefit the Black community. For example, in Henry et al., *The Colour of Democracy*, the authors claim that, as a result of the United Way stand, "19 out of 22 members of its Black and Caribbean Fundraising Committee resigned" (222). Anne Golden, the president, stated that the claim was blatantly untrue.

74 Amartya Sen, *New York Review of Books*, 40 no. 7 (8 April 1993), 27.

75 Arch Puddington, "Black Anti-Semites and How It Grows," *Commentary*, 97 no. 4 (April 1994), 23.

76 Ibid., 19.

77 Ibid., 23.

78 Ibid., 24.

79 Cf. Michel Feher, "The Schisms of '67: On Certain Restructurings of the American Left, from the Civil Rights Movement to the Multiculturalist Constellation," in Berman, ed., *Blacks and Jews*, 175–6.

80 I believe that this is essentially Charles Taylor's thesis in Amy Gutman, Charles Taylor, Susan Wolf, Steven Rockefeller, and Michael Walzer, *Multiculturalism* (Princeton, NJ: Princeton University Press, 1994), an expanded edition of the 1992 version.

81 Both quotes are taken from Podhoretz, "My Negro Problem," and his postscript, when it was republished in Berman, ed., *Blacks and Jews*, 96.

82 Leon Wiesentieler, "Taking Yes for an Answer," in Berman, ed., *Blacks and Jews*, 255.

83 "Free of ties with his own people, the foreigner feels 'completely free.' Nevertheless, the consummate name of such a freedom is solitude . . . Available, freed of everything, the foreigner has nothing, he is nothing. But he is ready for the absolute, if an absolute would choose him . . . The foreigner longs for affiliation, the better to experience, through a refusal, its untouchability." Kristeva, *Strangers*, 12.

84 Cf. Frances Henry, *The Dynamics of Racism in Toronto* (Toronto: York University, 1978).

85 "While Jews, who along with the Italians and the Irish, have in most of the century's renderings of American history been assigned the role of 'immigrant,' and as such, are permitted a history *before* America, Negroes were made in America. That left us with a blank place where history should be: no place to put our peoplehood and few ways to understand the situation. So we patched our wounds with the pages of the Bible. So in church, our hospital, we tell the tale over and over again: how much we resemble the ancient Jews, how we too are slaves waiting deliverance." Joe Wood, "The Problem Negro and Other Tales," in Berman, ed., *Blacks and Jews*, 110.

86 As quoted in ibid., 114.

87 Clayborne Carson, "The Politics of Relations between African-Americans and Jews," in Berman, ed., *Blacks and Jews*, 141.

88 West, *Keeping Faith*, 11.

89 Cf. Michel Feher, "Schisms," 265, for a fuller description of this thesis.

90 Cf. Earl Rabb, "Anti-Semitism in the 1980's," *Midstream*, 38 no. 2 (1994), 11–18.

Matt Cohen's "Cosmic Spine": Recovering Spadina Avenue's Jewish Landscape

NORMAN RAVVIN

During a long career as a working writer—roughly thirty–five years dedicated to the writing of fiction, children's books, to translating between French and English, as well as to guiding Canada's nascent Writers Union—Matt Cohen never gained the celebrity or readership of such iconic figures as Margaret Atwood, Timothy Findley, Leonard Cohen, or Mordecai Richler. In some ways, his career had more in common with the former two: he was Ontario-born, set much of his fiction in Toronto, and formed his voice and writer's network in the context of the renewed Canadian nationalism and national culture, whose expression in the English language was largely forged in a few square miles of downtown Toronto, in the years after 1965.

Things shifted in surprising ways for Cohen in the final years of his life. His fine last novels, *Last Seen* and *Elizabeth and After,* were critical and popular

Canada has few public monuments to contemporary writers, but the Bloor-Spadina area of Toronto has its share of sites commemorating writers who contributed to the cultural ferment of the late 1960s and early 1970s. Matt Cohen Park, at the corner of Bloor and Spadina, may be the most impressive of these. Created through cooperation by the city and Cohen's friends, it includes a number of plaques displaying substantial excerpts from his works. Though the chosen corner is a number of blocks distant from the Jewish Spadina that appears in Cohen's writing, it is near to the part of town where he lived and worked.

PHOTOS BY NORMAN RAVVIN.

successes, the latter winning the Governor General's Award for fiction; the former dubbed by Margaret Atwood a "Best Book" of 1996. News of his terminal lung cancer contributed to a growing sense—especially among writers and critics—that Cohen deserved better than he'd received. Most striking was a shift toward a more public and heartfelt celebration of his role in the Canadian cultural scene—an elevation, though it was short-lived, to iconic status as a cultural leader and worker who had helped to change the country's view of itself. Robert Fulford, a journalist whose views receive national notice, viewed this shift with a certain cynicism, or at least sarcasm, suggesting that "[c]louds of piety surrounded Matt Cohen in the last months of his life"[1] One does find such clouds, lightly drifting through the memorial volume *Uncommon Ground: A Celebration of Matt Cohen,* to which friends and admirers contributed memoir and criticism as a summation of Cohen's oeuvre. But the book that offers the most revealing response to shifts in Cohen's reception, is Matt Cohen's own *Typing: A Life in 26 Keys.* Completed in his final months and published, after his death, in 2000, *Typing* is a far-reaching and angry portrait of the artist as a young man, as well as being a chronicle of a young man's progress toward a wary, late-middle-aged view of himself. *Typing* offers the best record we have of the cultural excitement—should we say revolution?—that flourished in downtown Toronto during the late 1960s and early '70s. But its aims are greater than this. Using his own experience and accomplishments as a prism, Cohen challenges the Canadian literary establishment over what he viewed as its narrowness, its resistance to non-mainstream voices, and, ultimately, for its rejection of Jewishness as part of its broader cultural character. Of that character, circa 1974, and its legacy today, Cohen writes that many

> of those writers now considered to be our greatest—
> Robertson Davies, Timothy Findley, Margaret Laurence,
> Margaret Atwood, Alice Munro—gained unprecedented
> audiences, sales, international recognition, and most of
> all a dominant place in the Canadian public imagination.
> All of them were writing out of a conservative, small-
> town, restrained, Protestant tradition that found a
> tremendous echo of self-recognition across the country.
> These writers were, in effect, writing the secret diaries of
> their readers . . . .
>
> But for writers of a slightly younger generation, for
> example the offbeat, very unconservative unProtestant
> unrestrained offspring of a completely different cultural
> and religious tradition, which I happened to be, no such
> echo was to be found. The readers, critics and teachers who

would have provided it simply didn't exist—at least not in very large numbers.[2]

Needless to say, Cohen did not make himself any friends with this parting effort. Most notably, Fulford fired off an angry response in his column in the *National Post* newspaper, concentrating on the mistakes in *Typing* rather than on its accomplishments, and ducking the key issue—Jewishness in Canadian literature—in favour of the softer question of whether Cohen made a success of himself or not. Here is Fulford on the subject of whether the writer had a right to be bitter:

> How did Cohen convince himself, against all the evidence, that he was rejected? From his beginnings as a writer he was adopted by those who were powerful or soon would be. In 1967 the renowned philosopher George Grant saw his promise and hired him at McMaster University, but Cohen discounts that because Grant was "a kind of cult leader who demanded perfect faith and perfect fidelity." His first publisher was the House of Anansi, where his colleagues included Margaret Atwood and Dennis Lee . . . .
>
> But soon he was publishing with the most eminent firm, McClelland and Stewart; later, with Knopf Canada. The universities of Alberta and Western Ontario made him writer-in-residence for a year each, and the University of Victoria made him a visiting professor. His peers elected him head of the Writers' Union. The Canada Council gave him two senior arts fellowships. He was three times a finalist for the Governor General's Award for fiction and he won it the third time, accepting it just two weeks before he died.
>
> Many writers will see this as an enviable record; many more will consider it beyond their dreams. Why, then,

does he write as if he had been forced to observe the party of Canadian literature thought the window with his face pressed against the glass?[3]

Margaret Atwood offers her own prickly form of rebuttal in her contribution to the Cohen memorial volume, *Uncommon Ground*. Referencing Greek myth and Carl Jung in order to psychologize Cohen's presentation of his own life and career, she characterizes him as "the artist as odd little outsider and grumbling isolate." Atwood reads Cohen in such a way as to duck his notion of the place of Jewishness in the Canadian literary tradition.[4] Fulford is only slightly more concerned with this challenge, and offers the following as counter-evidence:

> it happens that when [Cohen] started his career, the leading figures in Canadian literature included Mordecai Richler, Leonard Cohen and Irving Layton, none of them a notorious Protestant; the year before Matt Cohen's first book appeared, the Governor General's judges awarded the fiction prize to Richler and the poetry prize to Leonard Cohen.[5]

In an effort to rebuff the argument in *Typing*, Fulford must take us back more than thirty years, to a time when Leonard Cohen and Richler won their prizes, and, as Fulford admits, to the moment when Matt Cohen was just starting out. Leonard Cohen's presence on the literary scene could be said to have ended in 1984, with the little-read *Book of Mercy*, his last full-fledged collection of new poetry. Richler continued as a singular voice until his death, but with arguably little influence over what might be called a Canadian Jewish literary tradition.

Still, there is something more disturbing in these responses to *Typing* than the willingness of leading writers and critics to dismiss Cohen's view of the Canadian literary scene. That is their lack of willingness, or their inability to take note of the singular reading Matt Cohen offers in *Typing* of his Spadina Avenue neighbourhood. In this, he makes an uncanny reclamation of this strip of downtown Toronto, calling it the city's "cosmic spine," while moving towards a reclamation of Spadina as not just a source for much of Canada's English language counterculture, but as a Jewish landscape.[6]

Matt Cohen begins his reminiscences of Spadina in the winter of 1965, only a few years before Richler and Leonard Cohen were offered their respective Governor General's Awards. Noting the passing of his birthday on December 30 of that year, Matt Cohen revels in what he recalls as

> the great good fortune to be living in the centre of the universe, on Spadina Road.
>
> Spadina was Toronto Central, the cosmic spine. On its southern stretch, you could breakfast at the Crest Grill, lunch at Switzer's, dine, drink beer and listen to jazz at Grossman's Tavern. You could shoot pool on Spadina, walk with girlfriends on Spadina . . . . I myself had already lived at three Spadina addresses, eaten at a dozen Spadina restaurants, dressed in Spadina-bought clothes, even gone to my grandfather's funeral at a Spadina Avenue funeral chapel.[7]

Cohen's celebration of Spadina for its cultural and social delights captures a moment at the onset of the countercultural scene that would soon sweep the city, celebrating

> an infinity of delectable possibilities, an adolescent theme park throbbing with folk music, jazz, drugs, protest marches, idealists of all ages, delusions of grandeur, delusions of wealth, delusions of righteousness.[8]

But he hints, too, at the Spadina of an earlier time, when Jewish immigrant life spawned a main street whose remnants include delicatessens, clothing outlets for the garment industry, and funeral chapels established by a Yiddish-speaking working class, which, by 1965, had largely abandoned Spadina and the Kensington Market area for the city's northern suburbs. In *Typing*, passages like this are fleeting, gone before the reader can take much notice, but Cohen manages to portray himself as a young man who, to a degree, ate, dressed, and even buried in the style of his immigrant ancestors. Spadina's Jewish pedigree is, in fact, deeper and more glorious than Matt Cohen lets on. And it takes a Polish-born Yiddish writer to tell us so. In the late 1930s Isaac Bashevis Singer was living and writing in New York City, and decided it was time to get himself full American citizenship. To do so, he left New York for Canada, in order to return through an American immigration office at the border. Singer traveled to Toronto, where he spent a few days before traveling back to America to present himself to the immigration officers at Niagara Falls. In Toronto he stayed at a good hotel, and, typically, brought along a woman with whom he was unhappy. But out of this anxious trip came a wonderful portrait of Spadina as a Jewish main street:

> I was told that Spadina Avenue was the center of Yiddishism in Toronto, and there we went. I again strolled on Krochmalna Street—the same shabby buildings, the same pushcarts and vendors of half-rotten fruit, the familiar smells of the sewer, soup kitchens, freshly baked bagels, smoke from the chimneys. . . .
>
> . . . the restaurant we entered—a kind of Jewish Polish coffeehouse—was crowded with young men and women. They all conversed—or rather, shouted—in Yiddish. The tables were strewn with Yiddish newspapers and magazines. I heard the names of Jewish writers, poets, and politicians. This place was a Canadian version of the Warsaw Writers' Club. . . .
>
> It was odd that having crossed the Atlantic and smuggled myself over the border I found myself in a copy of Yiddish Poland.[9]

This is forgotten Spadina; Torontonians do not have the same relationship with the old neighbourhood as do Montrealers, who continue to feel a degree of attachment to St. Lawrence Boulevard, once known as the Main. And there is no Canadian literature, except for untranslated Yiddish work, that maintains the link between a Jewish immigrant past and Spadina Avenue. Montreal's St. Urbain Street has its share of rememberers, in photography, in film, and of course in the written word, where Mordecai Richler asserted himself as Montreal's Great Rememberer. In *Typing*, Matt Cohen moves edgewise, obliquely and subtly, toward a remembrance of old Spadina. He loves the street for all its charms, among which he includes its past.

Critics and readers took little interest in this aspect of *Typing*. *Who cares?* they seemed to pronounce with their silence. The funeral chapels and *landsmannschaftn*? This, it seems, was the real dead archaeology. What the critics did respond to was Cohen's claims—not unrelated to his remembrance of an older Toronto—that his Jewishness had plagued his efforts at Canadian literary success. Unknowingly, Cohen writes, he was striving to enter a "Canadian literary establishment" that "too often played to very confined groups of people."[10]

Cohen says little in *Typing* about the late stage of his career—the post–1996 period when Knopf published his last two highly regarded novels, *Last Seen* and *Elizabeth and After,* and when the "[c]louds of piety," in Fulford's words, began to gather.[11] He focuses, instead, on a period between 1984 and 1990, when he published what he called a "multi-century triptych" on Jewish themes.[12] This trio of books included *The Spanish Doctor* (1984), *Nadine* (1986), and *Emotional Arithmetic* (1990). He credits his editor, the Hungarian born Anna Porter, with having pressed him to go in this direction: Why, she asked him, "don't you write something that reveals more about yourself? Your books are always so distant. Why don't you write something about being Jewish?"[13] What followed was an historical novel based on the phenomenon of Spanish marranos—hidden Jews—and two novels investigating Jewish identity after the Holocaust. Although these novels were well received abroad, Cohen viewed their reception at home as a dead loss: "had I known the reception they would have in Canada, I certainly would have been afraid to publish them."[14] In an interview he gave in 1990, a decade before the publication of *Typing*, Cohen expressed his dissatisfaction over the Canadian reception of his triptych:

They thought I had gone insane. The book critic of the *Toronto Star* wrote a piece about three thousand words long—basically an open letter to me—pleading with me to regain my senses and go back to my normal kind of writing! Many other critics assumed that either it was a comedy, or I had done it for the money. . . . Finally I came to understand that *The Spanish Doctor* had come as such a shock to so many of my readers, especially the critics, because of their sense that I betrayed my Canadianness by writing about being Jewish. It tells you something uncomfortable about people's conception of what it means to be Canadian. Even after *Nadine* was published, people would say to me: "Are you going to write about Canada again?" I would answer that most of *Nadine* takes place in Canada, and that her being Jewish doesn't mean she isn't Canadian. Then they would be offended, as if I'd made a hostile remark.[15]

It is true that by 2000, when *Typing* appeared, the claim that the "white, conservative middle-class and Protestant values of the literary establishment" marginalized writers outside this context was outdated.[16] In particular, writers of South Asian descent had moved to the forefront of Canadian literature. But in 1990, as Cohen struggled to understand the response to his overtly "Jewish" novels, this multicultural variety had not yet asserted itself as strongly as it has since; and with the rejection of his triptych, he naturally saw the mainstream voices of Davies, Findley, Atwood, alongside such critical kingpins as Robert Weaver and Robert Fulford, as the representatives of a literary establishment who would have him, but only on very particular terms.

Cohen's 1990 musings about mainstream Canadian critics, writers, and readers allow us to dismiss Fulford's denigration of *Typing* as a "work of revenge," or, as the headline of his 2000 newspaper piece had it, a "Hate letter from Beyond."[17] Cohen grappled with the Canadian reception offered his more overtly Jewish writing from the vantage point of its completion, and his comments in *Typing* simply reiterate his earlier views. Unfortunately, the reception of *Typing* confirms these views, as critics proved themselves either unwilling or unable to express curiosity about Cohen's unearthing of an older Jewish Spadina, or to explore in what way this presentation of the past related to his misgivings about his novels' reception. The backlash against the latter aspect of *Typing* is remarkable, considering the "[c]louds of piety" that did, in fact, hover about Cohen's head in his final months and after his death.[18] Out of those clouds came the remarkable Matt Cohen Park, which was carved out of a small outjutting of land at the corner of Bloor and Spadina, near to where Cohen lived for much of his adult life. There, the makers of the park chose passages from his work to lay out on plaques—longish quotes from stories and novels— that capture the variety of Cohen's idiosyncratic output.

Included among these excerpts is a darkly funny passage from the 1978 story "The Universal Miracle," which appeared in a collection entitled *Night Flights*. Here Cohen portrays the funeral of his narrator's grandfather, which takes place at a chapel on Spadina, amidst a certain low-rent squalor. And here we find intimations, not from Cohen's death year, but from twenty-odd years before, of the complex web of nostalgia and diffidence with which he viewed all things Spadina:

> As the service started, old drunks at the back of the chapel chanted and muttered in company. These derelicts, unknown of course to the family, were a compulsory part of the funeral, and in accordance with the mortician's instructions Harvey had tried to pay for their good graces, handing out a whole pocketful of two-dollar bills.
>
> He was so tired that even the harsh music of the prayers was soothing. He had been forced to study Hebrew, learned to read and write the characters so he could follow in the book, but he didn't actually understand more than a few words. . . . With his hands in his pockets, shoulders hunched and bent, tears beginning to collect, Harvey rocked back and forth on his bench, trying to remember his grandfather.[19]

NOTES

1   Robert Fulford, "Hate Letter from Beyond," *National Post,* Oct. 10 2000, p. B1.

2   Matt Cohen, *Typing: A Life in 26 Keys* (Toronto, 2000), pp. 157–158.

3   Fulford, "Hate Letter," p. B1.

4   Margaret Atwood, "The Wrong Box: Matt Cohen, Fabulism, and Critical Taxonomy." *Uncommon Ground: A Celebration of Matt Cohen.* Ed. G. Gibson, et al. (Toronto, 2002), pp. 67–69.

5   Fulford, "Hate Letter," p. B1.

6   Cohen, *Typing,* p. 42.

7   Cohen, *Typing,* pp. 42–43.

8   Cohen, *Typing,* pp. 44–45.

9   Isaac Bashevis Singer, *Love and Exile: An Autobiographical Trilogy* (New York, 1997), pp. 317–319.

10 Cohen, *Typing,* pp. 159–160.

11 Fulford, "Hate Letter," p. B1.

12 Cohen, *Typing,* p. 201.

13 Cohen, *Typing,* p. 194.

14 Cohen, *Typing,* p. 202.

15 Mervin Butovsky, "Interview 6." *Uncommon Ground,* pp. 254–255. Margaret Atwood, in her contribution to *Uncommon Ground,* weirdly calls Cohen's triptych his "'European Jews' trilogy." "The Wrong Box," p. 72.

16 Cohen, *Typing,* p. 231.

17 Fulford, "Hate Letter," p. B1.

18 Fulford, "Hate Letter," p. B1.

19 Matt Cohen, "The Universal Miracle," *The Expatriate: Collected Short Stories* (Toronto, 1982), 242–243.

Contributors

HOWARD ADELMAN

Currently a Visiting Fellow at Princeton University, Howard Adelman was a professor of Philosophy at York University in Toronto from 1966–2003, where he founded and was the first Director of the Centre for Refugee Studies and was editor of *Refuge* until the end of 1993. He has written over one hundred academic articles and chapters in books as well as authored or co-edited twenty-one books. In addition to his writings on refugees, he has written on the Middle East, humanitarian intervention, membership rights, ethics, early warning and conflict management. In 1999, he and Astri Suhrke co-edited *The Path of a Genocide: The Rwanda Crisis from Uganda to Zaire*. His latest volume is *Humanitarian Intervention in Zaire*.

PIERRE ANCTIL

Pierre Anctil obtained a Ph.D. in Social Anthropology at the New School for Social Research in New York, and has completed a post-doctoral fellowship at the Jewish Studies Department of McGill University. Besides holding several positions in the Quebec government in recent years, he is currently Director of the Canadian Studies programme at the University of Ottawa. Anctil has written several books on the Montreal Jewish community, including *Le rendez-vous manqué: les Juifs de Montréal face au Québec de l'entre-deux-guerres, Tur Malka: flâneries sur les cimes de l'histoire juive montréalaise* and *Saint-Laurent: la Main de Montréal*. He has also translated into French the memoirs of Yiddish Canadian writers Israel Medres, Simon Belkin and Hirsch Wolofsky.

FRANKLIN BIALYSTOK

Franklin Bialystok is a part-time lecturer in the Department of History at the University of Toronto and the University of Waterloo. He has published numerous articles on the Holocaust in various journals and edited collections, as well as *Delayed Impact: The Holocaust and the Canadian Jewish Community.*

MARLENE BONNEAU

Marlene Bonneau received her Ph.D. in Religious Studies from Concordia University in Montreal. Her areas of research include: marriage and burial ritual practices in Quebec, the history of wedding rings, and religion and art in Southeast Asia. She is a counsellor at Notre-Dame-des-Neiges Cemetery in Montreal and lectures in the Department of Religion at Concordia University.

MICHAEL BROWN

Michael Brown is professor emeritus and a past Director of the Centre for Jewish Studies at York University. He writes about Canadian Jewry and other aspects of modern Jewish history and literature. He is the editor of the journal *Canadian Jewish Studies/Études Juives Canadiennes* and, together with Ira Robinson and the late Daniel Elazar, the recently published *Not Written in Stone: Jews, Constitutions, and Constitutionalism in Canada.*

BRENDA COSSMAN

Brenda Cossman is a professor in the Faculty of Law at the University of Toronto. Her teaching and scholarly interests include family law, freedom of expression, feminist legal theory, law and sexuality, and law and development. Her publications include the co-authored *Bad Attitudes on Trial: Pornography, Feminism and the Butler Decision; Subversive Sites: Feminist Engagements with Law in India;* and *Secularism's Last Sigh?: Hindutva and the (Mis)Rule of Law.* She is the co-editor of *Privatization, Law and the Challenge to Feminism.*

ETAN DIAMOND

Etan Diamond, an American social historian, is a senior research associate at The Polis Center in Indianapolis, Indiana. He holds a Ph.D. from Carnegie Mellon University. He is also the author of *And I Will Dwell in Their Midst: Orthodox Jews in Suburbia.*

ANGELA GROSSMANN

Angela Grossmann was born in London, England in 1955. She studied journalism and painting in Canada, and has taught at the Emily Carr College of Art in Vancouver, as well as at the University of British Columbia. Her career was launched by the groundbreaking 1985 "*Young Romantics*" show at the Vancouver Art Gallery, which focused on a group of five painters. Over the years, her work has been influenced by motifs and images associated with the Second World War, including her *Affaires d'Enfants* series, which involved painting on the insides of suitcases, and a later series of paintings of prisoners, who were not themselves Holocaust survivors but whose appearance was evocative of the treatment of Jews by the Nazis. Grossmann lives in Vancouver where she paints and teaches.

About *Remainders* (2000), which appears in detail on the cover of this volume, Angela Grossmann writes, "I made this piece while thinking of my father who meets regularly in a North Toronto *Konditerei*, with his friends Egon and Alfred. They discuss the merits of streudel over streusel, they reminisce; they remember fondly the songs and stories of their boyhood in Dusseldorf. Of course they don't discuss the terrible things; of course they have not forgotten those, and though they are not my memories, I cannot forget either."

MARLEE KLINE

Marlee Kline was a professor at the University of British Columbia in the Faculty of Law at the time of her death in 2001. Despite passing at the tragically young age of 41, she established herself as a pioneer in the areas of child welfare law, law and the welfare state, and explored, in some of her writing, the relationship between racism, anti-Semitism and gender. After her death, the *Canadian Journal of Women and the Law* devoted an issue to the themes in Kline's work.

REBECCA MARGOLIS

Rebecca Margolis received her B.A. at McGill University in Montreal and is completing her doctorate in Yiddish Studies at Columbia University in New York. She has taught and lectured in and about Yiddish at the community and university levels in New York, Montreal, Toronto and Charlotte. She was recently the Scholar-In-Residence at the Institute for Canadian Jewish Studies, Concordia University, and taught a course entitled "The Yiddish Experience in Montreal." Her publications include *"Les écrivains yiddish de Montréal et leur ville"* in *Juifs et Canadiens français dans la société québécoise* and "Jewish Print Culture in Canada" in *History of the Book in Canada, Vol. III (1918–1980)*.

RICHARD MENKIS

Richard Menkis is an associate professor at the University of British Columbia, where he teaches Jewish history. He was the founding editor of the journal *Canadian Jewish Studies/Études juives canadiennes*. Special issues of that journal included *New Perspectives on Canada: The Holocaust and Survivors*, co-edited with Paula Draper, as well as *Jews and Judaism in Canada: A Bibliography of Works Published After 1965*, co-compiled with Michael Brown, Ben Schlesinger and Stuart Schoenfeld. A native of Toronto, Richard Menkis has published on anti-Semitism in Canada and on the history of Canadian Jewish identities. His current research focuses on historical writing and historical memory in the Canadian Jewish community. He has served as Scholar-in-Residence at Concordia University's Institute for Canadian Jewish Studies, as well as a fellow at the American Jewish Archives in Cincinnati.

NORMAN RAVVIN

Norman Ravvin is a writer of fiction, criticism and journalism. His essays on Jewish literature appeared in *A House of Words: Jewish Writing, Identity and Memory*. His fiction publications include two novels—*Café des Westens* and *Lola by Night*— and a story collection titled *Sex, Skyscrapers and Standard Yiddish*. He is also the author of *Hidden Canada: An Intimate Travelogue*, and the editor of *Not Quite Mainstream: Canadian Jewish Short Stories* and *Great Stories of the Sea*. His fiction and non-fiction have appeared in magazines across the country, as well as on CBC radio. He chairs Concordia University's Institute for Canadian Jewish Studies, where he is the general editor of a series devoted to Canadian Jewish Studies, published in partnership by Red Deer Press and the Institute for Canadian Jewish Studies.

IRA ROBINSON

Ira Robinson is a professor of Judaic Studies in the Department of Religion at Concordia University in Montreal. He is past president of the Association for Canadian Jewish Studies and the Jewish Public Library of Montreal. He has published numerous articles in the area of Canadian Jewish history and has co-edited several volumes in this field. The latest of them to be published is *Not Written in Stone: Jews, Constitutions and Constitutionalism in Canada.*

JANICE ROSEN

Janice Rosen has been the Archives Director of the Canadian Jewish Congress National Archives in Montreal since 1989. She has a Masters degree in Cultural Anthropology from the University of Virginia, and has done fieldwork in Ouezzane, Morocco. Her publications include three surveys of Jewish archival repositories in Canada for *Canadian Jewish Studies/Études juives canadiennes* (1993, 1995 and 1996–1997), and the editing of two books of historical photographs published by Canadian Jewish Congress: *The Canadian Jewish Agenda, 1995,* and *The Canadian Jewish Congress Agenda, 2001.* Prior to her current position, she researched Sephardic Jewish culture in Montreal for a national museum exhibit ("A Coat of Many Colours" at the Canadian Museum of Civilization.) She has recently completed the English translation of a book about Moroccan Jewish marriage customs, which is entitled *Mariage à Mogador.*

BARB SCHOBER

Barb Schober is a Ph.D. candidate at the University of British Columbia. Her M.A. thesis dealt with the development of Holocaust commemoration in Vancouver. Her essay in this volume is adapted from that work. Currently, she is researching the Vancouver section of the National Council of Jewish Women. In 2003, she won one of six "Jewish Women Making Community" fellowships from the Jewish Women's Archives.

FAYDRA L. SHAPIRO

Faydra L. Shapiro is an assistant professor in the department of Religion and Culture at Wilfrid Laurier University in Waterloo. She has written several articles on Israel experience programs and the construction of Jewish identities, and is completing a book on the subject.

HENRY SREBRNIK

Henry Srebrnik is a professor in the Department of Political Studies at the University of Prince Edward Island in Charlottetown, P.E.I., and associate editor of the *Canadian Review of Studies in Nationalism*. His recent publications include "Birobidzhan on the Prairies: Two Decades of Pro-Soviet Jewish Movements in Winnipeg," in Daniel Stone, ed., *Jewish Radicalism in Winnipeg, 1905–1960*, and "Diaspora, Ethnicity, and Dreams of Nationhood: North American Jewish Communists and the Soviet Birobidzhan Project," in Gennady Estraikh and Mikhail Krutikov, eds., *Yiddish and the Left*. His book on London Jews and British Communism was published in 1995.

HAROLD TROPER

Harold Troper is best known for *None Is too Many: Canada and the Jews of Europe 1933–1948*, which he co-wrote with Irving Abella. He is also the author of *Immigrants: A Portrait of the Urban Experience*, with Robert Harney, and *Old Wounds: Jews, Ukrainians and the Hunt for Nazi War Criminals in Canada*, with Morton Weinfeld. He is a professor of History at the Ontario Institute for Studies in Education in Toronto.

GERALD TULCHINSKY

Gerald Tulchinsky, professor emeritus at Queen's University in Kingston, Ontario, is the author of *Taking Root: The Origins of the Canadian Jewish Community, Branching Out: The Transformation of the Canadian Jewish Community*, and shorter pieces in various journals and anthologies. His work on Canadian economic history includes *The River Barons: Montreal Businessmen and the Growth of Industry and Transportation, 1837–1853*.

MIRIAM WADDINGTON

Miriam Waddington (1917–2004) was a leading Canadian poet, well known for her poems of the prairie landscape and her commitment to expressing social concerns. A product of the secular Yiddish Peretz School in Winnipeg, she made direct contributions to Canadian Jewish culture with her poetry on Jewish themes, her pioneering critical appraisal of A.M. Klein, her fine anthology of Canadian Jewish stories, her translations from Yiddish, as well as her excellent autobiographic pieces and essays, such as the one included here from her collection *Apartment Seven.*

MORTON WEINFELD

Morton Weinfeld is a professor of Sociology and holds the Chair in Canadian Ethnic Studies at McGill University in Montreal. He has published extensively in the field of ethnic and race relations in general, and modern Jewish studies in particular. His most recent book is *Like Everyone Else . . . But Different: The Paradoxical Success of Canadian Jews.* Among his other works are *The Canadian Jewish Mosaic,* with William Shaffir and Irwin Cotler, *The Jews in Canada,* with Robert Brym and William Shaffir, *Trauma and Rebirth: Intergenerational Effects of the Holocaust,* with John Sigal, and *Still Moving: Recent Jewish Migration in Comparative Perspective,* with Daniel Elazar.

Adelman, Howard. "Blacks and Jews: Racism, Anti-Semitism, and *Show Boat.*" From *Multiculturalism, Jews, and Canadian Identity.* The Magnes Press, 1996. Copyright © Howard Adelman. Used by permission.

Anctil, Pierre. "A. M. Klein: The Poet and His Relations with French Quebec." From *The Jews of North America.* Wayne State University Press, 1987. Copyright © Pierre Anctil. Used by permission.

Bialystok, Franklin. "Were things that bad?" The Holocaust Enters Community Memory." From *Delayed Impact: The Holocaust and the Canadian Jewish Community* by Franklin Bialystok. McGill-Queen's University Press, 2000. Copyright © Franklin Bialystok. Reprinted by permission of McGill-Queen's University Press.

Bonneau, Marlene. "Getting Married in Montreal with Two Wedding Rings." Copyright © Marlene Bonneau. Used by permission.

Brown, Michael. "The Empire's Best Known Jew and Little Known Jewry." From *Community and the Individual Jew: Essays in Honor of Lavy M. Becker.* Reconstructionist Rabbinical College Press, 1986. Copyright © Michael Brown. Used by permission.

Cossman, Brenda and Marlee Kline. "And if not now, when?": Feminism and Anti-Semitism Beyond Clara Brett Martin." Copyright © 1992 by Brenda Cossman and the Estate of Marlee Kline. Used by permission. From *Canadian Journal of Women and the Law* 5 (1992).

Diamond, Etan. "Sanctifying Suburban Space." From *And I Will Dwell in Their Midst: Orthodox Jews in Suburbia* by Etan Diamond. University of North Carolina Press, 2000. Copyright © Etan Diamond. Reprinted by permission of University of North Carolina Press.

Margolis, Rebecca. "A Tempest in Three Teapots: Yom Kippur Balls in London, New York and Montreal." Copyright © Rebecca Margolis. Used by permission.

Menkis, Richard. "Introduction: Jewish Cultures, Canadian Cultures." Copyright © Richard Menkis. Used by permission. "Historiography, Myth and Group Relations: Jewish and Non-Jewish Québécois on Jews and New France." Copyright © 1991 by Richard Menkis. Used by permission. From *Canadian Ethnic Studies* 23.2 (1991).

Ravvin, Norman. "Eli Mandel's Family Architecture: Building A House of Words on the Prairies." From *A House of Words: Jewish Writing, Identity and Memory* by Norman Ravvin. McGill-Queen's University Press, 1997. Copyright © McGill-Queen's University Press. Used by permission. "Matt Cohen's "Cosmic Spine": Recovering Spadina Avenue's Jewish Landscape." Copyright © Norman Ravvin. Used by permission.

Robinson, Ira. ""A Letter from the Sabbath Queen": Rabbi Yudel Rosenberg Addresses Montreal Jewry." From *An Everyday Miracle: Yiddish Culture in Montreal.* Véhicule Press, 1990. Copyright © Ira Robinson. Used by permission.

Rosen, Janice. "Moroccan Jewish Saint Veneration: From the Maghreb to Montreal." Copyright © Janice Rosen. Used by permission.

Schober, Barb. "The Vancouver Holocaust Monument that Wasn't: Arnold Belkin's "Warsaw Ghetto Uprising" Mural." Copyright © Barb Schober. Used by permission.

Shapiro, Faydra L. "Learning to be a Diaspora Jew through the Israel Experience." Copyright © 2001 by Faydra L. Shapiro. Used by permission. From *Studies in Religion/Sciences Religieuses* 30.1 (2001).

Srebrnik, Henry. "Red Star Over Birobidzhan: Canadian Jewish Communists and the "Jewish Autonomous Region" in the Soviet Union." Copyright © 1999 by Henry Srebrnik. Used by permission. From *Labour/Le travail* 44 (Fall, 1999).

Troper, Harold and Morton Weinfeld. "Two Solitudes: The Legacy of the War." From *Old Wounds: Jews, Ukrainians and the Hunt for Nazi War Criminals in Canada* by Harold Troper and Morton Weinfeld. Copyright © Harold Troper and Morton Weinfeld. Used by permission.

Tulchinsky, Gerald. "Goldwin Smith: Victorian Canadian Antisemite." From *Antisemitism in Canada: History and Interpretation*. Wilfrid Laurier University Press, 1992. Copyright © Gerald Tulchinsky. Used by permission.

Waddington, Miriam. "Mrs Maza's Salon." Copyright © The Estate of Miriam Waddington. Used by permission.